A TEXT BOOK OF

DATA COMMUNICATION

For

Semester - II

SECOND YEAR DEGREE COURSE IN COMPUTER ENGINEERING AND INFORMATION TECHNOLOGY

As Per The New Revised Syllabus of
North Maharashtra University, Jalgaon, June 2013

G. R. PATIL
M. E. (Electronics),
Associate Professor in E & TC Department,
Army Institute of Technology,
Dighi, PUNE.

R. C. JAISWAL
M. E. (E & TC),
Asst. Professor, E & TC Department,
Pune Institute of Computer Technology,
Dhankwadi, PUNE.

NIRALI PRAKASHAN

N3098

DATA COMMUNICATION (S.E. COMPUTER ENGINEERING / I.T.)　　　　**ISBN 978-93-83971-04-6**

First Edition　：　January 2014

©　　　　：　**Authors**

Published By :
NIRALI PRAKASHAN
Abhyudaya Pragati, 1312, Shivaji Nagar,
Off J.M. Road, PUNE – 411005
Tel - (020) 25512336/37/39, Fax - (020) 25511379
Email : niralipune@pragationline.com

DISTRIBUTION CENTRES

PUNE

Nirali Prakashan
119, Budhwar Peth, Jogeshwari Mandir Lane
Pune 411002, Maharashtra
Tel : (020) 2445 2044, 66022708
Fax : (020) 2445 1538
Email : niralilocal@pragationline.com

MUMBAI

Nirali Prakashan
385, S.V.P. Road, Rasdhara Co-op. Hsg. Society Ltd.,
Girgaum, Mumbai 400004, Maharashtra
Tel : (022) 2385 6339 / 2386 9976,
Fax : (022) 2386 9976
Email : bookorder@pragationline.com

DISTRIBUTION BRANCHES

NAGPUR

Pratibha Book Distributors
Above Maratha Mandir, Shop No. 3, First Floor,
Rani Jhanshi Square, Sitabuldi, Nagpur 440012,
Maharashtra, Tel : (0712) 254 7129

JALGAON

Nirali Prakashan
34, V. V. Golani Market, Navi Peth, Jalgaon 425001,
Maharashtra, Tel : (0257) 222 0395
Mob : 94234 91860

BENGALURU

Pragati Book House
House No. 1, Sanjeevappa Lane, Avenue Road Cross,
Opp. Rice Church, Bengaluru – 560002.
Tel : (080) 64513344, 64513355,
Mob : 9880582331, 9845021552
Email:bharatsavla@yahoo.com

KOLHAPUR

Nirali Prakashan
New Mahadvar Road,
Kedar Plaza, 1st Floor Opp. IDBI Bank
Kolhapur 416 012, Maharashtra. Mob : 9855046155

CHENNAI

Pragati Books
9/1, Montieth Road, Behind Taas Mahal, Egmore,
Chennai 600008 Tamil Nadu, Tel : (044) 6518 3535,
Mob : 94440 01782 / 98450 21552 / 98805 82331
Email : bharatsavla@yahoo.com

RETAIL OUTLETS
PUNE

Pragati Book Centre
157, Budhwar Peth, Opp. Ratan Talkies,
Pune 411002, Maharashtra
Tel : (020) 2445 8887 / 6602 2707, Fax : (020) 2445 8887

Pragati Book Centre
Amber Chamber, 28/A, Budhwar Peth,
Appa Balwant Chowk, Pune : 411002, Maharashtra,
Tel : (020) 20240335 / 66281669
Email : pbcpune@pragationline.com

Pragati Book Centre
676/B, Budhwar Peth, Opp. Jogeshwari Mandir,
Pune 411002, Maharashtra
Tel : (020) 6601 7784 / 6602 0855

PBC Book Sellers & Stationers
152, Budhwar Peth, Pune 411002, Maharashtra
Tel : (020) 2445 2254 / 6609 2463

MUMBAI

Pragati Book Corner
Indira Niwas, 111 - A, Bhavani Shankar Road, Dadar (W), Mumbai 400028, Maharashtra
Tel : (022) 2422 3526 / 6662 5254
Email : pbcmumbai@pragationline.com

www.pragationline.com　　　　　　　　info@pragationline.com

Preface ...

It gives us immense pleasure to present this book on "Data Communication".

The book is written mainly for the second year students of Computer Engineering and Information Technology courses of North Maharashtra University for the subject **"Data Communication"**. It is written as per the revised syllabus of North Maharashtra University (w.e.f. 2012).

In recent years communication has become an important part of our life. It has become essential to understand the basic concept of communication almost for every engineer. This text is designed to explain the basic concepts in Data Communication.

The text includes information about basic concepts of Data Communication. Various building blocks of the data communication systems are explained in detail. Mathematical treatment of various concepts are given wherever necessary. Number of Solved Problems, Exercises and University Questions are included in each unit.

Unit I provides the Concepts of Introduction of Data Communication and Signals.

Unit II provides the Concepts of Digital Transmission and Analog Transmission.

Unit III provides the Concepts of Multiplexing and Transmission Media.

Unit IV provides the Concepts of Switching and Multiple Access.

Unit V provides the Concepts of Error Control and Data Link Control.

Nirali Prakashan put the book, what we thought into reality. Our sincere thanks to Shri. Dineshbhai Furia, Shri, Jignesh Furia and Shri. M. P. Munde. The books could be completed in time, due to sincere and hard work of Nirali Prakashan's staff namely Mr. Malik Shaikh, Miss Pallavi Kumari and Miss Chaitali Takale. We thanks them all.

Valuable suggestions from our esteemed readers to improve the text will be most welcome and highly appreciated.

January 2014
Pune.

Authors

Syllabus ...

1. Introduction to Data Communication and Signals (08 Hours, 16 Marks)

(a) Basics of Data Communication: Characteristics and Components

(b) Data Representation and Data Flow

(c) Networks, Introduction to ISO-OSI Reference model

(d) Introduction to Signals and Transmission Impairments: Analog and Digital

(e) Periodic Analog Signals, Digital Signals

(f) Transmission impairment, Data rate limits, Performance.

2. Digital Transmission and Analog Transmission (08 Lectures, 16 Marks)

(a) Digital to Digital Conversion

(b) Analog to Digital Conversion

(c) Transmission Modes

(d) Digital-to-analog Conversion

3. Multiplexing and Transmission Media (08 Hours, 16 Marks)

(a) Multiplexing

(b) Guided Media

(c) Unguided Media

4. Switching and Multiple Access (08 Hours, 16 Marks)

(a) Circuit-switched Networks

(b) Datagram networks

(c) Virtual-circuit networks

(d) Multiple Access

5. Error Control and Data Link Control (08 Hours, 16 Marks)

(a) Types of errors

(b) Block coding

(c) Linear block codes

(d) Cyclic codes

(e) Checksum

(f) Flow and Error control

***

Contents ...

***

Unit I

INTRODUCTION TO DATA COMMUNICATION AND SIGNALS

1.1 Introduction to Data communication

Data Communications is the transfer of data or information between a source and a receiver. The source transmits the data and the receiver receives it. The actual generation of the information is not part of Data Communications nor is the resulting action of the information at the receiver. Data Communication is interested in the transfer of data, the method of transfer and the preservation of the data during the transfer process.

In Local Area Networks, we are interested in "connectivity", connecting computers together to share resources. Even though the computers can have different disk operating systems, languages, cabling and locations, they still can communicate to one another and share resources.

The purpose of Data Communications is to provide the rules and regulations that allow computers with different disk operating systems, languages, cabling and locations to share resources. The rules and regulations are called protocols and standards in Data Communication.

The distance over which data moves within a computer may vary from a few thousandths of an inch, as is the case within a single IC chip, to as much as several feet along the backplane of the main circuit board. Over such small distances, digital data may be transmitted as direct, two-level electrical signals over simple copper conductors. Except for the fastest computers, circuit designers are not very concerned about the shape of the conductor or the analog characteristics of signal transmission.

Frequently, however, data must be sent beyond the local circuitry that constitutes a computer. In many cases, the distances involved may be enormous. Unfortunately, as the distance between the source of a message and its destination increases, accurate transmission becomes increasingly difficult. This results from the electrical distortion of signals travelling through long conductors and from noise added to the signal as it propagates through a transmission medium. Although some precautions must be taken for data exchange within a computer, the biggest problems occur when data is transferred to devices outside the computer's circuitry. In this case, distortion and noise can become so severe that information is lost.

Data communication is the exchange of data between two devices via some form of transmission medium. When we communicate, we are sharing information. This sharing can be local or remote. Data Communications concerns the transmission of digital messages to devices external to the message source. "External" devices are generally thought of as being independently powered circuitry that exists beyond the chassis of a computer or other digital message source. As a rule, the maximum permissible transmission rate of a message is directly proportional to signal power and inversely proportional to channel noise. It is the aim of any communications system to provide the highest possible transmission rate at the lowest possible power and with the least possible noise.

Data communications through the telephone network can reach any point in the world. The volume of overseas fax transmissions is increasing constantly, and computer networks that link thousands of businesses, governments and universities are pervasive. Transmissions over such distances are not generally accomplished with a direct-wire digital link, but rather with digitally-modulated analog carrier signals. This technique makes it possible to use existing analog telephone voice channels for digital data, although at considerably reduced data rates compared to a direct digital link.

1.2 Components of Data Communication

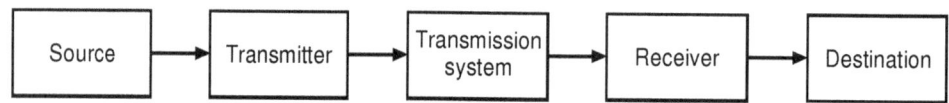

Fig. 1.1: Components of Data Communication

The main purpose of communication system is to exchange data between two points by electric means. Fig. 1.1 shows exchange of the data between workstation and server on telephone lines. Following are the different blocks of communication system.

1. Source: Source generates the data which is to be transmitted. Examples of sources are telephone and personal computers.

Examples: 1. Terminal, 2. Computer, 3. Mainframe.

2. Transmitter: Data from the source are not transmitted in the same form which are generated by source, transmitter converts and encodes the data so as to produce electromagnetic signals.

Modem is used to convert incoming data stream into analog signals that can be handled by telephone network.

3. Transmission system: It is a single transmission line or network connecting source and destination.

Examples: 1. Cabling, 2. Microwave, 3. Fiber optics.

4. Receiver: Function of the receiver is to accept the information from transmission line or network and converting it into digital data in the form of stream so that destination computer can handle the data.

Example: Printer terminal.

5. **Destination:** Destination is a device like computer that receives the data.

Following are the some key terms which are used in communication system.

1. **Transmission system utilization:** It is a measure of use of transmission facilities that are shared among the number of communicating devices.

Various multiplexing techniques are used to share total capacity of transmission medium with number of users.

2. **Synchronization:** Receiver must be able to detect when transmission begins and when it ends. Synchronization between receiver and transmitter should be achieved using handstaking signals.

3. **Error detection and Correction:** Transmitted signal may get distorted when it travels long distance through medium. For example, a file from one computer can be transmitted to other should be accompanied by error detection code.

4. **Exchange management:** Besides the nature and timing of signals, there are various requirement for communication between two parties that comes under the term exchange management.

5. **Message formatting:** Two parties should have some agreement about format of data to be exchanged or transmitted. Binary code for characters is to be adopted universally.

1.3 Data Representation

A binary digit has only two states i.e. 0 and 1 and can be represented by only two symbols. In communication between computers requires much larger set of symbols.

For example:

1.   52 capital and Small letters.

2.   10 Humerals from 0 to 9.

3.   Special symbols.

A group of bits are used as code to represent a symbols. The code is usually 5 to 8 bits long.

For example:

5-bit code can have 2^5 = 32 combinations and can therefore, represent 32 symbols.

8-bit can represent 2^8 = 256 bits.

A code set is a set of these codes that represents the symbols. Following two code sets are commonly used:

(1) American standard Code for Information Interchange (ASCII).

(2) Extended Binary Coded Decimal Interchange Code (EBCDIC).

1. American Standard Code for Information Inerchange (ASCII)

American National Standards Institute (ANSI) defines ASCII code. The code sit is consist of 96 graphic symbols and 32 control symbols. Control symbols are codes reserved for special function. ASCII is often used with an eight bit called as parity bit. This bits are utilized for detecting errors that occurs during transmission.

2. Extended Binary Coded Decimal Interchange code (EBCDIC)

It uses 8 bit code. That is 256 possible combinations. All combinations are not used and have also not been defined. There is no parity bit for error detecting in the basic code. Graphical symbols of EBCDIC code is approximately same as ASCII but several difference in the control character.

In data communication information comes in different forms such as text, images, audio, video and numbers.

1. Text: It represented as a bit pattern. The sequence of bits is 0's or 1's. It consist of number of bit patterns. They are represents text symbols. Each set of bit pattern is called as a code and process of representing symbols is called as **coding**. The pentavalent loading system is called as **Unicode** which uses 32 bits to represent symbols or characters.

2. Images: It is also represented by bit patterns. Image is composed of a matrix of pixels. While each pixel is a small dot. The pixel size is depends upon the resolution. Image is divided into pixels and each pixel is assigned a bit patterns. Size of the pattern is depends on the image.

3. Audio: It is refers to the recording or broadcasting of sound. Audio is continuous, not discrete. It is by nature different from text, numbers, images.

4. Video: It is refers to recording or broadcasting of a picture or movie. Video can be combination of images, each a discrete entity arranged to convey the idea of the motion.

5. Numbers: Numbers are represented by bit patterns.

1.4 Direction of Data Flow

- Communication between two devices can be simplex, half-duplex or full duplex.

1.4.1 Simplex

- In simplex mode, the communication is unidirectional, as on a one-way street.
- Only one of the two devices on a link can transmit; the other can only receive.

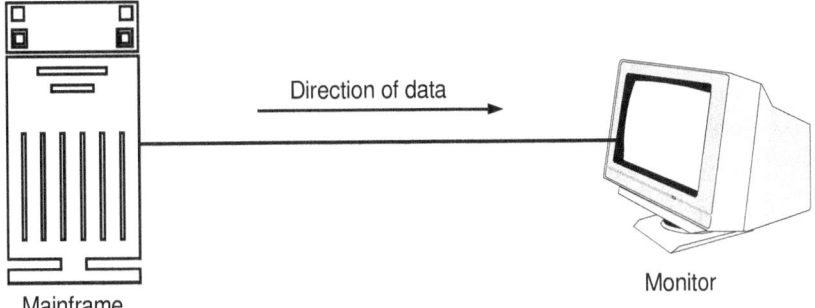

Fig. 1.2: Simplex

Simplex means communication runs in one direction. The examples include

- TV and radio broadcasting or pager.

- Keyboards and traditional monitors are both examples of simplex devices. The keyboard can only introduce input; the monitor can only accept output.

Simplex is a form of communication in which signals are sent in only one direction. This is different from duplex transmission, in which signals can simultaneously be sent and received by a station, and from half-duplex transmission, in which signals can be sent or received but not both at the same time.

Simplex transmission occurs in many common communication applications, the most obvious being broadcast and cable television. It is not used in true network communication because stations on a network generally need to communicate both ways. Some forms of network communication might seem to be simplex in nature, such as streaming audio or video, but the communication actually takes place using bidirectional network traffic, usually Transmission Control Protocol (TCP) traffic.

1.4.2 Half-Duplex

In *half-duplex mode*, each station can both transmit and receive, but not at the same time. For half-duplex, both end devices can send and receive (they must alternate).

When one device is sending, the other can only receive, and vice versa.

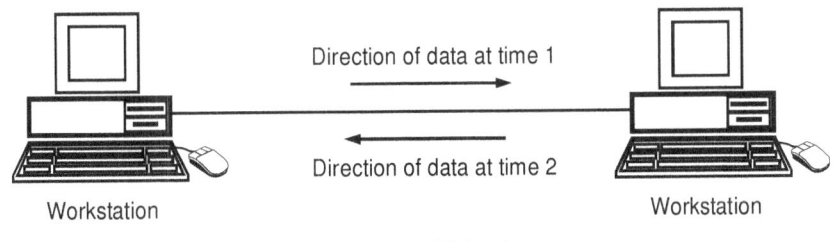

Fig. 1.3: Half duplex

In a half duplex transmission, the entire capacity of a channel is taken over by whichever of the two devices is transmitting at the time. For example, Walkie-talkies.

The simplest example is a walkie-talkie: You have to press a button to talk and release the button to listen. When two people use walkie-talkies to communicate, at any given moment, only one of them can talk while the other listens. If both try to talk simultaneously, a collision occurs and neither hears what the other says.

Communication through traditional Ethernet networks is another example of half-duplex communication. When one station on an Ethernet transmits, the other stations detect the carrier signal and listen instead of transmitting. If two stations transmit signals simultaneously, a collision occurs and both stations stop transmitting and wait random intervals of time before retransmitting.

In contrast, full-duplex communication enables stations to transmit and receive signals simultaneously, with the advantage of providing twice the bandwidth of equivalent half-duplex technologies. However, full-duplex requires two communication channels to achieve these results - one to transmit and one to receive signals

1.4.3 Full-Duplex

In *full duplex mode* (also called *duplex*), both stations can transmit and receive simultaneously.

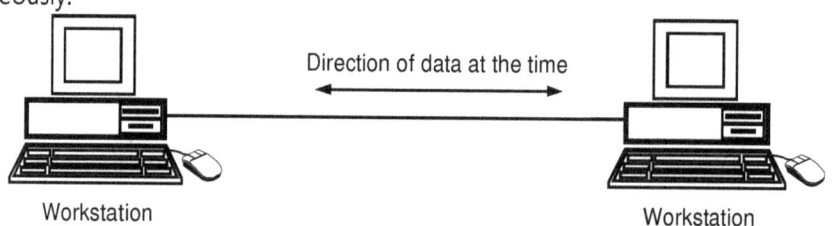

Workstation   Workstation

Fig. 1.4: Full-duplex

The full-duplex mode is like a two way street with traffic flowing in both direction at the same time.

In full-duplex mode, signals going in either direction share the capacity of the link.

Sharing of link can occur in two ways: Either the link must contain two physically separate transmission paths, one for sending and the other for receiving; or the capacity of the channel is divided between signals travelling in both directions.

One common example of full duplex communication is the telephone network. When two people are communicating by a telephone line, both can talk and listen at the same time.

In full-duplex communication, both stations send and receive at the same time, and usually two communication channels are required. However, you can also achieve full-duplex communication using a multiplexing technique whereby signals traveling in different directions are placed into different time slots. The disadvantage of this technique is that it cuts the overall possible transmission speed by half.

1.5 Network

We will see different terminologies of concept 'Network'.

- Computers are information tools and networks are how the computers exchange that information.
- A network is a set of devices (often referred as nodes) connected by communication links. A node can be a computer, printer, or any other device capable of sending and/or receiving data generated by other nodes on the network.
- A network is a set of computers, which are linked together on a permanent basis. This can mean two computers cabled together on the same desk, or thousands of computers across the world.
- Networked computers can share data and peripherals (resource sharing), allowing people in an organization to communicate better and more effectively use their hardware resources.

1.5.1 Computer Network

"A group of computers connected in some fashion in order to share resources".

OR

"A collection of autonomous computers interconnected by a single technology". Two computers are said to be interconnected if they are able to exchange information.

A network consists of two or more computers that are linked in order to share resources (such as printers and CD-ROMs), exchange files, or allow electronic communications. The computers on a network may be linked through cables, telephone lines, radio waves, satellites or infrared light beams.

Network is a group of computers and associated peripheral devices connected by a communications channel capable of sharing files and other resources among several users. A network can range from a peer-to-peer network connecting a small number of users in an office or department, to a LAN connecting many users over permanently installed cables and dial-up lines, to a MAN or WAN connecting users on several networks spread over a wide geographic area.

The purpose of a computer network is to link two or more "clients" together in order to exchange information.

1.5.2 Uses of Computer Network

1. **Resource Sharing:**
   Enables users to share hardware like scanners and printers. This reduces costs by reducing the number of hardware items bought.

Resources are available to anyone on the network without regard to the physical location of the resource and the user.

For example: Printers, scanners, CD burners, etc.

2. **Information Sharing:**

   Allows users **access to data** stored on others' computers. This keeps everyone up-to-date on the latest data, since it's all in the same file, rather than having to make copies of the files, which are immediately out-of-date.

   For example: files, database, records etc.

3. **Person-to-person communication:**

   For example, e-mail (electronic mail), Videoconferencing etc.

4. **Electronic business:**

   Users can place orders electronically as needed.

5. **Interactive entertainment:**

   Real-time simulation games, like flight simulators, Age of empires etc.

1.5.3 Advantages of Network

1. **Speed:** Networks provide a very rapid method for sharing and transferring files. Without a network, files are shared by copying them to floppy disks, than carrying or sending the disks from one computer to another. This method of transferring files (referred to as sneaker-net) is very time-consuming.

2. **Cost:** Networkable versions of many popular software programs are available at considerable savings when compared to buying individually licensed copies. Besides monetary savings, sharing a program on a network allows for easier upgrading of the program. The changes have to be done only once, on the file server, instead of on all the individual workstations.

3. **Security:** Files and programs on a network can be designated as "copy inhibit," so that you do not have to worry about illegal copying of programs. Also, passwords can be established for specific directories to restrict access to authorized users.

4. **Centralized Software Management:** One of the greatest benefits of a network is the fact that all of the software can be loaded on one computer (the *file server*). This eliminates the need to spend time and energy installing updates and tracking files on independent computers throughout the building or campus.

5. **Resource Sharing:** Sharing resources is another area in which a network exceeds stand-alone computers. Most organizations cannot afford enough laser printers, fax machines, modems, scanners, and CD-ROM players for each computer. However, if these or similar peripherals are added to a network, they can be shared by many users.

6. **Electronic Mail:** The presence of a network provides the hardware necessary to install an e-mail system. Due to e-mail systems, person to person communication became easy.

7. **Flexible Access:** Some organization's networks allow authorized users to access their files from computers throughout the network of organization.

8. **Workgroup Computing:** Workgroup software (such as *Microsoft BackOffice*) allows many users to work on a document or project concurrently. For example, educators located at various schools within a state could simultaneously contribute their ideas about new curriculum standards to the same document and spreadsheets.

1.5.4 Disadvantages of Network

1. **Expensive to Install**: Although a network will generally save money over time, the initial costs of installation can be prohibitive. Cables, network cards and software are expensive, and the installation may require the services of a technician.

2. **Requires Administrative Time:** Proper maintenance of a network requires considerable time and expertise.

3. **File Server May Fail:** Although a file server is no more susceptible to failure than any other computer, when the files server "goes down," the entire network may come to a halt. When this happens, the entire organization may lose access to necessary programs and files.

1.6 Network Criteria

To be considered effective and efficient, a network must meet a number of criteria. The most important of these are performance, reliability and security.

1. Performance:

It can be measured in many ways, including transit time and response time. Transit time is the amount of time required for a message to travel from one device to another. Response time is the elapsed time between an enquiry and a response.

The performance of a network depends on a number of factors, including the number of users, the type of transmission medium, the capabilities of the connected hardware and the efficiency of the software.

(i) Type of transmission medium: The medium defines the speed at which data can travel through a connection. Today's networks are moving to faster and faster transmission media, such as fiber-optic cabling, a medium that can carry data at only 10 megabits per second. However, the speed of light imposes an upper bound on the data rate.

(ii) Software: The software used to process data at the sender, receiver, and intermediate nodes also affects network performance. Moving a message from node to node through a network requires processing to transform the raw data into transmittable signals, to route these signals to the proper destination, to ensure error-free delivery and to recast the signals into a form the receiver can use.

The software that provides these services affects both the speed and the reliability of a network link. Well-designed software can speed the process and make transmission more effective and efficient.

(iii) Number of users: Having a large number of concurrent users can slow response time in a network not designed to coordinate heavy traffic loads. The design of a given network is based on an assessment of the average number of users that will be communicating at any one time. In peak load periods, however, the actual number of users can exceed the average and thereby decrease performance. How a network responds to loading is measure of its performance.

(iv) Hardware: The types of hardware included in a network affect both the speed and capacity of transmission. A higher-speed computer with greater storage capacity provides better performance.

2. Reliability:

In addition to accuracy of delivery, network reliability is measured frequency of failure, the time it takes a link to recover from a failure and the network's robustness in a catastrophe.

(i) **Frequency of failure:** All networks fail occasionally. A network that fails often, however, is of little value to a user.

(ii) **Catastrophe:** Networks must be protected from catastrophic events such as fire, earthquake or theft. One protection against unforeseen damage is a reliable system to back up network software.

(iii) **Recovery time of a network after a failure:** How long does it take to restore service? A network that recovers quickly is more useful than one that does not.

3. Security:

Network security issues include protecting data from unauthorized access and viruses.

(i) **Viruses:** Because a network is accessible from many points, it can be susceptible to computer viruses. A virus is an illicitly introduced code that damages the system. A good network is protected from viruses by hardware and software designed specifically for that purpose.

(ii) **Unauthorized access:** For a network to be useful, sensitive data must be protected from unauthorized access. Protection can be accomplished at a number of levels. At the lowest level are user identification codes and passwords. At a higher level are encryption techniques. In these mechanisms, data are systematically altered in such a way that if an unauthorized user intercepts them, they will be unintelligible.

1.7 Network Hardware and Software

Computer networks are made up of both hardware and software.

Hardware consists of the computers, terminals, NIC, communication media, hubs, bridges, switches, routers, gateways, front end processor, concentrators, controllers, protocol converters, and etc.

Hardware devices remain relatively stable; the software changes whenever upgrades are made to the network.

Some of the functions of software include communication with terminals, terminal definition, error checking, flow control and network access.

In describing the basics of networking technology, it will be helpful to explain the different types of networks in use.

1.7.1 Local Area Networks (LANs)

A network is any collection of independent computers that exchange information with each other over a shared communication medium. Local Area Networks or LANs are usually confined to a limited geographic area, such as a single building or a college campus. LANs can be small, linking as few as three computers, but can often link hundreds of computers used by thousands of people. The development of standard networking protocols and media has resulted in worldwide proliferation of LANs throughout business and educational organizations.

- Typically connects computer in a single building or campus.
- Developed in 1970s.
- Medium: optical fibres, coaxial cables, twisted pair, wireless.
- Low latency (except in high traffic periods).
- High speed networks (0.2 to 100 Mb/sec).
- Speeds adequate for most distributed systems.
- Problems: Multi media based applications.
- Typically buses or rings.
- Ethernet, Token Ring

Table 1.1

Network Type	Data Transfer Rate
Ethernet	10 (upto 100) Mbits/s
FDDI	100 Mbits/s
Token Ring	4 or 16 Mbits/s
Apple LocalTalk	0.23 Mbits/s
Wireless	1-3 Mbits/s

1.7.2 Wide Area Networks (WANs)

Often elements of a network are widely separated physically. Wide area networking combines multiple LANs that are geographically separate. This is accomplished by connecting the several LANs with dedicated leased lines such as a T1 or a T3, by dial-up phone lines (both synchronous and asynchronous), by satellite links and by data packet carrier services. WANs can be as simple as a modem and a remote access server for employees to dial into or it can be as complex as hundreds of branch offices globally linked. Special routing protocols and filters minimize the expense of sending data over vast distances.

Wide Area Networks (WAN) refers to the technologies used to connect offices at remote locations. The size of a network is limited due to size and distance constraints. However, networks may be connected over a high speed communications link (called a WAN link) to link them together and thus become a WAN. WAN links are usually:

- **Dial up connection.**
- **Dedicated connection:** It is a permanent full-time connection. When a dedicated connection is used, the cable is leased rather than a part of the cable bandwidth and the user has exclusive use.
- **Switched network:** Several users share the same line or the bandwidth of the line. There are two types of switched networks:
  1. **Circuit switching:** This is a temporary connection between two points such as dial-up or ISDN.
  2. **Packet switching:** This is a connection between multiple points. It breaks data down into small packets to be sent across the network. A virtual circuit can improve performance by establishing a set path for data transmission. This will share some overhead of a packet switching network. A variant of packet switching is called cell-switching where the data is broken into small cells with a fixed length.

1.7.3 WAN Connection Technologies

- **X.25**: This is a set of protocols developed by the CCITT/ITU which specifies how to connect computer devices over a internetwork. These protocols use a great deal of error checking for use over unreliable telephone lines. Their speed is about 64 Kbps. Normally X.25 is used on packed switching PDNs (Public Data Networks). A line must be leased from the LAN to a PDN to connect to an X.25 network. A PAD (packet assembler/ disassembler) or an X.25 interface is used on a computer to connect to the X.25 network. CCITT is an abbreviation for International Telegraph and Telephone Consultative Committee. The ITU is the International Telecommunication Union.
- **Frame Relay:** Error checking is handled by devices at both sides of the connection. Frame relay uses frames of varying length and it operates at the data link layer of the OSI

model. A permanent virtual circuit (PVC) is established between two points on the network. Frame relay speed is between 56 Kbps and 1.544 Mbps. Frame relay networks provide a high-speed connection upto 1.544 Mbps using variable-length packet-switching over digital fiber-optic media.

- **Switched Multi-megabit Data Service (SMDS)** - Uses fixed length cell switching and runs at speeds of 1.533 to 45Mbps. It provides no error checking and assumes devices at both ends provide error checking.

- **Telephone connections**
  - Dial up.
  - **Leased lines:** These are dedicated analog lines or digital lines. Dedicated digital lines are called digital data service (DDS) lines. A modem is used to connect to analog lines, and a Channel Service Unit/Data Service Unit or Digital Service Unit (CSU/DSU) is used to connect to digital lines. The DSU connects to the LAN and the CSU connects to the line.
  - **T Carrier lines:** Multiplexors are used to allow several channels on one line. The T1 line is basic T Carrier service. The available channels may be used separately for data or voice transmissions or they may be combined for more transmission bandwidth. The 64 Kbps data transmission rate is referred to as DS-0 (Digital Signal level 0) and a full T1 line is referred to as DS-1.
  - T1 and T3 lines are the most common lines in use today. T1 and T2 lines can use standard copper wire. T3 and T4 lines require fiber-optic cable or other high-speed media. These lines may be leased partially called fractional T1 or fractional T3 which means a customer can lease a certain number of channels on the line. A CSU/DSU and a bridge or router is required to connect to a T1 line.
  - **Integrated Services Digital Network (ISDN):** Comes in two types and converts analog signals to digital for transmission.
    - **Basic Rate ISDN (BRI):** Two 64 Kbps B-channels with one 16 Kbps D channel. The D-channel is used for call control and setup.
    - **Primary Rate ISDN (PRI):** 23 B-channels and one D channel.
    A device resembling a modem (called an ISDN modem) is used to connect to ISDN. The computer and telephone line are plugged into it.
  Switched-56-A switched line similar to a leased line where customers pay for the time they use the line.

- **Asynchronous Transfer Mode (ATM):** May be used over a variety of media with both baseband and broadband systems. It uses fixed length data packets of 53 bytes called cell switching. 5 bytes contain header information. It uses hardware devices to perform the switching of the data. Speeds of upto 622 Mbps can be achieved. Error checking is done at the receiving device, not by ATM. A permanent virtual connection is established (PVC).

- **Synchronous Optical Network (SONET):** A physical layer standard that defines voice, data and video delivery methods over fiber optic media. It defines data rates in terms of Optical Carrier (OC) levels. The transmission rate of OC-1 is 51.8 Mbps. Each level runs at a multiple of the first. The OC-5 data rate is 5 times 51.8 Mbps which is 259 Mbps. SONET also defines Synchronous Transport Signals (STS) for copper media which use the same speed scale of OC levels. STS-3 runs at the same speed of OC-3. Mesh or ring topology is used to support SONET. SONET uses multiplexing. The ITU has incorporated SONET into their Synchronous Digital Hierarchy (SDH) recommendations.

Following are some concepts related with WAN:

  - Developed in 1960s.
  - Generally covers large distances (states, countries, continents).
  - Medium: communication circuits connected by routers.
  - Routers forwards packets from one to another following a route from the sender to the receiver. Store-and-Forward
  - Hosts are typically connected (or close to) the routers.
  - Typical latencies: 100ms - 500ms.
  - Problems with delays if using satellites.
  - Typical speed: 20 - 2000 Kbits/s.
  - Not (yet) suitable for distributed computing.
  - New standards are changing the landscape.

1.7.4 Wireless Local Area Networks (WLANs)

Wireless LANs, or WLANs, use Radio Frequency (RF) technology to transmit and receive data over the air. This minimizes the need for wired connections. WLANs give users mobility as they allow connection to a local area network without having to be physically connected by a cable. This freedom means users can access shared resources without looking for a place to plug in cables, provided that their terminals are mobile and within the designated network coverage area. With mobility, WLANs give flexibility and increased productivity, appealing to both entrepreneurs and to home users. WLANs may also enable network administrators to connect devices that may be physically difficult to reach with a cable.

The Institute for Electrical and Electronic Engineers (IEEE) developed the 802.11 specification for wireless LAN technology. 802.11 specifies over-the-air interface between a wireless client and a base station, or between two wireless clients. WLAN 802.11 standards also have security protocols that were developed to provide the same level of security as that of a wired LAN. The first of these protocols is Wired Equivalent Privacy (WEP). WEP provides security by encrypting data sent over radio waves from end point to end point.

The second WLAN security protocol is Wi-Fi Protected Access (WPA). WPA was developed as an upgrade to the security features of WEP. It works with existing products that are WEP-enabled but provides two key improvements: improved data encryption through the temporal key integrity protocol (TKIP) which scrambles the keys using a hashing algorithm. It has means for integrity-checking to ensure that keys have not been tampered with. WPA also provides user authentication with the extensible authentication protocol (EAP).

Table 1.2: Wireless Protocols

Specification	Data Rate	Modulation Scheme	Security
802.11	1 or 2 Mbps in the 2.4 GHz band	FHSS, DSSS	WEP and WPA
802.11a	54 Mbps in the 5 GHz band	OFDM	WEP and WPA
802.11b/High Rate/Wi-Fi	11 Mbps (with a fallback to 5.5, 2, and 1 Mbps) in the 2.4 GHz band	DSSS with CCK	WEP and WPA
802.11g/ Wi-Fi	54 Mbps in the 2.4 GHz band	OFDM when above 20Mbps, DSSS with CCK when below 20Mbps	WEP and WPA

1.7.5 Metropolitan Area Networks (MAN)

- Generally covers towns and cities (50 kms).
- Developed in 1980s.
- Medium: optical fibres, cables.
- Data rates adequate for distributed computing applications.
- A typical standard is DQDB (Distributed Queue Dual Bus).
- Typical latencies: < 1 msec.
- Message routing is fast.

1.7.6 Physical Structure

In network two or more device connected through links. Link is nothing but the communication path way between network devices. For communication two devices must be connected in some way at same time. There are two connections are used:

1. Multiple connection and 2. Point-to-point connection.

1.7.7 Network Topology

- Two or more devices connect to a link; two or more links form a topology. The physical topology of a network refers to the configuration of cables, computers, and other peripherals.

- The topology of a network is the geometric representation of the relationship of all the links and linking devices (usually called *nodes*) to one another. A node is an active device connected to the network, such as a computer or a printer. A node can also be a piece of networking equipment such as a hub, switch or a router.

- Topology defines the physical or logical arrangement of links in a network.

- A topology defines how nodes/stations are connected.

- **Topology** The map of a network. Physical topology describes where the cables are run and where the workstations, nodes, routers, and gateways are located. Networks are usually configured in bus, ring, star, or mesh topologies. Logical topology refers to the paths that messages take to get from one user on the network to another.

- In short, topology is the physical layout of computers, cables, switches, routers, and other components of a network. This term can also refer to the underlying network architecture, such as Ethernet or Token Ring. The word "topology" comes from topos, which is Greek for "place."

- When you design a network, your choice of topology will be determined by the size, architecture, cost, and management of the network. Basic network topologies include the following:

  - **Bus topology:**

    The stations are connected in a linear fashion. An example is the 10Base2 form of Ethernet.

  - **Star topology:**

    The stations are connected to a single concentrating device called a hub (Ethernet) or a Multistation Access Unit, or MAU (Token Ring physical topology).

  - **Ring topology:**

    The stations are connected in a ring. Examples are Fiber Distributed Data Interface, or FDDI (logical and physical ring), and Token Ring (logical ring and physical star).

  - **Mesh topology:**

    The stations are connected in a complex, redundant pattern. This topology is generally used only in wide area networks (WANs) in which different networks are connected using routers.

Note: The term "topology" can refer to either a network's physical topology, which is the actual physical layout or pattern of the cabling, or its logical topology, which is the path that signals actually take around the network. This difference is most evident in Token Ring networks, whose cabling is physically arranged in a star, but whose signal flows in a ring from one component to the next. The term "topology" without any further description is usually assumed to mean the physical layout.

Now we will study above topologies in detail.

Types of network topologies

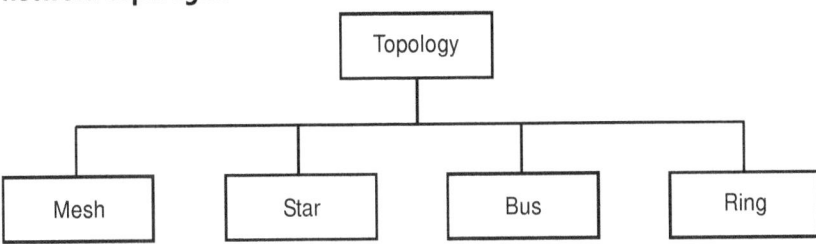

Fig. 1.5: Categories of topologies

1. Ring Topology:

- Each device has a dedicated point-to-point line configuration only with the two devices on either side of it. (Dedicated means that the link carries traffic only between the two devices is connects.) Nodes form a ring by point-to-point links to adjacency neighbours.

- A signal is passed along the ring in one dirn, from device to device, until it reaches its destination.

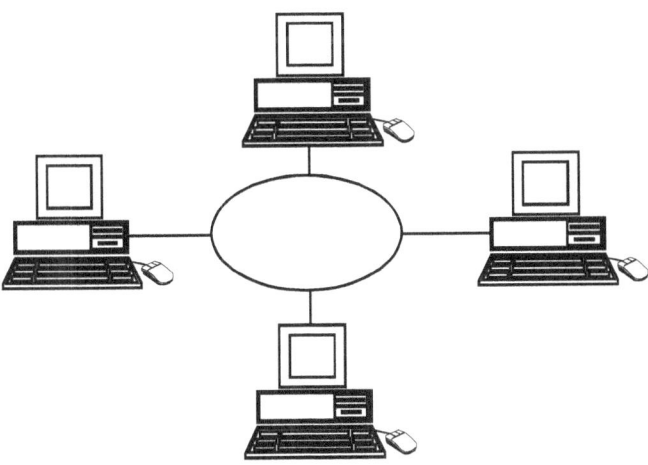

Fig. 1.6: Ring Topology

- Each device in the ring incorporates a repeater. When a device receives a signal intended for another device, its repeater regenerates the bits and passes them along.

- Computers are connected on a single circle of cable. Each computer acts as a repeater and keeps the signal strong, that is, there is no need for repeaters on a ring topology. Token passing is used in Token Ring networks. The token is passed from one computer to the next, only the computer with the token can transmit. The receiving computer strips the data from the token and sends the token back to the sending computer with an acknowledgment. After verification, the token is regenerated.

- Ring topology is a network topology in the form of a closed loop or circle, with each node in the network connected to the next. Messages move in one direction around the system. When a message arrives at a node, the node examines the address information in the message. If the address matches the node's address, the message is accepted; otherwise, the node regenerates the signal and places the message back on the network for the next node in the system. It is this regeneration that allows a ring network to cover greater distances than star networks or bus networks. Ring networks normally use some form of token-passing protocol to regulate network traffic. The failure of a single node can disrupt network operations; however, fault tolerant techniques have been developed to allow the network to continue to function in the event one or more nodes fail.

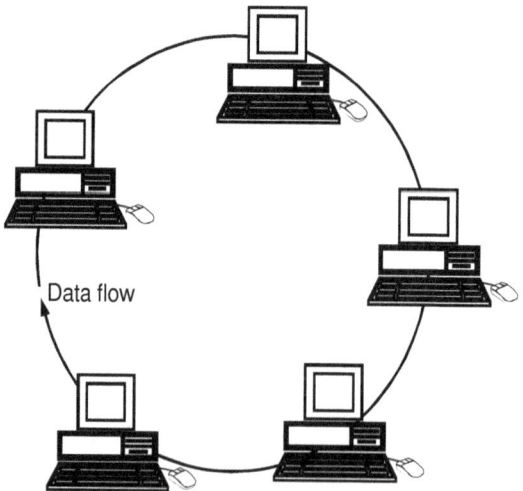

Fig. 1.7: Ring network

- Ring topology usually seen in a Token Ring or FDDI (fiber optic) network.

- **Example of ring topology:** In ring topology each node functions as a repeater. Suppose ring operates in clockwise direction i.e. data is transferred from one node to another in clockwise direction and node "B" wants to transmit data to node "A". Node "B" will first prepare the frame, then forward it towards node "C". Node "C" examines the frame and ignore it. Node "C" simply forward it to node "A". Node "A" accepts the frame, because its intended for it.

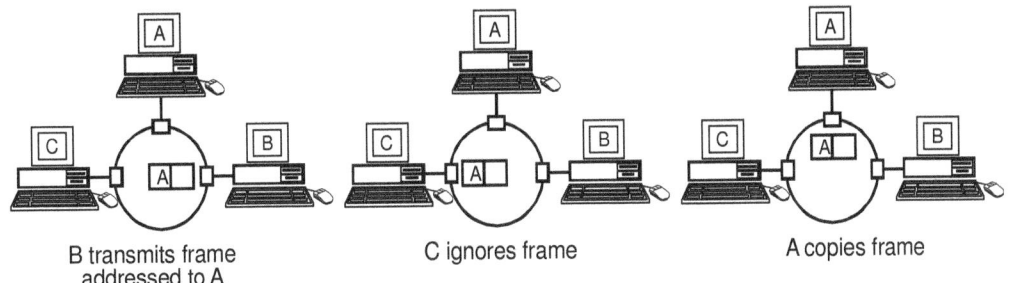

B transmits frame   C ignores frame   A copies frame
addressed to A

Fig. 1.8: Example of Ring topology

The major disadvantage of a physical ring topology is its sensitivity to single link failure. If one connection between two stations fails or a bypass for a particular inactive station is malfunctioning, the ring traffic is down.

➢ **Advantages**
1. Require less cabling so is less expensive.
2. Fault isolation is simplified. Generally in a ring, a signal is circulating at all times. If one device does not receive a signal within a specified period, it can issue an alarm. The alarm alerts the network operator to the problem and its location.

➢ **Disadvantages**
1. Traffic is unidirectional.
2. If one node goes down, it takes down the whole network.
3. Slow.
4. Reconfiguration: To add one node, whole network must be down first.

2. Bus Topology (or Linear bus topology, or Horizontal topology))
In networking, a topology that allows all network nodes to receive the same message through the network cable at the same time is called as bus topology.
- The **bus** pattern connects the computer to the same communications line. In bus topology all nodes/stations are connected to common link/medium.
- Communications goes both directions along the line.
- It is a multipoint configuration.

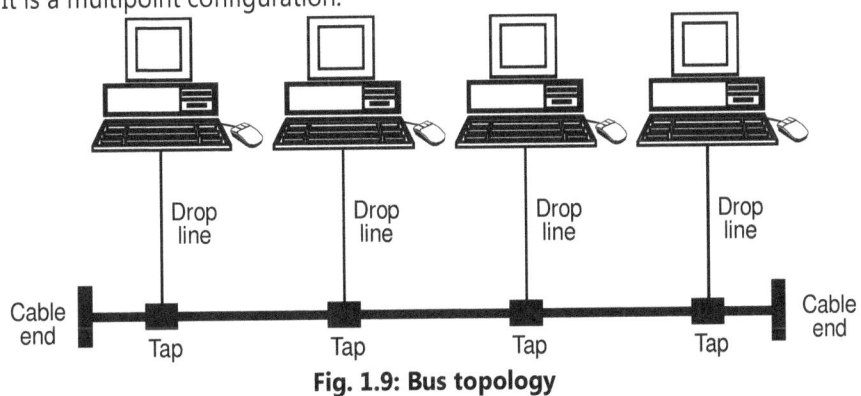

Fig. 1.9: Bus topology

- One long cable acts as a backbone to link all the devices in a network.
- Nodes are connected to the bus by drop lines and tap.
- A drop line is a connection running between a device and the main cable.
- A tap is a connector that either splices into the main cable or punctures the sheathing of a cable to create a contact with the metallic core.
- A bus topology consists of a main run of cable with a terminator at each end. All nodes (file server, workstations, and peripherals) are connected to the linear cable. Ethernet and LocalTalk networks use a linear bus topology.
- A network that uses a bus topology is referred to as a "Bus Network."

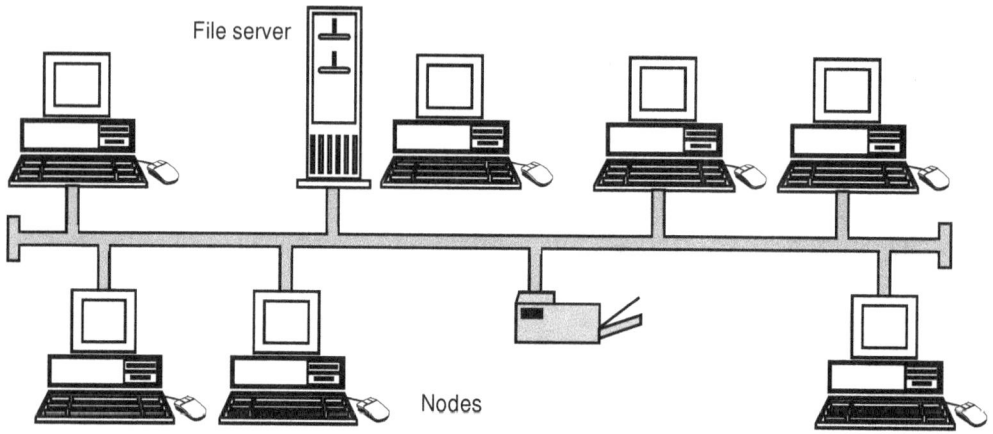

Fig. 1.10: A Bus network

- As a signal travels along the backbone, some of its energy is transformed into heat. Therefore, it becomes weaker and weaker as it has to travel farther and farther. For this reason there is limit on the number of taps a bus can support and on the distance between those taps.
- Bus topology is the cheapest way of connecting computers to form a workgroup or departmental LAN, but it has the disadvantage that a single loose connection or cable break can bring down the entire LAN.
- Bus consists of a single linear cable called a trunk. Data is sent to all computers on the trunk. Each computer examines EVERY packet on the wire to determine whom the packet is for and accepts only messages addressed to them. Bus is a passive topology. Performance degrades as more computers are added to the bus. Signal bounce is eliminated by a terminator at each end of the bus. Barrel connectors can be used to lengthen cable. Repeaters can be used to regenerate signals. Usually bus topology uses *Thinnet* or *Thicknet*. Both of these require 50-ohm terminator. Bus topology is good for a temporary, small (fewer than 10 people) network. But it's difficult to isolate malfunctions and if the backbone goes down, the entire network goes down.

Example of Bus topology: Suppose node "A" wants to transfer data to node "D" as shown in Fig. In bus topology all nodes will receive the packet sent by node "A" to node "D" bcoz of common/same medium/link used by all nodes. Node "B" and node "C" will reject the packet while node "D" will accept the packet.

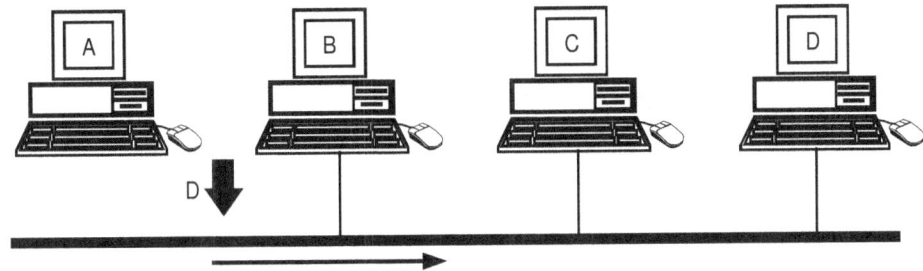

Fig. 1.11: Example of Bus topology

➢ **Advantages**
   1. Easy to install. It's very easy to connect a computer or peripheral to a bus.
   2. Requires less cabling length so cheaper.
   3. Any one computer or device being down does not affect the others.
   4. Fast as compare to ring topology.

➢ **Disadvantages**
   1. Can't connect a large number of computers.
   2. Difficult faulty isolation. A fault or break in the bus cable stops all transmission. Difficult to identify the problem if the entire network shuts down.
   3. Collision may occur.
   4. Signal reflection at the taps can cause degradation in quality.
   5. Entire network shuts down if there is a break in the main cable.
   6. Terminators are required at both ends of the backbone cable.
   7. Not meant to be used as a stand-alone solution in a large building.

3. **Star Topology**
   ▪ The devices are not directly linked to one another. A star topology does not allow direct traffic between devices.
   ▪ Each device has a dedicated point-to-point link to central controller, usually called a **hub** or **switch.**
   ▪ The controller acts as an exchange: If one device wants to send data to another, it sends the data to the controller, which then relays the data to the other connected device.

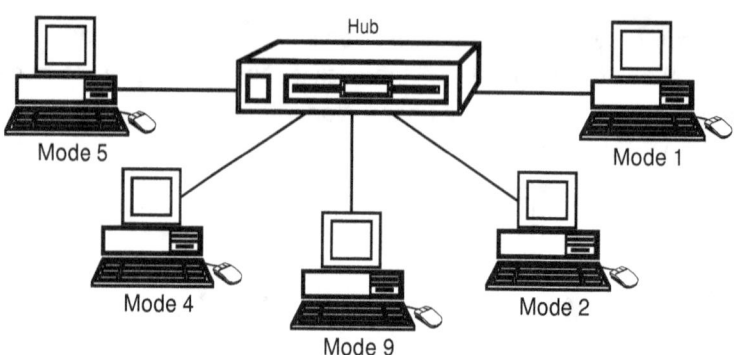

Fig. 1.12: Star Topology

At the center of the star is a wiring hub or concentrator, and the nodes or workstations are arranged around the central point representing the points of the star. Wiring costs tend to be higher for star networks than for other configurations, because each node requires its own individual cable. Star networks do not follow any of the IEEE standards.

A star topology is designed with each node (file server, workstations, and peripherals) connected directly to a central network hub or concentrator. Data on a star network passes through the hub or concentrator before continuing to its destination. The hub or concentrator manages and controls all functions of the network. It also acts as a repeater for the data flow. This configuration is common with twisted pair cable; however, it can also be used with coaxial cable or fiber optic cable.

The protocols used with star configurations are usually *Ethernet* or *LocalTalk*. Computers are connected by cable segments to a centralized hub. Signal travels through the hub to all other computers. Star topology requires more cable. If hub goes down, entire network goes down. If a computer goes down, the network functions normally.

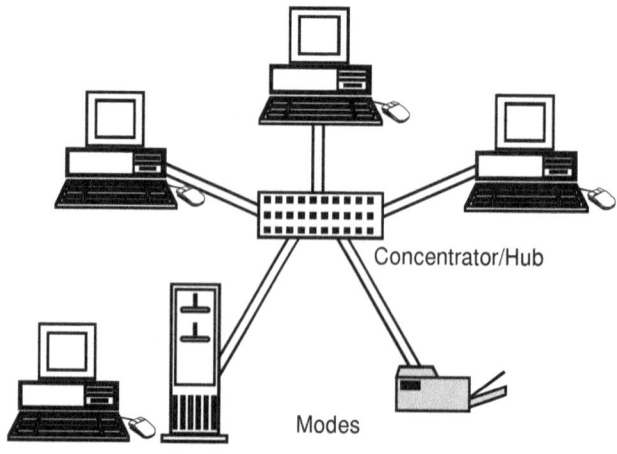

Fig. 1.13 (a): Star network

- **Example of star topology:** In star topology each station or node attached to central node (may be hub or switch). Suppose node "C" wants to transfer data to node "A". If hub is use as a central node then it will broadcast packet to each every other node but only station/node "A" copies the packet and all other nodes discard the packet. But if switch is used as a central node then it will directly sent the packet only to node "A".

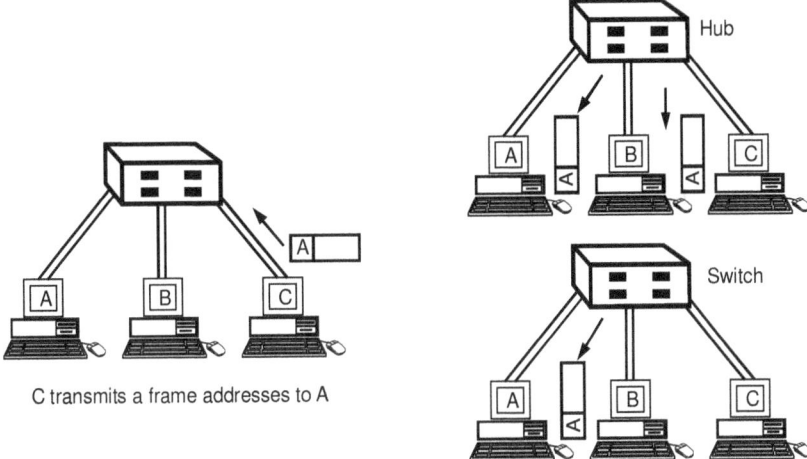

Fig. 1.13 (b): Example of star topology

➢ **Advantages**
1. Easy to install, reconfigure and wire.
2. Robustness: If one link fails, only that link is affected.
3. Fast as compare to ring topology.
4. Multiple devices can transfer data without collision.
5. Eliminates Traffic problem.
6. No disruptions to the network then connecting or removing devices.
7. Easy to detect faults and to remove parts.
8. Supported by several hardware and software venders.

➢ **Disadvantages**
1. If central node (hub or switch) goes down then entire network goes down.
2. More cabling is required than bus topology, so expensive than bus topology.
3. More expensive than bus topologies because of the cost of the concentrators (hub or switch).

4. **Tree Topology (or Hierarchical topology)**

A *tree topology* is variation of a star topology. In tree topology not every device plugs to the central hub. The majority of devices connect to a secondary hub that in turn is connected to the central hub.

> **Advantages**

1. Easy to install, reconfigure and wire.
2. Robustness: If one link fails, only that link is affected.
3. Fast as compare to ring topology.
4. Multiple devices can transfer data without collision.
5. Eliminates Traffic problem.
6. No disruptions to the network then connecting or removing devices.
7. Easy to detect faults and to remove parts.
8. Supported by several hardware and software venders.

> **Advantages in addition to star topology:**

1. More devices can be attached due to secondary hub or switch.
2. Due to secondary devices distance signal can travel are increases.

Disadvantages

1. If central node (hub or switch) goes down then entire network goes down.
2. More cabling is required than bus topology, so expensive than bus topology.
3. More expensive than bus topologies because of the cost of the concentrators (hub or switch).

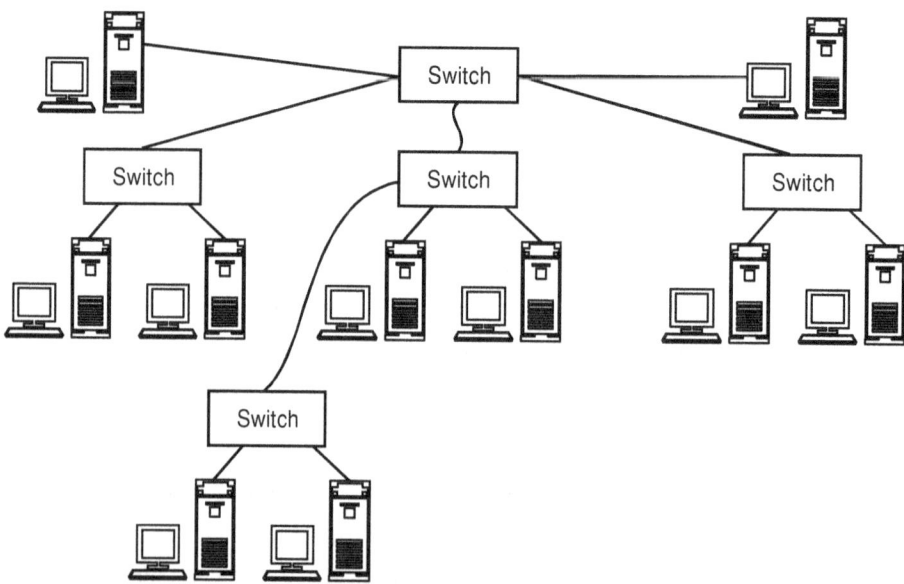

Fig. 1.14: Tree Topology

A tree topology can also combines characteristics of linear bus and star topologies. It consists of groups of star-configure workstations connected to a linear bus backbone cable. Tree topologies allow for the expansion of an existing network, and enable schools to configure a network to meet their needs.

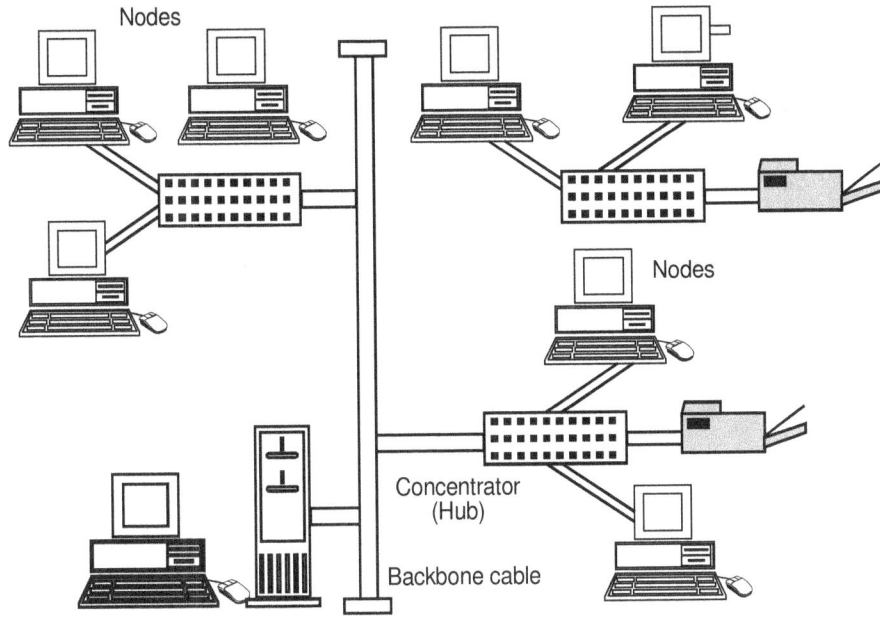

Fig. 1.15: A tree network

5. Mesh Topology

- Each device has a dedicated point-to-point link to every other device.
- The mesh topology connects each computer on the network to the others.

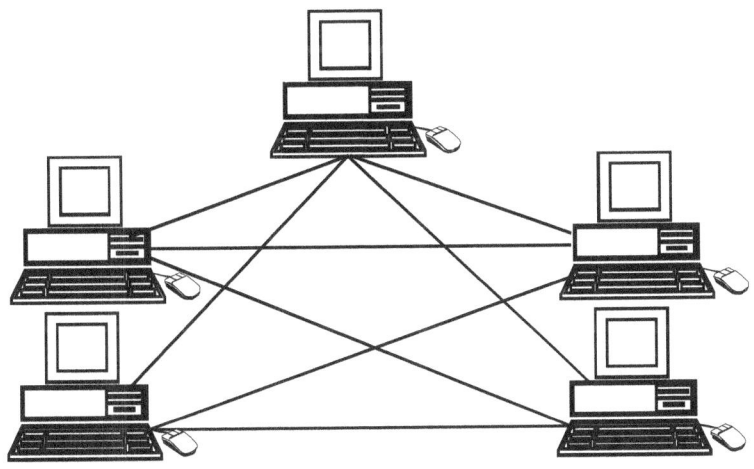

Fig. 1.16: Mesh Topology

- Fully connected mesh network has *n(n-1)/2* links for *n* devices.
- To accommodate n(n-1)/2 links, every device on the network must have *n-1 input/output (I/O) ports.*

- Meshes use a significantly larger amount of network cabling than do the other network topologies, which makes it more expensive.
- The mesh topology is highly fault tolerant. That is, every computer has multiple possible connection paths to the other computers on the network, so a single cable break will not stop network communications between any two computers.

A network topology in which every device is connected by a cable to every other device on the network. Multiple links to each device are used to provide network link redundancy.

Mesh Network

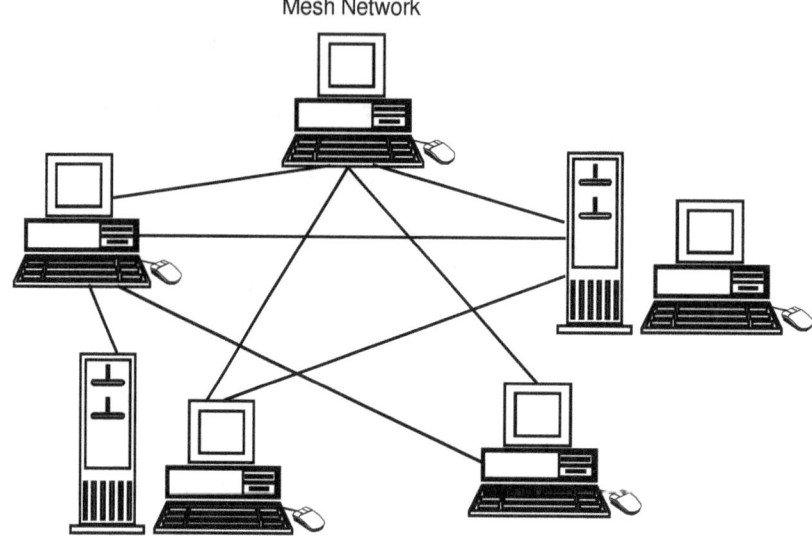

Fig. 1.17: Mesh network

➢ **Advantages**

1. Each connection can carry its own data load due to dedicated link.
2. Eliminates Traffic problem.
3. Mesh topology is robust. If one link becomes unusable, it doesn't affect other systems.
4. Privacy or security bcoz of dedicated line.
5. Point-to-point link make fault identification easy.

➢ **Disadvantages**

1. More cables are required than other topologies
2. N-1 Input/Output ports are required for N devices.
3. Installation and reconfiguration is very difficult bcoz each device must be connected to every other device.
4. Expensive due to hardware requirements such as cables and input/output ports.

6. Hybrid Topology

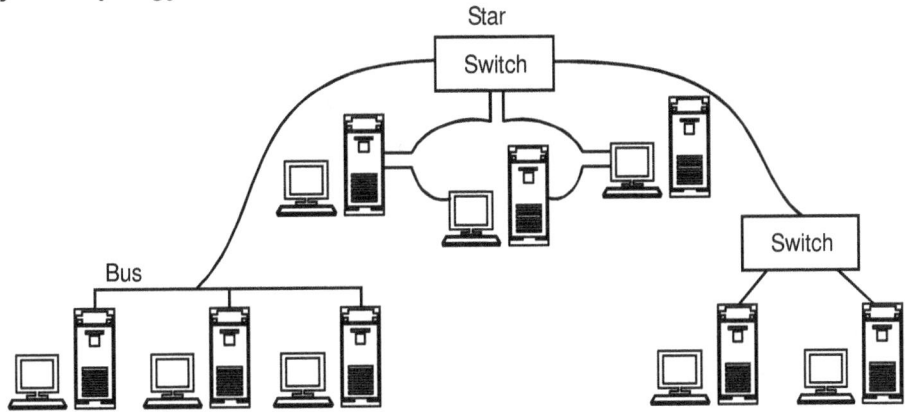

Fig. 1.18: Hybrid Topology

Considerations When Choosing a Topology:

- **Money:** A bus network may be the least expensive way to install a network; you do not have to purchase concentrators.
- **Length of cable needed:** The linear bus network uses shorter lengths of cable.
- **Future growth:** With a star topology, expanding a network is easily done by adding another concentrator.
- **Cable type:** The most common cable in organization is unshielded twisted pair, which is most often used with star topologies

Table 1.3: Summary chart

Physical Topology	Common Cable	Common Protocol
Linear Bus (or Bus)	Twisted Pair, Coaxial, Fiber	Ethernet LocalTalk
Star	Twisted Pair, Fiber	Ethernet LocalTalk
Tree	Twisted Pair, Coaxial, Fiber	Ethernet

1.7.8 Categories of Networks

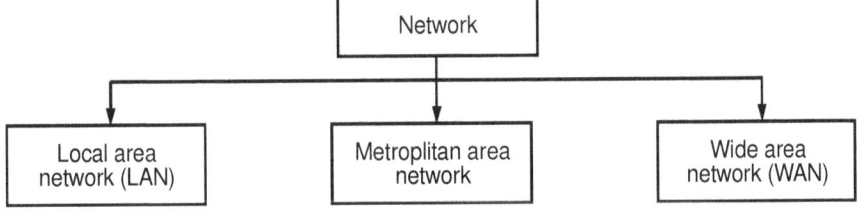

Fig. 1.19: Types of Networks

- Its size, its ownership, distance it covers, and its physical architecture can determine types of network.

1. Local Area Network (LAN)

- A group of computers and associated peripheral devices connected by a communications channel, capable of sharing files and other resources among several users.
- **LAN** is usually privately owned and links the devices in a single office, building, or campus.
- LAN can be as simple as two PCs and a printer. Local area networks or LANs enable computer-based equipment to communicate and share resources. The products that make up a LAN consist of computers, adapters, media and software.
- LAN size is limited to few kilometers. One of the main capabilities of a local area network is resource sharing, such as data and expensive peripherals. This ability to share resources can mean a decrease in the cost of an individual workstation, since not every workstation may need its own printer or hard disk.
- LAN is a group of computers located in the same room, on the same floor, or in the same building that are connected to form a single network. Local area networks (LANs) allow users to share storage devices, printers, applications, data, and other network resources. They are limited to a specific geographical area, usually less than 2 kilometers in diameter. They might use a dedicated backbone to connect multiple subnetworks, but they do not use any telecommunication carrier circuits or leased lines except to connect with other LANs to form a wide area network (WAN).
- A network is any collection of independent computers that communicate with one another over a shared network medium. LANs are networks usually confined to a geographic area, such as a single building or a college campus. LANs can be small, linking as few as three computers, but often link hundreds of computers used by thousands of people. The development of standard networking protocols and media has resulted in worldwide proliferation of LANs throughout business and educational organizations.
- LANs are distinguished from other types of networks by their transmission media and topology. In general, a given LAN will use one type of transmission medium. The most common LAN topologies are bus, ring and star.

Characteristics of LAN

- Confined within geographical area.
- Relatively high data rate.
- Under single management
- Ingredients
  - *Topology:* bus, star, ring.
  - *Medium:* Twisted pair, coaxial, fiber optic cable, wireless.
  - *Medium access techniques:* protocols to access or coordinate the medium.

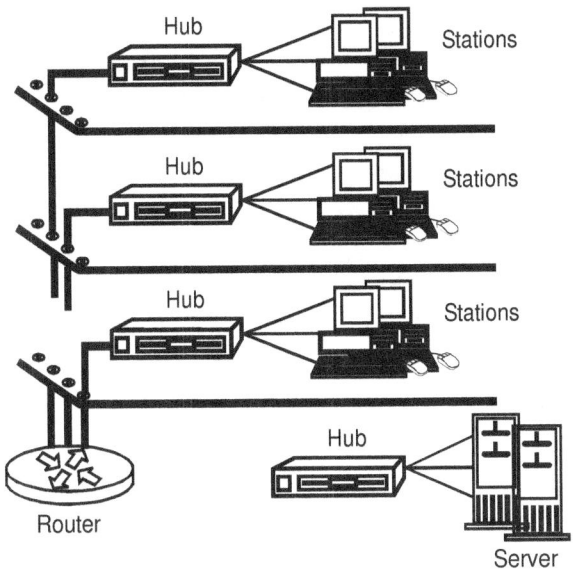

Fig. 1.20: LAN

- LAN have data rate 10 to 100 Mbps.

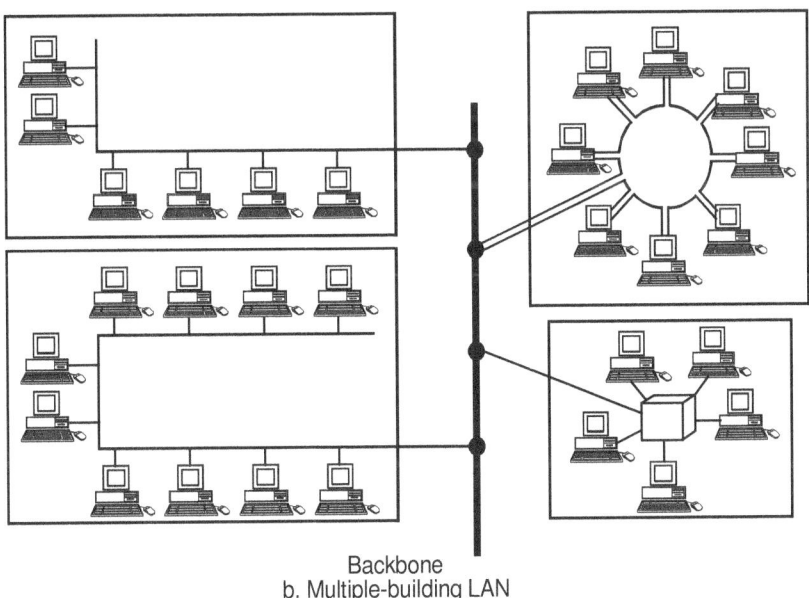

Backbone
b. Multiple-building LAN

Fig. 1.21: LAN

How It Works?

Before you can link computers into a LAN, you must install a network-aware operating system on them to enable them to share resources. The choice of operating system depends on whether the network will be a peer-to-peer network or a server-based network. Microsoft Windows 98 is a good choice for peer-to-peer workgroup LANs, while Windows NT and Windows 2000 offer the security and scalability needed to support a server-based network.

Next, you choose a networking architecture. (The vast majority of LANs use Ethernet.) Then you must install a suitable network interface card (NIC) in an available slot on the motherboard of each node (computer) in the network. You must also install a software driver to control the card's functions. You use cabling to join the NICs in order to enable the computers to communicate with each other. The most common type of cabling used in LANs is unshielded twisted-pair (UTP) cabling. The cabling is installed in some kind of topology or layout, the most popular of which is the cascaded star topology used in the 10BaseT version of Ethernet. You then choose a protocol to enable the nodes on the network to speak a common "language"; the most popular protocol is TCP/IP, especially for Internet connectivity, although for small stand-alone workgroup LANs that use Windows 95 or Windows 98/Me, NetBEUI is still popular.

Wireless LANs

Fig. 1.22: Wireless LAN

Not all networks are connected with cabling; some networks are wireless. Wireless LANs use high frequency radio signals, infrared light beams, or lasers to communicate between the workstations and the file server or hubs. Each workstation and file server on a wireless network has some sort of transceiver/antenna to send and receive the data. Information is relayed between transceivers as if they were physically connected. For longer distance, wireless communications can also take place through cellular telephone technology, microwave transmission, or by satellite.

Wireless networks are great for allowing laptop computers or remote computers to connect to the LAN. Wireless networks are also beneficial in older buildings where it may be difficult or impossible to install cables.

2. Metropolitan Area Network (MAN)

A public, high-speed network, capable of voice and data transmission over a distance of up to 80 kilometers (50 miles). A MAN is smaller than a wide-area network (WAN) but larger than a local-area network (LAN). **MAN** is designed to extend over an entire city. Multiple local area networks (LANs) that are connected on a campus or industrial complex using a high-speed backbone. Multiple networks that are connected within the same city to form a citywide network for a specific government or industry. Any network bigger than a LAN but smaller than a wide area network (WAN) is called as MAN. Fiber Distributed Data Interface

(FDDI) is a good network technology for building a metropolitan area network (MAN). A MAN may be wholly owned and operated by a private company. Number of LANs connected so that resources may be shared LAN-to-LAN as well as device-to-device. For e.g. Cable television network.

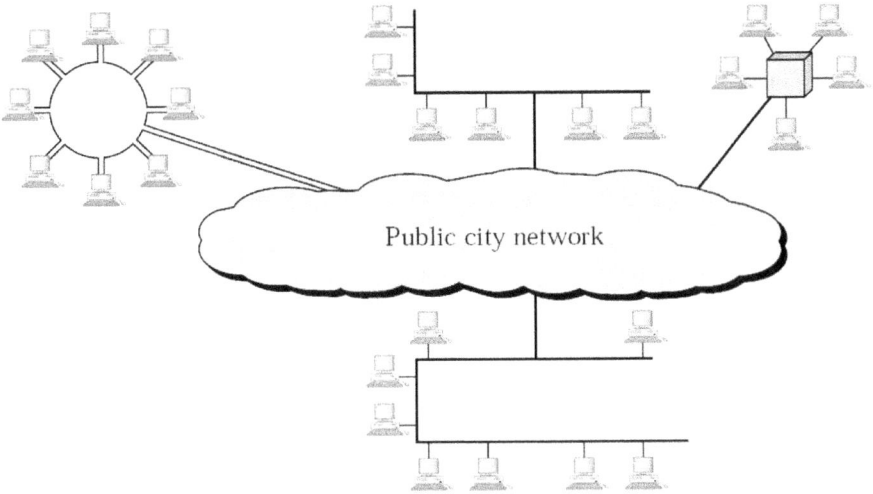

Fig. 1.23: MAN

3. Wide Area Network (WAN)

- A network that connects users across large distances, often crossing the geographical boundaries of cities or states.
- A **WAN** provides long-distance transmission of data, voice, image, and video information over large geographical areas that may comprise a country, or even whole world.
- A geographically distributed network composed of local area networks (LANs) joined into a single large network using services provided by common carriers. Wide area networks (WANS) are commonly implemented in enterprise networking environments in which company offices are in different cities, states, or countries or on different continents.

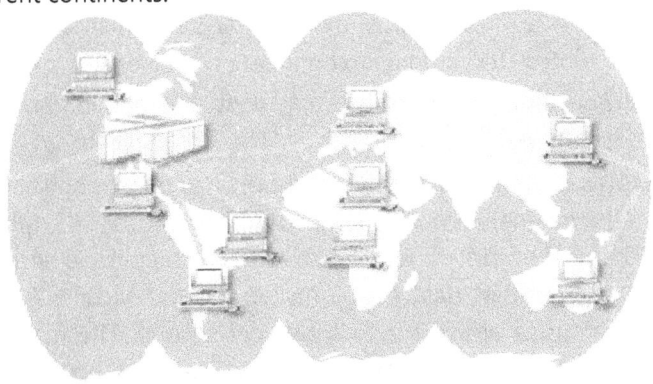

Fig. 1.24: WAN

- WANs utilize public, leased, or private communication devices.
- A WAN that is wholly owned and used by a single company is often referred to as an enterprise network.
- Wide area networking combines multiple LANs that are geographically separate. This is accomplished by connecting the different LANs using services such as dedicated leased phone lines, dial-up phone lines (both synchronous and asynchronous), satellite links, and data packet carrier services. Wide area networking can be as simple as a modem and remote access server for employees to dial into, or it can be as complex as hundreds of branch offices globally linked using special routing protocols and filters to minimize the expense of sending data sent over vast distances.
- WAN's span more than one geographical area and are used to connect remote offices to each other. Basically, a WAN is comprised of two or more LAN's joined together by routers. Routers are hardware devices that direct traffic from one LAN to another. A WAN would be found in medium to large sized businesses with more than one office location. For example, a software company might have its headquarters in Dallas, but also have remote office locations in Austin and Ft. Worth. The LAN in the Dallas office would be connected to the LAN in the remote offices forming a WAN.
- WAN technologies were previously limited to expensive leased lines such as T1 lines, slow packet-switching services such as X.25, cheap but low-bandwidth solutions such as modems, and dial-up Integrated Services Digital Network (ISDN) connections, but this has changed considerably in recent years. Frame relay services provide high-speed packet-switching services that offer more bandwidth than X.25, and virtual private networks (VPNs) created using Internet Protocol (IP) tunneling technologies enable companies to securely connect branch offices by using the Internet as a backbone service. Intranets and extranets provide remote and mobile users with access to company resources and applications and provide connectivity with business partners and resellers. Wireless networking technologies allow roaming users to access network resources by using cell-based technologies. Digital Subscriber Line (DSL) services provide T1 speeds at much lower costs than dedicated T1 circuits. These and other new technologies continue to evolve and proliferate, allowing enterprise network administrators to implement and administer a highly diverse range of WAN solutions.
- LAN's and WAN's come in many different flavors. The most popular type of network is Ethernet. Ethernet networks have speeds of 10 Mbps, 100 Mbps, or 1 Gbps. A 10 Mbps Ethernet network transmits data at 10 million bits per second. A 100 Mbps Ethernet network transmits data at 100 million bits per second. A 1 Gbps Ethernet network transmits data at 1000 million bits per second. The majority of networks today operate at 100Mbps. 1Gbps networks, however, are becoming more common as technology and bandwidth demand increases.

1.8 Protocol hierarchy

In data communication, the communication occurs between entities in different systems. The Entity is capable for sending or receiving the data or information between network devices. For communication the entity must agree on a protocol. A protocol defines:

1. What is communicated?
2. How is communicated?
3. When it is communicated?

A protocol is a set of rules that govern data communication.

A protocol consists of:

1. **Syntax:** It is refers to structure of the data and meaning the order in which they are presented.
2. **Timing:** It is refers to two characters. When data should be sent and how fast they can be sent.
3. **Semantics:** It is refers to the meaning of the each section of bits.

In Open Systems Architecture (OSI), the distribution of network protocol among the various layers of the network.

1.8.1 Open Systems Architecture

The layered hierarchical structure, configuration or model of a communications or distributed data processing system that:

(a) Enables system description, design, development, installation, operation, improvement and

(b) Allows each layer to provide a set of accessible functions that can be controlled and used by the functions in the layer above it.

(c) Enables each layer to be implemented without affecting the implementation of other layers and

(d) Allows the alteration of system performance by the modification of one or more layers without altering the existing equipment, procedures and protocols at the remaining layers.

1.8.2 Network

An interconnection of three or more communicating entities.

An interconnection of usually passive electronic components that performs a specific function (which is usually limited in scope), e.g., to simulate a transmission line or to perform a mathematical function such as integration or differentiation.

1.8.3 Protocol

A formal set of conventions governing the format and control of interaction among communicating functional units.

Note: Protocols may govern portions of a network, types of service, or administrative procedures. For example, a data link protocol is the specification of methods whereby data communications over a data link are performed in terms of the particular transmission mode, control procedures, and recovery procedures.

In layered communications system architecture, a formal set of procedures that are adopted to facilitate functional interoperation within the layered hierarchy.

Set of rules and formats, semantic and syntactic, permitting information systems (IS's) to exchange information.

1.9 Design Issues for the Layer

- To reduce design complexity, most networks are organised as a series of layers or levels. Each one built upon the one below it.

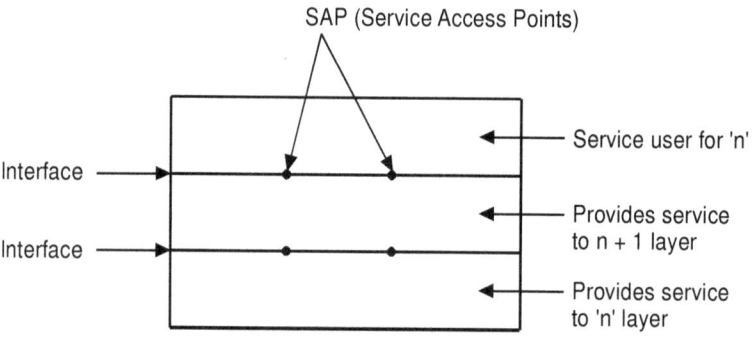

Fig. 1.25

- The number of layers, the name of each layer, the contents of each layer, and the function of each layer differs from network to network. However, in all networks, the purpose of each layer is to offer certain services to the higher layer.
- The function of each layer is to provide services to the layer above it. The active elements in each layer are often called entities. Entity can be software entity or hardware entity.
- The layered architecture concept redefines the way networks are conceived and creates significant cost savings and managerial benefits.
- Instead of building a separate network for each service, user can have multiple services sharing a common core network.
- Adding new services and managing the network infrastructure must be easy.
- That is why the layered architecture concept will become increasingly important for user.
- It offers opportunities to reduce capital and operating expenditure by offering a smooth step-by-step migration to IP.

- Key advantage is that network resources can be used more effectively in terms of simplicity and fewer equipment sites leading to lower total cost of ownership.
- Also, the need for transmission connections in the network can, in many cases, be reduced by more than 50 percent.

1.9.1 Benefits of Layered Designs

- Segmentation of high-level from low-level issues. Complex problems can be broken into smaller more manageable pieces.
- Since, the specification of a layer says nothing about its implementation, the implementation details of a layer are hidden (abstracted) from other layers.
- Many upper layers can share the services of a lower layer. Thus layering allows us to reuse functionality.
- Development by teams is aided because of the logical segmentation.
- Easier exchange of parts at a later date.

1.9.2 Downsides of Layered Designs

- The trouble with layers of computer software is that sooner or later you loose touch with reality. Layers are abstraction boundaries and the more they encapsulate their works the more one is unaware of the application's inner works.
- Layering is a form of information hiding. A "layering violation" occurs in situations where a layer uses knowledge of the implementation details of another layer in its own operations. At the limit this leads to changes to one layer resulting in changes to every other layer, which is an expensive and error prone proposition.
- Layering can lead to poor performance. To avoid this penalty, in situations where an upper layer can optimize its actions by knowing what a lower layer is doing, we can reveal information that would normally be hidden behind a layer boundary.
- The layers must be engineered at the outset, before the system is built.

1.10 Network Architecture Model

A set of layers and protocols is called **network architecture**.

Network's architecture can be described in two ways: peer to peer and client-server. A peer-to-peer network is a grouping of personal computers that all share information between each other. Peer-to-peer networks are usually comprised of less than ten computers.

This type of network fulfills the needs of users that require very little computer services and security. File storage is scattered among the computers, and security is extremely low. Peer-to-peer networks are very susceptible to hackers and other malicious users because there is no solid security policy enforced. A more organized approach to networking is client-server architecture. A client-server network is a network comprised of several workstations and one or more servers. Clients (users) log in to the server and gain access to their files. In client-server networks, an administrator can control the privileges of each user. Files are stored centrally, simplifying data backup. Security policies are implemented that protect users' information. Client-server architecture has become the de-facto standard in small, medium, and large businesses because of the advantages it offers.

Designing the architecture of a system requires model. A model helps in visualizing and understanding the structure of the system.

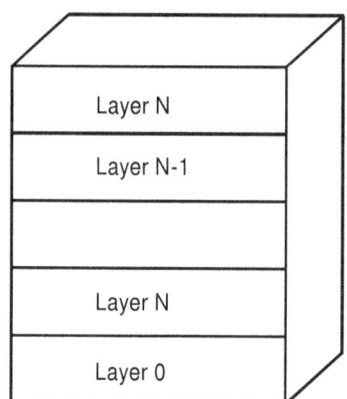

Fig. 1.26: Layered Architecture of a Computer Network

Each layer has an active element, a piece of hardware or software, which carries out the layer functions. It is called **layer entity**.

A *service* is a set of primitives (operations) that a layer provides to the layer above it.

Functionality of the Layered Architecture

Hierarchical communication: Communication between adjacent layers of a system. The messages exchanged between the adjacent layers during hierarchical communication are called Interface Control Information (ICI).

Peer-to-Peer communication: Communication between peer layers for carrying out an assigned set of functions.

Need for Standardization of Network Architecture

   IBM's System Network Architecture (SNA).

   Digital's Digital Network Architecture (DNA).

   Open System Interconnection (OSI) Reference Model developed by ISO (International Organization for Standardization).

   SNA and DNA are vendor-specific layered architecture while the OSI Model has been accepted as an international standard.

1.11 ISO/OSI Reference Model

- ISO/OSI is the organization. ISO/OSI is the model. In general, ISO/OSI defines standards by which computers can communicate together. ISO/OSI describes the architecture, protocols, and services that are needed to achieve this goal. There are multiple ISO/OSI standards. Some of these are complete, while others are still evolving.
- The term open system in ISO/OSI defines a computer system that can communicate with another computer system using the OSI protocol. What this means is that computer systems, having different operating systems which process data differently, can still communicate and interpret information upon receipt, if the information that passes between their processors conforms to the ISO international standards.
- The foundation of the ISO/OSI architecture is a layering concept, called the ISO/OSI Reference Model. Each layer in the ISO/OSI Reference Model has a name, a number, protocols that provide specific functions, and defined services. Because the various intended uses of ISO/OSI are very broad, spanning terminals, personal computers, and very large mainframes, different services and protocol options are available at each layer. This range of support can accommodate different connection requirements and environments.
- The Reference Model defined by ISO/OSI is also an excellent model to understand how networks work. Although there are many different architectures, standards and models the ISO/OSI Reference Model is mostly used to explain the different functions implemented in protocols from different layers and how these protocols work together.

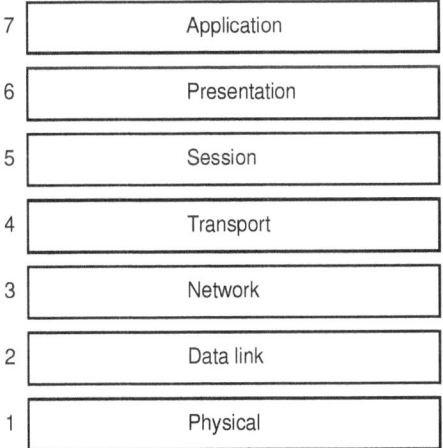

Fig. 1.27: The ISO/OSI Reference Model

- It is a layered framework for the design of network systems that allows for communication across all types of computer systems.
- International Standards Organization (ISO) specifications for network architecture.
- Called the Open Systems Interconnect or OSI model.
- Seven layered model, higher layers have more complex tasks.
- Each layer provides services for the next higher layer.

- Each layer communicates logically with its associated layer on the other computer.
- Packets are sent from one layer to another in the order of the layers, from top to bottom on the sending computer and then in reverse order on the receiving computer.
- Each layer performs a unique, generic, and well-defined function.
- Layer boundaries are designed so that the amount of information flowing between any two adjacent layers is minimized. This is accomplished by having each layer within an open system use the services provided by the layer below. Conversely, each layer provides a sufficient number of services to the layer immediately above it.

1.11.1 Layered Architecture of the OSI Reference Model

Each interface defines what information and services a layer must provide for the layer above it.

Layer 1, 2, and 3 are the network support layers; they deal with physical aspect of moving data from one device to another (such as electrical specification, physical connection) Layer 4, ensures end-to-end reliable data transmission. Layers 5, 6, and 7 are user support layer.

The upper OSI layers are almost always implemented by software; lower layers are a combination of hardware and software, except physical layer, which is mostly hardware.

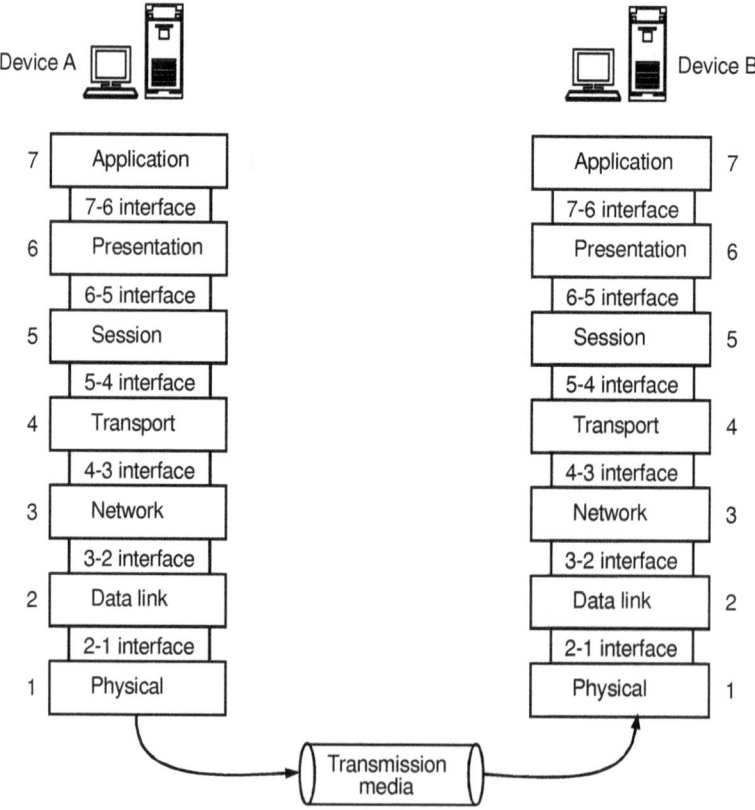

Fig. 1.28: Layered architecture of the ISO/OSI model

This layered approach was selected as a basis for the OSI Reference Model to provide flexibility and open-ended capability through defined interfaces. The interfaces permit some layers to be changed while leaving other layers unchanged. In principle, as long as standard interfaces to the adjacent layers are adhered to, an implementation can still work.

For example, a system implementation could use either HDLC or local area network protocols as the data link layer. Similarly, a particular layer such as the presentation layer, can be implemented as a null layer for the time being. This means the layer is functionally empty, providing only the mandatory interfaces between the upper and lower layers (application and session layers respectively).

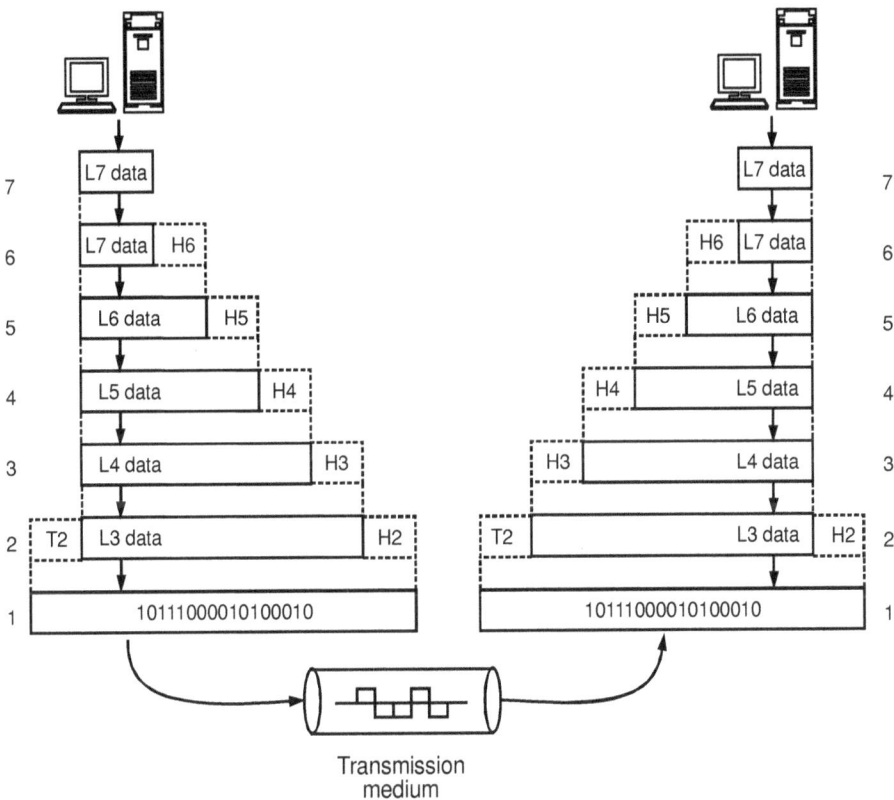

Fig. 1.29: Example of OSI Model

1.11.2 Functions of the ISO/OSI Layers

1. **Physical Layer**
   - Transmits the unstructured raw bit stream over a physical medium.
   - Relates the electrical, optical mechanical and functional interfaces to the cable.
   - Defines how the cable is attached to the network adapter card.
   - Defines data encoding and bit synchronization.

Physical layer deals with the mechanical and electrical specifications of the interface and transmission medium.

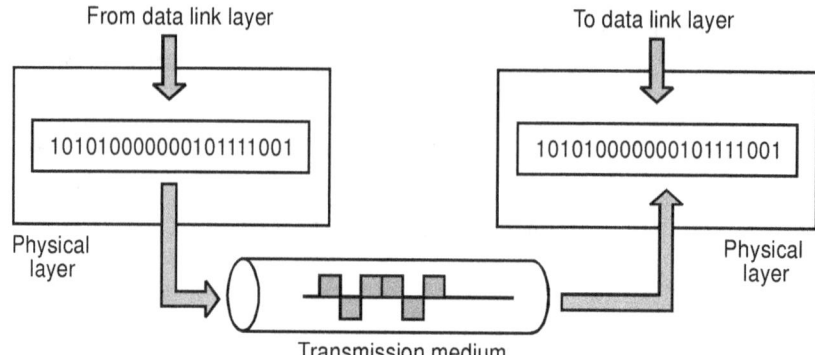

Fig. 1.30: Physical Layer

The physical layer concerned with the following:

- **Physical characteristics of interfaces and media:** Defines type of transmission medium.
- **Representation of bits:** Data consist of a stream of bits (0's and 1's). To be transmitted, bits must be encoded into signals-electrical or optical. The physical layer defines the type of **encoding**.
- **Data rate:** The **transmission rate**- the number of bits sent per second.
- **Synchronization of bits:** The sender and receiver clocks must be synchronized.
- **Physical topology:** It defines how devices are connected to make a network. For ex: a *star topology* (devices are connected through a central device), a *ring topology* (every device is connected to the next).
- **Transmission mode:** It defines direction of transmission between two devices: simplex, half-duplex, or full-duplex.

2. **Data Link Layer**
   - Sends data frames from the Network layer to the Physical layer.
   - Packages raw bits into frames for the Network layer at the receiving end.

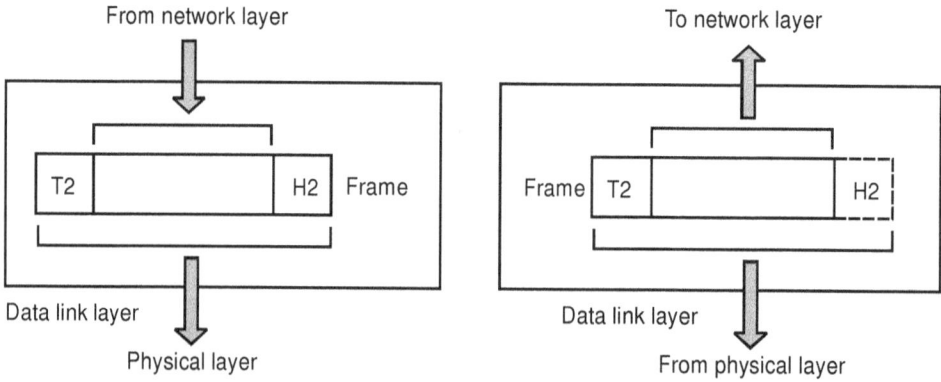

Fig. 1.31: Data Link Layer

- Responsible for providing error free transmission of frames through the Physical layer.

It makes the physical layer appear error free to the upper layer.

Responsibilities of the data link layer are as follows:

- **Framing:** The data link layer divides the stream of bits received from the network layer into manageable data units called frames.
- **Physical addressing:** If frames are distributed to different system on the network, the data link layer adds header to the frame to define the **physical address** of the sender (source address) and receiver address (destination address) of the frame. If the frame is intended for the system outside the sender's network, the receiver address is the address of device that connects one network to the next.
- **Flow control:** If the rate at which the data are absorbed by receiver is less than the rate produced in the sender, the data linker layer imposes a flow control mechanism.
- **Error control:** It adds reliability to the physical layer by adding mechanism to detect and retransmit damaged or lost frames. It also prevents duplication of frames.
- **Access control:** When two or more devices are connected to the same link, data link layer protocols determine which device has control over the link at any given time.

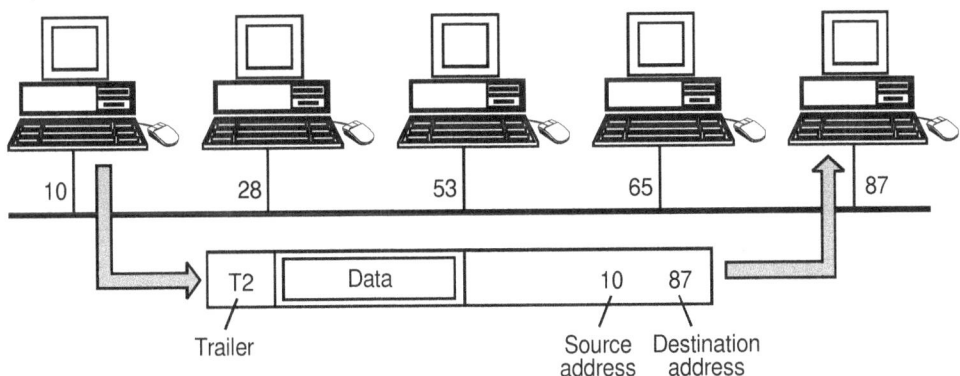

Fig. 1.32: Example of Data Link Layer

3. Network Layer
- Responsible for addressing messages and translating logical addresses and names into physical addresses.
- Determines the route from the source to the destination computer.
- Manages traffic such as packet switching, routing and controlling the congestion of data. The network layer is responsible for the source-to-destination delivery of a packet possibly across multiple networks (links). Whereas the data link layer oversees the delivery of the packet between two systems on the same network (links). If two systems are connected to the same link, there is usually no need for a network layer.

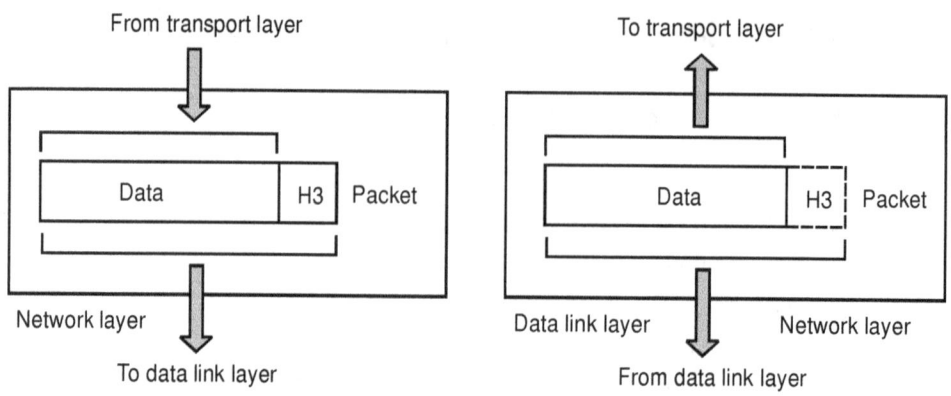

Fig. 1.33: Network Layer

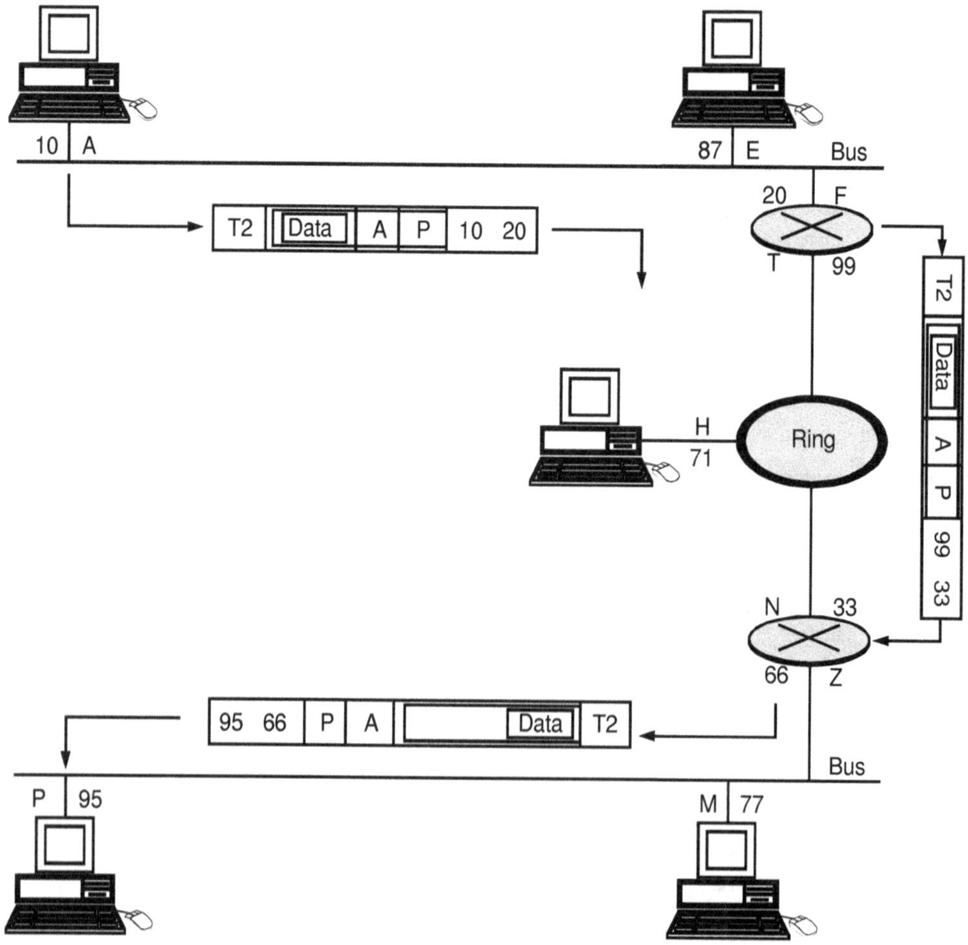

Fig. 1.34: Example of Network Layer

Responsibilities of Network layer:

- **Logical addressing:** The physical addressing implemented by the data link layer handles the addressing problem locally. If a packet passes the network boundary, then need of another addressing system to help to distinguish the source and destination systems.
- **Routing:** When independent networks or links are connected together to create an internetwork (a network of networks), the connecting devices (called router or gateway) route the packets to their final destination.

Example of Network Layer: The network (logical) address remains same from original source to the final destination (A, and P respectively). They will not change when packet moves network to network. However, the physical address will change when packet moves from one memory write to another.

4. **Transport Layer**
   - Responsible for packet creation.
   - Provides an additional connection level beneath the Session layer.
   - Ensures that packets are delivered error free, in sequence with no losses or duplications.
   - Unpacks, reassembles and sends receipt of messages at the receiving end.
   - Provides flow control, error handling and solves transmission problems.

The **transport layer** is responsible for **source-to-destination** (end-to-end) **delivery** of the entire message.

Network layer treats each packet independently, as though each packet belonged to a separate message, whether or not it does. Whereas the transport layer ensures that the whole message arrives intact and in order, overseeing both error control and flow control at the source-to-destination level.

Responsibilities of the transport layer are as follows:

Service-point addressing: Computers often run multiple programs at the same time. Source-to-destination delivery means delivery not only from one computer to the next but also from a specific process (running program) on the other. The transport layer header therefore must include a type of address called a service-point address (or **port address**).

The network layer delivers each packet to the correct destination computer; the transport layer delivers the entire message to the correct process on that computer.

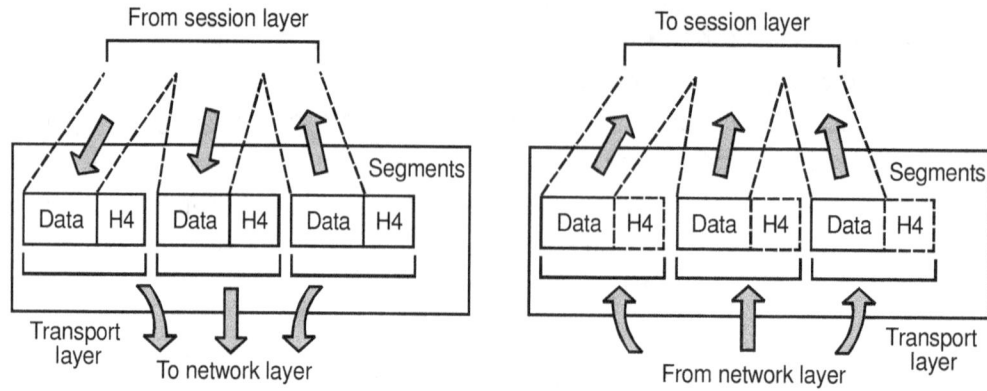

Fig. 1.35: Transport Layer

Segmentation and Reassembly: A message is divided into transmittable segments, each segment containing a sequence number. These numbers enable the transport layer to reassemble the message correctly upon arriving at the destination and to identify and replace packets that were lost in the transmission.

Connection control: It creates a connection between the two end ports. A connection is a single logical path between the source and destination that is associated with all packets in a message.

Flow control: Flow control at this level is performed end to end rather than across a single link.

Error control: Error control at this level is performed end to end rather than across a single link. The transport layer makes sure that the entire message arrives at the receiving transport layer without error (damage, loss or duplication).

Example of the transport layer:

Data coming from the upper layers have port addresses j and k (j is the address of the sending application and k is the address of the receiving application). If data size is larger than network layer can handle, the data are split into two packets.

Then in the network layer, network addresses are added to each packet. The packets may travel on different paths and arrive at the destination either in order or out of order.

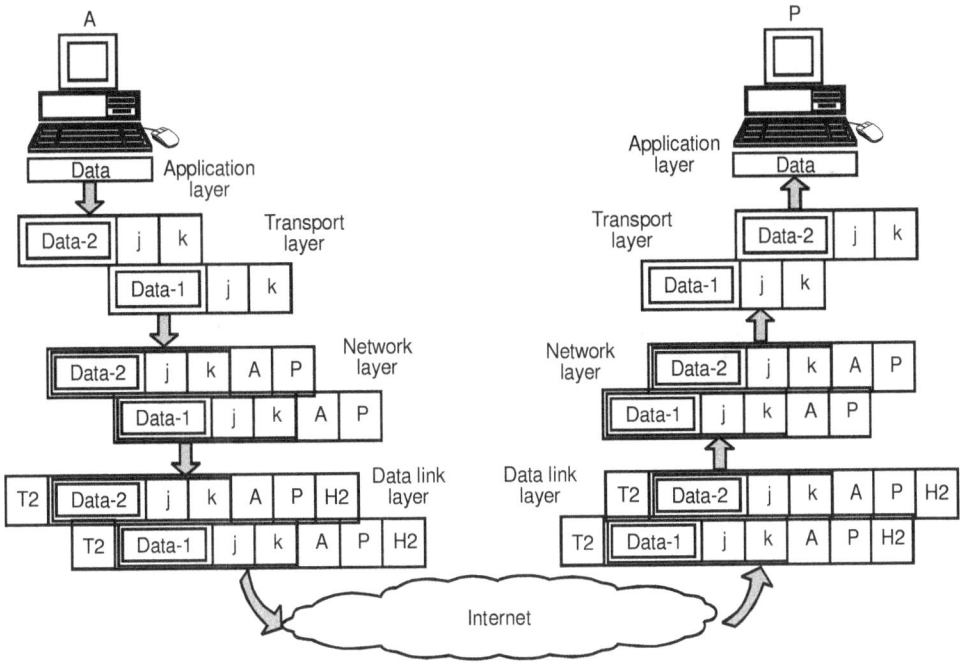

Fig. 1.36: Example of the transport layer

5. **Session layer**
   - Allows two applications running on different computers to establish use and end a connection called a Session.
   - Performs name recognition and security.
   - Provides synchronization by placing checkpoints in the data stream.
   - Implements dialog control between communicating processes.

The **session layer** is the network *dialog controller.* It establishes, maintains, and synchronizes the interaction between communicating systems.

Responsibilities of the session layer
   - **Dialog control:** It allows two systems to enter into a dialog by keeping track of whose turn it is to transmit.
   - **Token management:** Preventing two parties from attempting the same critical operation at the same time.
   - **Synchronization:** It allows a process to add checkpoints (synchronization points) into a stream of data. Use of Checkpoints for long transmission allow them to continue from where they were after a crash.

For example, if a system sending a file of 2000 pages and process inserts checkpoints after every 100 pages to ensure that each 100-page unit is received and acknowledged independently. If crash happens during transmission of page 545, retransmission begins at page 501; pages 1 to 500 need not be retransmitted.

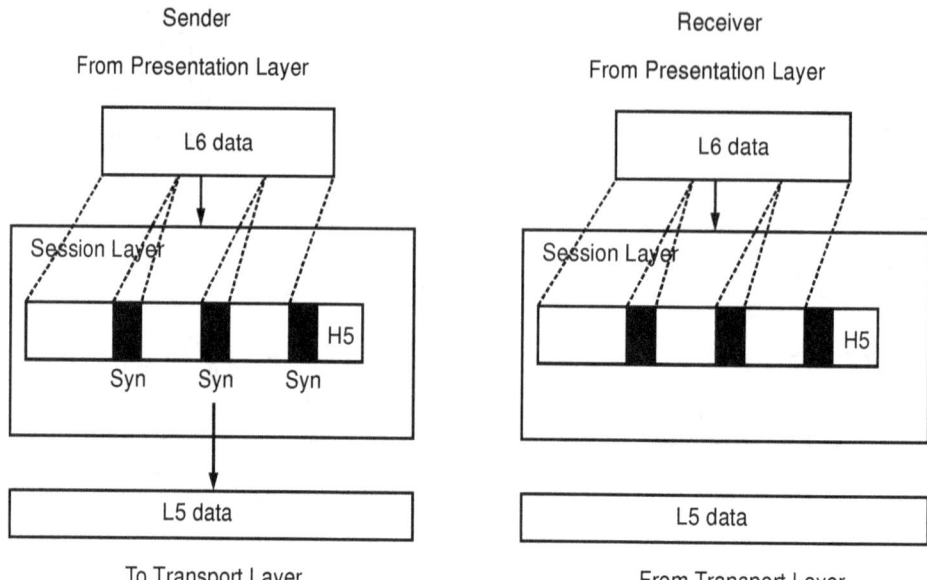

Fig. 1.37: Session layer

6. Presentation Layer:
- Determines the format used to exchange data among the networked computers.
- Translates data from a format from the Application layer into an intermediate format.
- Responsible for protocol conversion, data translation, data encryption, data compression, character conversion, and graphics expansion.
- Redirector operates at this level.

The **presentation layer** is concerned with the syntax and semantics of the information exchanged between two system. The presentation layer is concerned with the representation of user or system data. This includes necessary conversions (For example, printer control characters) and code translation (for example, ASCII to or from EBCDIC).

Responsibilities of the Presentation layer:
- **Translations:** Different computers use different encoding systems, the presentation layer is responsible for interoperability between these different encoding methods. The presentation layer at the sender changes the information from its sender-dependant format into a common format. The presentation layer at the receiving machine changes the common format into its receiver-dependant format.
- **Encryption:** The process of rendering a message (or data) unusable to all but the intended recipients, who have the ability to decrypt it.
- **Compression:** reduces the number of bits to be transmitted. Saves network bandwidth.

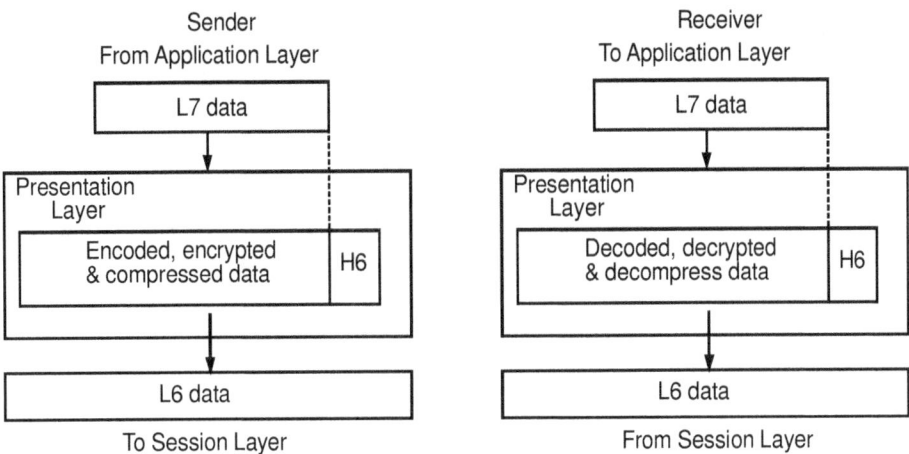

Fig. 1.38: Presentation layer

7. Application Layer
- Serves as a window for applications to access network services.
- Handles general network access, flow control and error recovery
- The application layer enables the user, whether human or software, to access the network.

Services provided by the Application Layer.
- **Network virtual terminal:** It allows a user to log on to a remote host.
- **File transfer, access and management (FTAM):** This application allows a user to access files in remote computer (to make changes or read data), to retrieves files from a remote computer and to manage or control files in a remote computer.
- **Mail service:** This application provides the basis for e-mail forwarding and storage.
- **HTTP (HyperText Transfer Protocol):** A standard Internet protocol that specifies the client/server interaction processes between Web browsers such as Microsoft Internet Explorer and Web servers such as Microsoft Internet Information Services (IIS).

1.11.3 Summary of OSI Layer Functions

Table 1.4: Summary of ISO/OSI model layers

OSI LAYER	FUNCTIONS
APPLICATION Message/data	Service advertisement, service availability. Manages communications between applications. (FPDAM) File, Print, Database, Application, and Messaging services. Allows applications to use the network. Handles network access, flow control and error recovery.

OSI LAYER	FUNCTIONS
PRESENTATION Message/data	Translation, compression, encryption, data conversion. Translates data into a form usable by the application layer. The redirector operates here. Responsible for protocol conversion, translating and encrypting data, and managing data compression.
SESSION Message/data RPC (Remote Procedure calls) functions here.	Connection establishment, data transfer, connection release (Half duplex, full duplex, simplex). Allows applications on connecting systems to establish a session. Provides synchronization between communicating computers.
TRANSPORT Segments (or Datagrams)	Service addressing, segmentation and transport control, flow control, end-to-end data integrity. Responsible for packet handling. Ensures error-free delivery. Repackages messages, divides messages into smaller packets and controls error handling.
NETWORK Packets (or Datagrams)	Logical addressing, switching, routing, network control. Translates system names into addresses. Determines routes for sending data and manages network traffic problems, packet switching, routing, data congestion and reassembling data.
DATA LINK Frames	Sends data from network layer to physical layer. Manages physical layer communications between connecting systems. LLC Layer (Logical Link Control): flow control and timing (802.2). Manages link control and defines SAPs (Service Access Points). MAC Layer (Media Access Control): framing and physical addressing (802.3, 802.4, 802.5, 802.12). Communicates with adapter card.
PHYSICAL Bits Is concerned with definition of low level functions (voltage, media types)	Transmits data over a physical medium. Defines cables, cards and physical aspects as well as electrical properties, transmission media, transmission devices, physical topology, data signaling, data synchronization and data bandwidth. Manages data placement on and data removal from the network media.

1.11.4 OSI Model Enhancements

The bottom two layers - Data Link and Physical - define how multiple computers can simultaneously use the network without interfering with each other.

- Divides the Data-link layer in to the Logical Link Control and Media Access Control sublayers.
- **Logical Link Control**
  - Manages **error and flow control** and
  - Defines logical interface points called Service Access Points (SAP's). These SAP's are used to transfer information to upper layers

- **Media Access Control**
  - Communicates directly with the network adapter card.
  - Decides which station will get access to medium.
  - Is responsible for delivering error-free data between two computers.
    - Categories
    - 802.3 (CSMA/CD – **Ethernet)**
    - 802.4 (Token Bus LAN (ARCnet))
    - 802.5 (**Token Ring** LAN) and
    - 802.12 (**Demand Priority** Access LAN, 100 Base VG - AnyLAN) define standards for both this sublayer and the Physical layer.

1.12 Signals

Signal is an electrical transmission of Alternating Current (AC) on network cabling that is generated by a networking component such as a Network Interface Card (NIC).

Signals can be either analog or digital.

An *analog signal* is a continuous wave form that changes smoothly over time. An analog signal can take on any value in a specified range of values. As the wave moves from value A to B, it passes thro and includes an infinite number of values along its path. A simple example is Alternating Current (AC), which continually varies between about +110 volts and –110 volts in a sine wave fashion 60 times per second. A more complex example of an analog signal is the time-varying electrical voltage generated when a person speaks into a dynamic microphone or telephone. Analog signals such as telephone speech contain a wealth of detail, but are not readily accessible to computers unless they are converted to digital form using a device such as an Analog-to-Digital converter (ADC). Analog signals are usually specified as a continuously varying voltage over time and can be displayed on a device known as an oscilloscope. The maximum voltage displacement of a periodic (repeating) analog signal is called its amplitude, and the shortest distance between crests of a periodic analog wave is called its wavelength.

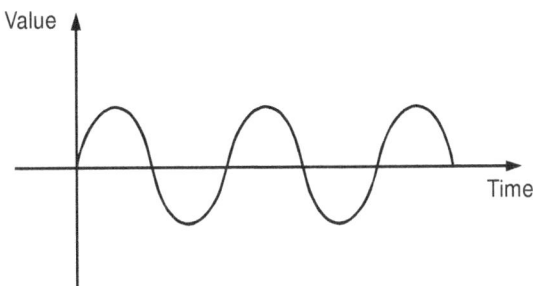

Fig. 1.39: Analog Signal

A *digital signal* is discrete. It can have only a limited number of definite values, often as simple as 1 and 0.

Digital signal: Transmission of signals that vary discretely with time between two values of some physical quantity, one value representing the binary number 0 and the other representing 1. *With copper cabling, the variable quantity is typically the voltage or the electrical potential. With fiber-optic cabling or wireless communication, variation in intensity or some other physical quantity is used.*

Digital signals use discrete values for the transmission of binary information over a communication medium such as a network cable or a telecommunications link. On a serial transmission line, a digital signal is transmitted 1-bit at a time.

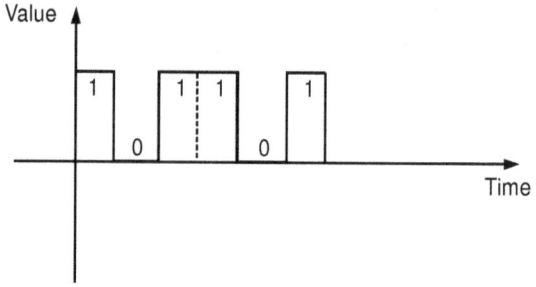

Fig. 1.40: Digital Signal

The opposite of digital signal is analog signal, in which information is transmitted as a continuously varying quantity. An analog signal might be converted to a digital signal using an analog-to-digital converter (ADC) and vice versa using a digital-to-analog converter (DAC). ADCs use a method called "quantization" to convert a varying AC voltage to a stepped digital one.

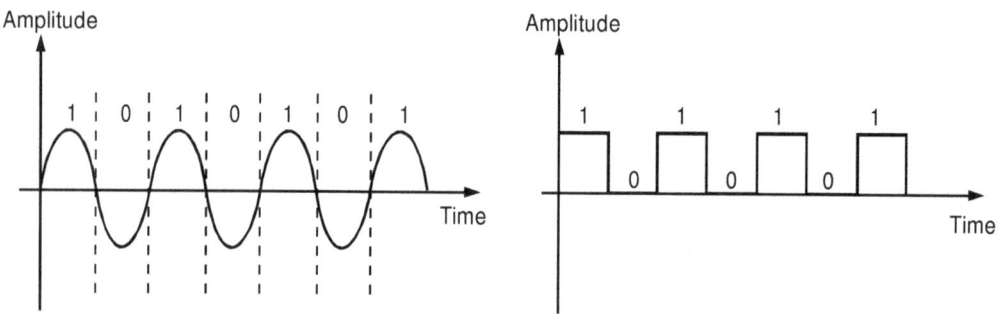

Fig. 1.41: Analog Vs Digital Signal

An electrical transmission of Alternating Current (AC) on network cabling that is generated by a networking component such as a Network Interface Card (NIC).

Signals are purposeful transmissions, as opposed to noise, which is an undesirable transmission from other components or the environment.

An analog signal is a (continuous) electromagnetic wave that is propagated over twisted pair, coaxial cable, fiber optic cable, the atmosphere, etc.

A digital signal is a sequence of pulses, with different pulses corresponding to 1, 0, e.g., positive and negative pulses. Must be propagated over a conducted or guided medium. Digital signals cannot be propagated over wireless medium since they are easily distorted. *Data can be analog or digital.*

An example of *analog data* is the human voice. When somebody speaks, a continuous wave is created in the air. Analog data -- voice, video -- continuously varying patterns of different intensity (amplitude). Another example of analog data is video. Typical bandwidth 4 MHz.

An example of *digital data* is data stored in memory of a computer in the form of 0's and 1's. For example, a 1 can be encoded as a positive voltage and a 0 as zero voltage. Digital data -- text, digitized images -- takes discrete values, usually binary (0,1). Example of digitized text is the ASCII code. 7 - bits so 128 patterns - upper and lower case characters, integers 0-9, special characters including some "control" characters used in communication such as NAK, SYN, EOT, etc.

BOTH analog and digital data may be represented by EITHER analog or digital signals.

In the networking environment, all electrical signals are digital except when the following devices are used:

- **Modems:**

Convert the digital signal from the serial port of a computer to an analog signal for transmission as audible sound waves over a phone line.

- **Digital cellular phones:**

Convert the analog signal of sound waves produced by human speech into digital electrical pulses by sampling the sound wave at discrete intervals.

Digital signals are essentially square waves, but they must also be encoded using line code, which represents binary information using discrete voltages. Line coding is a method of placing digital signals on a wire. Line coding specifies the relationship between the binary information in a data bitstream and the square-wave voltage variations on the wire that represent this information electrically.

Bit interval and **baud rate** are used to describe digital signals.

The bit interval is the time required to send one single bit. The *bit rate* is the number of bit intervals per second. This means that the bit rate is number of bits sent in one second, usually expressed in bits per second (bps).

Baud rate refers to the number of signal units per second that are required to represent those bits. Baud rate is less than or equal to the bit rate.

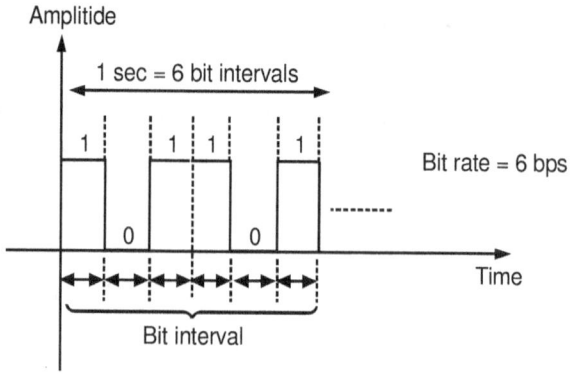

Fig. 1.42: Bit rate and Bit Interval

Example 1.1: A signal carries three bits in each signal element. If 1200 signal elements are sent per second, find the baud rate and the bit rate.

Solution: Baud rate = Number of signal elements

= 1200 bps

Bit rate = baud rate × Number of bits per signal element

= 1200 × 3

= 3600 bps.

Example 1.2: The bit rate of a signal is 2000. If each signal element carries five bits, what is the baud rate?

Solution: Baud rate = Bit rate / Number of bits per signal element

= 2000 / 5

= 400 bps.

1.13 Analog And Digital Transmission

- **ANALOG TRANSMISSION:** A means of transmitting ONLY analog signals.
- Data could be analog or digital; signal is always analog.
- Propagation could be over guided or unguided medium (space, atmosphere).
- Analog signal will become weaker in signal strength (attenuate) over distance. Will also be impaired by noise.
- An AMPLIFIER will boost the energy of the signal but also the noise. Noise is a undesirable random electrical transmission on network cabling that is generated by networking components such as Network Interface Cards (NICs) or induced in cabling by proximity to electrical equipment that generates electromagnetic interference (EMI).
- Analog data on an analog signal can tolerate more noise distortion and still be intelligible; however, this is not the case for digital data on an analog signal.

- **DIGITAL TRANSMISSION:** a means of transmitting BOTH digital and analog signals. Usually assume the signal is carrying digital (or digitized) data.
- Can only be propagated a limited distance before attenuation distorts the signal and compromises the data integrity.
- A REPEATER retrieves the (digital) signal; recovers the (digital) data, e.g., a pattern of 1's and 0's; retransmits a new signal.
- A similar technique used for the analog signal where we assume that the data is digital or digitized; repeater recovers the (digital or digitized) data and amplifies only the data and retransmits.
- Digital transmission is the preferred method for several reasons:
  1. Equipment for digital transmission is cheaper as compared to analog transmissions equipments.
  2. Use of repeaters, which recover the data and retransmit, are preferred over amplifiers, which boost both signal and noise. Errors are not cumulative and so it is possible to transmit over longer distances, using lower quality guided medium with better data integrity.
  3. Multiplexing -- transmission links have high bandwidth and must propagate multiple signals simultaneously to utilize the bandwidth. In digital transmission, we use time-division multiplexing -- signals share the same medium over different time slots. This is easier than analog transmission where the analog signals occupy different frequency spectrum (frequency-division).
  4. Encryption of signal possible for security and privacy
  5. By assuming that analog and digital signals all carry digital (or digitized) data, all signals are treated uniformly. Allows integration of voice, video, digital, image, and other data.

1.14 Periodic Analog Signals

1. Periodic analog signals are classified as:

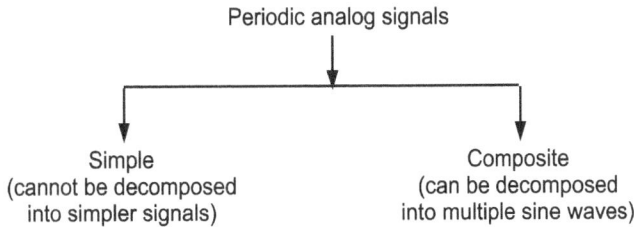

2. The example of **simple** periodic analog signals which cannot be decomposed into simpler signals is sine wave.

3.   The examples of **composite** periodic analog signals which can be decomposed into multiple sine waves are:

   •   Square wave (duty cycle = 50%).

   •   Pulse wave (duty cycle ≠ 50%)

   •   Triangular waveform.

   •   RAMP waveform (positive or negative RAMP).

4.   Let's see the characteristics of sine wave in detail.

5.   Also we will discuss the remaining signal waveforms in brief.

1.14.1 Sine Wave Signal

   •   A sine wave has the same shape as the graph of the sine function used in trigonometry. Sine waves are produced by rotating electrical machines such as dynamos, power station turbines and electrical energy is transmitted to the consumer in this form.

   •   In electronics, sine waves are among the most useful of all signals in testing circuits and analyzing system performance.

   •   Sine wave in more detail is shown in Fig. 1.43.

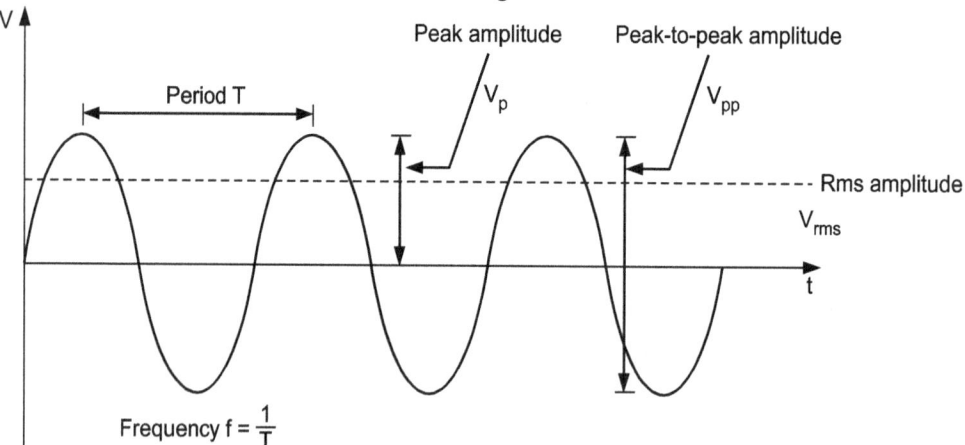

Fig. 1.43: Periodic Sine Wave Signal

The terms defined below are needed to describe sine waves and other waveforms precisely:

1. **Period (T):**

   •   The period is the time taken for one complete cycle of a repeating waveform.

   •   The period is often thought of as the time interval between peaks, but can be measured between any two corresponding points in successive cycles.

2. Frequency (f):

- Frequency is the number of cycles completed per second.
- The measurement unit for frequency is the **hertz, Hz**. 1 Hz = 1 cycle per second.
- If you know the period, the frequency of the signal can be calculated from

$$f = \frac{1}{T}$$

Conversely, the period is given by

$$T = \frac{1}{f}$$

- Signals you are likely to use vary in frequency from about 0.1 Hz, through values in **kilohertz, kHz** (thousands of cycles per second) to values in **megahertz, MHz** (millions of cycles per second).

Table 1.5: SI Multiples for Hertz (Hz)

Submultiples			Multiples		
Value	Symbol	Name	Value	Symbol	Name
10^{-1} Hz	dHz	decihertz	10^{1} Hz	daHz	decahertz
10^{-2} Hz	cHz	centihertz	10^{2} Hz	hHz	hectohertz
10^{-3} Hz	**mHz**	**millihertz**	10^{3} Hz	**kHz**	**kilohertz**
10^{-6} Hz	**µHz**	**microhertz**	10^{6} Hz	**MHz**	**megahertz**
10^{-9} Hz	nHz	nanohertz	10^{9} Hz	**GHz**	**gigahertz**
10^{-12} Hz	pHz	picohertz	10^{12} Hz	**THz**	**terahertz**
10^{-15} Hz	fHz	femtohertz	10^{15} Hz	PHz	petahertz
10^{-18} Hz	aHz	attohertz	10^{18} Hz	EHz	exahertz
10^{-21} Hz	zHz	zeptohertz	10^{21} Hz	ZHz	zettahertz
10^{-24} Hz	yHz	yoctohertz	10^{24} Hz	YHz	yottahertz
Common prefixed units are in bold face.					

- The **hertz** (symbol: **Hz**) is a unit of frequency.
- It is defined as the number of complete cycles per second. It is the basic unit of frequency in the International System of Units (SI). It is used worldwide in both general-purpose and scientific contexts.
- Hertz can be used to measure any periodic event; the most common uses of hertz are to describe radio and audio frequencies, more or less sinusoidal contexts in which case a frequency of 1 Hz is equal to one cycle per second.
- The unit hertz is defined by the International System of Units (SI).

3. **Amplitude:**

    - In electronics, the amplitude, or height, of a sine wave is measured in three different ways.
    - The **peak amplitude, V_p,** is measured from the X-axis, 0 V, to the top of a peak, or to the bottom of a trough. (In physics 'amplitude' usually refers to peak amplitude.)
    - The **peak-to-peak amplitude, V_{pp},** is measured between the maximum positive and negative values.
    - In practical terms, this is often the easier measurement to make. Its value is exactly twice **V_p**.
    - Although peak and peak-to-peak values are easily determined, it is often   more useful to know the **root mean square**, or **rms amplitude** of the wave, where:

$$V_{rms} = \frac{V_p}{\sqrt{2}} \text{ or } V_{rms} = 0.7 \times V_p$$

    and $V_p = \sqrt{2} \times V_{rms} \text{ or } V_p = 1.4 \times V_{rms}$

4. **Phase:**

    - It is sometimes useful to divide a sine wave into degrees, °, as follows:
    - Remember that sine waves are generated by rotating electrical machines. A complete 360° turn of the voltage generator corresponds to one cycle of the sine wave.
    - Therefore 180° corresponds to a half turn, 90° to a quarter turn and so on. Using this method, any point on the sine wave graph can be identified by a particular number of degrees through the cycle.

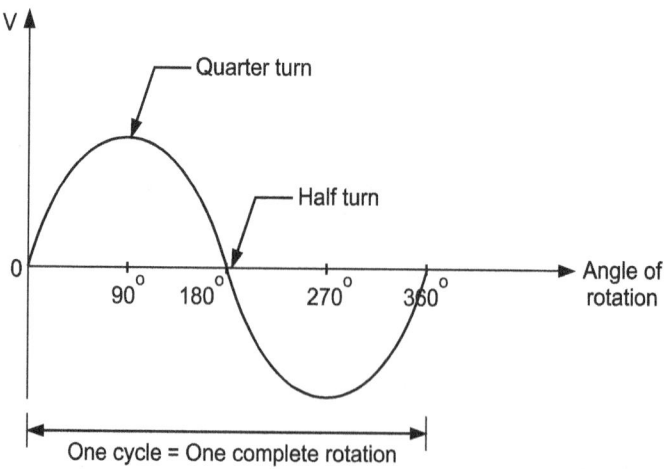

Fig. 1.44: Phase of Sine Wave

    - If two sine waves have the same frequency and occur at the same time, they are said to be **in phase**.

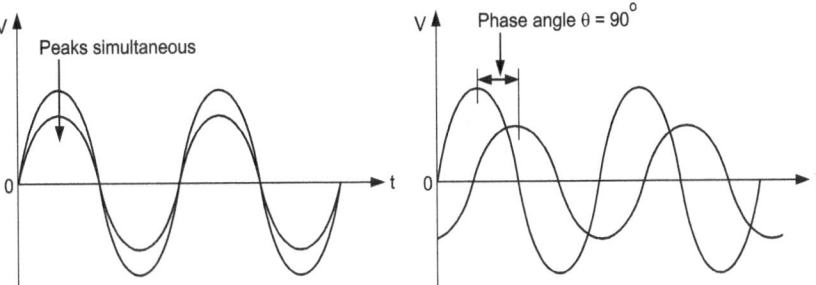

(a) Sine waves of the same frequency which are in phase　　　**(b) Sine waves of the same frequency which are a quarter cycle (90°) out of phase**

Fig. 1.45: In Phase and Out of Phase Sine Waves

- On the other hand, if the two waves occur at different times, they are said to be **out of phase**.
- When this happens, the difference in phase can be measured in degrees, and is called the **phase angle**, θ. As you can see, the two waves in part (b) are a quarter cycle out of phase, so the phase angle θ = 90°.
- The graphs below show waveforms of different frequency and amplitude.

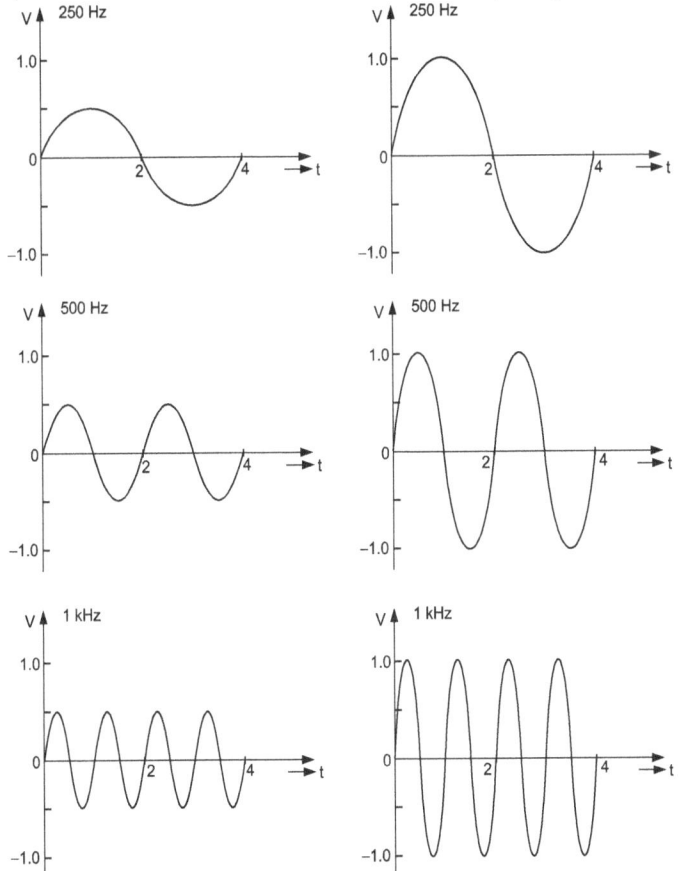

Fig. 1.46: Sine Waves of 250 Hz, 500 Hz and 1 kHz with different amplitudes

5. Wavelength:

- Wavelength is the characteristic of sine wave which binds the period or the frequency of sine wave to the propagation speed of the medium.

$$\boxed{\text{Wavelength} = \text{Propagation speed} \times \text{Period} = \frac{\text{Propagation speed}}{\text{Frequency}}}$$

where, propagation speed of electromagnetic signal $= 3 \times 10^8$ m/s.

Making of Waves:

- Sine waves can be mixed with DC signals, or with other sine waves to produce new waveforms. Here is one example of complex waveform.

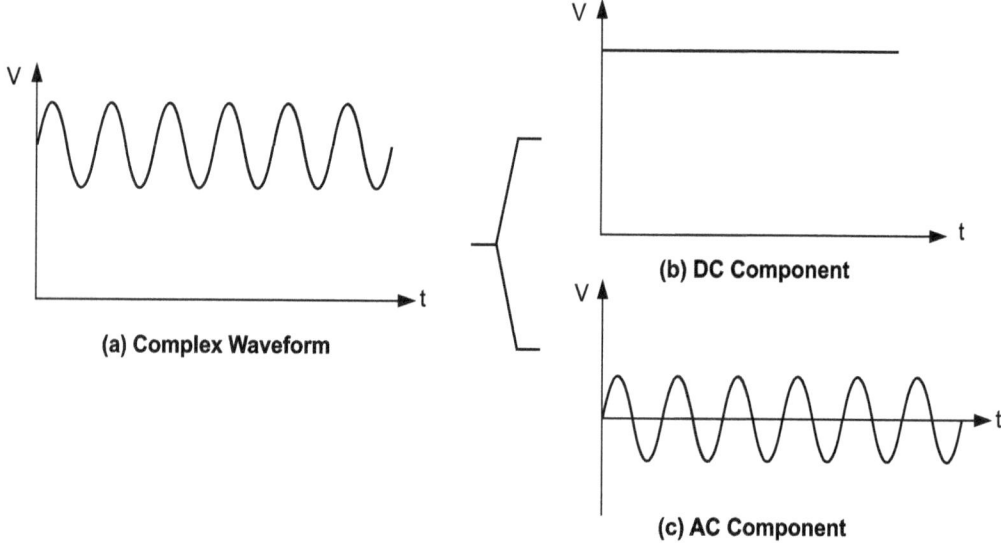

Fig. 1.47: DC Component Superimposed with AC Component

- 'Complex' does not mean difficult to understand. A waveform like this can be thought of consisting of a DC component with a superimosed AC component. It is quite easy to separate these two components using a **capacitor.**
- More dramatic results are obtained by mixing a sine wave of a particular frequency with exact multiples of the same frequency, in other words, by adding **harmonics** to the **fundamental** frequency. The V/t graphs below show what happens when a sine wave is mixed with its 3rd harmonic (3 times the fundamental frequency) at reduced amplitude, and subsequently with its 5th, 7th and 9th harmonics.

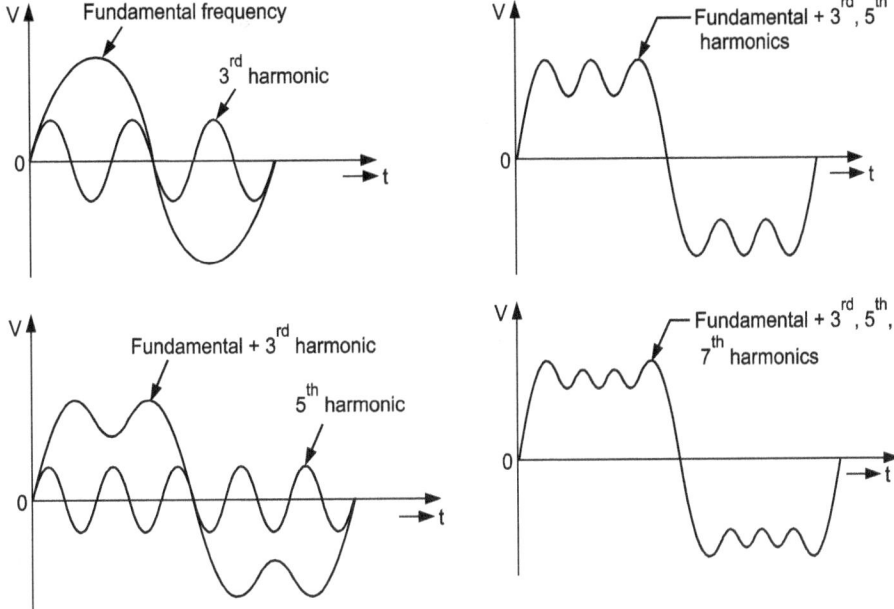

Fig. 1.48: Fundamental and Harmonic Waveforms

- As you can see, as more odd harmonics are added, the waveform begins to look more and more like a square wave.
- This surprising result illustrates a general principle first formulated by the French mathematician Joseph Fourier, namely that *any* complex waveform can be built up from a pure sine wave plus particular harmonics of the fundamental frequency.
- Square waves, triangular waves and sawtooth waves can be produced in this way.

1.14.2 Other Signals

This part of section outlines the other types of signal you are going to meet. Circuits which generate these signals are versatile building blocks.

1. **Square waves:**
   - Like sine waves, square waves are described in terms of period, frequency and amplitude as shown in Fig. 1.49.

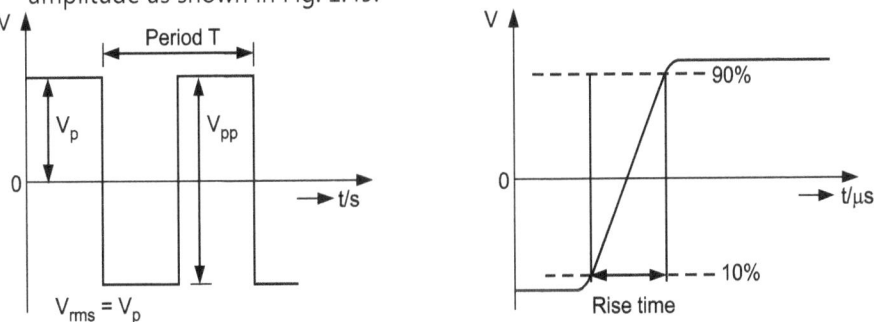

Fig. 1.49: Square Waveform

- Peak amplitude, V_p, and peak-to-peak amplitude, V_{pp}, are measured as you might expect.
- However, the rms amplitude, V_{rms}, is greater than that of a sine wave.
- Remember that the rms amplitude is the DC voltage which will deliver the same power as the signal. If a square wave supply is connected across a lamp, the current flows first one way and then the other.
- The current switches direction but its *magnitude* remains the same.
- In other words, the square wave delivers its maximum power throughout the cycle so that V_{rms} is equal to V_p. (If this is confusing, don't worry, the rms amplitude of a square wave is not something you need to think about very often.)
- Although a square wave may change very rapidly from its minimum to maximum voltage, this change cannot be instantaneous.
- The **rise time** of the signal is defined as the time taken for the voltage to change from 10% to 90% of its maximum value. Rise times are usually very short, with durations measured in nanoseconds (1 ns $= 10^{-9}$ s), or microseconds (1 µs $= 10^{-6}$ s), as indicated in the graph.

2. **Pulse waveforms:**

- Pulse waveforms look similar to square waves, except that all the action takes place above the X-axis.
- At the beginning of a pulse, the voltage changes suddenly from a LOW level, close to the X-axis, to a HIGH level, usually close to the power supply voltage.

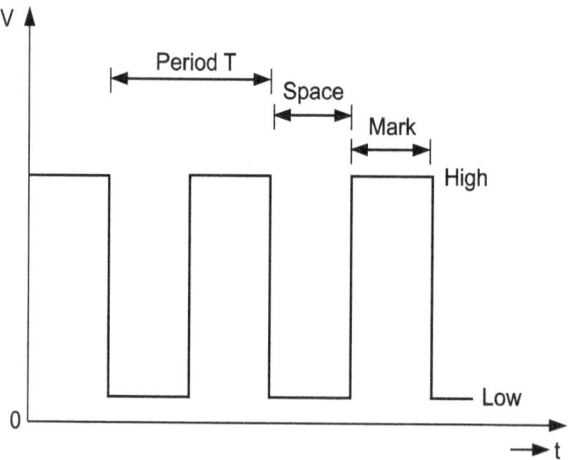

Fig. 1.50: Pulse Waveform

- Sometimes, the 'frequency' of a pulse waveform is referred to as its **repetition rate**. This means the number of cycles per second, measured in hertz, Hz.

- The HIGH time of the pulse waveform is called the **mark**, while the LOW time is called the **space**. The mark and space do not need to be of equal duration. The **mark space ratio** is given by,

$$\text{Mark space ratio} = \frac{\text{HIGH time}}{\text{LOW time}}$$

- A mark space ratio = 1.0 means that the HIGH and LOW times are equal, while a mark space ratio = 0.5 indicates that the HIGH time is half as long as the LOW time.

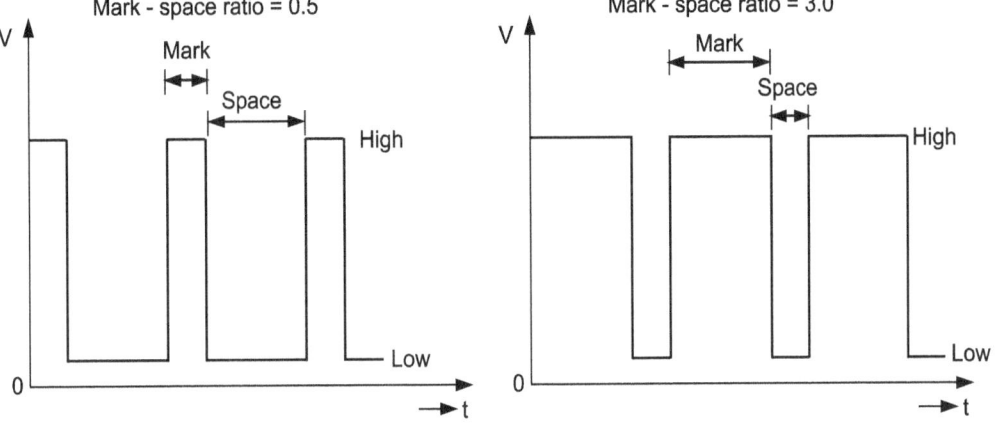

Fig. 1.51: Pulse Waveforms with Different Duty Cycles

- A mark space ratio of 3.0 corresponds to a longer HIGH time, in this case, three times as long as the space.
- Another way of describing the same types of waveform uses the **duty cycle**, where,

$$\text{Duty cycle} = \frac{\text{HIGH time}}{\text{Period}} \times 100\%$$

- When the duty cycle is less than 50%, the HIGH time is shorter than the LOW time, and so on.

3. Ramps:

- A voltage ramp is a steadily increasing or decreasing voltage, as shown in Fig. 1.52.

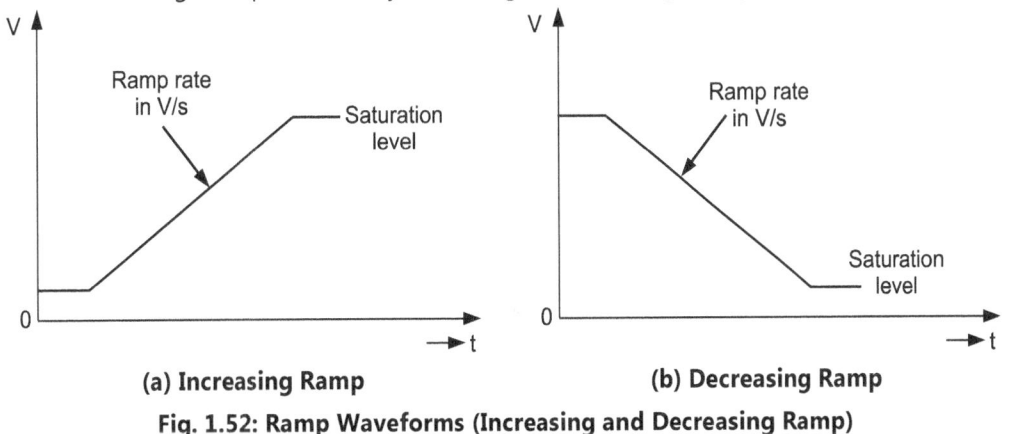

(a) Increasing Ramp   **(b) Decreasing Ramp**

Fig. 1.52: Ramp Waveforms (Increasing and Decreasing Ramp)

- The **ramp rate** is measured in units of volts per second, V/s. Such changes cannot continue indefinitely, but stop when the voltage reaches a **saturation level**, usually close to the power supply voltage.

4. **Triangular and sawtooth waves:**
   - These waveforms consist of alternate positive-going and negative-going ramps.
   - In a triangular wave, the rate of voltage change is equal during the two parts of each cycle, while in a sawtooth wave, the rates of change are unequal.
   - Sawtooth generator circuits are an essential building block in oscilloscope and television systems.

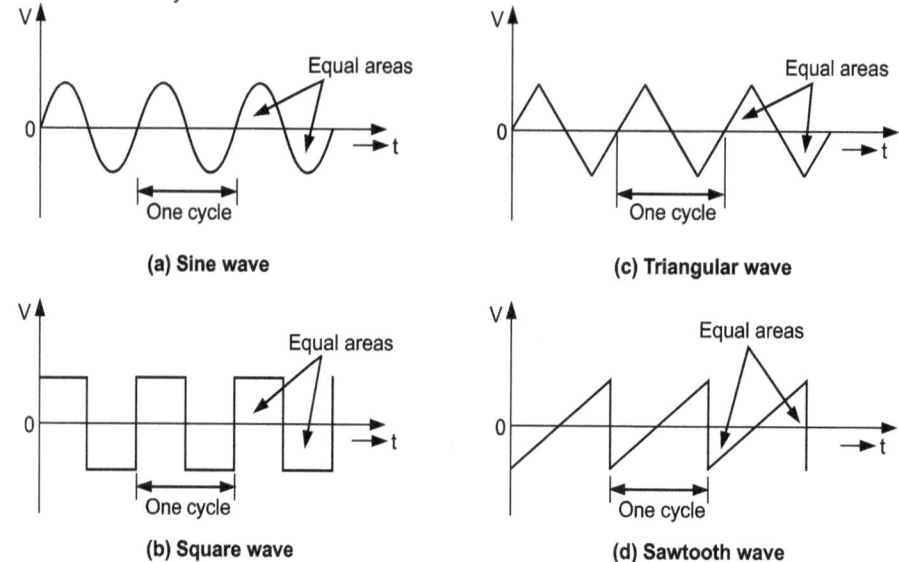

Fig. 1.53: Other Periodic Waves

- As you can see, the voltage levels change with time and are alternate between positive values (above the X-axis) and negative values (below the X-axis).
- Signals with repeated shapes are called **waveforms** and include **sine** waves, **square** waves, **triangular** waves and **sawtooth** waves.
- A distinguishing feature of alternating waves is that equal areas are enclosed above and below the X-axis.

5. **Audio signals:**

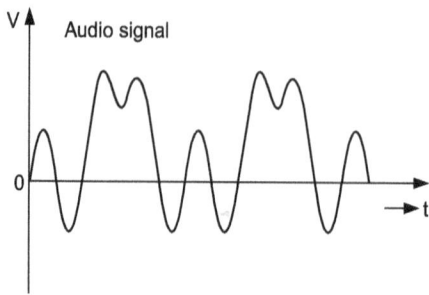

Fig. 1.54: Audio Signal (20 Hz to 20 kHz) Waveform

- As already mentioned, sound frequencies which can be detected by the human ear vary from a lower limit of around 20 Hz to an upper limit of about 20 kHz.
- A sound wave amplified and played through a loudspeaker gives a pure audio tone.
- Audio signals like speech or music consist of many different frequencies.
- Sometimes it is possible to see a dominant frequency in the V/t graph of a musical signal, but it is clear that other frequencies are present.

6. Noise:

- A noise signal consists of a mixture of frequencies with random amplitudes as shown in Fig. 1.55.

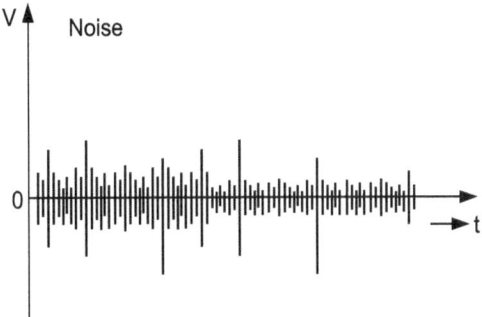

Fig. 1.55: Noise Waveform Signal

- Noise can originate in various ways.
- For example, heat energy increases the random motion of electrons and results in the generation of **thermal noise** in all components, although some components are 'noisier' than others.
- Additional sources of noise include radio signals, which are detected and amplified by many circuits, not just by radio receivers.
- Interference is caused by the switching of mains appliances and 'spikes' and 'glitches' are caused by rapid changes in current and voltage elsewhere in an electronic system.

1.14.3 Time and Frequency Domain

1. So far we have seen the amplitude, frequency and phase of the sine wave with respect to time axis, this is called as **time-domain** plot of sine wave.
2. The plot between amplitude and frequency of a wave is called as **frequency-domain** plot of a wave.
3. Thus, the complete sinewave of 3 Hz frequency in the time domain can be represented by one single spike in the frequency domain with (4 V peak amplitude).

4. Frequency domain plot is extremely useful and compact when we are dealing with more than one sine waves.

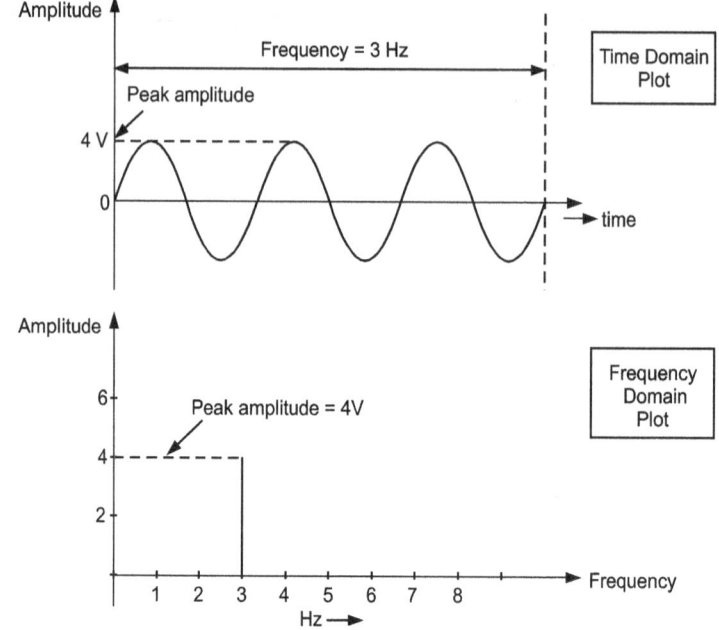

Fig. 1.56: Time and Frequency Domain Plot of the Sine wave

5. The time domain and frequency domain plot of 0 Hz, 4 Hz and 8 Hz sine waves are shown in Fig. 1.57.

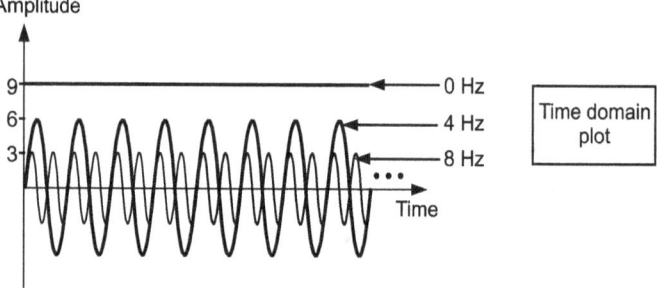

(a) Time-domain representation of three sine waves with frequencies 0, 4 and 8 Hz

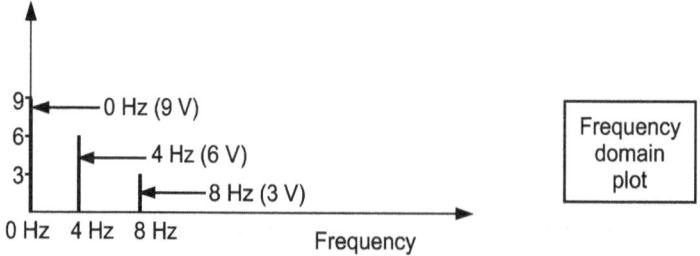

(b) Frequency-domain representation of the same three signals

Fig. 1.57: Time Domain and Frequency Domain Plot of 0 Hz, 4 Hz and 8 Hz Sine waves

6.   If you consider the data communication application, we are required to deal with **composite signals** like square waveform signal.

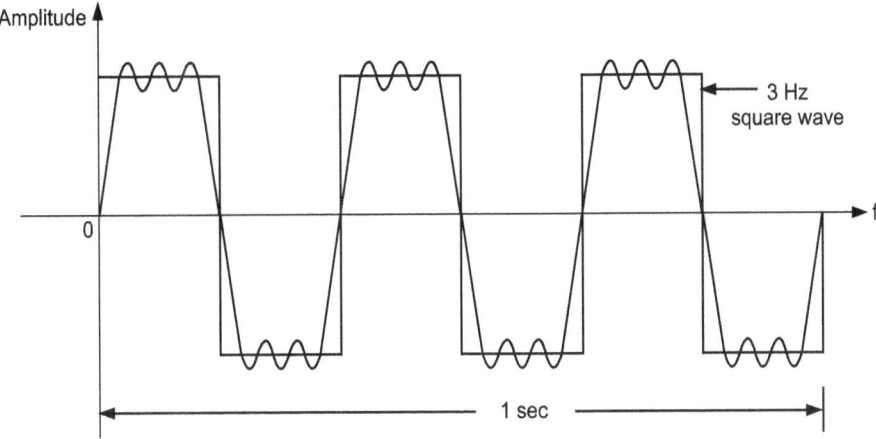

Fig. 1.58: Square Waveform of 3 Hz (Composite and Periodic Wave is drawn)

7.   According to Fourier analysis, any composite signal is a combination of simple sine waves with different frequencies, amplitudes and phases.

8.   If the composite signal is periodic, then its decomposition gives a series of signals with discrete frequencies.

9.   If the composite signal is non-periodic then the decomposition gives a combination of sine waves with continuous frequencies.

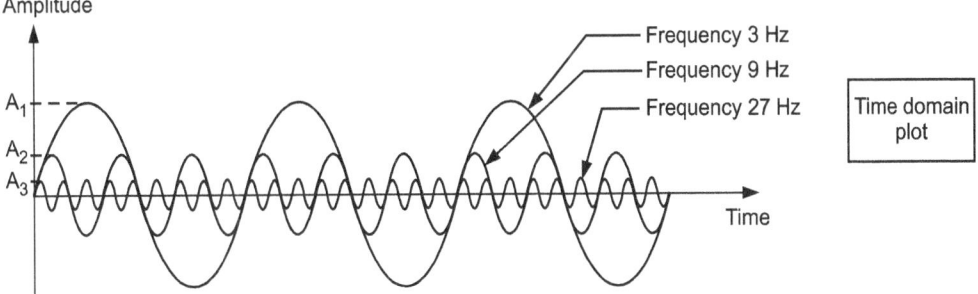

(a) Time-domain decomposition of a composite signal of 3 Hz square wave

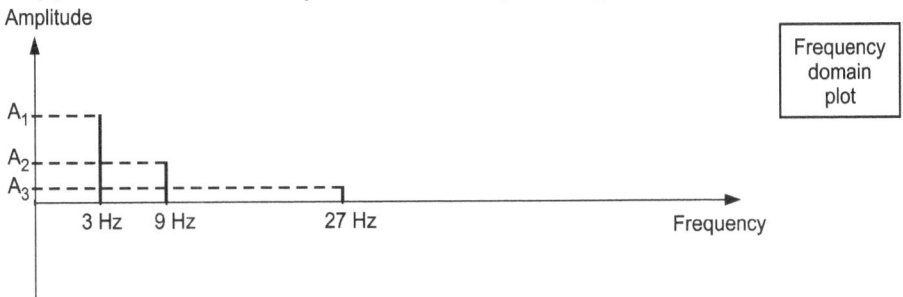

(b) Frequency-domain decomposition of a composite signal of 3 Hz square wave
Fig. 1.59: Time Domain and Frequency Domain Plot of 3 Hz Composite Square Wave Signal

10. Hence, we can say that, the square wave signal of 3 Hz is composed of the fundamental frequency = 3 Hz (or known as first harmonic), 3rd harmonic is of 9 Hz and 9th harmonic is of 27 Hz. Thus, it is integral multiple of 1, 3 and 9 but it is not float number multiple.

11. Thus, for non-periodic signal, the time domain and frequency domain plots are as shown in Fig. 1.59 (c).

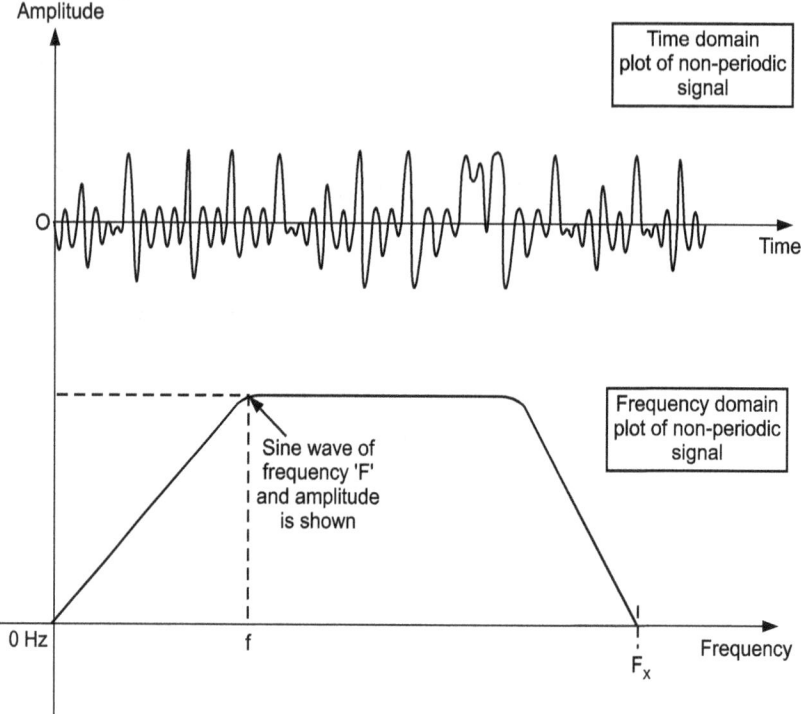

Fig. 1.59 (c): Time Domain and Frequency Domain Plot of Non-periodic signal

12. **The Bandwidth of Composite signal** can be given as the range of the frequencies contained in a composite signal.

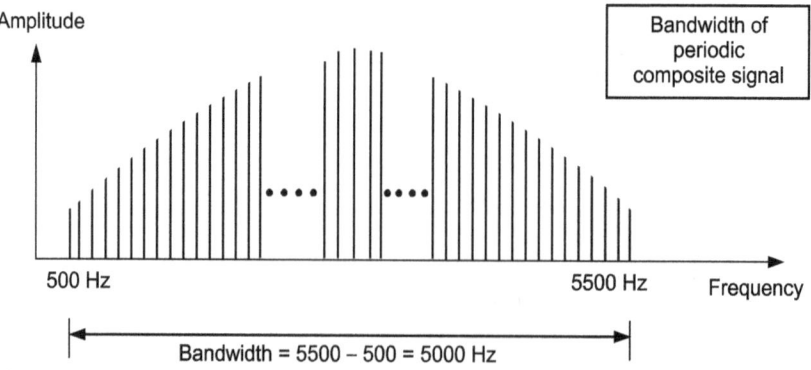

(a) Bandwidth of a periodic signal contains all integer frequencies between 500 Hz and 5500 Hz [i.e. 500, 501, 502, 503, 504 ... 5500 etc.]

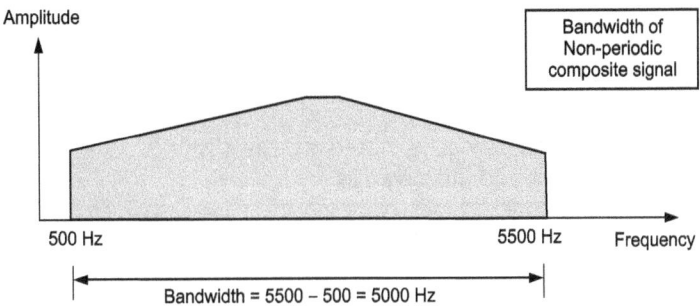

**(b) Bandwidth of a non-periodic signal has
same range but the frequencies are continuous**

Fig. 1.60: Bandwidth of Periodic and Non-periodic Composite Signals

13. Thus, the bandwidth of a periodic composite signal contains all integer frequencies between 500 Hz and 5500 Hz (i.e. 500 Hz, 501 Hz, 502 Hz, 503 Hz, 504 Hz ... 5500 Hz, etc.).

14. Also the bandwidth of a non-periodic composite signal contains same range but the frequencies are continuous as shown in Fig. 1.60.

1.15 Digital Signals

1. We know that digital signals has discrete values.
2. Also digital signal can have more than two levels.
3. Two level and four level digital signals are shown in Fig. 1.61.

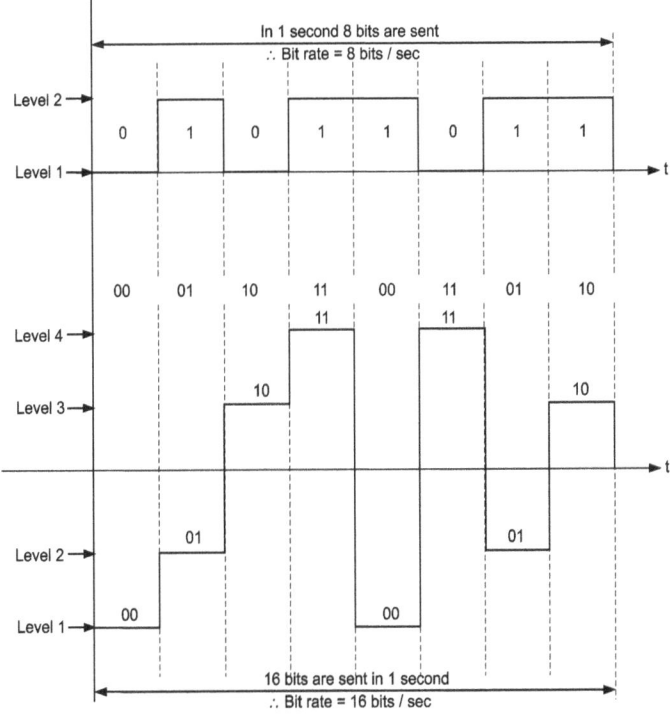

Fig. 1.61: Two Level and Four Level Digital Signals

4. **Bit Rate** of digital signal is given as number of bits sent in one second. Hence, bit rate is given in bps.

$\therefore$ | Bit rate = Bits/sec |

5. **Bit Length** of digital signal is stated as the distance one bit occupies on the transmission medium and it is given as,

| Bit length = Propagation speed × Bit duration |

1.15.1 Digital Signal as Composite Analog Signal

1. We have already seen that fourier series analysis can be used to decompose a digital signal.
2. If digital signal is periodic, decomposed signal has infinite bandwidth of discrete frequencies.
3. If digital signal is non-periodic, decomposed signal has infinite bandwidth of continuous frequencies.
4. The time domain and frequency domain analysis details are shown in Fig. 1.62.

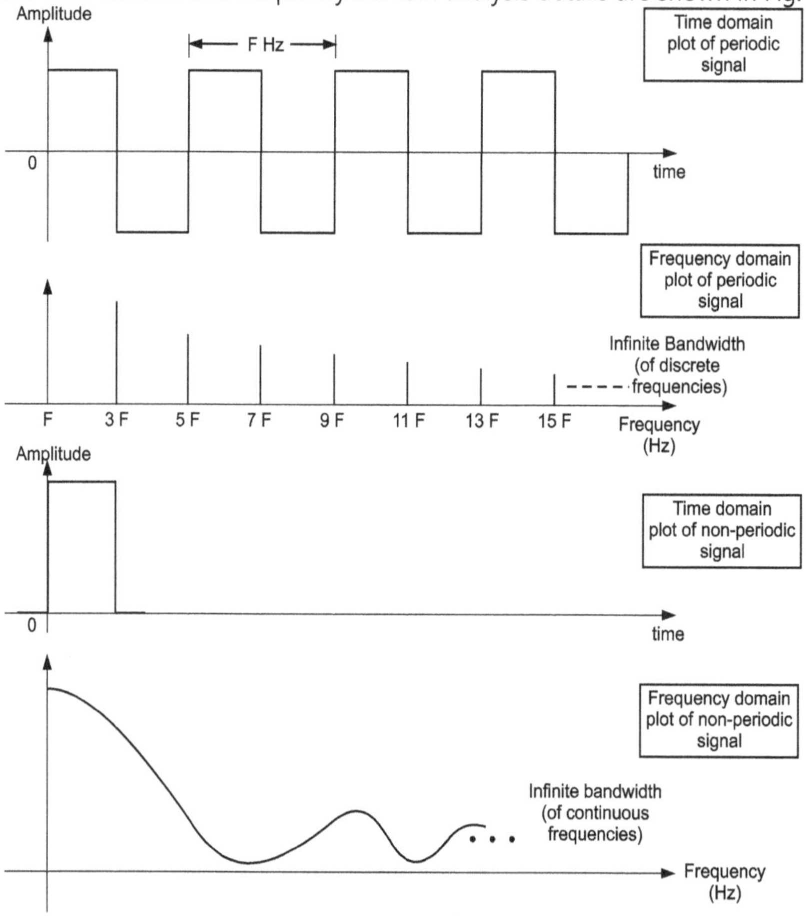

Fig. 1.62: Time Domain/Frequency Domain Plot of Periodic Digital Signal and Non-periodic Digital Signal

1.15.2 Transmission of Digital Signals

Case 1: Physical medium bandwidth is high:

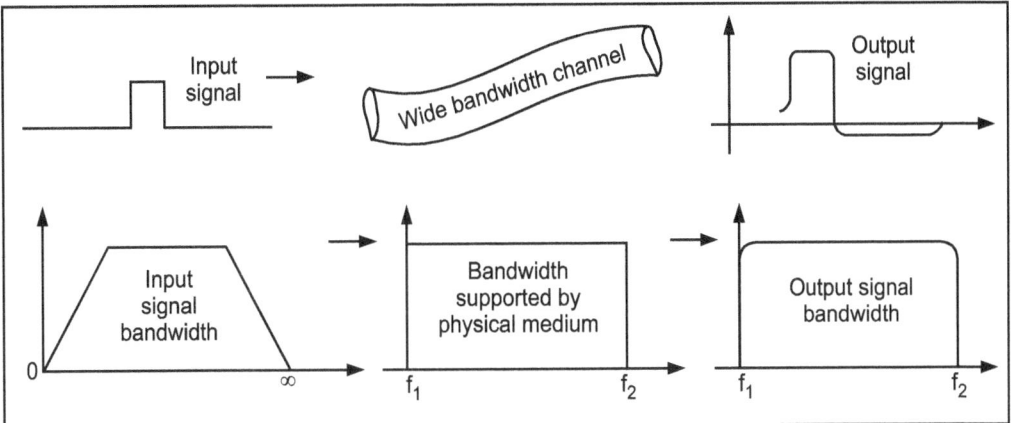

Case 2: Physical medium bandwidth is low:

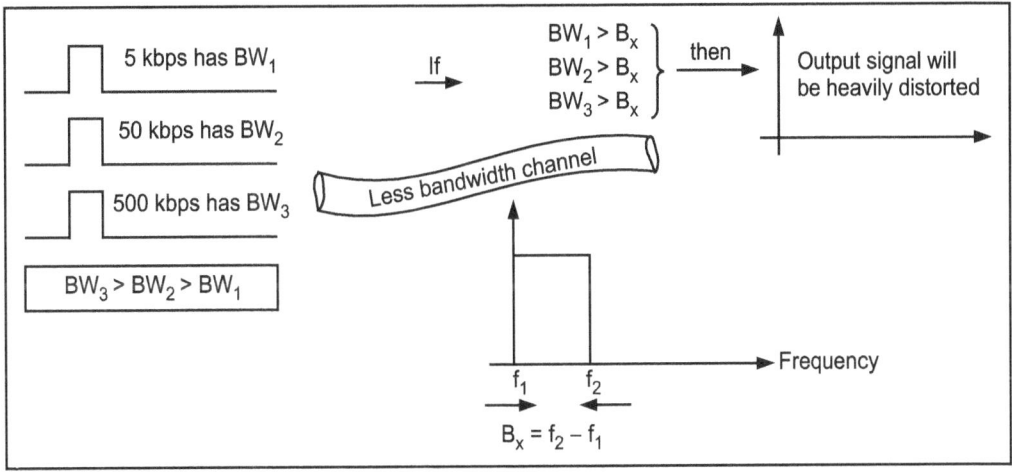

Fig. 1.63: Digital Signal Transmission using Different Bandwidth Medium

1. The transmission of digital signal is possible in two ways:

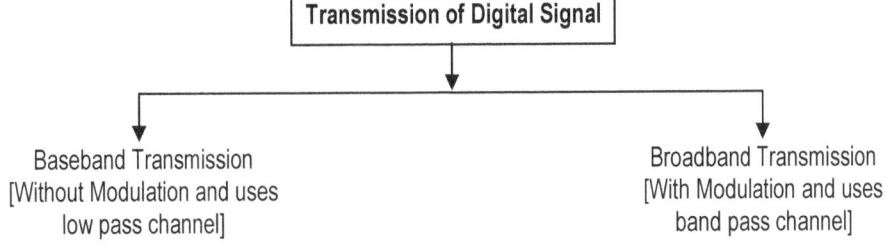

2. In Fig. 1.63, we have considered the baseband transmission of the digital signal (which is always non-periodic in nature practically, in data communication).

3. Here we have considered two cases:

    Case 1: Wide bandwidth channel is used.

    Case 2: Narrow bandwidth channel is used.

4. In case 1, small amount of distortion takes place and output signal is less distorted as shown.

5. Whereas in case 2, it is clearly shown that if bit rate of input baseband signal increases, then bandwidth requirement to transfer this data also increases.

6. In such case 2, if the narrow bandwidth channel is used then output signal will be heavily distorted or may not be available at output.

7. The bandwidth requirement for different data rates and for different harmonic values is as shown in Table 1.6.

Table 1.6: Bandwidth requirement for different data rates and different harmonic values

Bit Rate (N)	Harmonic 1 and required BW = N/2	Harmonics 1 and 3 and required BW = 3N/2	Harmonics 1, 3 and 5 and required BW = 5N/2
N = 5 kbps	2.5 kHz	7.5 kHz	12.5 kHz
N = 50 kbps	25 kHz	75 kHz	125 kHz
N = 500 kbps	250 kHz	750 kHz	1250 kHz

8. Thus, for proper digital signal transmission with more bit rate, the bandwidth requirement of medium channel increases and if not used, then signal may be heavily distorted or may even be lost.

9. **Now second way of digital signal transmission is with modulation. [i.e. No baseband transmission]. It is known as broadband transmission.**

10. Thus, Fig. 1.64 drawn is self explanatory.

11. In this figure, we can see that modulation process allows us to use a bandpass channel (a channel with bandwidth which doesn't start from zero i.e. starts at f_1 and ends at f_2).

12. Here, D to A conversion and A to D conversion are basically different concepts.

13. D to A conversion is digital continuous wave modulation. For example, ASK (Amplitude Shift Keying), FSK (Frequency Shift Keying) or PSK (i.e. Phase Shift Keying).

14. Due to this digital continuous wave modulation, which gives analog output in nature, has limited bandwidth = $f_2 - f_1$ and is less practical.

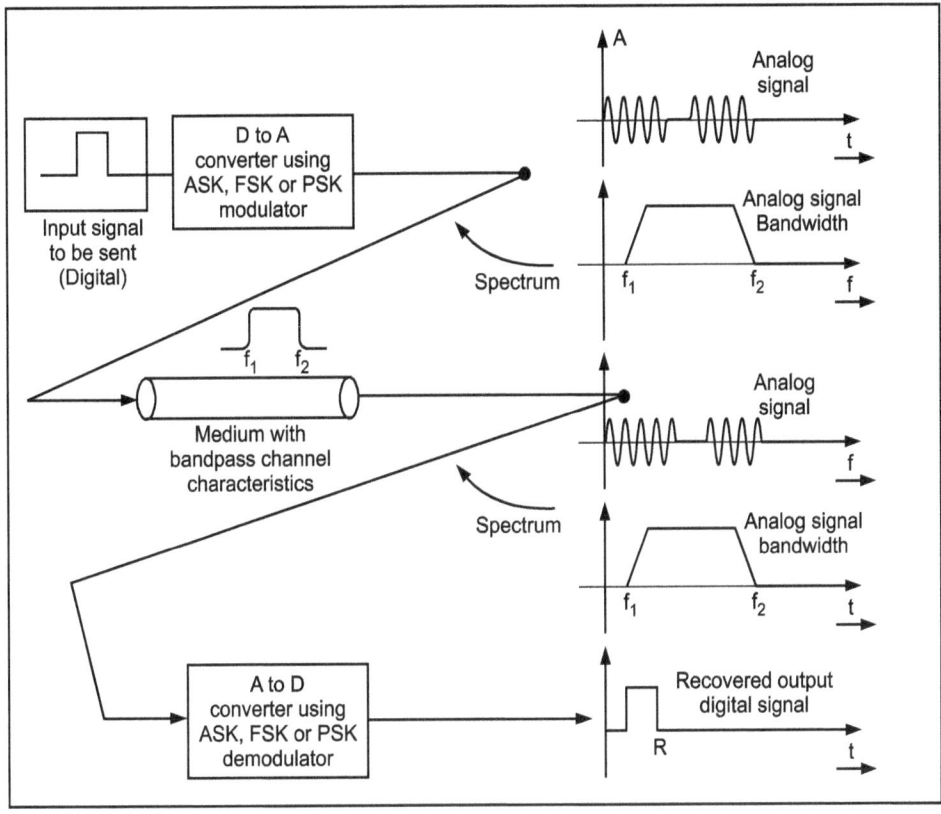

Fig. 1.64: Transmission and Reception of
Modulated Broadband Signal over Bandpass Channel Medium

15. This bandwidth of signal is easily passed through the medium with bandpass channel characteristics and has almost negligible distortion at medium (channel) output as shown.

16. Thus, now this analog signal is given to A to D converter at receiver end to recover original unmodulated digital signal as shown.

17. At receiver end, A to D converter is basically a ASK, FSK or PSK demodulator.

18. This ASK, FSK or PSK modulator/demodulator will be studied in Unit 2 of this book, in detail.

1.16 Transmission Impairment

1. Transmission impairment means, due to imperfections of medium, signal sent from transmitter is not equal to signal received from receiver.

2. There are three causes of impairment:
   - Attenuation
   - Distortion
   - Noise

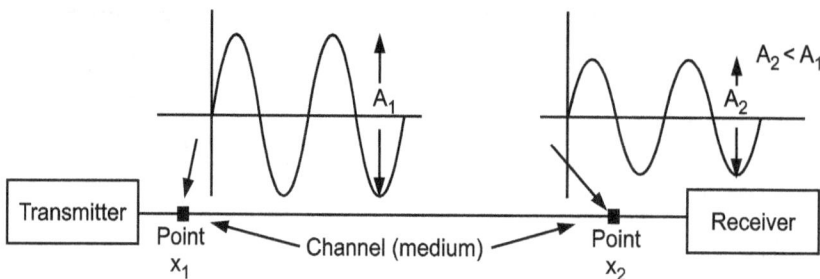

Fig. 1.65: Attenuation Impairment

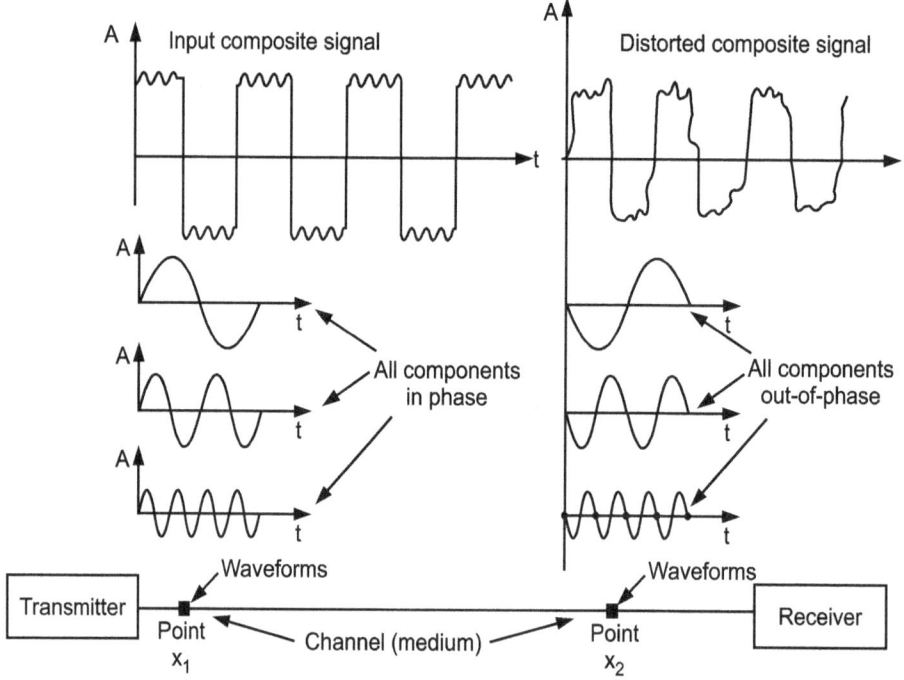

Fig. 1.66: Distortion Impairment

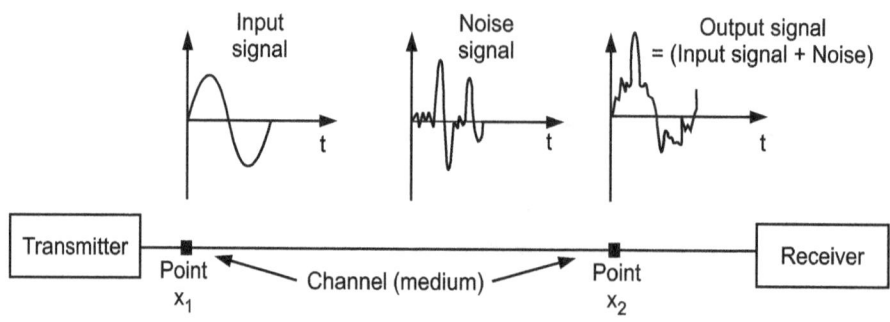

Fig. 1.67: Noise Impairment

3. Attenuation impairment is shown in Fig. 1.65. Distortion impairment is shown in Fig. 1.75 and Noise impairment is shown in Fig. 1.67.

4. Attenuation means loss of electrical signal energy in the form of heat due to channel resistance. Thus, energy lost is given as,

$$E_L = I^2 (R)$$

where, I is the current flowing through medium and R = channel resistance.

Also power loss in decibels is given as,

$$P_L = \log_{10} \frac{P_2}{P_1}$$

where, P_2 is the power at point x_2 and P_1 is the power at point x_1.

5. Distortion means the received signal at receiver end changes its shape or its form. This distortion is different in different frequencies due to different propagation speed of signal frequencies in medium. Thus, phases of received waveforms are changed and distortion occurs in received signal.

6. Electrical disturbances interfere with the input signal and produce noise. Noise always limits the performance of communication system. In electrical terms, any unwanted introduction of energy tending to interfere with the proper reception and reproduction of transmitted signal.

7. Noise is classified as external noise and internal noise. External noise is due to atmosphere, extraterrestrial noise or industrial noise.

8. The different types of internal noises are thermal noise, shot noise, partition noise and low frequency or flicker noise.

9. Signal to noise ratio of system is given by,

$$SNR = \frac{\text{Average signal power}}{\text{Average noise power}}$$

$$SNR_{dB} = 10 \log_{10} (SNR)$$

1.17 Data Rate Limits

1. In data communication system, the Data Rate depends upon three factors:

    (a) Available bandwidth (of medium).

    (b) Signal level (amplitude of signal).

    (c) Quality of medium (channel) (Noise amplitude).

2.   There are two formulae to calculate the data rate.

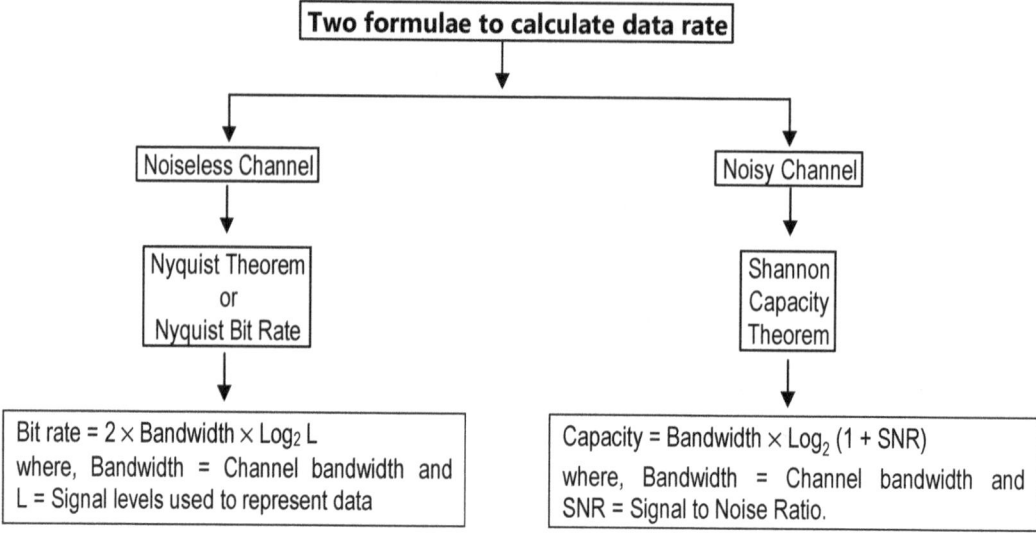

Bit rate = 2 × Bandwidth × Log₂ L
where, Bandwidth = Channel bandwidth and
L = Signal levels used to represent data

Capacity = Bandwidth × Log₂ (1 + SNR)
where, Bandwidth = Channel bandwidth and
SNR = Signal to Noise Ratio.

1.18 Performance

In this section, we will discuss the following things:

    (a)   QoS (Quality of Service).
    (b)   Bandwidth.
    (c)   Throughput.
    (d)   Delay
    (e)   Jitter.
    (f)   Bandwidth-delay product.

1.18.1 Problems in Data Communication

1.   When the Internet was first deployed many years ago, it lacked the ability to provide Quality of Service guarantees due to limits in router computing power.

2.   It therefore ran at default QoS level, or "best effort".

3.   Many things can happen to packets as they travel from origin to destination, resulting in the following problems as seen from the point of view of the sender and receiver:

(i)   **Dropped packets :** The routers might fail to deliver (**drop**) some packets if they arrive when their buffers are already full. Some, none, or all of the packets might be dropped, depending on the state of the network, and it is impossible to determine what will happen in advance. The receiving application must ask for this information to be retransmitted, possibly causing severe delays in the overall transmission.

(ii) **Delay:** It might take a long time for a packet to reach its destination, because it gets held up in long queues, or takes a less direct route to avoid congestion. Alternatively, it might follow a fast, direct route. Thus delay is very unpredictable.

(iii) **Jitter:** Packets from source will reach the destination with different delays. This variation in delay is known as jitter and can seriously affect the quality of streaming audio and/or video.

(iv) **Out-of-order delivery:** When a collection of related packets is routed through the Internet, different packets may take different routes, each resulting in a different delay. The result is that the packets arrive in a different order to the one with which they were sent. This problem necessitates special additional protocols responsible for rearranging out-of-order packets to an isochronous state once they reach their destination. This is especially important for video and VoIP streams where quality is dramatically impacted by both latency or lack of isochronicity.

(v) **Error:** Sometimes packets are misdirected, or combined together, or corrupted, while enroute. The receiver has to detect this and, just as if the packet was dropped, ask the sender to repeat itself.

1.18.2 Applications Requiring QoS

A defined Quality of Service may be required for certain types of network traffic, for example:

- Streaming multimedia may require guaranteed throughput.
- IP telephony or Voice over IP (VoIP) may require strict limits on jitter and delay.
- Video Teleconferencing (VTC) requires low jitter.
- Alarm signalling (e.g. Burglar alarm).
- Dedicated link emulation requires both guaranteed throughput and imposes limits on maximum delay and jitter.
- A safety-critical application, such as remote surgery may require a guaranteed level of availability (this is also called *hard QoS*).

1.18.3 QoS Introduction

1. Quality of Service (QoS) for networks is an industry-wide set of standards and mechanisms for ensuring high-quality performance for critical applications.

2. By using QoS mechanisms, network administrators can use existing resources efficiently and ensure the required level of service without reactively expanding or over-provisioning their networks.

3. Traditionally, the concept of quality in networks meant that all network traffic was treated equally.

4. The result was that all network traffic received the network's best effort, with no guarantees for reliability, delay, variation in delay, or other performance characteristics.

5. With best-effort delivery service, however, a single bandwidth-intensive application can result in poor or unacceptable performance for all applications.
6. The QoS concept of quality is one in which the requirements of some applications and users are more critical than others, which means that some traffic needs preferential treatment.

1.18.4 Network Characteristics Managed by QoS

The goal of QoS is to provide preferential delivery service for the applications that need it by ensuring sufficient bandwidth, controlling latency and jitter, and reducing data loss. Table 1.7 describes these network characteristics.

Table 1.7: Network characteristics managed by QoS

Network Characteristics	Description
Bandwidth	The rate at which traffic is carried by the network.
Latency	The delay in data transmission from source to destination.
Jitter	The variation in latency.
Reliability	The percentage of packets discarded by a router.

1.18.5 QoS provides the Following Benefits

1. Gives administrators control over network resources and allows them to manage the network from a business, rather than a technical perspective.
2. Ensures that time-sensitive and mission-critical applications have the resources they require, while allowing other applications access to the network.
3. Improves user experience.
4. Reduces costs by using existing resources efficiently, thereby delaying or reducing the need for expansion or upgrades.

1.18.6 Bandwidth

Bandwidth is a central concept in many fields, including information theory, radio communications, signal processing and Telecom Networks.

Definition 1:

Bandwidth is a measure of frequency range, measured in hertz.

Example: The range of frequencies within which the performance of the antenna, with respect to some characteristics, conforms to a specified standard. (2.4-2.5 GHz antenna has 100 MHz bandwidth).

As an example, the 3 dB bandwidth of the function depicted in Fig. 1.68 is $f_2 - f_1$, whereas other definitions of bandwidth would yield a different answer.

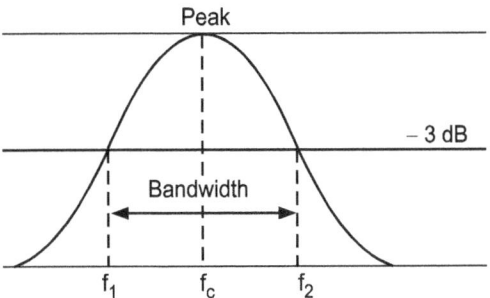

Fig. 1.68: 3 dB Bandwidth in Analog System

Definition 2:

Bandwidth is the amount of data that can be transmitted in a fixed amount of time, expressed in bits per second (bps) or bytes per second.

Example: A V.90 modem supports a maximum theoretical bandwidth of 56 kbps. Fast Ethernet supports a maximum theoretical bandwidth of 100 Mbps.

Bit Rates in Multimedia Communications:

(i) Audio (MP3):

- 32 kbits/s – MW (AM) quality.
- 96 kbits/s – FM quality.
- 128-160 kbits/s – Decent quality, difference can sometimes be obvious.
- 192 kbits/s – Good quality, difference can only be heard by a few.
- 224-320 kbits/s – High quality, nearly lossless quality.

(ii) Other Audio:

- 4 kbits/s – Minimum necessary for recognizable speech (using special-purpose speech codec).
- 8 kbits/s – Telephone quality (using speech codec).
- 500 kbits/s – 1 Mbits/s – Lossless audio as used in formats such as FLAC (free lossless audio codec), WavPack or Monkey's Audio.
- 1411 kbits/s – PCM (WAV) sound format of Compact Disc Digital Audio.

(iii) Video (MPEG2):

- 16 kbits/s – Videophone quality (minimum necessary for a consumer-acceptable "talking head" picture).
- 128-384 kbits/s – Business-oriented videoconferencing system quality.
- 1 Mbits/s – VHS quality.
- 5 Mbits/s – DVD quality.
- 15 Mbits/s – HDTV quality.

1.18.7 Throughput

1. In Data communication networks, **throughput** is the amount of digital data per unit time that is delivered to a certain terminal in a network, from a network node, or from one node to another, for example via a communication link.
2. The throughput is usually measured in bit per second (bit/s or bps).
3. The **system throughput** or **aggregate throughput** is the sum of the data rates that are delivered to all terminals in a network.
4. Often **maximum throughput** is implied by the term **throughput**. The maximum **throughput** of a node or communication link is synonym to its **capacity**.
5. The **maximum throughput** is defined as the **asymptotic throughput** when the load (the amount of incoming data) is very large.
6. In packet switched systems where the load and throughput are equal (where there are no packet drops), the maximum throughput may be defined as the load in bit/s when the delivery time (the latency) asymptotically reaches infinity.
7. The concept is applicable for all Telecom Networks.

1.18.8 Delay (Latency)

- The flow of a compressed voice circuit is shown in Fig. 1.69.
- The analog signal from the telephone is digitized into pulse code modulation (PCM) signals by the voice coder-decoder (codec).
- The PCM samples are then passed to the compression algorithm, which compresses the voice into a packet format for transmission across the WAN.
- On the far side of the cloud the exact same functions are performed in reverse order. The entire flow is shown in Fig. 1.69.

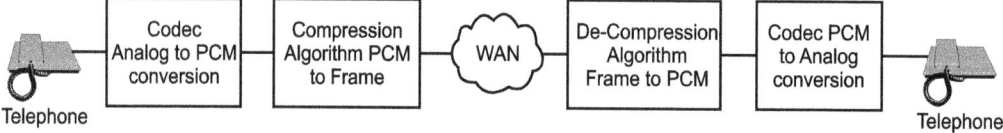

Fig. 1.69: End-to-End Voice Flow

- Based on how the network is configured, the router/gateway can perform both the codec and compression functions or only one of them.
- **Fixed delay components** add directly to the overall delay on the connection.
- **Variable delays arise** from queuing delays in the egress trunk buffers on the serial port connected to the WAN.
- **Different Delays are:**
    1. Coder (Processing) Delay
    2. Algorithmic Delay
    3. Packetization Delay
    4. Serialization Delay

5.   Queuing/Buffering Delay
6.   Network Switching Delay
7.   De-Jitter Delay

- **Thus, Latency (Delay)** = Propagation time + Transmission Time + Queuing time + Processing delay
  Where propagation time = Distance / Propagation speed.
- Transmission time = Message Size / Bandwidth.

1.18.9 Jitter

- Simply stated, *jitter* is the variation of packet interarrival time.
- Jitter is one issue that exists only in packet-based networks.
- While in a packet voice environment, the sender is expected to reliably transmit voice packets at a regular interval (for example, send one frame every 20 ms).
- These voice packets can be delayed throughout the packet network and not arrive at that same regular interval at the receiving station (for example, they might not be received every 20 ms; see Fig. 1.70).
- The difference between the time at which the packet is expected and the time at which it is actually received is *jitter*.
- In Fig. 1.70, you can see that the amount of time it takes for packets A and B to send and receive is equal ($D_1 = D_2$).
- Packet C encounters delay in the network, however, it is received *after* it is expected.
- This is why a *jitter buffer*, which conceals interarrival packet delay variation,   is necessary.
- Voice packets in IP networks have highly variable packet-interarrival intervals.

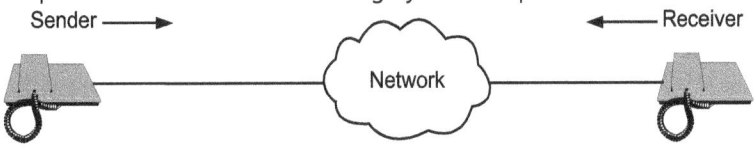

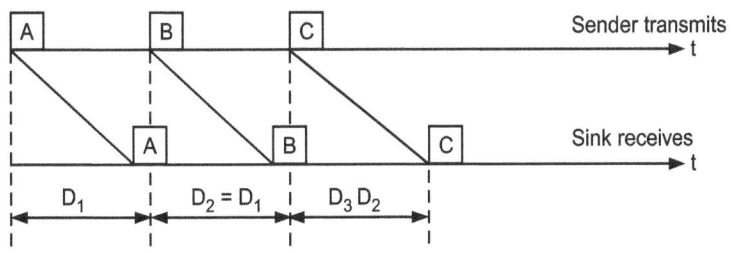

Fig. 1.70: Variation of Packet Arrival Time (Jitter)

- Recommended practice is to count the number of packets that arrive late and create a ratio of these packets to the number of packets that are successfully processed.
- You can then use this ratio to adjust the jitter buffer to target a predetermined, allowable late-packet ratio. This adaptation of jitter buffer sizing is effective in compensation of delays.
- Note that jitter and total delay are *not* the same thing, although having plenty of jitter in a packet network can increase the amount of total delay in the network.
- This is because the more jitter you have, the larger jitter buffers are needed to compensate for the unpredictable nature of the packet network.
- Most Digital Signal Processors do not have infinite jitter buffers to handle excessive network delays.
- Sometimes it is better to just drop packets or have fixed-length buffers instead of creating unwanted delays in the jitter buffers.
- If your data network is engineered well and you take the proper precautions, jitter is usually not a major problem and the jitter buffer does not significantly contribute to the total end-to-end delay.

1.18.10 Bandwidth-Delay Product

- In data communications, **bandwidth-delay product** refers to the product of a data link's capacity (in bits per second) and its end-to-end delay (in seconds).
- The result, an amount of data measured in bits (or bytes), is equivalent to the maximum amount of data on the network circuit at any given time, i.e. data that has been transmitted but not yet received.
- Sometimes it is calculated as the data link's capacity times its round trip time.
- Obviously, the bandwidth-delay product is higher for faster circuits with long-delay links such as GEO satellite connections.
- The product is particularly important for protocols such as TCP that guarantee reliable delivery, as it describes the amount of yet-unacknowledged data that the sender has to duplicate in a buffer memory in case the client requires it to retransmit a garbled or lost packet.
- A network with a large bandwidth-delay product is commonly known as a **long fat network** (shortened to **LFN** and often pronounced "elephant").
- A network is considered an LFN if its bandwidth-delay product is significantly larger than 10^5 bits (~12 kB).

Examples:
- Customer on a DSL link, 1 Mbit/s, 200 ms one-way delay: 200 kbit = 25 kB.
- High-speed terrestrial network: 100 Mbit/s, 100 ms: 10 Mbit = 1.25 MB.
- Server on a long-distance 1 Gbit/s link, average one-way delay 300 ms = 300 Mbit = 37.5 MB total required for buffering.

SOLVED EXAMPLES

Example 1.3:

Calculate the time periods of following frequency components.

    (a) 50 Hz   (b) 60 Hz   (c) 1 kHz   (d) 10 MHz

Solution:

(a)
$$T = \frac{1}{50 \text{ Hz}} = 0.02 \text{ s} = 20 \text{ ms}$$

(b)
$$T = \frac{1}{60 \text{ Hz}} = 0.016 \text{ s} = 16.66 \text{ ms}$$

(c)
$$T = \frac{1}{1 \text{ kHz}} = 1 \times 10^{-3} \text{ s} = 1 \text{ ms}$$

(d)
$$T = \frac{1}{10 \text{ MHz}} = 1 \times 10^{-6} \text{ s} = 1 \text{ μsec.}$$

Example 1.4:

Calculate the wavelength of the following signals.

    (a) Audio signal = 5 kHz   (b) Bass frequency signal = 300 Hz
    (c) Speech signal = 3400 Hz   (d) Ultrasonic signal = 30 kHz
    (e) Video signal = 5.5 MHz   (f) Microwave signal = 1 GHz
    (g) Violet colour signal = 790 THz = 790×10^{12} Hz
    (h) Red colour signal = 405 THz = 405×10^{12} Hz.

Solution:

(a) Audio signal wavelength $\lambda = \dfrac{3 \times 10^8}{f} = \dfrac{3 \times 10^8}{5 \text{ kHz}}$
$$= 60 \times 10^3 \text{ meters}$$

(b) Bass frequency signal $\lambda = \dfrac{3 \times 10^8}{300} = 1 \times 10^6 \text{ meters}$

(c) Speech signal $\lambda = \dfrac{3 \times 10^8}{3400} = 88.235 \times 10^3 \text{ meters}$

(d) Ultrasonic signal $\lambda = \dfrac{3 \times 10^8}{30 \times 10^3} = 10{,}000 \text{ meters}$

(e) Video signal $\lambda = \dfrac{3 \times 10^8}{5.5 \times 10^6} = 54.54 \text{ meters}$

(f) Microwave signal $\lambda = \dfrac{3 \times 10^8}{1 \times 10^9} = 0.3 \text{ meters}$

(g) Violet colour signal $\lambda = \dfrac{3 \times 10^8}{790 \times 10^{12}} \cong 380 \text{ nanometers} = 380 \text{ nm}$

(h) Red colour signal $\lambda = \dfrac{3 \times 10^8}{405 \times 10^{12}} = 740 \text{ nm}$

Example 1.5:

A periodic signal is decomposed into five sine waves with frequencies of 50, 150, 250, 350, 450 Hz. What is the bandwidth ? Draw the spectrum, assuming all components have a maximum amplitude of 21 V.

Solution:

$$B.W = f_H - f_L$$
$$\text{Bandwidth} = 450 \text{ Hz} - 50 \text{ Hz} = 400 \text{ Hz}$$

∴ $\boxed{B.W. = 400 \text{ Hz}}$

∵   Spectrum is as given.

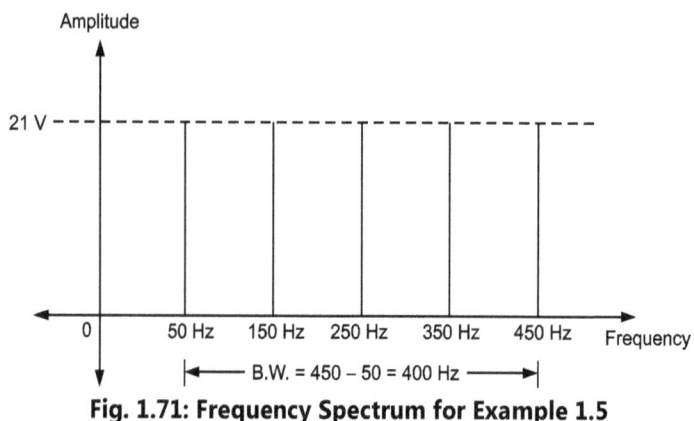

Fig. 1.71: Frequency Spectrum for Example 1.5

Example 2.4:

A periodic signal has a B.W. of 30 Hz. The highest frequency is 90 Hz. What is the lowest frequency ? Draw the spectrum if the signal contains all frequencies of the amplitude = 21 volts.

Solution:

$$B.W. = f_H - f_L$$
$$30 = 90 - f_L$$
$$f_L = 90 - 30 = 60 \text{ Hz}$$

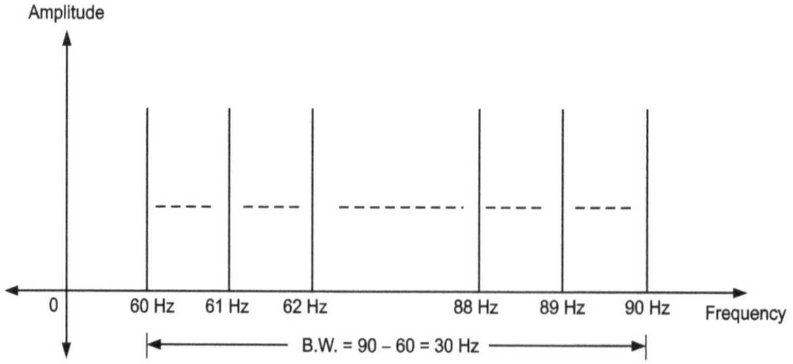

Fig. 1.72: Spectrum for Example 1.6

Example 1.7:
A non-periodic composite signal has a B.W. = 200 MHz, with a middle frequency of 200 MHz and peak amplitude of 40 V. The two extreme frequencies have an amplitude of 0 V. Draw the frequency spectrum of a given signal specification.
Solution:

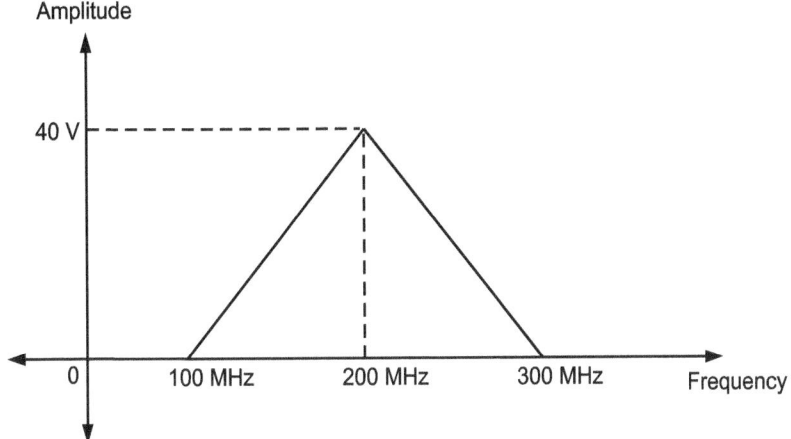

Fig. 1.73: Spectrum for Example 1.7

Example 1.8:
A digital signal has 16 levels. How many bits are needed per level?
Solution:

Number of bits/level $= \log_2 (16) = 4$.

Example 1.9:
A digital signal has 256 levels. How many bits are needed per level?
Solution:

Number of bits/level $= \log_2 (256)$

$$= \frac{\log_{10} (256)}{\log_{10} (2)} = 8$$

Example 1.10:
We have a low pass channel with bandwidth = 200 kHz. What is the maximum bit rate of this channel?
Solution:

1st harmonic of 200 kHz = 200 kHz

∴   Bit rate $= 2 \times 1^{st}$ harmonic

Bit rate $= 2 \times 200$ kHz = 400 kbps

Example 1.11:
Suppose a signal travels through a transmission medium and its power is reduced to one-third i.e. $P_2 = \frac{1}{3} P_1$. Calculate attenuation.

Solution:

$$\text{Attenuation} = 10 \log_{10}\left(\frac{P_2}{P_1}\right) = 10 \log_{10}\left(\frac{\frac{1}{3}P_1}{P_1}\right)$$

$$\text{Attenuation} = 10 \log_{10}(0.333) = -4.77 \text{ dB.}$$

Example 1.12

A signal travels through an amplifier and its power is increased to 15 times. This means that $P_2 = 15\ P_1$. Calculate the gain.

Solution:
$$\text{Gain} = 10 \log_{10}\left(\frac{P_2}{P_1}\right) = 10 \log_{10}\left(\frac{15\ P_1}{P_1}\right)$$

$$\text{Gain} = 10 \log_{10}(15) = 11.76 \text{ dB.}$$

Example 1.13:

Convert the -60 dB_m power in watts.

$$\text{dB}_m = 10 \log_{10}(P_m)$$

$$-60 = 10 \log_{10}(P_m)$$

$$\log^{-1}\left[\frac{-60}{10}\right] = P_m$$

$$\boxed{P_m = 1 \times 10^{-6} \text{ watts}}$$

Example 1.14:

The power of a signal is 100 mW and the power of the noise is 10 µW. Calculate SNR and SNR_{dB}.

Solution:

$$\text{SNR} = \frac{S}{N} = \frac{100 \times 10^{-3}}{10 \times 10^{-6}} = 10000$$

$$\text{SNR}_{dB} = 10 \log_{10}(\text{SNR}) = 10 \log_{10}(10000)$$

$$\text{SNR}_{dB} = 40 \text{ dB}$$

$$\boxed{\begin{array}{l} \therefore \quad \text{SNR} = 10000 \\ \text{SNR}_{dB} = 40 \text{ dB} \end{array}}$$

Example 1.15:

Consider a noiseless channel with a B.W. of 4000 Hz transmitting a signal with two signal levels. Calculate maximum bit rate. Also calculate the bit rate if 6 signal levels are decided.

Solution:

Bit rate for 2 signal levels $= 2 \times 4000 \times \log_2 2 = 8000 \text{ bps.}$

Bit rate for 6 signal levels $= 2 \times 4000 \times \log_2 6 = 20679.7 \text{ bps.}$

Example 1.16:

Calculate the theoretical highest bit rate of a telephone line if bandwidth assigned for data communication is 3400 Hz and SNR = 3200.

Solution:

$$B = 3400$$

$$SNR = 3200$$

$$\text{Bit rate} = B \log_2 (1 + SNR)$$

$$= 3400 \times \log_2 (1 + 3200)$$

$$= 3400 \times \frac{\log 3201}{\log 2}$$

$$= 3400 \times 11.64430$$

$$\boxed{\text{Bit rate} = 39590.644 \text{ bps}}$$

Example 1.17:

Calculate bit rate for above example if SNR_{dB} = 30 dB, SNR_{dB} = 40 dB.

Solution: $SNR_{dB} = 30 \text{ dB} = 10 \log_{10} (SNR)$

$$\therefore \qquad SNR = 1000$$

$$SNR_{dB} = 40 \text{ dB} = 10 \log_{10} (SNR)$$

$$SNR = 10,000$$

$$\text{Bit rate for SNR} = 1000 \text{ is} = 3400 \log_2 (1 + 1000)$$

$$\boxed{\text{Bit rate} = 33888.56 \text{ bps}}$$

$$\text{Bit rate for SNR} = 10,000$$

$$\therefore \qquad \text{Bit rate} = 3400 \log_2 (1 + 10000)$$

$$\boxed{\text{Bit rate} = 45178.713 \text{ bps}}$$

Example 1.18:

Calculate the bit rate if bandwidth assigned for telephone line is = 1 MHz and SNR_{dB} = 40 dB.

Solution:

$$\text{Bit rate} = B \cdot \log_2 (1 + SNR), B = 1 \times 10^6 \text{ Hz}$$

$$\therefore \qquad SNR_{dB} = 10 \log_{10} (SNR)$$

$$40 \text{ dB} = 10 \log_{10} (SNR)$$

$$\therefore \qquad \boxed{SNR = 10000}$$

$$\therefore \qquad \text{Bit rate} = 1 \times 10^6 \times \log_2 (1 + SNR)$$

$$= 1 \times 10^6 \times \log_2 (1 + 10000)$$

$$\text{Bit rate} = 13.28 \times 10^6 \text{ bits/sec.}$$

$$\boxed{\text{Bit rate} = 13.28 \text{ Mbps}}$$

Example 1.19:

Calculate the maximum data rate by Shannon formula and required levels using Nyquist formula for a data communication link for B.W. = 1.2 MHz and SNR = 64.

Solution:

Shannon formula $\boxed{C = B \log_2 (1 + \text{SNR})}$

$$= 1.2 \times 10^6 \log_2 (1 + 64)$$

$\boxed{C = 7.226 \text{ Mbps}}$, $\boxed{C = 2 B \log_2 L}$ is Nyquist formula

$$7.226 \times 10^6 = 2 \times 1.2 \times 10^6 \cdot \log_2 (L)$$

$$\frac{7.225 \times 10^6}{2 \times 1.2 \times 10^6} = \log_2 (L)$$

$$L = 8.06$$

$$\boxed{L = 8 \text{ levels}}$$

Example 1.20:

A network with B.W. of 12 Mbps can pass only an average of 14,000 frames per minute with each frame carrying an average of 12,000 bits. What is the throughput of this network?

Solution: 1 minute = 60 sec.

$$\text{Throughput} = \frac{14000 \times 12000}{60 \text{ sec}} = 2.8 \text{ Mbps}$$

Example 1.21:

What is the propagation time if the distance between the two points is 14,000 km? Assume the propagation speed to be 2.4×10^8 m/s in cable.

Solution:

$$14000 \text{ km} = 14000 \times 1000 = 14 \times 10^6 \text{ meters}$$

$$\text{Propagation time} = \frac{14000 \times 1000}{2.4 \times 10^8} = 58.33 \text{ msec.}$$

$$\boxed{\text{Propagation time} = 58.33 \text{ msec.}}$$

Example 1.22:

What are the propagation time and the transmission time for a 3.5 kbyte message sent by an email, if the B.W. of the network is 2 Gbps? Assume that the distance between the transmitter and receiver is 14000 km and that light travels at 2.4×10^8 m/s.

Solution:

$$3.5 \text{ kbyte} = 3.5 \times 10^3 \times 8 = 28000 \text{ bits}$$

$$14000 \text{ km} = 14000 \times 1000 = \text{meters}$$

$$\therefore \qquad \text{Propagation time} = \frac{14000 \times 1000}{2.4 \times 10^8} = 58.33 \text{ msec}$$

$$\therefore \qquad \text{Transmission time} = \frac{3500 \times 8}{2 \times 10^9} = 0.014 \text{ msec.}$$

Example 1.23:

What are the propagation time and the transmission time for a 6 Mbyte message sent by an email if the B.W. of network is 1.2 Mbps? Assume that the distance between the sender and the receiver is 14000 km and that light travels at 2.4×10^8 m/sec.

Solution:
$$6 \text{ Mbyte} = 6 \times 10^6 \times 8 = 48 \times 10^6 \text{ bits}$$
$$\text{Distance} = 14000 \text{ km} = 14000 \times 1000 = 14 \times 10^6 \text{ meters}$$

∴
$$\text{Propagation time} = \frac{14000 \times 1000}{2.4 \times 10^8} = 58.33 \text{ msec.}$$

∴
$$\text{Transmission time} = \frac{6 \times 10^6 \times 8}{1.2 \times 10^6} = 40 \text{ sec.}$$

Propagation time = 58.33 msec.
Transmission time = 40 sec

EXERCISE

1. Describe data communication.
2. List out various components of data communication.
3. Explain data representation.
4. Write short note on: Direction of flow.
5. Define Network. Explain computer network.
6. Explain:
    (i)   Advantages of network.
    (ii) Uses of computer network.
7. Describe network criteria.
8. Briefly describe network hardware and software.
9. Define protocol and it's hierarchy.
10. List out various network topologies.
11. Write short notes on:
    (i)   Ring topology
    (ii) Mech topology
    (iii) Star topology
    (iv) Bus topology
12. With neat diagram explain hybrid topology.
13. List out different categories of networks.
14. Describe:
    (i)   LAN
    (ii) WAN
    (iii) MAN

15. Explain design issues for layer.
16. Describe network architecture.
17. With the neat diagram explain ISO/OSI reference model.
18. List out different layers of ISO/OSI model with their functions.
19. Define signal.
20. Explain Analog and Digital signal with suitable diagram.
21. Compare digital and analog signal.
22. Describe:
    (i)   Analog transmission.
    (ii) Digital transmission.
23. Define the following :
    (a)   Analog signal
    (b)   Digital signal
    (c)   Analog data
    (d)   Digital data
24. Draw and explain the periodic analog signal.
25. What is composite signal?
26. What is duty cycle of square waveform and pulse waveform ?
27. Draw and explain the time domain and frequency domain representation of sine wave signal.
28. Draw and explain the time domain and frequency domain representation of the composite signal.
29. Draw time and frequency domain plot of non-periodic signal.
30. Comment on bandwidth of composite signal with suitable example.
31. Write short notes on :
    (a)   Digital signals
    (b)   Digital signal as composite analog signal
32. Explain the limitation of transmitting baseband digital signal over the channel.
33. Write a short note on transmission impairment.
34. What factors are responsible for limiting data rates in data communication system?
35. Explain Nyquist bit rate and Shannon capacity theorem.
36. What is QoS (Quality of Service)?
37. Write short notes on:
    (a) Bandwidth   (b) Throughput
    (c) Delay   (d) Jitter
    (e) Bandwidth-delay product

UNIVERSITY QUESTIONS

NOVEMBER-DECEMBER 2011

1. (a) (i) Define data communication? What are the network criteria for an effective data communication. **(5)**

    (ii) Draw and explain ISO-OSI reference model. **(5)**

   (b) Define the following terms: **(10)**

    (i) Throughput and frequency

    (ii) Analog signals and digital signal

    (iii) Periodic and Non-periodic signal

   (c) Write short notes on:

    (i) Characteristics and component

    (ii) Transmission modes.

MAY-JUNE 2011

2. What are the direction of flow in data communication? Also state the characteristics of data communication system. **(5)**

3. Explain in detail various data rate limits of transmission impairments. **(5)**

4. (i) The power of signal is 100 mW and the power of noise is 1 mW. What are the values of SNR and SNR dB? **(5)**

   (ii) Compare the neat diagram of network hardware and network software. **(10)**

   (iii) A system has 10 watts of signal power, 1 watt of noise power and the bandwidth of 1 kHz. What should be the channel capacity?

NOVEMBER-DECEMBER 2010

5. Explain ISO-OSI reference model. Also explain function of each layer in short. **(10)**

6. What is transmission impairment? Also explain cause of impairment. **(5)**

7. Explain the component of data communication with neat diagram. **(10)**

MAY-JUNE 2010

8. What is communication, telecommunication, data, data communication and data representation? **(5)**

9. Explain design issues of layers. **(5)**

10. What is signal, analog signal and digital signal. **(10)**

11. What is data rate limits, transmission impairment throughput, propagation speed, propagation time, wavelength? **(10)**

NOVEMBER-DECEMBER 2009

12. Define the following terms: **(10)**
    (i)   Throughput
    (ii) Propagation speed
    (iii) Wavelength
    (iv) Transmission impairment
    (v)   Propagation time

13. What are different types of signals used in data communication? Compare them.   **(10)**

14. Explain with diagram OSI reference model.   **(10)**

MAY-JUNE 2009

15. (i) What are the basic components of any data communication system? How do they work?   **(5)**

    (ii) A system has 100 watt of signal power going into the channel with noise of 100 watt. In order to send 10,000 bits/sec, how much bandwidth is needed?

16. Compare with the help of neat diagram network hardware and network software.   **(10)**

17. (i) A telephone line has a bandwidth of 3000 Hz, the signal to noise ratio is 3162. What is the channel capacity?   **(5)**

    (ii) What is various form of data representation?   **(5)**

✳✳✳

Unit II

DIGITAL TRANSMISSION AND ANALOG TRANSMISSION

Introduction

The basic classification of various conversions is as follows:

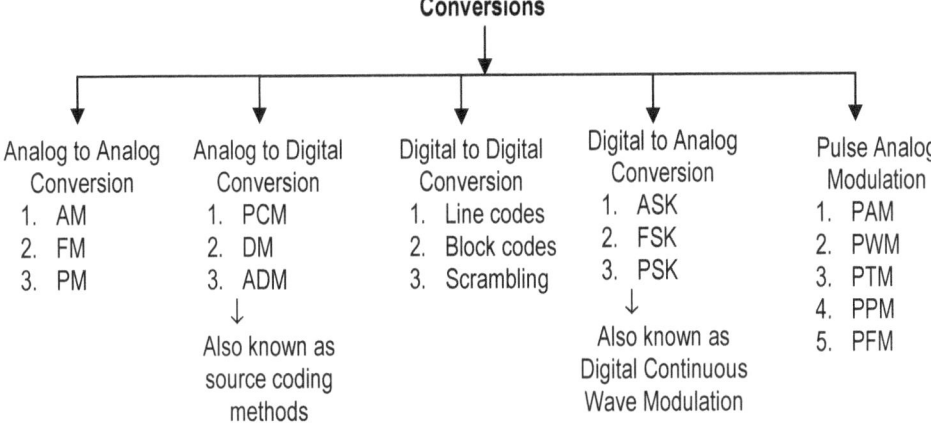

2.1 Digital to Digital Conversion

In Data Communication, a line code (also called digital baseband modulation) is a code chosen for use within a communication system for baseband transmission purposes. Line coding is often used for digital data transport. Here in this section we can represent the digital data by using digital signals. **The conversion involves three techniques like Line coding, block coding and scrambling**.

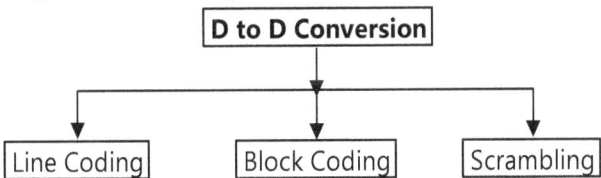

2.2 Line Coding Fundamental Theory

1. Line coding consists of representing the digital signal to be transported by an amplitude and time-discrete signal that is optimally tuned for the specific properties of the physical channel (and of the receiving equipment). The waveform pattern of voltage or current used to represent the 1s and 0s of a digital signal on a transmission link is called *line encoding*. The common types of line encoding are unipolar, polar, bipolar and Manchester encoding.

2. For reliable clock recovery at the receiver, one usually imposes a maximum runlength constraint on the generated channel sequence, i.e. the maximum number of consecutive ones or zeros is bounded to a reasonable number. A clock period is recovered by observing transitions in the received sequence, so that a maximum runlength guarantees such clock recovery, while sequences without such a constraint could seriously hamper the detection quality.

3. After line coding, the signal is put through a "physical channel", either a "transmission medium" or "data storage medium". Sometimes the characteristics of two very different-seeming channels are similar enough that the same line code is used for them. The most common physical channels are:
    - The line-coded signal can directly be put on a transmission line, in the form of variations of the voltage or current (often using differential signalling).
    - The line-coded signal (the "baseband signal") undergoes further pulse shaping (to reduce its frequency bandwidth) and then modulated (to shift its frequency bandwidth) to create the "RF signal" that can be sent through free space.
    - The line-coded signal can be used to turn on and off a light in Free Space Optics, most commonly infrared remote control.
    - The line-coded signal can be printed on paper to create a bar-code.
    - The line-coded signal can be converted to magnetized spots on a hard drive or tape drive.
    - The line-coded signal can be converted to pits on optical disc.

4. Unfortunately, most long-distance communication channels cannot transport a DC component. The DC component is also called the disparity, the bias, or the DC coefficient. The simplest possible line code is called unipolar because it has an unbounded DC component which gives too many errors on such systems.

5. Most line codes eliminate the DC components such codes are called DC balanced, zero-DC, zero-bias or DC equalized etc. There are two ways of eliminating the DC component:
    - **Use a constant-weight code:** In other words, design each transmitted code word such that every code word that contains some positive or negative levels also contain enough of the opposite levels, such that the average level over each code word is zero. For example, Manchester code and Interleaved 2 of 5.
    - **Use a paired disparity code:** In other words, design the receiver such that every code word that averages to a negative level is paired with another code word that averages to a positive level. Design the receiver so that either code word of the pair decodes to the same data bits. Design the transmitter to keep track of the running DC buildup, and always pick the code word that pushes the DC level back towards zero. For example, AMI, 8B10B, 4B3T, etc.

6. Line coding should make it possible for the receiver to synchronize itself to the phase of the received signal. If the synchronization is not ideal, then the signal to be decoded will not have optimal differences (in amplitude) between the various digits

or symbols used in the line code. This will increase the error probability in the received data.

7. It is also preferred for the line code to have a structure that will enable error detection.

8. Note that the line-coded signal and a signal produced at a terminal may differ, thus requiring translation.

9. A line code will typically reflect technical requirements of the transmission medium, such as optical fiber or shielded twisted pair. These requirements are unique for each medium, because each one has different behaviour related to interference, distortion, capacitance and loss of amplitude.

10. Each of the various line formats has a particular advantage and disadvantage. It is not possible to select one, which will meet all needs. The format may be selected to meet one or more of the following criteria:

   • Minimize transmission hardware

   • Facilitate synchronization

   • Ease error detection and correction

   • Minimize spectral content

   • Eliminate a DC component.

2.3 Line Coding Technical Theory

1. Digital data is converted into digital signal in line coding.

2. Digital data can be voice, video, image, text or numbers which are stored as a bit sequence in digital storage.

3. Typical line coding and line decoding mechanism is as shown in Fig. 2.1.

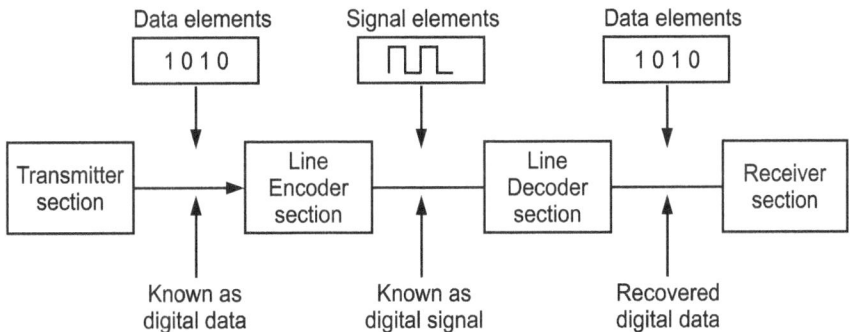

Fig. 2.1: Data Elements and Signal Elements in
Line Encoding and Line Decoding Mechanism

4. **Thus, the block schematics clearly explain that data elements are being carried and signal elements are the carriers.**

5. | The ratio r_{ds} is given as, $r_{ds} = \dfrac{\text{Data elements}}{\text{Signal elements}}$

6. Thus, for different values of r_{ds}, Fig. 2.2 clearly indicates the waveform.

7. The different values of r_{ds} are:

$r_{ds} = 1$, $r_{ds} = \dfrac{1}{2}$, $r_{ds} = 2$, $r_{ds} = \dfrac{3}{4}$ and $r_{ds} = \dfrac{4}{3}$.

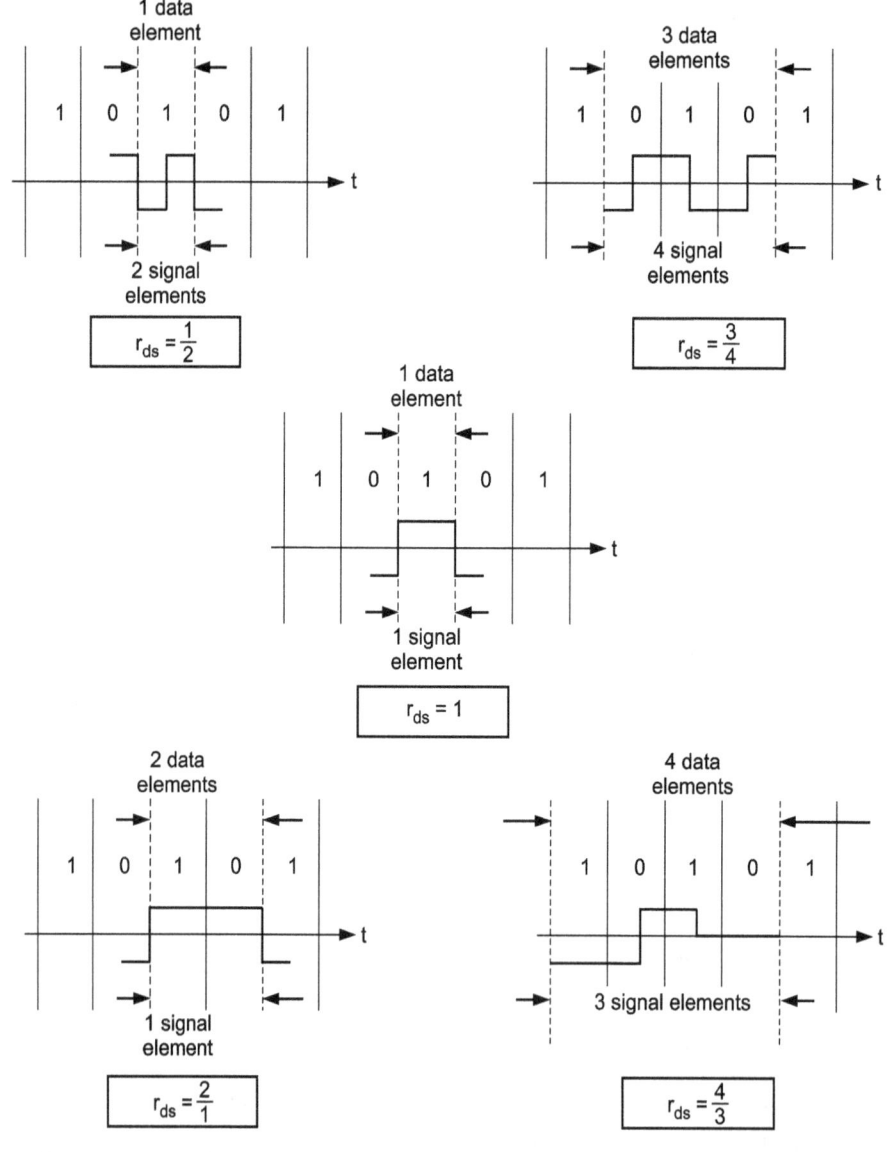

Fig. 2.2: Ratio of Data Elements to Signal Elements and Related Waveforms

8. Thus, data rate can be defined as, the number of data elements sent in 1s. The unit of data rate is bps.
9. Signal rate can be defined as, the number of signal elements sent in 1s. The unit of signal rate is baud.
10. Sometimes data rate is called as bit rate and signal rate is called as pulse rate or modulation rate or also baud rate.
11. The final target or goal in data communication is to increase the data rate while decreasing the signal rate.
12. Thus, increase in data rate increases the speed of transmission.
13. Thus, decrease in signal rate decreases the bandwidth requirement.
14. And we know that bandwidth spectrum is limited, hence expected thing is data rate should be high with limited signalling rate.

$$\boxed{S \;=\; \frac{C}{r_{ds}} \times N \;\; \text{bauds}}$$

where,
$$S \;=\; \text{Signal rate}$$
$$N \;=\; \text{Data rate}$$
$$C \;=\; \text{Case factor}$$
$$r_{ds} \;=\; \frac{\text{Data elements}}{\text{Signal elements}}$$

15. We have also seen that actual bandwidth of a digital signal is infinite, but the effective bandwidth is finite (Thus, in effective bandwidth, the upper frequency component with negligible amplitudes can be ignored. Hence, called as effective bandwidth).

16.   Thus, Bandwidth $= C \times N \times \dfrac{1}{r_{ds}}$

∴ $$\boxed{B_{min} \;=\; C \times N \times \frac{1}{r_{ds}}}$$

∴ $$\boxed{N_{max} \;=\; \frac{1}{C} \times B \times r_{ds}}$$

17. Finally, compare this N_{max} with Nyquist formula.

∴ $$\boxed{N_{max} \;=\; \frac{1}{C} \times B \times r_{ds} \;=\; 2B \times \log_2(L)}$$

18. **Baseline wandering:** Receiver calculates average received signal power while decoding the line codes. This average is known as baseline. If '0' and '1' string is long then drifting in baseline is possible, which is called as **baseline wandering.** Due to which decoding becomes difficult and incorrect. Good line codes should prevent the baseline wandering.
19. **DC component:** Telephone lines cannot pass frequencies below 210 Hz, so in line codes, if digital level '0' or '1' is constant for long time, which generates low frequencies around zero. This DC component saturate the core of coupling transformers in communication path.

20. **Self synchronization:** Transmitter and receiver clock should be matched otherwise, data error occurs or misinterpreting of data is possible. In self synchronization the timing information is added alongwith data.

21. Thus, good line codes must have built-in error detection and correction capabilities. Also, it should have good immunity to noise and interference. But more level line code is complex in nature and it is costly.

2.4 Types of Line Coding

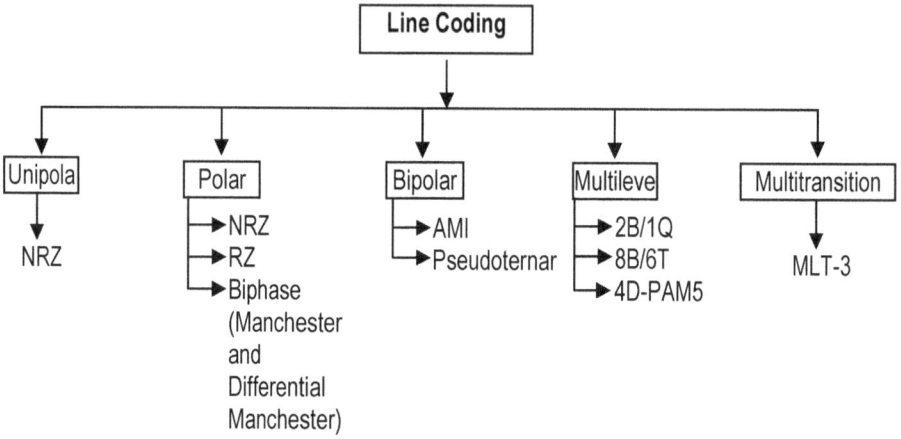

2.5 Line Coding in Detail

As we have seen there are basically five categories of studying line coding like:

- Unipolar
- Polar
- Bipolar
- Multilevel
- Multitransition.

Let's study one by one in detail.

2.5.1 Unipolar Scheme / NRZ (Non-Return-to-Zero)

1. In unipolar line coding scheme, all voltage levels or signal levels are on one side of the time axis. The signal level can be below or above of time axis.

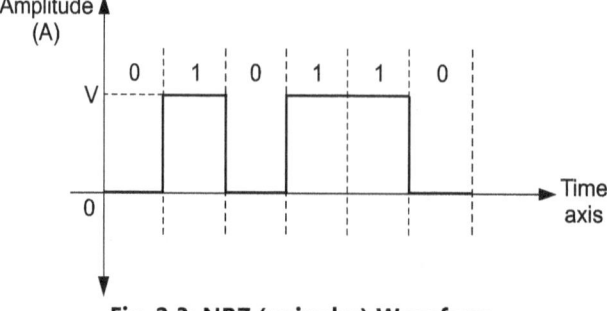

Fig. 2.3: NRZ (unipolar) Waveform

2. Positive voltage defines bit '1' and zero voltage defines bit '0'.

3. Here signal does not return to zero at the middle of the bit, hence called as NRZ (Non-Return-to-Zero).

4. Normalized power is given as $\frac{1}{2}(V)^2 + \frac{1}{2}(0)^2 = \frac{1}{2}V^2$

    i.e. Normalized power required to send 1 bit/unit line resistance is double as compared to polar NRZ. Hence NRZ unipolar scheme is costly.

2.5.2 Polar Schemes [NRZ-L, NRZ-I, RZ]

1. Polar NRZ (NRZ-L and NRZ-I) uses two levels of voltage amplitude.

2. NRZ-L stands for NRZ-level and NRZ-I stands for NRZ-Invert.

3. In NRZ-L, the level of voltage determines the value of the bit.

4. In NRZ-I, the change or lack of change in the level of voltage determines the value of bit, if there is no change the bit is '0' and if there is change the bit is '1'.

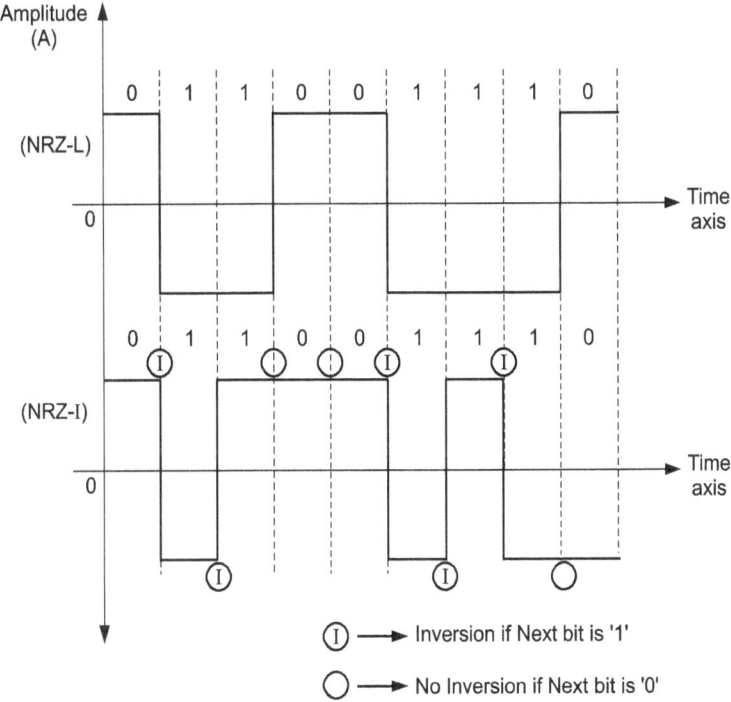

Fig. 2.4: NRZ-L and NRZ-I Waveforms

5.   The NRZ-L and NRZ-I comparison is as given in Table 2.1.

Table 2.1

NRZ-L	NRZ-I
1. Baseline wandering problem is severe in NRZ-L.	1. It is less as compared to NRZ-L.
2. The average signal power is less if long sequence of '0' or '1' is present.	2. This problem occurs only for a long sequence of '0'.
3. Synchronization problem exists and it is severe in NRZ-L.	3. Synchronization problem exists and it is less as compared to NRZ-L.
4. NRZ-L gives more problem if there is a sudden change of polarity in the system.	4. NRZ-I does not have this problem.
5. Average signal rate $(S_{avg}) = \dfrac{N}{2}$ bauds.	5. Average signal rate $(S_{avg}) = \dfrac{N}{2}$ bauds.
6. DC component carrying high level of energy, gives DC component problem.	6. DC component carrying high level of energy, gives DC component problem.
7. Normalized bandwidth graph is as shown below: 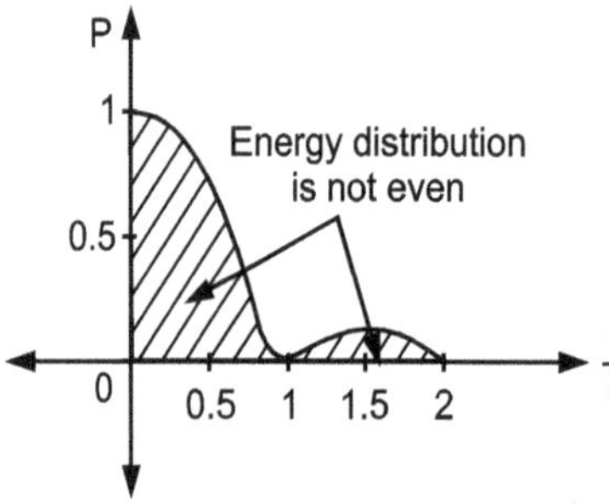 Fig. 2.5 (a): NRZ-L bandwidth curve for $\left[r = 1,\ S_{avg} = \dfrac{N}{2}\right]$	7. Normalized bandwidth graph is as shown below: 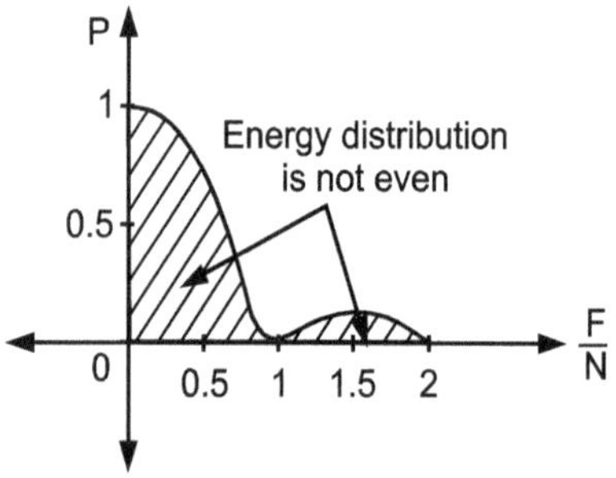 Fig. 2.5 (b): NRZ-I bandwidth curve for $\left[r = 1,\ S_{avg} = \dfrac{N}{2}\right]$

6.   **RZ (Return to Zero) Scheme:** Synchronization problems are solved in RZ scheme. Receiver understands start and end of next bit.

7.   In NRZ-L and NRZ-I, receiver does not understand the start and end of next bit.

8.   RZ uses three values:
   *   Positive
   *   Zero
   *   Negative.

9. **In RZ, the signal does not change between the bits but it changes during the bits.**

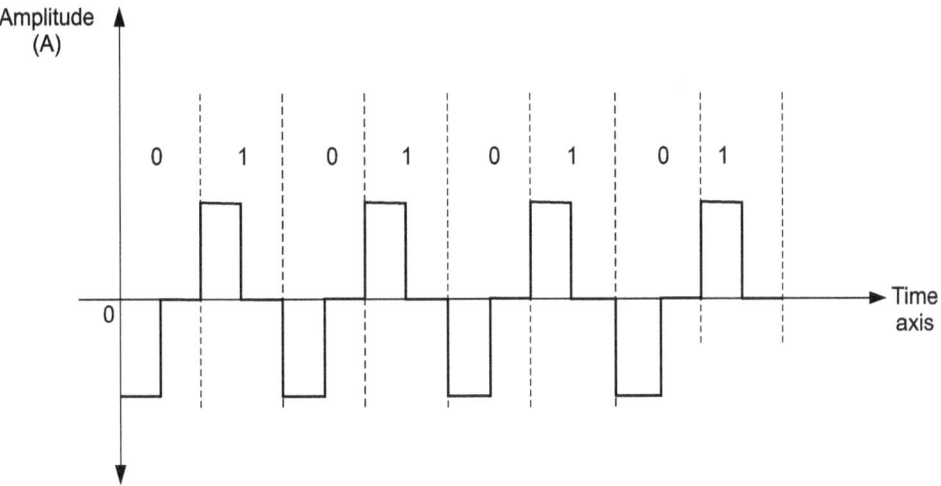

Fig. 2.6: RZ Waveform

10. Thus, in RZ, signal goes to zero in the middle of each bit. It does not change until the beginning of the next bit (0 or 1 bit).

11. In RZ, it occupies two signal changes to encode a bit and hence has more signalling rate and hence occupies more bandwidth as shown in Fig. 2.7.

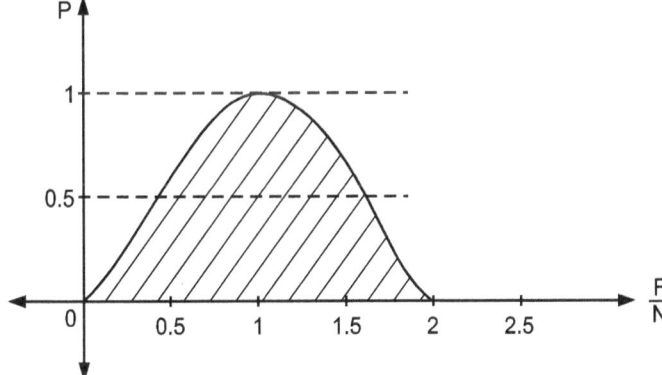

Fig. 2.7: Normalized bandwidth of RZ $\left[\text{for } r = \dfrac{1}{2}, S_{avg} = N \right]$

12. Also RZ gives more problem if there is sudden change of polarity in the system (i.e. '0' will be accepted as '1' and vice versa).

13. In RZ, there is no DC component problem.

14. RZ system is complex because three levels are used.

15. Thus, due to all these problems, RZ is not used as it is.

16. **To overcome these problems, RZ has been replaced by the Manchester and differential Manchester methods.**

17. Manchester and differential Manchester methods are also known as **Biphase line coding techniques**.
18. **Manchester scheme = RZ scheme + NRZ (L) scheme:**
    The idea of transition at the middle of the bit in RZ and NRZ (L) are combined to give Manchester line coding technique.
19. **Differential Manchester scheme = RZ scheme + NRZ (I) scheme**:
    The transition at the middle of the bit in RZ and NRZ (I) idea are combined to give differential Manchester line coding technique.
20. Manchester and differential Manchester line coding waveforms are shown in Fig. 2.8.

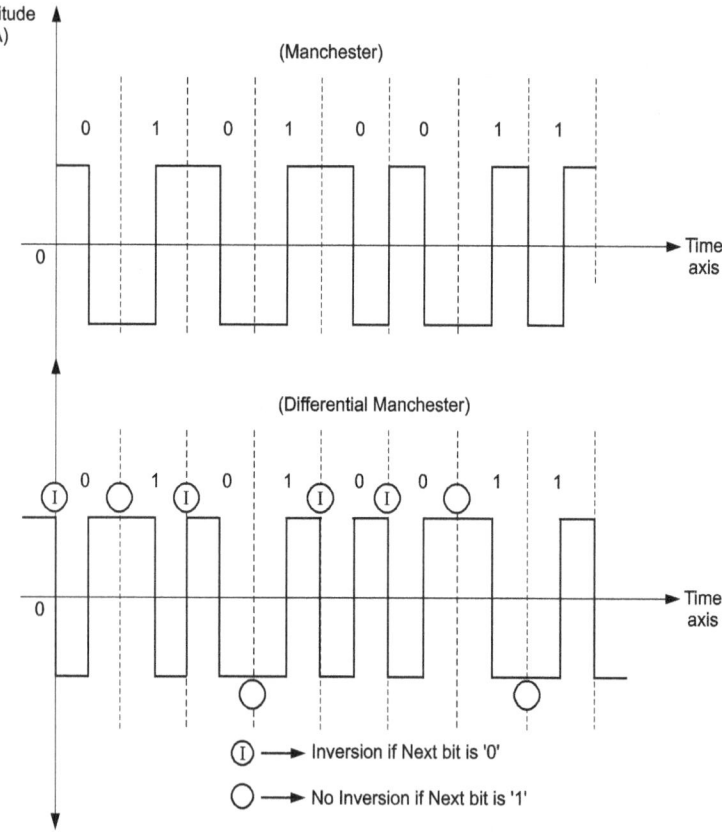

Fig. 2.8: Manchester and Differential Manchester Line Coding

21. Manchester method overcomes the problem of NRZ-L and differential Manchester method overcomes the problem of NRZ-I line coding techniques.
22. Advantages of Manchester and differential Manchester method:
    • No baseline wandering.
    • Absence of DC component (each bit has positive and negative voltage contribution).
23. Disadvantage of Manchester and differential Manchester method:
    Bandwidth required = 2 × NRZ bandwidth.

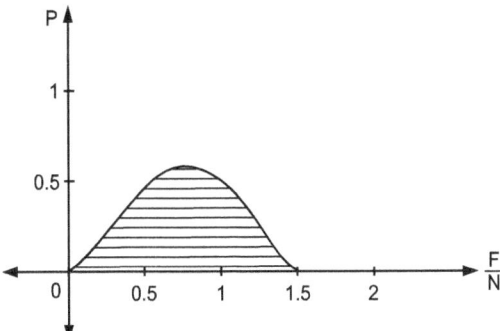

Fig. 2.9: Normalized Bandwidth of Manchester and Differential Manchester Line Coding

$$\text{Techniques}\left[\text{for } r = \frac{1}{2}, \; S_{avg} = N\right]$$

2.5.3 Bipolar Line Coding (AMI and Pseudoternary)

1.   **AMI stands** for Alternate Mark Inversion.

   Binary '0' → Zero volts (Neutral).

   Binary '1' → Alternate positive and negative voltages.

2.   In Pseudoternary,

   Binary '1' → Zero volts (Neutral).

   Binary '0' → Alternate positive and negative voltages.

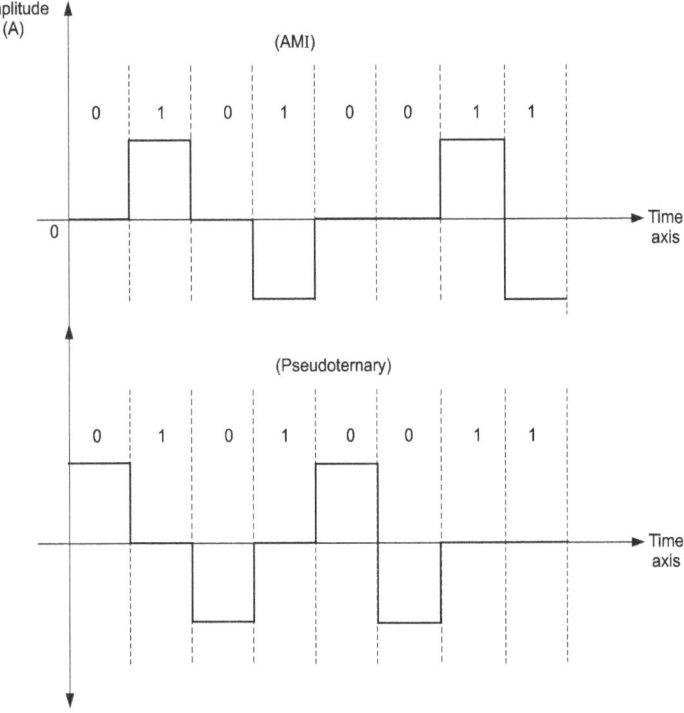

Fig. 2.10: AMI and Pseudoternary Line Coding Techniques

3. Typical normalized bandwidth curve for bipolar line coding method is shown in Fig. 2.11.

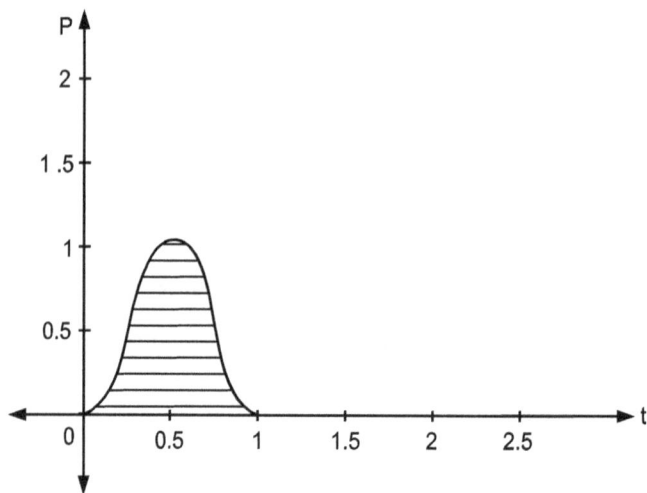

Fig. 2.11: Normalized Bandwidth for Bipolar Line Coding $\left[\text{for r = 1 and } S_{avg} = \dfrac{N}{2} \right]$

4. In AMI, long stream of '0' and in Pseudoternary, long stream of '1' cannot produce DC components because these are neutral zero voltages, which cannot create DC components.

5. **AMI is commonly used in long-distance communication applications.**

6. AMI has synchronization problems in communication.

7. **Comparison between Bipolar and Polar NRZ:**

Table 2.2

Bipolar Method	Polar NRZ
1. Bipolar method was developed as alternative to NRZ.	1. Polar NRZ method was developed as alternative to unipolar NRZ.
2. Bipolar signal rate = Polar NRZ signal rate.	2. Same as Bipolar.
3. It has no DC component problem for long '0' and '1' data.	3. It has DC component problem for long '0' and '1' data.
4. Bipolar methods has most of its energy concentrated around frequency $= \dfrac{N}{2}$.	4. NRZ method has most of its energy concentrated near zero frequency, so unsuitable for transmission.
5. Normalized bandwidth curve is as shown in Fig. 2.12 (a).	5. Normalized bandwidth curve is as shown in Fig. 2.12 (b).

Bipolar Method	Polar NRZ
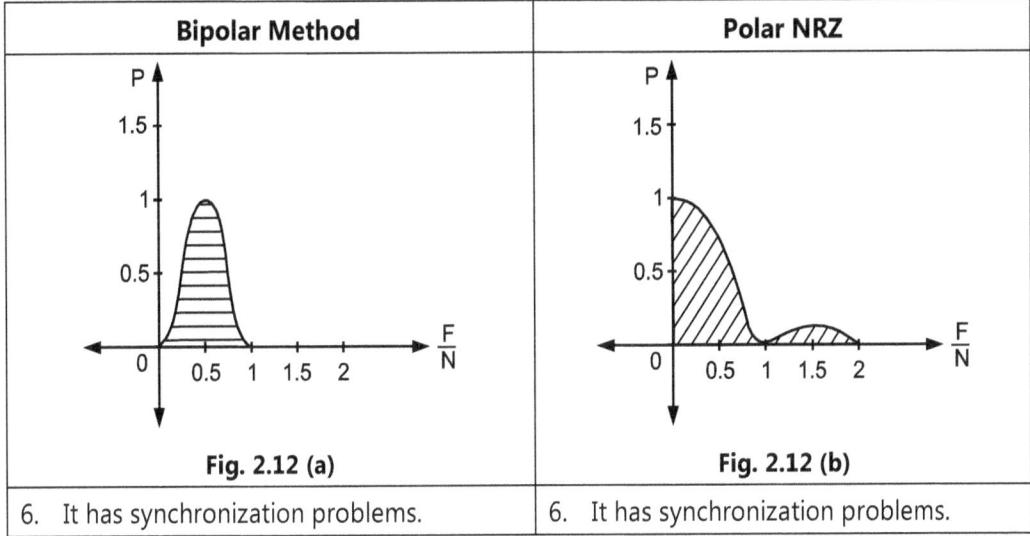	
Fig. 2.12 (a)	Fig. 2.12 (b)
6. It has synchronization problems.	6. It has synchronization problems.

2.6 Multilevel Line Coding [2B/1Q, 8B/6T, 4D-PAM5]

1. Multilevel line coding techniques has following advantages:
    - Increase in data speed or decrease in required bandwidth.
    - Prevents baseline wandering to provide synchronization.
    - Error detection possible.

2. For this coding the designers have classified these types as **mBnL**.

    where,   m = Length of binary pattern

                               B = Binary data

                               n = Length of the signal pattern

                               L = Number of levels in signalling

    $$L = 2 \rightarrow \text{Binary}$$
    $$L = 3 \rightarrow \text{Ternary}$$
    $$L = 4 \rightarrow \text{Quaternary}$$

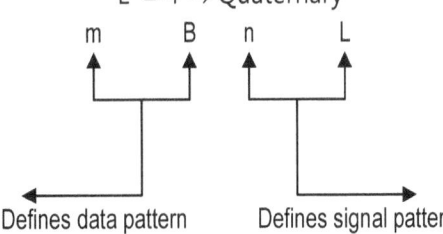

Defines data pattern   Defines signal pattern

3. In **mBnL** method, a pattern of 'm' data elements is encoded as a pattern of 'n' signal elements in which $2^m < L^n$. Because data encoding is not possible if $2^m > L^n$, as some of the data patterns cannot be encoded.

2.6.1 2B1Q Coding

1. 2B1Q stands for two binary, one quaternary method.

2. It uses data patterns size = 2 and encodes the 2 bit patterns as one signal element belonging to a four-level signal.

3. The 2B1Q (two binary, one quaternary) line encoding scheme was intended to be used by the ISDN DSL and SDSL applications.

4. This code is a four-level line code in which two binary bits (2B) represent one quaternary symbol (1Q).

5. The 2B1Q line coding was seen as a major enhancement over the original T1 line coding, because 2B1Q encoded two bits per signal change instead of just one per change.

2B1Q Coding Rules

1. 2B1Q is a 4-level code. It takes two 2-level bits and converts them into one 4-level baud (quat) as indicated in Table 2.3.

2. This conversion effectively doubles the period of the symbol. Since the period is inversely proportional to frequency (i.e., $f = 1/T$) the frequency on the line is reduced. With every advantage there is always drawback and the 2B1Q is no exception.

3. A 4-level code results in reduced distance between decision levels, thus increasing the required SNR for a given performance level (BER). However, the baud rate reduction and narrower bandwidth result in performance gains which outweigh this drawback.

4. The important elements of the transmit quat are its sign, and its amplitude. The values assigned to the levels are set so that there is equal spacing between the four levels.

5. Levels can be chosen to be +1, +0.33, -0.33 and −1. In order to eliminate the decimals, we will choose the four levels to be +3, +1, −1, and −3. The 2B1Q conversion table is shown in Table 2.3.

6. The first bit of the dibit is called the "sign-bit". If it is 0, the output quat will have a negative sign. If the first bit is 1, then the output quat will have a positive sign.

7. The second bit of the dibit is called the amplitude bit, and it determines the magnitude of the output quat. If it is 0, then the output level has an amplitude of 3.

8. If the second bit of the dibit is 1, then the output amplitude is 1. This provides for a very simple means of encoding a binary bit stream into a 4-level code. An example of 2B1Q coding is shown in Fig. 2.13.

Table 2.3: 2B1Q Coding Rules

Dibit	Output Quat
10	+3
11	+1
01	−1
00	−3

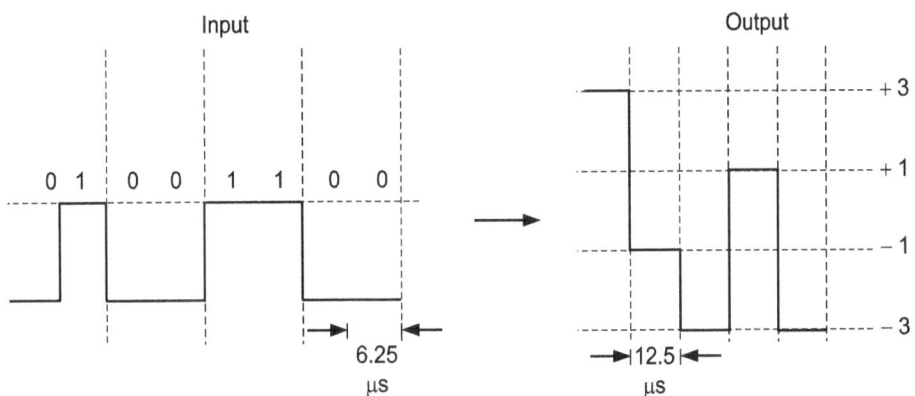

2-Level, Binary Data, 160 kbit/s　　　　4-Level, Quaternary Data, 80 kbaud/s

Fig. 2.13: 2B1Q Line Coding Example, 2 Binary, 1 Quaternary

Performance

1. The transmit baud rate of the 2B1Q system is one half the rate of linear codes (80 kbaud/s vs 160 kbaud/s). This puts the bandwidth of the 2B1Q system in a lower frequency region of the Power Spectral Density (PSD) graph. It also produces a bandwidth which is much narrower than that for Biphase.

2. Fig. 2.14 shows comparison of filtered PSD plots. Telephone transmission lines act as a low pass filter with attenuation varying directly with frequency. Lower bandwidth codes will experience less attenuation, thus achieving greater reach.

3. A limiting factor to most linear line codes is the performance in the presence of Near End Crosstalk (NEXT). NEXT is generated onto a transmission line from the adjoining twisted pairs that are found in a bundle of cable.

4. The signal on the adjoining pair will induce a signal on the line. The magnitude of the induced signal will increase proportionally with frequency. Therefore, if you lower a signal bandwidth (i.e., lower frequency content) you reduce the effect of NEXT.

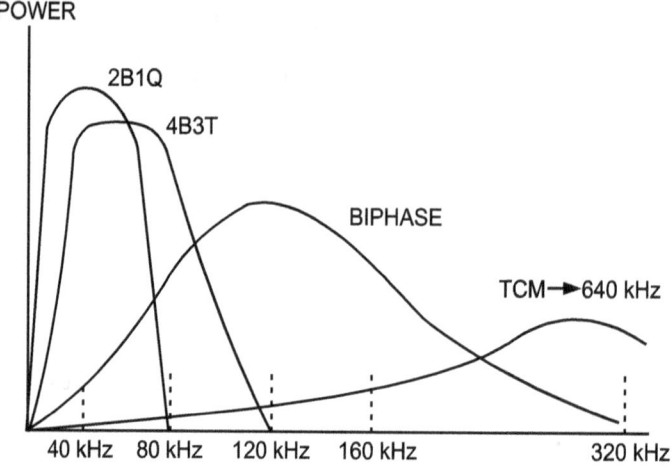

Fig. 2.14: 2B1Q Power Spectral Density Comparison

Complexity

1. One drawback of low frequency transmission is that the pulse output on the line tend to develop long "tails", or pulse responses caused by excessive group delay.

2. Several consecutive pulses will tend to have effect on its neighbours, resulting in Inter Symbol Interference (ISI).

3. This ISI must be compensated in order to ensure valid data recovery. Decision Feedback Equalization (DFE) is a technique which can be used to remove the effect of ISI.

4. A DFE is simply a finite impulse response filter which performs convolution of the loop impulse response with the received data.

5. This convolution will provide an estimate of the effects of ISI which can be removed from the received signal.

2.6.2 8B6T Coding

1. Some Encoding schemes for Ethernets are:

   - 10Mbps Ethernet (*Manchester encoding*).
   - 100baseTX (*MLT-3, 2 pair cat5, 4B5B*).
   - 100BaseFX (*NRZ-I, 2 pair fiber, 4B5B*).
   - 100BaseT4 (3 level 1V, 0V, & -1V, 4 pair cat 3, *8B/6T*).
   - Token Ring (*Differential Manchester*).

2. 100Base-T4 is designed to produce a 100 Mbps data rate over lower-quality voice grade, or Category 3, cable. The advantage of this is that in many existing buildings, there is an abundance of voice-grade cabling and very little else. Thus, if this cabling can be used, installation costs are minimized.

3. With present technology, a data rate of 100 Mbps over one or two Category 3 pairs is impractical. Instead, 100Base-T4 specifies that the data stream to be transmitted is divided into three separate data streams. Four twisted pairs are used.

4. Data are transmitted using three pairs and received using three pairs. Thus, two of the pairs must be configured for bidirectional transmission.

5. As with 100Base-X, a simple NRZ encoding scheme is not used for 100Base-T4. This would require a signalling rate of 33 Mbps on each twisted pair and does not provide synchronization.

6. Instead, a ternary signalling scheme known as 8B6T is used. With ternary signalling, each signal element can take on one of three values-positive voltage, negative voltage, or zero voltage.

7. A pure ternary code is one in which the full information-carrying capacity of the ternary signal is exploited. However, pure ternary is not attractive for the same reason for which pure binary (NRZ) code is rejected the lack of synchronization.

8. The 8B6T code is designed to approach the efficiency of ternary and overcome this disadvantage.

9. With 8B6T, the data to be transmitted is handled in 8-bit blocks. Each block of 8 bits is mapped into a code group of 6 ternary symbols. The stream of code groups is then transmitted in round-robin fashion across the three output channels.

10. In 8B6T line encoding technique,

- The data to be transmitted are handled in 8-bit blocks.
- Each block of 8 bits is mapped into a code group of 6 ternary symbols.
- The stream of code groups is then transmitted in round-robin fashion across the three output channels.
- Thus, the ternary transmission rate on each output channel is $(6/8) \times 33.333 = 25$ Mbaud.

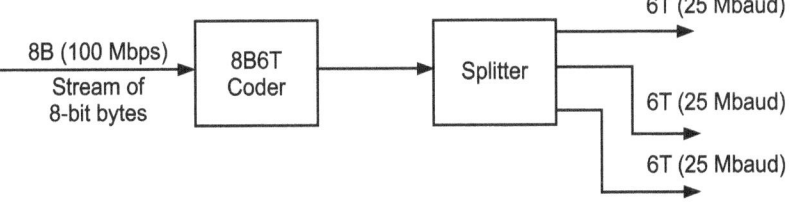

Fig. 2.15: Transmission Scheme

Table 2.4: Portion of 8B6T Code Table

Data octet	6T code group	Data octet	6T code group	Data octet	6T code group	Data octet	6T code group
00	+ – 0 0 + –	10	+ 0 + – – 0	20	0 0 – + + –	30	+ – 0 0 – +
01	0 + – + – 0	11	+ + 0 – 0 –	21	– – + 0 0 +	31	0 + – – – + 0
02	+ – 0 + – 0	12	+ 0 + – 0 –	22	+ + – 0 + –	32	+ – 0 – + 0
03	– 0 + + – 0	13	0 + + – 0 –	23	+ + – 0 – +	33	– 0 + – + 0
04	– 0 + 0 + –	14	0 + + – – 0	24	0 0 + 0 – +	34	– 0 + 0 – +
05	0 + – – 0 +	15	+ + 0 0 – –	25	0 0 + 0 + –	35	0 + – + 0 –
06	+ – 0 – 0 +	16	+ 0 + 0 – –	26	0 0 – 0 0 +	36	+ – 0 + 0 –
07	– 0 + – 0 +	17	0 + + 0 – –	27	– – + + + –	37	– 0 + + 0 –
08	– + 0 0 + –	18	0 + – 0 + –	28	– 0 – + + 0	38	– + 0 0 – +
09	0 – + + – 0	19	0 + – 0 – +	29	– – 0 + 0 +	39	0 – + – + 0
0A	– + 0 + – 0	1A	0 + – + + –	2A	– 0 – + 0 +	3A	– + 0 – + 0
0B	+ 0 – + – 0	1B	0 + – 0 0 +	2B	0 – – + 0 +	3B	+ 0 – – + 0
0C	+ 0 – 0 + –	1C	0 – + 0 0 +	2C	0 – – + + 0	3C	+ 0 – 0 – +
0D	0 – + – 0 +	1D	0 – + + + –	2D	– – 0 0 + +	3D	0 – + + 0 –
0E	– + 0 – 0 +	1E	0 – + 0 – +	2E	– 0 – 0 + +	3E	– + 0 + 0 –
0F	+ 0 – – 0 +	1F	0 – + 0 + –	2F	0 – – 0 + +	3F	+ 0 – + 0 –

11. Table 2.4 shows a portion of the 8B6T code table; the full table maps all possible 8-bit patterns into a unique code group of 6 ternary symbols. The mapping was chosen with two requirements in mind:

    synchronization and DC balance

12. For synchronization, the codes were chosen to maximize the average number of transitions per code group. The second requirement is to maintain DC balance, so that the average voltage on the line is zero.

13. For this purpose, all of the selected code groups either have an equal number of positive and negative symbols or an excess of one positive symbol. To maintain balance, a DC balancing algorithm is used.

14. In essence, this algorithm monitors the cumulative weight of all code groups transmitted on a single pair. Each code group has a weight of 0 or 1.

15. To maintain balance, the algorithm may negate a transmitted code group by changing all plus symbols to minus symbols and all minus symbols to plus symbols so that the cumulative weight at the conclusion of each code group is always either 0 or 1.

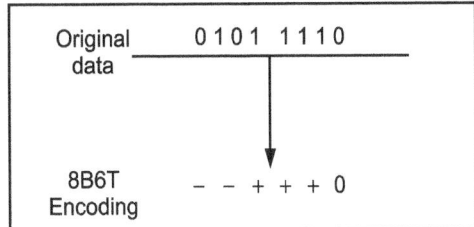

Fig. 2.16: 8 bits of Data Encoded into a Sequence of Six Ternary Codes

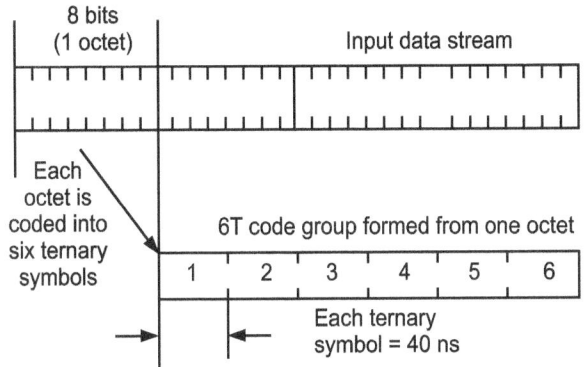

Fig. 2.17: 8B6T Coding

16. 8B6T coding, as used with 100BASE-T4 signalling, maps data octets into ternary symbols. Each octet is mapped to a pattern of 6 ternary symbols, called a 6T code group. The 6T code groups are fanned out to three independent serial channels. The effective data rate carried on each pair is one third of 100 Mbps, which is 33.333... Mbps. The ternary symbol transmission rate on each pair is 6/8 times 33.33 Mbps, or precisely 25.000 MHz.

17. Also for different Ethernet, different line coding techniques used are as follows:

Table 2.5

Standard	Name	Media Type	Encoding	Line	Network Size
10GEthernet	10GBASE-SR	Two 50/125 µm MMF, 850 nm	64B/66B	NRZ	2/550 m
IEEE 802.3ae	10GBASE-SW	Two 62.5/125 µm MMF, 850 nm	64B/66B	NRZ	2/33 m
	10GBASE-LX4	Two 50/125 µm MMF, 4xDWM signal	8B/10B	NRZ	300 m
	10GBASE-LX4	Two 62.5/125 µm MMF, 4xDWM signal	8B/10B	NRZ	300 m
	10GBASE-LX4	Two 8-10 µm SMF, 1310 nm, 4xDWM signal	8B/10B	NRZ	10 km
	10GBASE-LR	Two 8-10 µm SMF, 1310 nm	64B/66B	NRZ	10 km

Standard	Name	Media Type	Encoding	Line	Network Size
	10GBASE-LW	Two 8-10 µm SMF, 1310 nm	64B/66B	NRZ	10 km
	10GBASE-ER	Two 8-10 µm SMF, 1550 nm	64B/66B	NRZ	2/40 km
	10GBASE-EW	Two 8-10 µm SMF, 1550 nm	64B/66B	NRZ	2/40 km
Gigabit Ethernet IEEE 802.3z/ab	1000BASE-ZX	Two 8-10 µm SMF, 1310 nm	8B/10B	NRZ	80 km
	1000BASE-LX	Two 8-10 µm SMF,1310 nm	8B/10B	NRZ	5 km
	1000BASE-LX	Two 50/125 µm MMF, 1310 nm	8B/10B	NRZ	550/2000 m
	1000BASE-LX	Two 62.5/125 µm MMF, 1310 nm	8B/10B	NRZ	550/1000 m
	1000BASE-SX	Two 50/125 µm MMF, 850 nm	8B/10B	NRZ	500/750 m
	1000BASE-SX	Two 62.5/125 µm MMF, 850 nm	8B/10B	NRZ	220/400 m
	1000BASE-CX	Two pairs 150 Ohm STP (twinax)	8B/10B	NRZ	25 m
	1000BASE-T	Four pair UTP 5 (or better)	4D-PAM5	PAM5	<100 m
Fast Ethernet IEEE 802.3u	100BASE-Fx	Two optical 50/125 µm SMF	4B/5B	NRZI	40 km
	100BASE-Fx	Two optical 62.5/125 µm MMF	4B/5B	NRZI	2 km
	100BASE-Tx	Two pairs of STP cables	4B/5B	MLT3	200 m
	100BASE-Tx	Two pairs of UTP 5 (or better)	4B/5B	MLT3	<100 m
	100BASE-T4	Four pairs of UTP 3 (or better)	8B/6T	MLT3	<100 m
	100BASE-T2	Two pairs of UTP 3 (or better)	PAM5x5	PAM5	<100 m
Ethernet IEEE 802.3a-t	10BASE-FB	Two optical 62.5 /125 µm MMF sync hub	4B/5B	Manchester	<2000 m
	10BASE-FP	Two optical 62.5/125 µm MMF passive hub	4B/5B	Manchester	<1000 m
	10BASE-FL	Two optical 62.5/125 µm MMF asyn hub	4B/5B	Manchester	2000 m
	10BASE-T	Two pairs of UTP 3 (or better)	4B/5B	Manchester	<100 m
	10Broad36	One 75 Ohm coaxial (CATV)	4B/5B	Manchester	<3600 m
	10BASE-2	One 50 Ohm thin coaxial cable	4B/5B	Manchester	<185 m
	10BASE-5	One 50 Ohm thick coaxial cable	4B/5B	Manchester	<500 m

2.6.3 The 4D-PAM5 Line Coding

1. 4D-PAM5 **encoding** is a four-dimensional, five-level pulse amplitude modulation.

2. This is a way of encoding bits on copper wires to get a 1 GB per second transfer rate when the maximum rate of a single wire is 125 MHz. This is done by employing a multilevel amplitude signal.

3. A five-level signal, called pulse amplitude modulation 5, is used.

4. This works in a similar manner to MLT-3 except the levels are −2V, −1V, 0V and 2V.

    The transmitted signal on each wire is a five-level pulse modulation symbol.

5. Four symbols transmitted simultaneously on the four pairs of wire forms the 4D-PAM5 code group that represents an 8-bit frame octet.

6. The symbols to be transmitted are selected from a four-dimensional (4D) code group of five-level symbols.

7. Because there are four separate pairs being used for transmission and reception of data, there are 625 possible codes to choose from when using all four pairs. Therefore, all 8 bits can be transferred using only one 4D-PAM5 symbol.

8. The data signals have distinct and measurable amplitude and phases, allowing more data bits per cycle.

9. This type of encoding is used by Gigabit Ethernet, whereby 1000 Mbps is squeezed into 125 MHz signals.

10. The electronics are more complex and the technology is more susceptible to noise.

11. Actually, only four levels are used for data; the 0V level is used to recover the transmitted signal from high noise. This fifth level of coding is used for error detection and correction.

1000BASE-T Architecture

1. A twisted-pair version was introduced by the IEEE in 1999 under the name IEEE 802.3ab. The physical layer was specified as UTP Cat. 5 cabling in order to guarantee easy integration with existing 10BASE-T and 100BASE-T networks.

2. 1000BASE-T over UTP is usually the preferred option for horizontal cabling and desktop connection. This is an alternative to 1000BASE-CX, which is rarely used in practice.

3. The physical layer is split into the Physical Coding Sublayer (PCS) which controls logic functions, and the Physical Medium Attachment (PMA) sublayer which performs analogue-digital mixed signal functions.

Physical Coding Sublayer (PCS):

1000BASE-T operates over Cat. 5 (or better) cabling systems by using all four pairs, sending and receiving a 250 Mbps data stream over each of the four pairs (4 × 250 Mbps = 1 Gbps) simultaneously (See Fig. 2.18).

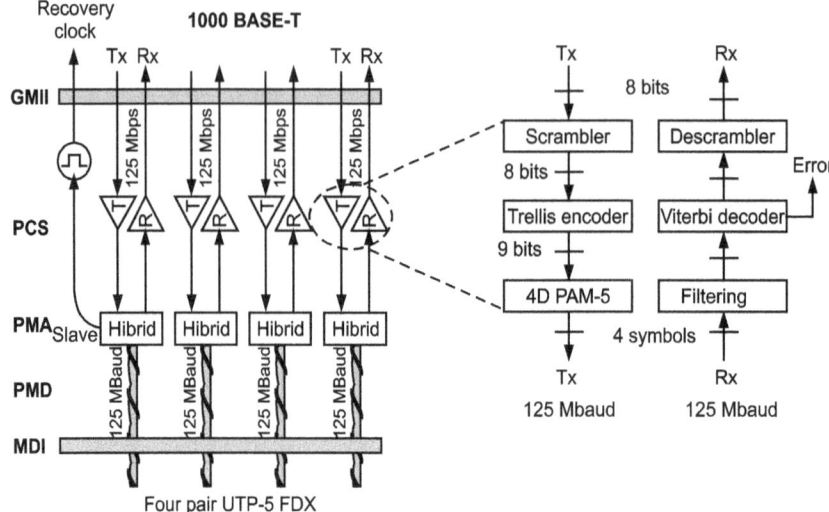

Fig. 2.18: 1000BASE-T Link Topology including Loop Timing Configuration

It is the combination of the signal level on all four twisted-pairs that defines a symbol. Each pair carries the equivalent of 125 MBaud (symbol/s), hence 250 Mbps.

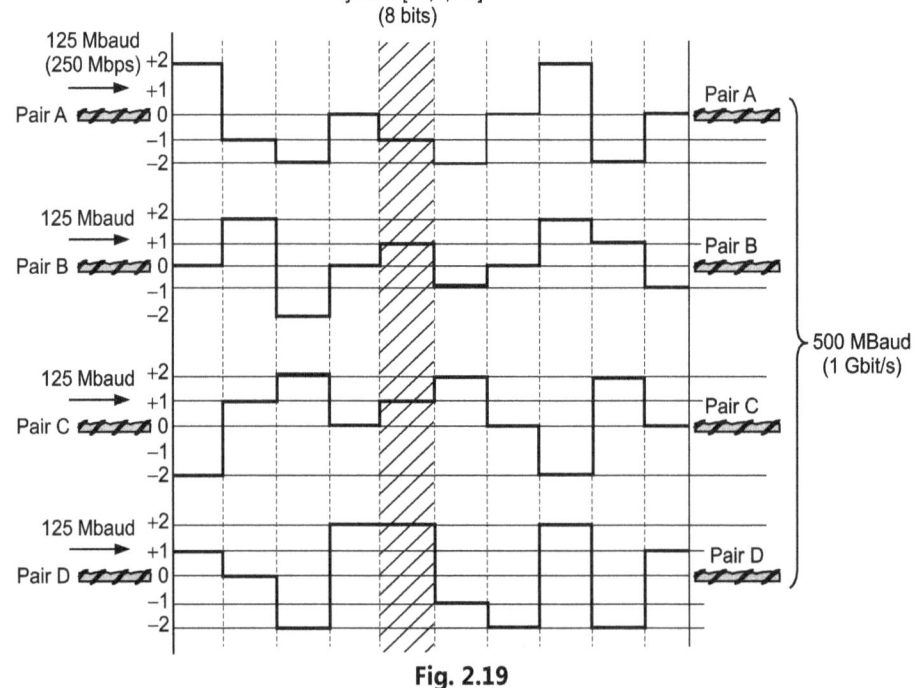

Fig. 2.19

In Fig. 2.19, each 8 bit byte is mapped into 4 level PAM5 symbols which consists of one signal level (−2, −1, 0, 1, 2) on each of the four twisted pairs (A, B, C, D). There are 625 possible symbols, leaving 512 patterns for data and 113 are for control codes such as idle, start of packet, end of packet.

The PCS sublayer performs the generation and processing of continuous code-groups to be transmitted or received over four channels. The process of converting data bits to code groups is called 4D-PAM5, (see Fig. 2.19). This modulation technique means:

- The four data lines (4 UTP wires) are used simultaneously to transmit/receive.
- Each byte is mapped into 4 pulse amplitude modulation (PAM) symbols.
  Five symbols form the PAM constellation being used {+2, +1, 0, −1, −2}.
- Data encoding needs only four levels (two bits per symbol), the fifth is used as forward error correction (FEC) coding.
- In the absence of data, IDLE symbols (restricted to {+2, 0, −2}) are used to keep the synchronization.
- 125 MBaud (1 Baud = 1 symbol/s) on each of the pairs.

As a result, each wire pair achieves 250 Mbps throughput using baseband signalling at 125 Mbaud - achieving 1 Gbps at a spectral power density similar to that of 100BASE-TX (See Fig. 2.20).

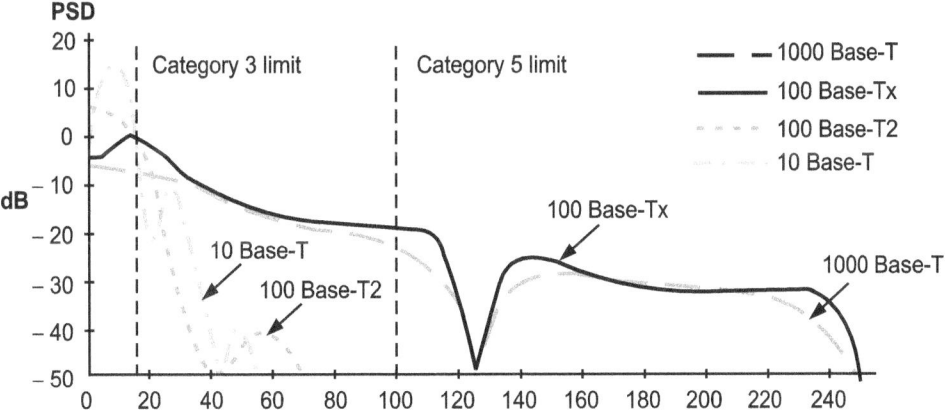

Fig. 2.20: Power Spectral Density (PSD) for 10/100/1000BASE-T Electrical Technologies

2.7 MLT-3 Line Coding

1. **MLT-3 encoding** (Multi-Level Transmit) is a line code (a signalling method used in a telecommunication system for transmission purposes) that uses three voltage levels.

2. An MLT-3 interface emits less electromagnetic interference and requires less bandwidth than most other binary or ternary interfaces that operate at the same bit rate, such as Manchester code or Alternate Mark Inversion.

3. MLT-3 cycles through the voltage levels −1, 0, +1, and 0. It moves to the next state to transmit a 1 bit, and stays in the same state to transmit a 0 bit.

4. Similar to simple NRZ encoding, MLT-3 has a coding efficiency of 1 bit/baud, however it requires four transitions (baud) to complete a full cycle (from low-to-middle, middle-to-high, high-to-middle, middle-to-low).

5. Thus, the maximum fundamental frequency is reduced to one fourth of the baud rate. This makes signal transmission more amenable to copper wires.

6. MLT-3 was first introduced by Cisco Systems as a coding scheme for FDDI copper interconnect (TP-PMD).

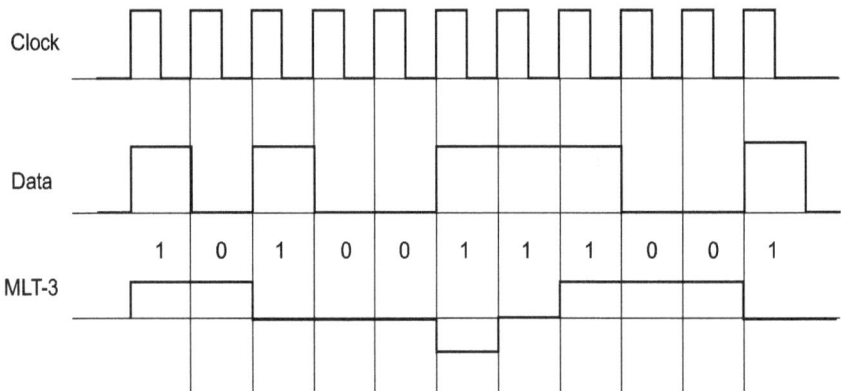

Fig. 2.21: Example of MLT-3 Encoding (Light-colored lines indicate two previous states)

7. Ethernet LANs use digital signals to share data among network devices. 10Base-T uses Manchester encoding to transmit the signal: transition occurs in the middle of each bit period. Two levels represent one bit.

8. A low to high transition in the middle of the bit represents a '1'. A high to low transition in the middle of the bit represents a '0'. There is no DC component. It uses positive/negative voltages.

9. 100-BaseTX uses 4B/5B encoding, where each 4-bit nibbles is being transferred, encoded as 5-bit symbols. The signaling model is a three level multi-level technique called MLT-3.

Table 2.6: Ethernet Encoding and Signaling

	10Base-T	100Base-TX
Data rate	10 Mbps	100 Mbps
Encoding	Manchester	4B/5B
Signaling	5V, differential	MLT-3
Cable	Cat. 3 UTP	Cat. 5 UTP

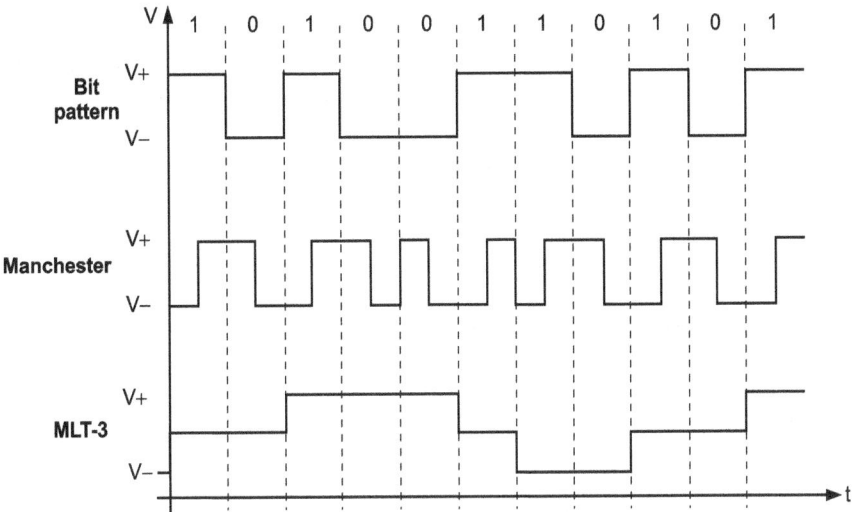

Fig. 2.22: Ethernet Encoding Schemes

10. It is also used by FDDI and TP-PMD to obtain 100 Mbps out of a 31.25 MHz signal. Where TP-PMD stands for Twisted Pair-Physical layer, Medium Dependent (TP-PMD) and FDDI stands for Fiber Distributed Data Interface backbone network.

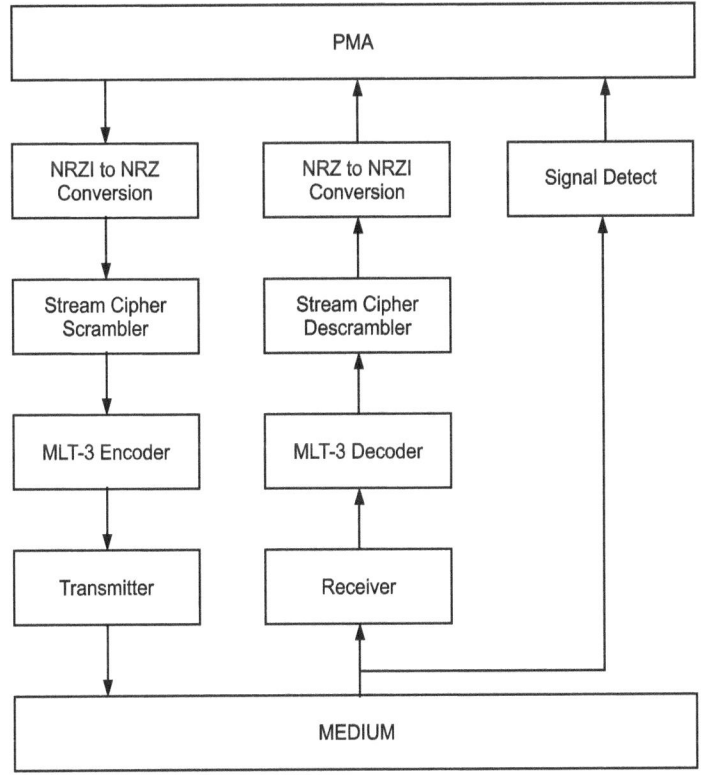

Fig. 2.23: TP-PMD Block Diagram (PMA: Physical Medium Attachment)

11. The mechanism chosen to overcome signaling rate issues is Multi-Level Transmit 3 (MLT-3). This is a tri-polar encoding mechanism based on three different signal levels. Its purpose within TP-PMD is to encode the data in such a manner that the signaling rate is reduced with the emissions that radiate from the cable.

12. MLT-3 encoding is essentially very simple, operating with a positive signal level, a negative one and a zero level. It does however require a binary input rather than the normal NRZI encoded signal normally passed from the PHY.

13. Therefore, an NRZI decoder is placed within the PMD to produce a binary output suitable for MLT-3.

14. The transition between levels is what differentiates between a binary 1_2 and 0_2. In addition to the ability to transition between three signal levels, a counter is required.

15. This can be a single bit counter as it is only necessary to determine between odd and even.

16. The rules for encoding are:
    - The transmitter can only transition between adjacent signal states i.e. from positive to zero, zero to negative, zero to positive. A transition from negative to positive is not allowed.
    - A transition only takes place when a 1_2 is transmitted. No transition takes place when a 0_2 is transmitted.
    - If a 1_2 is transmitted, the signal will transition from its current state to an adjacent state, i.e. from positive to zero, negative to zero.
    - If the current state is zero and a transition is required then it will be positive if the counter is even or negative if the counter is odd.
    - The counter is incremented when the zero state is left.

17. These rules are demonstrated in Fig. 2.24, which shows a example of MLT-3 encoding. The receiver function is opposite to that described above, with the decoded MLT-3 signal being passed through an NRZI encoder before being handed to the PHY.

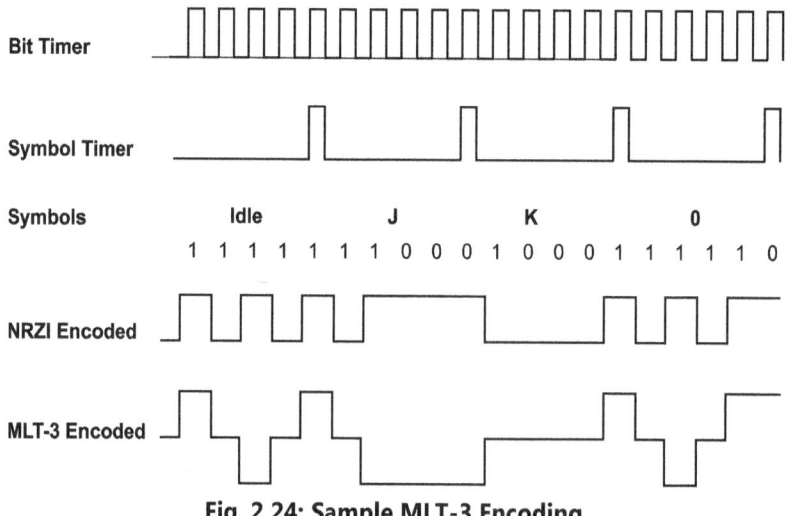

Fig. 2.24: Sample MLT-3 Encoding

18. The benefit produced by this system is the much reduced signaling rate, down from 125 MHz on fiber to 31.25 MHz over copper.
19. This produces much lower radiated emissions allowing the technology to stay well within published guidelines.

2.8 Summary of Line Coding

Table 2.7

Common Line Codes:	
Signal	**Comments**
NRZ-L	Non-return to zero level. This is the standard positive logic signal format used in digital circuits. 1 forces a high level 0 forces a low level
NRZ-M	Non-return to zero mark. 1 forces a transition 0 does nothing
NRZ-S	Non-return to zero space. 1 does nothing 0 forces a transition
RZ	Return to zero. 1 goes high for half the bit period 0 does nothing
Biphase-L	Manchester. Two consecutive bits of the same type force a transition at the beginning of a bit period. 1 forces a negative transition in the middle of the bit 0 forces a positive transition in the middle of the bit
Biphase-M	There is always a transition at the beginning of a bit period. 1 forces a transition in the middle of the bit. 0 does nothing.
Biphase-S	There is always a transition at the beginning of a bit period. 1 does nothing 0 forces a transition in the middle of the bit.
Differential Manchester	There is always a transition in the middle of a bit period. 1 does nothing 0 forces a transition at the beginning of the bit
Bipolar	The positive and negative pulses are alternate. 1 forces a positive or negative pulse for half the bit period. 0 does nothing.

Common Line Codes:

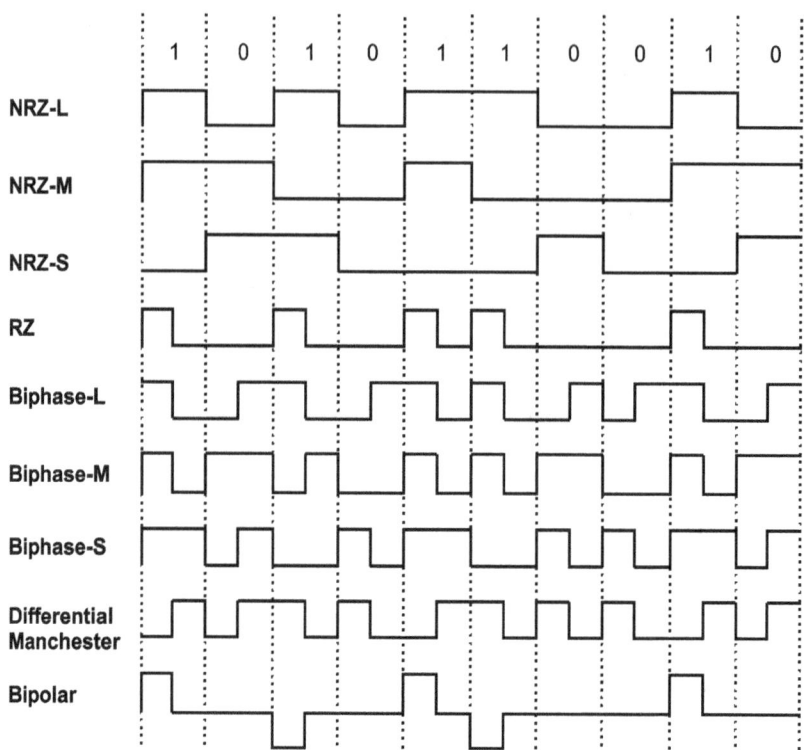

Fig. 2.25: Common Line Codes at a Glance

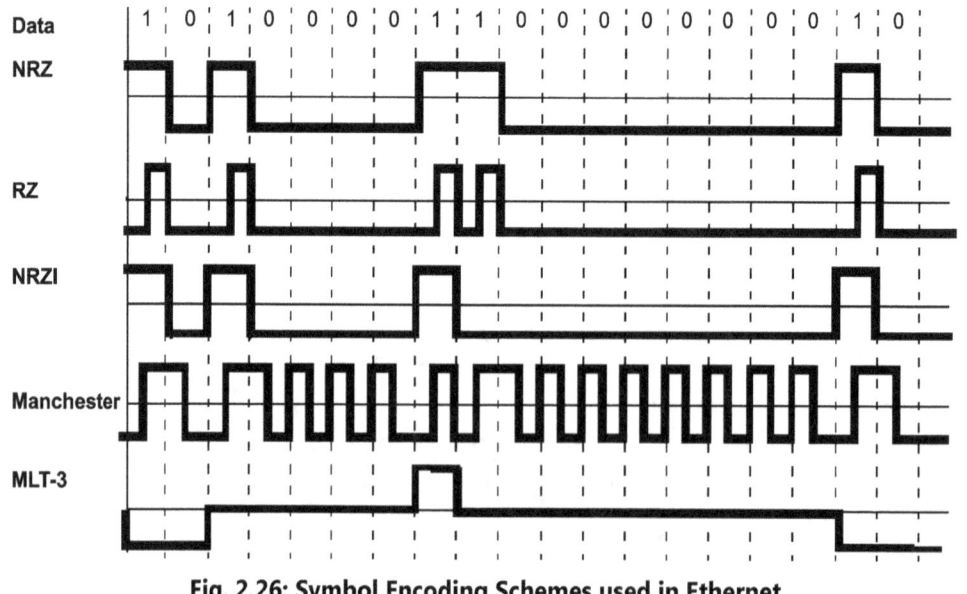

Fig. 2.26: Symbol Encoding Schemes used in Ethernet

2.8.1 Comparison of Line Coding Techniques

Table 2.8

Sr. No.	Main Technique	Type	Average Bandwidth B_{avg} =	Characteristics
1.	Unipolar Line coding	NRZ	N/2	DC component effect present. No self synchronization for long 0 & 1 bit streams. Implementation is costly.
2.	Polar Line coding	NRZ-L	N/2	DC component effect present. No self synchronization for long 0 & 1 bit streams.
		NRZ-I	N/2	DC component effect present. No self synchronization for long 0 bit streams.
		Biphase	N	DC component effect absent. Self synchronization is achieved.
3.	Bipolar Line coding	AMI	N/2	DC component effect present. No self synchronization for long 0 bit streams.
4.	Multilevel Line coding	2B1Q	N/4	No self synchronization for long same double bits.
		8B6T	3N/4	DC component effect absent. Self synchronization is achieved.
		4D-PAM5	N/8	DC component effect absent. Self synchronization is achieved.
5.	Multiline Line coding	MLT-3	N/3	DC component effect absent. No self synchronization for long 0 bit streams.

2.9 Block Coding

1. The performance of previous line codes studied is not adequate in advanced data communication applications.

2. We need redundancy to ensure the synchronization between transmitter and receiver.

3. We also need to incorporate the error detection mechanism, hence, new block coding concept comes into picture.

4. Block coding is indicated as mB/nB coding.

5. In block coding, each m-bit group is replaced with n-bit group.

6. Examples of block coding are:
   - 4B/5B.
   - 8B/10B.

7. In 4B/5B, (/) slash indicates block coding, whereas 8B6T is example of multilevel coding.

8. Block coding includes the following three steps.
   - Division step.
   - Substitution step.
   - Combination step.

9. In the division step, sequence of bits are divided into the groups of m-bits in block encoding.

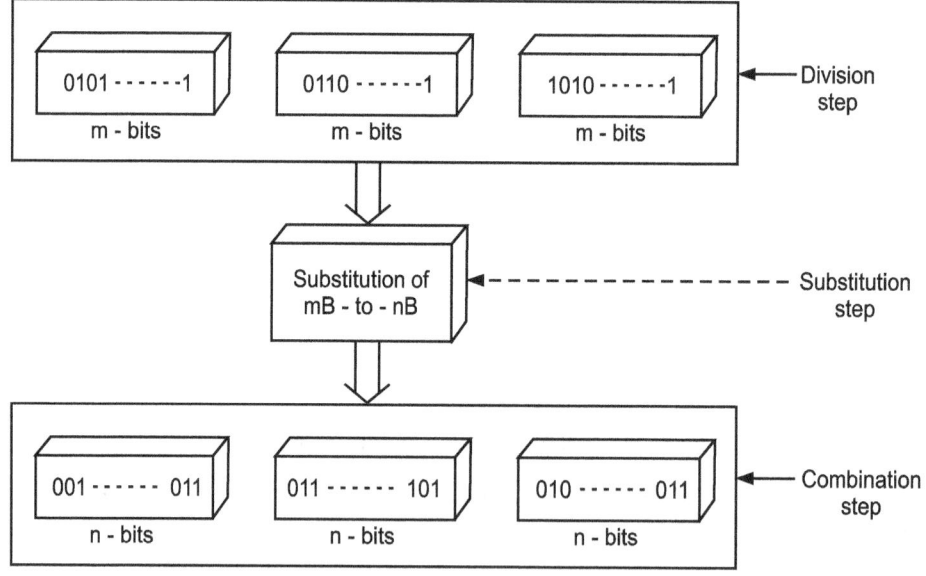

Fig. 2.27: Basic Block Encoding Steps

10. For example in 4B/5B, the bit sequence is divided into 4-bit groups, in block encoding.

11. In the substitution step, we substitute m-bit group for n-bit group, in block encoding.

12. For example, in 4B/5B, we substitute 4-bit code for a 5-bit group in block encoding.

13. In last or final step i.e. combination step, n-bit groups are combined together to form a block encoded stream output.

2.9.1 4B/5B Block Coding

1.   This 4B/5B technique was designed to be used in combination with NRZ-I line coding technique.

2.   In NRZ-I, there are two problems:

   •   DC component effect.

   •   Self synchronization problem for long stream of '0's.

3.   Also in NRZ, average bandwidth $B_{avg} = \dfrac{N}{2}$, i.e. it has good signalling rate (i.e. $\dfrac{1}{2}$ of Biphase coding).

4.   The solution over self-synchronization problem for long stream of '0's is to change the bit stream prior to encoding with NRZ-I, so that long bit stream of '0's will be cancelled.

5.   Thus, maximum number of consecutive '0's will be three only.

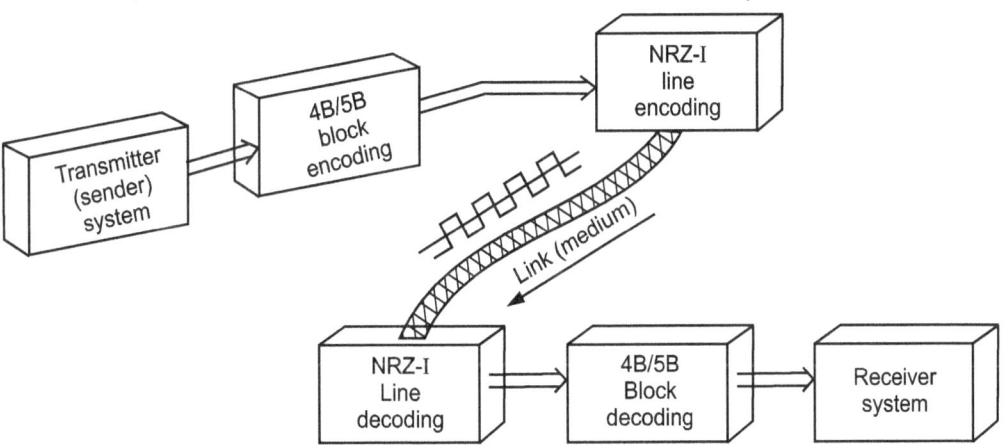

Fig. 2.28: 4B/5B Block Coding + NRZ-I Line Coding to improve Self-Synchronization and DC Component Effect

6.   Depending on the standard or specification of interest, there may be several 4B/5B characters left unused.

7.   The presence of any of the "unused" characters in the data stream can be used as an indication that there is a fault somewhere in the link.

8.   Therefore, the unused characters can actually be used to detect errors in the data stream.

9.   The use of only 16 of the possible 32 groups of 5 bits means that 4B/5B allows some errors to be detected as the error may change the group of 5 bits into one of the 16 unused groups and thus invalid combinations.

10. 4B/5B is used in the following standards:
   - 100BASE-TX standard defined by IEEE 802.3u in 1995.
   - MADI (Multichannel Audio Digital Interface)

Table 2.9: Encoding table of 4B/5B

Name	4B	5B	Description
0	0000	11110	hex data 0
1	0001	01001	hex data 1
2	0010	10100	hex data 2
3	0011	10101	hex data 3
4	0100	01010	hex data 4
5	0101	01011	hex data 5
6	0110	01110	hex data 6
7	0111	01111	hex data 7
8	1000	10010	hex data 8
9	1001	10011	hex data 9
A	1010	10110	hex data A
B	1011	10111	hex data B
C	1100	11010	hex data C
D	1101	11011	hex data D
E	1110	11100	hex data E
F	1111	11101	hex data F
Q	-NONE-	00000	Quiet (signal lost)
I	-NONE-	11111	Idle
J	-NONE-	11000	Start #1
K	-NONE-	10001	Start #2
T	-NONE-	01101	End
R	-NONE-	00111	Reset
S	-NONE-	11001	Set
H	-NONE-	00100	Halt

11. Note that normal data symbols begin with at most one 0 bit and end with at most two, so there can be most three 0 bits in a row.

12. Control symbols used in combinations that also preserve this rule. Thus, 4B/5B encoding is a (0, 3) RLL code.

13. FDDI and 100BASE-TX begin frames with a JK pair. FDDI ends frames with a TT pair, while 100BASE-TX uses a TR pair.

14. The following character sets are sometimes referred to as command characters.

Table 2.10: Control characters

Control Character	5B symbols	Purpose
JK	11000 10001	Sync, Start delimiter
II	11111 11111	Not Used
TT	01101 01101	FDDI end delimiter
TS	01101 11001	Not Used
IH	11111 00100	SAL
TR	01101 00111	100BASE-TX end delimiter
SR	11001 00111	Not Used
SS	11001 11001	Not Used
HH	00100 00100	HDLC0
HI	00100 11111	HDLC1
HQ	00100 00000	HDLC2
RR	00111 00111	HDLC3
RS	00111 11001	HDLC4
QH	00000 00100	HDLC5
QI	00000 11111	HDLC6
QQ	00000 00000	HDLC7

(HDLC = High-Level Data Link Control)

(FDDI = Fiber Distributed Data Interface)

15. Despite this 4B/5B does not guarantee at least one transition for each bit period, however there are enough transitions to allow the clock signal to be recovered.

16. Unfortunately the use of 5 bits to represent 4 bits does mean that the bandwidth needed to transmit the data is increased by 25%.

17. Substitution in 4B/5B block coding is as shown in Fig. 2.29.

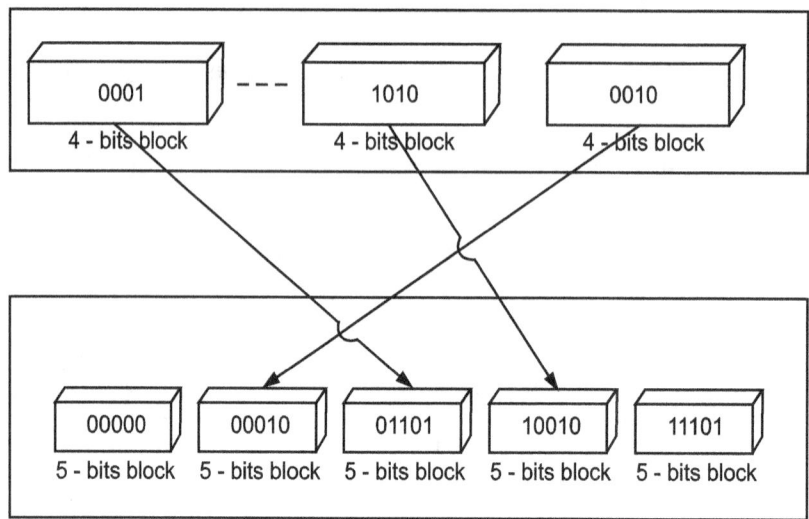

Fig. 2.29: 4B/5B Substitution Process

2.9.2 The 8B/10B Block Coding

1. The 8B/10B code is known as 8-Binary/10-Binary block coding technique.
2. The 4B/5B is similar to 8B/10B, except that a group of 8 bits of data is substituted by a 10 bit code.
3. It has greater error detection capability than 4B/5B block coding technique.
4. The 8B/10B is combination of 5B/6B and 3B/4B.

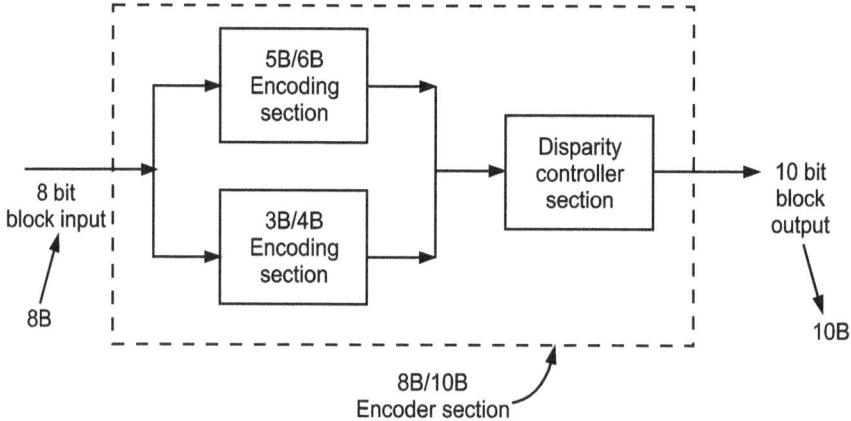

Fig. 2.30: The 8B/10B Block Coding Method

5. Disparity controller section minimizes/removes DC component effect due to long streams of consecutive '0' or '1's.
6. Thus, 8B/10B encoding also has better self-synchronization capacity as compared to 4B/5B block encoding.

Technologies that use 8b/10b

Following are the areas in which 8B/10B encoding finds application:

- PCI Express (Peripheral Component Interconnect Express).
- IEEE 1394b.
- Serial ATA (The serial ATA, or SATA computer bus, is a storage interface).
- SAS (Serial Attached SCSI) (Small Computer System Interface).
- Fibre Channel.
- SSA (Serial Storage Architecture).
- Gigabit Ethernet (except for the twisted pair based 1000Base-T).
- InfiniBand (InfiniBand is a switched fabric communication link primarily used in high-performance computing).
- XAUI (XAUI is a standard for extending the XGMII (10 Gigabit Media Independent Interface) between the MAC and PHY layer of 10 Gigabit Ethernet (10GbE). XAUI is pronounced "zowie", a concatenation of the roman numeral X, meaning ten, and the initials of "Attachment Unit Interface".
- Serial RapidIO (The RapidIO architecture is a high-performance packet-switched, interconnect technology for interconnecting chips on a circuit board, and also circuit boards to each other using a backplane.)
- DVI (Digital Visual Interface) and HDMI (Transition Minimized Differential Signaling) (High-Definition Multimedia Interface).
- DVB (Asynchronous Serial Interface (ASI)) (Digital Video Broadcasting).
- DisplayPort Main Link.
- HyperTransport.
- Common Public Radio Interface (CPRI).
- USB 3.0.

Digital Audio Applications

Encoding has a heavy use in digital audio applications which use this modulation scheme:

- Digital Audio Tape.
- Digital Compact Cassette (DCC).

A differing but related scheme is used for audio CDs and CD-ROMs:

- Compact Disc Eight-to-Fourteen Modulation.

Exceptions

- For 10 Gigabit Ethernet's 10GBASE-R Physical Medium Dependent (PMD) interfaces, 64B/66B encoding is used.

- This scheme is considerably different in design to 8B/10B encoding, but was created with similar considerations of DC balance, maximum run length, transition density and electromagnetic emission minimization.
- Note that 8B/10B is the encoding scheme, not a specific code. While many applications do use the same code, there exist some incompatible implementations; for example, Transition Minimized Differential Signalling, which also expands 8 bits to 10 bits, has some subtle differences.

Encoding Tables

- Note that in the following tables, "A" and "a" are the least significant bit. The bits are sent low to high: a → b → c → d → e → i → f → g → h → j (i.e. the 5B/6B code followed by the 3B/4B code). With that the uniqueness of the special bit sequence in the comma codes is ensured.
- The residual effect on the stream to the number of zero and one bits transmitted is maintained as the Running Disparity (RD) and the effect of slew is balanced by the choice of encoding for following symbols.
- Each 6 or 4 bit code word has either equal numbers of '0' and '1' bits (a disparity of 0), or comes in a pair of forms, one with two more '1' bits than '0' bits (four '1' bits and two '0' bits, or three '1' bits and one '0' bit, respectively) and one with two less.
- When a 6 or 4 bit code is used that has a non-zero disparity (count of '1' bits minus count of '0' bits, i.e. −2 or +2), the choice of positive or negative disparity encodings must be the one that toggles the running disparity. i.e. the non-zero disparity codes are alternate.
- This encoding is used by Fibre Channel, Gigabit Ethernet, 10 Gigabit Ethernet, and ATM (Asynchronous Transfer Mode) transmission interfaces. Example format:

Table 2.11: Data Encoding

-	Data Byte	8B/10B	5B/6B	3B/4B
00	0000 0000	011000 1011	011000	0100
01	0000 0001	100010 1011	100010	1001
02	0000 0010	010010 1011	010010	0101
04	0000 0101	001010 1011	001010	0010
07	0000 0111	000111 0100	000111	0001
08	0000 1000	000110 1011	000110	--
0F	0000 1111	101000 1011	101000	--
F0	1111 0000	100100 1110	--	--
FF	1111 1111	010100 1110	--	--

Running Disparity

- Running Disparity is a concept used in the 8B/10B encoding to keep the number of 1s and 0s that are transmitted "down the wire" roughly equal.
- This scheme only needs two states for Running Disparity of +1 and −1. It starts at −1.
- For each 5B/6B and 3B/4B code with an unequal number of 1s and 0s, there are two bit patterns that can be used to transmit it. One with two more 1 bits and one with all bits inverted and thus two more 0s.
- Depending on the current running disparity of the signal, the encoding engine selects which of the two possible 6 or 4 bit sequences to send for the given data. (Obviously, if the 6 or 4 bit code has equal numbers of 1s and 0s, there is no choice to make, as the disparity would be unchanged.)

Table 2.12: Rules for Running Disparity

Previous RD	Disparity of 6 or 4 Bit Code	Disparity chosen	Next RD
−1	0	0	−1
−1	± 2	+2	+1
+1	0	0	+1
+1	± 2	−2	−1

2.10 Scrambling

1. Properties of Biphase line codes are:
   - No DC component.
   - Self-synchronization capacity.
   - High bandwidth requirement.
2. Biphase technique can be used in LAN environment of short distance communication.
3. It cannot be used for long distance communication because of their wide bandwidth requirement.
4. DC component problem does not allow combination of block coding + NRZ coding. Also synchronization problems for long stream of '0' occur.
5. To avoid synchronization problems, we can use Bipolar AMI for long distance.
6. But scrambling can give you synchronization that substitutes long '0' level pulses with a combination of other levels.
7. Thus, part of AMI can be modified to include scrambling as shown in Fig. 2.31.
8. There are two scrambling techniques:
   (i) B8ZS.
   (ii) HDB3.

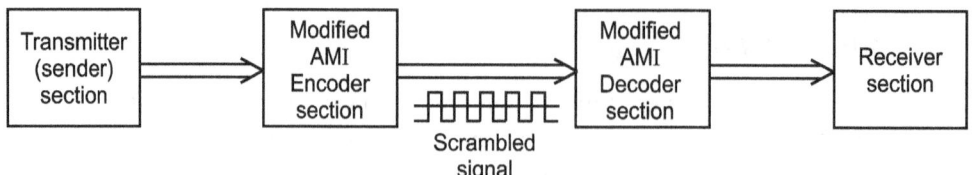

Fig. 2.31: Modified AMI – Scrambling Technique

2.10.1 Bipolar with 8-zeros Substitution (B8ZS) Signal Encoding

The bipolar-AMI encoding supplemented with a scrambling scheme, which uses two code violations to ensure synchronization in runs of 0's.

- Replace '00000000' with '000+−0−+', if the preceding voltage pulse was positive.

- Replace '00000000' with '000−+0+−', if the preceding voltage pulse was not positive.

- The amount of data remains unchanged.

- The spectrum graph shows that there is no DC component, with most of the energy concentrating in a relative sharp spectrum, making the encoding suitable for high-rate transmissions.

- Used mainly in North America.

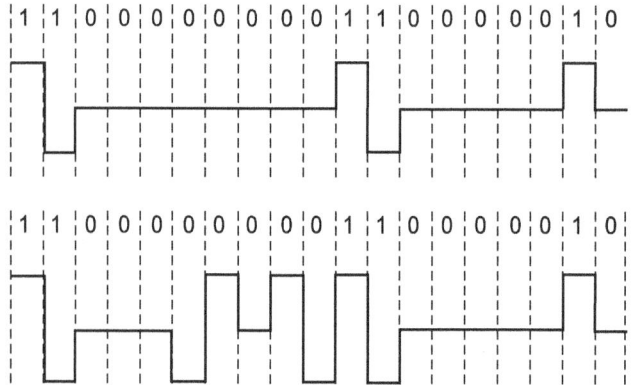

Fig. 2.32: Bipolar with 8-zeros Substitution (B8ZS) Signal Encoding

Following data for B8ZS encoding is very important

1. **B8ZS** is an abbreviation for bipolar with eight-zeros substitution, which is a method of line coding used in the T-carrier system which allows full 64 kbps per channel, though it does not allow for Clear Channel Capability (CCC - 64 kbps) in and of itself.

2. The service would still have to be point-to-point (P2P) and not switched throughout digital switching network.

3.   The standard is to use B8ZS as the line encoding option when providing P2P circuits and services.
4.   The older AMI scheme was implemented in channel cards that always robbed a bit for signalling regardless if the service on that channel was switched or P2P. B8ZS cards can be optioned not to rob that bit.
5.   On a T1, ones are sent by applying voltage to the wire, where a zero is sent by having no voltage on the wire. Sending excessive zeros in a row could cause receiving equipment to lose synchronization with sending equipment, so it is important that such a pattern is not sent.
6.   The original standard of line coding, Alternate Mark Inversion, specifies that there are three states of the line, no voltage is a zero, positive voltage is a one (or mark), and negative voltage is also a one (or mark).
7.   Because of the inversion of the voltage for each "mark," or one, sent, the receiving equipment can easily determine the data rate of the line and not lose synchronization.
8.   B8ZS builds upon this, by using violations of this rule to replace a pattern of eight zeros in a row.

Original signal:							
0	0	0	0	0	0	0	0
B8ZS encoded signal (V = Bipolar violation)							
0	0	0	V	1	0	V	1
Signal Polarity (assuming that the previous mark was negative)							
0	0	0	−	+	0	+	−

9.   B8ZS is used in the North American hierarchy at the T1 rate. When European E1 was developed much later than T1, it was then common knowledge that forcing 'ones' into a DS0 would corrupt data. E1 uses another method called High Density Bipolar Three (HDB3) code.

2.10.2 High-Density Bipolar 3-Zeros (HDB3) Signal Encoding

The bipolar-AMI encoding is supplemented with the following substitution scheme for '0000' runs.

- Used in Europe and Japan.
- Successive violations are of alternate polarity to avoid dc component.

Polarity of preceding pulse	Number of bipolar pulses (ones) since last substitution	
	odd	even
−	000−	+00+
+	000+	−00−

The HDB3 signal encoding is shown in Fig. 2.33.

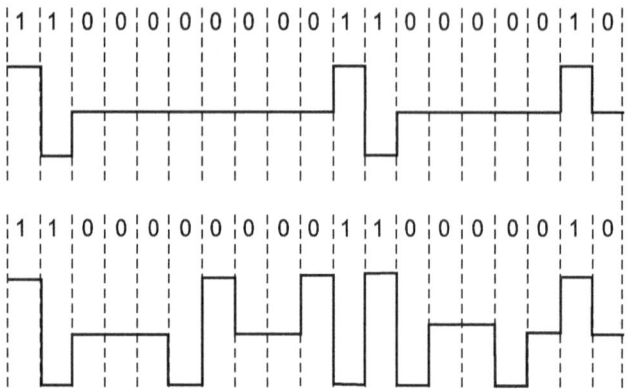

Fig. 2.33: High-Density Bipolar 3-Zeros (HDB3) Signal Encoding

Based on the AMI code (alternating the levels of voltage when transmitting "1"), this limits the maximum number of consecutive zeros transmitted to three. The basic idea consists of replacing series of four bits that are equal to "0" with a code word "000V" or "B00V", where "V" is a pulse that violates the AMI law of alternate polarity and is rectangular or some other shape. The rules for using "000V" or "B00V" are as follows:

- "B00V" is used when up to the previous pulse, the coded signal presents a DC component that is not null (the number of positive pulses is not compensated for by the number of negative pulses).

- "000V" is used under the same conditions as above when up to the previous pulse the DC component is null.

- The pulse "B" ("B" for balancing), which respects the AMI alternancy rule, has positive or negative polarity, ensuring that two successive V pulses will have different polarity.

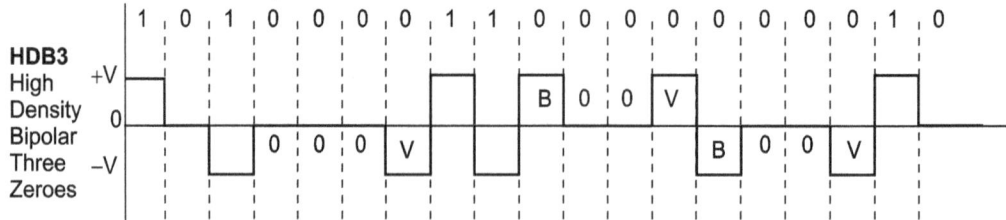

Fig. 2.34: The HDB3 Coding Waveforms

The HDB3 code has the following characteristics:

- The timing information is preserved by embedding it in the line signal even when long sequences of zeros are transmitted, which allows the clock to be recovered properly on reception.

- The DC component of a signal that is coded in HDB3 is null.

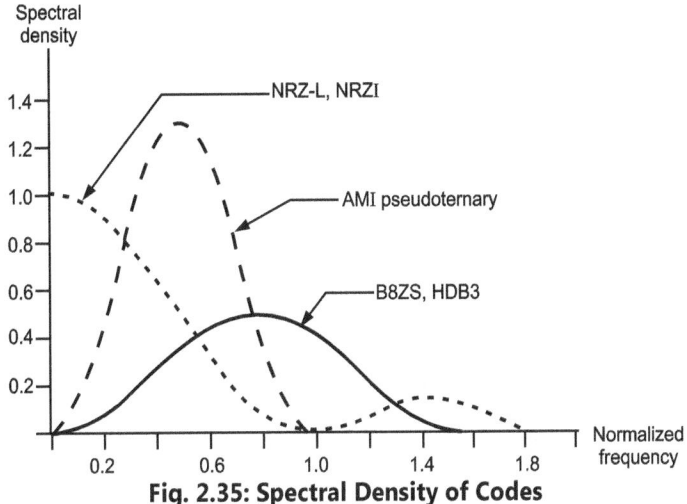

Fig. 2.35: Spectral Density of Codes

2.11 Analog-To-Digital Conversion

1. Digital signals has superior quality as compared to analog signals.
2. As we have already seen the classification of different conversions i.e. Analog to Analog conversion, Analog to Digital conversion, Digital to Analog conversion and Digital to Digital conversion etc.
3. The different techniques to convert analog signals into digital are as follows:
   (a) PCM (b) DM

2.12 PCM (Pulse Code Modulation) Transmitter

1. The process of converting analog signals into digital data is called as Digitization.
2. One of the technique used for digitization is PCM.
3. The basic components of PCM transmitter are:
   - Sampling section.
   - Quantizing section.
   - Encoding section.
   - PISO (Parallel Input-Serial Output) Converter.
4. The block diagram of PCM transmitter is as shown in Fig. 2.36.

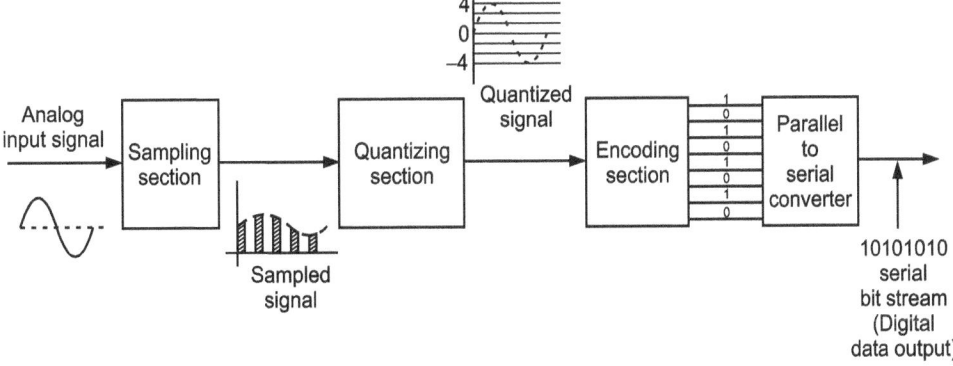

Fig. 2.36: PCM Transmitter Section

5.　Following processes are done in PCM transmitter section:
- Analog signal is sampled using sampling section.
- Sampled signal is quantized using quantizing section.
- Quantized signal is converted into parallel bit stream using encoding section.
- Parallel bit stream converted into serial bit stream using PISO (Parallel Input Serial Output) converter section

and finally Digital data is available at output.

2.12.1 Sampling

1.　The analog input signal is sampled every T_s seconds, where T_s is the sample interval or period.

2.　Sampling frequency $f_s = \dfrac{1}{T_s}$ Hz.

3.　There are three types of sampling:
　　(a) Ideal sampling　　　　(b) Natural sampling　　　　(c) Flat-top sampling.

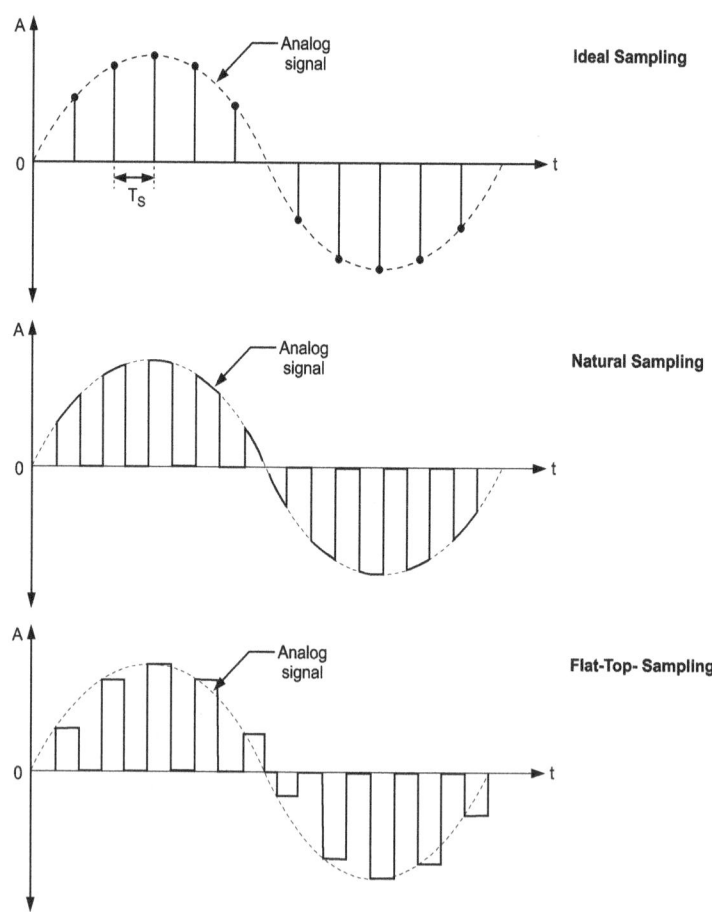

Fig. 2.37: Sampling Methods for PCM System

4. In ideal sampling, the pulses from the analog signal are sampled and is difficult to implement.

5. In natural sampling method, high speed switch is tuned on for small period of time when sampling is applied.

6. In flat-top-sampling method, sampled level is held using capacitor-based switching circuit. This is widely used sampling method.

7. The process of sampling is also called as PAM (Pulse Amplitude Modulation).

8. **Nyquist theorem:** To recover original signal with minimum distortion, sampling rate must be ≥ 2 times the highest frequency contained in the analog input signal.

9. Thus, Nyquist rate for low-pass and bandpass signal is as shown in Fig. 2.38.

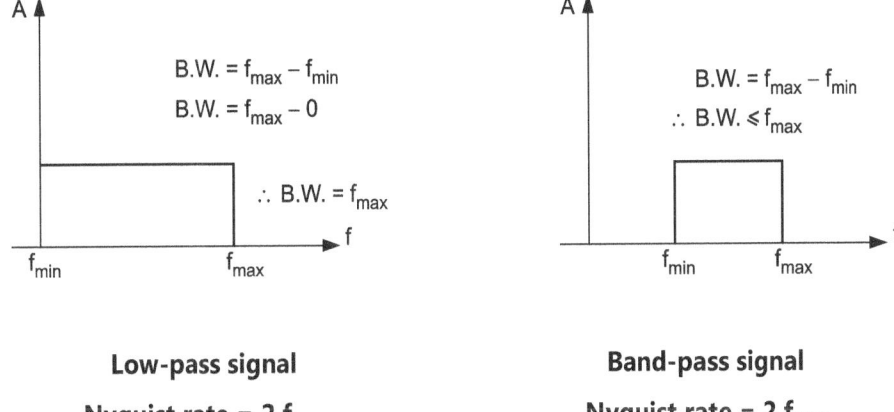

Low-pass signal

Nyquist rate = 2 f_{max}

Band-pass signal

Nyquist rate = 2 f_{max}

Fig. 2.38: Nyquist Rate for Low-pass and Band-pass Signal

10. Thus, we can sample the signal only if the signal is band limited i.e. signal of infinite bandwidth cannot be sampled. Thus, requirement is $f_s \geq 2\, f_{max}$.

11. Also, if input sine wave signal is sampled with the sampling frequency $f_s = f$, then recovered signal at receiver end gives distorted output.

12. If $f_s = 2f$, then recovered signal at receiver end gives good output (i.e. with minimum distortion).

13. If $f_s = 4f$, then recovered signal at receiver end will be exact replica of input signal i.e. it gives best output at receiver end.

14. These input signals and recovered signals are as shown in Fig. 2.39.

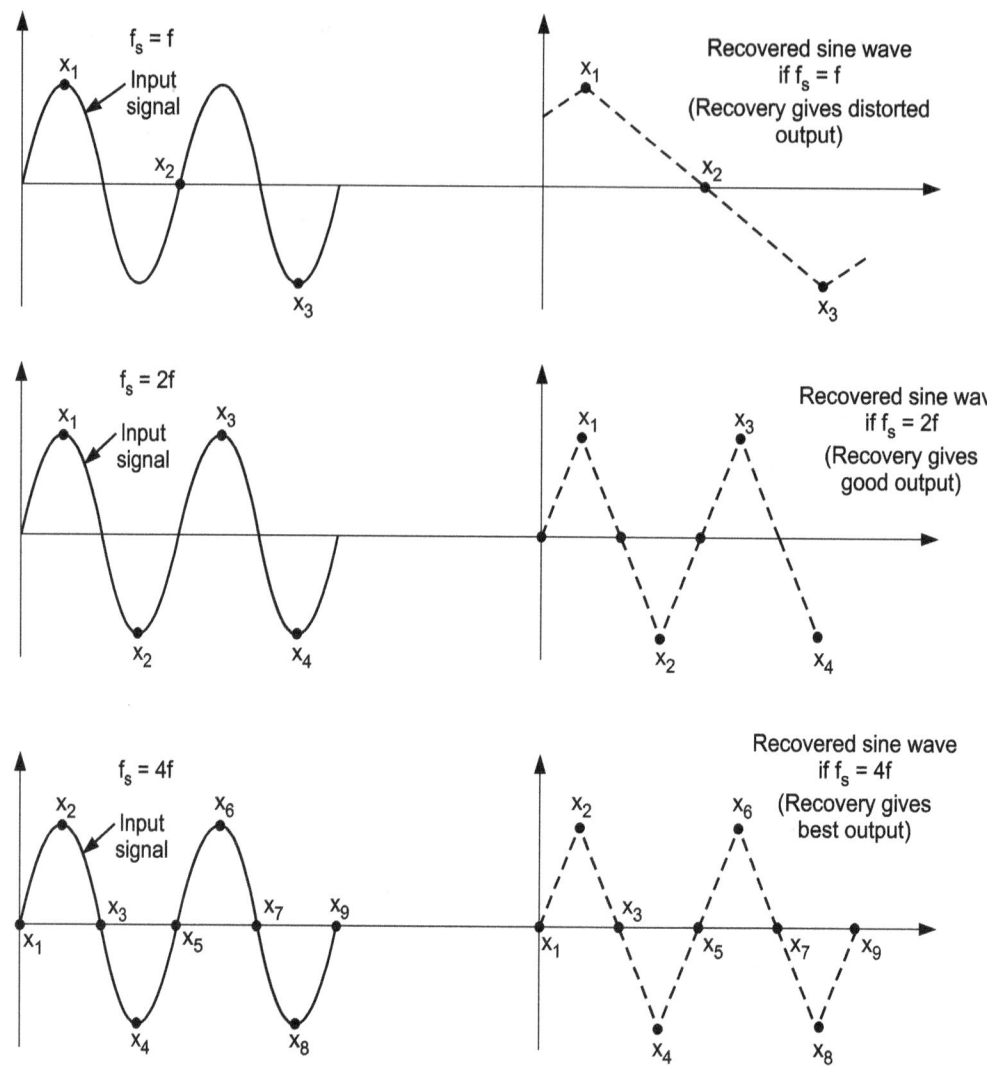

**Fig. 2.39: Different Sine Wave Analog Signals are Sampled at f_s= f, f_s = 2f and f_s = 4f.
Also Recovered Signals at Receiver End are Shown**

2.12.2 Quantization

1. Quantization is basically a process of approximation. This is also like rounding off procedure i.e., if the sampled voltage level is 3.45 then rounding off value = 3.5. If sampled voltage level is 5.78 then rounding off value = 5.8.

2. Thus, quantizer converts the sampled signal level into an approximated quantized voltage level, which is nearest to the predecided standard voltage level.

3. **These nearest predecided standard voltage levels are called as "quantization levels".**

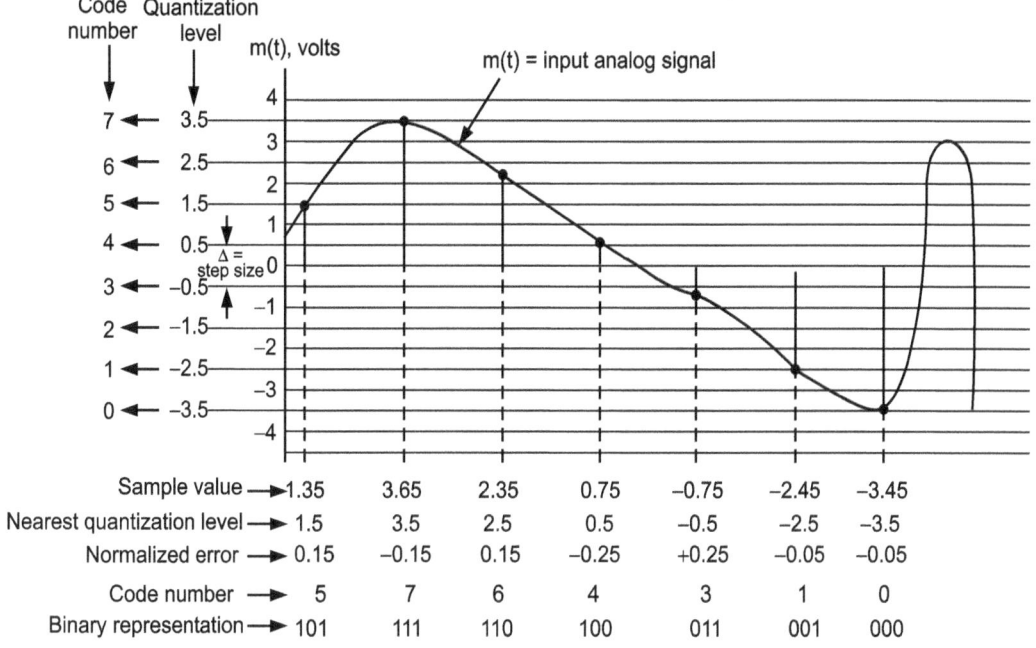

Sample value →	1.35	3.65	2.35	0.75	−0.75	−2.45	−3.45
Nearest quantization level →	1.5	3.5	2.5	0.5	−0.5	−2.5	−3.5
Normalized error →	0.15	−0.15	0.15	−0.25	+0.25	−0.05	−0.05
Code number →	5	7	6	4	3	1	0
Binary representation →	101	111	110	100	011	001	000

Fig. 2.40: Sampled value, Quantized level, Normalized error,

Code number and Binary code representation for the given signal

4. Here we assume that the original analog signal has amplitudes between E_{min} and E_{max}. Here the signal voltage is instantaneous.

5. In Fig. 2.40, E_{max} = 4 V and E_{min} = −4 V. This entire range has been divided into 'L' equal intervals each having equal size = Δ.

6. Hence, step size = Δ = $\dfrac{E_{max} - E_{min}}{L}$

    Here, in Fig. 2.40,   L = 8

    E_{max} = 4V

    E_{min} = −4V

7. At the centre of these steps the quantization levels are located as shown.

8. The difference between quantized level and sampled value is known as:

    • Normalized error.

    • or Quantization error.

    • or Quantization noise.

9. Quantization error should be as small as possible. Thus, maximum quantization error Q_E is always $-\Delta/2 \leq Q_E \leq \Delta/2$.

10. Thus, to minimize the quantization error, we must reduce step size.

11. Step size can be reduced by increasing the number of quantization levels.

12. Thus, if we use 3 bit PCM, then quantization levels will be $2^N = 2^3 = 8 = L =$ Levels.

13. If N = 4 bit i.e., 4 bit PCM, then

Quantization levels $= L = 2^N = 2^4 = 16$ levels.

14. To increase quantization levels, number of bits are increased and hence bit rate in PCM increases, hence bandwidth requirement of the channel increases.

15. In audio communication, normally we use 8-bit PCM, hence $2^8 = 256$ levels. In video communication, the number of levels are in thousands.

16. Thus, if number of levels are more then bandwidth required increases.

    If number of levels are less then quantization error increases.

17. Hence, compromise is done always, while selecting number of levels.

18. Signal to noise ratio is given as,

$$\boxed{SNR_{dB} = 6.02 \times N_b + 1.76 \text{ dB}}$$

where, N_b = Number of bits/sample

19. There are two types of quantizers:

    (i) Uniform quantizer.

    (ii) Non-uniform quantizer.

20. In uniform quantizer the representation levels or quantized levels are uniformly spaced.

21. In non-uniform quantizer the representation levels or quantized levels are spaced non-uniformly.

22. Also the quantizer characteristics are categorized in two forms as follows:

    (i) Midtread type quantizer.

    (ii) Midrise type quantizer.

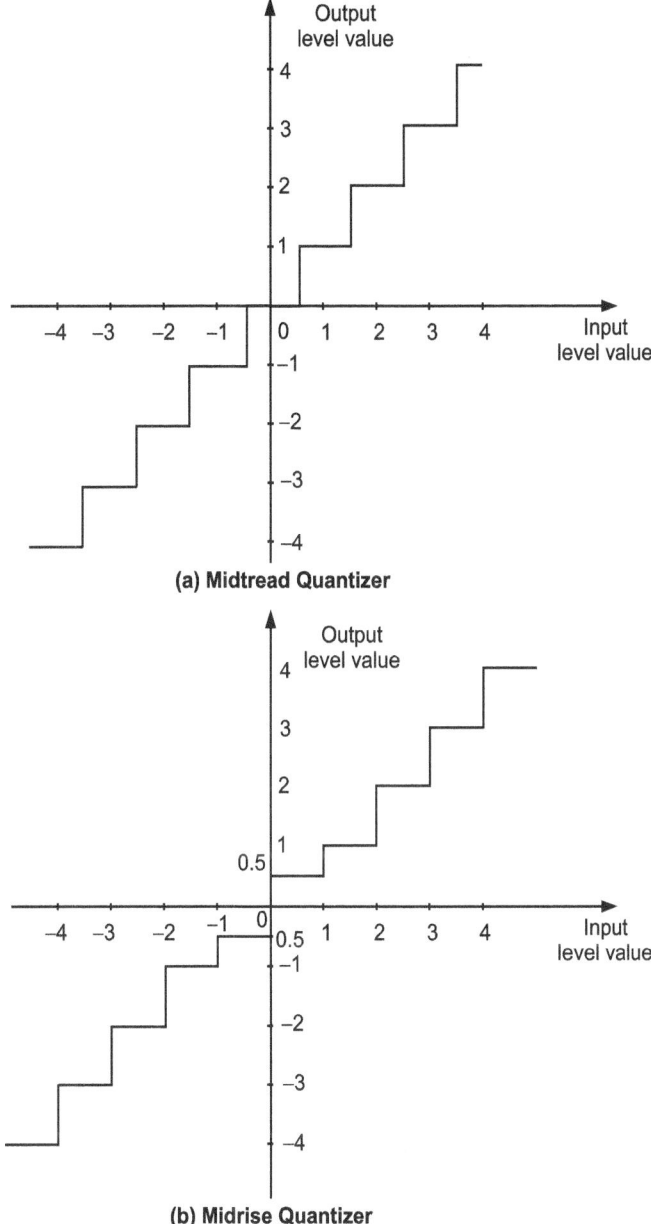

Fig. 2.41: Midtread and Midrise Quantizers

2.12.3 Encoding and Parallel to Serial Converter

1. In PCM sampling → quantizing is the previous step which we have seen in detail.
2. Each quantized level is given a separate code number. For example, code 0, 1, 2, 3, 4, 5, 6, 7, etc.
3. Thus, in encoding process each code number is represented by the digital code or binary code.

Table 2.13: Code number represented in Binary code

Code Number	Binary Code
0	000
1	001
2	010
3	011
4	100
5	101
6	110
7	111

4. Thus, available binary code is in parallel bits form.
5. This parallel bit stream is converted into serial bit stream using parallel to serial converter.
6. Thus, output bit rate is given by,

$$\text{Bit rate} = \text{Sampling rate} \times \text{Number of bits/sample}$$
$$= f_s \times N_b$$

2.13 PCM Receiver

1. The PCM transmitter and PCM receiver block diagram is given in Fig. 2.42 and Fig. 2.43 respectively.

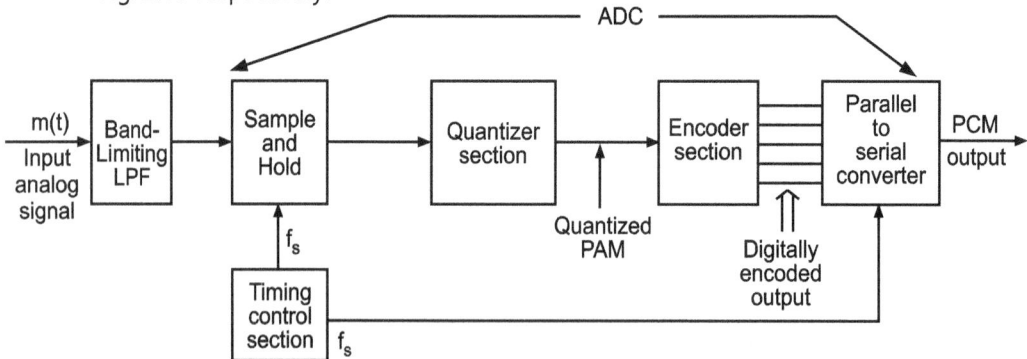

Fig. 2.42: PCM Transmitter (Generalized Block Diagram)

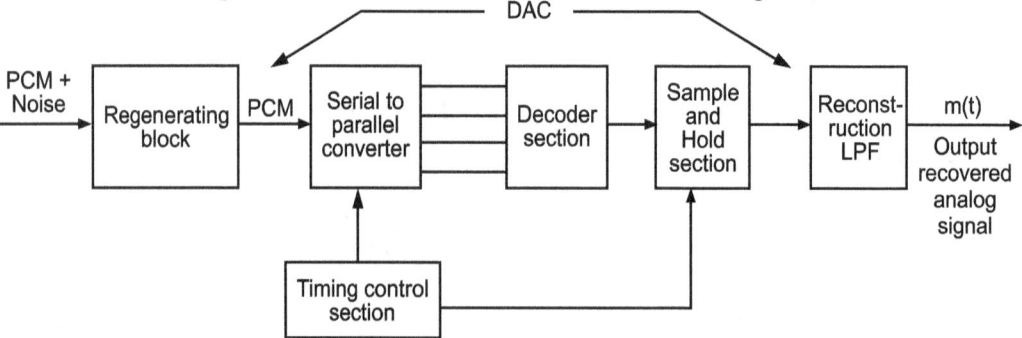

Fig. 2.43: PCM Receiver (Generalized Block Diagram)

2.   The PCM receiver consists of the following blocks:
     •   Regeneration block.
     •   Serial to parallel converter.
     •   Decoder section.
     •   Sample and hold section.
     •   Reconstruction LPF section.
3.   Regeneration block removes the noise from incoming PCM signal and gives noisefree PCM to serial to parallel converter of DAC section.
4.   Parallel bit streams are given to decoder section and then to sample and hold section, which is used to make and connect samples.
5.   Thus, decoder + sample and hold section convert the codewords into a pulse that holds the amplitude until the next pulse.
6.   Finally, after the staircase signal is completed, it is passed through a LPF section to smooth the staircase signal into a required original analog signal.

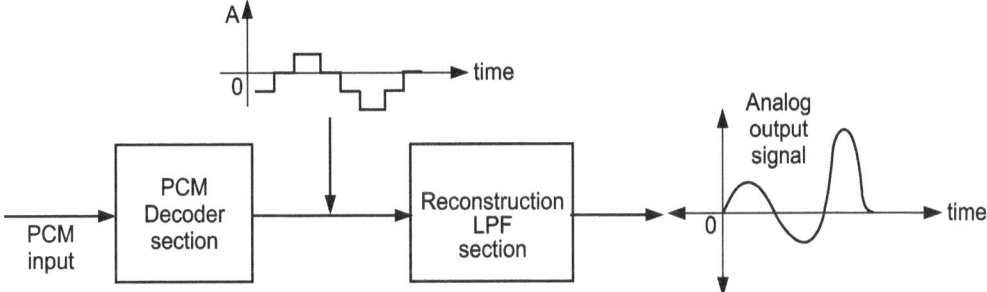

Fig. 2.44: Typical Staircase Waveform converted into Smooth Analog Output Signal

7.   The reconstruction filter has cut-off frequency equal to (≅) signal frequency sent by transmitter.
8.   **PCM Bandwidth** is given by,

$$B_{min} = N_b \times B_{analog}$$

9.   Also **Maximum Data Rate of a channel** is given by,

$$D_{R_{max}} = 2 \times B \times \log_2 (L) \quad \text{in bits/sec}$$

     where, $D_{R_{max}}$ = Maximum data rate of channel

                              B = Signal bandwidth

                              L = Number of levels

     This is stated by Nyquist theorem for data rate calculation.

10. Also **Minimum Required Bandwidth** is given by,

$$B_{min} = \frac{D_R}{2 \times \log_2 (L)} \quad \text{in Hz}$$

2.14 Delta Modulation

1. The basic disadvantage of the PCM system is complexity. Transmitter as well as Receiver has complex processing steps in PCM system. Another A to D conversion techniques are:
   - DM (Delta Modulation).
   - ADM (Adaptive Delta Modulation).
2. In PCM, every sampled value is quantized and every quantized level gives you binary bit stream output whereas, in DM, instead of code words or bit stream, bits are sent one after the another.
3. The **DM modulator** block diagram is as shown in Fig. 2.45.

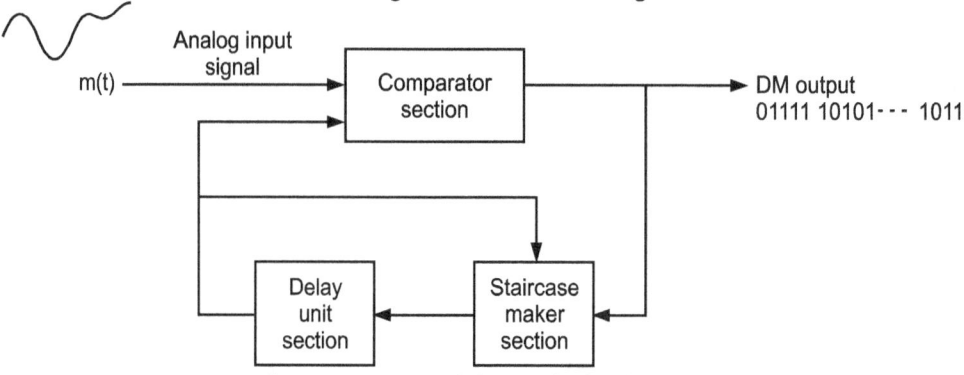

Fig. 2.45: DM Modulator Block Diagram

4. The **DM Demodulator** block diagram is as shown in Fig. 2.46.

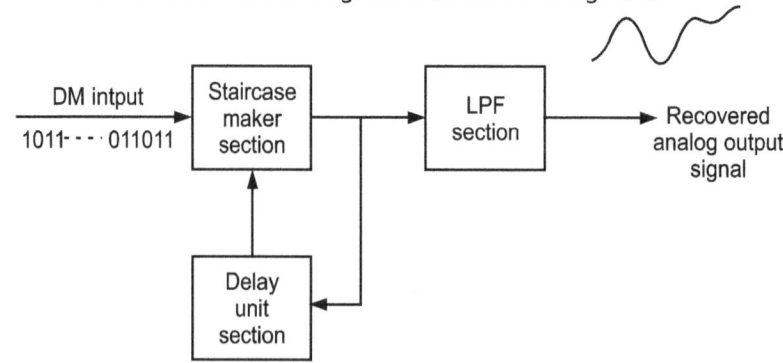

Fig. 2.46: DM Demodulator Block Diagram

5. In delta modulation process, it checks and records the small negative and positive changes known as 'δ'.
6. Input signal m(t) is approximated to step signal by the delta modulator system, represented as D(t).
7. This step size is always fixed. The negative changes are −δ and +ve changes are known as 'δ'.
8. The difference between m(t) and D(t) is positive then, approximate or D(t) signal is increased by one step i.e., 'δ' and thus, '1' is transmitted.

9.   The difference between m(t) and D(t) is negative then, approximate or D(t) signal is decreased by one step i.e. 'δ' and thus '0' is transmitted.

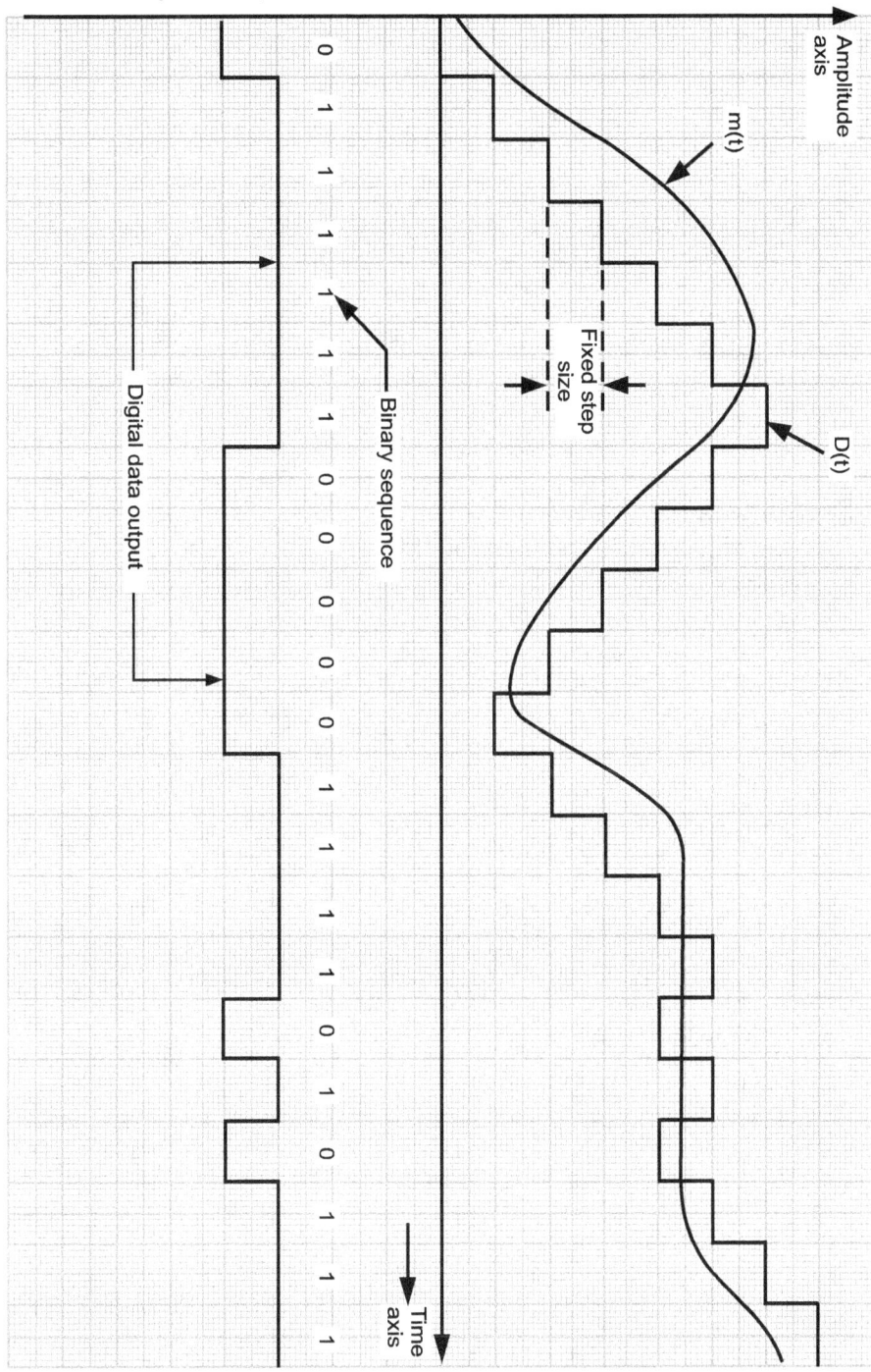

Fig. 2.47: DM (Delta Modulation), Analog Input and Digital Output Waveform

10. Thus, in delta modulation, for every sample, only one binary bit i.e. either '1' or '0' is transmitted depending upon difference between m(t) and D(t).

11. In other words, if the amplitude of the analog signal is larger, then the next bit in the digital data is '1', otherwise it is '0'.

12. Also, delay unit section is required to hold the staircase function for a period between two comparisons we have discussed.

13. In DM demodulator, digital data bit stream is applied to staircase maker section.

14. Staircase maker section and Delay unit section creates the analog signal, which is not smooth in nature.

15. Thus, final required analog signal which is smooth in nature, is available at the output of low-pass-filter section.

2.14.1 Advantages of DM

1. Delta modulator gives only one bit for every sample. Hence, bit rate as well as channel bandwidth requirement is less.

2. Simplest transmitter and receiver circuitry reduces the cost.

2.14.2 Disadvantages of DM

1. There are two distortions occurring in DM.
   - Slope overload distortion.
   - Granular noise distortion (Hunting effect).

2. These distortions are as shown in Fig. 2.48.

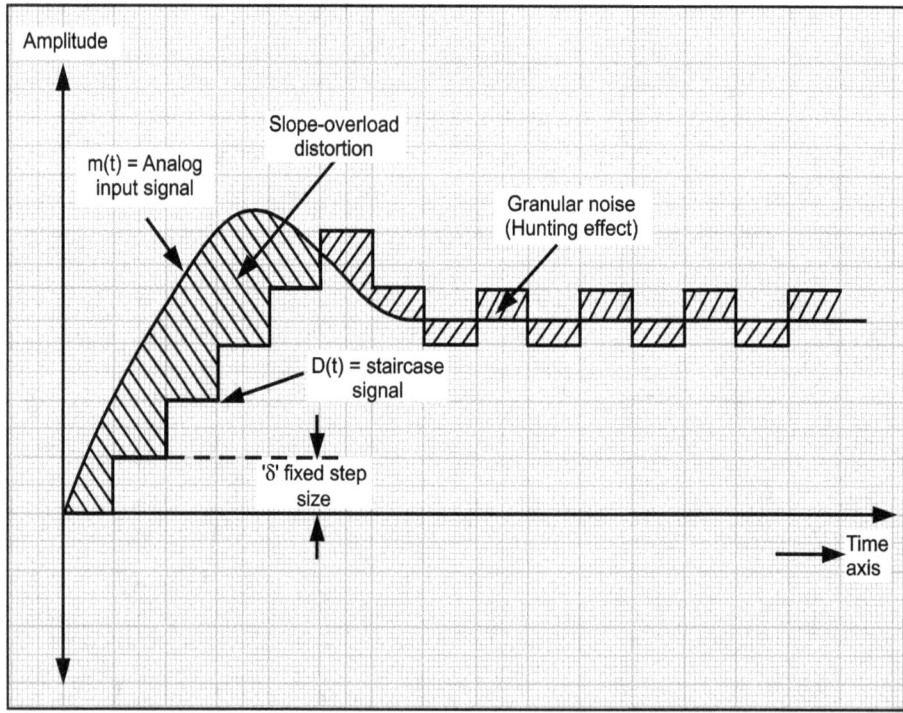

Fig. 2.48: Slope Overload and Granular Noise Distortions in DM

3.　If the rise rate of input signal m(t) is high, then staircase signal can not approximate it or predict it because step size 'δ' is fixed and small for staircase signal D(t) to follow the analog signal m(t).

4.　Due to which there is large error between m(t) and D(t) signal. This large error is known as **slope overload distortion.**

5.　To reduce this **slope overload error**, step size should be increased when slope or rising rate of analog signal m(t) is high. This can be achieved with new technique known as **Adaptive Delta Modulation.**

6.　Thus, in ADM (Adaptive Delta Modulation), the value of step size 'δ' changes according to the amplitude of the input analog signal m(t).

7.　If analog input signal m(t) is flat in nature and step size of D(t) is having high 'δ' (step size), then staircase signal D(t) keeps on oscillating by ± δ around the signal. This difference or error between m(t) and D(t) is known as **granular noise** and this effect of oscillating by ± δ around the signal is known as **hunting effect.**

8.　To reduce the granular noise, ADM (Adaptive Delta Modulation) technique is used, which reduces step size 'δ' when signal m(t) becomes flat in nature.

9.　Finally, ADM technique uses variable step size to overcome slope-overload noise and granular noise.

10.　The waveform of ADM technique to reduce slope-overload noise and granular noise is as shown in Fig. 2.49.

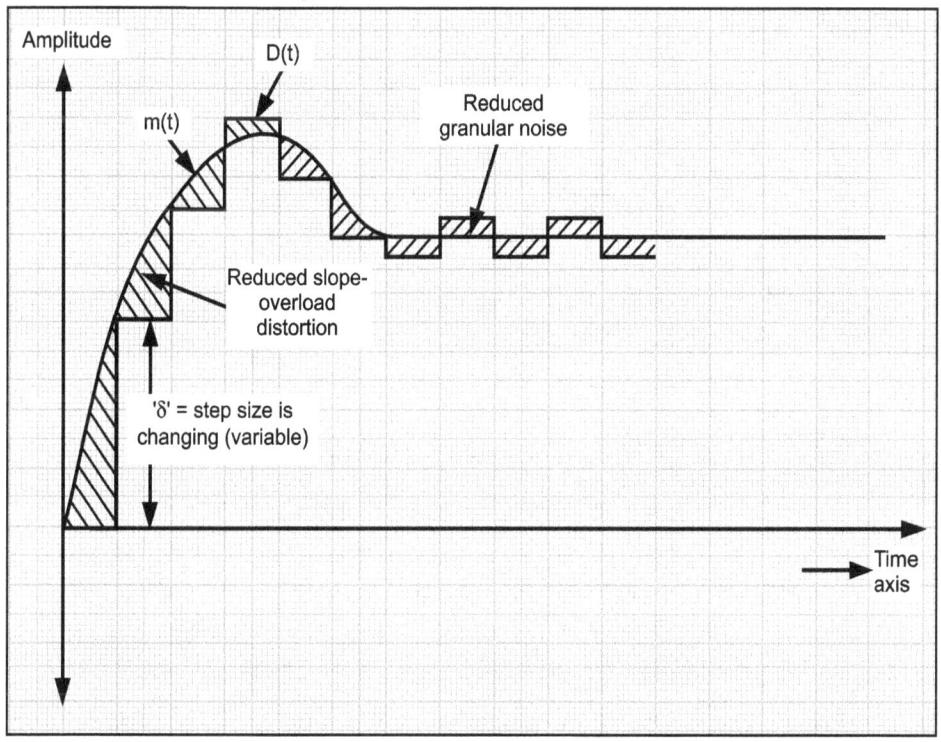

Fig. 2.49: ADM (Reduced Slope-Overload Noise and Granular Noise)

11. Thus, following are the advantages of ADM:
    - SNR is better than DM.
    - Bandwidth utilization is better than DM.
    - Dynamic range is better than DM.

2.15 Transmission Modes

1. Transmission modes are classified as:

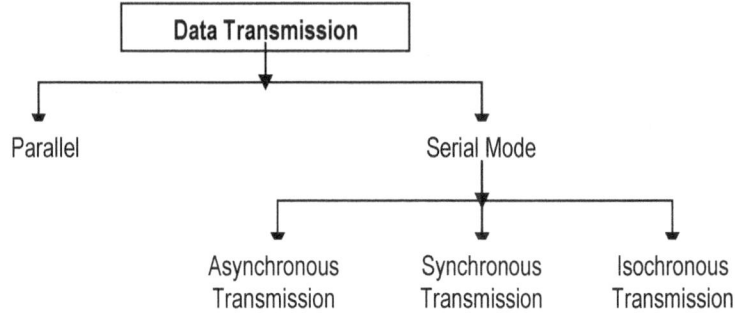

2. **Parallel mode of transmission:** In parallel mode, a group of 'n' bits are formed and simultaneously send from one device to other. This is called as parallel data transmission.

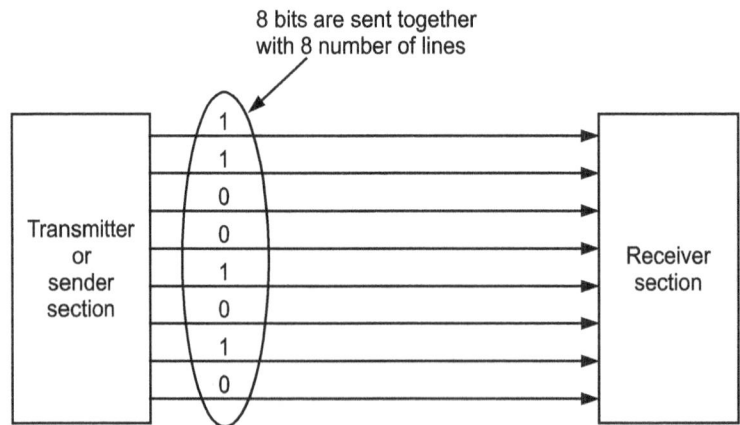

Fig. 2.50: Parallel Transmission Mode

3. 'n' wires are used to send 'n' number of bits at a time.
4. Thus, on 'n' wires, 'n' bits are ready and with one clock transition 'n' bits will be transferred from transmitter and will be received by receiver.
5. In parallel transmission mode 'n' wires or here 8 wires are bundled in a cable with connector at each end.

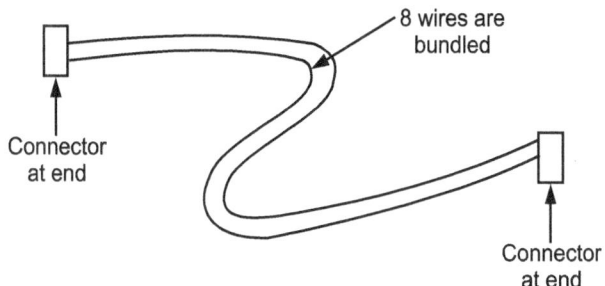

Fig. 2.51: Wires are Bundled in Parallel Transmission

6. Advantages of parallel transmission mode:

    • Speed is high.

    • Simple method.

7. Disadvantages of parallel transmission mode:

    • Cost increases because of 'n' number of wires.

    • Complexity increases if 'n' increases and maintenance becomes difficult.

    • Due to expensive and complex property, it is used for small distance communication.

8. **Serial mode of transmission:**

    There are three types of serial transmission:

    • Asynchronous mode.

    • Synchronous mode.

    • Isochronous mode.

9. In serial communication, only one channel is used for communication. Thus, digital data is transferred between transmitter and receiver using only one communication channel instead of 'n' channels in parallel mode.

10. The cost of serial communication reduces by factor 'n' as compared to parallel one.

11. In serial communication, parallel to serial converter is required at transmitter end and serial to parallel converter is required at receiver end.

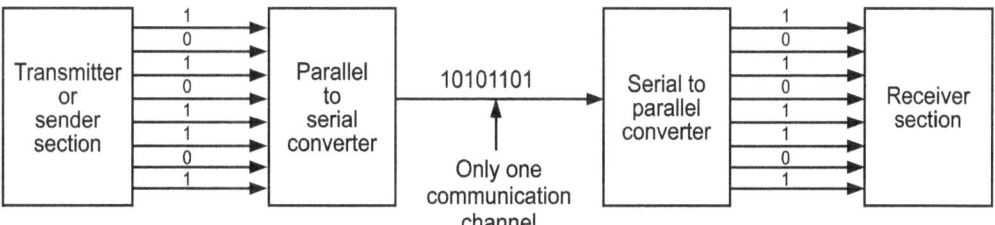

Fig. 2.52: Serial Mode of Transmission

12. Asynchronous serial communication is as shown in Fig. 2.53.

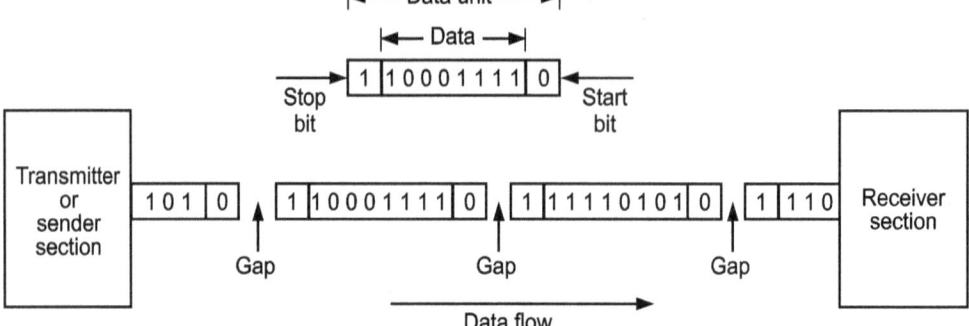

Fig. 2.53: Asynchronous Serial Communication

13. Typical synchronous serial communication is as shown in Fig. 2.54.

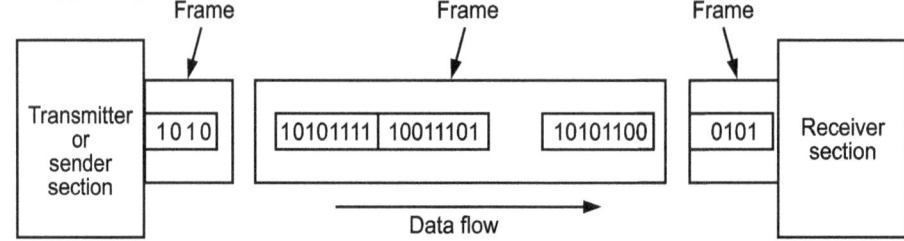

Fig. 2.54: Synchronous Serial Communication

14. In asynchronous communication system:
    - Importance is not given to timing of signal.
    - Grouping of bit stream is done i.e. 1 byte = 8 bits group.
    - Extra start bit is added at the beginning of each byte for synchronization.
    - Extra stop bit is added at the end of each byte for synchronization.
    - Start bit alerts receiver that the byte has arrived.
    - Stop bit informs receiver that the byte has finished.
    - Varying gap is maintained between two bytes.
    - Gap is either stream of additional stop bits or idle channel.
    - Here the asynchronous effect is present at byte level but the bits are fully synchronized.
    - Presence of gaps between two bytes reduces speed of communication.
    - Keyboard to computer CPU is an example of asynchronous communication.

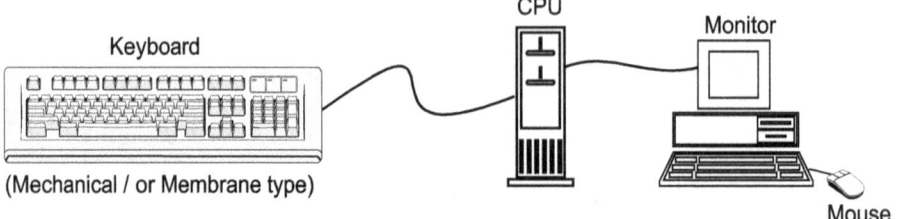

Fig. 2.55: Example of Asynchronous Communication

15. In synchronous communication system:
    - Multiple bytes are combined into longer frames.
    - Data bits are transmitted as an unbroken stream of '1' and '0'.
    - Receiver performs the separation of bit stream, converting into bytes for decoding purpose.
    - Start and stop bits are not added in synchronous communication.
    - Synchronization is maintained and is must between transmitter and receiver section.
    - Gaps are not provided between bytes by transmitter and hence, higher speed is achieved in synchronous communication system.
    - Synchronization between transmitter and receiver is maintained and handled by data link layer protocol working at both ends.
    - Gaps are absent between individual bits, but there can be gaps between two frames.
    - This synchronous communication system fails when uneven delays between frames are not acceptable.
    - For example, in TV broadcast of PAL system, 25 frames of each picture or 25 images/second are required to be transmitted and viewed at the same rate. Then and then only picture can be displayed without loss or distortion in TV receiver display. This is not possible because of uneven gaps present between different frames.

16. In isochronous communication system,
    - It is used in real time audio, video and multimedia applications.
    - Data arrival at fixed rate is guaranteed and delays between frames are absent.

SOLVED EXAMPLES

Example 2.1:

A signal is carrying data in which one data element is encoded as one signal element ($r_{ds} = 1$). If the bit rate is 200 kbps, what is the average value of the baud rate if C = 0.5?

Solution:

$$r_{ds} = 1$$
$$N = 2,00,000 \text{ bps} = 200 \text{ kbps} = 200 \times 10^3$$
$$C = 0.5$$
$$S = ?$$

$\therefore$
$$S = C \times N \times \frac{1}{r_{ds}}$$

$$= 0.5 \times 200 \times 10^3 \times \frac{1}{1}$$

$$= 100 \times 10^3 \text{ baud}$$

$$\boxed{S = 100 \text{ kbaud}}$$

Example 2.2:

In a digital transmission, the receiver clock is 0.2% faster than the sender clock. How many extra bits per second does the receiver receive if the data rate is 2 kbps ? How many if the data rate is 2 Mbps?

Solution:

$$C_1 = 2 \text{ kbps} = 2000 \text{ bps}$$

$$C_2 = 2 \text{ Mbps} = 20,00,000 \text{ bps}$$

(a)

$$100 - 0.2\%$$

$$2000 - ?$$

∴

$$\frac{2000 \times 0.2}{100} = 4 \text{ bits extra received}$$

(b)

$$100 - 0.2$$

$$20,00,000 - ?$$

∴

$$\frac{20,00,000 \times 0.2}{100} = 4000 \text{ bits extra received}$$

∴ Hence for 200 kbps data rate = 2,00,000 + 4 = 200004 bits received.
Hence for 2 Mbps data rate = 20,00,000 + 4,000 = 2004000 bits received.

Example 2.3:

A system is using NRZ-I to transfer 2 Mbps data. What are the average signal rate and minimum B.W.?

Solution:

$$\text{Average signal rate } S = \frac{N}{2} = \frac{2 \times 10^6}{2} = 1 \text{ Mbaud.}$$

$$B_{min} = S = 1 \text{ MHz.}$$

Example 2.4:

Calculate the SNR_{dB} for the following system:

(a)   PCM with 8 levels
(b)   PCM with 32 levels
(c)   PCM with 64 levels

Solution:

$$SNR_{dB} = 6.02 \cdot N_b + 1.76 \text{ dB}$$

(a) $SNR_{dB} = 6.02 \times 8 + 1.76 = 49.92 \text{ dB}$
(b) $SNR_{dB} = 6.02 \times 32 + 1.76 = 194.4 \text{ dB}$
(c) $SNR_{dB} = 6.02 \times 64 + 1.76 = 387.04 \text{ dB}$

Example 2.5:

Calculate the minimum number of bits per sample for the PSTN line having following different SNR_{dB}.

(a)   PSTN line with $SNR_{dB} = 35 \text{ dB}$
(b)   PSTN line with $SNR_{dB} = 38 \text{ dB}$
(c)   PSTN line with $SNR_{dB} = 48 \text{ dB}$

Solution:

$$SNR_{dB} = 6.02 \cdot N_b + 1.76 \text{ dB}$$

(a)
$$35 = 6.02 \times N_b + 1.76$$

$$\boxed{N_b = 5.52 \text{ i.e. use 6 bits}}$$

(b)
$$38 = 6.02 \times N_b + 1.76$$

$$\boxed{N_b = 6.019 = \text{use 7 bits}}$$

(c)
$$48 = 6.02 \times N_b + 1.76$$

$$\boxed{N_b = 7.68 = \text{use 8 bits}}$$

Example 2.6:

Calculate the sampling rate and bit rate for the 8 bit PCM system, if voice signal to be sampled is of 4 kHz.

Solution:

∴ $\quad$ Sampling rate $= 2 \times 4$ kHz $= 8000$ samples/sec

∴ $\quad$ Bit rate $=$ Sampling rate $\times$ 8 bits/sample

$$= 8000 \times 8$$

Bit rate $= 64000$ bps

∴ $\quad$ $\boxed{\text{Bit rate} = 64 \text{ kbps}}$

Example 2.7:

Calculate the minimum B.W. of 8 bit PCM system, if we have audio input frequency of 3800 Hz.

Solution:

$$B.W. = ?$$
$$N_b = 8$$
$$B_{analog} = 3800 \text{ Hz}$$

∴ $\quad BW_{minimum} = N_b \times B_{analog}$

∴ $\quad \boxed{BW_{min} = 8 \times 3800 = 30400 \text{ Hz}}$

2.16 Digital to Analog Conversion [or Digital Continuous Wave (DCW) Modulation]

1. In Digital to Analog conversion (or in digital continuous wave modulation), the amplitude, frequency or phase of sine wave carrier is changed according to digital input data '1' or '0'.

2. There are four types of Digital to Analog conversion systems.

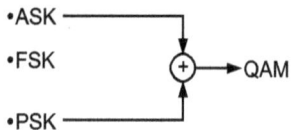

3. Thus, four types can be given as follows :
   - ASK
   - FSK
   - PSK
   - QAM
4. Typical Digital to Analog conversion is given as,

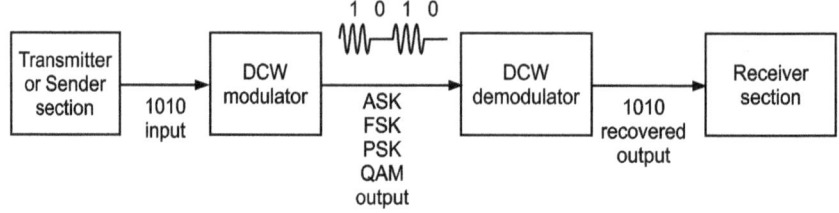

Fig. 2.56: Typical Digital to Analog Conversion (or DCW Modulation) System

5. The following points revision is required before proceeding to next section.
   - Data elements Vs. Signal element.
   - Data rate Vs. Signal rate.
6. We have covered these points in Chapter 3.
7. Thus, recall that and we can write,

$$S = N \times \frac{1}{r_{ds}} = \text{(bauds)}$$

where,   S = Signal rate

                N = Data rate

                r_{ds} = Number of data elements carried in one signal element

∴ $r_{ds} = \log_2 (L)$

where,   L = Type of signal element, not the level = $(2)^{r_{ds}}$

8. Thus, Bit rate is number of bits/sec and Baud rate is number of signal elements/sec.
9. In DCW communication, baud rate ≤ bit rate always.

Example 2.8:

An analog signal carries 5 bits per signal element. If 2000 signal elements are sent per second, find the bit rate of system.

Solution:

$$r_{ds} = 5$$
$$S = 2000$$
$$N = ?$$

∴ $S = N \times \frac{1}{r_{ds}}$

∴ $N = S \times r_{ds}$

$$= 2000 \times 5$$

$$\boxed{N = 10000 \text{ bps}}$$

Example 2.9:

An analog signal has a bit rate of 9000 bps and a baud rate of 900 baud. How many data elements are carried by each signal element? How many signal elements do we need?

Solution:

$$S = 900 \text{ baud}$$

$$N = 9000 \text{ bps}$$

$$r_{ds} = ?, \; L = ?$$

$$S = N \times \frac{1}{r_{ds}}$$

$$\boxed{r_{ds} = \frac{N}{S} = \frac{9000}{900} = 10 \text{ bits/baud}}$$

∴

$$r_{ds} = \log_2 L$$

∴

$$L = 2^{r_{ds}}$$

$$= 2^{10}$$

∴

$$\boxed{L = 1024}$$

2.17 ASK (Amplitude Shift Keying)

1. In ASK technique, amplitude of sine wave carrier signal is varied to create signal elements by keeping frequency and phase of carrier signal unchanged (or constant).

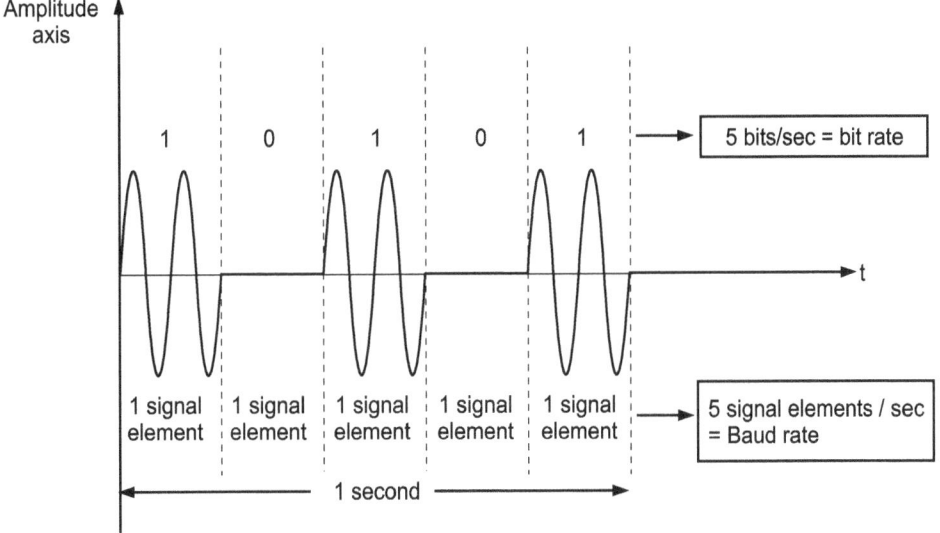

Fig. 2.57: ASK Digital to Analog Conversion or DCW Technique

2. Bandwidth calculation for ASK technique is given by formula

$$B.W. = (1 + D) \times S$$

where,   S = Signal rate

          D = Factor which depends upon modulation and filtering process

3. Practical implementation of ASK system is done with the help of multiplier unit as shown in Fig. 2.58.

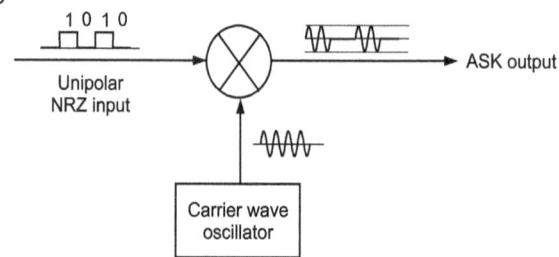

Fig. 2.58: ASK Generation using Multiplier

4. The typical waveform for ASK generation is as shown in Fig. 2.59.

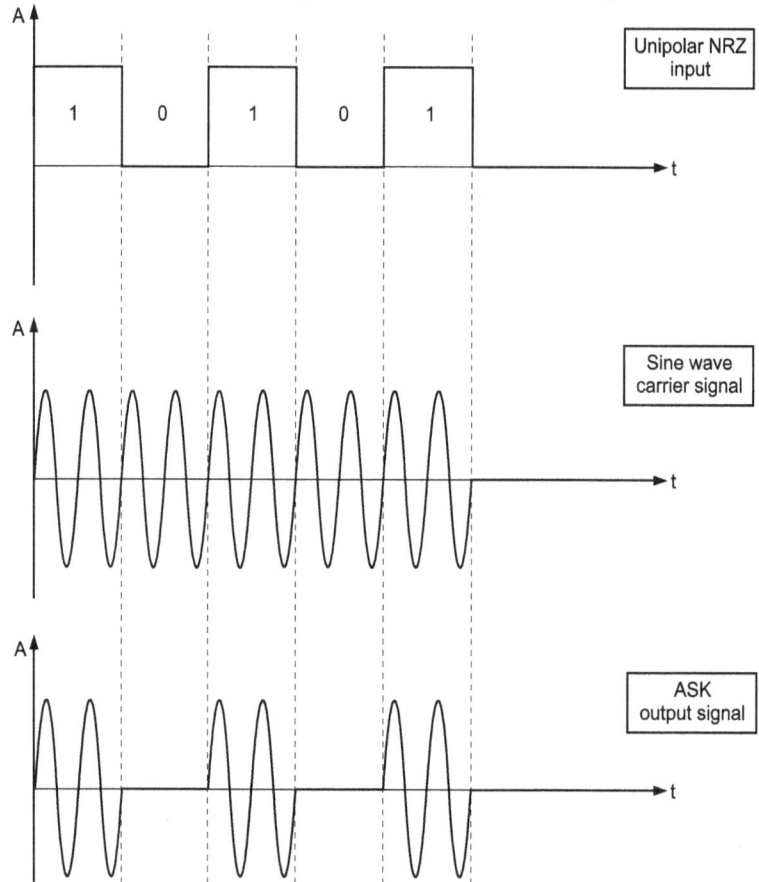

Fig. 2.59: ASK Generation from Unipolar NRZ and Sine Wave Signal

Example 2.10:

Available bandwidth of 150 kHz which spans from 300 to 400 kHz. What are the carrier frequency and bit rate if ASK modulation is used and if d = 1?

Solution:

$$\text{Bandwidth B} = 150 \text{ kHz}$$

$$f_c = \frac{300 + 400}{2}$$

$$= 350 \text{ kHz} = \text{Carrier frequency}$$

$$\therefore \qquad B = 2 \times N \times \frac{1}{r_{ds}}$$

$$\therefore \qquad r_{ds} = d = 1$$

$$\therefore \qquad N = \frac{B \times r_{ds}}{2} = \frac{150 \text{ kHz} \times 1}{2}$$

$$\boxed{N = 75 \text{ kbps}}$$

Example 2.11:

Draw frequency spectrum of typical full duplex ASK communication system.

Solution:

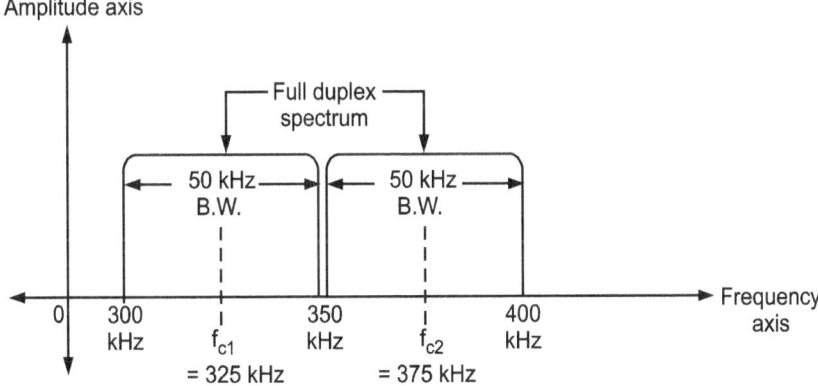

Fig. 2.56: Typical Full Duplex ASK Spectrum

2.17.1 Multilevel ASK

1. Previous section discusses about only two levels of amplitude i.e. '0' and '1'.
2. In multilevel ASK, more than two amplitude levels can be used.
3. If we use data using 2, 3, 4 or more bits at a time, in this case, it will give

$$r_{ds} = 2$$
$$r_{ds} = 3$$
$$r_{ds} = 4$$

4. This multilevel ASK concept is applicable in QAM (or Quadrature Amplitude Modulation) system.

2.18 FSK (Frequency Shift Keying)

1. In FSK technique, frequency of sine wave carrier signal is varied to create signal elements by keeping amplitude and phase of carrier signal unchanged (or constant).

2. Here, two carrier frequencies are selected for '0' and '1' input, i.e. f_1 and f_2 respectively.

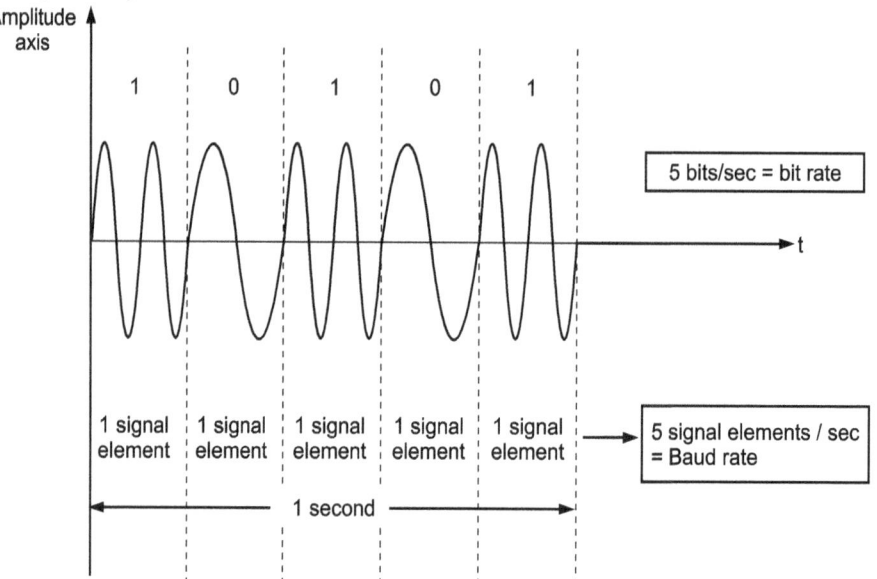

Fig. 2.57: FSK Digital to Analog Conversion or DCW Technique

3. Bandwidth calculation for FSK technique is given by formula,

$$B.W. = (1 + D) \times S + 2\Delta f$$

where, S = Signal rate

D = Factor which depends upon modulation and filtering process

4. Here in above formula required $2\Delta f$ is calculated from Fig. 2.58.

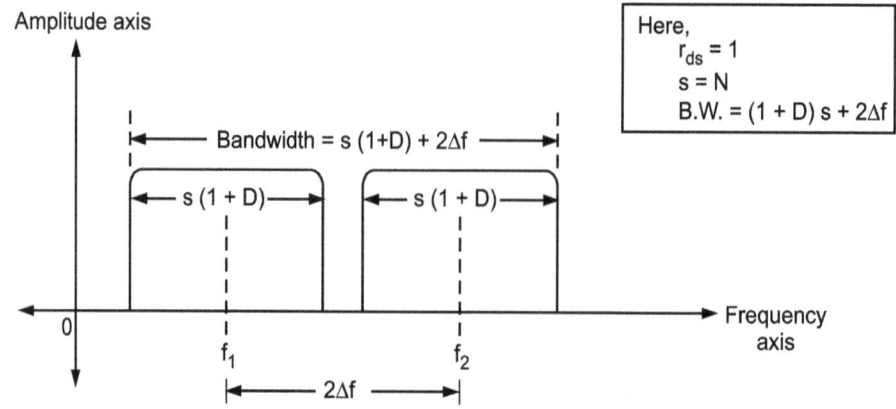

Fig. 2.58: $2\Delta f$ calculation using f_1 and f_2 (or difference between f_1 and f_2)

5. Practical implementation of FSK system is done with the help of VCO (Voltage Controlled Oscillator) section.

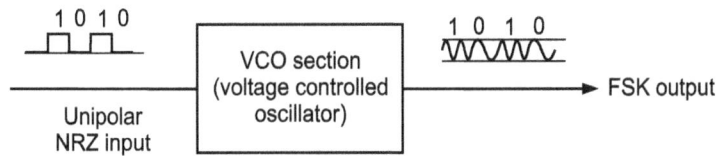

Fig. 2.59: FSK Generation using VCO (Voltage Controlled Oscillator)

6. The typical waveform for FSK generation is as shown in Fig. 2.60.

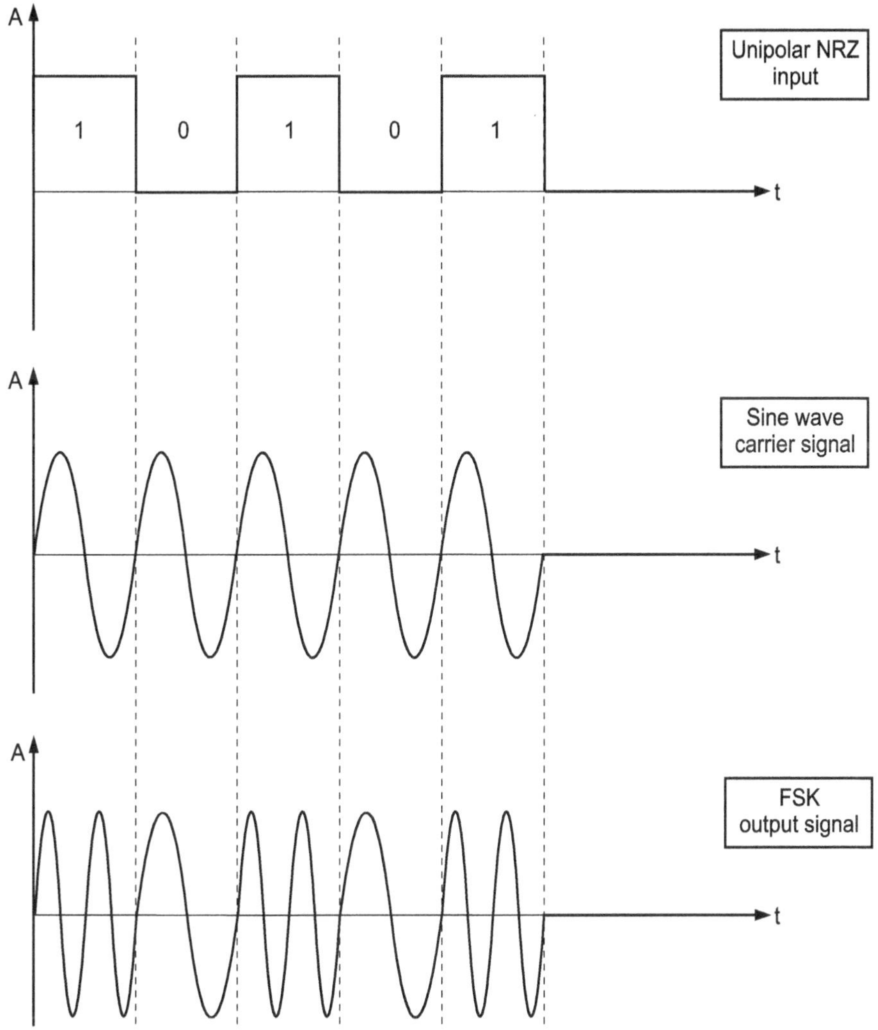

Fig. 2.60: FSK Generation from Unipolar NRZ and Sine Wave Signal

2.18.1 Multilevel FSK

1. Previous section of FSK discusses only two frequencies i.e. f_1 and f_2.

2. In multilevel FSK, we can use f_1, f_2, f_3 and f_4 to send 2 bits at a time.

3. In multilevel FSK, we can use f_1, f_2, f_3, f_4, f_5, f_6, f_7, f_8 frequencies to send 3 bits and so on.

4. However, the basic condition is frequencies should be $2\Delta f$ apart.

5. For proper working/operation of FSK modulator and FSK demodulator section, the minimum value of $2\Delta f$ needs to be S.

6. Thus, we can show :

$$\text{for } D = 0$$
$$\text{B.W.} = (1 + D) \times S + (L - 1)\, 2\Delta f$$
$$\boxed{\text{B.W.} = L \times S}$$

Example 2.12:

Available bandwidth of 150 kHz, which spans from 300 kHz to 400 kHz. What should be the carrier frequency and the bit rate if FSK modulation with $D = 1$ is taken?

Solution: We choose, $\quad 2\Delta f = 75$ kHz

$$\text{B.W.} = 150$$
$$\therefore \qquad \text{B.W.} = (1 + D) \times S + 2\Delta f = 150$$
$$\text{B.W.} = (2) \times S + 2\Delta f = 150$$
$$\therefore \qquad 2S = 75 \text{ kHz}$$
$$\therefore \qquad \boxed{S = 37.5 \text{ kbaud}}$$
$$\therefore \qquad \boxed{N = 37.5 \text{ kbps}}$$

Example 2.13:

We need to send data of 4 bits at a time at a bit rate of 4 Mbps. The carrier frequency is 20 MHz. Calculate the number of levels (different frequencies), the baud rate and the bandwidth.

Solution:

$$f_c = 20 \text{ MHz}$$
$$\therefore \qquad L = 2^4 = 16$$
$$\therefore \qquad \text{Baud rate} = S = \frac{4 \text{ Mbps}}{4} = 1000 \text{ Mbaud}$$
$$\therefore \qquad 2\Delta f = 1 \text{ MHz apart}$$
$$\therefore \qquad \text{Baudwidth} = L \times S = 16 \times 1000$$
$$= 16000 \text{ Hz}$$
$$= 16 \text{ MHz}$$

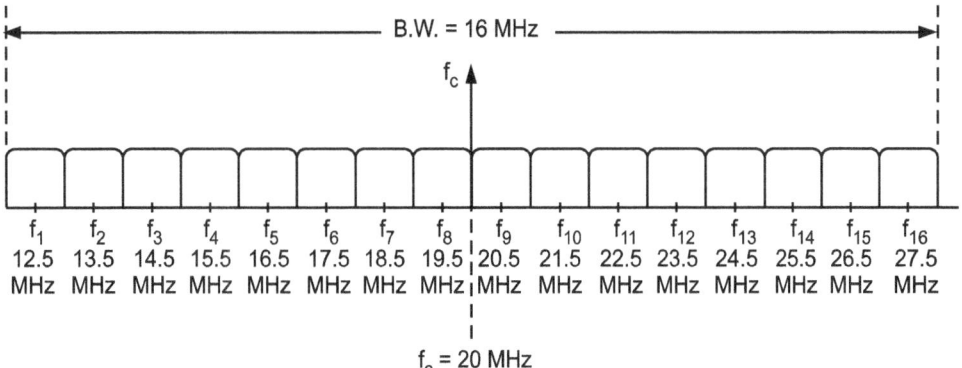

$f_c = 20$ MHz

Fig. 2.61: Multilevel FSK Example

2.19 PSK (Phase Shift Keying)

1. In PSK technique, phase of sine wave carrier signal is varied to create signal elements by keeping amplitude and frequency of carrier signal unchanged (or constant).
2. PSK technique is widely used as compared to ASK and FSK.
3. In PSK, we have only two signal elements, one with θ_1 = Phase = $0°$ and other with θ_2 = Phase = $180°$.
4. PSK is better than ASK, because PSK is less susceptible to noise than ASK (or PSK is highly immune to noise).
5. PSK is better than FSK, because FSK requires two frequencies f_1 and f_2 whereas PSK requires one frequency only.

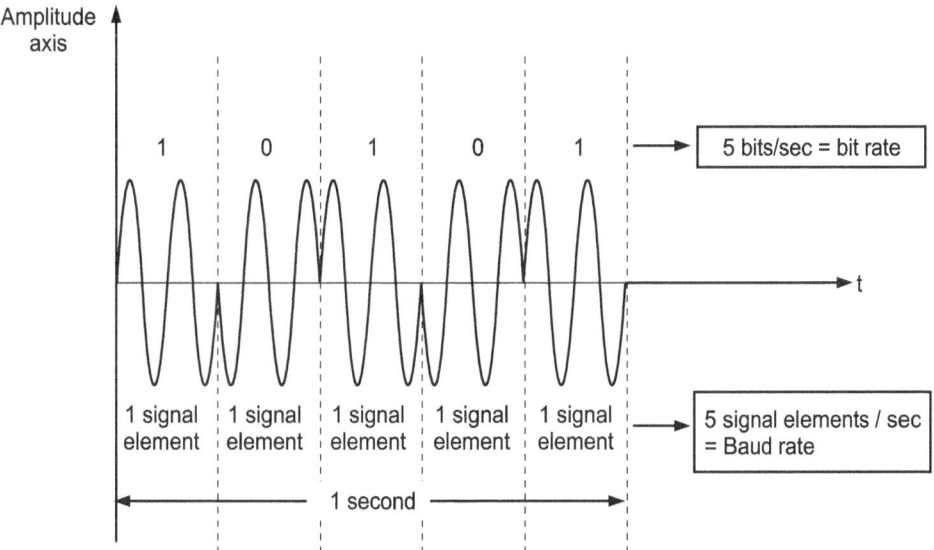

Fig. 2.62: PSK Digital to Analog Conversion or DCW Technique

6. Bandwidth calculation for PSK technique is given by formula,

   $$B.W. = (1 + D) \times S$$

   where,   S = Signal rate

              D = Factor which depends upon modulation and filtering process.

7. Bandwidth of PSK system is given as,

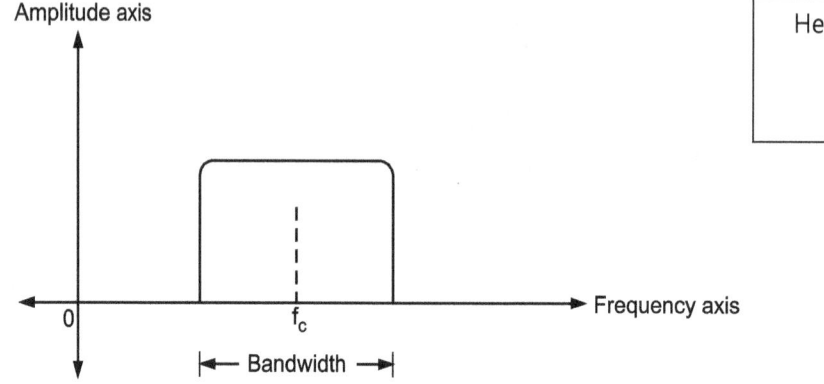

Here, r_{ds} = 1

S = N

B.W. = (1 + D) S

Fig. 2.63: Bandwidth Spectrum for PSK

8. Practical implementation of PSK system is done with the help of multiplier and carrier oscillator section.

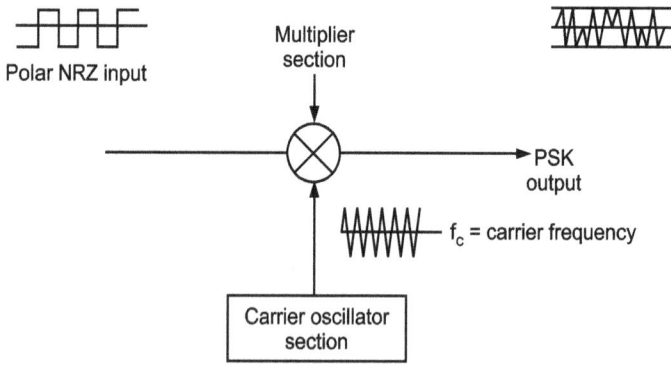

Fig. 2.64: PSK Generation using Multiplier Section

9. The typical waveform for PSK generation is as shown in Fig. 2.65.

10. As compared to BASK, here polar NRZ is used instead of unipolar NRZ.

11. Polar NRZ signal is multiplied by carrier signal f_c, the '1' bit (+ve voltage) is represented by a phase starting at 0° and bit '0' (–ve voltage) is represented by a phase starting at 180°.

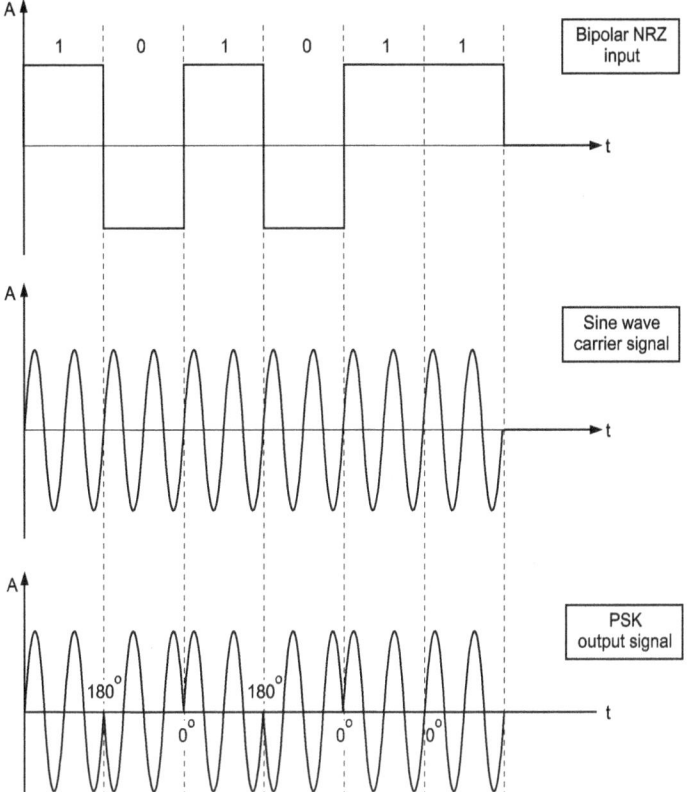

Fig. 2.65: PSK Generation from Bipolar NRZ and Sine Wave Signal

2.19.1 QPSK (Quadrature PSK)

1. In BPSK or Binary PSK system which we have seen earlier, it uses 2 bits at a time in each signal element i.e. $r_{ds} = \dfrac{2}{1} = 2$.

2. This decreases the baud rate and hence decreases the required bandwidth also.

3. QPSK uses two separate BPSK modulations.
    *   One is in phase.
    *   Other in quadrature (Out-of-phase).

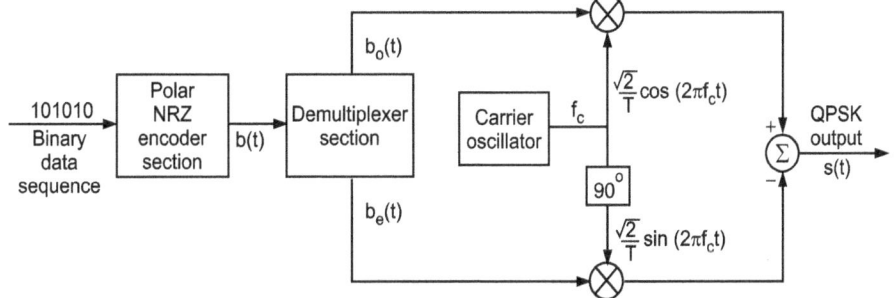

Fig. 2.66: QPSK Generation System

4. Thus, this is basically bandwidth conserving modulation technique for digital transmission.

5. The information carried by the signal is available in phase form.

6. There are four ways to change the phase of carrier frequency.

7. Two successive bits are combined to form 4 different levels, when the level 0 is changed the phase of carrier changes by 45°.

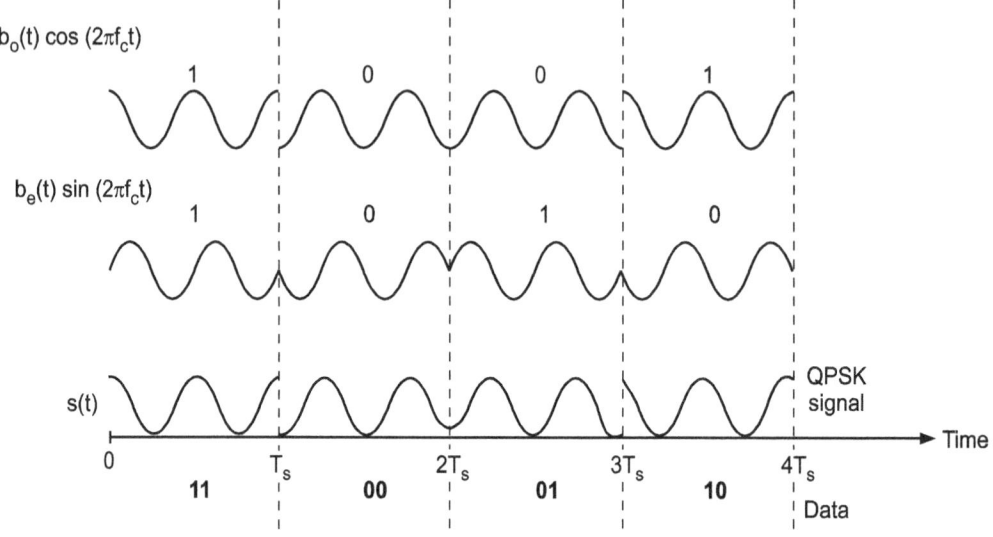

Fig. 2.67: QPSK Waveforms

8. The two different composite signals created by each multiplier are sine waves with the same frequency, but having the different phases.

9. The resultant output of the adder is s(t) which is a sine wave with one of four possible phases i.e. 45°, –45°, 135° and –135°.

10. Now there are four kinds of signal elements in the output signal.

11. This indicates L = 4 and hence we can send 2 bits per signal element i.e. $r_{ds} = \frac{2}{1}$.

2.20 Constellation Pattern Or Constellation Diagram

1. So far, we have seen the following techniques :
    *   ASK or Binary ASK.
    *   FSK or Binary FSK.
    *   PSK or Binary PSK.

2. Constellation diagram is very useful when we are working with multilevel ASK, PSK or QAM.

3. Constellation pattern or constellation diagram helps us to define the phase and amplitude of a signal element, specially when we use two carriers in which one is in phase and other is in quadrature.

4. In this diagram, signal element type is represented as a dot.

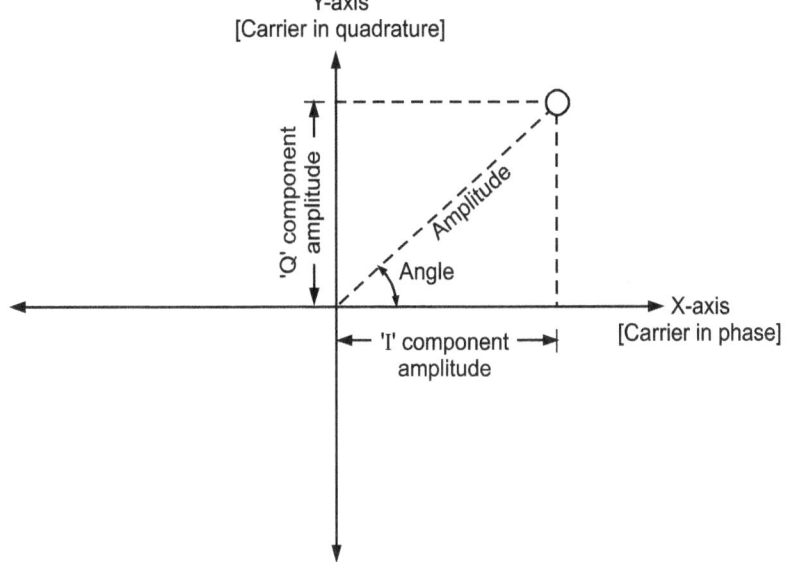

Fig. 2.68: Constellation Diagram Basics

5. Fig. 2.68 is self explanatory and every information we want is displayed in the constellation diagram.

6. Following are the constellation diagrams for the :
    *   Binary ASK
    *   Binary PSK
    *   Quadrature PSK.

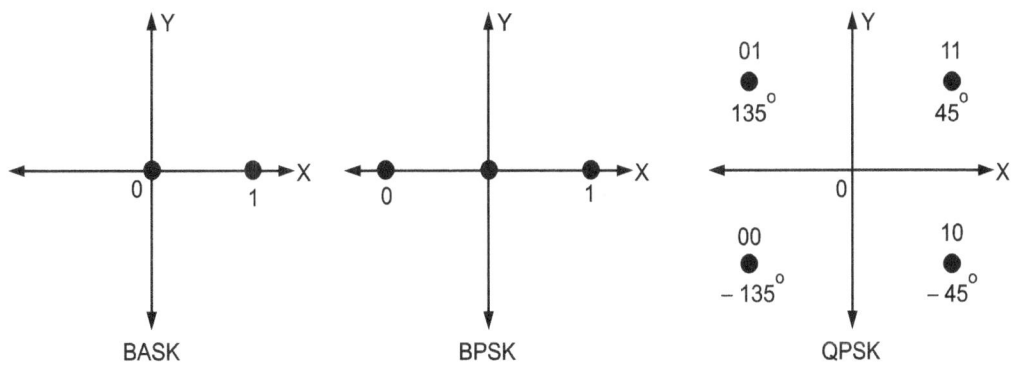

Fig. 2.69: Constellation Pattern for BaSK, BPSK and QPSK Systems

7. In Binary ASK

    - Binary '0' has an amplitude of 0 V. $\biggr\}$ Using only in phase carrier
    - Binary '1' has an amplitude of 1 V.

8. In Binary PSK, two different signal elements are present:
    - One with amplitude 1 V and in phase.
    - Other with amplitude 1 V and 180° out of phase.

9. In QPSK system, two carriers are used :
    - One carrier is in phase and other carrier is in quadrature.
    - All signal elements amplitude = $2^{\frac{1}{2}}$ and phases are 45°, 135°, −135° and −45°.

2.21 QAM (Quadrature Amplitude Modulation)

1. In Binary PSK system, Bit rate is limited due to small difference in phase of two different signal elements.
2. In BASK, BFSK or BPSK, only one characteristic of the carrier is changed.
3. QAM system is a combination of ASK and PSK.
4. The different varieties of QAM systems are as shown below.

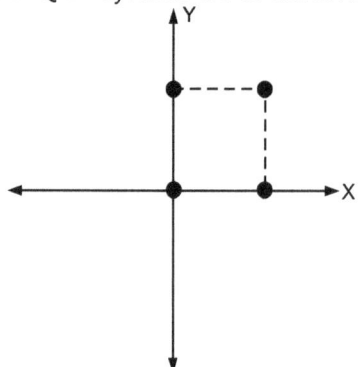

Fig. 2.70: 4-QAM using Unipolar NRZ Signal to Modulate each Carrier

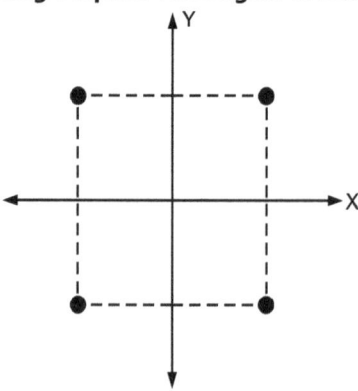

Fig. 2.71: 4-QAM using Polar NRZ Signal to Modulate each Carrier

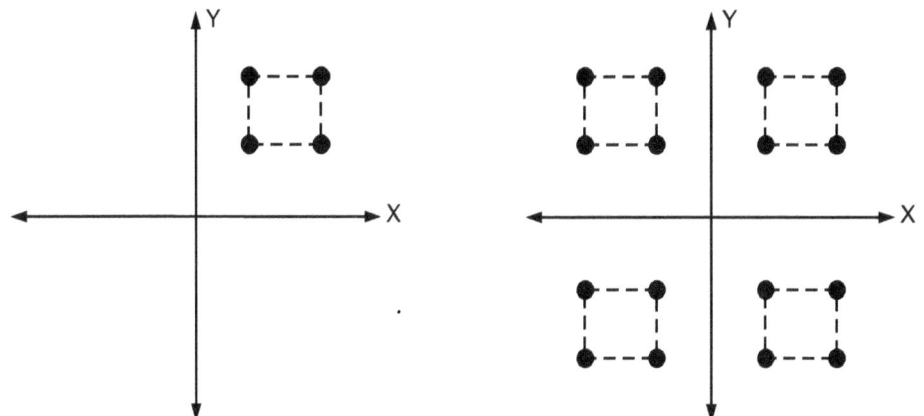

Fig. 2.72: 4-QAM in which Signal with Two Positive Levels is used to Modulate each of the Two Carriers

Fig. 2.73: 16-QAM Signal with Eight levels, Four Positive and Four Negative

5. Bandwidth requirement in QAM system is,
    B.W. of QAM = B.W. of ASK = B.W. of PSK
6. Also QAM has all advantages of PSK over ASK system.
7. QAM system is very useful in data networks like modem equipments etc.

EXERCISE

1. Classify the different conversion systems for signal and data.
2. Explain the applications of line codes.
3. How to eliminate DC components in line coding?
4. List the different line coding format selection criteria.
5. What is the difference between data element and signal element.
6. What is the concept of data element/signal element ratio?
7. Explain the term signalling rate in communication.
8. Explain the following terms in detail:
    (a) Baseline wandering.
    (b) DC component.
    (c) Self synchronization.
9. Classify the different line coding techniques.
10. Write short notes on:
    (a) Unipolar (NRZ) line code
    (b) Polar line codes (NRZ, RZ and Biphase)

(c)   Bipolar (AMI and Pseudoternary) code

(d)   Multilevel code (2B/1Q, 8B/6T and 4D-PAM5)

(e)   Multitransition line codes.

11. Compare NRZ-L Vs. NRZ-I.

12. Compare Bipolar method Vs. Polar NRZ.

13. Explain 2B1Q coding rules.

14. Write short notes on following:

(a)   Block coding

(b)   4B/5B block coding

(c)   8B/10B block coding.

15. What are the different technologies that use 8B/10B coding?

16. What is running disparity? What are the rules for running disparity?

17. What is scrambling? Explain the following scrambling techniques in detail:

(a)   B8ZS

(b)   HDB3

18. Draw and explain the block diagram of PCM transmitter and receiver.

19. Write short notes on following:

(a)   Sampling

(b)   Quantizing

20. Draw and explain block diagram of DM transmitter and DM receiver.

21. What are the different advantages and disadvantages of DM system?

22. What is the advantage of variable step size in adaptive DM? Explain with typical waveform.

23. Write short notes on:

(a)   Parallel mode of transmission

(b)   Serial mode of transmission

24. What are the different types of serial communication? Explain each technique in detail.

25. Write short notes on the following:

(a) Binary ASK	(b) Binary PSK
(c) Binary FSK	(d) QAM system
(e) Constellation patterns	(f) QPSK system
(g) Multilevel ASK and Multilevel FSK.	

UNIVERSITY QUESTIONS

NOVEMBER-DECEMBER 2011

1. (a) (i) Define line coding? Explain the characteristics of line coding schemes in detail.
   (5)

   (ii) We want to digitize the human voice. What is the bit rate, assuming the 16-bit per sample.
   (5)

   (b) (i) Explain parallel and serial mode of transmission in detail.
   (10)

   (ii) What is QAM? Draw amplitude verses phase diagram of 4 QAM and 8 QAM?
   (5)

   (iii) Draw the signal waveform for all line coding schemes for the following data stream 10010011.
   (5)

MAY-JUNE 2011

2. (a) (i) What is modulation? Explain with neat diagrams AM and FM?
   (7)

   (ii) A network with bandwidth of 10 Mbps can pass only art-average of 12,000 frames per minutes with each frame carrying an average of 10,000 bits. What is the throughput of the network in Mbps.
   (3)

   (b) (i) A telephone line has bandwidth of 3,000 Hz, the signal-to-noise is 3162, what is the channel capacity?
   (2)

   (ii) State various schemes used for binary to digital encoding. Explain the block coding schema.
   (8)

   (c) (i) Explain with neat diagram ASK, FSK and PSK? Also explain hat is QAM?
   (10)

NOVEMBER-DECEMBER 2010

3. Explain the line coding schemes with suitable example in detail.
   (10)

4. Explain PCM in detail.
   (10)

5. Compare AM, FM and PM.
   (10)

MAY-JUNE 2010

6. Explain what is line coding? Also explain with the help of neat waveforms unipolar scheme, polar scheme, bipolar scheme and other scheme.
   (10)

7. Explain in detail block coding.
   (10)

8. (a) Compare ASK with FSK.
   (5)

   (b) What is modulation? Why modulation is needed? What are the types of modulation? Explain.
   (5)

NOVEMBER-DECEMBER 2009

9. What are different digital modulation techniques? Explain any one in detail. **(10)**

10. (i) An analog signal has bit rate of 8000 bps and a band rate 1000 band. How many data elements are carried by each signal element? How many signal elements do we needed? **(10)**

    (ii) Define with comparison of bit rate and band rate.

MAY-JUNE 2009

11. (a) For the following bit pattern 01001110 draw the waveforms for all line coding schemes? **(6)**

    (b) What is analog and digital transmission? **(2)**

    (c) Calculate the period of sine wave for the power which has frequency of 60 Hz. **(2)**

12. (a) A digitized voice channel is mode by digitizing a 4 kHz bandwidth analog voice signal, signal is sampled at twice the highest frequency, assume each sample required 8-bits. What is the required bit rate? **(10)**

    (b) (i) Compare AM, FM and PM. **(6)**

         (ii) What is RZ and NRZ? **(4)**

    (c) (i) What is 2-PSK and 4-PSK schemes. **(5)**

         (ii) A network with bandwidth of 10 Mbps can pass only an average of 12,000 frame per minutes with each frame carrying an this network in Mbps? **(5)**

✱✱✱

Unit III

MULTIPLEXING AND TRANSMISSION MEDIA

3.1 Introduction to Multiplexing

Various Definitions of Multiplexing:

Multiplexing is a set of techniques that allows the simultaneous transmission of multiple signals across a single transmission link.

Multiplexing is the transmission of multiple data communication sessions over a common wire or medium.

Multiplexing is the process to combine multiple signals (analog or digital) for transmission over a single line or media. A common type of multiplexing combines several low speed signals for transmission over a single high speed connection.

Multiplexing is a technique for sending more than one information signal at a time over a single communication path (e.g. medium, circuit or channel).

Thus, multiplexing is loosely referred to many into one as shown in Fig. 3.1.

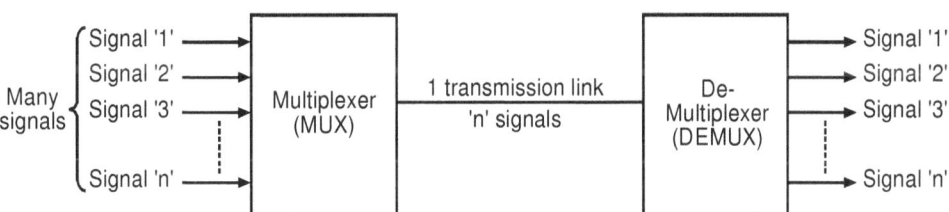

Fig. 3.1: Multiplexer and Demultiplexer

The reverse procedure of multiplexing is called as demultiplexing referred to as one into many. Whenever the transmission capacity of a medium linking two devices is greater than the transmission needs of the devices, the transmission link can be shared in order to maximize the utilization of the link. For example, one cable can carry hundred channels of TV in cable TV system.

   Types of Multiplexing: There are two basic techniques: (1) Frequency Division Multiplexing (FDM) and (2) Time Division Multiplexing (TDM).

   Generally, FDM is used for analog signal multiplexing and TDM is used for digital signal multiplexing. The classification of multiplexing techniques can be given as:

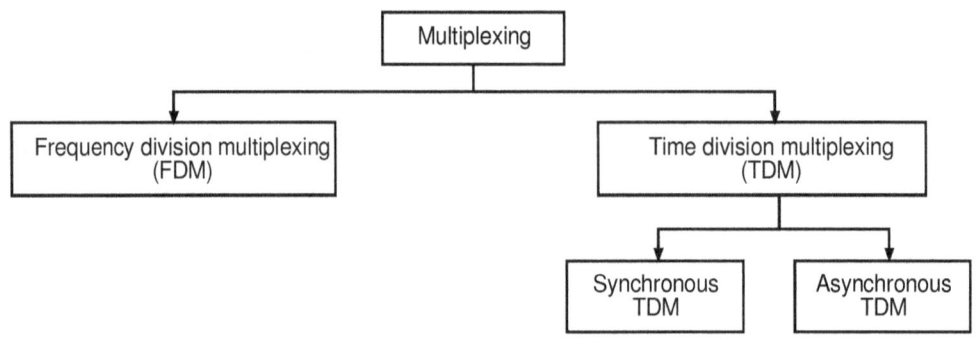

Fig. 3.2

3.2 Frequency Division Multiplexing (FDM)

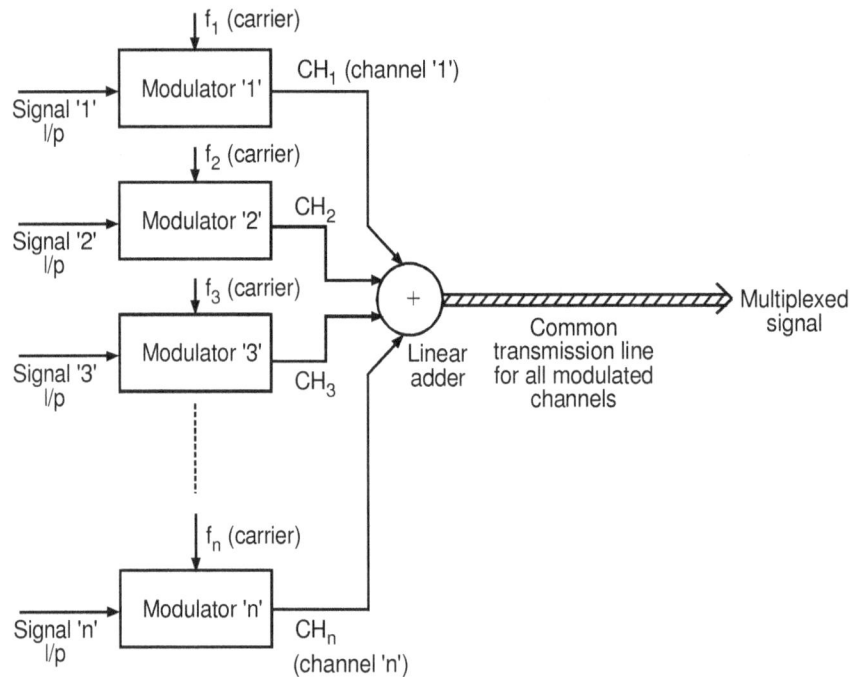

Fig. 3.3: FDM transmitter block diagram

In FDM, total bandwidth available to the system is divided into several frequency sub-bands on one transmission line. The signals to be transmitted simultaneously will modulate a separate carrier. The modulation method can be AM, FM, PM, SSB (Single Sideband Technique) or VSB (Vestigial Sideband Technique) etc. Then different modulated signals are added using the simple adder circuit. Thus, this added signal acts as multiplexed signal and then transmitted over a single or common transmission line as shown in Fig. 3.3.

The operation of FDM transmitter is as follows:

1. Signal 1 is going to modulate carrier 1 and channel 1 will be available. Signal 2 is going to modulate carrier 2 and channel 2 will be available. Each modulated channel will be having specific bandwidth.

2. Algebric addition of different channels are done in the linear adder circuit. Thus multiplexed signal is available and transmitted on a common transmission line.

3. Thus every channel will have specific frequency band. There is always guard band separating these channels. This is an unused band of frequencies. This band reduces the overlapping of frequencies and effect of "cross talk" that may occur between different channels.

4. Frequency spectrum for FDM signal in frequency domain is as shown in Fig. 3.4.

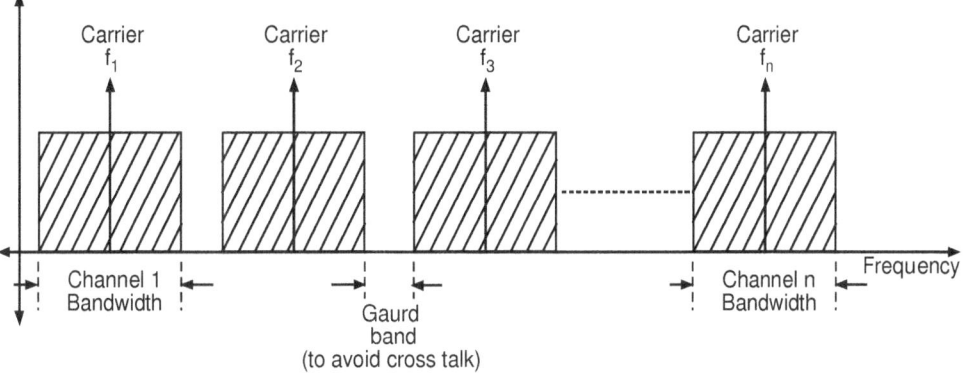

Fig. 3.4: Frequency spectrum of FDM signal (in frequency domain)

3.2.1 FDM Receiver

In FDM receiver, the multiplexed signal is given to the first stage from common transmission line as shown in Fig. 3.4.

The operation of FDM receiver is as follows:

1. Channel 1 is filtered out using BPF_1. Channel 2 is filtered out using BPF_2. Cut-off frequencies of band pass filters are sharp enough to avoid the overlapping or mixing of adjacent channels.

2. BPF_1 output is given to CH_1 demodulator. BPF_2 output is given to CH_2 demodulator. Thus demodulator output will be original signal 1 and signal 2 respectively.

3. Thus center frequency of each band pass filter is corresponding to the carrier of respective channel.

4. Thus each filter will pass only its own channel and rejects the other channels.

5. Thus, using FDM receiver, the FDM multiplexed signal in frequency domain is demultiplexed and original signal is recovered.

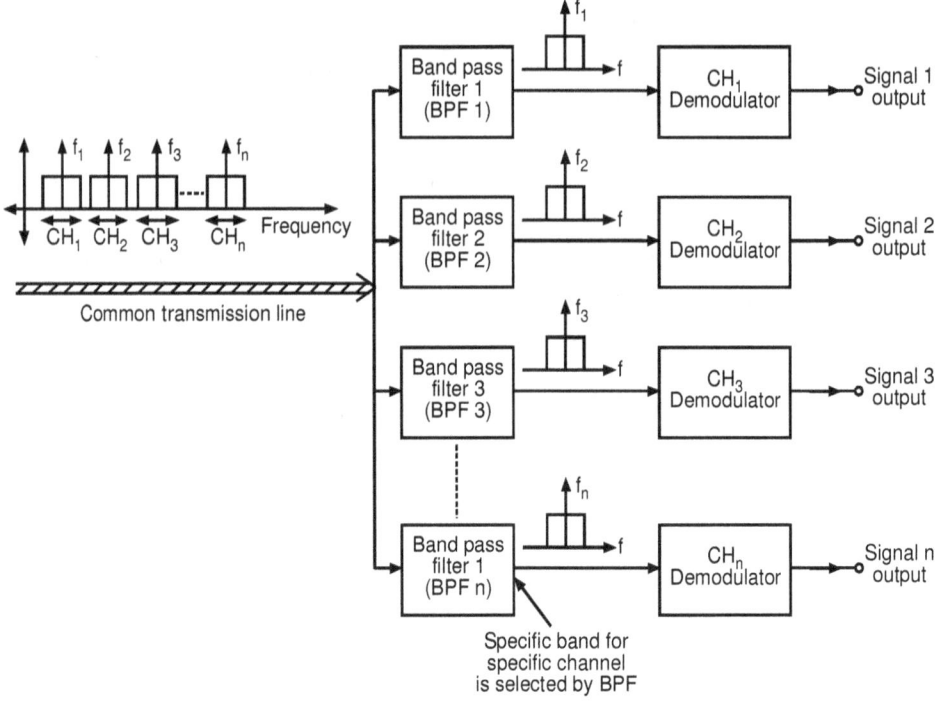

Fig. 3.5: FDM receiver block diagram

FDM Applications:

- Radio broadcast
- Mobile radio
- Wireless communication
- TV broadcast
- Fiber optic channel communication
- Analog telephony

3.2.2 Application of FDM in Analog Telephony or Telephone System

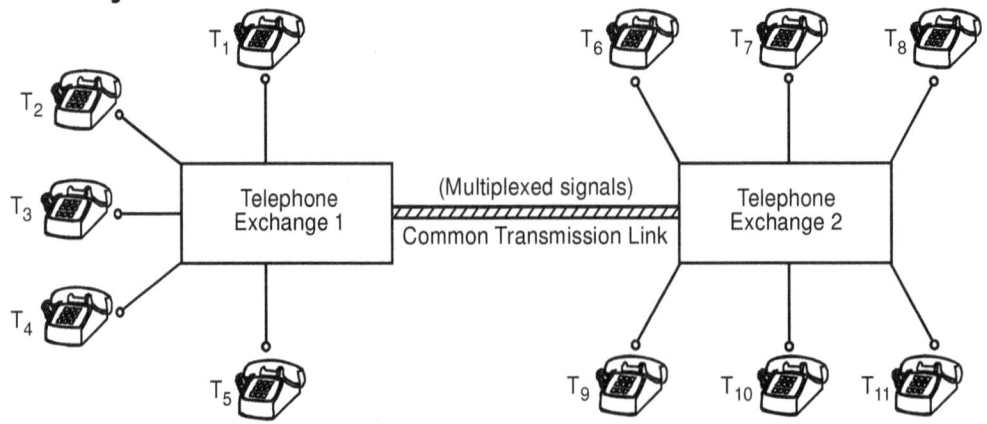

Fig. 3.6: Multiplexed signal transmission across telephone exchange

Telephone system is basically used for voice communication. The range of voice frequency is 300 Hz to 3400 Hz. In real world telephone communication, each telephone is connected to the telephone exchange. These connections of telephones to the telephone exchange follows the star topology. In this connection layout, the telephone exchange is at center position as shown in Fig. 3.6.

At telephone exchange, these voice channels modulate different sub-carriers. These modulated sub-bands are then added together. There are several levels of multiplexing as shown in Table 3.1.

Table 3.1: Levels of multiplexing process

Levels	Groups (Service)	Multiplexed channels	Total voice channels
Level (1)	1 Basic group	12 Voice channels	12
Level (2)	1 Super group	5 Basic groups	60
Level (3)	1 Master group	10 Super groups	600
Level (4)	1 Jumbo group	6 Master groups	3600

Though the voice frequency range given is 300 to 3400 Hz, considering guard band, the frequency band for one voice channel is 4 kHz. Accordingly the bandwidth for Basic group, Super group, Master group and Jumbo group is calculated and shown below:

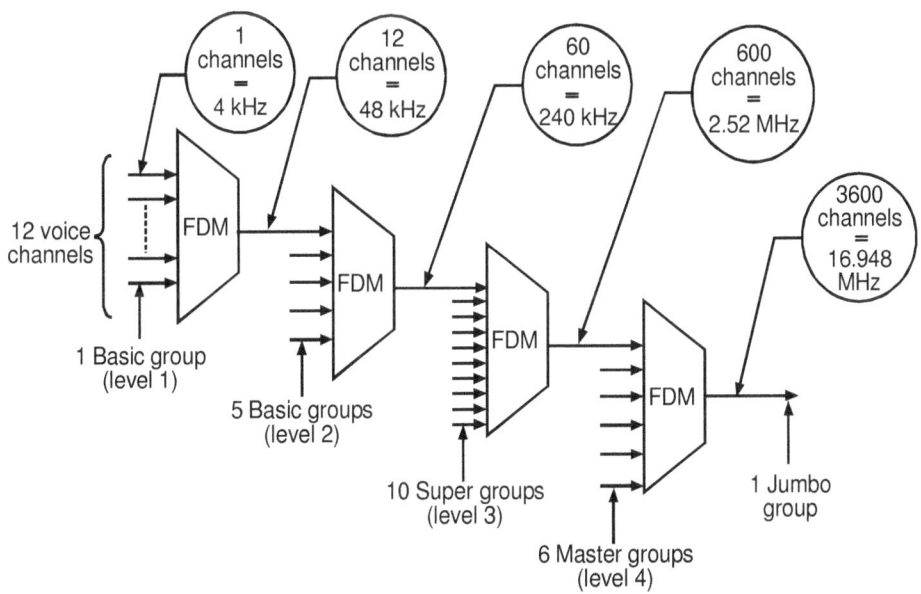

Fig. 3.7: Levels of multiplexing process

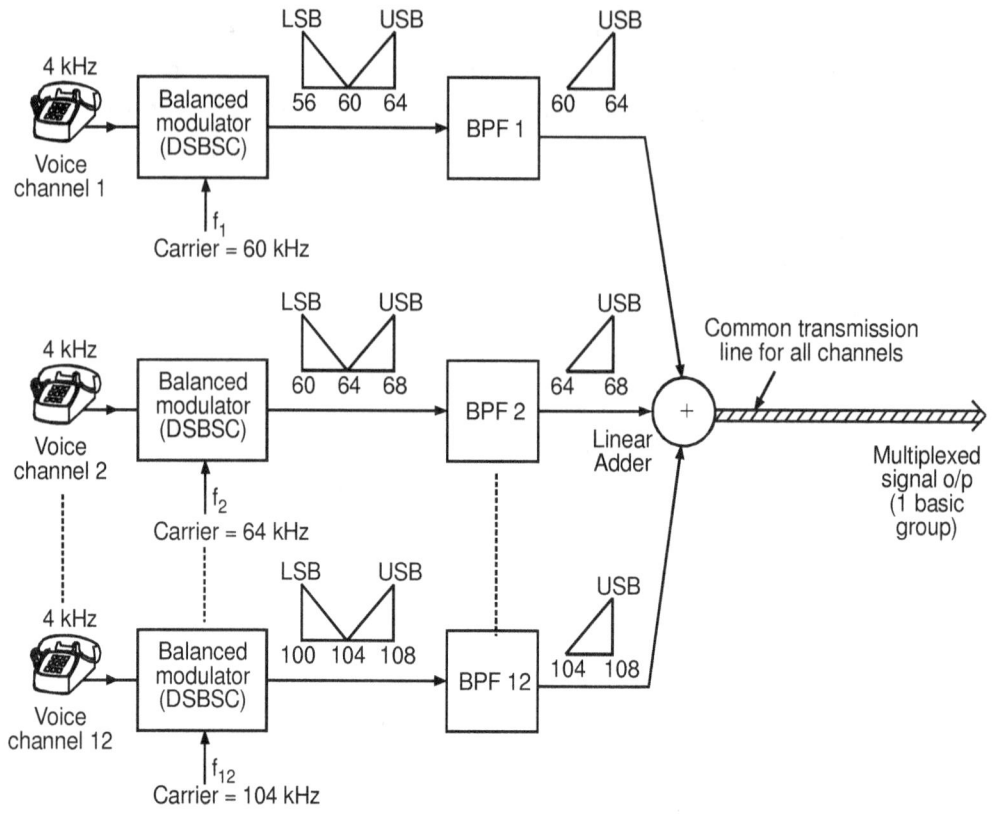

Fig. 3.8: FDM transmitter for 1 basic group (12 voice channels)

At telephone exchange, these voice channels modulate different sub-carriers. These modulated sub-carriers are then added together as shown in Fig. 3.8. This modulation at telephone exchange is given for basic group only.

Operation of FDM transmitter is as follows:

1. In this system, 12 voice channels of 4 kHz bandwidth each is used.
2. 12 voice channels are used to modulate 12 different carrier frequencies. Voice channel 1 is used to modulate 60 kHz carrier frequency. Voice channel 2 is used to modulate 64 kHz carrier frequency. And voice channel 12 is used to modulate 104 kHz carrier frequency. Carrier frequencies are spaced at 4 kHz from each other.
3. SSB modulation technique is used to save the bandwidth and power output of balanced modulator having lower sideband as well as upper sideband.
4. Using bandpass filter only upper sideband (USB) is selected. These sidebands are added using a linear adder. This added signal is nothing but the multiplexed signal output of 1 basic group i.e. 12 voice channels.

Thus, this multiplexed signal is used as one input to a super group which is already shown in levels of multiplexing in Fig. 3.7. Lets see the spectrum for the 12 voice channels which are multiplexed in frequency domain.

The frequency spectrum for multiplexed 12 voice channels is shown in Fig. 3.9.

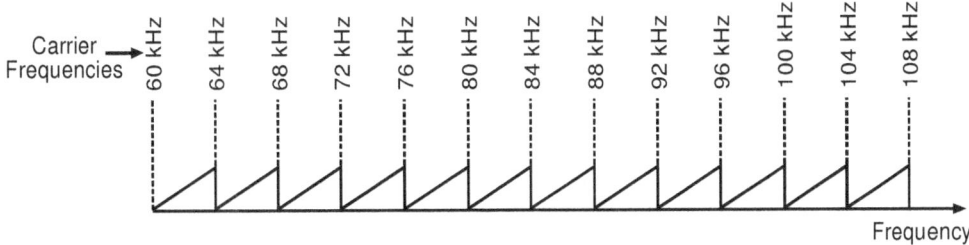

Fig. 3.9: Frequency spectrum for frequency division multiplexed 12 voice channels

Lets see the FDM receiver for 1 basic group which is given in Fig. 3.10.

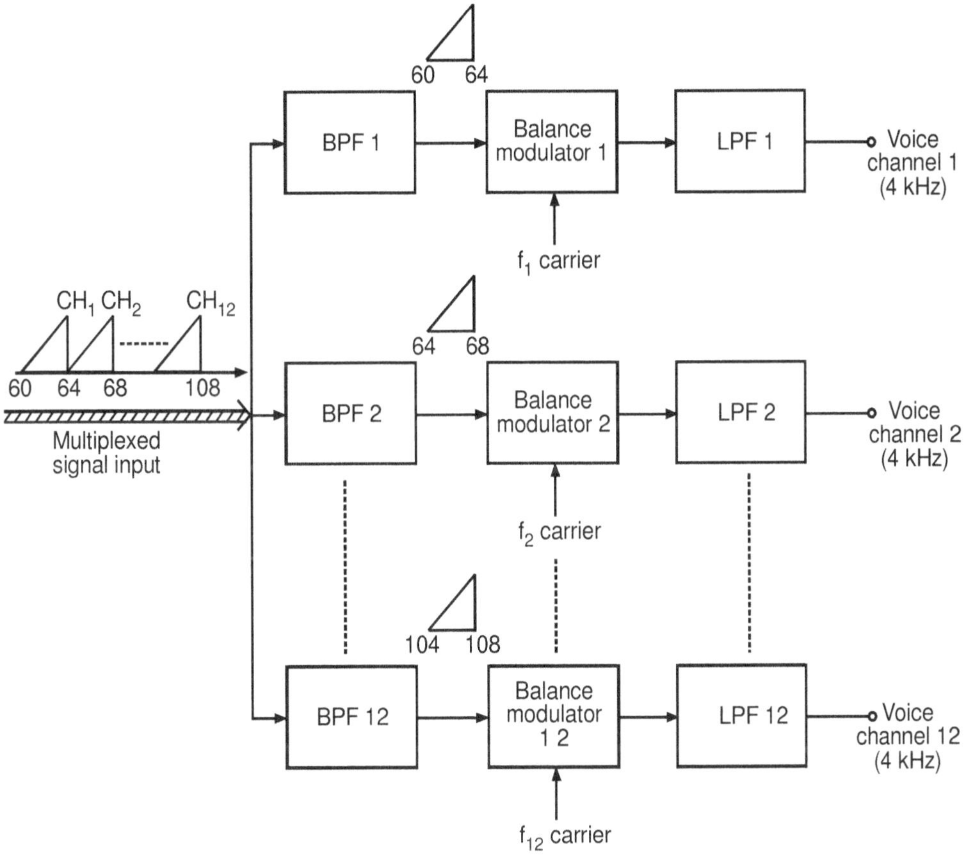

Fig. 3.10: FDM receiver (Demultiplexing of signal)

Operation of the FDM receiver is as follows:

1.   This FDM receiver unit is known as demultiplexer.

2.   Band pass filters are used to separate the basic group signals which are multiplexed.

3.   BPF$_1$ is used to select the 1st multiplexed channel, BPF$_2$ is used to select the 2nd multiplexed channel and likewise BPF$_{12}$ is used to select the 12th multiplexed channel.

4.   Balanced modulator is acting as SSB demodulator. Thus demodulated signal is filtered by low pass filter, which is nothing but original voice channel of 4 kHz.

Thus FDM system for multiplexing ordinary telephone calls is widely used. It is purely analog system that is based on repeated amplitude modulation. SSB is one of the type of AM. FDM system is used in a telephone exchange office to transmit phone calls to another telephone exchange office, where the phone calls are demultiplexed by filtering and demodulation. The pilot signals are used at the receiving end to generate carriers of the correct frequencies. Thus demultiplexed signals are then further distributed, some of them possibly multiplexed again to be transmitted to another exchange office.

The system is obviously one-directional, while phone calls are two-directional. Therefore, those systems are used in pairs, one system for each direction.

3.2.3 Time Division Multiplexing (TDM)

TDM allows multiple conversations to take place by the sharing of medium or channel in **time**. A channel is allocated the whole of the line bandwidth for a specific period of time. This means each sub-carrier is allocated a time slot. Time division multiplexing is a technique where a short time sample of each channel is inserted into the multiplexed data stream. Each channel is sampled in turn, and then the sequence is repeated. TDM is used for digital signal multiplexing only. It cannot be used to multiplex the analog signals. TDM can be implemented in two ways. Synchronous TDM and asynchronous TDM.

3.2.4 Synchronous TDM

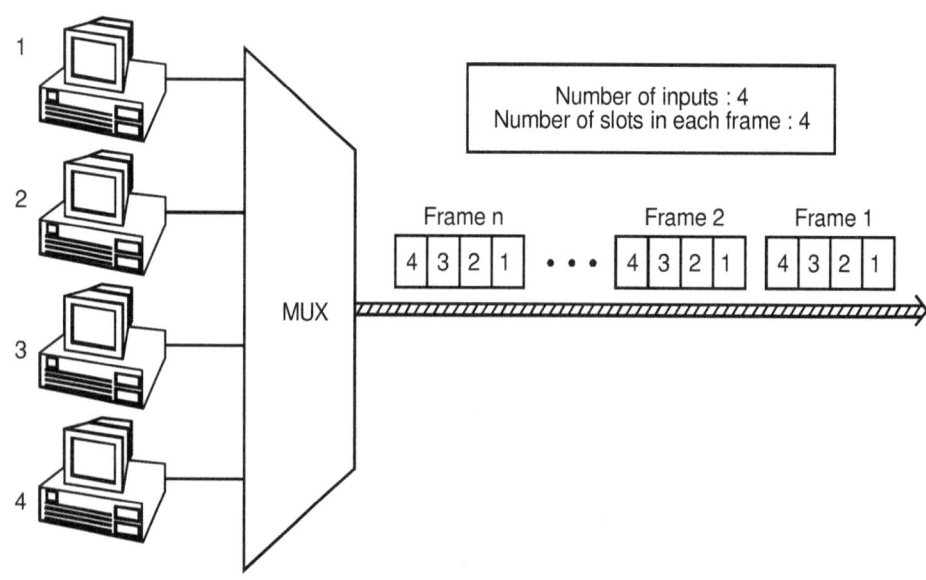

Fig. 3.11: Basic synchronous TDM system

The multiplexer allocates exactly the same time slot to each device at all times, whether or not a device has anything to transmit. Time slot 1, for example, is assigned to device 1 alone and cannot be used by any other device as shown in Fig. 3.11.

In above Fig. 3.11, a frame consists of one complete cycle of time slots. Thus the number of slots in the frame is equal to the number of inputs.

Multiplexing and demultiplexing processes in synchronous TDM system are clearly shown in Fig. 3.12 (a) and (b).

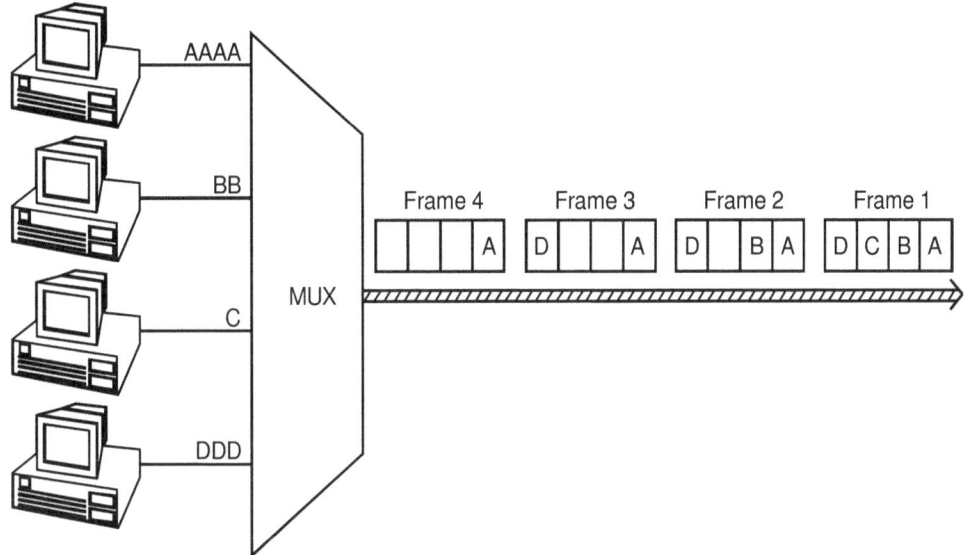

Fig. 3.12 (a): Synchronous TDM: Multiplexing process

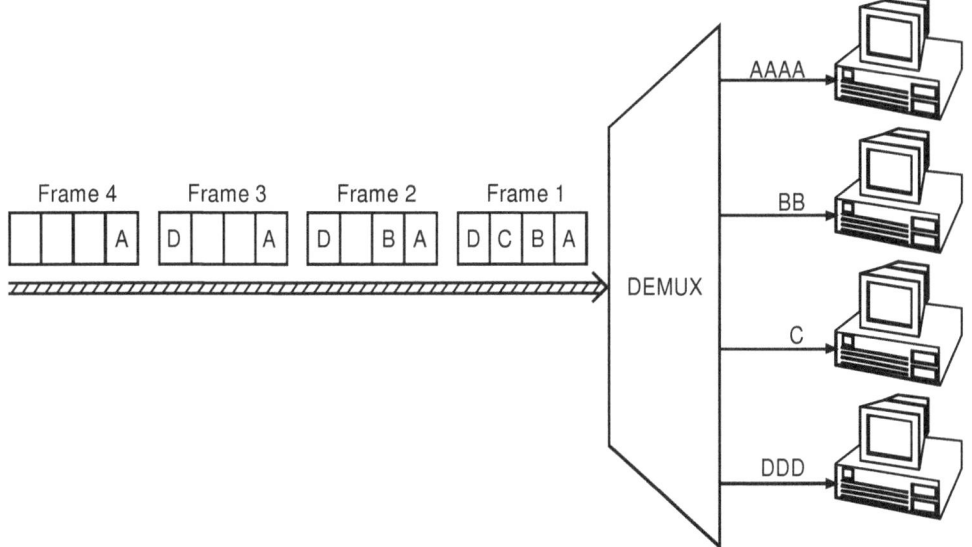

Fig. 3.12 (b): Synchronous TDM: demultiplexing process

Synchronous TDM (Multiplexing and Demultiplexing) system can also be explained with Fig. 3.13 (a) and (b).

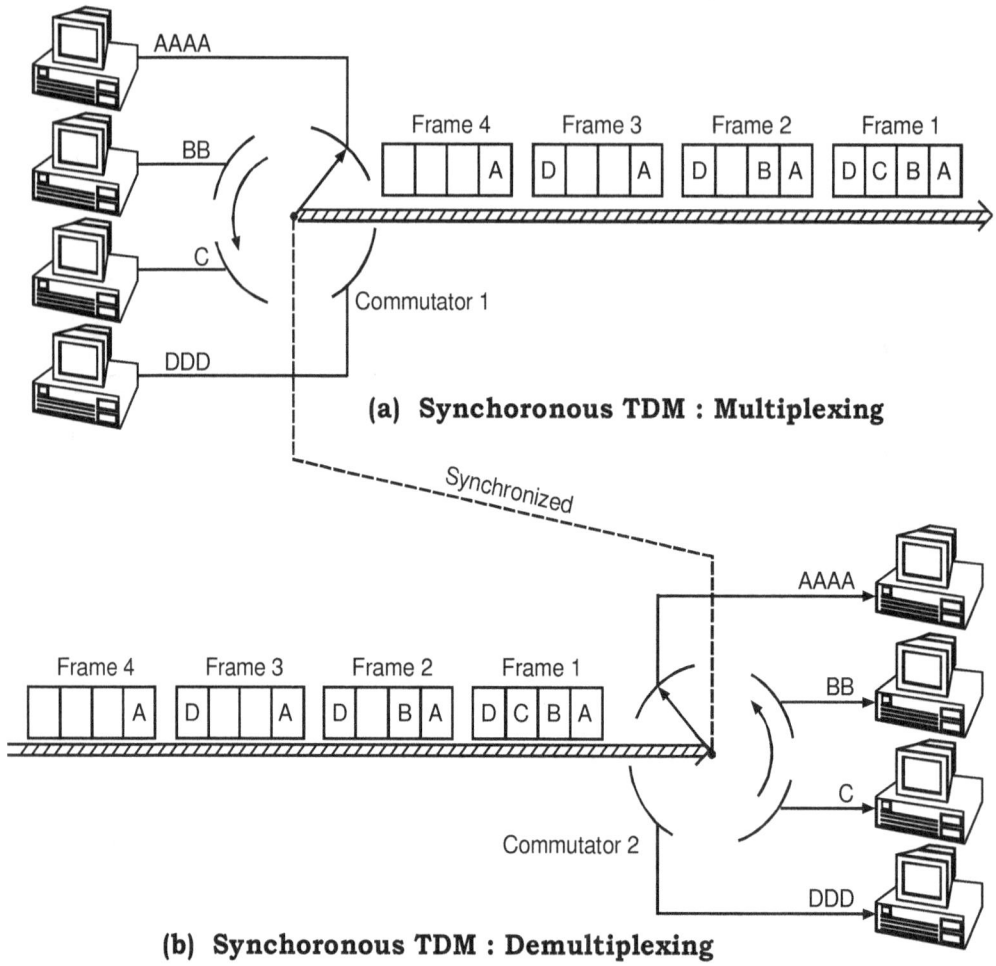

(a) **Synchoronous TDM : Multiplexing**

(b) **Synchoronous TDM : Demultiplexing**

Fig. 3.13: Synchronous TDM (Multiplexing and Demultiplexing)

[Showing mux as commutator]

Commutator: Single pole rotating switch (Mechanical or electronic)

In synchronous TDM systems, the following points are important:

- Both transmitter and receiver must be synchronized.
- This synchronization causes fixed cycle operation.
- The channel is divided into time slots and each user is allocated a slot - whether it is empty or not.
- The slots are rotated among the attached users.
- Access to channel is granted at specific time slots.

1. Time Slots and Frames

The data flow of each input connection is divided into units in synchronous TDM. Each input occupies one input time slot. A unit can be 1 bit, one character or one block of data. Each input unit becomes one output unit and occupies one output time slot. Fig. 3.14 shows an example of synchronous TDM where n is 3. The duration of an output time slot is n times shorter than the duration of an input time slot. If an input time slot is T s, the output time slot is T/n s, where n is the number of connections.

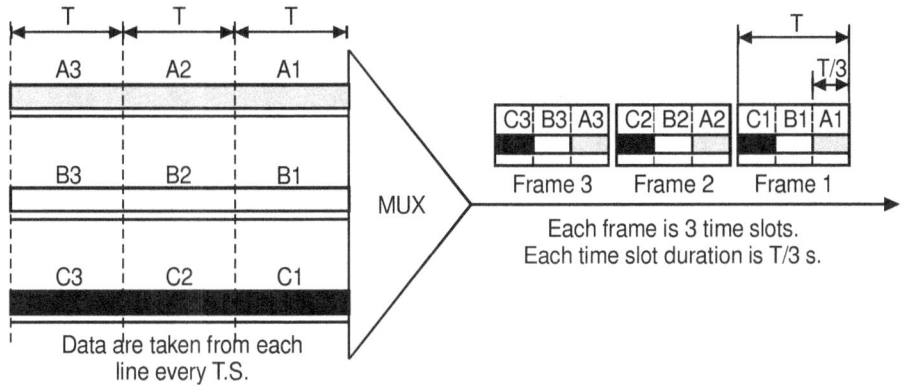

Fig. 3.14: Synchronous time-division multiplexing

Data rate of the output link must be n times the data rate of a connection to guarantee the flow of data. Fig. 3.14, the data rate of the link is 3 times the data rate of a connection; likewise, the duration of a unit on a connection is 3 times that of the time slot. In the Fig. 3.14 user represent the data prior to multiplexing as 3 times the size of the data after multiplexing. This is just to convey the idea that each unit is 3 times longer in duration before multiplexing than after.

If user have n connections, a frame is divided into n time slots and one slot is allocated for each unit, one for each input line. The duration of the input unit is T, the duration of each slot is T/n and the duration of each frame is T.

In synchronous TDM, the data rate of the link is n times faster and the unit duration is n times shorter.

Number of time slots are grouped into frames. A frame consists of one complete cycle of time slots, with one slot dedicated to each sending device. In a system with n input lines, each frame has n slots, with each slot allocated to carrying data from a specific input line.

2. Interleaving

Fig. 3.15 shows the interleaving process. In Fig. 3.15, user assume that no switching is involved and that the data from the first connection at the multiplexer site go to the first connection at the demultiplexer in Fig. 3.15.

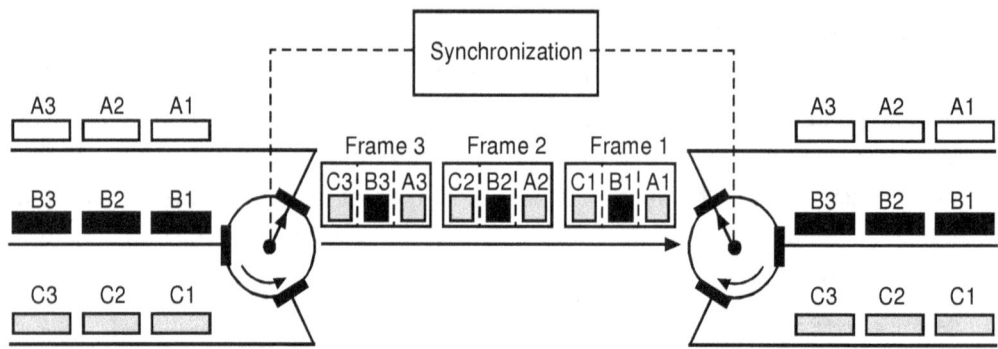

Fig. 3.15: Interleaving

TDM can be visualized as two fast-rotating switches, one on the multiplexing side and the other on the demultiplexing side. Switches are synchronized and rotate at the same speed, but in opposite directions. On the multiplexing side, as the switch opens in front of a connection, that connection has the opportunity to send a unit onto the path. This process is called interleaving. On demultiplexing side, as the switch opens in front of a connection, that connection has the opportunity to receive a unit from the path.

3. Empty Slots

Fig. 3.16 shows a case in which one of the input lines has no data to send and one slot in another input line has discontinuous data. If a source does not have data to send, the corresponding slot in the output frame is empty.

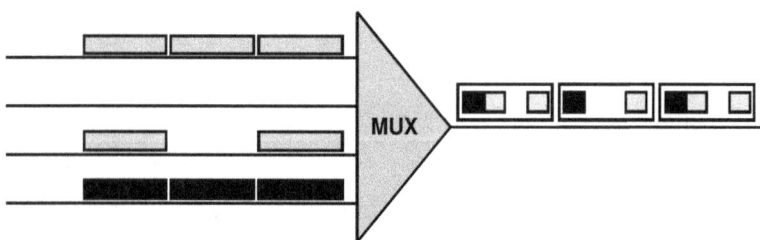

Fig. 3.16: Empty slots

First output frame has three slots filled, the second frame has two slots filled, and the third frame has three slots filled. No frame is full.

4. Data Rate Management

TDM consist of a problem i.e. is how to handle a disparity in the input data rates. User assumed that the data rates of all input lines were the same.

If data rates are not the same, three strategies or a combination of them, can be used. We call these three strategies **multilevel multiplexing, multiple-slot allocation** and **pulse stuffing**.

Multilevel Multiplexing: It is a technique used when the data rate of an input line is a multiple of others. For example, in Fig. 3.17, we have two inputs of 40 kBps and three inputs of 20 kBps. The first two input lines can be multiplexed together to provide a data rate equal to the last three. A second level of multiplexing can create an output of 140 kBps.

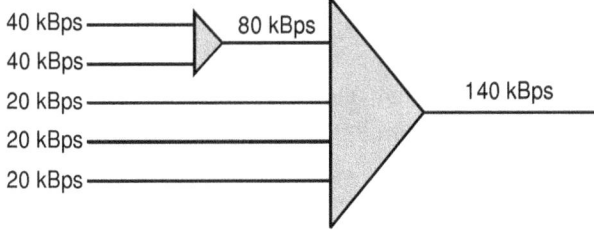

Fig. 3.17: Multilevel multiplexing

Multiple-slot Allocation: It is more efficient to allot more than one slot in frame to single input line. In Fig. 3.18, the input line with a 50-kBbs data rate can be given two slots in the output. We insert serial-to-parallel converter in the line to make two inputs out of one.

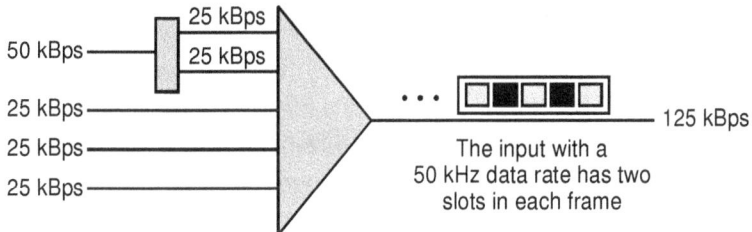

Fig. 3.18: Multiple-slot multiplexing

5. Pulse Stuffing or Bit Padding

The bit rates of sources are not multiple integers of each other. Therefore, neither of the above two techniques can be applied. One solution is to make the highest input data rate the dominant data rate and then add dummy bits to the input lines with lower rates. This will increase their rates. This technique is called **pulse stuffing, bit padding**, or bit stuffing. The input with a data rate of 46 is pulse-stuffed to increase the rate to 50 kBbs. Now multiplexing can take place.

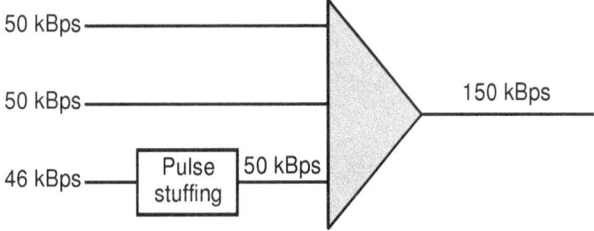

Fig. 3.19: Pulse stuffing or bit padding

6. Frame Synchronizing

Implementation of TDM is not as simple as that of FDM. Synchronization between the multiplexer and demultiplexer is a major issue.

If the multiplexer and demultiplexer are not synchronized, a bit belonging to one channel may be received by the wrong channel. For this reason, one or more synchronization bits are usually added to the beginning of each frame. These bits, called **framing bits**. Framing bits follow a pattern, frame to frame, that allows the demultiplexer to synchronize with the incoming stream so that it can separate the time slots accurately. Fig. 3.20 shows synchronization information consists of 1 bit per frame, alternating between 0 and 1.

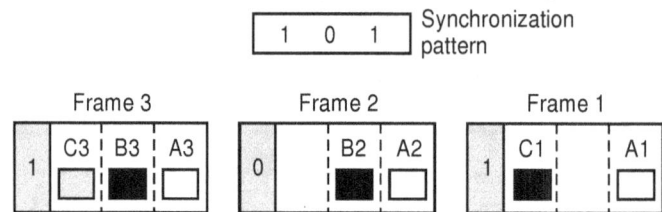

Fig. 3.20: Framing bits

3.2.5 Asynchronous TDM (or Statistical Time Division Multiplexing)

In asynchronous TDM, each slot in a frame is not dedicated to the fix device. Each slot contains an index of the device to be sent to and a message. Thus, the number of slots in a frame can be allocated for an input device. This technique allows a number of lower speed input lines to be multiplexed to a single higher speed line (transmission link) as shown in Fig. 3.21.

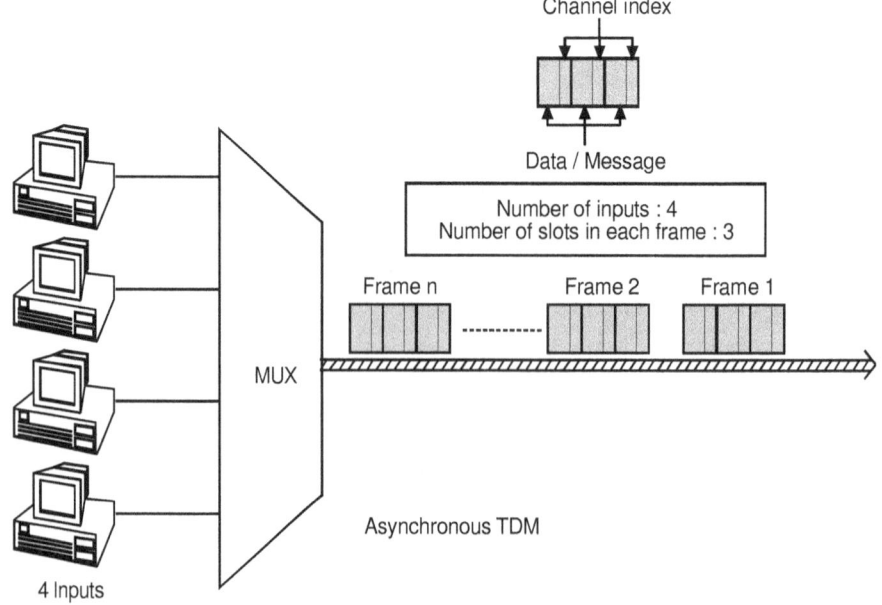

Fig. 3.21: Basic asynchronous TDM system

In Fig. 3.21 a frame contains a fix number of time slots. Each slot has an index of which device to receive.

Multiplexing and demultiplexing processes in asynchronous TDM system are clearly shown in the Fig. 3.22 (a) and (b).

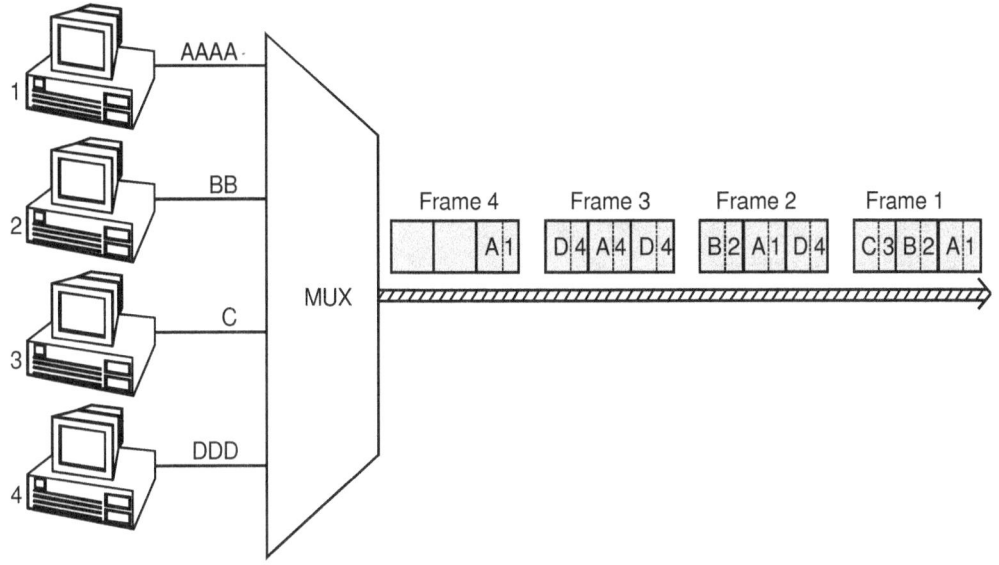

(a) Asynchronous TDM: Multiplexing process

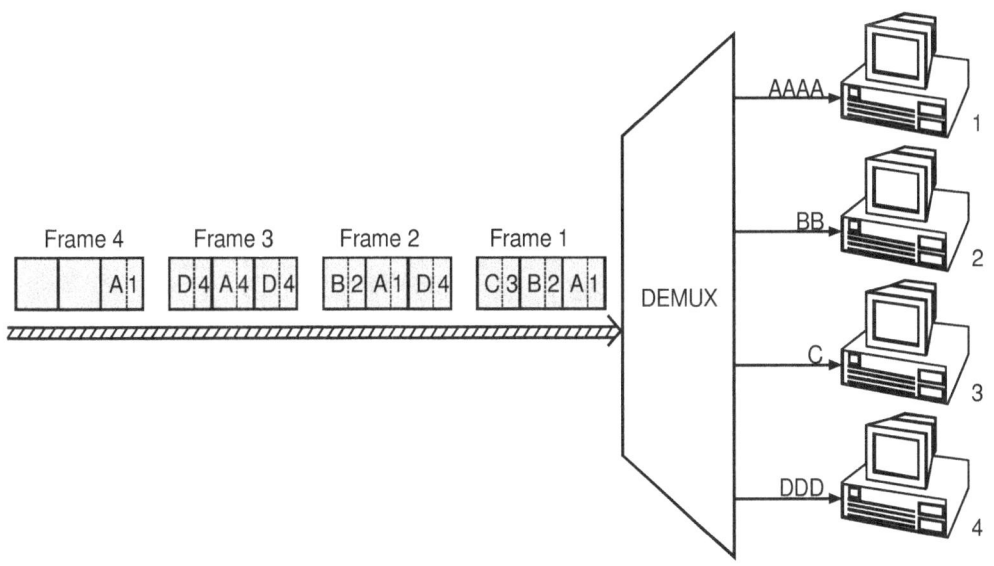

(b) Asynchronous TDM: Demultiplexing process

Fig. 3.22: Asynchronous TDM (Multiplexing and demultiplexing)

Asynchronous TDM (Multiplexing and demultiplexing) system can also be explained with Fig. 3.23 (a) and (b).

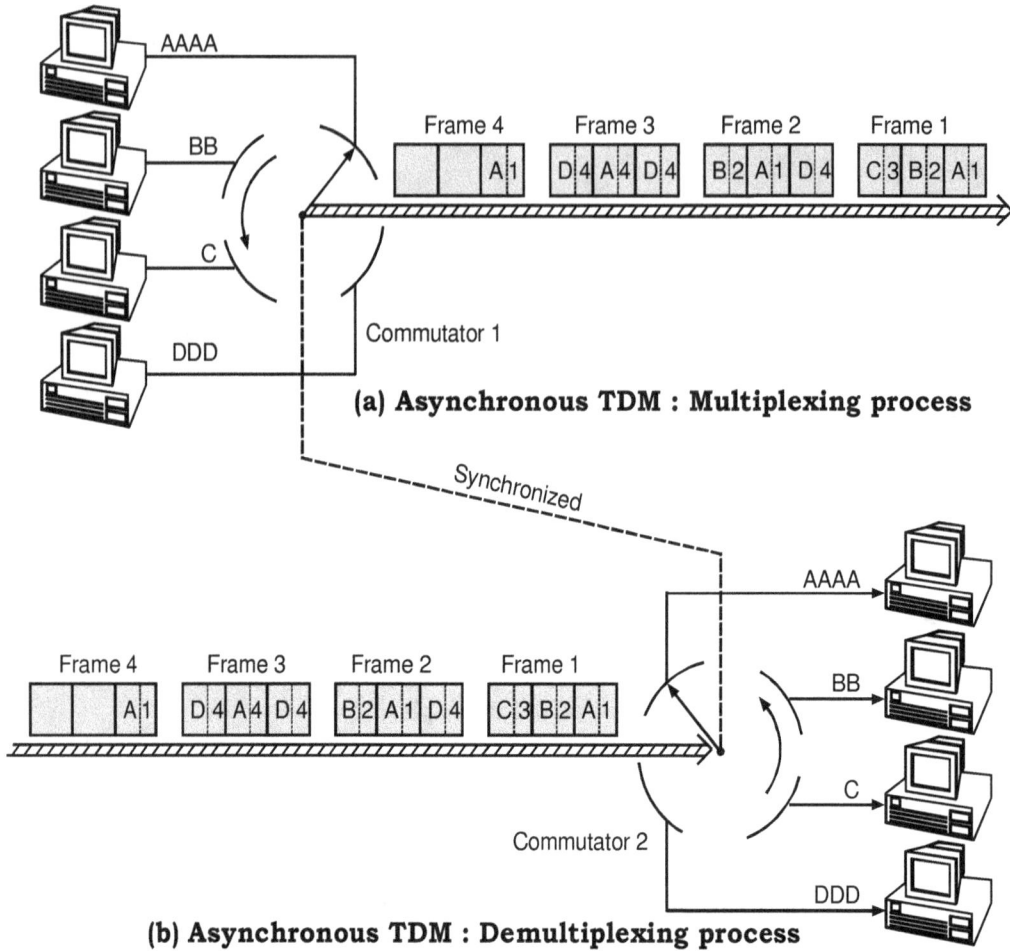

(a) Asynchronous TDM : Multiplexing process

(b) Asynchronous TDM : Demultiplexing process

Fig. 3.23: Asynchronous TDM (Multiplexing and Demultiplexing)
[Showing mux as commutator]
Commutator: Single pole rotating switch (Mechanical or electronic)

In asynchronous TDM systems, following points are important:

*   Time slots are allocated on demand instead of a fixed cycle.
*   Allows unused slots to be allocated to active users. The devices wanting to transmit must request a slot, which is granted for the duration of the transmission.
*   Many devices can be connected and provide more efficient use of the available bandwidth.
*   This system performs best with bursty sources. (i.e. not continuously sending).

- Thus asynchronous TDM system provides some advanced capabilities like:
  1. Data compression,
  2. Line priority,
  3. Mixed speed lines,
  4. Automatic speed detection, etc.

Applications of TDM:
- Digital telephony,
- Data communication,
- Satellite access,
- Cellular radio.

3.3 Comparison of FDM and TDM Techniques

S.N.	FDM	TDM
1.	The signals, which are to be multiplexed, occupy different slots in frequency domain.	The signals, which are to be multiplexed, are send by dividing time domain slots, in which one slot for each signal is given.
2.	Generally FDM is used for analog signals.	Generally TDM is used for digital data.
3.	Synchronization between transmitter and receiver is not required for proper operation.	Synchronization between transmitter and receiver is must for proper operation.
4.	Circuit complexity is more in FDM system.	Circuit for transmitter and receiver is not complex.
5.	A problem of cross talk (or frequency overlapping) exists in the FDM system. This is due to BPF characteristics used in circuit.	In TDM, there is no problem of cross-talk.
6.	In FDM, it requires modulators, filters (LPF and BPF), adder and demodulators for their operation.	In TDM, it requires a commutator which is one pole fast rotating mechanical or electronic switch.
7.	Applications of FDM: • Radio broadcast • TV broadcast • Mobile radio • Fiber optic channel communication • Wireless communication • Analog telephony	Applications of TDM: • Data communication • Satellite access • Cellular radio • Digital telephony

3.4 TDM used in Voice Communication

3.4.1 Introduction

1. The second method of dividing the capacity of a transmission channel among several separate signal sources is to allocate a very short period on the channel in a repeating pattern to each signal. This technique is called time-division multiplexing.

2. It is well suited to binary signals consisting of pulses representing a 1 or a 0. These pulses can be made of very short duration and still convey the desired information; therefore, many of them can be squeezed into the time available on a digital carrier channel.

3. The original signal can be an analog wave that is converted to binary form for transmission (as in the case of speech signals in the telephone network), or the original signal can already be in binary form (as in the case of a business machine).

4. The electronic systems that perform this TDM process are called digital carrier systems.

5. As with the analog carrier systems, there is a standard hierarchy of digital carrier systems in the public telephone network, as shown in Table.

6. The digital signals listed in Table reference the type of signal that a particular digital line transports to include applicable framing.

7. For example, a T1 line transports a DS1 digital signal, which consists of 24 voice circuits whose aggregate operating rate is 1.544 Mbps.

Carrier System	Digital Signal No.	No. of Voice Circuits/Channels	Bit Rate, Mbps
T1	DS1	24	1.544
T2	DS2	96	6.312
T3	DS3	672	44.736
T4	DS4	4,032	274.176

3.4.2 What is T-Carrier System?

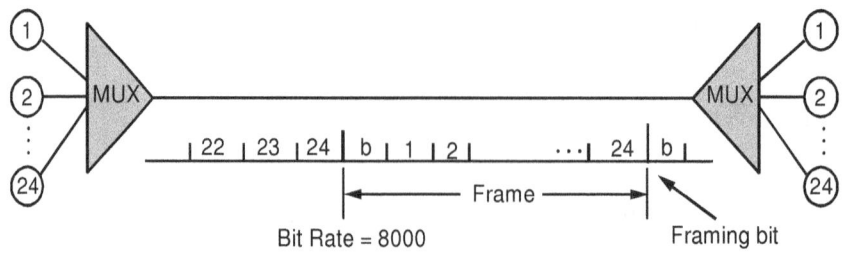

Fig. 3.24: Indicated the typical T carrier system

- Digital Telephone System uses TDM.
- PCM voice channel is basic unit for TDM.
  1 channel = 8 bits/sample × 8000 samples/sec. = 64 kbps
- T-1 carrier carries Digital Signal 1 (DS-1) that combines 24 voice channel into a digital stream.
- **T-carrier** is the generic designator for any of several digitally multiplexed telecommunications carrier systems originally developed by Bell Labs and used in North America and Japan.
- The basic unit of the T-carrier system is the DS0, which has a transmission rate of 64 kbit/s, and is commonly used for one voice circuit.
- The **E-carrier system**, where **'E' stands for European**, is incompatible with the T-carrier and is used just about everywhere else in the world besides North America and Japan.
- The most common legacy of this whole system is the line rate designations.
- A **"T1"** now seems to mean any data circuit that runs at the original 1.544 Mbit/s line rate.
- Originally the T1 format carried 24 pulse-code modulated, time-division multiplexed speech signals each encoded in 64 kbit/s streams, leaving 8 kbit/s of framing information which facilitates the synchronization and demultiplexing at the receiver.
- T2 and T3 circuit channels carry multiple T1 channels multiplexed, resulting in transmission rates of up to 44.736 Mbit/s

3.4.3 North American Digital Multiplexing Hierarchy System

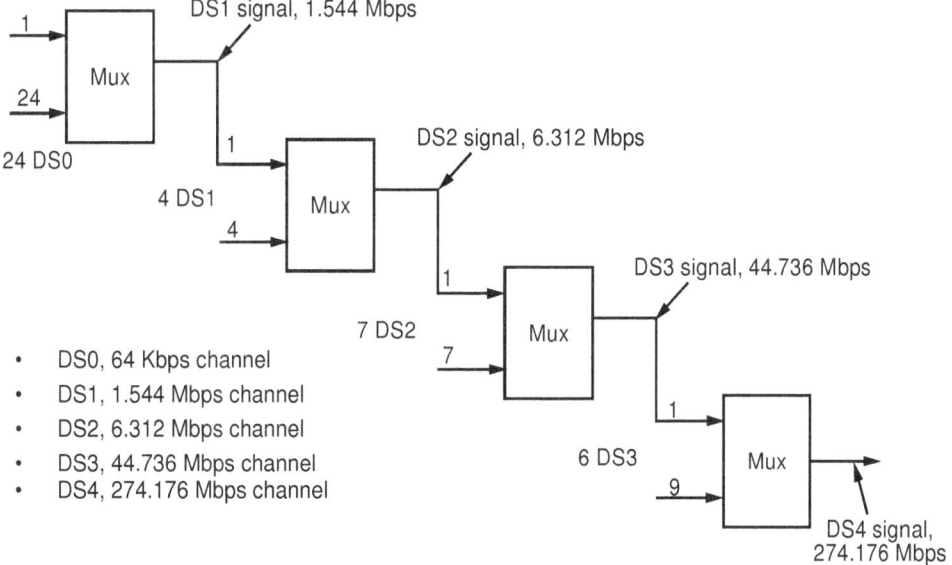

- DS0, 64 Kbps channel
- DS1, 1.544 Mbps channel
- DS2, 6.312 Mbps channel
- DS3, 44.736 Mbps channel
- DS4, 274.176 Mbps channel

Fig. 3.25: North American digital multiplexing Hierarchy

3.4.4 CCITT Digital Multiplexing Hierarchy System

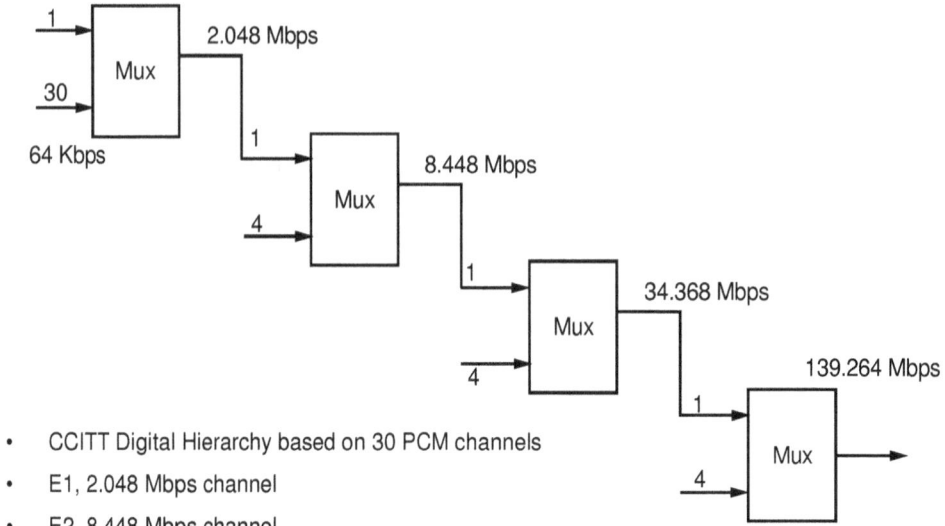

- CCITT Digital Hierarchy based on 30 PCM channels
- E1, 2.048 Mbps channel
- E2, 8.448 Mbps channel
- E3, 34.368 Mbps channel
- E4, 139.264 Mbps channel

Fig. 3.26: CCITT digital multiplexing hierarchy

Note: Here we will discuss regarding North American Digital Multiplexing Hierarchy only.

3.4.5 Using Pulse Code Modulation

1. In North America, the DS1 is commonly referred to as a T1 line or circuit.
2. That circuit was developed to relieve cable congestion in metropolitan areas by providing a transport mechanism for 24 digitized voice conversations to be simultaneously carried over one cable.

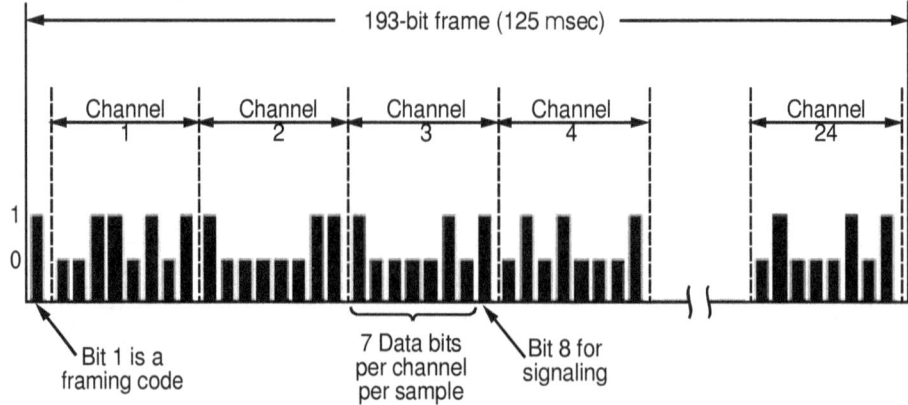

Fig. 3.27: The T1 carrier (1.544 Mbps)

Thus,

- Audio Signal = 4 kHz.
- Nyquist Rate = 2 × 4 kHz = 8 kHz = 8000 samples/seconds.
- At lower rate information would be lost.
- At higher one no extra information would be gained.
- Analog Signals are digitized in the end office by device called CODEC producing 7 or 8 bit number using PCM.
- CODEC makes 8000 samples/sec.
- 1 Frame = 24 Channels × * bit = 192 Bits + 1 Frame Synchronization Bit.
- 1 Frame = 193 bits in every 125 microseconds.
- Data Rate = 193 × 8000 samples/sec. = 193/125 µs = 1.544 Mbps.

3. To do so, each voice conversation is digitized using a technique called Pulse Code Modulation (PCM). Under PCM, an analog voice conversation is digitized at 64 Kbps.

4. To provide information that enables one conversation to be distinguished from another and switched into and out of a group of conversations, framing bits must be added to the T1 data flow.

5. Those framing bits operate at 8000 bps and carry control information, error-detection information, and a limited data-link capability.

6. This capability, for example, enables two private branch exchanges (PBXs) to communicate with one another while transporting 24 voice conversations on a T1 circuit interconnecting the PBXs.

7. The 24 channels, each operating at 64 Kbps, result in an operating rate of 1.536 Mbps. When the 8 Kbps framing information is added to the T1 line, its operating rate becomes 1.544 Mbps.

8. The 64 Kbps circuit, in turn, is connected to a channel on a carrier's T1 line, which represents the basic backbone infrastructure used for transporting voice, data, and video across North America.

9. However, unlike T1 and T3 circuits that are commercially available, DS2 and DS4 signals are only internally used by communications carriers, which explains the absence of commercially available T2 and T4 circuits.

3.4.6 PCM-TDM used in Voice Communication

The most important advantage of digital communication is time division multiplexing. Using this technique, we can transmit signals from more than one source using same channel. When an analog signal is sampled, there will be a time interval between the two samples which can be utilized to transmit samples from other sources. This is called time division multiplexing. A PCM-TDM transmitter and receiver are shown in Fig. 3.28 (a) and (b).

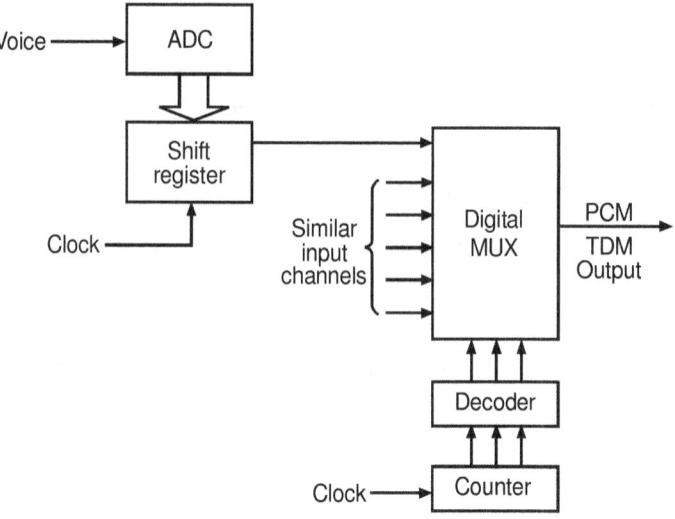

Fig. 3.28 (a): PCM-TDM transmitter

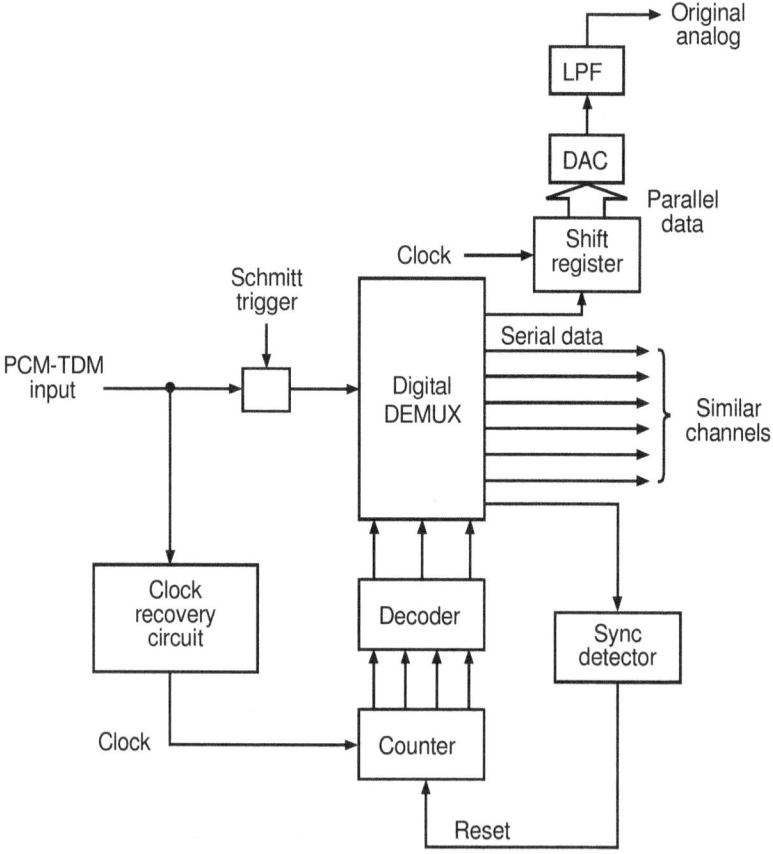

Fig. 3.28 (b): PCM-TDM receiver

In telephone communication T_1 system is used for TDM. The T_1 system multiplexes 24 voice channels on to a single line using TDM technique. In this system each voice channel is sampled at rate of 8 kHz. Each sample is encoded into 8 bits. The duration between two samples of same channel is equal to $\frac{1}{8000}$ = 125 μs. In between these samples, 23 other channels are accommodated. Hence, there will be 24 × 8 = 192 bits in 125 μs. One additional bit is added to this for synchronization. Hence, there will be 193 bits in one frame. The bit rate for multiplexed signal will be equal to $\frac{193}{125}$ μs = 1.544 Mbps.

3.5 T Lines

DS-0, DS-1 and so on are the names of the services. To implement these services, the telephone companies use T lines (T-1 to T-4). These are lines with capacities precisely matched to the data rates of the DS-1 to DS-4 services. (See Table 3.2)

Table 3.2: DS and T Lines

Service	Line	Rate (Mbps)	Voice Channels
DS-1	T-1	1.544	24
DS-2	T-2	6.312	96
DS-3	T-3	44.736	672
DS-4	T-4	274.176	4032

T-1 is used to implement DS-1, T-2 is used to implement DS-2 and so on. From Table 3.2, DS-0 is not actually used as a service. Telephone companies believe that customers needing the level of service would be found in DS-0 can use DDS.

T Lines for Analog Transmission

T lines are digital lines used for the transmission of digital data, voice or audio signals. T lines are also used for analog transmission, provided the analog signals are sampled first, then time division multiplexed.

Earlier, when an organization wanted 24 separate telephone lines, it needed to run 24 twisted pair cables from the company to the central exchange. Today, that same organization can combine the 24 lines into one T-1 line and run only the T-1 to the exchange. Fig. 3.29 shows how 24 voice channels can be multiplexed onto one T-1 line.

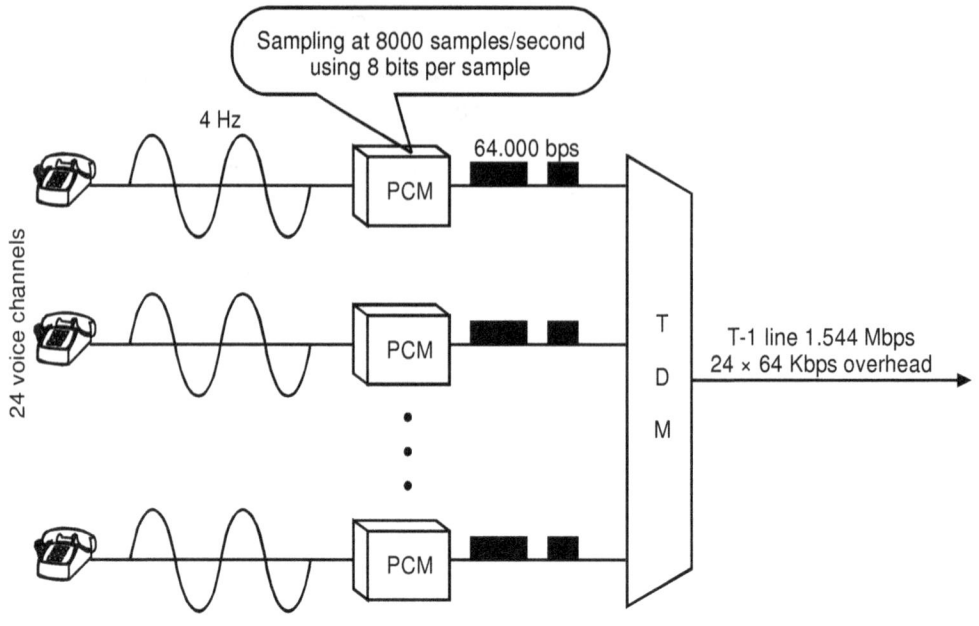

Fig. 3.29: T-1 Line for Multiplexing Telephone Line

The T-1 Frame:

As noted above, DS-1 requires 8 kbps of overhead. To understand how this overhead is calculated, we must examine the format of 24 voice channel frame.

The frame used on a T-1 line is usually 193 bits divided into 24 slots of 8 bits each plus one extra bit for synchronization ($24 \times 8 + 1 = 193$); see Fig. 3.30. In other words, each slot contains 1 signal segment from each channel; 24 segments are interleaved in one frame. If a T-1 line carries 8000 frames, the data rate is 1.544 Mbps ($193 \times 8000 = 1.5444$ Mbps) the capacity of the line.

Fractional T Lines:

Many subscribers may not need the entire capacity of a T line. To accommodate these customers, the telephone companies have developed **fractional T line** service, which allow several subscribers to share one line by multiplexing their transmissions.

For example, a small business may need only one fourth of the capacity of a T-1 line. If four businesses of that size have offices in the same building, they can share T-1 lines. To do so, they direct their transmissions through a device called digital service unit/channel service unit (DSU/CSU). This device divide the capacity of the line into four interleaved channels. (See Fig. 3.31)

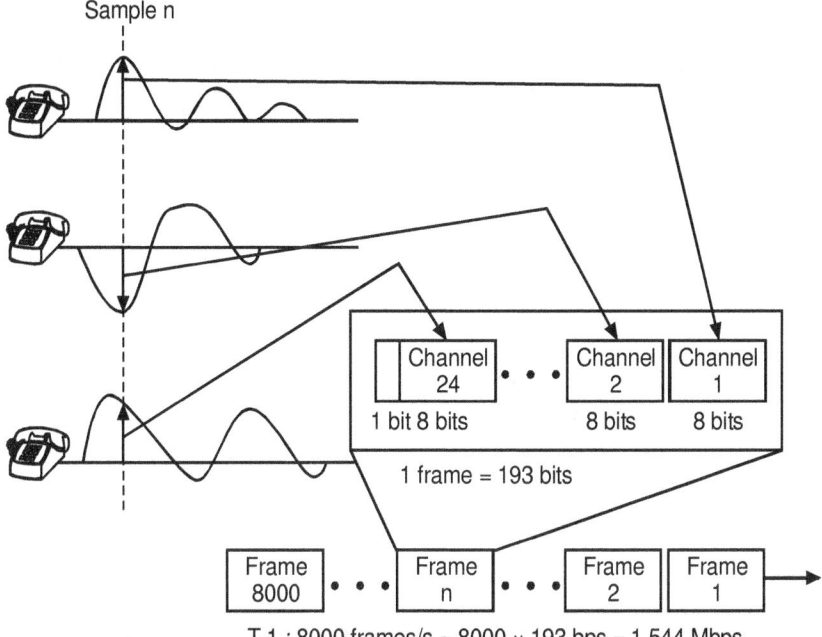

Fig. 3.30: T-1 Frame Structure

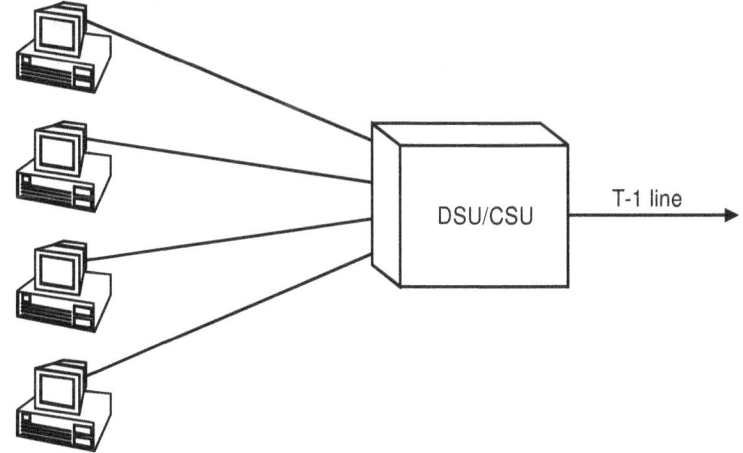

Fig. 3.31: Fractional T-1 Line

3.6 Digital Subscriber Line (DSL)

The Digital Subscriber Line (DSL) is a technology that uses the existing telecommunication networks such as the local loop telephone line to accomplish high-speed delivery of data, voice, video and multimedia.

The different technologies of DSL are discussed here.

Asymmetric Digital Subscriber Line (ADSL):

This line is asymmetrical, which means it provides higher bit rates in the down stream direction (from the telephone central office to the subscriber's site) than the upstream direction (from subscriber site to telephone central office). Subscriber want to receive high volume files quickly from the internet, but they usually have small files, such as a short e-mail message, to send.

ADSL divides the bandwidth of a twisted pair cable (one megahertz) into three bands. The first band, normally between 0 and 25 kHz, is used for regular telephone service (POTS). This service uses only 4 kHz of this band and remaining is used as a guard band to separate voice channel from the data channels. The second band, usually between 25 and 200 kHz is used for upstream communication. The third band, usually 250 kHz to 1 MHz, is used for downstream communication. Fig. 3.32 shows the guard bands.

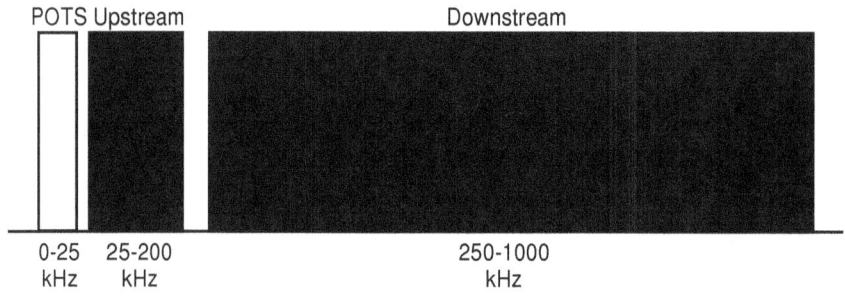

Fig. 3.32: Bands for ADSL

Rate Adaptive Asymmetrical Digital Subscriber Line (RADAL):

This is a technology based on ADSL. It allows different data rates depending on the type of communication; voice, data, multimedia and so on. Differing rates may also be assigned to subscribers based on their demand of the bandwidth. This is beneficial to the customer because the cost is based on the data rate needed.

High Bit Rate Digital Subscriber Line (HDSL):

This line was designed as an alternative to the T-1 line (1.544 Mbps). The T-1 line **uses** AMI encoding, which is very susceptible to attenuation at high frequencies. This limits the length of T-1 line to 1 km. For longer distance, amplifier is necessary, which means increased costs. HDSL uses 2 BIQ encoding, which is less susceptible to attenuation. A data rate of almost 2 Mbps can be achieved without repeaters upto the distance of 3.6 km. HDSL uses twisted pair wires to achieve full duplex transmission.

Symmetric Digital Subscriber Line (SDSL):

This line is same as HDSL but uses one single twisted pair cable, available to most residential subscribers to achieve the same data rate as HDSL.

Very High Bit Rate Digital Subscriber Line (VDSL):

This line is similar to ADSL, uses coaxial, fiber-optic, or twisted-pair cable for short distances. The modulating technique is DMT with a bit rate of 50 to 55 Mbps downstream and 1.5 to 2.5 Mbps upstream.

3.7 Application

1. The Telephone System:

The essential tool of telephone industry is the multiplexing.

The different parts of the world use different systems.

The North American telephone system include many **common carriers** that gives local and long distance services to subscribers.

Local companies – Pacific Bell.

Long-distance providers – AT and T, MCI and Sprint.

For this purpose, these various carriers as a single entity called **telephone network**, and the line connecting a subscriber to that network as a **service line** as shown in Fig. 3.33.

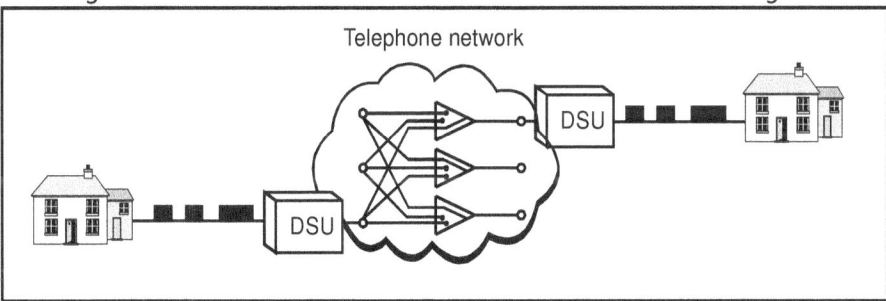

Fig. 3.33: Switched/56 service

2. Digital Data Service (DDS):

Digital Data Service (DDS) is the digital version of an analog leased line, it is a digital leased line with a maximum data rate of 64 kbps.

Like switched/56, DDS also requires the use of a DSU as shown in Fig. 3.34.

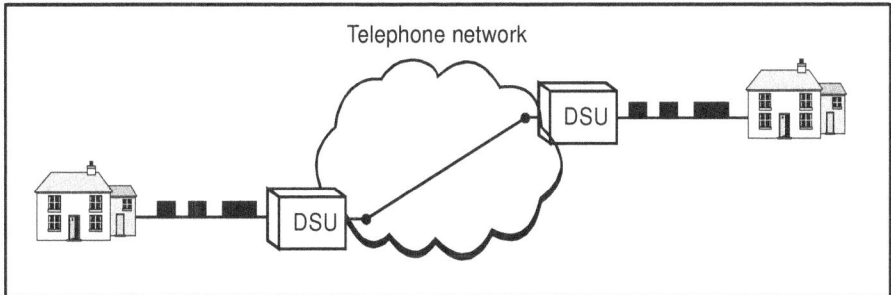

Fig. 3.34: DDS Service

3. Digital Signal Service (DSS):

Digital Signal Service (DSS), is a hierarchy of digital signals. As shown in Fig. 3.35, the data rates are supported by each level.

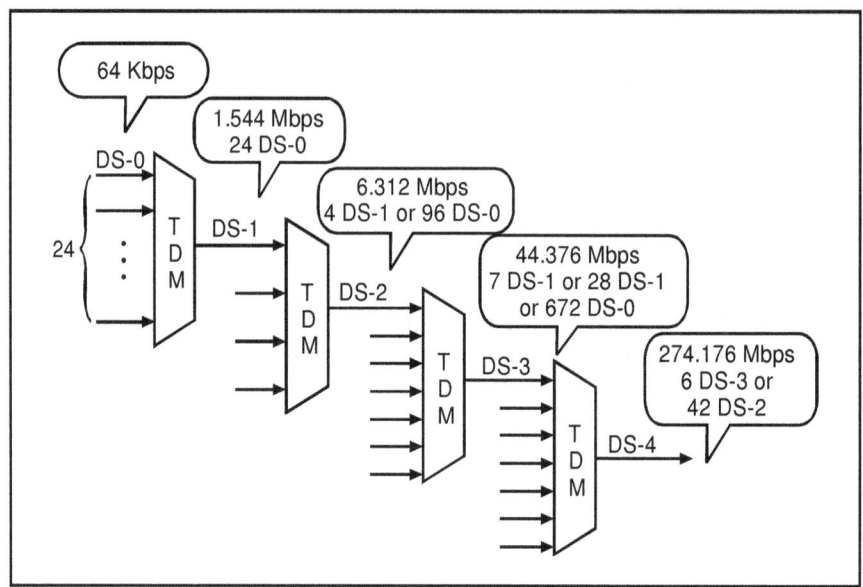

Fig. 3.35: DSS hierarchy

- A DS-0 service resembles DDS. It is a single digital channel of 64 kbps.
- DS-1 is a 1.544-Mbps service. It can be used as a single service for 1.5444 Mbps transmission or to multiplex 24 DS-0 channel.
- DS-2 is a 6.312 Mbps service. It can be used to multiplex 4 DS-1 channels. 96 DS-0 channels or combination.
- DS-3 is a 44.376 Mbps service. It can be used to multiplex 7 DS-2 channel, 28 DS-1 channel, 672 DS-0 channel or combination.
- DS-4 is a 274.176 Mbps service. It can be used to multiplex 6 DS-3 channel, 42 DS-2 channels, 168 DS-1 channels, 4032 DS-0 channels or combination.

3.8 Wavelength Division Multiplexing (WDM)

WDM used for the high rate data transmission using fiber optic cable. The data transfer rate of optical fiber is higher than other metallic transmission cable.

WDM is conceptually similar to FDM except the multiplexing and demultiplexing involves optical signals transmitted through fiber-optic channels. WDM combines various and different signals of different frequencies.

Following Fig. 3.36 shows the conceptual view of WDM multiplexer and demultiplexer.

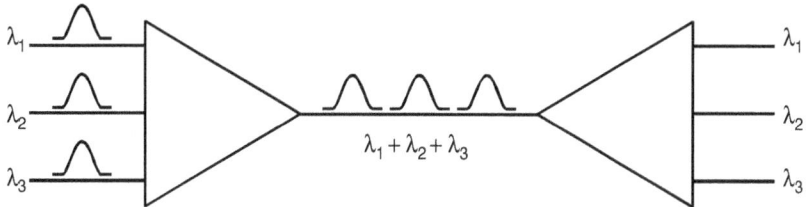

Fig. 3.36: WDM

The basic idea of WDM is very simple. WDM combines multiple light sources into a one single light at the multiplexer and then reverse at the demultiplexer. Combining and splitting of light sources are easily handled by a prism. Using Prism technique a multiplexer can be made to combine several input beams of light, each light beam containing narrow band of frequencies into one output beam of a wider band of frequencies. Fig. 3.37 shows the Prism technology used in WDM.

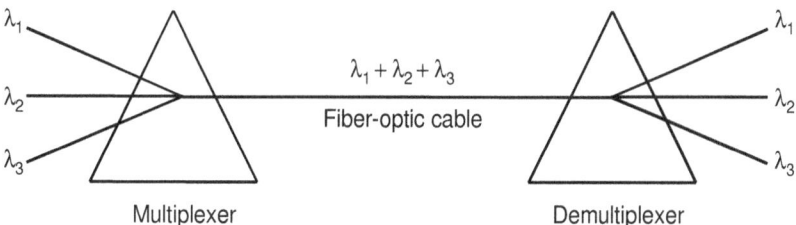

Fig. 3.37

3.9 PHYSICAL MEDIA

1. In computers, media refers to whatever medium is used to communicate data.
2. Media is usually the copper or fiber optic glass cables but data can also be sent through the air via electromagnetic frequencies such as infrared, micro waves or radio waves.
3. Media is important because it is often half the cost of the network.
4. **Important factors in determining media include :**
    *   Required speed.
    *   Distance.
    *   Ease of installation and maintenance access.
    *   Technical expertise required to install and utilize.
    *   Resistance to internal EMI (Electromagnetic Interference) inside the cable, especially the cross talk of parallel wires.
    *   Resistance to external EMI outside the cable.
    *   Resistance to other environmental hazards such as workers carelessly drilling into walls, fire and the weather.

- *Bandwidth* : The range of frequencies that the cable can accommodate. LANs generally carry data rates of 1 to 100 megabits per second and require moderately high bandwidth.
- *Attenuation* characteristics : Attenuation describes how cables reduce the strength of a signal with distance. Resistance is one factor that contributes to signal attenuation.
- *Cost.*

5. When data is sent across the network it is converted into electrical signals.
6. These signals are generated as electromagnetic waves (analog signaling) or as a sequence of voltage pulses (digital signaling).
7. To be sent from one location to another, a signal must travel along a physical path.
8. The physical path that is used to carry a signal between a signal transmitter and a signal receiver is called the **transmission medium**.
9. **There are two types of transmission media : guided and unguided.**

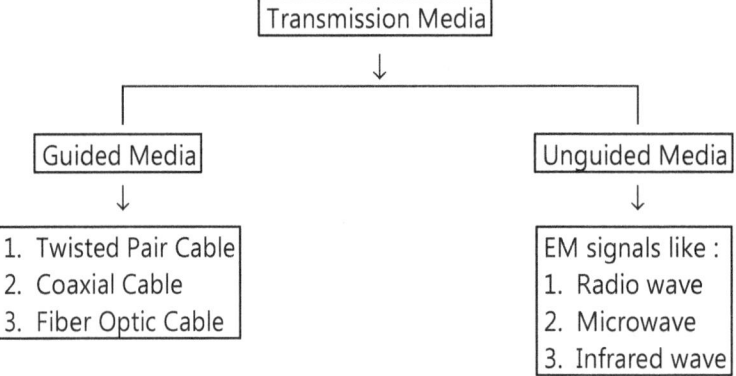

Fig. 3.38 : Classification of Transmission Media

3.10 Guided Media

1. Guided media are manufactured so that signals will be confined to a narrow path and will behave predictably.
2. The three most commonly used types of guided media are twisted-pair wiring, coaxial cable, and optical fiber cable.
3. Each type is suited to specific applications and network topologies.

3.10.1 Unshielded Twisted Pair (UTP) Cable and Shielded Twisted Pair (STP) Cable

Unshielded Twisted Pair (Utp) Cable

1. Twisted pair has become the most popular network cabling media today.

2.   Twisted pair cabling is used in a star or star tree topology for Ethernet networks.

3.   Maximum number of network devices is 1,024, with a maximum cable length of 100 meters for individual devices and a total distance of 500 meters of cabling between the farthest two devices, including links between data closets.

4.   The signal from a network hub can be repeated three times, giving you a maximum of four data closets.

5.   The distance between closets can be extended by switching to a star bus topology and using fiber optic cable for links between closets.

6.   **Twisted pair copper cable** is perhaps the oldest and certainly still the most commonly used transmission medium.

7.   A twisted pair consists of two insulated copper cables, typically about 1 mm in diameter, twisted together to reduce electrical interference between adjacent pairs of wires (two pairs of parallel wires can act as a crude antenna).

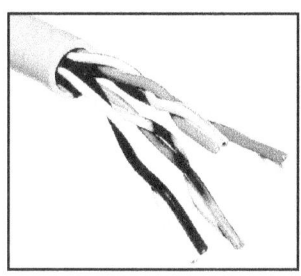

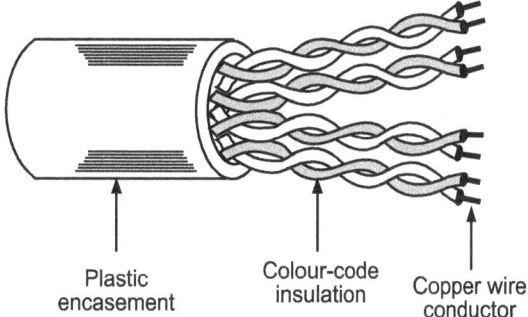

Plastic encasement · Colour-code insulation · Copper wire conductor

Fig. 3.39: Unshielded Twisted pair cable   **Fig. 3.40: Four pair UTP cable used in LAN (Local Area Network)**

8.   Twisted pair cable is still used in the public telephone system, specifically in the subscriber loop, the link from a domestic or business telephone subscriber to the local telephone exchange.

9.   These links are good for several kilometers without amplification, but longer runs need repeaters.

10. The local subscriber loop is essentially an analogue transmission medium, but twisted pair cables can also be used for digital transmission.

11. The data rate (or *bandwidth*) for twisted pair depends on factors such as the diameter of wire used and the length of the transmission line, but several megabits per second (Mbps) can be achieved over a few kilometers.

12. Low cost and ease of installation have kept twisted pair in widespread use both in the telephone system and in Local Area Networks (LANs).

13. The type of twisted pair cables used in LANs fall into two main categories.

14. **Category 3** twisted pair cable is the type you will normally find connected to your domestic telephone outlet and consists of two insulated wires twisted gently twisted together. Typically, four pairs are grouped together within a plastic sheath which serves both as protection and to keep the eight wires together.

15. **Category 5** twisted pairs, introduced in the late eighties, are similar to category 3 twisted pair but with more twists per centimeter and Teflon-based insulation.

16. This results in a further reduction in crosstalk and a better quality signal over long distances, which makes them more suitable for high-speed data communication.

17. Both types are referred to as *Unshielded Twisted Pair* (UTP). A summary of the twisted pair categories is given below.

Category 1 : Used for traditional telephone voice communication (but not data) - most telephone cable used before 1983 were category 1.

Category 2 : Four twisted pairs - suitable for data rates of up to 4 Mbps.

Category 3 :

- Four twisted pairs with three twists per foot - suitable for data rates of up to 10 Mbps.
- In the beginning of twisted pair technology, some networks were set up utilizing spare pairs on existing phone systems or cabled with Category 3.
- These networks are only capable of 10Base-T (10 megabits per second) data transfer, and most of them set up on spare pairs of existing phone wiring run for slower than that.
- These networks have been obsolete for some time and cannot match the network speeds of today. New Category 3 should only be installed for phone systems.

Category 4 : Supports data transmission of up to 20 Mbps.

Category 5 :

- Four twisted pairs with a higher number of twists per foot than previous categories and Teflon based outer coating.
- Category 5 is generally accepted as the cable to install because of its higher transmission rate and better noise immunity.
- Testing of these cables assumes that only two pairs will be used - one to transmit (T_X) and one to receive (R_X).
- Falling costs in recent years have made category 5 twisted pair a more cost-effective option.
- The predominant type of twisted pair installed in the majority of commercial buildings is unshielded Category 5.
- It is most commonly used for 100 Base T Ethernet networks, giving data transfer rates of 100 megabits per second.

- In addition, the IEEE has approved a network standard for 1000 BASE T Ethernet networks (data transfer of 1,000 megabits per second) which can utilize most existing Category 5 cabling when it has been properly installed and certified.
- In addition to unshielded Category 5, there is also a shielded version, which provides some protection against electromagnetic interference.
- A typical application might be for a heavy manufacturing plant where interference from large electric motors could present a problem.
- For the vast majority of existing offices and smaller industrial plants, unshielded Category 5 is the most commonly found cable.

Category 5e :

- **Enhanced category 5** - more comprehensive testing is carried out on all four pairs to measure the effect of transmitting data, particularly with regard to crosstalk.
- This category is primarily intended for use in Gigabit Ethernet networks.
- Over the last several years, Category 5e has become the replacement for Category 5.
- There are two main types, known as "Little e" and "Big E", capable of 155 and 350-megabit transmission respectively.
- Although there are no network standards to support these speeds, the increased bandwidth does enhance this cable's ability to run gigabit Ethernet.
- With the price drop of Category 5e over the last few years, it has become the most common choice for new network installation.

Category 6 :

- A proposed standard for cable having a transmission frequency of 200 MHz, with all components coming from one manufacturer (i.e. no "mixing").
- With the ever increasing speed of networks today, Category 6 is becoming more common in new office installations that demand reliable gigabit network speed.
- It is a viable choice today for a new network installation in a commercial space where the tenants plan to stay for an extended length of time.
- In addition, gigabit switches and network cards are also beginning to drop in price, so the cost of the hardware necessary to set up a true gigabit network is becoming less expensive as well.

Category 7 : A proposed standard for cable having a transmission frequency of 600 MHz using fully shielded cables, i.e. shielding is to be provided for both individual pairs and for the grouped pairs. A new connection type is also proposed.

18. The maximum recommended cable run for unshielded twisted pair is 100 meters.

19. UTP cables are terminated with RJ45 connectors, similar in design to the connectors used to connect telephones into a wall socket outlet (RJ11).

20. Twisted pair cables are most commonly used to connect workstations to hubs or MAUs.
21. The standard connector for unshielded twisted pair cabling is RJ-45 connector.
22. This is a plastic connector that looks like a large telephone-style connector.
23. A slot allows the RJ-45 to be inserted only one way.
24. RJ stands for Registered Jack, implying that the connector follows a standard borrowed from the telephone industry.
25. This standard designates which wire goes with each pin inside the connector.

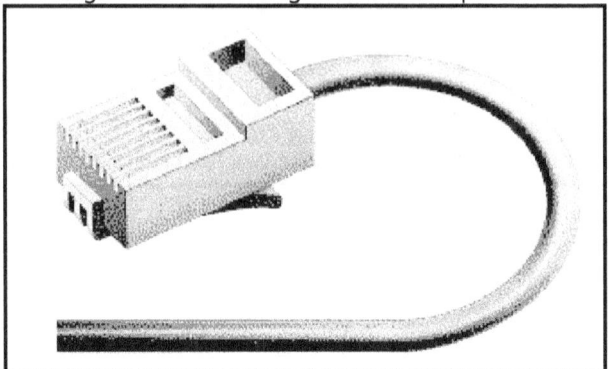

Fig. 3.41: RJ-45 Connector and UTP Cable

Shielded Twisted Pair Cable

1. *Shielded Twisted Pair* (STP) cable was introduced in the 1980s by IBM as the recommended medium for their Token Ring network technology, and has a characteristic impedance of 150 ohms.
2. Each cable consists of two pairs, with each pair individually foil shielded, and an overall braided shield.
3. Because STP was specified by IBM, many users thought that it was required for reliable data transfer.

Fig. 3.42: Shielded Twisted Pair Cable　　　**Fig. 3.43: Typical two pair Shielded Twisted Pair Cable (STP Cable)**

4. Since this is not in fact the case its popularity has declined due to :
    *   The high cost of the cable and connectors (much more complex than UTP).
    *   The increased bulk of cable and connectors compared to UTP.
    *   The increased time required for installation compared to UTP.
    *   **Ground loops** - These arise when the ground voltage at each end of a cable run is different, causing a current to flow in the cable's shield and creating a magnetic field, which induces, current (noise) in the same cable the shielding is designed to protect.
    *   The same cable length restrictions apply (100 meters maximum) as for UTP.
    *   STP is limited for data communication to IBM machines and Token Ring networks - there is no standard for STP for Ethernet, ISDN or analog telephones.
    *   Shielded twisted pair is now manufactured to the same standard as Unshielded Twisted Pair.

Thus following points summarize the features of STP cable :
*   Speed and throughput—10 to 100 Mbps
*   Average cost per node—Moderately expensive
*   Media and connector size—Medium to large
*   Maximum cable length—100 m (short)

When comparing UTP and STP, keep the following points in mind :
*   The speed of both types of cable is usually satisfactory for local-area distances.
*   These are the least-expensive media for data communication. UTP is less expensive than STP.
*   Because most buildings are already wired with UTP, many transmission standards are adapted to use it, to avoid costly rewiring with an alternative cable type.

Table 3.3: Categories of Unshielded Twisted Pair

Type	Bandwidth	Use
Category 1	< 1 MHz	Voice Only (Telephone Wire).
Category 2	1 MHz	Data to 4 Mbps (Local Talk) and Telephone, T_1 lines etc.
Category 3	16 MHz	Data to 10 Mbps (Ethernet), Telephone, 10Base-T, Token Ring, LAN applications.
Category 4	20 MHz	Data to 20 Mbps (16 Mbps Token Ring), 10Base-T, LAN application.
Category 5	100 MHz	Data to 100 Mbps (Fast Ethernet), 10Base-T, 100Base-T, LAN applications.
Category 5e	350 MHz	125 Mbps, Data Networks.
Category 6	550 MHz	Proposed standard for cable having a data rate of 200 Mbps, LAN applications.
Category 7	600 MHz	Proposed standard for cable having a data rate of 600 Mbps using fully shielded cables, LAN applications.

Some advantages of twisted pair wiring are as follows :
- Reasonable cost.
- High speed.
- Easy to add additional network devices.
- Supports large number of network devices.
- Telephone cable standards are mature and well established. Materials are plentiful, and a wide variety of cable installers are familiar with the installation requirements.
- It may be possible to use in-place telephone wiring if it is of sufficiently high quality.
- UTP represents the lowest cost cabling. The cost for STP is higher and is comparable to the cost of coaxial cable.

Some disadvantages of twisted pair are as follows :
- High attenuation (signal loss) limits individual runs to 100 meters.
- Susceptible to EMI/RFI (except shielded type).
- STP can be expensive and difficult to work with.
- Compared to fiber optic cable, all Twisted Pair cable is more sensitive to EMI. UTP especially may be unsuitable for use in high-EMI environments.
- Twisted Pair cables are regarded as being less suitable for high-speed transmissions than coax or fiber optic. Technology advances, however, are pushing upward the data rates possible with Twisted Pair. Cable segment lengths are also more limited with Twisted Pair.

3.10.2 Coaxial Cable

1. A coaxial cable consists of a central copper wire core, which is surrounded by an insulating material.
2. The insulator is surrounded by braided metal shielding which helps to absorb external electronic signals (noise) and prevents it from interfering with the data signal.
3. A plastic sheath protects the outer conductor. A durable plastic or Teflon jacket coats the cable to prevent damage. Fig. 3.44 diagram illustrates the basic construction of a coaxial cable.

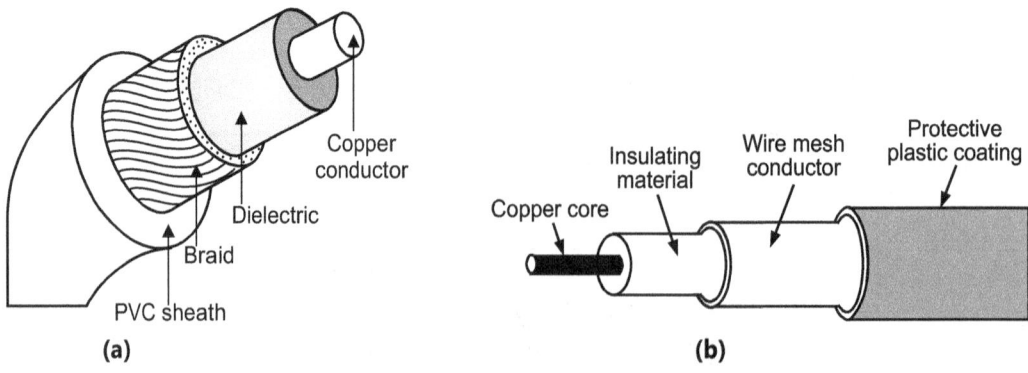

(a)   **(b)**

Fig. 3.44: Coaxial cable construction

4. The construction and shielding of coaxial cable provides a high degree of immunity to noise, and coax can be used over longer distances (upto 500 meters) than twisted pair cable.

5. Coaxial cable runs are used to provide the network backbone cable segments in networks having a **bus topology**, and require a terminating resistor at each end of the cable in order to prevent interference due to signal reflection.

6. Coax has many desirable characteristics. It is highly resistant to EMI and can support high *bandwidths*.

7. Some types of coax have heavy shields and center conductors to enhance these characteristics and to extend the distances, so that signals can be transmitted reliably.

8. A wide variety of coax cable is available. You must use cable that exactly matches the requirements of a particular type of network.

9. Coax cables vary in a measurement known as the *impedance* (measured in a unit called the ohm), which is an indication of the cable's resistance to current flow.

10. The specifications of a given cabling standard indicate the required impedance of the cable.

11. Two types of coaxial cable can be used in computer networks :
    * **Thinnet or Cheapernet (also known as Baseband Coax - RG-58)**
    * **Thicknet**

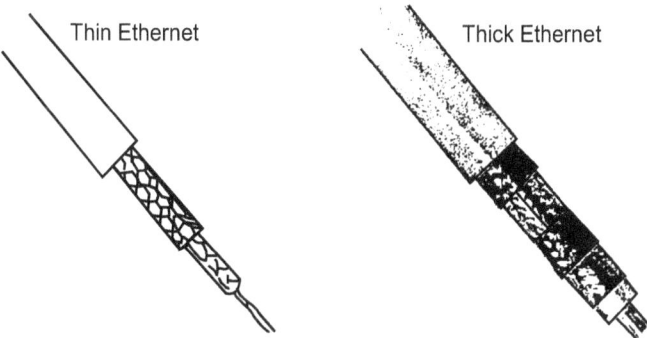

Fig. 3.45: Thin Ethernet and Thick Ethernet

12. Thinnet (10Base2) is so called because of the thin, inexpensive coaxial cabling it uses, and is fairly flexible, being 0.25 inches in diameter.

13. The IEEE specification refers to this type of cable as 10Base2, referring to its main specifications of 10 Mbps data rate, baseband transmission type, and 185 (nearly 200) meter maximum segment length.

14. The cable between computers must be at least 0.5 meters (20 inches) long.

15. An IEEE standard for Thinnet doesn't allow a drop cable to be used from the bus T-connector to a workstation.

16. Instead, the T-connector fits directly onto the network adapter card using a BNC connector.

17. **A Thinnet network** can support a maximum of 30 nodes per cable segment, and up to five segments can be connected using repeaters, of which three segments may be populated, allowing up to 90 nodes to be supported (based on the IEEE 802.3 specification).

18. **Thicknet cable** (also known as **Standard Ethernet**) is relatively rigid, being 0.5 inches in diameter.

19. **The IEEE specification refers to this type of cable as 10Base5, referring to its main specifications of 10 Mbps data rate, baseband transmission type, and 500-metre maximum segment length.**

20. Thicknet is generally used to provide the network backbone and can support up to 100 nodes per backbone segment.

21. The minimum cable length between connections (or taps) on a Thicknet cable segment is 2.5 meters (about 8 feet).

22. Thicknet cable has a data rate of 10 Mbps and can carry a signal for 500 meters before a repeater is required.

23. The grade of coaxial cable used will depend on where it is used.

24. Normal PVC coaxial cable is flexible, easy to work with, and may be used in exposed areas of offices, but because it gives of poisonous fumes when it burns, it is against the fire regulations in many countries for it to be installed in floor and ceiling voids which are also used to allow air to circulate around the building.

25. Thick coax was the transmission medium originally used by Xerox for their Ethernet network, although it was later superceded by thin coax.

26. Although still used in many networks, coaxial cable is gradually being replaced by fiber optic and UTP cable - fiber optic is normally used for the network backbone, with UTP being used to connect workstations to hubs or MAUs.

27. Here are some common examples of coaxial cables used in LANs, along with their impedances, and the LAN standards with which they are associated :

    • RG-8 and RG-11 are 50-ohm cables required for thick wire Ethernet. (10Base5 - ThikNet).

    • RG-58 is a smaller 50-ohm cable required for use with thin wire Ethernet. (10Base2 – ThinNet).

    • RG-59 is a 75-ohm cable most familiar when used to wire cable TV. RG-59 is also used to cable broadband 802.3 Ethernet.

    • RG-62 is a 93-ohm cable used for ARCnet. It is also commonly employed to wire terminals in an IBM SNA network.

Some advantages of coaxial cable are as follows :

- Low cost due to less total footage of cable, hubs not needed.
- Lower attenuation than twisted pair.
- Good immunity to EMI/RFI / Highly insensitive to EMI.
- Supports high bandwidths.
- Heavier types of coax are sturdy and can withstand harsh environments.
- Represents a mature technology that is well understood and consistently applied among vendors.

Coaxial cable also has some disadvantages including the following :

- Limited in network speed.
- Limited in size of network.
- One bad connector can take down entire network.
- Although fairly insensitive to EMI, coax remains vulnerable to EMI in harsh conditions such as factories.
- Coax can be bulky.
- Coax is among the most expensive types of wire cables.

3.10.3 Fiber Optic Cable

1. Data transmission over optical fiber has greatly increased over the last few years, although fiber to the desktop has not really caught on as expected.
2. However, fiber optic plays an important role in many networks.
3. In addition, it has some outstanding advantages over copper cabling for certain applications.
4. There are a number of network topologies and standards based on fiber optic, such as 10 BASE FL and FDDI, which apply mainly to the backbone cabling of very large facilities and campus environments.
5. The discussion will be limited here to the uses of fiber optic in star bus Ethernet network topologies.
6. When used as a link in a star bus topology, multi-mode fiber optic cable can transmit a maximum distance of 2,000 meters between all data closets, using a less expensive LED light source.
7. While single mode fiber can transmit up to 3,000 meters, it requires a more expensive laser light source.
8. By using fiber optic to link closets, it is possible to greatly extend the distance limitations in Ethernet networks using twisted pair only.
9. Fiber optic is an outstanding choice for linking buildings together.
10. In addition to the much greater distances possible, it is completely immune to over currents from lightning strikes and ground potential problems.

11. There is literally nothing metallic in a fiber optic cable to conduct current. It is an excellent choice for heavy manufacturing environments, such as a foundry, due to its immunity to EMI/RFI.

12. Finally, it is the best choice where data of a highly sensitive nature is being transmitted.

13. Fiber optic cable radiates no electrical signal at all, and the cable would be down for quite some time if someone tried to splice into it.

Construction of Optical Fiber:

- Optical fiber cable carries light signals instead of electric signal.
- Each fiber has inner core of either plastic or glass that carries light.
- The inner core is surrounded by cladding, a layer of plastic or glass that reflects the light back into core.
- Fiber optic cable can have single fiber or bundle of fibers at the centre of the cable. The refractive index of the core is relatively high.
- Refractive index is low. Cladding material is lossy.
- This entire optical core-cladding assembly is then coated with protective inner jacket and outer plastic jacket as shown in Fig. 3.46.

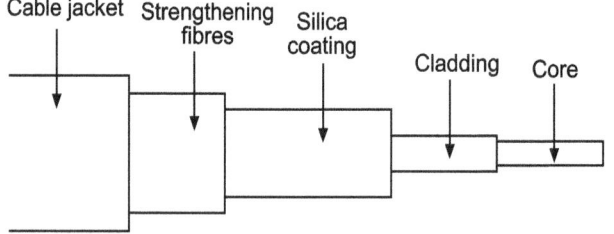

Fig. 3.47: Construction of Fiber Optic Cable

The cross-section of a fiber illustrating the different layers is as shown in Fig. 3.47.

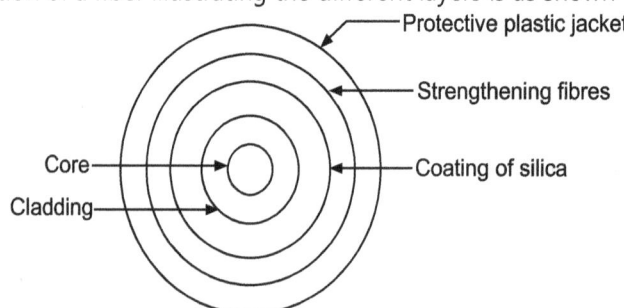

Fig. 3.47: A Cross-Section of a Fiber illustrating the Different Layers

The core is surrounded by cladding surface and entire thing is coated with silicon oil and organic material with silica. External plastic jacket is to provide mechanical strength and optical fiber is protected from mechanical wear and tear.

Typical optical fiber communication is shown in Fig. 3.48.

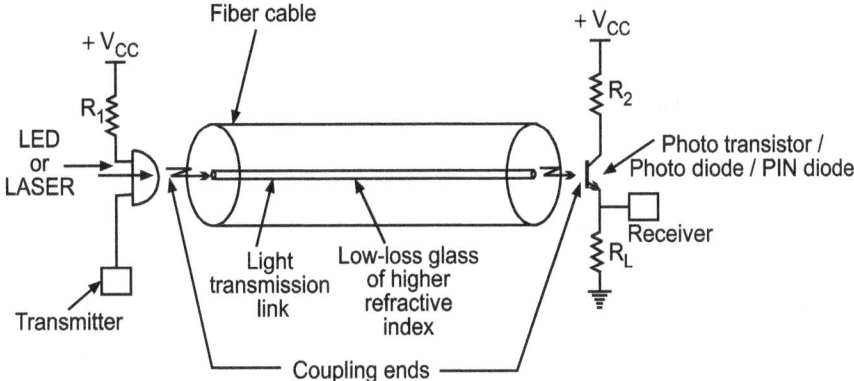

Fig. 3.48: Typical Fiber Optic Communication System

The basic point-to-point fiber optic communication system consists of three basic units.

1. Optical transmitter unit   2. Fiber optic cable unit

3. Optical receiver unit.

Optical Transmitter Unit: The transmitter converts applied electrical, analog or digital signal into a corresponding light signal. The source of the light signal can be either a light emitting diode, or a solid-state laser diode.

Fiber Optic Cable Unit: Converted signal travels in the form of light from one end of fiber to other end of fiber. This is also called as light transmission link. If the distance between transmitter and receiver is in kilometers, then two or more fiber optic cables can be joined together.

Optical Receiver: The receiver converts the optical signal into the original electrical signal. This optical receiver uses the photodetectors like avalanche type photodiode or PIN type of photodiode (P type-Intrinsic-N type material is used).

Optical fibers can be classified in two ways as shown.

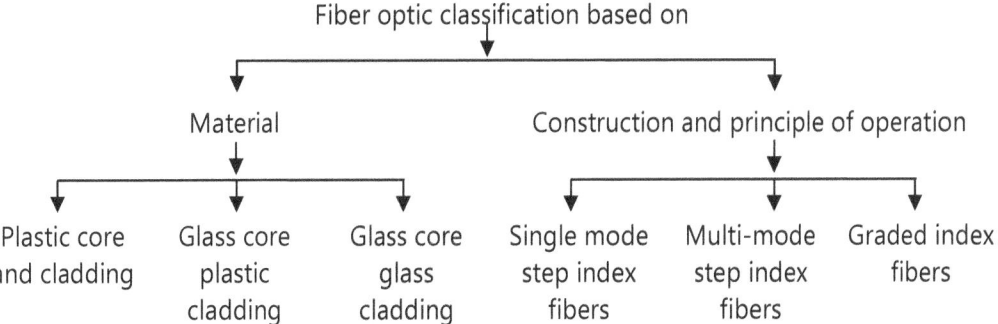

Plastic core and cladding: These type of fibers are more rugged than glass. They are less expensive. They provide high attenuation characteristics and can be used within a single building or a building complex. Less attenuation when exposed to external radiation.

Glass core with plastic cladding: These type of fibers are more effectively used in military applications.

Glass core and glass cladding: These type of fibers are least rugged and are more susceptible to increase in attenuation when exposed to external radiation compared to above both optical fibers.

Single mode step index fiber has following properties:

- Support only one mode of operation.
- Use of LASER is must, makes power launching difficult.
- Fiber coupling is difficult due to less diameter size of core which is approximately ≈ 8 to 12 μm.

Multi-mode step index fiber has following properties:

- Supports hundreds of modes of propagation.
- LED can be used as optical transmitter, so power launching becomes easy.
- Fiber coupling is easy because moderate core diameter which is approximately ≈ 50 to 200 μm.
- In this fiber the pulse which is sent at transmitter end spreads in time, when it is received at receiver end. This pulse distortion is called as intermodal dispersion.

Graded index fiber :

- The intermodal dispersion of pulse is reduced in the graded index fiber due to its construction itself.
- Graded index fibers have larger bandwidth than step index fibers.

Construction of the monomode or single mode step index fiber is given in Fig. 3.49 (a).

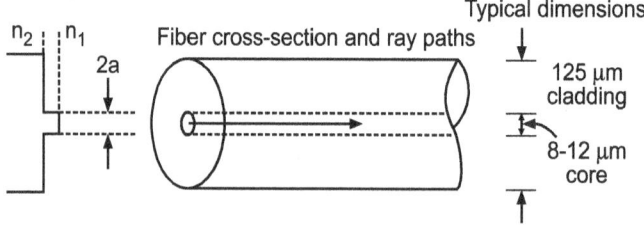

Fig. 3.49 (a): Monomode or Single Mode Step Index Fiber

Construction of the multi-mode step index fiber is given in Fig. 3.49 (b).

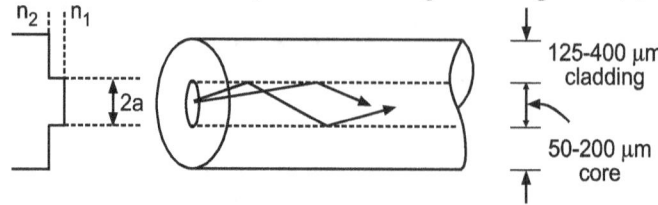

Fig. 3.49 (b) : Multi-mode Step Index Fiber

Construction of the graded index fiber is given in Fig. 3.49 (c).

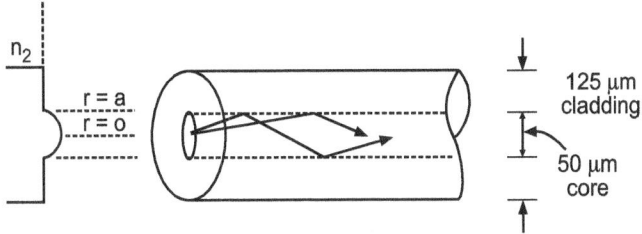

Fig. 3.49 (c): Graded Index Fiber

Thus fiber optic transmission line confines light energy within its surface and guides the light in a direction parallel to its axis.

In previous figures,

n_1 = refractive index of the core

n_2 = refractive index of cladding

Main advantages of fiber optic cable:
- High data rate and wide bandwidth.
- Immunity to EMI/RFI and lightning damage.
- No ground loops.
- Low attenuation (Low data loss).
- Longer distance - 2 and 5 km with multi-mode fiber and over 25 km with single mode fiber.
- Small cable diameter fits anywhere.
- Light weight.
- No sparks if cut.
- No shock hazard.
- Secure communication.
- Safe and easy installation.
- Low system cost.
- Longer life expectancy than copper or coaxial cable.
- Cabling of the future.

Main disadvantages of fiber optic cable are as follows:
Cost:
Despite the fact that the raw material for making optical fibers is abundant and cheap, optical fibers are still more expensive per meter than copper.

Special Skills:
Optical fibers cannot be joined together as easily as copper. It requires additional training for person. Expensive precision splicing and measurement equipment are also required.

Installation and Maintenance Cost:
Initial installation of the fiber optic system is more and maintenance is expensive.

Table 3.4: Summary of Cable Characteristics

Cable Type	Cable Cost	Installation Cost	EMI Sensitivity	Data Bandwidth
UTP	Lowest	Lowest	Highest	Lowest
STP	Medium	Moderate	Low	Moderate
Coax	Medium	Moderate	Low	High
Fiber Optic	Highest	Highest	None	Very high

- Thus choosing the correct type of cabling depends on what type of network you have or intend to have, the number of network devices used, expected future growth, the speed requirements of your applications and the physical layout of your facility.

- Make this decision with the assistance of a professional, licensed and insured network cabling company and a good information technology consultant.

Table 3.5: Characteristic comparison of guided media

	Twisted Pair	Coaxial Cable	Fiber Optic Cable
1.	It uses electrical signal for transmission.	It uses electrical signal for transmission.	It uses optical signal for transmission.
2.	Affected by EMI and noise.	Less affected by EMI and noise.	Not affected by EMI and noise.
3.	Bandwidth is low which is 3 to 4 MHz.	Bandwidth is high which is 300 to 400 MHz.	Bandwidth is very high which is 2 to 3 GHz.
4.	Used for analog and digital transmission.	Used for analog and digital transmission.	Used for analog and digital transmission.
5.	Supports low data rates upto 4 Mbps.	Supports high data rates upto 400 to 500 Mbps.	Supports very high data rates upto 3 Gbps.
6.	Cost is very less.	Cost is moderate.	More costly.
7.	For long distance communication, repeaters are required after every 2 km distance.	For long distance communication, repeaters are required after every 1 km distance.	For long distance communication, repeaters are required after every 10 km distance.
8.	Signal attenuation is more.	Signal attenuation is moderate.	Signal attenuation is least.
9.	Installation is easiest.	Installation is easy.	Installation is difficult.
10.	Signal to noise ratio is less.	Signal to noise ratio is moderate.	Signal to noise ratio is very high.

Twisted Pair	Coaxial Cable	Fiber Optic Cable
11. Crosstalk is more.	Crosstalk is moderate.	No crosstalk is present.
12. Losses like copper losses and radiation losses are present.	Losses like copper losses and radiation losses are present.	Losses like microbending and macrobending losses are present.

3.11 Unguided Media

3.11.1 Introduction

1. Unguided media are natural parts of the earth's environment that can be used as physical paths to carry electrical signals.

2. The atmosphere and outer space are examples of unguided media that are commonly used to carry signals.

3. **These media can carry such electromagnetic signals as microwaves, infrared light waves, and radio waves.**

4. Network signals are transmitted through all transmission media as a type of waveform.

5. When transmitted through wire and cable, the signal is an electrical waveform.

6. When transmitted through fiber-optic cable, the signal is a light wave : either visible or infrared light.

7. When transmitted through earth's atmosphere or outer space, the signal can take the form of waves in the radio spectrum, including VHF and microwaves, or it can be light waves, including infrared or visible light (for example, lasers).

8. Recent advances in radio hardware technology have produced significant advancements in wireless networking devices : the cellular telephone, wireless modems, and wireless LANs.

9. These devices use technology that in some cases has been around for decades but until recently was too impractical or expensive for widespread consumer use.

10. The next few sections explain technologies unique to unguided media that are especially of concern to networking.

11. There are a variety of wireless network media, each of which uses a different transmission protocol. Typically, a wireless network uses infrared light or radio transmissions to distribute data.

12. **Infrared networks** communicate by using beams of infrared light. They have a maximum range of 100 meters. Theoretically, they can transmit at 10 Mbps, but 1-3 Mbps is more typical.

13. **Narrow band radio networks** can cover an area up to 5,000 square meters at up to 4.8 Mbps. Their disadvantage is that they offer little security.

14. **Spread-spectrum radio networks** use multiple frequencies. These multiple channels provide network security. They can transmit data at up to 1 Mbps at a range of 800 feet indoors, though 300 kbps is more typical.

15. Some common applications of wireless data communication include the following :
    - Accessing the Internet using a cellular phone.
    - Establishing a home or business Internet connection over satellite.
    - Beaming data between two hand-held computing devices.
    - Using a wireless keyboard and mouse for the PC.

3.11.2 The Electromagnetic Spectrum

1. All electromagnetic waves travel at the speed of light (300,000,000 metres per second) in a vacuum, whatever their frequency (in copper or fibre), the speed drops to approximately two thirds of this value, and is slightly frequency dependent.

2. The relationship between frequency, wavelength and the speed of light (C) in a vacuum is given by :

$$F \lambda = C$$

3. Since C is a constant, if wavelength is known, then frequency can be calculated and vice versa.

4. Thus, a frequency of 1 MHz would give a wavelength of approximately 300 meters, and a 1 cm wavelength would give a frequency of approximately 30 GHz. The Electromagnetic Spectrum is shown in Fig. 3.50.

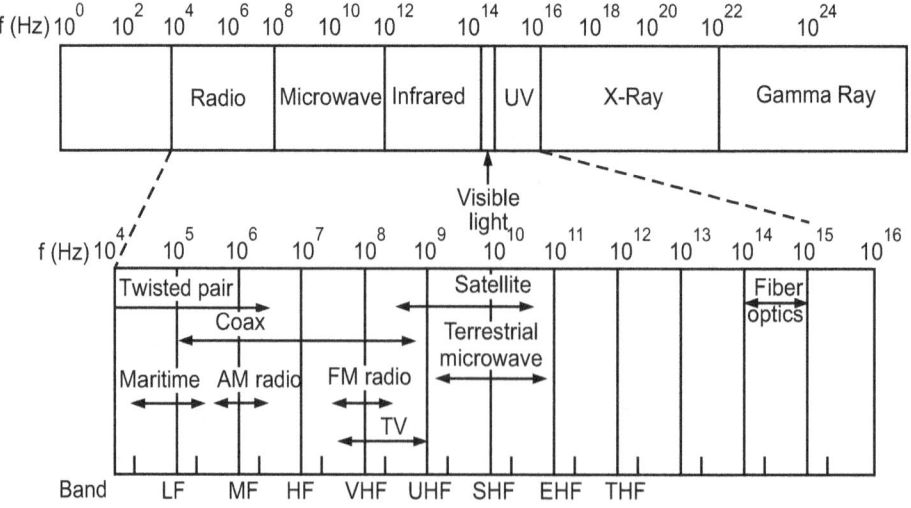

Fig. 3.50: The Electromagnetic Spectrum

5. The parts of the electromagnetic spectrum which can be used for transmitting information using amplitude, frequency or phase modulation are shown using a darker shading and include radio, microwave, infrared and visible light.

3.12 Radio Transmission

1. Radio waves are widely used for both indoor and outdoor communication because they are easy to generate, can travel over long distances, and can penetrate buildings easily.
2. Because they travel in all directions from the transmitter (i.e. they are omni directional), the transmitter and receiver do not need to be carefully aligned.
3. The properties of radio waves are dependent on frequency.
4. At low frequencies, they pass through obstacles well, but the power falls off sharply as the distance from the transmitter increases.
5. At high frequencies, radio waves tend to travel in straight lines and bounce off obstacles.
6. They are also absorbed by rain.
7. At all frequencies, they are subject to electromagnetic interference from electrical equipment such as electric motors.
8. The ability to travel over large distances means that radio transmissions can also interfere with each other, which is one of the main reasons why the use of radio transmitters is tightly controlled by governments.
9. In the very low to medium frequency bands, radio waves follow the ground, as illustrated below, and can be detected at distances of about 1000 kilometers. (Also called as Ground Wave Propagation)
10. Radio waves at these frequencies can easily pass through buildings and are subsequently widely used by terrestrial radio stations.
11. The relatively low bandwidth, however, means that they are not suitable for data communication.

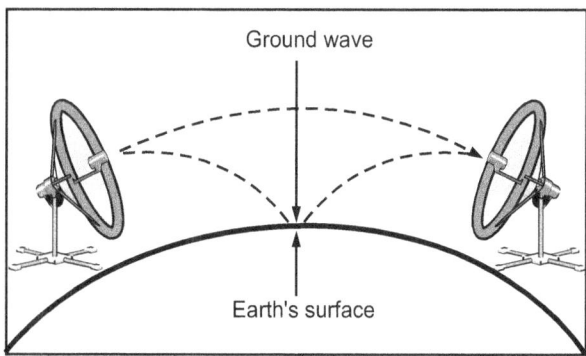

Fig. 3.51: Radio Transmission using Ground Wave Propagation

12. RF is part of electromagnetic spectrum that ranges from 3 Hz-300 GHz.

13. Radio wave is radiated by an antenna and produced by alternating currents fed to the antenna.

14. RF is used in many standard as well as proprietary wireless communication systems.

15. **RF has been used since long time for radio and TV broadcasting, wireless local loop, mobile communication, and amateur radio.**

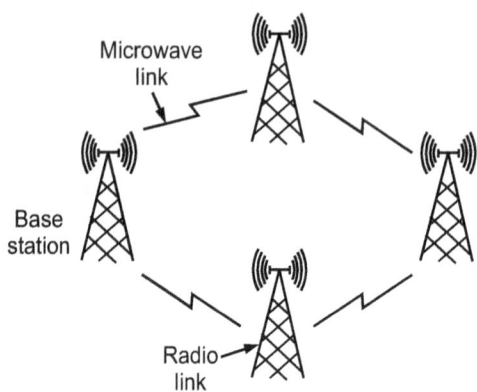

Fig. 3.52: Radio waves radiated by a Base Station's antenna

16. High (HF) and very high (VHF) frequency radio waves that reach the ionosphere, which is a layer of charged particles approximately 100-500 km above the earth's surface, are refracted by it and sent back to earth.

17. These bands are used by amateur radio operators to talk over long distances, and are also used for military radio communication.

18. **Radio waves** have virtually no distance limitations. However the radio waves are government regulated, expensive, and can be tapped into. This can be used across continents.

3.13 Microwave Transmission

1. At frequencies of 1 GHz and above, electromagnetic waves travel in straight lines and can be narrowly focused. Microwave is the upper part of RF spectrum. Because of the availability of larger bandwidth in microwave spectrum, microwave is used in many applications such as wireless PAN, wireless LAN, fixed broadband wireless access (wireless MAN), satellite communications, radar, and as backhaul in cellular networks.

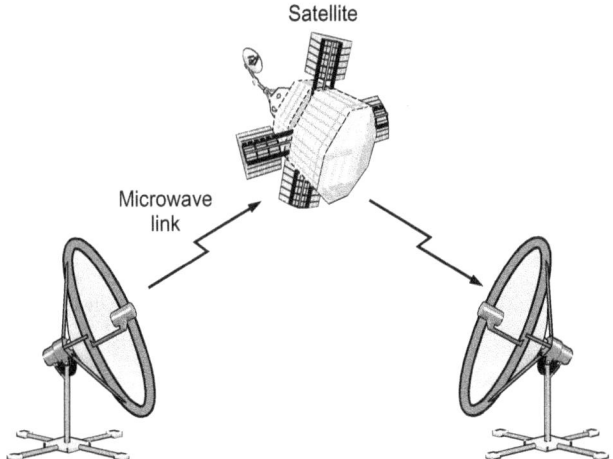

Fig. 3.53: Typical example of Microwave Link using Dish Antenna and Satellite

2. A parabolic dish antenna can be used to focus the transmitted power into a narrow beam to give a high signal to noise ratio, and before the advent of optical fiber, some long distance telephone transmission systems were heavily dependent on the use of a series of microwave towers.

3. Because microwaves travel in a straight line, the curvature of the earth limits the maximum distance over which microwave towers can transmit, so repeaters are needed to compensate for this limitation. As a general rule, the higher the towers are, the further apart they can be.

4. At these higher frequencies, the transmitted waves do not easily pass through buildings.

5. In addition, however well focused the transmitter may be, some waves may be refracted by low-lying atmospheric layers, and will take longer to arrive at their destination than direct waves.

6. The delayed waves may therefore arrive out of phase with the direct waves and cancel out the signal. This effect is known as multipath fading.

7. Rain can also be a problem, as frequencies around 8 GHz are absorbed by water.

8. At higher frequencies, more expensive electronics are required, and transmissions can be subject to interference from radar installations and microwave ovens.

9. **Microwave does, however, have several advantages over fiber.**

10. Obstacles such as roads, railways and rivers may make laying cables difficult whereas these problems do not exist for microwave, and rights of way are not an issue.

11. Erecting simple towers or mounting antenna on top of tall buildings is usually far cheaper than laying several kilometers of cable.

12. Microwave also removes the need for reliance on telephone companies.

13. In addition, governments worldwide have set aside the frequency band from 2.400 GHz to 2.484 GHz for unlicensed transmissions, so use of these frequencies does not require a license, and is therefore popular for various forms of short range wireless networking.

14. **Microwaves** have a medium distance limitation and require line of sight. This is good between buildings or between satellites and satellite dishes. Weather and solar conditions may affect transmission.

15. Microwaves are used for long distance communication like cellular phones, garage door openers, and much more.

16. Microwave transmission is line of sight transmission. The transmitting station must be in visible contact with the receiving station.

17. This sets a limit on the distance between stations depending on the local geography. Typically the line of sight due to the Earth's curvature is only 50 km to the horizon ! Repeater stations must be placed so the data signal can hop, skip and jump across the country.

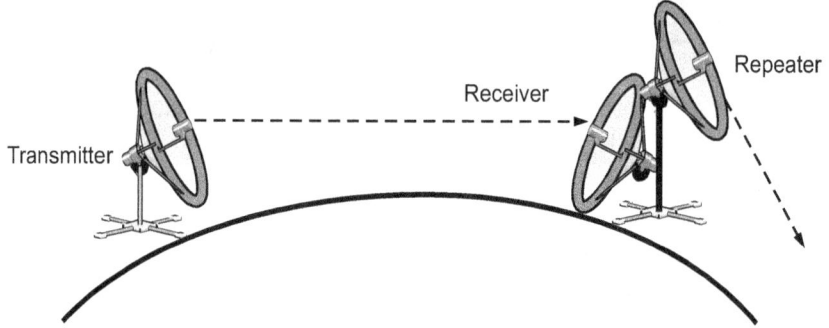

Fig. 3.54: Other example of Microwave Transmission

18. Microwaves operate at high operating frequencies of 3 to 10 GHz. This allows them to carry large quantities of data due to the large bandwidth.

3.13.1 Terrestrial Microwave Transmission

1. Communication is accomplished through line of sight parabolic dish antenna located on elevated sites.
2. Long distance communication is possible by using a series of relay stations.
3. The distance between the stations is dependent on the height above the ground.
4. Used for voice, television transmission, private communications and telephone networks e.g. emergency services, utilities etc.
5. Utilizes a wide frequency band, 2 to 40 GHz but is susceptible to attenuation and interference.
6. Attenuation can rise markedly in poor atmospheric conditions e.g. rain, but adversely affects the higher end of the frequency band, which is only used for short distance transmission.
7. Natural noise severely affects transmission frequencies below 2GHz.
8. Quick to install and overcomes the problems of laying cables in congested locations or over difficult terrain.

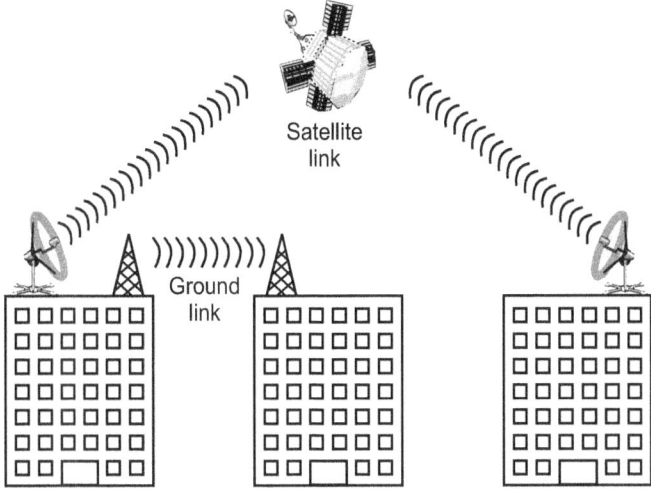

Fig. 3.55: Typical Example of Terrestrial and Satellite Microwave Links

3.13.2 Satellite Microwave Transmission

1. Overcomes the line of sight problems of terrestrial microwave and can be used for point-to-point or broadcast transmission.

2. Uses an uplink and downlink frequency, a common frequency set is referred to as the 4/6 range which uses a downlink frequency of 4 GHz and an uplink frequency of 6 GHz.

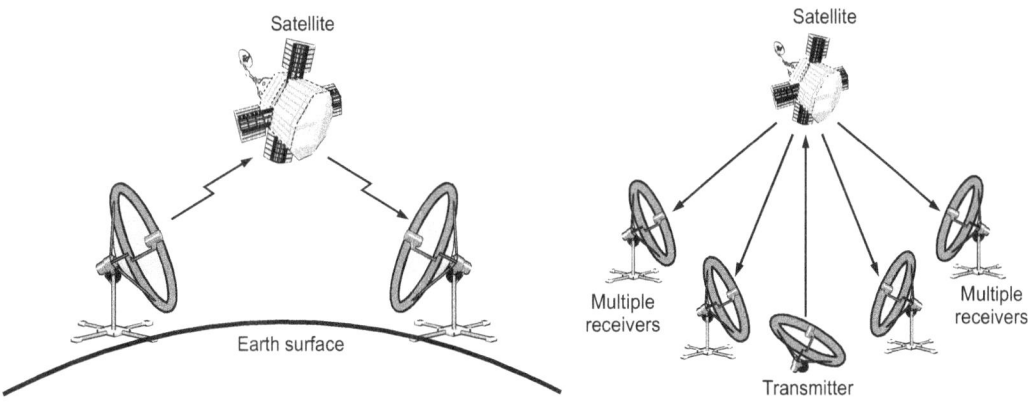

Fig. 3.56: Point-to-Point Link   **Fig. 3.57: Broadcast Link**

via Satellite Microwave   **via Satellite Microwave**

3.   Typical uses of satellite microwave - television distribution, long distance telephone transmission, private business networks for global organizations.
4.   Suffers the same attenuation problems as terrestrial microwave.
5.   Microwave transmitters and receivers, especially satellite systems, are commonly used to transmit network signals over great distances.
6.   A microwave transmitter uses the atmosphere or outer space as the transmission medium to send the signal to a microwave receiver.
7.   The microwave receiver then either relays the signal to another microwave transmitter or translates the signal to some other form, such as digital impulses, and relays it on another suitable medium to its destination.

Fig. 3.58 shows a satellite microwave link.

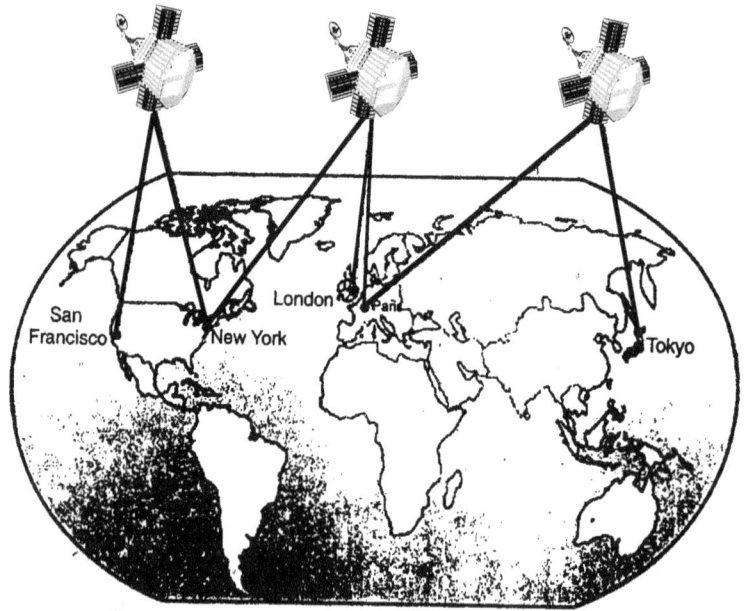

Fig. 3.58: Satellite Microwave Link for Worldwide Communication

8.   Originally, this technology was used almost exclusively for satellite and long-range communication.
9.   Recently, however, there have been developments in cellular technology that allow you complete wireless access to networks, intranets, and the Internet.
10.   IEEE 802.11 defines a MAC and physical access control for wireless connection to networks.
11.   Used for TV distribution, long-distance telephone, and business networks.

Advantages:
(a)   They require no right of way acquisition between towers.

(b) They can carry high quantities of information due to their high operating frequencies.

(c) Low cost land purchase : each tower occupies small area.

(d) High frequency/short wavelength signals require small antenna.

Disadvantages:

(a) Attenuation by solid objects : birds, rain, snow and fog.

(b) Reflected from flat surfaces like water and metal.

(c) Diffracted (split) around solid objects.

(d) Refracted by atmosphere, thus causing beam to be projected away from receiver.

3.14 Infrared Transmission

1. Unguided infrared waves are widely used for short-range communication. **Infrared** technology allows computing devices to communicate via short-range wireless signals. With infrared, computers can transfer files and other digital data bidirectionally. The infrared transmission technology used in computers is similar to that used in consumer product (television and VCRs) remote control units.

2. Used for very short line of sight transmission, remote car locking systems, wireless security alarms.

3. **Infrared** light is part of electromagnetic spectrum that is shorter than radio waves but longer than visible light. Computer infrared network adapters both transmit and receive data through ports on the rear or side of a device. Infrared adapters are installed in many laptops and handheld personal devices.

4. Its frequency range is between 300 GHz and 400 THz, that correspond to wavelength from 1 mm to 750 nm.

5. Infrared has long been used in night vision equipment and TV remote control.

6. Infrared is also one of the physical media in the original wireless LAN standard, that is IEEE 802.11. Infrared networks were designed to support direct two-computer connections only, created temporarily as the need arises. However, extensions to infrared technology also support more than two computers and semi-permanent networks.

7. Infrared use in communication and networking was defined by the IrDA (Infrared Data Association).

8. **Using IrDA specifications, infrared can be used in a wide range of applications, e.g. file transfer, synchronization, dial-up networking, and payment.**

9. However, IrDA is limited in range (up to about 1 meter). It also requires the communicating devices to be in LOS (Line of Sight) and within its 30-degree beam-cone. Infrared technology used in local networks exists in three different forms:

   • IrDA-SIR (slow speed) infrared supporting data rates up to 115 kbps.

   • IrDA-MIR (medium speed) infrared supporting data rates up to 1.15 Mbps.

- IrDA-FIR (fast speed) infrared supporting data rates up to 4 Mbps.

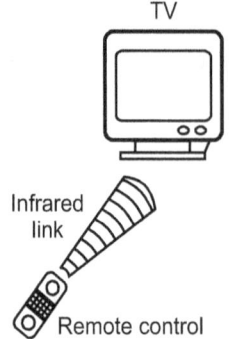

Fig. 3.59: TV Remote Control Uses Infrared

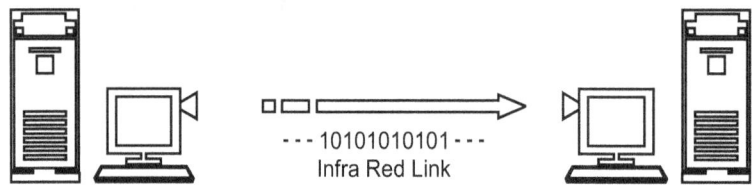

Fig. 3.60: Computer Communication uses Infrared

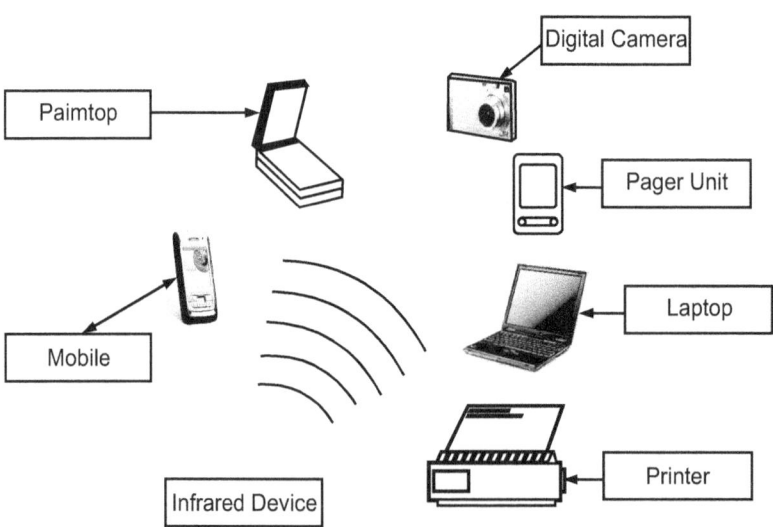

Fig. 3.61: Devices Communicate using Infrared

10. Infrared transmitters are (relatively) directional, cheap, and easy to manufacture. Infrared data and communication is a mode of communication that now plays an important role in wireless data communication. It suits the use of laptop computers, wireless data communication and other digital equipment such as personal assistants, cameras, mobile telephones and pagers.

11. The major drawback is that infrared waves will not pass through solid objects. The communication between the devices requires that each have a transceiver (a combination of a transmitter and a receiver) in order to communicate. This capability is provided by microchip technology. However, devices may also require further, specialized software allowing communication to be synchronized.

12. On the plus side, an infrared system in one room of a building will not interfere with similar systems in nearby rooms, and the possibility of eavesdropping is far lower than with radio-based systems. IR can be used over longer interconnections and has applicability to local area networks (LANs). However, the maximum effective distance is approximately 1 mile, with a maximum bandwidth of 16 Mbps.

13. Infrared is therefore a realistic alternative for indoor wireless LANs, and the computers and offices within a building can be equipped with infrared transmitters and receivers which can be designed to be either directional or *diffuse*.

14. In the latter case, signals bounce off walls and other objects to reach the receiver.

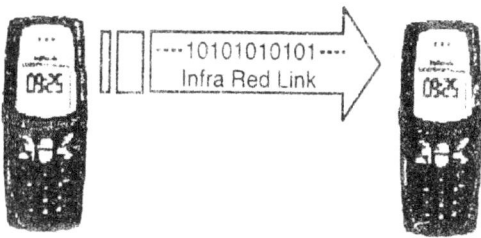

Fig. 3.62: Mobile Handsets Communicate using Infrared

15. As you can see from the two examples infrared communications work by sending and receiving pulses of infrared light.

16. These pulses consist of periods of light and darkness.

17. In the case of a TV or stereo, these pulses are nothing more than recognized patterns.

18. However, in the case of computing devices, the pulses are binary code.

19. When the infrared emitter is on, it is essentially sending a binary one.

20. Likewise, when the infrared emitter is dark, it is considered to be sending a binary zero.

21. This is where the need for infrared-based protocols comes in.

22. The protocol regulates the timing of the infrared signal.

23. It makes sure that the receiving device is checking the on/off status of the emitter at the same frequency the emitter intends.

24. For example, if the emitter sent pulses at 4-millisecond intervals, but the receiver was expecting 2-millisecond pulses, then a single pulse of light could be mistaken for two pulses.

25. The protocols must also negotiate things such as packet length (where one segment of binary code ends and the next one begins).

26. For example, suppose the sender sent the following two packets: 10101100 00110010.

27. Without proper timing, the receiver might pick up part of both packets and think it was a single packet.

28. For example, if the receiver picked up the last four bits of the first packet and the first four bits of the second packet, it would receive the code as 11000011.

29. As you can see, this is much different from the intended message.

30. Infrared transmitters are similar to microwave systems: they use the atmosphere and outer space as transmission media.

31. However, because they transmit light waves rather than radio waves, they require a line-of-sight transmission path.

32. Infrared and laser transmissions are useful for signaling across short distances where it is impractical to lay cable for instance, when networks are at sites a few miles apart.

33. Because infrared signals are in the light spectrum, rain, fog, and other environmental factors can cause transmission problems.

34. Infrared communication is now common as a means of wireless communication between devices. It will not penetrate buildings and therefore is secure.

35. Infrared communication is more secure than other options, such as radio, but it cannot be used outside due to interference by the Sun.

3.14.1 Applications of IR

As mentioned above, the short distance of interconnection drives the main application of this technology between appliances. Thus, according to the IrDA, at present, the main benefits and applications are:

- Sending a document from your notebook computer to a printer.
- Co-ordinating schedules and telephone books between desktop and hand-held (notebook) computers.
- Sending faxes from a hand-held computer, via a public telephone, to a distant fax machine.
- Beaming images from digital cameras to a desktop computer.
- Exchanging messages, business cards, and other information between hand-held personal computers.

For some of these functions, an interconnection between the hand-held or laptop computer and the desktop PC/printer in the form of an IR port, is required. Alternatively an IR adapter can be used.

3.14.2 The Future of IR Technology

1.　Infrared technology claims to be as secure as cable applications.

2.　For example, the access to LANs requires the user to be an authorised user of the network.

3.　Also, it claims to be more reliable than wired technology as it obviates wear and tear on the hardware used.

4.　In the future, it is forecast that this technology will be implemented in copiers, fax machines, overhead projectors, bank ATMs, credit cards, game consoles and headsets.

5.　All of these have local applications and it is really here where this technology is best suited, owing to the inherent difficulties in its technological process for interconnecting over distances.

EXERCISE

1.　Define multiplexing and it's different types.

2.　With a neat diagram explain FDM.

3.　With a neat diagram explain TDM.

4.　List out different　　　applications of FDM.

5.　Write short note on: FDM receiver.

6.　Describe synchronous TDM.

7.　Explain asynchronous TDM.

8.　Compare TDM and FDM.

9.　What is T-carrier system.

10.　Write short notes on:

　　(i)　Time slots

　　(ii)　Frames

　　(iii)　Interleaving

　　(iv)　Bit padding

11.　Explain frame synchronizing.

12.　Describe T-lines.

13.　Explain Digital Subscriber Line (DSL).

14. With neat diagram explain WDM.

15. Classify the different transmission media.

16. Write notes on :

    (a) UTP cable

    (b) STP cable

    (c) Coaxial cable

17. What are the Cat 3, Cat 4, Cat 5, Cat 5e cables?

18. Explain Cat 6 and Cat 7 wires in detail.

19. What is the difference between thin Ethernet cable and thick Ethernet cable ?

20. Draw and explain the construction of fiber cable.

21. Explain the typical fiber optic communication system.

22. Classify the fiber optic cable depending upon material and principle of operation.

23. Explain the advantages and disadvantages of fiber optic cable.

24. Compare Coaxial cable Vs. Fiber optic cable.

25. Draw and explain typical electromagnetic spectrum.

26. What is radio transmission?

27. Explain the concept and types of microwave communication.

28. Write short notes on:

    (a) Infrared transmission

    (b) Terrestrial and satellite microwave transmission.

UNIVERSITY QUESTIONS

NOVEMBER-DECEMBER 2011

1. State types of multiplexing. Explain the types of multiplexing in detail.   **(10)**

2. Explain why fiber optic cable is superior than co-axial cable for long distance communication.   **(10)**

3. Figure shows synchronous TDM with a data stream for each input and one data stream for the output. The unit of data is 1 bit.

    Find: (i) The input bit duration, (ii) The output bit duration, (iii) The output bit rate, (iv) output frame rate.

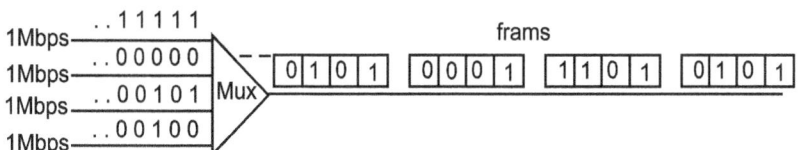

Fig.

MAY-JUNE 2011

4. What is multiplexing? What are the factors on which the choice of multiplexing depends? What are the types of multiplexing?   **(14)**

5. Explain FDM in detail.   **(6)**

6. Write a short note on coaxial and fibre-optical cable.   **(10)**

NOVEMBER-DECEMBER 2010

7. (a) (i) Discuss the need of multiplexing. Explain in detail WDM.   **(6)**

    (ii) Five channels each with 100 kHz bandwidth are to be multiplexing together what is the minimum bandwidth of the link if there is a need for a guard band of 10 kHz between the channel to prevent interference?   **(4)**

    (b) Explain the terms: **(10)**

         (i) DSS

         (ii) Microwave

         (iii) Radiowave

         (iv) Infrared

    (c) Write short notes on: **(10)**

         (i) Fiber optic cable

         (ii) Inverse TDM

         (iii) Co-axial cable

         (iv) Twisted pair.

MAY-JUNE 2010

8. (a) Compare FDM with TDM.   **(5)**

    (b) Explain STDM in short.   **(5)**

9. (a) Compare WDM with TDM.   **(5)**

    (b) Compare radiowave, microwaves and infrared.   **(10)**

NOVEMBER-DECEMBER 2009

10. Explain with neat diagram FDM.   **(10)**

11. Explain the following terms with neat diagram.   **(10)**
    (i)   Time slot and frames
    (ii) Interleaving

12. (a) On which factors the choice of multiplexing depends.   **(5)**
    (b) What are the advantages of coaxial cable over the twisted pair cable.

✳✳✳

Unit IV

SWITCHING AND MULTIPLE ACCESS

4.1 Switching Introduction

1. When multiple devices want to communicate with each other, then the simple solutions are:

- Mesh network formation.
- Bus network formation.

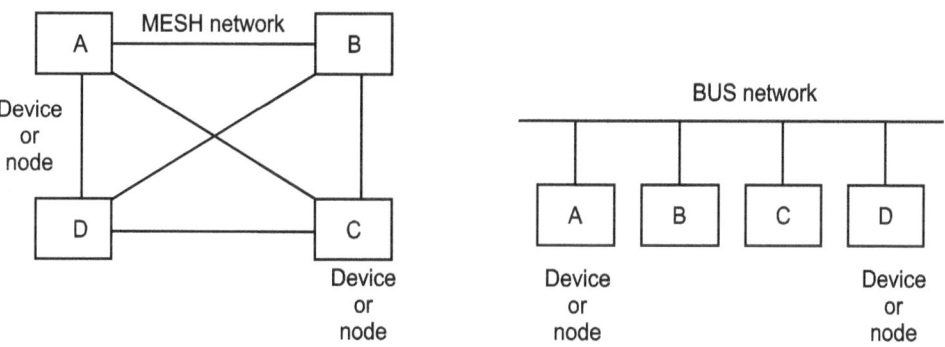

Fig. 4.1: Interdevice communication

2. When the above techniques are employed, it becomes impractical and wasteful when the network size increases.

3. Also network cost and maintenance becomes difficult for large network of devices.

4. Then the solution to the above problems is to use the switching system.

5. Typical use of switch and switching system is as shown in Fig. 4.2.

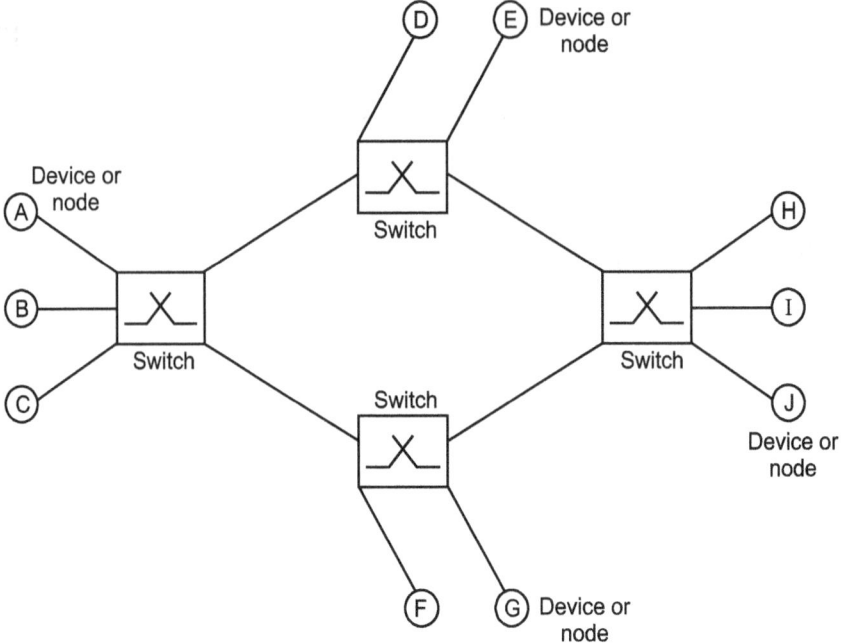

Fig. 4.2: Typical switch based network

6. Thus, different devices/nodes can communicate with each other with the help of switches connected in the typical switch based network.
7. The switches work on the principle of switching system.

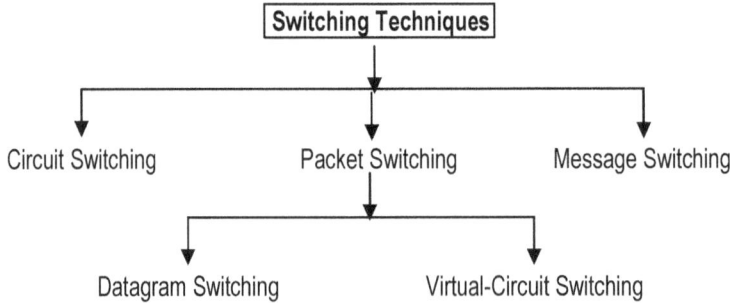

4.2 Circuit Switching Networks

1. In circuit switching networks, nodes or devices are connected to each other by physical links via switches.
2. Typical circuit switched network is as shown in Fig. 4.3.

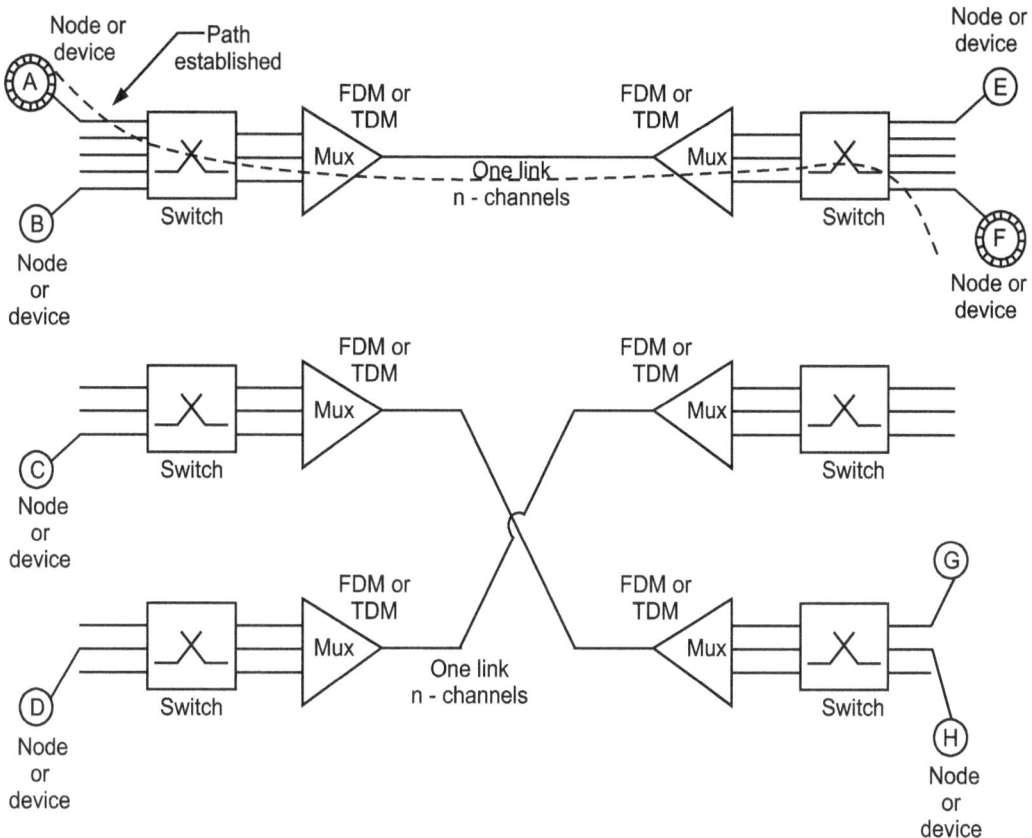

Fig. 4.3: Typical Circuit Switched Network and
Communication between Two End Systems A and F

3. In this diagram, the multiplexer (MUX) symbol is explicitly shown and it is implicitly included in the switch fabric itself.

4. The end system can be a computer node or a device like a telephone set.

5. In Fig. 4.3, the communication between the two end systems A and F is highlighted.

6. In circuit switched network, the communication between node 'A' and node 'F' is done through 3 phases as follows:

    •   **Set-up phase (also known as connection establishment).**

    •   **Data transfer phase.**

    •   **Teardown phase (also known as connection release).**

7. **In set-up phase a dedicated circuit** (i.e. combination of channels in links) needs to be established. For this node 'A' sends set-up request through a switch fabric including a multiplexer, to node 'F'. Then node 'F' receives this request and sends acknowledgement

to node 'A' through the same dedicated path. Thus, only after receiving this acknowledgement from node 'F', we can say that the connection is established or set-up phase is completed. In this circuit switched network, the end systems use addresses in TDM network whereas they use telephone numbers in FDM network.

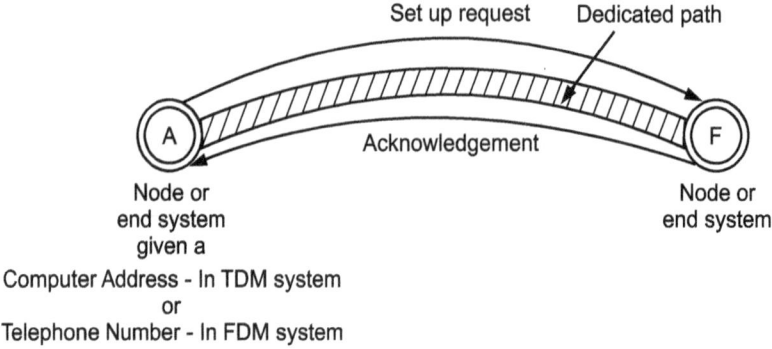

Fig. 4.4: Typical set-up phase between end systems A and F

8. **In data transfer phase**, the end systems 'A' and 'F' can transfer data (or communication between two end systems is done).

9. **In teardown phase (or connection release process)**, either the 'A' system or 'F' system can stop the communication and release the common resources like dedicated link and switch etc.

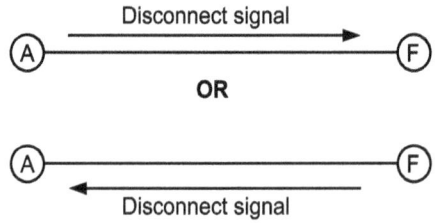

Fig. 4.5: Teardown phase (or connection release process)

10. **The circuit switched network is less efficient as compared to others** because network resources (switch and link) are allocated to 'A' and 'F' node and cannot be used by others or other connections are deprived.

11. The total delay in communication between 'A' and 'F' end systems is given as:

Total delay	=	Connection establishment delay	+	Data transfer delay	+	Connection release delay

12. Data transfer delay is also given as:

Data transfer delay = Propagation time delay + Data transfer time delay

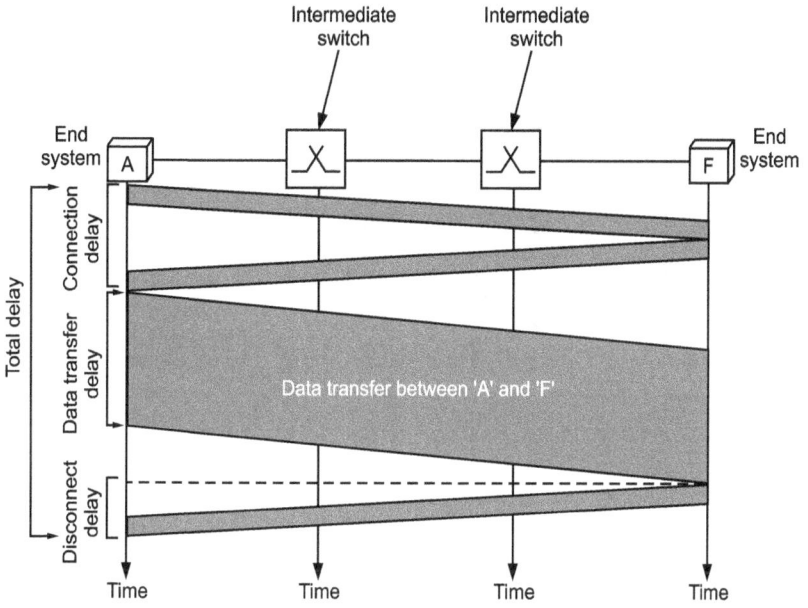

Fig. 4.6: Typical delays in circuit switched network

(Here between two end systems like 'A' and 'F')

13. Thus, typical example or application of a circuit switched network in a telephone communication is as shown in Fig. 4.7.

14. There is a common misunderstanding that circuit switching is used only for connecting voice circuits (analog or digital). The concept of a dedicated path persisting between two communicating parties or nodes can be extended to signal a content other than voice. Its advantage is that it provides for non-stop transfer without requiring packets and without most of the overhead traffic usually needed, making maximal and optimal use of available bandwidth for that communication. The disadvantage of inflexibility tends to reserve it for specialized applications, particularly with the overwhelming proliferation of Internet-related technology.

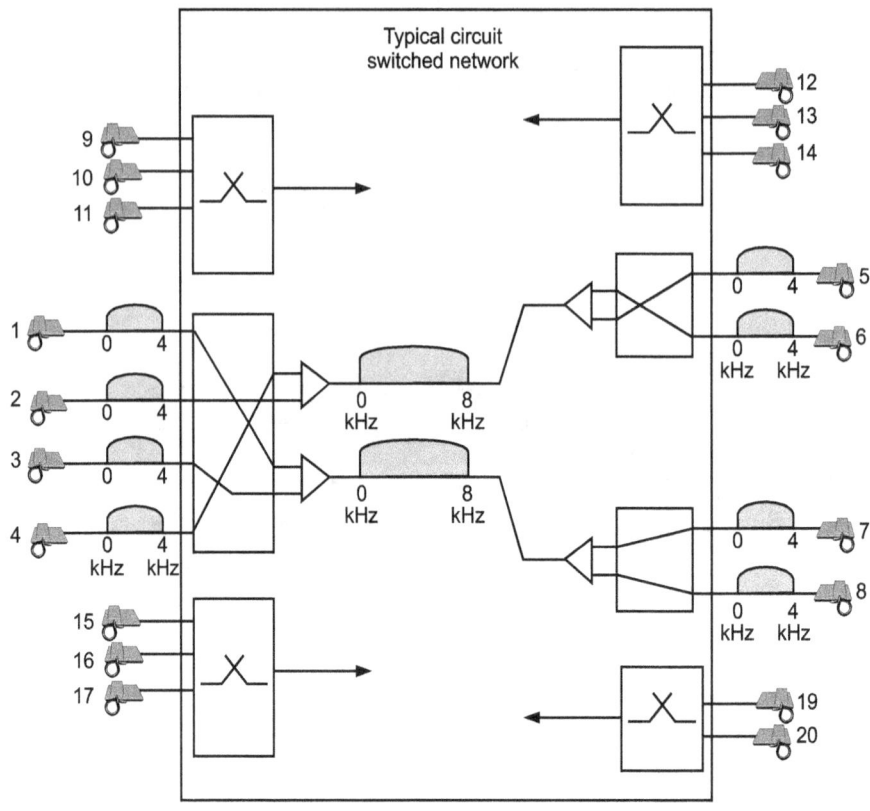

Fig. 4.7: Typical circuit switched network example

15. For call set-up and control (and other administrative purposes), it is possible to use a separate dedicated signaling channel from the end node to the network. **ISDN** is one such service that uses a separate signaling channel while **Plain Old Telephone Service (POTS)** does not.

16. The method of establishing the connection and monitoring its progress and termination through the network may also utilize a separate control channel as in the case of links between telephone exchanges which use SS7 packet-switched signaling protocol to communicate the call set-up and control information and use TDM to transport the actual circuit data. **Signaling System Number** 7 (SS7) is a set of telephony signaling protocols which are used to set-up most of the world's public switched telephone network telephone calls. The main purpose is to set-up and tear down telephone calls.

17. Early telephone exchange is a suitable example of circuit switching. The subscriber would ask the operator to connect to another subscriber, whether on the same exchange or via an inter-exchange link and another operator. In any case, the end result was a physical

electrical connection between the two subscribers telephones for the duration of the call. The copper wire used for the connection could not be used to carry other calls at the same time, even if the subscribers were in fact not talking and the line was silent.

18. Thus, generally, resources are frequency intervals in a **Frequency Division Multiplexing (FDM)** scheme or more recently time slots in a **Time Division Multiplexing (TDM)** scheme.

   - The set of resources allocated for a connection is called a **circuit.**
   - A path is a sequence of links located between nodes called *switches*.
   - The path taken by data between its source and destination is determined by the circuit on which it is flowing and does not change during the lifetime of the connection.
   - The circuit is *terminated* when the connection is closed.

19. In circuit switching, resources remain allocated during the full length of a communication, after a circuit is established and until the circuit is terminated and then the allocated resources are freed.

   - Resources remain allocated even if no data is flowing on a circuit, hereby wasting link capacity when a circuit does not carry as much traffic as the allocation permits.
   - This is a major issue since frequencies (in FDM) or time slots (in TDM) are available in infinite quantity on each link and establishing a circuit consumes one of these frequencies or slots on each link of the circuit.
   - As a result, establishing circuits for communication that carry less traffic than allocation permits can lead to resource exhaustion and network saturation, preventing further connections from being established.
   - If no circuit can be established between a sender and a receiver because of a lack of resources, the connection is *blocked*.

20. A second characteristic of circuit switching is the time cost involved when establishing a connection.

   - In a communication network, circuit-switched or not, nodes need to lookup in a *forwarding table* to determine on which link to send incoming data, and to actually send data from the input link to the output link.
   - Performing a lookup in a forwarding table and sending the data on an incoming link is called *forwarding*.
   - Building the forwarding tables is called *routing*. In circuit switching, routing must be performed for each communication, at circuit establishment time.

- During circuit establishment, the set of switches and links on the path between the sender and the receiver is determined and messages are exchanged on all the links between the two end hosts of the communication in order to make the resource allocation and build the routing tables.
- In circuit switching, forwarding tables are hardwired or implemented using fast hardware, making data forwarding at each switch almost instantaneous.
- Therefore, circuit switching is well suited for long-lasting connections where the initial circuit establishment time cost is balanced by the low forwarding time cost.

21. The circuit identifier (a range of frequencies in FDM or a time slot position in a TDM frame) is changed by each switch at forwarding time so that switches do not need to have a complete knowledge of all circuits established in the network but rather only local knowledge of available identifiers at a link.

- Using local identifiers instead of global identifiers for circuits also enables networks to handle a larger number of circuits.

22. *Traffic Engineering* (TE) consists in optimizing resource utilization in a network by choosing appropriate paths followed by flow of data, according to static or dynamic constraints.

- A main goal of traffic engineering is to balance the load in the network, i.e., to avoid congestion on links on a network while other links are under-utilized.
- To achieve such goals, traffic engineering methods can vary from offline capacity planning algorithms to automatic, dynamic changes.
- Since circuit switching allocates a fixed path for each flow, circuits can be established according to traffic engineering algorithms.

23. On the other hand, circuit switching networks are not reactive when a network topology change occurs.

- For instance, on a link failure, all circuits on a failed link are cut and communication is interrupted.
- Special mechanisms that handle such topological changes have to be devised. Traffic engineering can alleviate the consequences of a link failure by pre-planning failure recovery.
- A back-up circuit can be established at the same time or after the primary circuit used for a communication is set-up, and traffic can be rerouted from the failed circuit to the back-up circuit if a link of the primary circuit fails.
- Circuit switching networks are intrinsically sensitive to link failures and rerouting must be performed by additional traffic engineering mechanisms.

Examples of Circuit Switched Networks

- Public Switched Telephone Network (PSTN).
- ISDN B-channel.
- Circuit Switched Data (CSD) and High-Speed Circuit-Switched Data (HSCSD) service in cellular systems such as GSM.
- Datakit [It supports file transfers, remote login, remote printing, and remote command execution. At the physical layer, it can operate over multiple media, from slow speed EIA-232 to 500 Mbit fiber optic links (called FIBERKIT)].
- X.21 (Used in the German DATEX-L and Scandinavian DATEX circuit switched data network).

4.3 Datagram Switching Networks

1. In packet switching networks, voice, video or data is converted into packet. Packet can be of a fixed size or a variable size, decided by the network used and the protocol used at both ends.
2. In datagram switching, there is no resource allocation for a packet travelling from sender to receiver.
3. This means there is no bandwidth reservation on links and no scheduled processing time for each packet.
4. Thus, resources are allocated on demand and this allocation is done on a first come first serve basis.
5. As a simple analogy consider two hotels (or restaurants). One which requires reservation and another that neither requires reservation nor accepts them.
6. For the hotel (or restaurant) which requires reservation, we have to go through the hassle of calling the person of the restaurant before we leave home and reach to the restaurant.
7. But when we arrive at the restaurant we get the table, can communicate with the waiter and order for food.
8. Thus, for the other restaurant which does not require reservation, we don't need to bother to reserve anything.
9. In this restaurant when we arrive, we may have to wait for a table, we may have to wait for communicating with the waiter to order the food.
10. Thus, the restaurant with reservation and without reservation, this analogy is applicable for circuit switched network and datagram switched network respectively.
11. The typical packet flow in datagram packet switched network is as shown in Fig. 4.8.

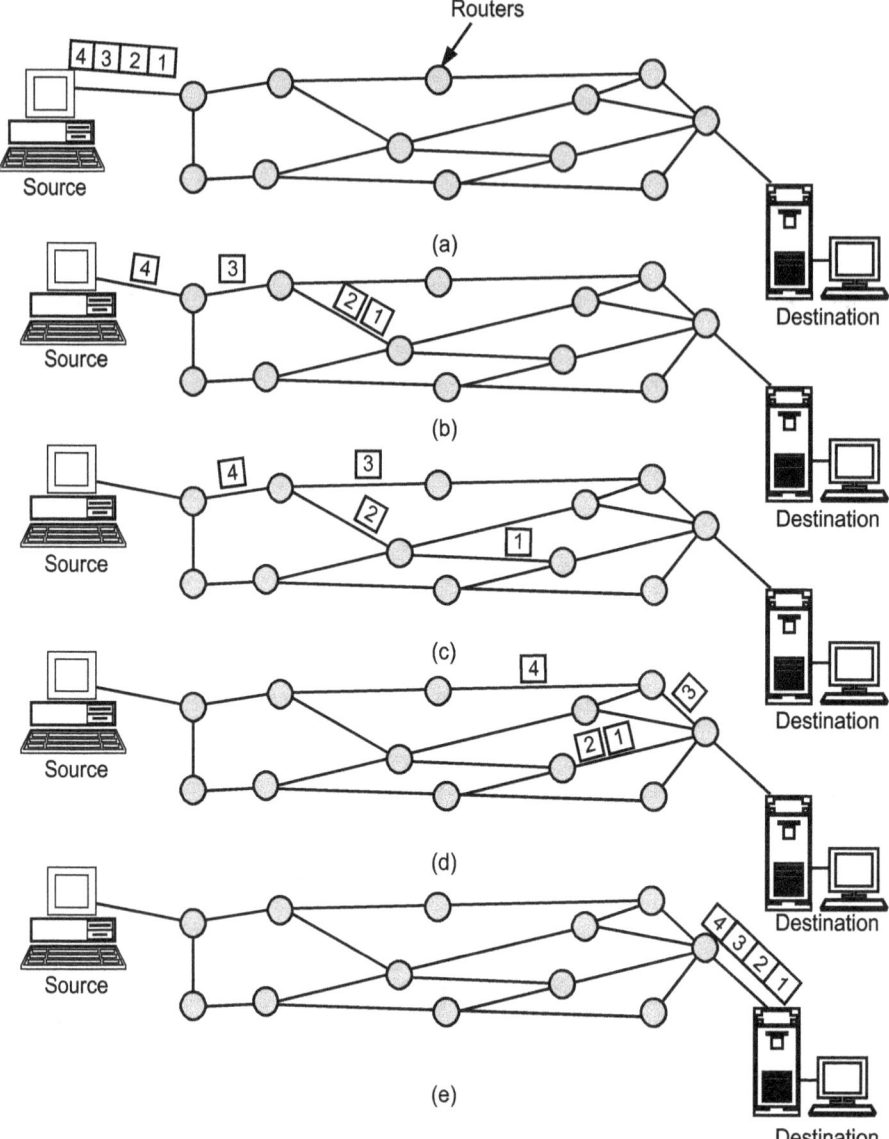

Fig. 4.8: Datagram network packet transfer from source to destination

12. Thus, in datagram packet networks, the following characteristics are important:
    - Each packet is treated independently.
    - Packets can take any practical route.
    - Packets may arrive out of order at destination router.
    - Packets may go missing in the datagram network journey.
    - Receiver at another end is responsible to re-order the packets and recover the missing packets.

- Transport layer at both (sender and receiver) ends is responsible to re-order the packet sequence and recover the missing packets.

13. We have already discussed the connection oriented and connectionless services in first chapter. Datagram based networks are also known as connectionless networks.

14. There is no set-up phase or teardown phase present in datagram switching network. When the data is ready, it is transferred with full source and destination address from sender to receiver. For this, each intermediate router maintains the routing table as shown in Fig. 4.9.

Routing Table maintained by Router Device

Table 4.1

Destination address	Output port
12347	1
34569	2
22130	3
⋮	⋮
⋮	⋮
⋮	⋮
75759	4

Fig. 4.9: Router device uses routing table based on destination address

15. The routing tables are dynamic in nature and are updated periodically. (Specific time is set by router administrator).

16. The destination address is carried by the header among other information (or control information) of packet. This address remains same during the entire journey of the packet from the source to the destination or the sender to the receiver.

17. Efficiency of datagram switch network is better than circuit switched network, because network resources are allocated only when there are packets to be transferred from source to destination.

18. If the source to the destination packet transfer is finished or delayed, then these resources can be used by other nodes or systems connected to this network.

19. The delay between sender and receiver is given by,

Total delay (T_D)	=	Transmission delay (T_t)	+	Propagation delay (T_p)	+	Waiting delay (T_w)

20. Typical datagram based packet switching network uses two routers in between the sender and the receiver as shown in Fig. 4.10.

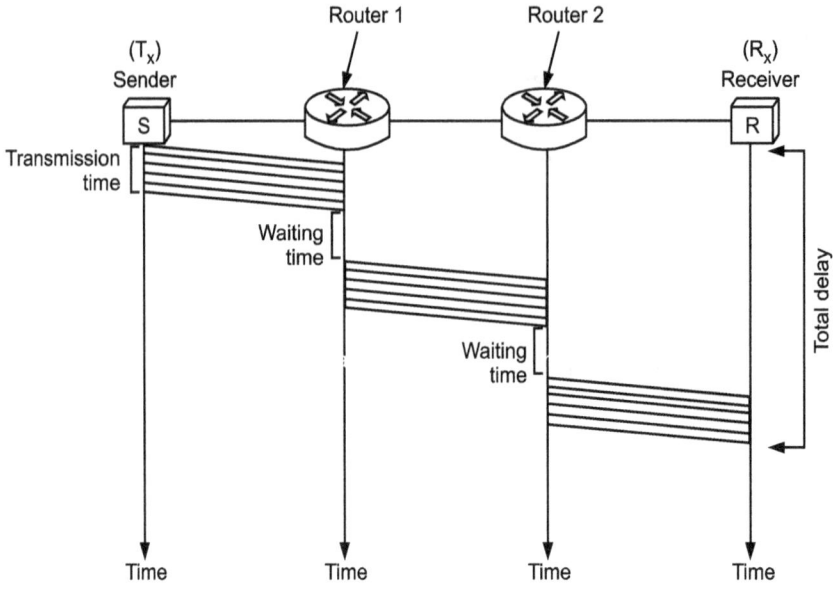

Fig. 4.10: Delay present in datagram network

21. Thus, total delay in the above typical datagram network is given as,

$$T_D = 3T_t + 3T_p + T_{w1} + T_{w2}$$

Where,

$3T_t$ = Three transmission times available (hence $3T_t$)

$3T_p$ = Three propagation delays available (hence $3T_p$)

$\left.\begin{array}{c} T_{w1} \\ T_{w2} \end{array}\right\}$ = Two waiting time delays available (hence T_{w1} and T_{w2})

22. The best example of datagram network is Internet or TCP/IP protocol based LAN or Internet communication.

23. Thus, a routing table contains a mapping between the possible final destination of packets and the outgoing link on their path to the destination.

   - Routing tables can be very large because they are indexed by possible destinations, making lookups and routing decisions computationally expensive and the full forwarding process relatively slow compared to circuit switching.

   - In datagram packet switching networks, each packet must carry the address of the destination host and use the destination address to make a forwarding decision.

- Consequently, routers do not need to modify the destination addresses of packets when forwarding packets.

24. Since each packet is processed individually by a router, all packets sent by a host to another host are not guaranteed to use the same physical links.

   - If the routing algorithm decides to change the routing tables of the network between the instants two packets are sent, then these packets will take different paths and can even arrive out of order.

25. Second, on a network topology change such as a link failure, the routing protocol will automatically recompute routing tables so as to take the new topology into account and avoid the failed link.

   - As opposed to circuit switching, no additional traffic engineering algorithm is required to reroute traffic.

   - Since routers make routing decisions locally for each packet, independent of the flow to which a packet belongs.

   - Therefore, traffic engineering techniques, which heavily rely on controlling the route of traffic, are more difficult to implement with datagram packet switching than with circuit switching.

26. There are three primary types of datagram packet switches:

   - **Store and forward:** Buffers data until the entire packet is received and checked for errors. This prevents corrupted packets from propagating throughout the network but increases switching delay.

   - **Fragment free:** Filters out most error packets but doesn't necessarily prevent the propagation of errors throughout the network. It offers faster switching speeds and lower delay than store-and-forward mode.

   - **Cut through:** Does not filter errors, it switches packets at the highest throughput, offering the least forwarding delay.

27. A datagram network is a best effort network. Delivery is not guaranteed. Reliable delivery must be provided by the end systems (i.e. user's computers) using additional protocols.

28. The most common datagram network is the Internet, which uses the IP network protocol.

   - Applications which do not require more than a best effort service can be supported by direct use of packets in a datagram network, using the User **Datagram Protocol (UDP)** transport protocol.

   - Applications like voice and video communications and notifying messages to alert a user that she/he has received new email are using UDP.

- Applications like e-mail, web browsing and file upload and download need reliable communications, such as guaranteed delivery, error control and sequence control.
- This reliability ensures that all the data is received in the correct order without errors.
- It is provided by a protocol such as the **Transmission Control Protocol (TCP)** or the **File Transfer Protocol (FTP)**.

4.4 Virtual Circuit Networks (VC Networks)

1. Virtual circuit network is another type of packet switched network.
2. Virtual circuit network is a cross between datagram switching network and circuit switching network. It has characteristics of both the networks.

Table 4.2

Characteristics of a Circuit Switched Network	Characteristics of a Datagram Network

1. It has three phases like:
  • Set-up phase (connection establishment).
  • Data transfer.
  • Teardown phase (connection release).
2. Resources can be allocated during the set-up phase or connection establishment phase.
3. All packets follow the same path established during set-up phase or connection establishment phase.
	1. Resource allocation can be on demand in VC networks.
	2. In datagram packet header, destination IP addresses are mentioned, whereas in VC packet header next switch VCI (Virtual Circuit Identifier) number is mentioned.

In today's technology • Circuit switched network is implemented in the physical layer. • Datagram switched network is implemented in the network layer. • VC switched network is implemented in the data link layer.	

3. In VC switched networks, two types of addressing used are as follows:

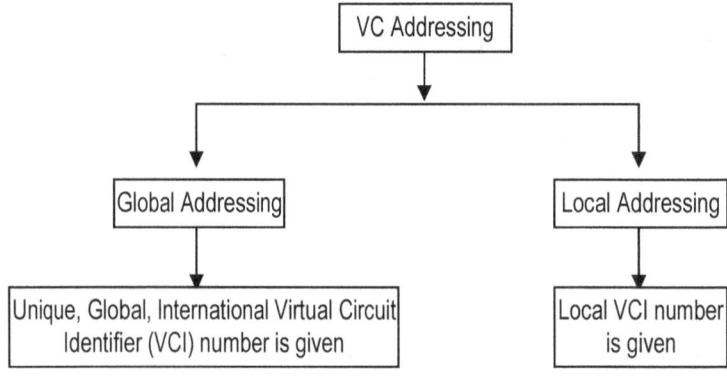

Virtual Circuit Packet Network

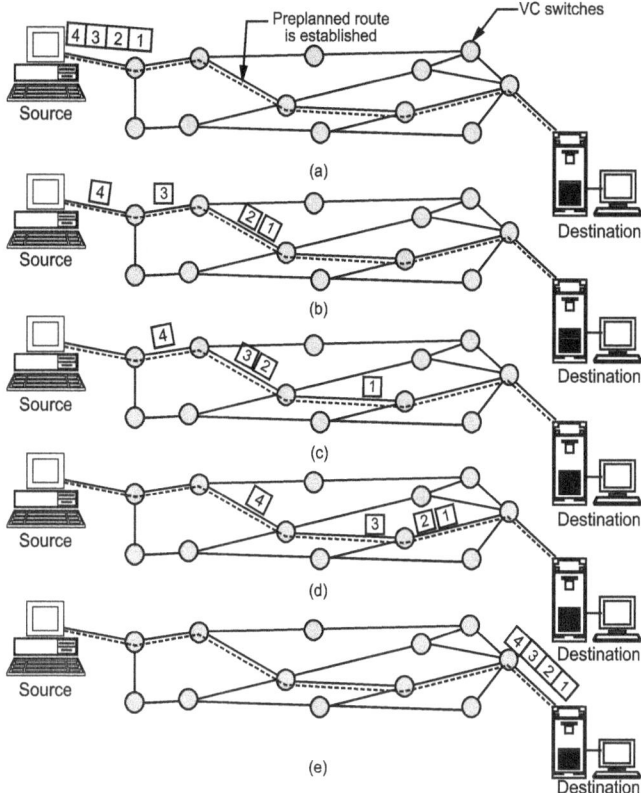

Fig. 4.11 (a): Packet flow in a typical virtual circuit packet switched network

4. Typical VC switched network is as shown in Fig. 4.11 (b).

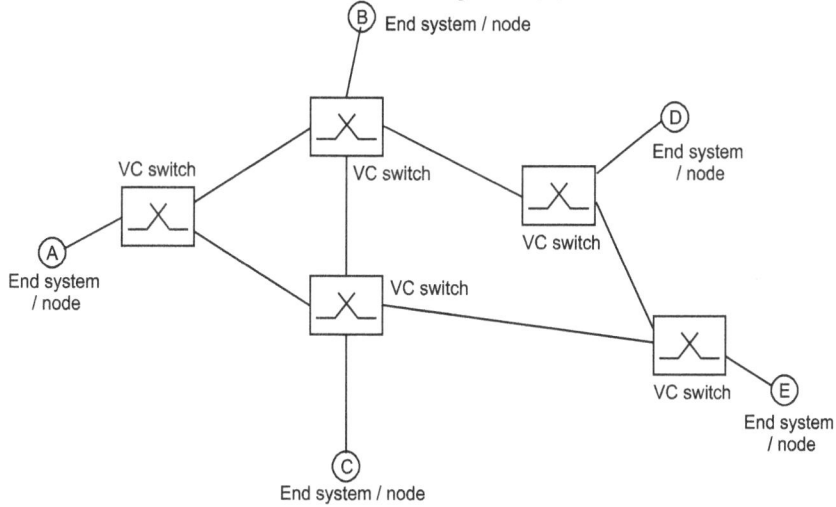

Fig. 4.11 (b): Typical VC switched network

5. **Virtual Circuit Identifier (VCI)** is used for data transfer from one end to another.

6. VCI is used by frames between two VC switches. When the frame arrives at one VC switch, it has a VCI, when it leaves it has a different VCI.

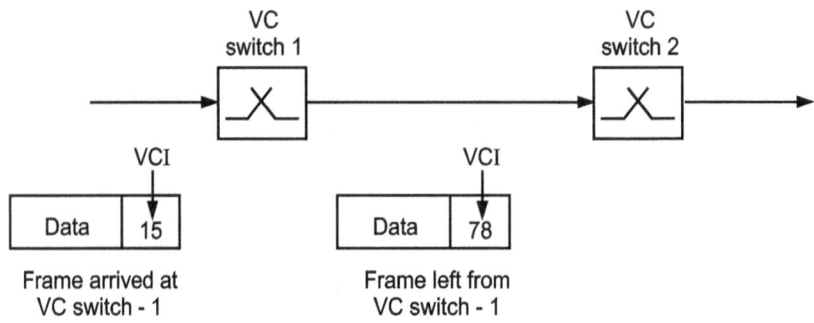

Fig. 4.12: VC Switch decides VCI number of frames

7. The VC switched network uses three steps for communication:

   • Set-up phase (connection establishment phase).

   • Data transfer phase.

   • Teardown phase (connection release phase).

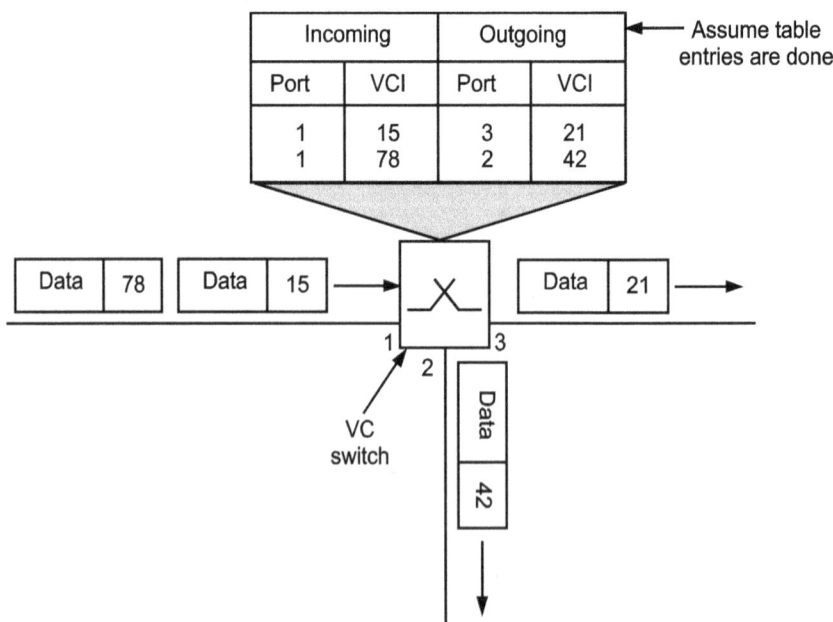

(a) Switching Table maintained by Typical VC Switch

(Assume that entries are done initially)

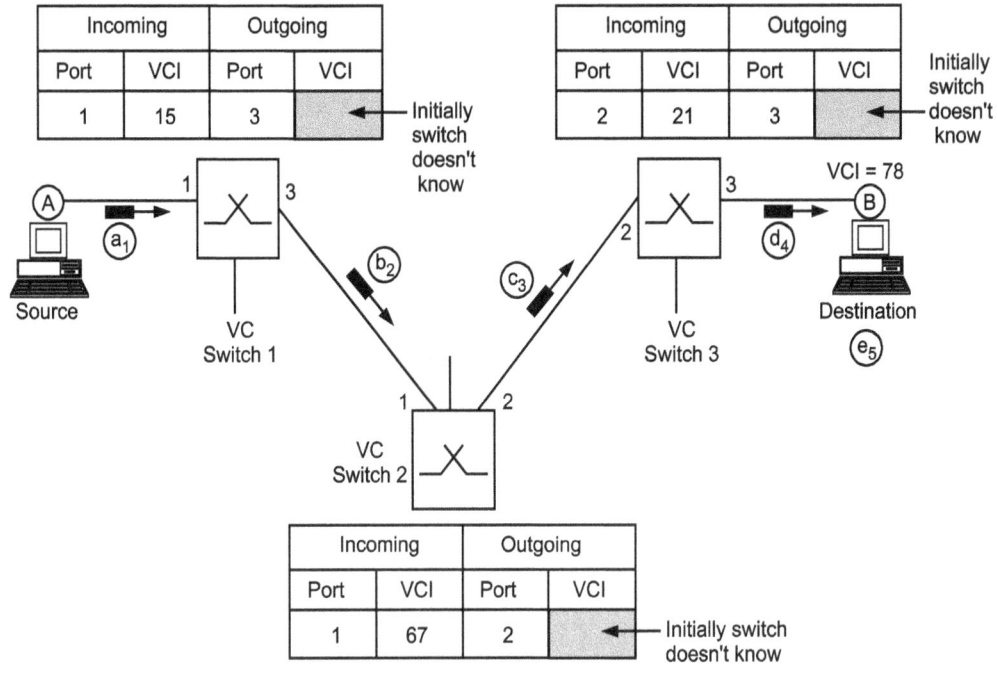

(b) Set-up request process from source 'A' to destination 'B'

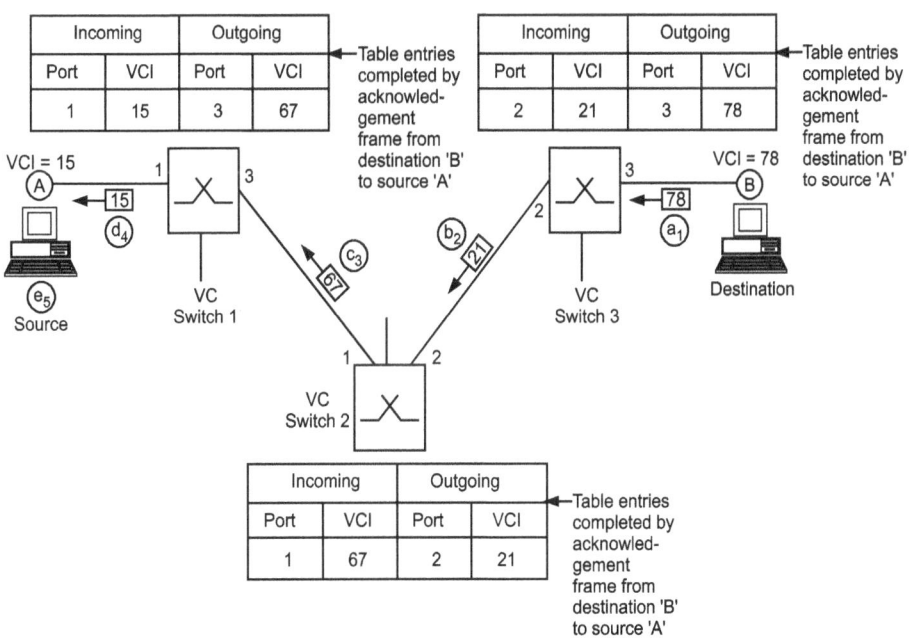

(c) Set-up acknowledgement process from destination 'B' to source 'A'

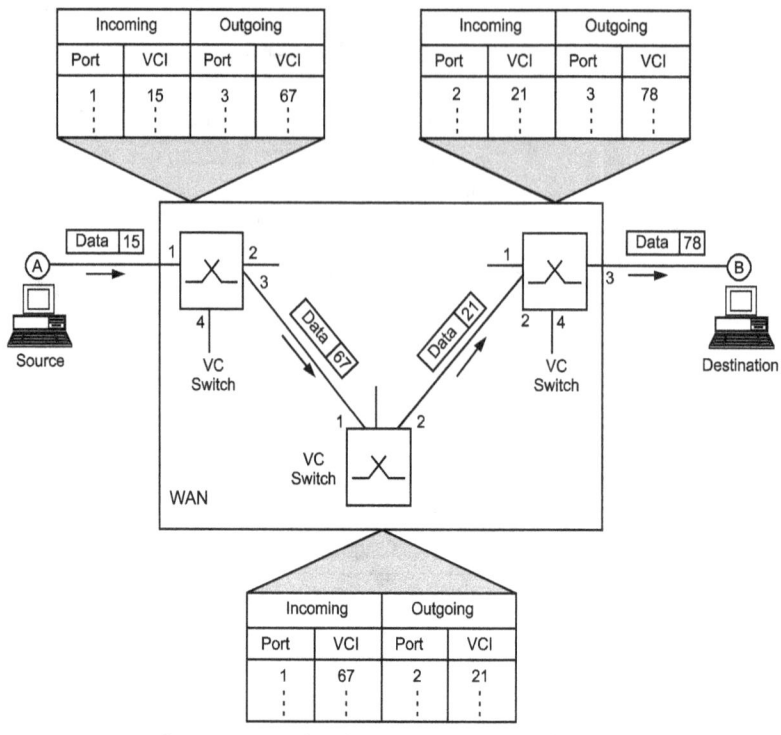

(d) Source to destination data transfer from

'A' to 'B' end system according to updated table entries

Fig. 4.13: Communication between Source 'A' and Destination 'B' in VC Switched Network

8. **Thus, Fig. 4.13 (a) says:**

When incoming frame 1 with VCI = 15 and frame 2 with VCI = 78 arrives to VC switch, depending upon switching table entries mentioned, frame 1-VCI is changed from 15 → 21 and sent on port 3. Also frame 2-VCI is changed from 78 → 42 and sent on port 2.

9. **Fig. 4.13 (b) says:**

 - Set-up request process from source 'A' to destination 'B'.
 - It clearly shows random incoming VCI number and undefined outgoing VCI numbers.
 - Set-up request starts from source 'A' → VC switch 1 → VC switch 2 → VC switch 3 → destination 'B'.

10. **Fig. 4.13 (c) says:**

 - Special acknowledgement frame is sent from destination 'B' to source 'A'.
 - This special acknowledgement frame completes the table entries like:

VC switch 3 →   Outgoing VCI = 78

                   Incoming VCI = 21

VC switch 2 → Outgoing VCI = 21

Incoming VCI = 67

VC switch 1 → Outgoing VCI = 67

Incoming VCI = 15

- Thus, source 'A' gets the VCI = 15 as source frame VCI number and hence source 'A' sends frame like | Data | 15 | to immediate VC switch 1 in data transfer phase.

11. **Thus, Fig. 4.13 (d) says:**

- Once table entries are confirmed the first frame generated from source 'A' is | Data | 15 | with VCI = 15.
- Thus, data transfer takes place from source 'A' → VC switch 1 → VC switch 2 → VC switch 3 → destination 'B'.

12. Hence, Fig. 4.13 shows communication between source 'A' and destination 'B' in VC switched network.

Where, set-up phase request process is given by Fig. 4.13 (b).

Set-up phase acknowledgement process is given by Fig. 4.13 (c).

Data transfer between 'A' and 'B' is given by Fig. 4.13 (d).

13. Finally, when the data transfer is completed between 'A' and 'B' systems, then the remaining process is teardown process or connection release process. In this process or in this phase source 'A' sends a special frame called a teardown request to destination 'B'. Destination 'B' also responds with teardown confirmation frame and sends to source 'A'. Thus, all corresponding switching table entries are deleted from VC switches.

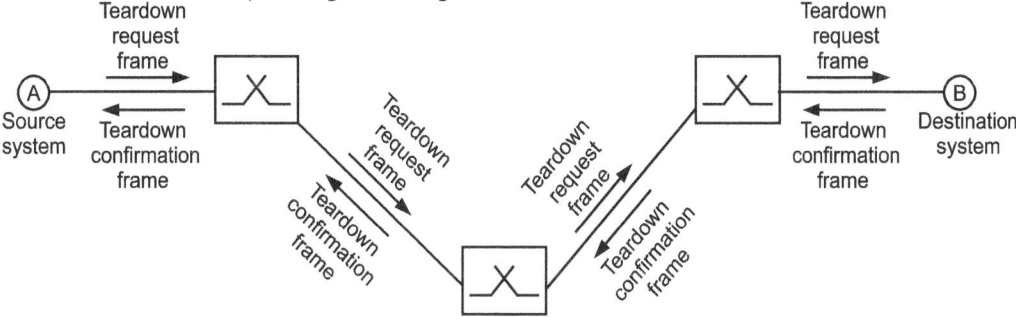

Fig. 4.14: Typical teardown request and confirmation set-up between source 'A' and destination 'B' after data transfer is over

14. Thus, the efficiency of the VC switched network is greater as compared to circuit switched network and datagram switched network.

15. This happens because the main advantage of VC switched network is even if resource allocation is on demand; the source can check availability of the resources without actually reserving it.

16. Thus, though the path between source 'A' and destination 'B' is same, packets may arrive at the destination with different delays if resource allocation is done on demand as we discussed.

17. The total delay in communication between source 'A' and destination 'B' is given by:

Total delay = Transmission delay + Propagation delay + Set-up delay + Teardown delay

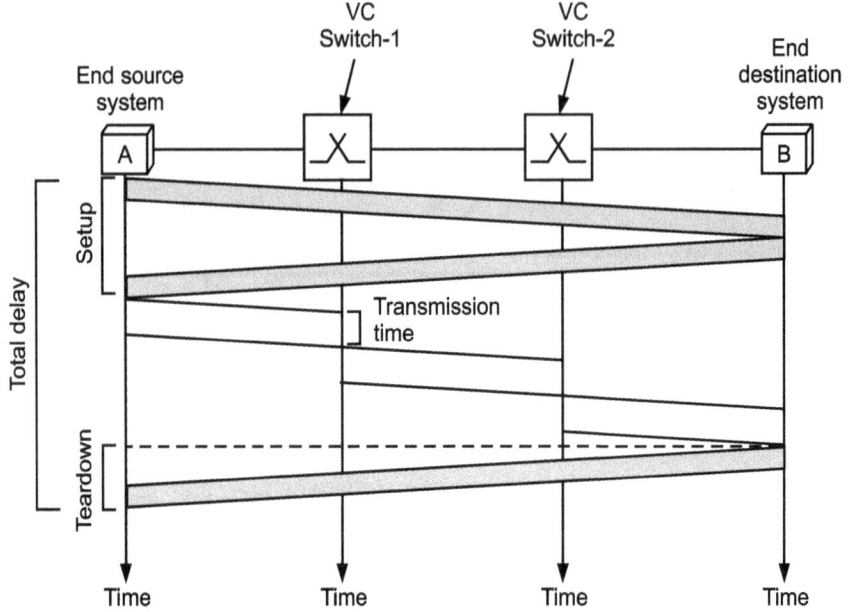

Fig. 4.15: Delay present in VC switched network

18. Thus, total delay in above typical VC switched network is given as,

$T_D = 3T_t + 3T_p$ + Set-up delay + Teardown delay

19. Where,

$$3T_t \;=\; \text{Three transmission times available (hence } 3T_t)$$
$$3T_p \;=\; \text{Three propagation delays available (hence } 3T_p)$$

Set-up delay consists of request + Acknowledged process delay.

Teardown delay consists of request + Acknowledged process delay.

20. Following are the typical VC switched networks:
    - X.25 VC switched networks.
    - Frame relay VC switched networks.
    - ATM (Asynchronous Transfer Mode) networks.
    - MPLS (Multiprotocol Label Switching) networks.

4.4.1 Concept of Virtual Circuit

1. A *virtual circuit* is a logical connection created to ensure reliable communication between two network devices.

2. A virtual circuit denotes the existence of a logical, bidirectional path from the sender device to another receiver device across a VC switched network.

3. Physically, the connection can pass through any number of intermediate nodes, such as VC switches.

4. Multiple virtual circuits (logical connections) can be multiplexed onto a single physical circuit (a physical connection).

5. Virtual circuits are demultiplexed at the remote end and data is sent to the appropriate destinations. Fig. 4.16 illustrates four separate virtual circuits being multiplexed onto a single physical circuit.

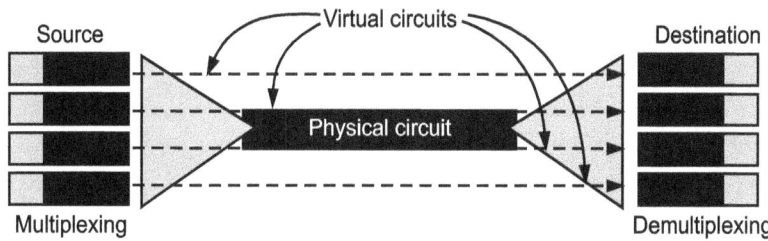

Fig. 4.16: Virtual circuits and physical circuit between source and destination

6. Thus, we have seen the trade-off between connection establishment and forwarding time costs that exist in circuit switching and datagram packet switching.

7. In VC switching, routing is performed at circuit establishment time to keep fast packet forwarding.

8. Other advantages of VC switching include the traffic engineering capability of circuit switching, and the resources usage efficiency of datagram packet switching.

9. Nevertheless, a main issue of VC switched networks is the behavior on a topology change.

10. As opposed to datagram packet switched networks which automatically recompute routing tables on a topology change like a link failure, in VC switching all virtual circuits that pass through a failed link are interrupted.

11. Hence, rerouting in VC switching relies on traffic engineering techniques.

4.4.2 Types of Virtual Circuits

1. Switched Virtual Circuits (Physical connection is always present temporary logical connection is to be established every time for the data transfer) *Switched Virtual Circuits* (SVCs) are temporary connections used in situations requiring only sporadic data transfer between DTE devices across the Frame Relay network.

2. Permanent Virtual Circuits (Physical connection is always present and permanent logical connection is already established so that any time data can be transferred) Permanent Virtual Circuits (PVCs) are permanently established connections that are used for frequent and consistent data transfers between DTE devices across the network. Communication across a PVC does not require the call set-up and termination states that are used with SVCs. PVCs do not require that sessions be established and terminated. Therefore, DTEs can begin transferring data whenever necessary because the session is always active.

4.4.3 Typical Applications of VC Switched Networks

- File Transfer:
    - Character-interactive traffic (For example, text editing).
    - High Resolution graphics.
- Access to Internet and Intranet.
- Multimedia, Real Time Voice, Video, Fax.
- LAN Peer-to-Peer, WAN Interconnection.
- Multi-protocol networking applications.
    - ATM, SNA, TCP/IP.
- Private backbone networks.

4.5 Comparison of Different Switching Techniques

1. Now, we have seen the following switching techniques in detail.
    - Circuit switching.
    - Datagram switching.
    - Virtual circuit switching.
2. Let's compare the following:
    - Circuit switching Vs. Packet switching.
    - Datagram switching Vs. Virtual circuit switching.
    - Circuit switching Vs. Datagram switching Vs. VC switching Vs. Message switching.

4.5.1 Circuit Switching Vs. Packet Switching

Table 4.3

Parameter	Circuit Switched	Packet Switched
Call set-up requirement	Required	Not required
Dedicated physical path requirement	Yes, it is required	No, it is not required
Whether each packet follows the same path (route)	Yes, it follows the same path (route)	No, it does not follow the same path (route)
Bandwidth Available for Transmission	It is fixed	It is dynamic
Congestion can occur at	Set-up time	On every packet
Bandwidth Wastage	Yes	No
Store and Forward transmission	Not available	Yes, it is available
Transparency in System	Yes, it is present	Not present
Charge applied	Per unit time	Per unit packet

4.5.2 Datagram (DG) Vs. Virtual Circuit (VC) Switching

Table 4.4

Parameter	Datagram (DG) Network	Virtual Circuit (VC) Network
Requirement of Circuit Set-up	Requirement of circuit set-up is not needed.	Requirement of circuit set-up is needed.
Routing of Packet	Each packet is routed independently.	Route is chosen when VC set-up is over and all packet follows the same
Router failure	None.	Less probability
If router fails	Packets are lost during the crash.	All VCs that passed through the failed router are terminated
Achievement of Quality of service	It is difficult here.	It is easy if enough resources can be allocated in advance for each VC
Congestion control	It is difficult over here.	It is easy if enough resources can be allocated in advance for each VC
Examples of network	TCP/IP internet network.	X.25, Frame Relay and ATM networks

4.5.3 Summary of Circuit Switched/Message Switched/ DG Packet Switched / VC Packet Switched

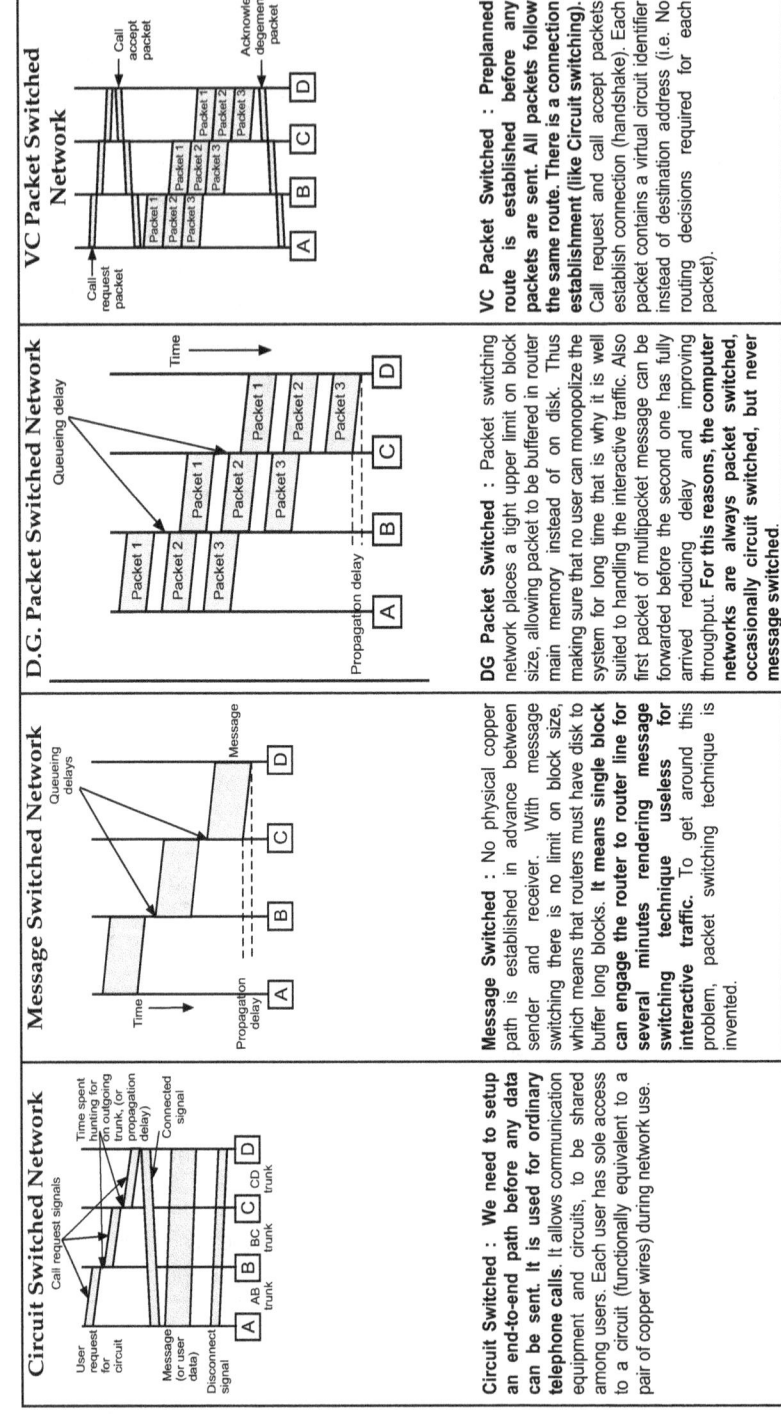

Circuit Switched : We need to setup an end-to-end path before any data can be sent. It is used for ordinary telephone calls. It allows communication equipment and circuits, to be shared among users. Each user has sole access to a circuit (functionally equivalent to a pair of copper wires) during network use.

Message Switched : No physical copper path is established in advance between sender and receiver. With message switching there is no limit on block size, which means that routers must have disk to buffer long blocks. It means single block can engage the router to router line for several minutes rendering message switching technique useless for interactive traffic. To get around this problem, packet switching technique is invented.

DG Packet Switched : Packet switching network places a tight upper limit on block size, allowing packet to be buffered in router main memory instead of on disk. Thus making sure that no user can monopolize the system for long time that is why it is well suited to handling the interactive traffic. Also first packet of multipacket message can be forwarded before the second one has fully arrived reducing delay and improving throughput. For this reasons, the computer networks are always packet switched, occasionally circuit switched, but never message switched.

VC Packet Switched : Preplanned route is established before any packets are sent. All packets follow the same route. There is a connection establishment (like Circuit switching). Call request and call accept packets establish connection (handshake). Each packet contains a virtual circuit identifier instead of destination address (i.e. No routing decisions required for each packet).

4.6 Structure of Different Switches

1.   Typical switches classification is as given below.

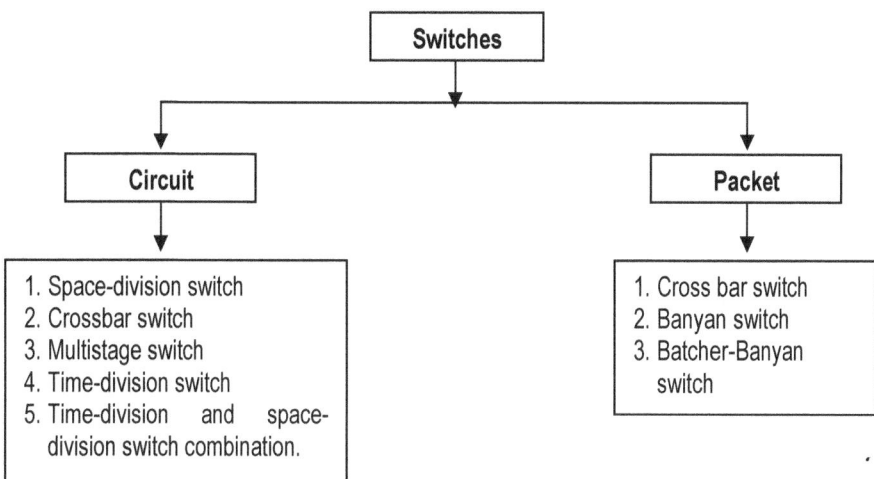

2.   Thus, circuit switching application uses the following switches as switching fabrics in their device architecture:
   •   Space-division switch.
   •   Crossbar switch.
   •   Multistage switch.
   •   Time-division switch.
   •   Time-division and space-division switch combination.
3.   The packet switching application uses the following switches as switching fabrics in their device architecture:
   •   Crossbar switch.
   •   Banyan switch.
   •   Batcher-Banyan switch.

4.7 Circuit Switches

1.   We have already classified the types of switches like:
   •   Circuit switches.
   •   Packet switches.
2.   Basically, there are two major types of switching used in telecommunication networks:
   •   Circuit switching.
   •   Packet switching.
3.   Basically the circuit switching is

- Developed for voice.
- Used nowadays also for data.
- Has well-specified delays.
- Faces echo problems.
- Uses TDM and FDM multiplexing.

4. The circuit switching is used in PSTN, ISDN and PCM networks.

5. In the circuit switching, following types of switches are used:

- Space-division switches
- Time-division switches
- Combination of both

6. Basically, the packet switching is

- Developed for data
- Used nowadays also for voice
- Faces traditionally variable delays
- Uses statistical multiplexing

7. Packet switching is used in IP (connectionless service), Frame relay (connection oriented service), ATM (connection oriented service), MPLS (connection oriented service) and X.25 (connectionless and connection oriented service) networks.

8. In the packet switching, following types of switches are used:

- Banyan switches
- Batcher-Banyan switches

9. We are interested in circuit switching and circuit switches now.

10. Hardware and/or software devices allowing temporary connections between two or more devices are known as switches.

11. Basic circuit switch device is as shown in Fig. 4.17.

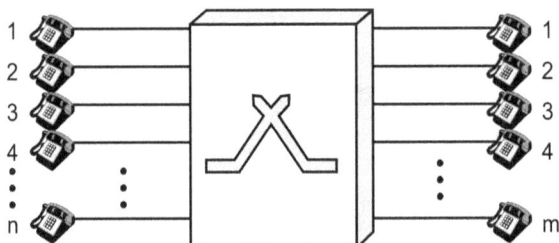

Fig. 4.17: Basic Circuit Switch Device

12. Basic circuit switch device contains:

- n inputs and m outputs; these do not have to be equal.
- These inputs and outputs create a temporary connection between an input link and output link.

13. Another circuit switch known as folded switch is shown in Fig. 4.18.

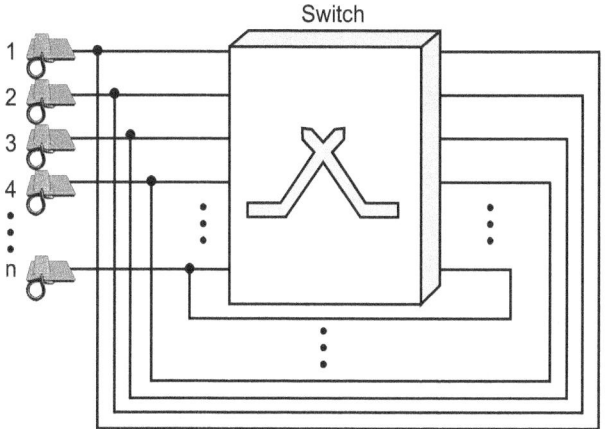

Fig. 4.18: An n-by-n Folded Switch allows every device to connect to every other device in Full-Duplex Mode

4.8 Space-Division switches and Switching

- In space-division switching paths between devices are separated from each other spatially.
- Space-division switching was originally used in analog networks; now it is used in both digital and analog networks.
- Crossbar switches and multistage switches are commonly used in space-division switching.

4.8.1 Crossbar Switches

1. Typical crossbar switch structure is as shown in Fig. 4.18.

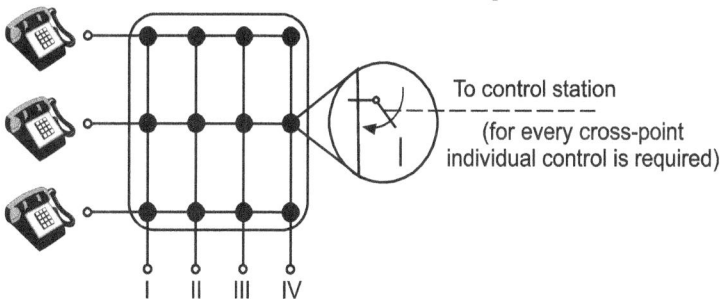

Fig. 4.19: Typical Crossbar Switch

2. Crossbar switch connects n inputs to m outputs in a grid using transistors at each crosspoint.

3.   Crossbar switch requires a significant number of crosspoints (for example   1000 inputs and 1000 outputs require the switch with 1000000 crosspoints), and crossbar with such number of crosspoints are not possible practically.

4.   Crossbar switch is inefficient; statistics says fewer than 25% of switches are in used at a given time and rest are idle.

4.8.2 Multistage Switches

1.   Typical multistage switch structure is as shown in Fig. 4.20.
2.   Multistage switch reduces the number of crosspoints in switch.
3.   Multistage switch combines crossbar switches in several stages.
4.   Multistage switch devices are linked to switches that are linked to a hierarchy of other switches.
5.   Middle stages of multistage switch usually have fewer switches than first and last stages.
6.   In multistage switch, crosspoints are fewer but still allowing multiple paths through the network which increases reliability.

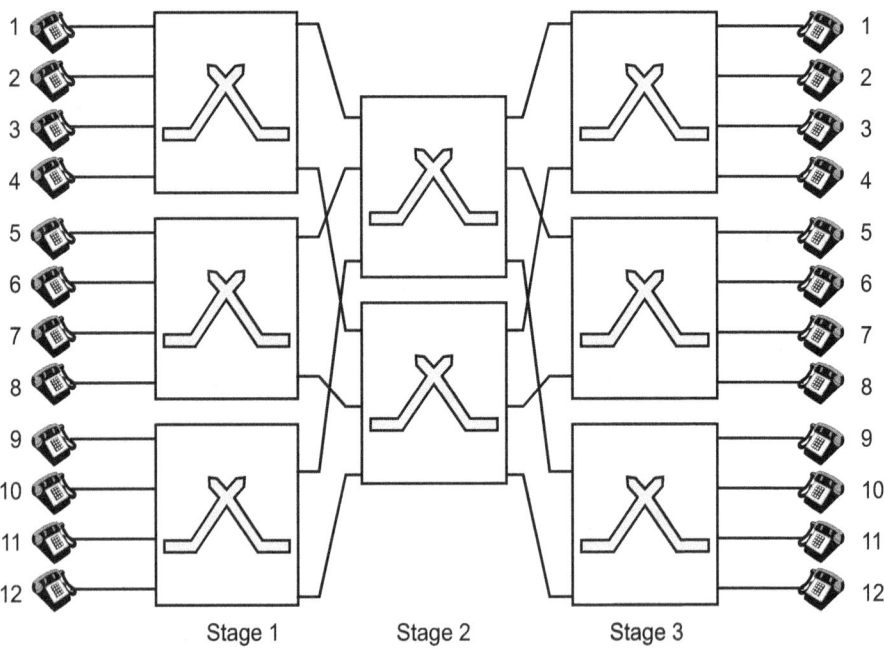

Fig. 4.20: Typical Multistage Switch Structure

7.   Multiple paths are established using multistage switch as shown in Fig. 4.21

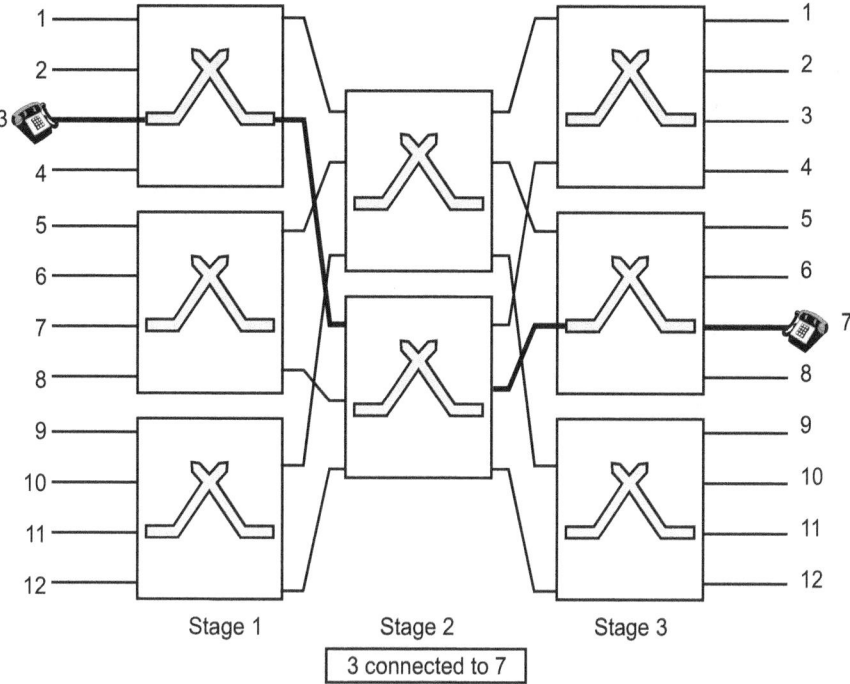

3 connected to 7

Fig. 4.21: Multiple Paths are established using Multistage Switch

8. Here in multistage switch, the concept of blocking is very important.

9. Reduced number of crosspoints may mean that at times of heavy traffic, an input may not be able to connect to an output if there is no path available (i.e. all switches are occupied).

10. Blocking does not occur in single-stage switch; a non-blocking path is always available.

4.9 Time-Division Switches and Switching

1. Time-division switches and switching uses time-division multiplexing to achieve switching.

2. There are two methods used in time-division switches and switching:
    *   Time-slot interchange
    *   TDM bus

3. Most modern switches use digital time-division techniques for establishing and maintaining circuits.

4. TD switching involves partitioning low speed bit stream into pieces that share higher speed stream.

5. TDM bus switching
   - Based on synchronous time division multiplexing (TDM).
   - Each station connects to high speed bus through controlled gates.
   - Time slot allows small amount of data onto bus.
   - Another line's gate is enabled for output at the same time.

4.9.1 Time Slot Interchanging (TSI)

1. Time division switching uses the time division multiplexing inside the switch. The most popular and widely used technology is known as **Time Slot Interchanging** (TSI).

2. Consider that the four equipments want to communicate with other four equipments using TSI method as shown in Fig. 4.22.

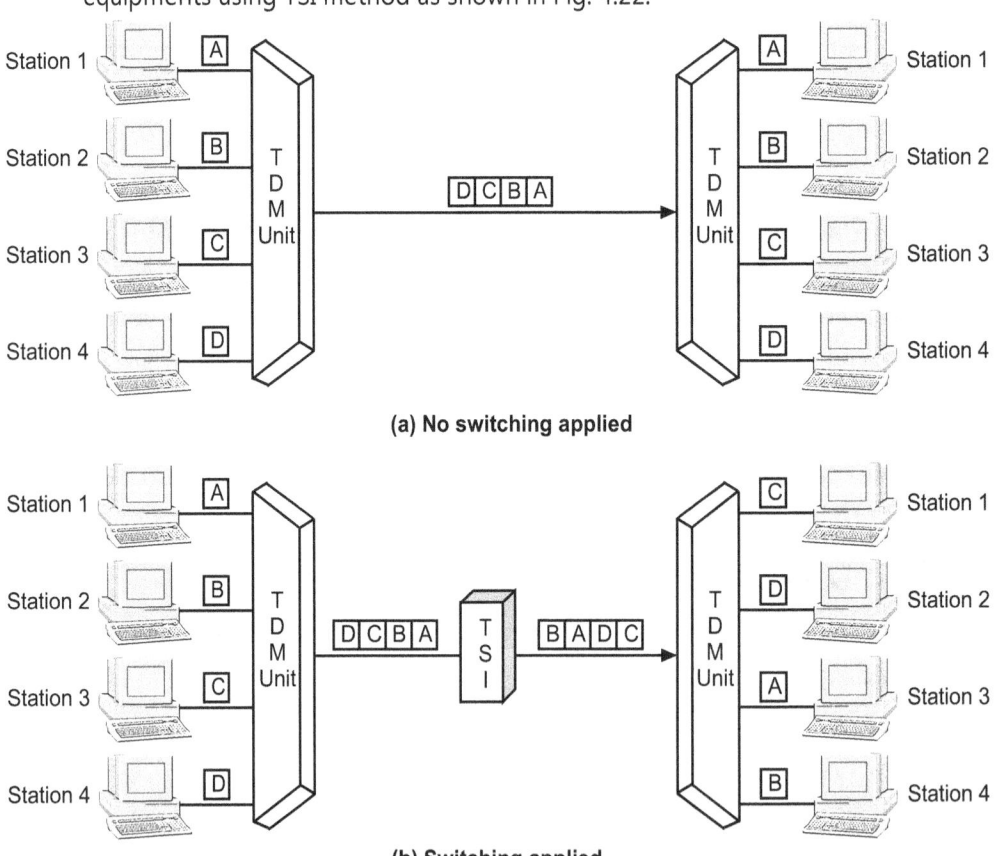

Fig. 4.22: Device which changes Ordering of
Slots based on Desired Connections

3. TSI system consists of RAM with several memory locations.

4. TSI system fills up with incoming data from time slots in order received.

5. In TSI system, slots are sent out in order based on control unit logic.

6. The TSI system is as shown in Fig. 4.23.

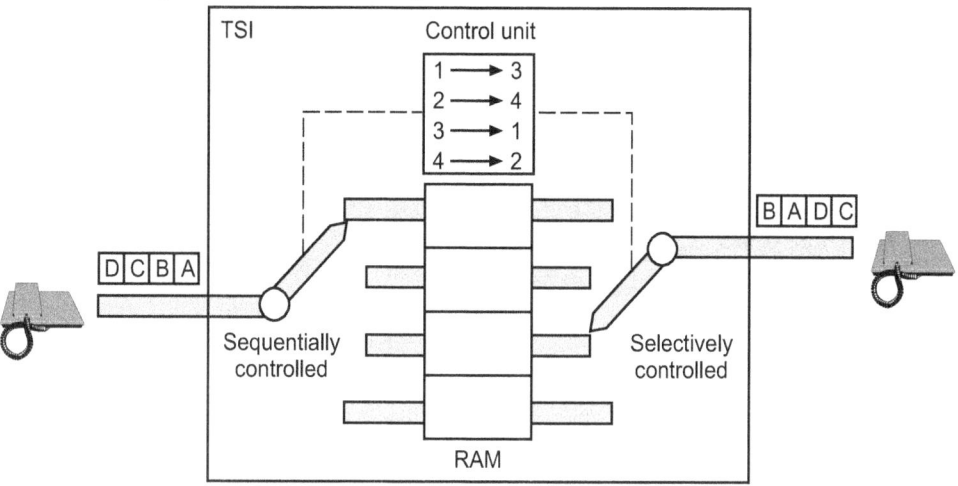

Fig. 4.23: The TSI System

4.9.2 TDM Bus Switching

1. In TDM bus switching system, input and output lines are connected to a high-speed bus through input and output gates.

2. In TDM bus switching system, control unit opens and closes gates as needed.

3. Typical TDM bus switching system is as shown in Fig. 4.24.

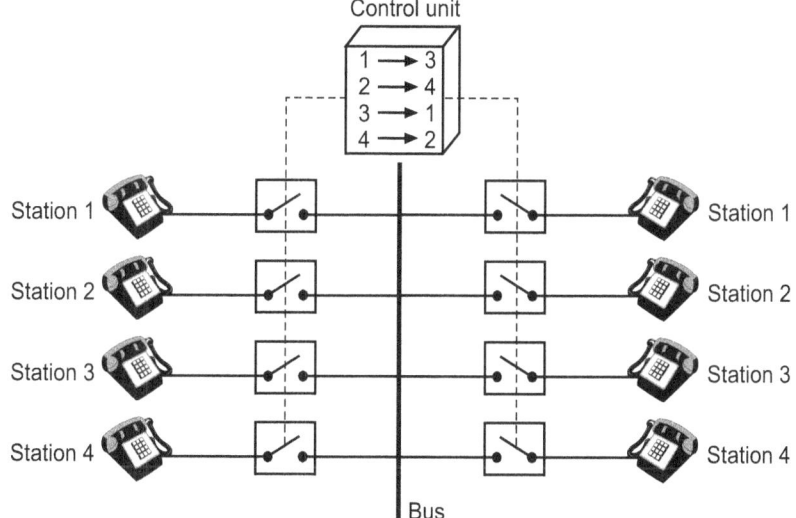

Fig. 4.24: Typical TDM Bus Switching System

4.10 Space- and Time-Division Switching Combinations

1. Advantage of space-division switching is, it is instantaneous; however, requires too many crosspoints.
2. Advantage of time-division switching is, it needs no crosspoints; however, processing connections create delays.
3. Combining them optimizes the number of crosspoints and reduces the amount of delay.
4. There are basically following types of combination switches:
   - Time-Space-Time (TST)
   - Time-Space-Space-Time (TSST)
   - Space-Time-Time-Space (STTS)
   - Others.
5. Typical T-S-T switch structure is as shown in Fig. 4.25.
6. It consists of two time stages and one space stage and has 12 inputs and 12 outputs.
7. Here in this T-S-T switch, instead of one time division switch, it divides the inputs into three groups of four inputs each and directs them to three time slot interchange to handle all 12 inputs applied.

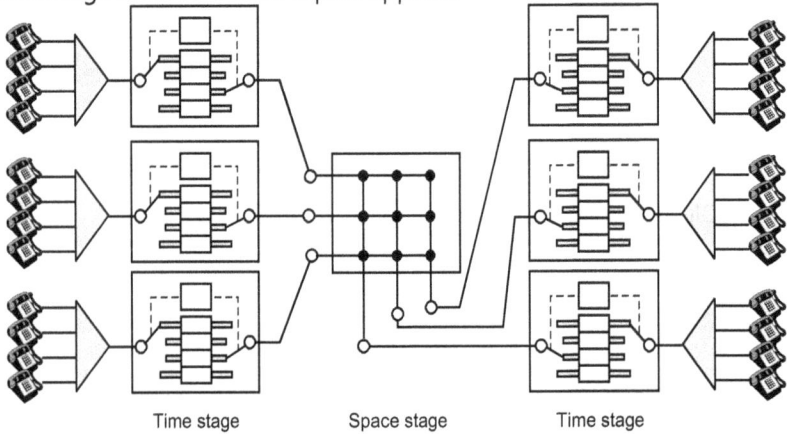

Time stage   Space stage   Time stage

Fig. 4.25: Typical T-S-T Switch Structure

4.11 Crosspoint Technology

1. For interconnecting different voice calls, usually switching system uses crosspoint switches.
2. The cost of switching system increases in direct proportion of size and cost of a crosspoint switches used in the system. Hence, reduction of size and cost using crosspoint switches are the major thrust of the crosspoint technology.

3. Crosspoint technology and its switches are as shown in Fig. 4.26.

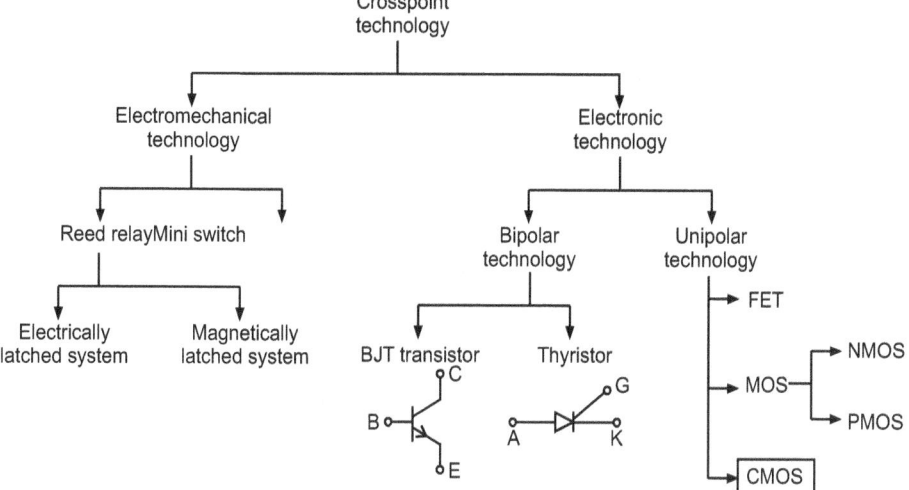

Fig. 4.26: Crosspoint Technology Advancements

4. The basic cross-point switch can be as shown in Fig. 4.27.

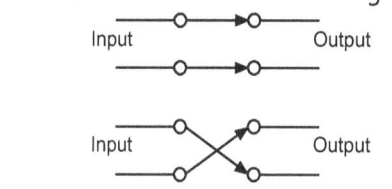

Fig. 4.27: Typical Crosspoint Mechanical Switch

5.

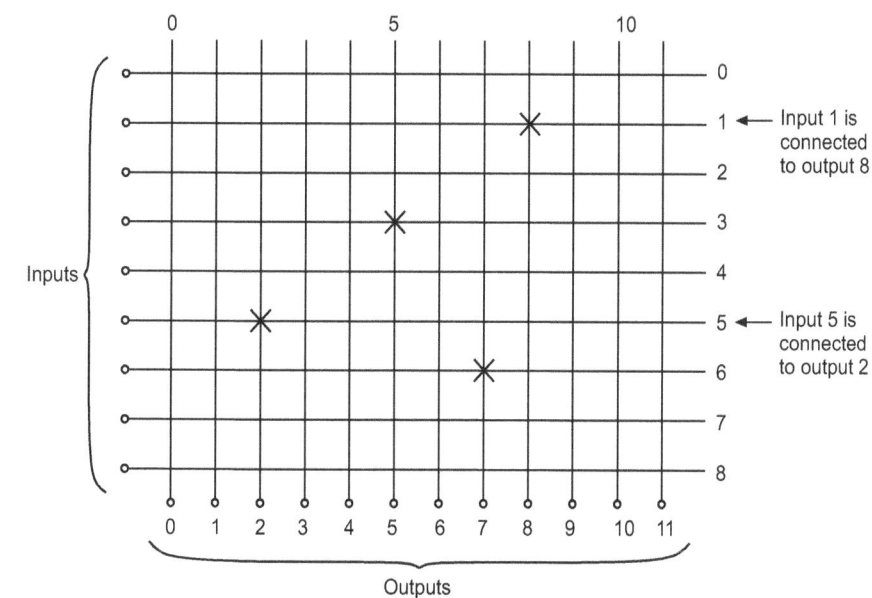

Fig. 4.28: Crosspoint is shown by 'X'

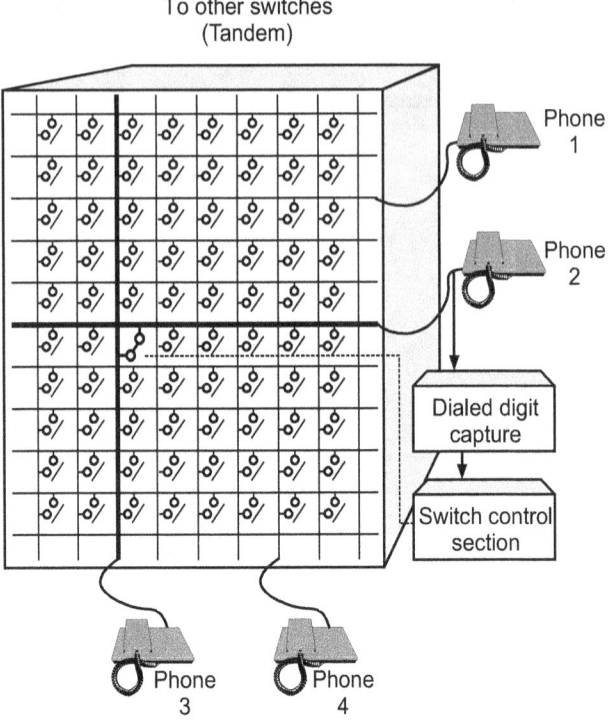

Fig. 4.29: Typical Telephone Units are connected using Crosspoints (Mechanically)

(Phone-2 is Mechanically connected to Phone-3)

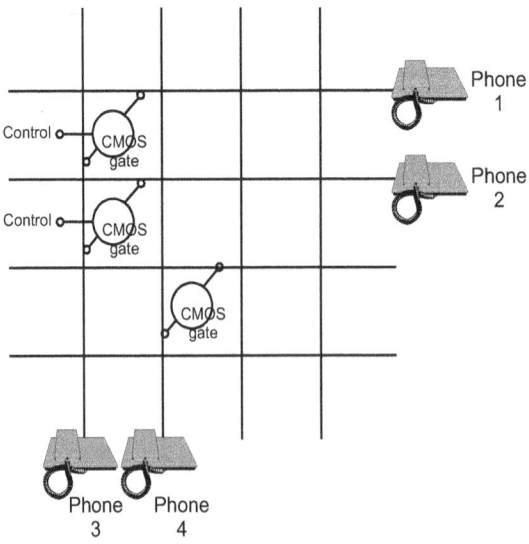

Fig. 4.30: Phone-2 is connected to Phone-3 through Crosspoint formed by CMOS Switch

4.11.1 CMOS Switch

1. A CMOS switch is shown in Fig. 4.31. The two MOSFETs are always in opposite operating states, as illustrated in the table below:

Table 4.5

Q_1 State	Q_2 State	Q_1 Resistance	Q_2 Resistance
On	Off	Low	High
Off	On	High	Low

2. When Q_1 is on and Q_2 is off, the resistance combination in the table results in an output that is very close to 0 V. When Q_1 is off and Q_2 is on, the resistance combination in the table results in an output very close to V_{SS}. This is why CMOS switches are used most of the times.

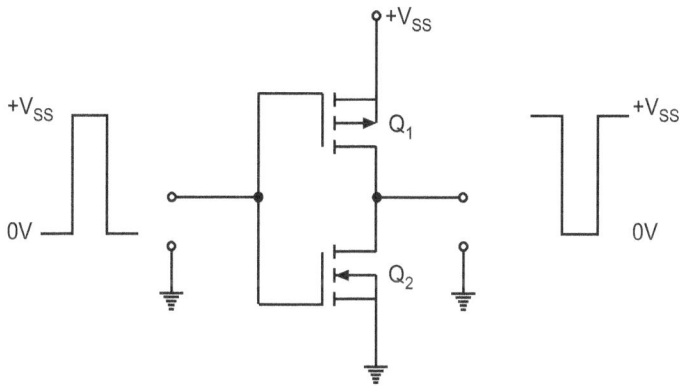

Fig. 4.31: The CMOS Switch

4.12 Structure of Packet Switches

1. Structure of packet switches is totally different as compared to circuit switches.
2. There are four components of typical packet switch:
    *   Routing processor.
    *   Switching fabric.
    *   Inputs ports.
    *   Output ports.

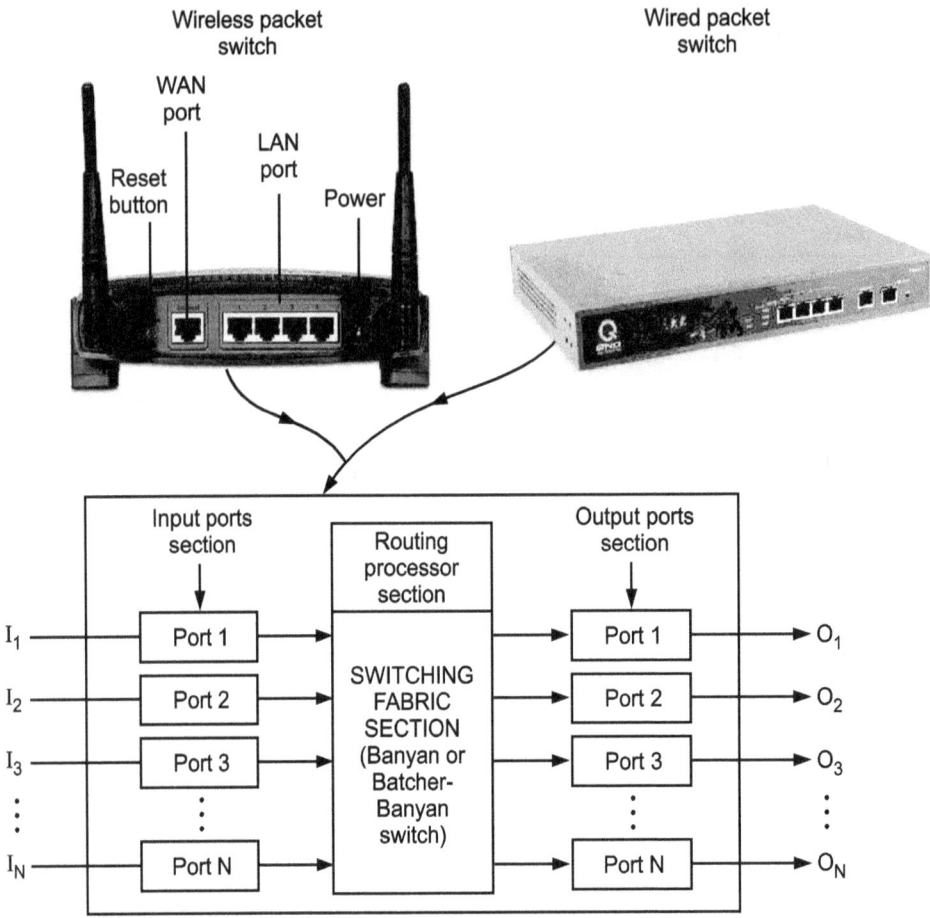

Fig. 4.32: Typical Components of Packet Switch

3. Basically switch works at datalink layer of ISI-OSI model.
4. Input signals are taken by the physical layer component at input ports.
5. Then bits are constructed from input signals and buffered in queue structure.
6. Error detection and correction is done and then given to the switching fabric section of switch.
7. Input and output port details are as shown in Fig. 4.33.
8. Output port and input port functioning is same, only output port works in reverse fashion.
9. Routing processor performs the function of network layer i.e. it takes care of:
    *   Routing.
    *   Routing algorithm.
    *   Network congestion.
    *   Network congestion control algorithm.
    *   Traffic shaping algorithm.

10. Switching fabrics is very important, where actual switching of the data packets is done.

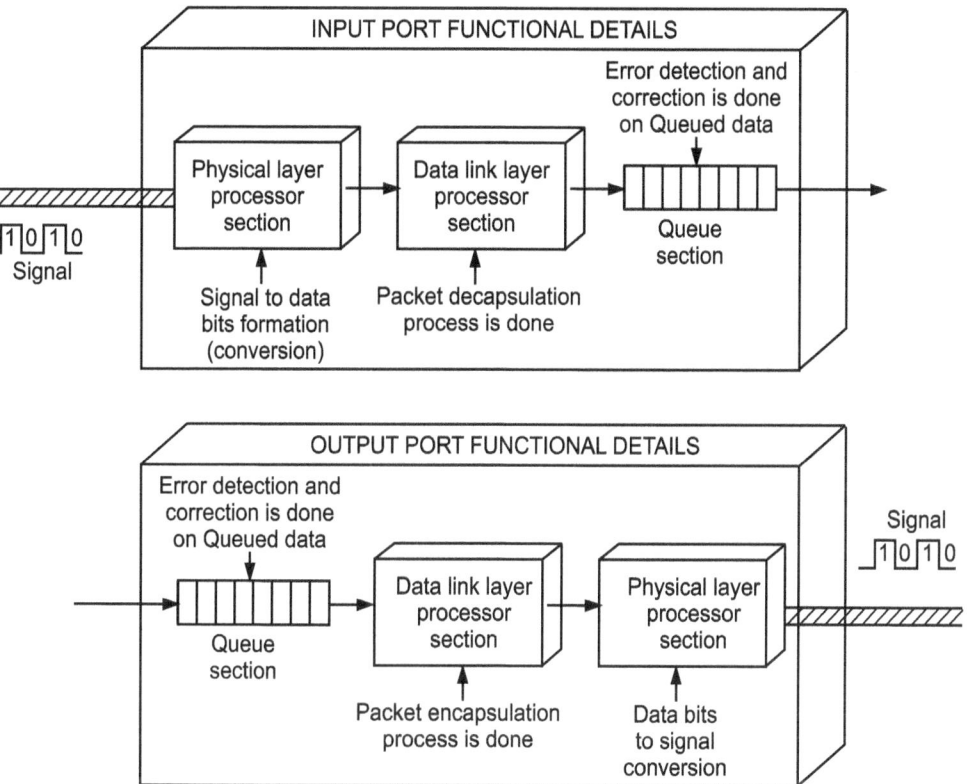

Fig. 4.33: Typical Input and Output Port Functional Details

4.13 Banyan Switch

1. In electronics, a **banyan switch** is a complex crossover switch used in electrical or optical switches.

2. It is named for its resemblance to the roots of the banyan tree which crossover in complex patterns. Logical banyan switches are used in logic or signal pathways to crossover switching of signals onto new pathways.

3. They can be mechanical MEMS (**Micro Electro Mechanical Systems**), electrical or optical NLO (**Nonlinear Optics**). Their complexity depends on the topology of the individual switches in a switch matrix (how wide it is by how many 'plies' or layers of switches it takes), to implement a desired crossover logic.

Design

1. Typical crossover matrices follow this formula: an N × N banyan switch uses (N/2) $\log_2$ N elements. Other formulas are used for differing number of crossover layers and scaling is possible, but becomes very large and complex with large N×N arrays.

CAD (**Computer-Aided Design**) and AI (**Artificial Intelligence**) can be used to take the drudgery out of creating these designs.

2. The switches are measured by how many stages, how many up/down sorters and crosspoints are used. Switches often have buffers built-in to speed up switching speeds.

3. A typical switch may have:
   - A 2 × 2 and 4 × 4 down sorter.
   - Followed by an 8 × 8 up sorter.
   - Followed by a 2 × 2 crosspoint banyan switch network.

This results in 3 level sorting for a 3 stage banyan network switch.

A Simple Example

1. Consider a 2 × 2 banyan switch, which requires (2/2) $\log_2 2 = 1$ switching element.

2. This switch takes two inputs, numbered 0 and 1, and two outputs, numbered 0 and 1. Every packet that comes in has a header that contains one bit indicating what its destination is (either 0 or 1).

3. If the switch reads the bit and it has value 0, it sends the packet to its higher output (which is 0 in this case), and to its lower output if the routing bit is one.

4. By connecting these switching elements in series and parallel it is possible therefore, to route packets in more complicated ways depending on the desired routes to establish.

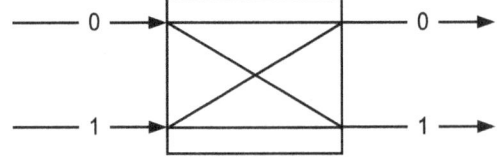

Fig. 4.34: Typical Banyan Switch

4.14 The Banyan Switch and Batcher-Banyan Switch

1. The Banyan switch is a multistage self-routing architecture which uses fewer elements than the minimum number required for a rearrangeable non-blocking design.

2. More specifically, an N×N Banyan switch uses (N/2) log N elements.

3. Consequently, the switch cannot be non-blocking; input-to-output permutations can be constructed that cannot be concurrently routed with the switch.

4. Therefore, smoothing buffers must lie inside the switch to achieve reasonably low packet loss rate.

5. The structure of an 8 × 8 Banyan switch is depicted in Fig. 4.35.

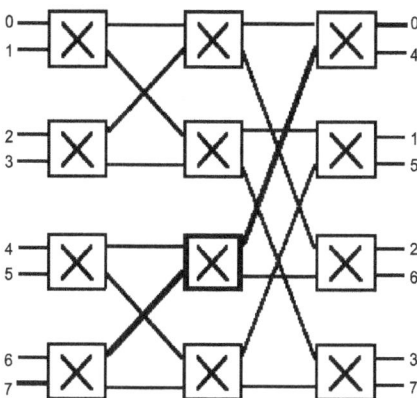

Fig. 4.35: The Structure of an 8 × 8 Banyan Switch

6.   We see that the elements are arranged in three columns of four elements each, in a pattern that resembles a grid of butterflies.

7.   The inputs to the switch are the inputs to the elements in the first column, and the outputs of the last column are the outputs from the switch. In each element, one output is connected to the input of the element just horizontally on its right, and the other goes to an element whose line number, represented in binary, differs in precisely the j's bit, where j is the column number of the element (counting from 0).

8.   For example, the outputs of element (2, 1) (bold in the diagram) are connected to the inputs of elements (2, 2) (horizontal connection) and (0, 2) (diagonal connection), as the numbers 2 and 0 differ in bit #1 of their binary representation.

9.   This simple rule also tells how to construct a path from any input to any output; in each column j, an appropriate element should be set in the "bar" state if the j's bits of the input and the output numbers equal, and in the "cross" state if those bits differ.

10. The path shown in bold in Fig. 4.35 illustrates how to connect input 7 to output 0. Since all the bits in the binary representation of the input and the output differ, all elements along the path are set to "cross". Note that every such path is unique.

11. Obviously, several paths cannot be routed concurrently unless they happen to require the same states of the elements.

12. Thus, in our case, once input 7 is connected to output 0, input 6 cannot be connected to outputs 2, 4, and 6, because any of these connections would require the element in the first column to be set to "bar".

13. Several remedies can be employed to attempt resolving this type of routing conflict: (1) Provide buffers within the elements, so that cells that cannot be immediately delivered are stored and their routing deferred according to some contention resolution policy; (2) Run the internal links at a rate that is a multiple of the cell arrival rate, sequentially establishing several paths within the duration of one cell.

14. To provide an insight to how good these techniques can be in reducing packet loss rate, it suffices to quote the results of a computer simulation for a large (1024 × 1024) Banyan switch run at full input load.

15. With the internal links running at twice the cell rate (hence capable of establishing two subsequent paths within one time slot) and a buffer size of 5 cells in each element, as many as 92 percent; of the input cells were delivered, compared to about 25 percent; for a simple unbuffered switch, and about 75 percent; for a double-rate unbuffered switch.

16. Still, to achieve reasonable packet loss rates (such as one packet per million), the input load would have to be reduced considerably.

17. **Typical Banyan Switch Topology is elaborated in Fig. 4.36.**

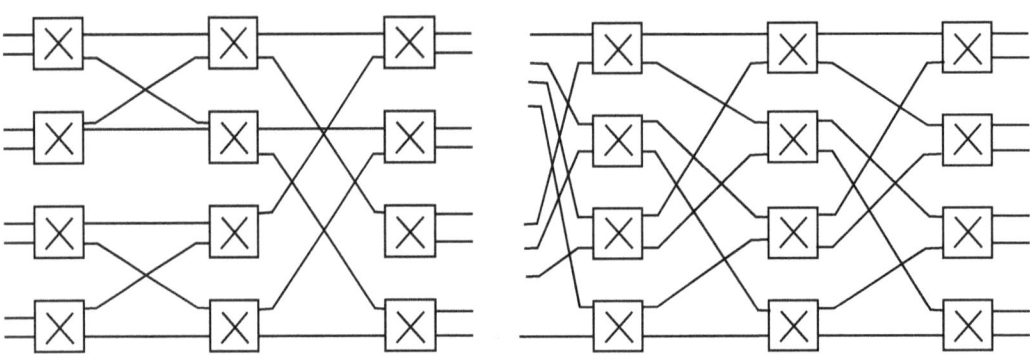

Fig. 4.36: Banyan 3 Stage Switch   **Fig. 4.37: Banyan 3 Stage Switch**

18. Banyan switches are based on crossbar switches that have been built into a binary tree topology.

19. There are many different configurations for Banyan switches. Two possible configurations for 3-stage Banyan switches are shown above.

20. Banyan switches are extremely efficient, but have the unfortunate problem of BLOCKING. This occurs when two inputs at a switching node are in contention for the same output and one of the inputs is forced to wait.

21. This situation can be avoided if the inputs are PRESORTED before entering the Banyan Tree Structure.

22. This topology is called the Batcher-Banyan switching topology and is the next topology on our list.

23. Typical **Batcher-Banyan Switch Topology is as shown in Fig. 4.38.**

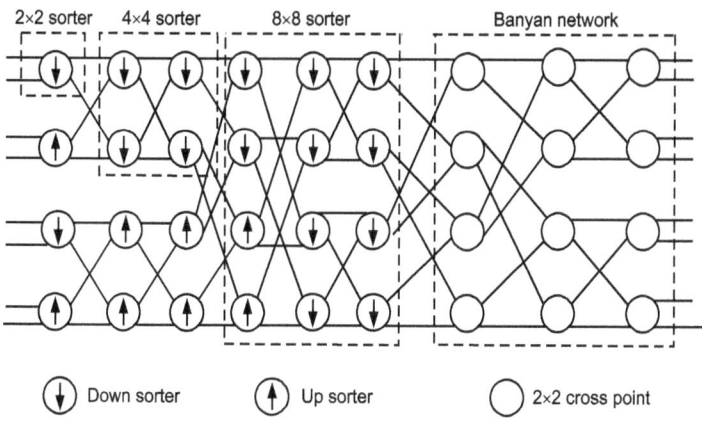

Fig. 4.38: Batcher-Banyan Switch

24. The Batcher sorting procedure involves 3 levels of sorting to produce NONBLOCKING input for a 3-stage Banyan network.
25. The price for removing the wait states in the Banyan network is more nodes (more cost) and a longer travel time through the greater number of nodes.
26. These switches are however much faster than simple Banyan switches, and of course, much more expensive.

4.15 Multiple Access Communications

When number of user share the same medium for transmission as shown in Fig. 4.39.

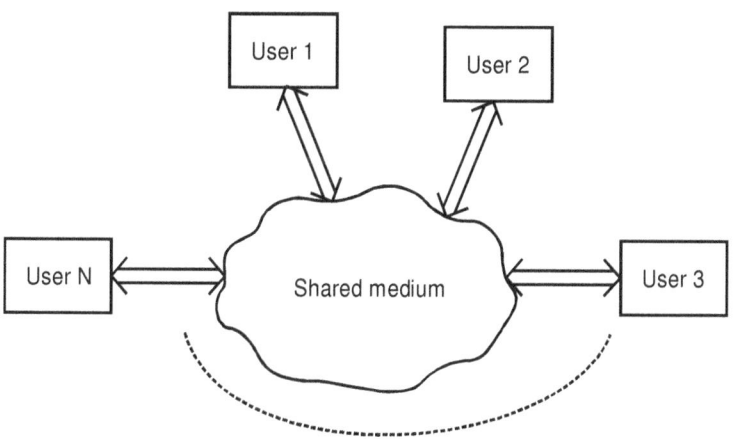

Fig. 4.39: Multiple Access Communication

All the stations sharing the medium can hear transmission from any given station.

If two or more stations try transmitting simultaneously their transmission will collide.

There are two schemes for allocating channels for transmission to a particular user.

(i) Static Channel Allocation:

It is static and collision free sharing of medium. If there are N users, the bandwidth of channel is divided into N sub channels and each user uses them separately. It is called Frequency Division Multiplexing (FDM).

FDM is efficient in case all the channels have continuous traffic and inefficient when traffic is bursty.

Another static channel allocation method is Time Division Multiplexing (TDM) where each user is allocated a fixed time slot for transmission.

(ii) Dynamic Channel Allocation:

In situations where user traffic is bursty the channel is allocated on a per frame basis. This is called **Medium Access Control Scheme**.

There are two approaches of implementing this scheme.

(i) Scheduling   (ii) Random Access

While allocating the channels dynamically, following assumptions are made.

(i)   There are N independent stations which generate frames for transmission randomly. Once a frame is generated station is blocked i.e. it does nothing until frame is successfully transmitted.

(ii) There is only one channel available.

(iii) If two frames are transmitted simultaneously, it results into collision.

(iv) Frame transmission can begin at any instant. Frames are transmitted in a fixed time slot.

(v)   Stations can sense if channel is in use. If it is sensed busy no station will attempt to use it.

Stations cannot serve channel before use. Only after transmission they decide whether transmission was successful or not.

4.16 Random Access (Multiple Access Protocols)

There are number of protocols for allocating multiple access channel. Some of the random access MAC procedures are described below.

4.16.1 ALOHA

- It is a random access scheme for transmitting information for terminals sharing the same channel.

-   It is simple in operation.
-   Information is transmitted over the shared channel as soon as it becomes available.
-   If there is collision because of more stations transmitting simultaneously, they will wait for random amount of time before transmitting the information again. It is called back-off.
-   Fig. 4.40 shows frame transmission using ALOHA.

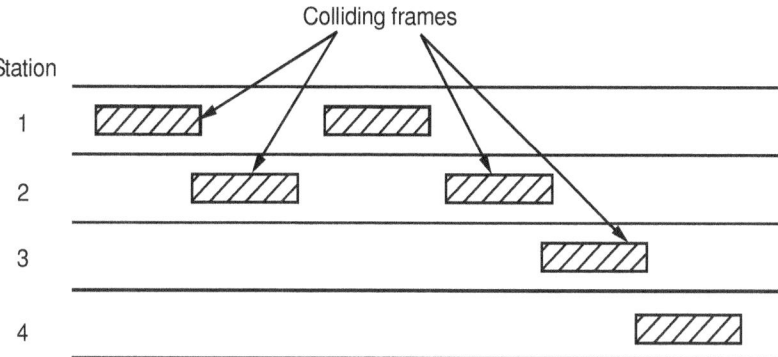

Fig. 4.40: ALOHA System

4.16.2 Efficiency of ALOHA

Let L be the length of frame (bits) (constant).

R be rate of transmission.

$$\therefore \qquad \text{Frame time} \ = \ X \ = \ \frac{L}{R}$$

Let some frame arrive at time t_0 and ends at $t_0 + X$.

This frame will collide if there is transmission from other stations between to $t_0 - X$ and $t_0 + X$ as shown in Fig. 4.41.

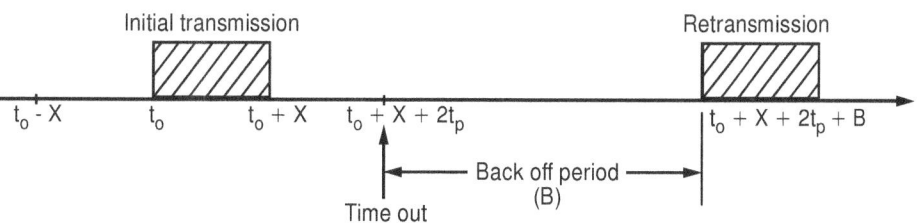

Fig. 4.41: ALOHA System

$$\bullet \qquad \text{Vulnerable time} \ = \ (t_0 + X) - (t_0 - X)$$
$$= \ 2X$$

Let G be the total arrival rate of the system in frames/X seconds. G is also throughput of system. Let G be total arrival rate of the system in frames/X seconds. G is also called total load of the system.

With the assumption that the back-off spreads retransmissions such that new and repeated frame transmission are equally likely to occur, the number of frames transmitted in a time interval has Poisson distribution with average number of arrivals of 2G arrivals/2X seconds. Hence, probability that k frames are generated during a given frame time are:

$$P[k \text{ transmissions in 2X seconds}] = \frac{(2G)^k}{k!} e^{-2G}$$

Hence, throughput S is equal to total arrival rate G times probability of successful transmission.

-        S = $P[\text{no collision}]$
  - = $P[0 \text{ transmissions in 2X seconds}]$
  - = $G\frac{(2G)^0}{0!} e^{-2G}$
  - = Ge^{-2G}

The plot of S versus G is shown in Fig. 4.42.

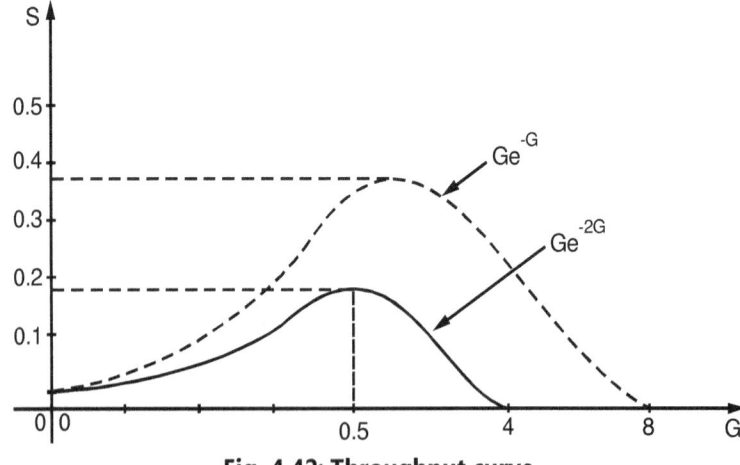

Fig. 4.42: Throughput curve

It can be seen that the maximum value of $S = \frac{1}{2e}$ at G = 0.5. That is system can achieve throughput of 18.4% only.

4.16.3 Slotted Aloha

Performance of ALOHA can be improved by putting a restriction on time of transmission i.e. stations will transmit only at a fixed time (Synchronise fashion). Thus, reducing the probability of collisions.

All stations keep track of transmission time slots and are allowed to initiate transmission only at beginning of slot.

Vulnerable time i.e. time of collision reduces to $t_o - X$ to X i.e. X second as shown in Fig. 4.43.

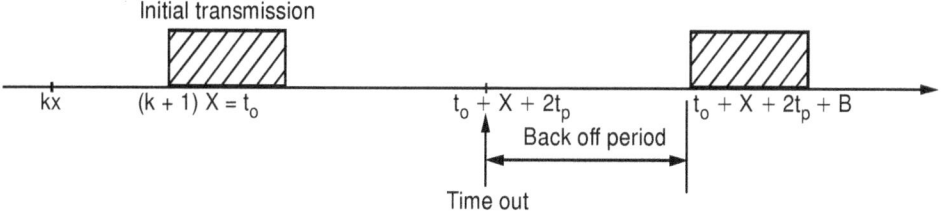

Fig. 4.43

There are G arrivals in X seconds, (G is total arrival rate)

$$S = G \times P \text{ [no collision]}$$
$$= G \times P \text{ [0 transmission in X seconds]}$$
$$= G \times \frac{(G)^0}{0!} e^{-G}$$
$$= Ge^{-G}$$

Above equation is plotted in Fig. 4.41. Slotted ALOHA has maximum throughput of $\frac{1}{e} =$ 36.8% at G = 1.

4.17 Carrier Sense Multiple Access Protocols

Protocols in which stations listen for carriers and take suitable action are called Carrier Sense Protocols. Following are some carrier sense protocols.

1. **1-Persistent CSMA**
   - When a station has some data to send it listens to the channel.
   - If channel is busy it waits until it becomes free or idle continuously sensing the channel.
   - If channel is idle it transmits the frame.
   - It is called 1-persistent because whenever channel is idle the station transmits with probability 1.

2. **Non-Persistent CSMA**
   - When station has some data to send, it listens to the channel and if channel is idle it sends data.
   - If channel is busy, it waits until it becomes free/idle.
   - But then it does not sense the channel continuously as in 1-persistent CSMA. It waits for random period and then again senses the channel.

3. P-Persistent CSMA

- It applies to slotted channels.
- When a station is needy to transit data and channel is idle it transmits with probability P and decides not to transmit with probability q = 1 – p until next slot. If that slot is also idle it decides to transmit or defer with probability p and q. This process is repeated until either frame is transmitted or another station has started transmission.
- If the channel is busy it waits until next slot and repeats above step.

4.17.1 Carrier Sense Multiple Access with Collision Detection (CSMA/CD)

A Shared Medium:

The Ethernet network may be used to provide shared access by a group of attached nodes to the physical medium which connects the nodes. These nodes are said to form a Collision Domain. All frames sent on the medium are physically received by all receivers, however the Medium Access Control (MAC) header contains a MAC destination address which ensure only the specified destination actually forwards the received frame (the other computers all discard the frames which are not addressed to them).

Consider a LAN with four computers each with a Network Interface Card (NIC) connected by a common Ethernet cable.

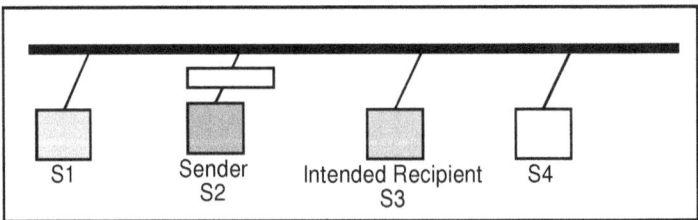

Fig. 4.44 (a)

One computer (S$_2$) uses a NIC to send a frame to the shared medium, which has a destination address corresponding to the source address of the NIC in the S$_3$ computer.

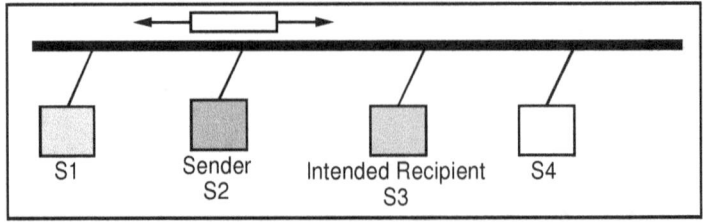

Fig. 4.44 (b)

The cable propagates the signal in both directions, so that the signal (eventually) reaches the NICs in all four of the computers. Termination resistors at the ends of the cable absorb the frame energy, preventing reflection of the signal back along the cable.

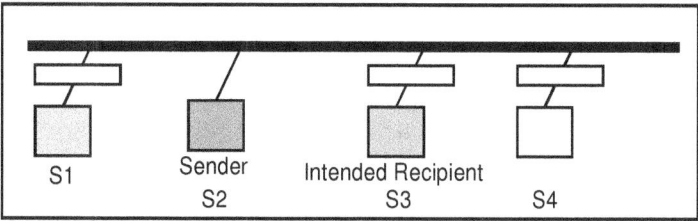

Fig. 4.44 (c)

All the NICs receive the frame and each examines it to check its length and checksum. The header destination MAC address is next examined, to see if the frame should be accepted, and forwarded to the network-layer software in the computer.

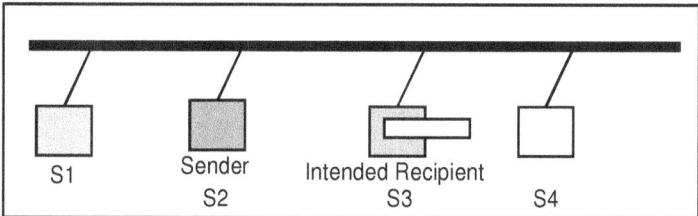

Fig. 4.44 (d)

Only the NIC in the computer S_3 recognises the frame destination address as valid and therefore this NIC alone forwards the contents of the frame to the network layer. The NICs in the other computers discard the unwanted frame.

The shared cable allows any NIC to send whenever it wishes, but if two NICs happen to transmit at the same time, a collision will occur, resulting in the data being corrupted.

4.17.2 ALOHA and Collisions

To control which NICs are allowed to transmit at any given time, a protocol is required. As seen earlier, the simplest protocol is known as ALOHA (this is actually an Hawaiian word, meaning "hello"). ALOHA allows any NIC to transmit at any time, but states that each NIC must add a checksum/CRC at the end of its transmission to allow the receiver(s) to identify whether the frame was correctly received.

ALOHA is therefore a best effort service, and does not guarantee that the frame of data will actually reach the remote recipient without corruption. It therefore relies on ARQ protocols to retransmit any data which is corrupted. An ALOHA network only works well when the medium has a low utilisation, since this leads to a low probability of the transmission colliding with that of another computer, and hence a reasonable chance that the data is not corrupted.

4.17.3 Carrier Sense Multiple Access (CSMA)

Ethernet uses a refinement of ALOHA, known as Carrier Sense Multiple Access (CSMA), which improves performance when there is a higher medium utilisation. When a NIC has data to transmit, the NIC **first** listens to the cable (using a transceiver) to see if a carrier (signal) is being transmitted by another node. This may be achieved by monitoring whether a current is flowing in the cable (each bit corresponds to 18-20 milliAmps (mA)). The individual bits are sent by encoding them with a 10 (or 100 MHz for Fast Ethernet) clock using Manchester encoding. Data is only sent when no carrier is observed (i.e. no current present) and the physical medium is therefore idle. Any NIC which does not need to transmit, listens to see if other NICs have started to transmit information to it.

However, this alone is unable to prevent two NICs transmitting at the same time. If two NICs *simultaneously* try transmit, then both could see an idle physical medium (i.e. neither will see the other's carrier signal), and both will conclude that no other NIC is currently using the medium. In this case, both will then decide to transmit and a *collision* will occur. The collision will result in the corruption of the frame being sent, which will subsequently be discarded by the receiver since a corrupted Ethernet frame will (with a very high probability) not have a valid 32-bit MAC CRC at the end.

4.17.4 Collision Detection (CD)

A second element to the Ethernet access protocol is used to detect when a collision occurs. When there is data waiting to be sent, each transmitting NIC also monitors its own transmission. If it observes a collision (excess current above what it is generating, i.e. > 24 mA for coaxial Ethernet), it stops transmission immediately and instead transmits a 32-bit jam sequence. The purpose of this sequence is to ensure that any other node which may currently be receiving this frame will receive the jam signal in place of the correct 32-bit MAC CRC, this causes the other receivers to discard the frame due to a CRC error.

To ensure that all NICs start to receive a frame before the transmitting NIC has finished sending it, Ethernet defines a minimum frame size (i.e. no frame may have less than 46 bytes of payload). The minimum frame size is related to the distance which the network spans, the type of media being used and the number of repeaters which the signal may have to pass through to reach the furthest part of the LAN. Together these define a value known as the *Ethernet Slot Time*, corresponding to 512 bit times at 10 Mbps.

When two or more transmitting NICs each detect a corruption of their own data (i.e. a collision), each responds in the same way by transmitting the jam sequence. The following sequence depicts a collision:

Fig. 4.45 (a)

At time t = 0, a frame is sent on the idle medium by NIC A.

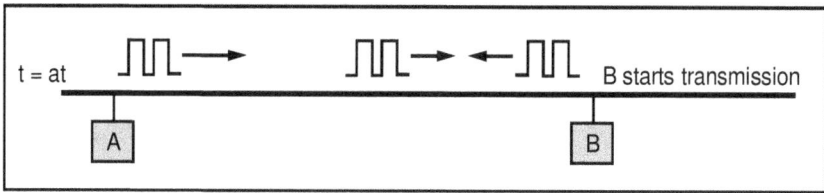

Fig. 4.45 (b)

A short time later, NIC B also transmits. (In this case, the medium, as observed by the NIC at B happens to be idle too).

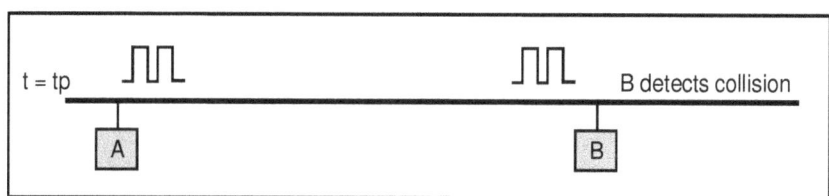

Fig. 4.45 (c)

After a period, equal to the propagation delay of the network, the NIC at B detects the other transmission from A, and is aware of a collision, but NIC A has not yet observed that NIC B was also transmitting. B continues to transmit, sending the Ethernet Jam sequence (32 bits).

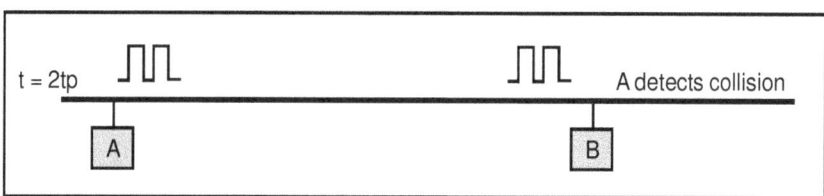

Fig. 4.45 (d)

After one complete round trip propagation time (twice the one way propagation delay), both NICs are aware of the collision. B will shortly cease transmission of the Jam Sequence, however A will continue to transmit a complete Jam Sequence. Finally the cable becomes idle.

4.17.5 Retransmission Back-Off

An overview of the transmit procedure is shown below. The transmitter initialises the number of transmissions of the current frame (n) to zero, and starts listening to the cable (using the carrier sense logic (CS) - e.g., by observing the Rx signal at transceiver to see if any bits are being sent). If the cable is not idle, it waits (defers) until the cable is idle. It then waits for a small Inter-Frame Gap (IFG) (e.g., 9.6 microseconds) to allow to time for all receiving nodes to return to prepare themselves for the next transmission.

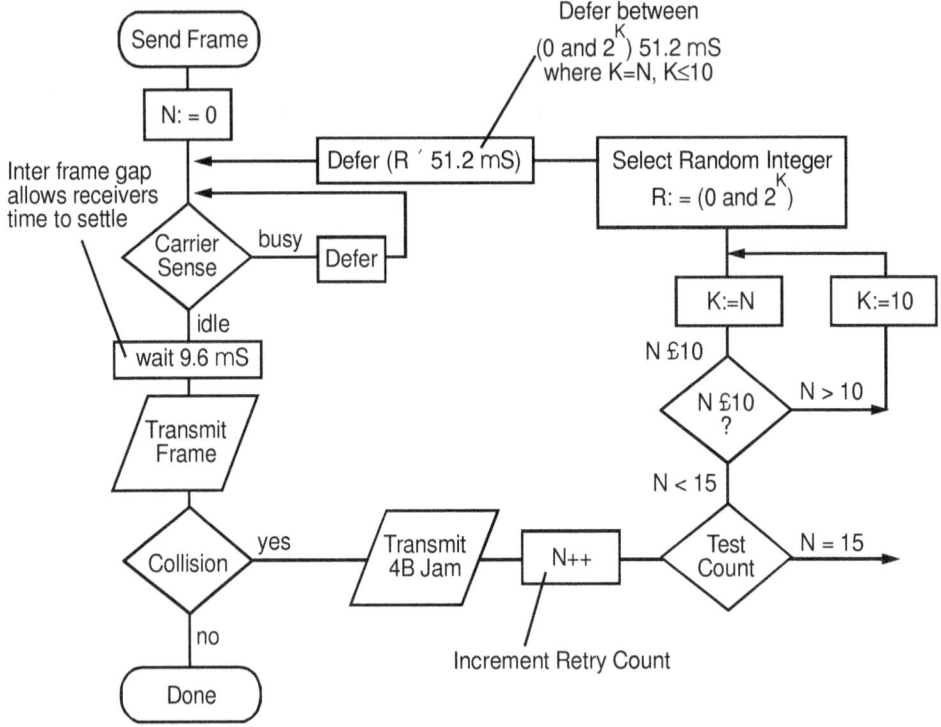

Fig. 4.46

Transmission then starts with the preamble, followed by the frame data and finally the CRC-32. After this time, the transceiver Tx logic is turned-off and the transceiver returns to passively monitoring the cable for other transmissions.

During this process, a transmitter must also continuously monitor the collision detection logic (CD) in the transceiver to detect if a collision occurs. If it does, the transmitter aborts the transmission (stops sending bits) within a few bit periods, and starts the collision procedure, by sending a Jam Signal to the transceiver Tx logic. It then calculates a retransmission time.

If all NICs attempted to retransmit immediately following a collision, then this would certainly result in another collision. Therefore a procedure is required to ensure that there is only a low probability of simultaneous retransmission. The scheme adopted by Ethernet uses a random back-off period, where each node selects a random number, multiplies this by the slot time (minimum frame period, 51.2 µS) and waits for this random period before attempting retransmission. The small Inter-Frame Gap (IFG) (e.g., 9.6 microseconds) is also added.

On a busy network, a retransmission may still collide with another retransmission (or possibly new frames being sent for the first time by another NIC). The protocol therefore counts the number of retransmission attempts (using a variable N in the above figure) and attempts to retransmit the same frame up to 15 times.

For each retransmission, the transmitter constructs a set of numbers:

{0, 1, 2, 3, 4, 5, ... L} where L is ([2 to the power (K)]–1) and where K = N; K <= 10;

A random value R is picked from this set, and the transmitter waits (defers) for a period.

R × (slot time) i.e. R x 51.2 Micro Seconds

For example, after two collisions, N = 2, therefore K = 2, and the set is {0, 1, 2, 3} giving a one in four chance of collision. This corresponds to a wait selected from {0, 51.2, 102.4, 153.6} micro seconds.

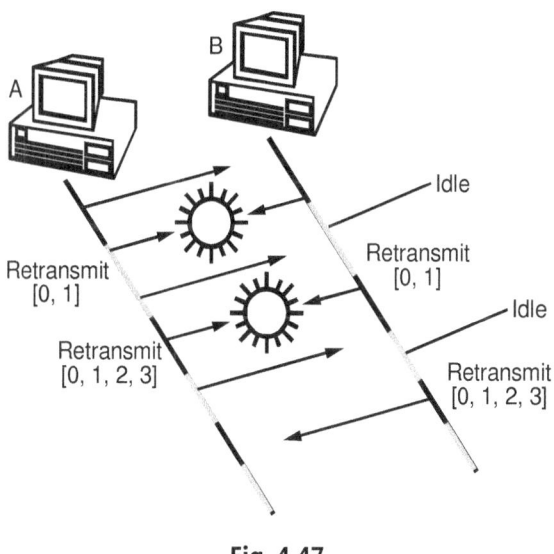

Fig. 4.47

After 3 collisions, N = 3, and the set is {0, 1, 2, 3, 4, 5, 6, 7}, that is a one in eight chance of collision.

But after 4 collisions, N = 4, the set becomes {0, 1, 2, 3, 4, 5, 6, 7, 8, 9, 10, 11, 12, 13, 14, 15}, that is a one in 16 chance of collision.

The scaling is performed by multiplication and is known as exponential back-off. This is what lets CSMA/CD scale to large numbers of NICs - even when collisions may occur. The first ten times, the back-off waiting time for the transmitter suffering collision is scaled to a larger value. The algorithm includes a threshold of 1024. The reasoning is that the more attempts that are required, the more greater the number of NICs which are trying to send at the same time, and therefore the longer the period which needs to be deferred. Since, a set of numbers {0, 1, ..., 1023} is a large set of numbers, there is very little advantage from further increasing the set size.

Each transmitter also limits the maximum number of retransmissions of a single frame to 16 attempts (N=15). After this number of attempts, the transmitter gives up transmission and discards the frame, logging an error. In practice, a network that is not overloaded should never discard frames in this way.

4.17.6 Late Collisions

In a proper functioning Ethernet network, a NIC may experience collision within the first slot time after it starts transmission. This is the reason why an Ethernet NIC monitors the CD signal during this time and use CSMA/CD. A faulty CD circuit, or misbehaving NIC or transceiver may lead to a late collision (i.e. after one slot time). Most Ethernet NICs therefore continue to monitor the CD signal during the entire transmission. If they observe a late collision, they will normally inform the sender of the error condition.

4.18 Performance of CSMA / CD

It is simple to calculate the performance of a CSMA/CD network where only one node attempts to transmit at any time. In this case, the NIC may saturate the medium and near 100% utilisation of the link may be achieved, providing almost 10 Mbps of throughput on a 10 Mbps LAN.

However, when two or more NICs attempt to transmit at the same time, the performance of Ethernet is less predictable (and not covered by this course). The fall in utilisation and throughput occurs because some bandwidth is wasted by collisions and back-off delays. In practice, a busy shared 10 Mbps Ethernet network will typically supply 2-4 Mbps of throughput to the NICs connected to it.

As the level of utilisation of the network increases, particularly if there are many NICs competing to share the bandwidth, an overload condition may occur. In this case, the throughput of Ethernet LANs reduces very considerably, and much of the capacity is wasted by the CSMA/CD algorithm, and very little is available for sending useful data. This is the reason why a shared Ethernet LAN should not connect more than 1024 computers. Many engineers use a threshold of 40% utilisation to determine if a LAN is overloaded. A LAN with a higher utilisation will observe a high collision rate, and likely a very variable transmission time (due to back off). Separating the LAN in to two or more collision domains using bridges or switches would likely provide a significant benefit (assuming appropriate positioning of the bridges or switches).

Shared networks may also be constructed using Fast Ethernet, operating at 100 Mbps. Since Fast Ethernet always uses fibre or twisted pair, a hub or switch is always required.

4.19 Ethernet Capture

A drawback of sharing a medium using CSMA/CD, is that the sharing is not necessarily fair. When each computer connected to the LAN has little data to send, the network exhibits almost equal access time for each NIC. However, if one NIC starts sending an excessive number of frames, it may dominate the LAN. Such conditions may occur, for instance, when one NIC in a LAN acts as a source of high quality packetised video. The effect is known as "Ethernet Capture".

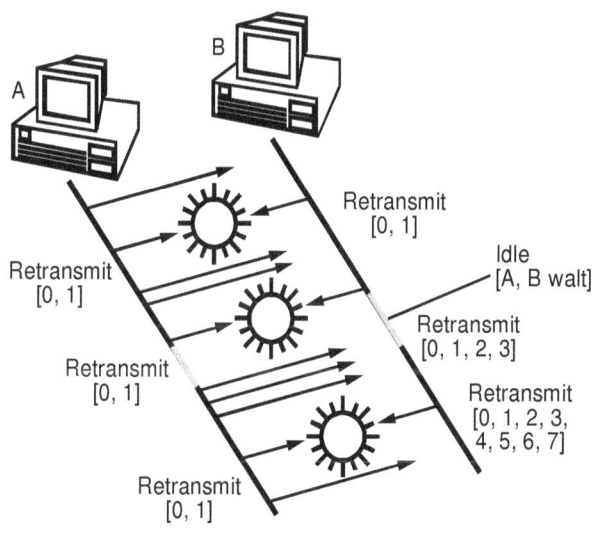

Fig. 4.48

Ethernet Capture by Node A.

The Fig. 4.48 illustrates Ethernet Capture. Computer A dominates computer B. Originally both computers have data to transmit. A transmits first. A and B then both simultaneously try to transmit. B picks a larger retransmission interval than A (shown in red) and defers. A sends, then sends again. There is a short pause, and then both A and B attempt to resume transmission. A and B both back-off, however, since B was already in back-off (it failed to retransmit), it chooses from a larger range of back-off times (using the exponential back-off algorithm). A is therefore more likely to succeed, which it does in the example. The next pause in transmission, A and B both attempt to send, however, since this fails in this case, B further increases its back-off and is now unable to fairly compete with A.

Ethernet Capture may also arise when many sources compete with one source which has much more data to send. Under these situations some nodes may be "locked out" of using the medium for a period of time. The use of higher speed transmission (e.g. 100 Mbps) significantly reduces the probability of Capture, and the use full duplex cabling eliminates the effect.

Ethernet LANs may be implemented using a variety of media (not just the coaxial cable described above). The types of media segments supported by Ethernet are:

- 10 Base 5 Low loss coaxial cable (also known as "thick" Ethernet).
- 10 Base 2 Low cost coaxial cable (also known as "thin" Ethernet).
- 10 Base T Low cost twisted pair copper cable (also known as Unshielded Twisted Pair (UTP)).
- 10 Base F Fibre optic cable.

The network design rules for using these types of media are summarised below:

Table 4.6

Segment type	Max Number of systems per cable segment	Max Distance of a cable segment
10 Base 5 (Thick Coax)	100	500 m
10 Base 2 (Thin Coax)	30	185 m
10 Base T (Twisted Pair)	2	100 m
10 Base F (Fibre Optic)	2	2000 m

Network Design Rules for Different types of Cable

There is also a version of Ethernet which operates using twisted pair cabling or fibre optic links at 100 Mbps and at 1 Gbps. 100 Mbps networks may operate full duplex (using a Fast Ethernet Switch) or half duplex (using a Fast Ethernet Hub). 1 Gbps networks usually operate between a pair of Ethernet Switches. Many LANs combine the various speeds of operation using dual-speed switches which allow the same switch to connect some ports to one speed of network, and other ports at another speed. The higher speed ports are usually used to connect switches to one another.

4.20 Collision Free Protocols

In CSMA/CD collision do not occur when station is busy transmitting. They occur during contention period i.e. when stations are trying to capture the channel. If cable is long (large Tp) and frames are short the collisions will affect systems performance. We can eliminate the collisions during contention period also.

Following protocols do this.

4.20.1 Bit Map Protocol

–   If there are N stations each contention period will have N slots reserved for each station.

–   Whoever has a frame to transmit, will announce in the contention slot by putting bit 1 in its slot. When transmission period starts the stations begin transmission in numerical order as shown in Fig. 4.49.

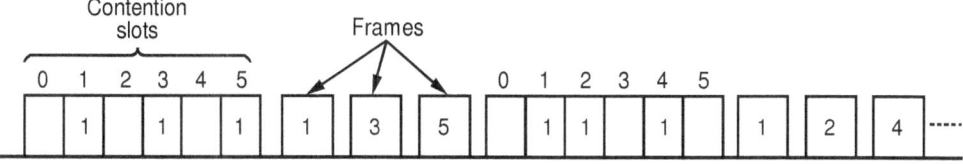

Fig. 4.49: Bit Map Protocol

Performance of Bit Map Protocol:

Let data frames = d units.

Number of stations = N.

High numbered stations must wait on the average 0.5 N slots.

Low numbered stations must wait on the average 1.5 N slots.

The mean for all stations is N slots.

At low load, overhead per frame is N bits.

$$\therefore \qquad \text{Efficiency} \;=\; \frac{d}{N + d}$$

At high load there will be 1 bit overhead per frame as N bit contention period is distributed over N frames.

$$\therefore \qquad \text{Efficiency} \;=\; \frac{d}{d + 1}$$

4.20.2 Binary Countdown

–   A station which wants to use channel broadcasts its address as binary string.

–   The bits in each addresses are ORed together and the station is decided.

–   e.g. let stations 0100, 1001, 1010 and 0010 trying to access the channel.

–   The first bits of each address are ORed e.g. 0 OR 1 OR 1 OR 0 = 1. Result is 1 it means high numbered station is competing for the channel so low numbered channels give up.

–   Stations 1001 and 1010 continue. Next bit is 0 both continue. Next bits are 0 and 1 and hence 1001 give up 1010 continues.

The station 1010 can transmit its frame.

The efficiency of this method is,

$$\eta = \frac{d}{d + \ln N}$$

If frame format is clearly chosen the $\ln N$ bits also will not be wasted and efficiency will be 100%.

4.20.3 Limited Contention Protocol

- For CSMA methods (including ALOHA and slotted ALOHA) light load is preferable. It gives higher efficiency.
- For collision free methods like Bit Map Protocol and Binary count down high load gives better efficiency.
- If we combine best properties of contention and collision free methods, a new method called limited contention protocol can be designed.
- The contention that will be used will make each station acquire channel with probability P, where P will be different for each station.
- Earlier contention protocols used the same probability P for each station.
- Probability of some station acquiring the channel can be increased only by decreasing amount of competition.
- The limited contention protocols divide the stations into groups.
- Stations from a group compete in the same slot.
- Appropriate division of stations into groups will reduce contention in each slot.
- Binary countdown had 1 station in 1 group hence there was no contention at all.
- If we assign two stations per group. The probability that both stations will try to transmit is p^2. For small p this is negligible.
- Extreme case will be all stations in same group which is same as slotted ALOHA.

4.20.4 Adaptive Tree Walk Protocol

- In this protocol, initially all stations are permitted to try and acquire the channel if one of them succeeds it is OK.
- If there is collision, only half the stations are permitted to complete. If one of them acquires channel the next slot is reserved for other half group. Otherwise half of first half are permitted to compete and so on.
- For this, we can divide the stations in a binary tree structure as shown in Fig. 4.50.

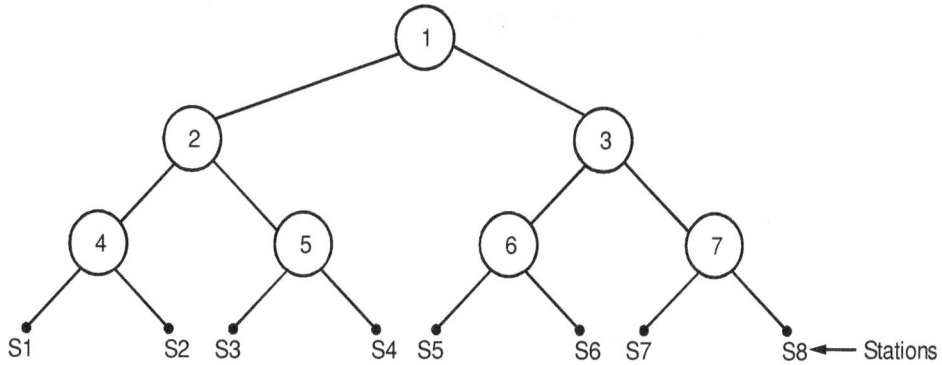

Fig. 4.50: Adaptive Tree Walk Protocol

- Initially, we consider all stations under node 1 (entire tree) for acquiring channel.
- In case of collision, we take nodes under left subtree and so on.
- In case of heavy load we can decide to start at higher level node in the tree instead of starting at the root node.

4.21 Wavelength Division Multiple Access Protocols (WDMA)

- It is a method of allocating channel by dividing it into sub-channels using Frequency Division Multiplexing (FDM) and Time Division Multiplexing (TDM) or both.
- Instead of allocating the sub-channels to fixed users or stations, they are dynamically allocated.
- This technique is used with fibre optic channel where different wavelengths (frequencies) can be used to transmit or receive information simultaneously.
- The spectrum is divided into wavelength bands or shown in Fig. 4.51 (a).

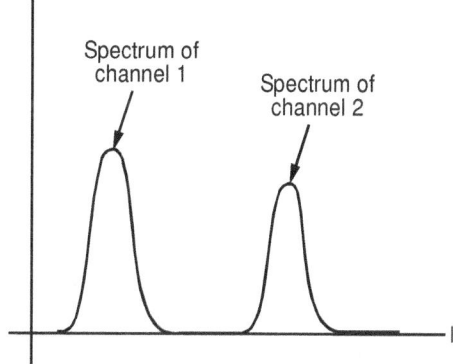

Fig. 4.51 (a): WDMA Spectrum

- Each station is assigned two channels as shown in Fig. 4.51 (b).

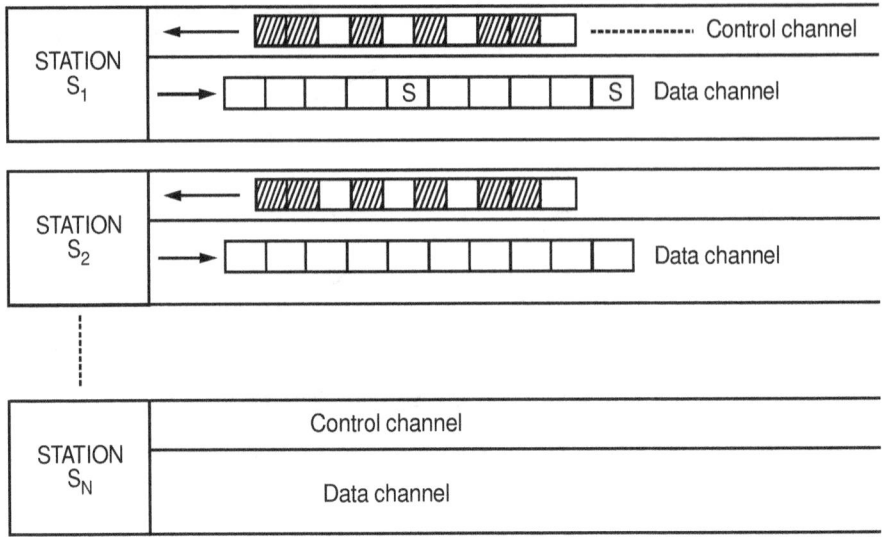

Fig. 4.51 (b) WDMA

(i)   Control channel
(ii) Data channel.
−   Control channel is narrow and it is used by other stations to contact the stations.
−   Data channel is wider and used to transmit data frames.
−   Each channel has number of time slots i.e. control channel has m time slots and data channel has n+1 line slots. n of these are data and the last one is used to report the status of which slots are free.
−   All channels are synchronized by a single global clock.
−   The protocol supports three types of traffic.
     (i)   Constant data rate connection oriented traffic (uncompressed video).
     (ii)   Variable data rate connection oriented traffic (file transfer).
     (iii) Datagram traffic i.e. UDP packets.
(i) Constant data rate:
       Connection oriented traffic: When station S1 wants communicate with S2 CONNECTION REQUEST frame is inserted by S1 in S2's control channel. If S2 accepts, communication starts.
       Each station has two transmitters and two receivers.
       (a) A fixed wavelength receiver for listening to its own control channel.
       (b) A tunable transmitter for sending an other station's control channel.
       (c) A fixed wavelength transmitter for outputting data frames.
       (d) A tunable receiver for selecting a data transmitter to listen to.
(ii) Variable data rate connection oriented traffic: Station S_1 tunes its data receiver to S_2 data channel and waits for status slot.
       S_1 picks one of the free control slot and inserts its CONNECTION REQUEST message in it.

Station S_2 looks into the request and assigns it the free requested slot to S_1. This assignment is transmitted in status slot of control channel.

To perform the file transfer, S_1 sends a control message to S_2, telling it in which slot the data will be available.

When S_2 gets control message, it tunes its receiver to S_1's output channel to read the data frame.

S_2 can use the same mechanism to acknowledge the received data.

(iii) **Datagram traffic:** This type of traffic sends a message like data for you in slot X instead of the CONNECTION REQUEST into the control slot.

If S_2 is free during next data slot X the transmission will take place otherwise data will be lost.

4.22 Frequency Division Multiple Access (FDMA)

The sub-bands of frequencies are allocated to different users on the continuous time basis. Thus, if each frequency band is treated as a channel. These channels are assigned to each user. Guard band is introduced between each channel to avoid interference between adjacent channels.

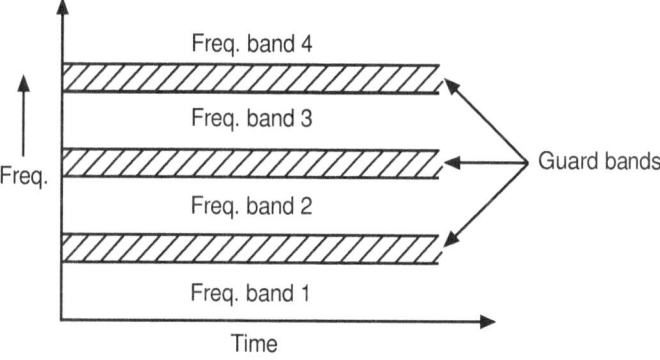

Fig. 4.52: FDMA

Example, BSNL uses FDMA technique for mobile communication.

The transponder operates upon these frequency bands simultaneously. The transponder consists of frequency converters and amplifiers. The amplifiers does not amplify all the frequencies equally. Because of this non-linearity, the frequency components of different users from different bands tends to interfere with each other.

Advantage: No time limit user can use the frequency band continuously.

In a situation where the number of earth stations is limited and there is continuous traffic between a pair of originating and receiving stations the traditional Frequency Division Multiplexing (FDM) or Time Division Multiplexing (TDM) techniques could be used where one slot is allocated to each station permanently. But in practice, the traffic may be much less. Moreover, the number of earth stations is usually much larger than the number of FDM or TDM slots that can be made available. This is particularly so in systems using DTU terminals.

In such a case, a free TDM or FDM slot needs to be allocated to an active station and deallocated as soon as the traffic ceases. The same slot may be allocated to another station thereafter. Such a scheme is known as Frequency Division Multiple Access (FDMA) or Time Division Multiple Access (TDMA), depending upon whether frequency or time division is used. The term **'multiple access'** is due to the fact that the same slot may be accessed by different stations at different times and a station may be allocated to different slots at different times. Multiple access may be preassigned or demand assigned. In preassigned schemes, a group of stations is identified with one or a group of FDM or TDM slots and given access only to these slots. In demand assigned multiple access (DAMA), scheme, there is a pool of space segment slots and any one of the available slot is assigned to a station when demanded by it.

Similar to FDMA and TDMA multiple access can be organised around code division multiplexing CDMA. In CDMA, individual bits of a message are encoded in terms of unique digital codes. Many stations, each having its unique code, transmit their signals simultaneously. The signals are discriminated by means of a cross correlator, using the code of the desired transmission as the reference code. Since, each transmitted symbol is encoded as a sequence of higher rate symbols, the scheme demands a much larger bandwidth for transmission and the technique is called code division multiple access, and hence is referred to as spread spectrum technique. The number of higher rate coding symbols per bit usually called chips, is an important parameter in CDMA and is referred to as processing gain or bandwidth spreading factor. The spectrum spreading property significantly reduces interference from other transmission. The codes used for CDMA are specifically selected to have good cross correlation properties so that interference from other unwanted signals simultaneously may be minimised. A family of Pseudo Random (PR) codes, known as GOLD codes have good cross correlation properties. CDMA may be used in two ways, one way is that every transmitting station uses its own PR sequence encoding data and a receiver station uses a separator correlator for each station it wishes to receive. The other way is for the transmitting station to choose the PR sequence of the destination station to encode its message. In this case each receiver station has only one correlator using its own PR code as the reference sequence. One of the applications, for which CDMA is very suitable is to transmit low bit rate data from a central station to any of a large number of receive only small stations. The capability of CDMA to selectively address the remote stations by use of different codes comes in very handy here. In India NICNET and RABMN use a CDMA access technique.

4.23 Time Division Multiple Access (TDMA)

In TDMA technique, each user is given a particular time slot regularly after fixed interval. During this slot, the user have the complete availability of satellite transponder. That is in this given time slot, the user can use the complete bandwidth of satellite transponder.

Guard band is inserted between each time slot to avoid interference from adjacent time slots.

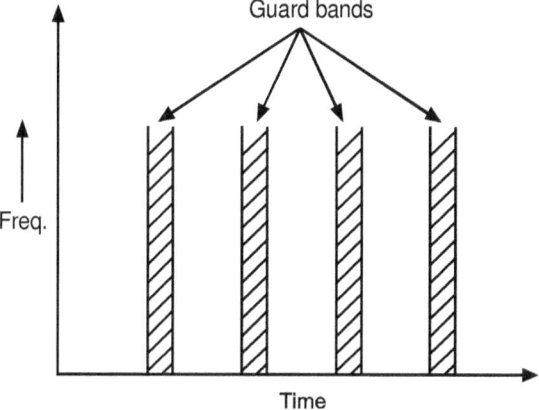

Fig. 4.53: TDMA

Time division multiplexing called **Time Division Multiple Access** (TDMA). As with standard time division multiplexing principles, channels are assigned time slot allocations. These time slots are separated by headers and guard bands. A typical TDMA frame is shown in Fig. 4.53. The frame contains 'N' number of bursts. These bursts are nothing but time slots allotted to the earth stations. Normally, one burst at the start of each frame is reserved for identification and synchronization. Thus, remaining (N – 1) bursts i.e. time slots are used by the ground station for transmission.

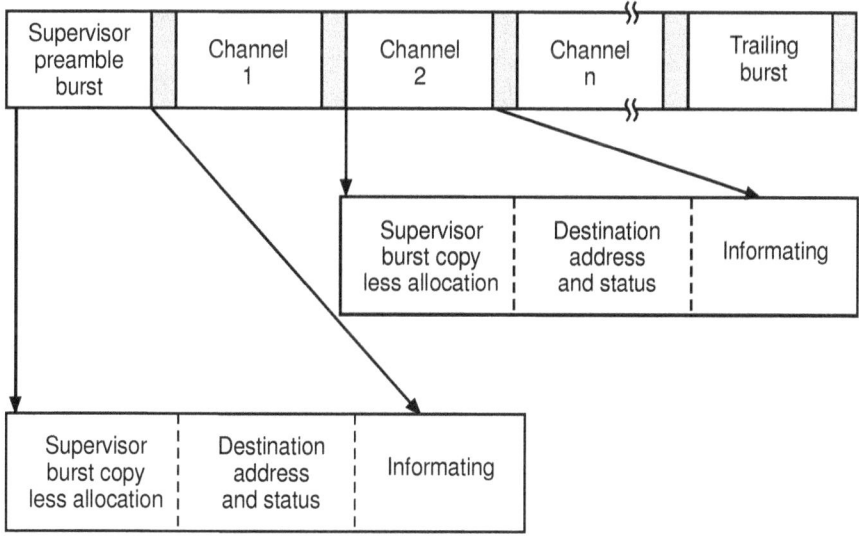

Fig. 4.54: TDMA frame

A supervisor burst of information precedes the transmission of channel information. The burst is used to establish symbol and burst timing. The first guard and band follows, and then the first channel's transmission. At the beginning the channel's block is header (or preamble), which repeats the supervisor burst and adds source and destination station addresses. Channel information completes the channel's block. Channel's are separated by guard bands to prevent overlaping between channels. A closing burst indicates the end of the transmission and reports status information about the transmission capacity and possible error occurrences.

Fig. 4.55 shows functional block diagram of a TDMA communications system. On the transmit side, the channels are multiplexed into their time slots and the control supervisor burst is added. This data stream modulates a 140 MHz intermediate carrier that is converted onto a 14 GHz carrier. The 14 GHz signal is sent to the satellite, arriving with a power of approximately 1 picowatt. The satellite transponder demodulates the 14 GHz for transmission back to earth. The 12 GHz signal is received by an earth station and is down converted to 140 MHz and demodulated. Finally, the demodulated information is demultiplexed to the various destination stations.

The disadvantage of TDMA is that user can use only in particular given time slot but not continuously.

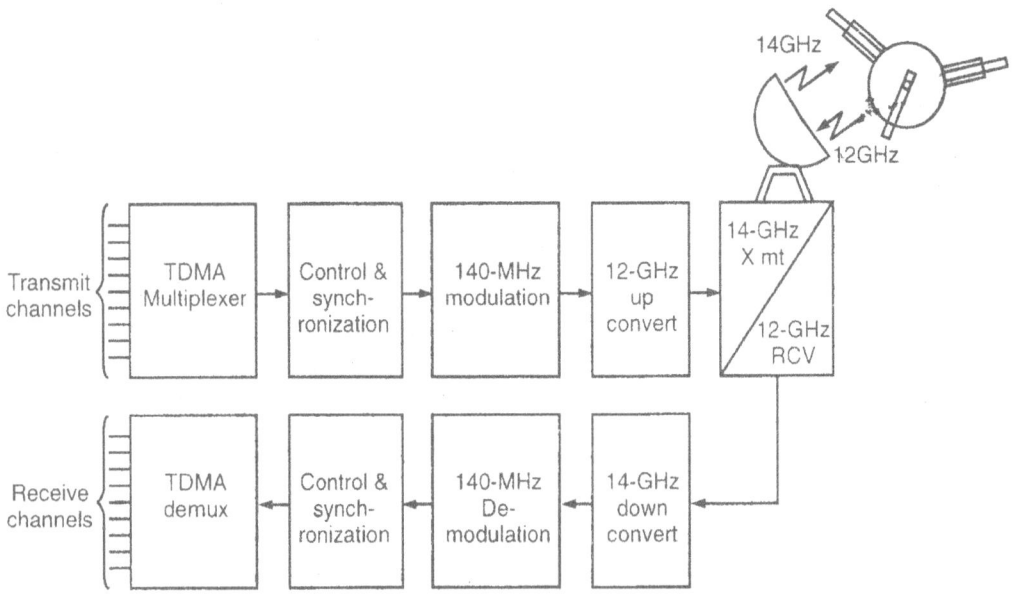

Fig. 4.55: TDMA communication system

4.24 Code Division Multiple Access (CDMA)

By combining TDMA and FDMA techniques, a hybrid technique formed called CDMA. Frequency hoping can be used so that the frequency bands assigned to the users are recorded in an essentially random manner.

Fig. 4.56 shows frequency time structure of CDMA technique.

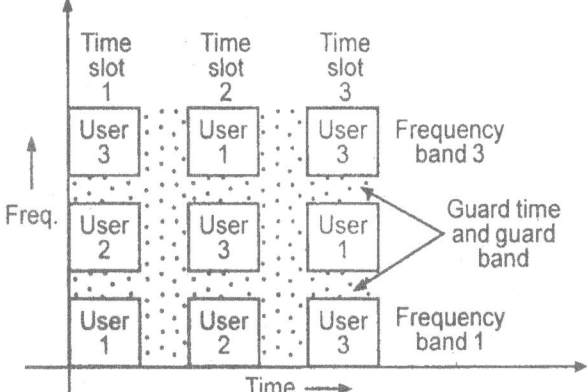

Fig. 4.56: CDMA structure

From structure, during time slot 1, user 1 occupies frequency band 1, user 2 occupies frequency band 2 and user 3 occupies frequency band 3. During second time slot, user 1 hops to frequency band 1, user 3 hops to band 2 and so on.

Example, suppose in a room, everyone is talking at once, then nothing can be understood. But if everyone is talking in different languages, then they can be understood.

Like this, CDMA has no channels but instead, every call is encoded by adding certain code (called psudo-noise code) that makes it different from other calls in frequency spectrum.

Advantages of CDMA:
1. Any external synchronization not required.
2. Noise reduction capability is better.

Comparison between FDMA, TDMA and CDMA:

Parameter	FDMA	TDMA	CDMA
1. Technique	Sharing of overall bandwidth of satellite transponder.	Sharing of time of the satellite transponder.	Sharing both time and frequency.
2. Synchronization	Not required.	Required.	Not required.
3. Code word	Not required.	Not required.	Required.
4. Power efficiency	Less.	Full power efficiency is possible.	Full power efficiency is possible.
5. Guard time and band.	Guard band required.	Guard time required.	Both guard time and band required.

4.25 IEEE 802.3 and Ethernet

- Very popular LAN standard.
- Ethernet and IEEE 802.3 are distinct standards but as they are very similar to one another these words are used interchangeably.
- A standard for a 1-persistent CSMA/CD LAN.
- It covers the physical layer and MAC sublayer protocol.

4.25.1 Ethernet Physical Layer A Comparison of Various Ethernet and IEEE 802.3 Physical-Layer Specifications.

Characteristic	Ethernet Value	IEEE 802.3 Values						
		10Base5	10Base2	10BaseT	10BaseF	10 Base -TX	100BaseT4
Data rate (Mbps)	10	10	10	10	10	100	100
Signaling method	Baseband	Baseband	Baseband	Baseband	Baseband	Baseband	Baseband
Maximum segment length (m)	500	500	185	100	2,000	100	100
Media	50-ohm coax (thick)	50-ohm coax (thick)	50-ohm coax (thin)	Unshielded twisted-pair cable	Fiber-optic	Cat 5 UTP	Unshielded twisted-pair cable
Nodes/segment	100	100	30	1024	1024		
Topology	Bus	Bus	Bus	Star	Point-to-point	Bus	Bus

10Base5 means it operates at 10 Mbps, uses baseband signaling and can support segments of up to 500 meters. The 10Base5 cabling is popularly called the **Thick Ethernet**. Vampire taps are used for their connections where a pin is carefully forced halfway into the co-axial cable's core as shown in the Fig. 4.57. The 10Base2 or Thin Ethernet bends easily and is connected using standard BNC connectors to form T junctions. In the 10Base-T scheme a different kind of wiring pattern is followed in which all stations have a twisted-pair cable running to a central hub. The difference between the different physical connections is shown in Fig. 4.57.

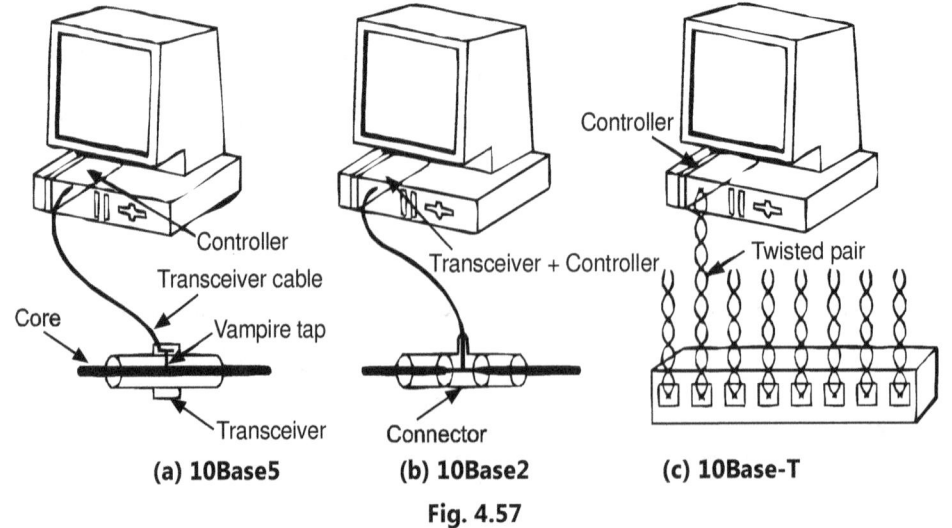

(a) 10Base5   (b) 10Base2   (c) 10Base-T

Fig. 4.57

All 802.3 baseband systems use Manchester encoding, which is a way for receivers to unambiguously determine the start, end or middle of each bit without reference to an external clock. There is a restriction on the minimum node spacing (segment length between two nodes) in 10Base5 and 10Base2 and that is 2.5 meter and 0.5 meter respectively. The reason is that if two nodes are closer than the specified limit then there will be very high current which may cause trouble in detection of signal at the receiver end. Connections from station to cable of 10Base5 (i.e. Thick Ethernet) are generally made using vampire taps and to 10Base2 (i.e. Thin Ethernet) are made using industry standard BNC connectors to form T junctions. To allow larger networks, multiple segments can be connected by repeaters as shown. A repeater is a physical layer device. It receives, amplifies and retransmits signals in either direction.

4.25.2 IEEE 802.3 Frame Structure

Preamble (7 bytes)	Start of Frame Delimiter (1 byte)	Dest. Address (2/6 bytes)	Source Address (2/6 bytes)	Length (2 bytes)	802.2 Header+Data (46-1500 bytes)	Frame Checksum (4 bytes)

Description of each of the fields:

- **Preamble:** Each frame starts with a preamble of 7 bytes, each byte containing the bit pattern 10101010. Manchester encoding is employed here and this enables the receiver's clock to synchronize with the sender's and initialise itself.
- **Start of Frame Delimiter:** This field containing a byte sequence 10101011 denotes the start of the frame itself.
- **Dest. Address:** The standard allows 2-byte and 6-byte addresses. Note that the 2-byte addresses are always local addresses while the 6-byte ones can be local or global.

2-Byte Address - Manually assigned address

Individual(0)/Group(1) (1 bit)	Address of the machine (15 bits)

6-Byte Address - Every Ethernet card with globally unique address

Individual(0)/Group(1) (1 bit)	Universal(0)/Local(1) (1 bit)	Address of the machine (46 bits)

- **Multicast:** Sending to group of stations. This is ensured by setting the first bit in either 2-byte/6-byte addresses to 1.

- **Broadcast:** Sending to all stations. This can be done by setting all bits in the address field to 1. All Ethernet cards (Nodes) are a member of this group.
- **Source Address:** Refer to Dest. Address. Same holds true over here.
- **Length:** The Length field tells how many bytes are present in the data field, from a minimum of 0 to a maximum of 1500. The Data and padding together can be from 46bytes to 1500 bytes as the valid frames must be at least 64 bytes long, thus if data is less than 46 bytes the amount of padding can be found out by length field.
- **Data:** Actually this field can be split up into two parts - Data(0-1500 bytes) and Padding (0-46 bytes).

Reasons for having a minimum length frame:

1. To prevent a station from completing the transmission of a short frame before the first bit has even reached the far end of the cable, where it may collide with another frame. Note that the transmission time ought to be greater than twice the propagation time between two farthest nodes.

   transmission time for frame > 2*propagation time between two farthest nodes

2. When a transceiver detects a collision, it truncates the current frame, which implies that stray bits and pieces of frames appear on the cable all the time. Hence to distinguish between valid frames from garbage, 802.3 states that the minimum length of valid frames ought to be 64 bytes (from Dest. Address to Frame Checksum).

- **Frame Checksum:** It is a 32-bit hash code of the data. If some bits are erroneously received by the destination (due to noise on the cable), the checksum computed by the destination would not match with the checksum sent and therefore the error will be detected. The checksum algorithm is a Cyclic Redundancy Checksum (CRC) kind. The checksum includes the packet from Dest. Address to Data field.

Ethernet Frame Structure

Preamble (8 bytes)	Dest. Address (2/6 bytes)	Source Address (2/6 bytes)	Type (2 bytes)	Data (46-1500 bytes)	Frame Checksum (4 bytes)

A brief description of the fields which differ from IEEE 802.3

- **Preamble:** The *Preamble* and *Start of Frame Delimiter* are merged into one in Ethernet standard. However, the contents of the first 8 bytes remains the same in both.
- **Type:** The length field of IEEE 802.3 is replaced by Type field, which denotes the type of packet being sent viz. IP, ARP, RARP, etc. If the field indicates a value less than 1500 bytes then it is length field of 802.3 else it is the type field of Ethernet packet.

4.26 IEEE 802.4: Token Bus Network

In this system, the nodes are physically connected as a bus, but logically form a ring with tokens passed around to determine the turns for sending. It has the robustness of the 802.3 broadcast cable and the known worst case behavior of a ring. The structure of a token bus network is as follows:

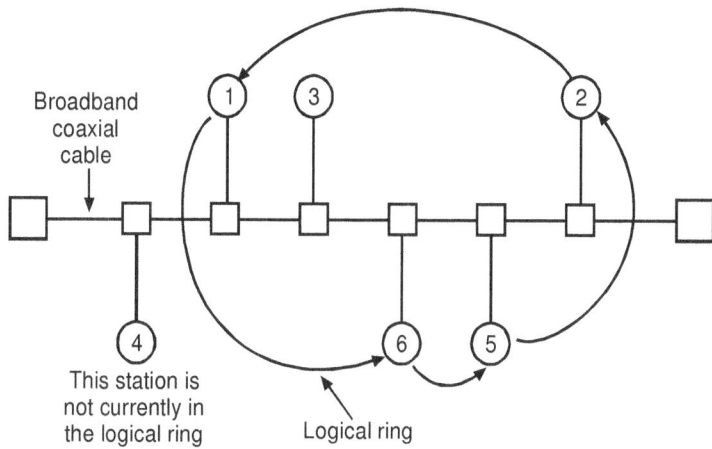

Fig. 4.58

8.12.1 Frame Structure

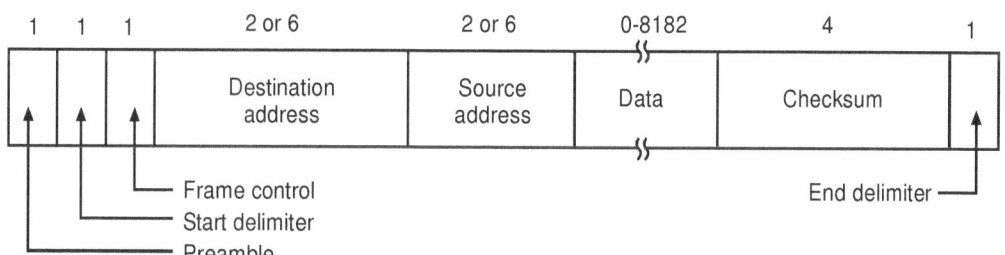

Fig. 4.59

A 802.4 frame has the following fields:

- **Preamble:** The Preamble is used to synchronize the receiver's clock.
- **Starting Delimiter (SD) and End Delimiter (ED):** The Starting Delimiter and Ending Delimiter fields are used to mark frame boundaries. Both of them contain analog encoding of symbols other than 1 or 0 so that they cannot occur accidentally in the user data. Hence no length field is needed.
- **Frame Control (FC):** This field is used to distinguish data frames from control frames. For data frames, it carries the frame's priority as well as a bit which the destination can set as an acknowledgement. For control frames, the Frame Control field is used to specify the

frame type. The allowed types include token passing and various ring maintenance frames.

- **Destination and Source Address:** The Destination and Source address fields may be 2 bytes (for a local address) or 6 bytes (for a global address).
- **Data:** The Data field carries the actual data and it may be 8182 bytes when 2 byte addresses are used and 8174 bytes for 6 byte addresses.
- **Checksum:** A 4-byte checksum calculated for the data. Used in error detection.

4.27 IEEE 802.5: Token Ring Network

- Token Ring is formed by the nodes connected in ring format as shown in the Fig. 4.60. The principle used in the token ring network is that a token is circulating in the ring and whichever node grabs that token will have right to transmit the data.
- Whenever, a station wants to transmit a frame it inverts a single bit of the 3-byte token which instantaneously changes it into a normal data packet. Because there is only one token, there can atmost be one transmission at a time.
- Since, the token rotates in the ring it is guaranteed that every node gets the token with in some specified time. So there is an upper bound on the time of waiting to grab the token so that starvation is avoided.
- There is also an upper limit of 250 on the number of nodes in the network.
- To distinguish the normal data packets from token (control packet) a special sequence is assigned to the token packet. When any node gets the token it first sends the data it wants to send, then recirculates the token.

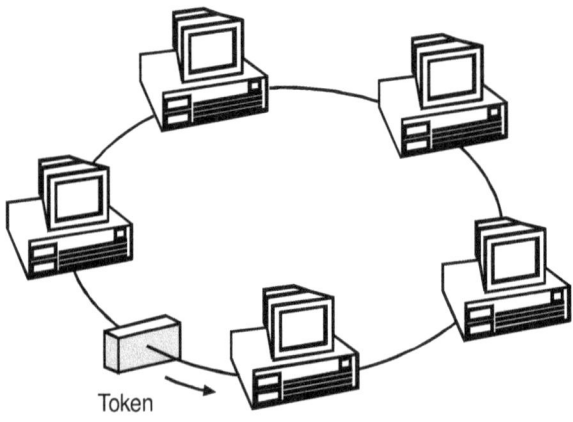

Token

Fig. 4.60

If a node transmits the token and nobody wants to send the data the token comes back to the sender. If the first bit of the token reaches the sender before the transmission of the last bit, then error situation araises. So to avoid this we should have:

Propagation delay + transmission of n-bits (1-bit delay in each node) > transmission of the token time.

A station may hold the token for the token-holding time. which is 10 ms unless the installation sets a different value. If there is enough time left after the first frame has been transmitted to send more frames, then these frames may be sent as well. After all pending frames have been transmitted or the transmission frame would exceed the token-holding time, the station regenerates the 3-byte token frame and puts it back on the ring.

4.27.1 Modes of Operation

1. Listen Mode: In this mode the node listens to the data and transmits the data to the next node. In this mode there is a one-bit delay associated with the transmission.

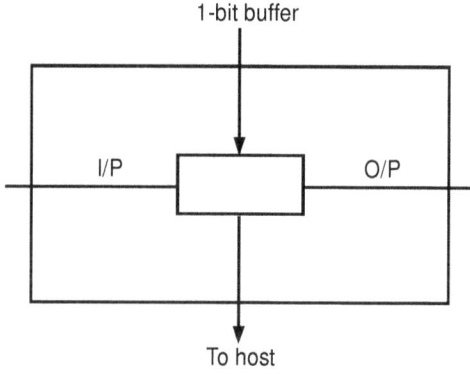

Fig. 4.61

2. Transmit Mode: In this mode the node just discards the any data and puts the data onto the network.

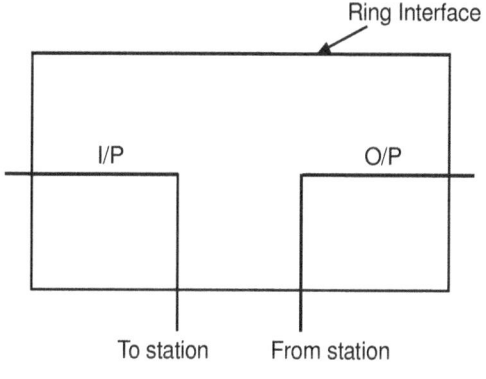

Fig. 4.62

3. By-pass Mode: In this mode reached when the node is down. Any data is just bypassed. There is no one-bit delay in this mode.

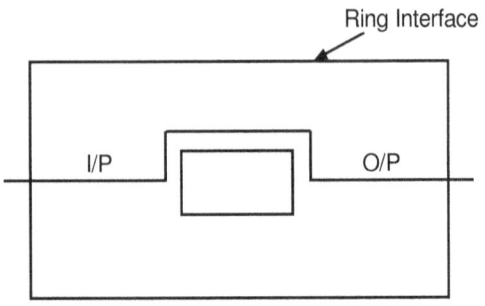

Fig. 4.63

4.27.2 Token Ring Using Ring Concentrator

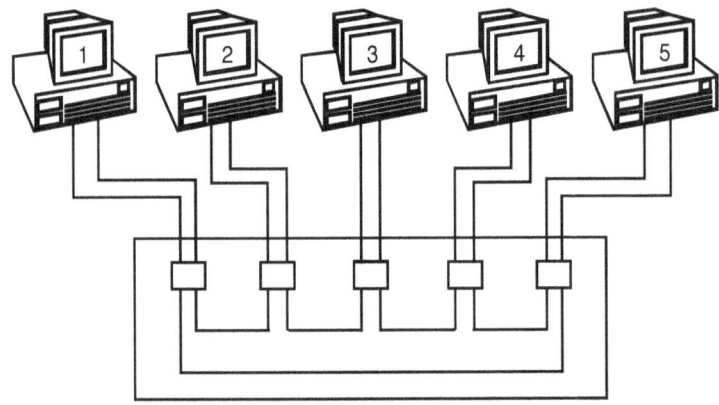

Fig. 4.64

One problem with a ring network is that if the cable breaks somewhere, the ring dies. This problem is elegantly addressed by using a ring concentrator. A Token Ring concentrator simply changes the topology from a physical ring to a star wired ring. But the network still remains a ring logically. Physically, each station is connected to the ring concentrator (wire center) by a cable containing at least two twisted pairs, one for data to the station and one for data from the station. The Token still circulates around the network and is still controlled in the same manner, however, using a hub or a switch greatly improves reliability because the hub can automatically bypass any ports that are disconnected or have a cabling fault. This is done by having bypass relays inside the concentrator that are energized by current from the stations. If the ring breaks or station goes down, loss of the drive current will release the relay and bypass the station. The ring can then continue operation with the bad segment bypassed.

4.27.3 Token Format

The token is the shortest frame transmitted (24 bit) MSB (Most Significant Bit) is always transmitted first - as opposed to Ethernet

SD AC ED

SD = Starting Delimiter (1 Octet)

AC = Access Control (1 Octet)

ED = Ending Delimiter (1 Octet)

Starting Delimiter Format:

J K O J K O O O

J = Code Violation

K = Code Violation

Access Control Format:

P P P T M R R R

T = Token

T = 0 for Token

T = 1 for Frame

When a station with a Frame to transmit detects a token which has a priority equal to or less than the Frame to be transmitted, it may change the token to a start-of-frame sequence and transmit the Frame

P = Priority

Priority Bits indicate tokens priority, and therefore, which stations are allowed to use it. Station can transmit if its priority as at least as high as that of the token.

M = Monitor

The monitor bit is used to prevent a token whose priority is greater than 0 or any frame from continuously circulating on the ring. If an active monitor detects a frame or a high priority token with the monitor bit equal to 1, the frame or token is aborted. This bit shall be transmitted as 0 in all frame and tokens. The active monitor inspects and modifies this bit. All other stations shall repeat this bit as received.

R = Reserved bits

The reserved bits allow station with high priority Frames to request that the next token be issued at the requested priority.

4.27.4 Ending Delimiter Format

J K 1 J K 1 1 E

J = Code Violation

K = Code Violation

I = Intermediate Frame Bit

E = Error Detected Bit

4.27.5 Frame Format

MSB (Most Significant Bit) is always transmitted first - as opposed to Ethernet

SD AC FC DA SA DATA CRC ED FS

SD = Starting Delimiter(1 octet)

AC = Access Control(1 octet)

FC = Frame Control (1 Octet)

DA = Destination Address (2 or 6 Octets)

SA = Source Address (2 or 6 Octets)

DATA = Information 0 or more octets up to 4027

CRC = Checksum(4 Octets)

ED = Ending Delimiter (1 Octet)

FS=Frame Status

Starting Delimiter Format:

J K 0 J K 0 0 0

J = Code Violation

K = Code Violation

Access Control Format:

P P P T M R R

T = Token

T = ?0? for Token,

T = ?1? for Frame

When a station with a Frame to transmit detects a token which has a priority equal to or less than the Frame to be transmitted, it may change the token to a start-of-frame sequence and transmit the Frame.

P = Priority

Bits Priority Bits indicate tokens priority, and therefore, which stations are allowed to use it. Station can transmit if its priority as at least as high as that of the token.

M = Monitor

The monitor bit is used to prevent a token whose priority is greater than 0 or any frame from continuously circulating on the ring. if an active monitor detects a frame or a high priority token with the monitor bit equal to 1, the frame or token is aborted. This bit shall be transmitted as 0 in all frame and tokens. The active monitor inspects and modifies this bit. All other stations shall repeat this bit as received.

R = **Reserved bits** the reserved bits allow station with high priority Frames to request that the next token be issued at the requested priority.

4.27.6 Frame Control Format

F F	CONTROL BITS (6 BITS)

FF = Type of Packet-Regular data packet or MAC layer packet Control Bits= Used if the packet is for MAC layer protocol itself

Source and Destination Address Format:

The addresses can be of 2 bytes (local address) or 6 bytes (global address).

local address format:

I/G (1 BIT)	NODE ADDRESS (15 BITS)

alternatively

I/G (1 BIT)	RING ADDRESS (7 BITS)	NODE ADDRESS (8 BITS)

The first bit specifies individual or group address.

Universal (global) address format:

I/G (1 BIT)	L/U (1 BIT)	RING ADDRESS (14 BITS)	NODE ADDRESS (32 BITS)

The first bit specifies individual or group address. The second bit specifies local or global (universal) address.

Local group addresses (16 bits):

| I/G (1 BIT) | T/B(1 BIT) | GROUP ADDRESS (14 BITS) |

The first bit specifies an individual or group address. The second bit specifies traditional or bit signature group address.

Traditional Group Address: $2Exp14$ groups can be defined.

Bit Signature Group Address: 14 groups are defined. A host can be a member of none or any number of them. For multicasting, those group bits are set to which the packet should go. For broadcasting, all 14 bits are set. A host receives a packet only if it is a member of a group whose corresponding bit is set to 1.

Universal group addresses (16 bits):

| I/G (1 BIT) | RING NUMBER | T/B (1 BIT) | GROUP ADDRESS (14 BITS) |

The description is similar to as above.

Data Format:

No upper limit on amount of data as such, but it is limited by the token holding time.

Checksum:

The source computes and sets this value. Destination too calculates this value. If the two are different, it indicates an error, otherwise the data may be correct.

4.27.7 Frame Status

It contains the A and C bits.

A bit set to 1: destination recognized the packet.

C bit set to 1: destination accepted the packet.

This arrangement provides an automatic acknowledgement for each frame. The A and C bits are present twice in the Frame Status to increase reliability in as much as they are not covered by the checksum.

Ending Delimiter Format:

| J | K | 1 | J | K | 1 | I | E |

J = Code Violation

K = Code Violation

I = Intermediate Frame Bit

If this bit is set to 1, it indicates that this packet is an intermediate part of a bigger packet, the last packet would have this bit set to 0.

E = Error Detected Bit

This bit is set if any interface detects an error.

This concludes our description of the token ring frame format.

4.27.8 Phase Jitter Compensation

In a token ring the source starts discarding all it's previously transmitted bits as soon as they circumnavigate the ring and reach the source. Hence, it's not desirable that while a token is being sent some bits of the token which have already been sent become available at the incoming end of the source. This behavior though is desirable in case of data packets which ought to be drained from the ring once they have gone around the ring. To achieve the aforesaid behavior with respect to tokens, we would like the ring to hold at least 24 bits at a time. How do we ensure this?

Each node in a ring introduces a 1 bit delay. So, one approach might be to set the minimum limit on the number of nodes in a ring as 24. But, this is not a viable option. The actual solution is as follows. We have one node in the ring designated as **"monitor"**. The monitor maintains a 24 bits buffer with help of which it introduces a 24 bit delay. The catch here is what if the clocks of nodes following the source are faster than the source? In this case the 24 bit delay of the monitor would be less than the 24 bit delay desired by the host. To avoid this situation the monitor maintains 3 extra bits to compensate for the faster bits. The 3 extra bits suffice even if bits are 10 % faster. This compensation is called Phase Jitter Compensation.

4.27.9 Handling Multiple Priority Frames

Each node or packet has a priority level. We don't concern ourselves with how this priority is decided. The first 3 bits of the Access Control byte in the token are for priority and the last 3 are for reservation.

P P P T M R R R

Initially the reservation bits are set to 000. When a node wants to transmit a priority n frame, it must wait until it can capture a token whose priority is less than or equal to n. Furthermore, when a data frame goes by, a station can try to reserve the next token by writing the priority of the frame it wants to send into the frame's Reservation bits. However, if a higher priority has already been reserved there, the station cannot make a reservation. When the current frame is finished, the next token is generated at the priority that has been reserved.

A slight problem with the above reservation procedure is that the reservation priority keeps on increasing. To solve this problem, the station raising the priority remembers the reservation priority that it replaces and when it is done it reduces the priority to the previous priority.

Note that in a token ring, low priority frames may starve.

4.27.10 Ring Maintenance

Each token ring has a monitor that oversees the ring. Among the monitor's responsibilities are seeing that the token is not lost, taking action when the ring breaks, cleaning the ring when garbled frames appear and watching out for orphan frames. An orphan frame occurs when a station transmits a short frame in it's entirety onto a long ring and then crashes or is powered down before the frame can be removed. If nothing is done, the frame circulates indefinitely.

- **Detection of orphan frames:** The monitor detects orphan frames by setting the monitor bit in the Access Control byte whenever it passes through. If an incoming frame has this bit set, something is wrong since the same frame has passed the monitor twice. Evidently it was not removed by the source, so the monitor drains it.

- **Lost Tokens:** The monitor has a timer that is set to the longest possible tokenless interval: when each node transmits for the full token holding time. If this timer goes off, the monitor drains the ring and issues a fresh token.

- **Garbled frames:** The monitor can detect such frames by their invalid format or checksum, drain the ring and issue a fresh token.

The token ring control frames for maintenance are:

Table 4.7

Control field	Name	Meaning
00000000	Duplicate address test	Test if two stations have the same address
00000010	Beacon	Used to locate breaks in the ring
00000011	Claim token	Attempt to become monitor
00000100	Purge	Reinitialize the ring
00000101	Active monitor present	Issued periodically by the monitor
00000110	Standby monitor present	Announces the presence of potential monitors

The monitor periodically issues a message "Active Monitor Present" informing all nodes of its presence. When this message is not received for a specific time interval, the nodes detect a monitor failure. Each node that believes it can function as a monitor broadcasts a "Standby Monitor Present" message at regular intervals, indicating that it is ready to take on the monitor's job. Any node that detects failure of a monitor issues a "Claim" token. There are three possible outcomes:

1. If the issuing node gets back its own claim token, then it becomes the monitor.
2. If a packet different from a claim token is received, apparently a wrong guess of monitor failure was made. In this case on receipt of our own claim token, we discard it. Note that our claim token may have been removed by some other node which has detected this error.

3. If some other node has also issued a claim token, then the node with the larger address becomes the monitor.

In order to resolve errors of duplicate addresses, whenever a node comes up it sends a **"Duplicate Address Detection"** message (with the destination = source) across the network. If the address recognize bit has been set on receipt of the message, the issuing node realizes a duplicate address and goes to standby mode. A node informs other nodes of removal of a packet from the ring through a **"Purge"** message. One maintenance function that the monitor cannot handle is locating breaks in the ring. If there is no activity detected in the ring (e.g. Failure of monitor to issue the **Active Monitor Present** token...) , the usual procedures of sending a claim token are followed. If the claim token itself is not received besides packets of any other kind, the node then sends **"Beacons"** at regular intervals until a message is received indicating that the broken ring has been repaired.

4.27.11 Other Ring Networks
The problem with the token ring system is that large rings cause large delays. It must be made possible for multiple packets to be in the ring simultaneously. The following ring networks resolve this problem to some extent:

Slotted Ring:
In this system, the ring is slotted into a number of fixed size frames which are continuously moving around the ring. This makes it necessary that there be enough number of nodes (large ring size) to ensure that all the bits can stay on the ring at the same time. The frame header contains information as to whether the slots are empty or full. The usual disadvantages of overhead/wastage associated with fixed size frames are present.

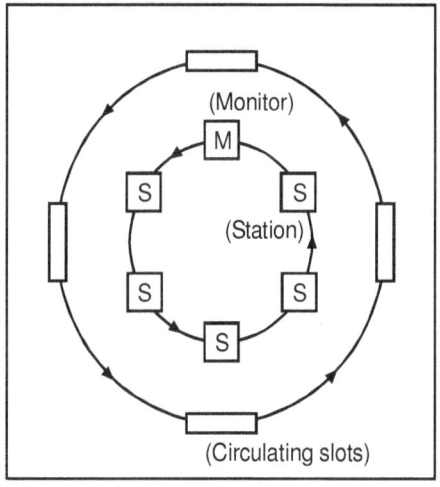

Fig. 4.65

Register Insertion Rings:

This is an improvement over slotted ring architecture. The network interface consists of two registers: a shift register and an output buffer. At startup, the input pointer points to the rightmost bit position in the input shift register. When a bit arrives it is in the rightmost empty position (the one indicated by the input pointer). After the node has detected that the frame is not addressed to it, the bits are transmitted one at time (by shifting). As new bits come in, they are inserted at the position indicated by the pointer and then the contents are shifted. Thus, the pointer is not moved. Once, the shift register has pushed out the last bit of a frame, it checks to see if it has an output frame waiting. In case yes, then it checks that if the number of empty slots in the shift register is at least equal to the number of bits in the output frame. After this the output connection is switched to this second register and after the register has emptied its contents, the output line is switched back to the shift register. Thus, no single node can hog the bandwidth. In a loaded system, a node can transmit a k-bit frame only if it has saved up a k-bits of inter frame gaps.

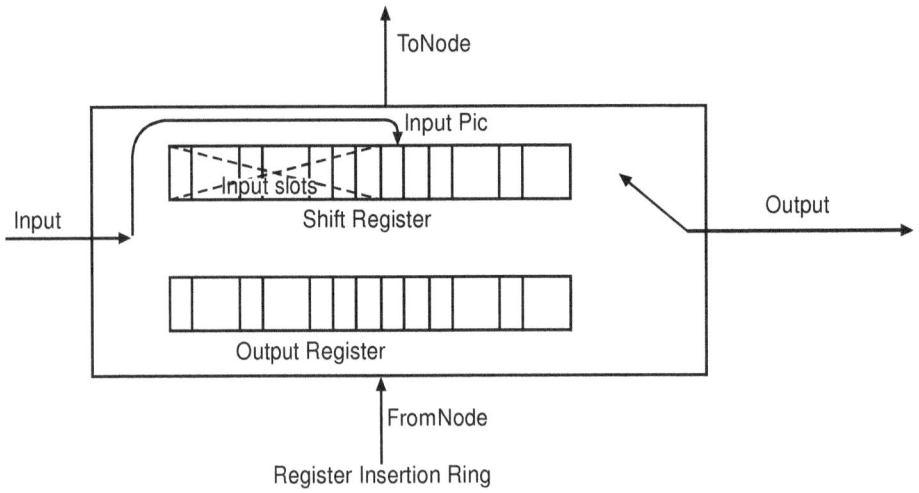

Fig. 4.65

Two major disadvantages of this topology are complicated hardware and difficulty in the detection of start/end of packets.

4.27.12 Contention Ring

The token ring has primarily two problems:

- On light loads, huge overhead is incurred for token passing.
- Nodes with low priority data may starve if there is always a node with high priority data.

A contention ring attempts to address these problems. In a contention ring, if there is no communication in the ring for a while, a sender node will send its data immediately, followed by a token. If the token comes back to the sender without any data packet in between, the sender removes it from the ring. However under heavy load the behavior is that of a normal token ring. In case a collision, each of the sending nodes will remove the others data packet from the ring, back off for a random period of time and then resend their data.

4.28 High Level Data Link Control (HDLC)
- It is the most widely used DLL protocol.
- It has a set of functions which provides communication service to network layer.
- HDLC supports variety of applications for which it has three types of stations, two link configurations and there three data transfer modes.

Types of Stations:
(i) **Primary stations:** It controls operation of link. It issues commands.
(ii) **Secondary station:** Primary station controls it by issuing command frames transmitted by secondary station.
(iii) **Combined station:** It has features of both primary and secondary stations i.e. it issues both commands and response.

Types of Configuration:
(i) **Unbalanced configuration:** It has one primary and one or more secondary stations. It supports both full duplex and half duplex configuration.
(ii) **Balanced configuration:** It consists of two combined stations supporting half duplex and full duplex transmission.

These configurations are shown in Fig. 4.67 (a) (b) and (c).

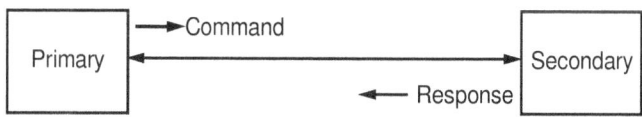

(a) Unbalanced Point-to-Point Link

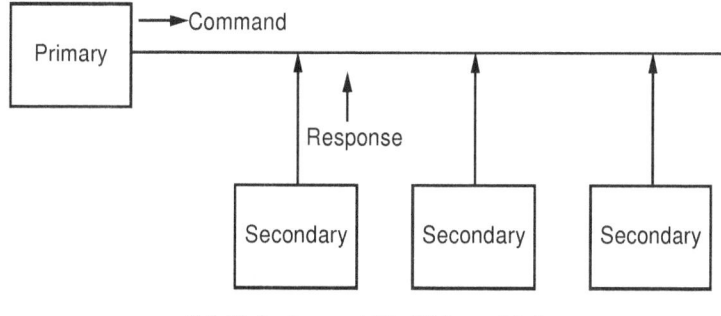

(b) Unbalanced Multidrop Link

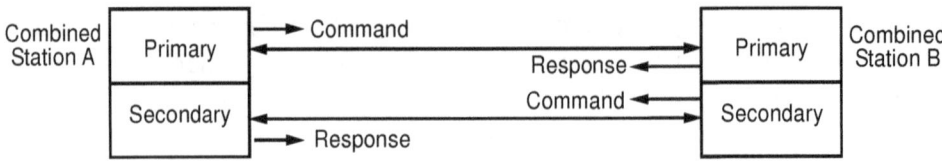

(c) Balanced Point-to-Point Link

Fig. 4.67

Types of data transfer modes:

(i) **Normal Response Mode (NRM):** Used with unbalanced configuration. Primary can initiate data transfer to a secondary. Secondary can only transfer data in response to command from primary.

(ii) **Asynchronous Balanced Mode (ABM):** Used with balanced configuration. Any one of the combined station can initiate transmission without the permission of other station.

(iii) **Asynchronous Response Mode (ARM):** Used with unbalanced configuration secondary can initiate transmission without permission from primary. But primary has control of the link.

NRM can be used on multidrop lines and point-to-point links. ABM is most widely used. ARM is rarely used.

4.28.1 HDLC Frame Format

- The functionality of a protocol depends on the control fields that are defined in the header and trailer.
- The various data transfer modes are determined by the frame structure.
- Fig. 4.68 shows HDLC frame format.

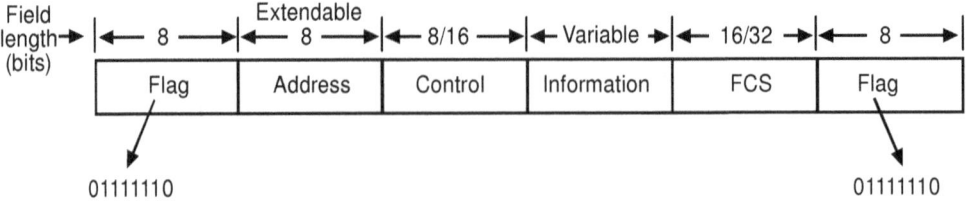

Fig. 4.68: HDLC frame format

- Information is attached with an header consisting of flag, address and control fields and a trailer consisting of checksum and flag.

- Flag fields which are 8 bit long delimit the frame at both ends with a pattern 01111110. Bit stuffing is used to achieve data transparency.
- The addressing function of DLL is identifying the station that transmitted the frame and the station that will be receiving the frame. The address field specifies this. It is extendable over more than 8 bits in multiples. If this field is all 1's, the frame is broadcast to all secondaries.
- There are three types of control fields to identify three types of frames.
    - **(i)** **Information frame (I-frame)** has 0 in the first bit of control field.
    - **(ii)** **Supervisory frame (S-frame)** has 10 in first two bits of control field.
    - **(iii)** **Unnumbered frame (U-frame)** has 11 in first two bits of control field.

Error control and flow control functions of DLL are provided by I-frame and S-frame. The three frame fields are shown in Fig. 4.69.

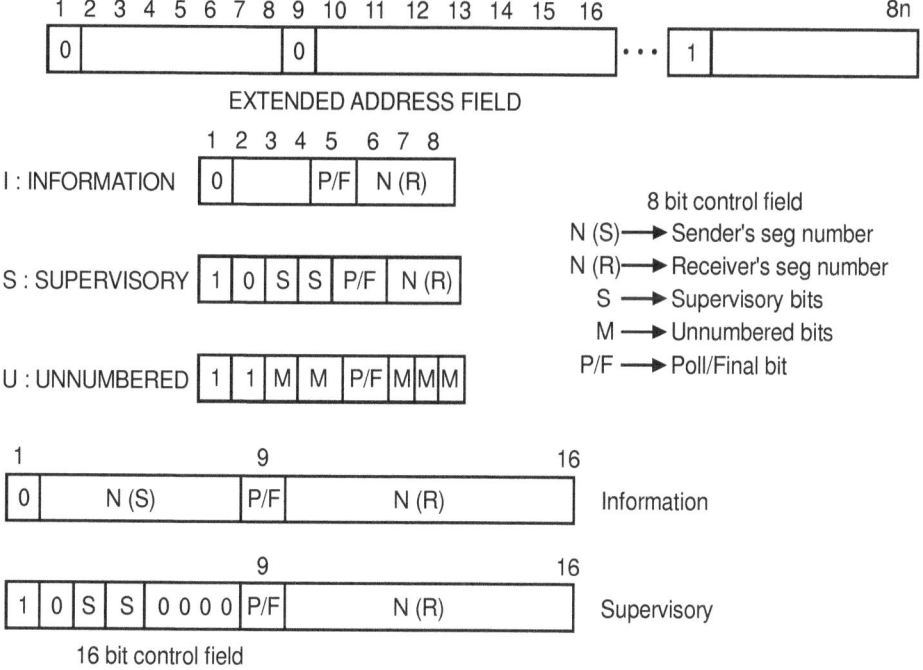

Fig. 4.69

Information field consists of 3 bit sequence number N(S) and N(R) of sender and acknowledgement number of receiver respectively (piggybacked). All frames have a P/F bit. Its uses depends on situation. In command frames it is called P bit and is set to 1 whenever a response frame is expected (Polled) from peer entity. In response frames it is called F bit and is set to 1 to indicate that the frame is response to a command frame (Poll). The length of information frame can be variable.

There are four types of supervisory frames decided by S-field.

If SS = 00. It is Receive Ready (RR) which acknowledges received frames in absence of piggybacking.

IF SS = 01. It is reject frame indicating negative acknowledgement and transmitter should go back and transmit frames N(R) onward.

SS = 10 means receive not ready (RNR). Buffer full condition.

SS = 11 indicates selective reject, where N(R) is frame to be retransmitted.

– Combination of I-frame and S-frame allows HDLC to implement ARQ techniques.

– The unnumbered frames implement number of control functions.

The M bits decide the function.

They are as below.

(i) **Set Asynchronous Balanced Mode (SABM):** To set up asynchronous balanced mode connection.

(ii) **Set Normal Response Mode (SNRM):** To set up normal response mode.

(iii) **Disconnect (DISC):** Indicates station wishes to disconnect connection.

(iv) **Unnumbered Acknowledgement (UA):** Acknowledges frames during call set up.

(v) **Frame Reject (FRMR):** Reject unacceptable frame.

– The information field contains sequence of bits in multiples of octets. Length of F-field is variable.

– Frame Check Sequence (FCS) field consists of error detecting code calculated from frame bits except flag fields. It has 16 bit CRC CCITT code.

4.28.2 Operation of HDLC

Let us now see how HDLC operates.

Connection Establishment and Release:

– Station A sends SAMB (Set Asynchronous Balanced Mode) frame indicating that it wants to establish a new connection.

– Station B sends unnumbered acknowledgement if it is ready to proceed. Otherwise it will REJECT the request by sending RNR frame.

– Whenever station wants to release connection it sends DISC frame and other stations sends unnumbered acknowledgement. It is shown in Fig. 4.70.

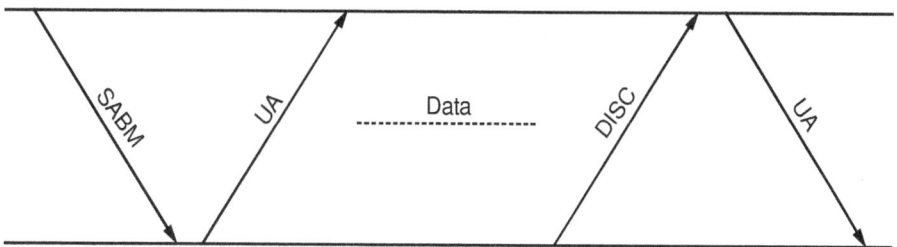

Fig. 4.70: HDLC Connection Establishment and Release

Exchange of Frames using Normal Response Mode:

Assuming that connection is established between Station A as primary and Station B and C as secondary, exchange of frames is shown in Fig. 4.71.

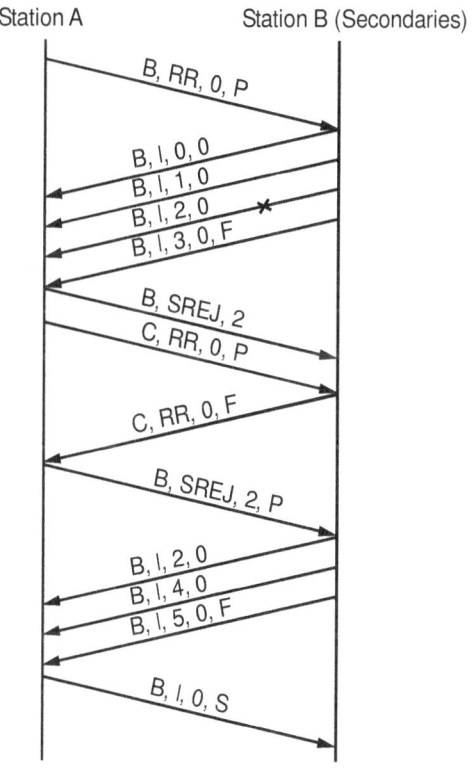

Fig. 4.71: Exchange of frames using NRM

- Station A polls B with N(R) = 0. Station B responds by sending frames 0, 1, 2, 3, with F bits set in last frame.

- Station A sends rejection of frame 2 and polls station C, which responds with receive ready frame.

- Station A again sends request to transmit frame 2 to B with poll bit set. Station B responds by sending frames 2, 4, 5 with F bit set in last frame.

- Station A sends information frame piggybacking acknowledgement of 5.

Exchange of frames using Asynchronous Balanced Mode (Refer Fig. 4.72).

Address field consists of address of receiving station, if it is information frame and address of transmitting station, if it is command frame or a response frame. Whenever frame is in error a REJ frame is send indicating number of bad frame so that transmitting station resends all the frames starting from that frame (Go back N) as is seen in case frame 1 rejected by station B.

Information frame consists of N(S) and N(R), where N(S) is transmitted frame number and N(R) is expected frame number i.e. piggy back acknowledgement. In case station does not have information frame to send it sends RR frame with acknowledgement of previously received frame.

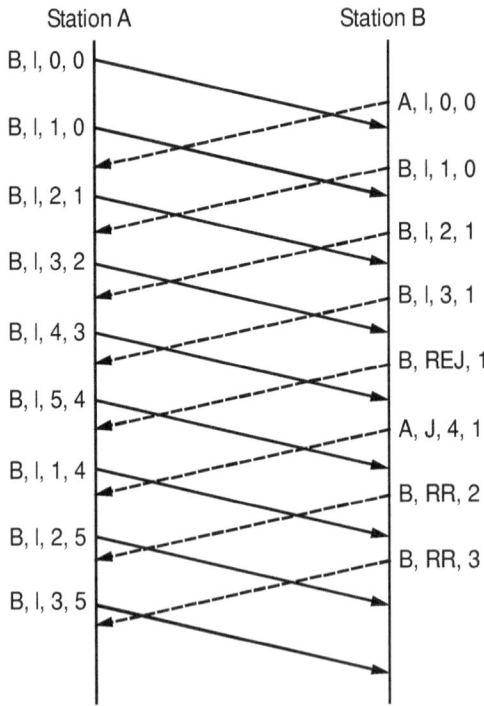

Fig. 4.72: Exchange of frames using ABM

4.29 X.21

It is a physical-layer protocol used in X.25 that defines the electrical and mechanical procedures for using the physical medium. The physical X.25 connector is 15 pins with some pins used as NULL given as follows.

Table 4.8

Line	NAME	From DTE	From DCE
G	GROUND	-	-
Ga	DTE common ground	Y	-
T	Transmit	Y	-
R	Receive	-	Y
C	Control	Y	-
I	Indication	-	Y
S	Signal Element Timing	-	Y
B	Byte Timing	-	Y

4.29.1 DTE Interface

DTE uses the Tx and Ctrl circuits to transmit data and control information, and the common ground for electrical purposes.

4.29.2 DCE Interface

DCE uses the Rx and Indication circuits for data and control. The DCE emits a timing signal stream on S to indicate bit-level timing to the DTE end. The DCE can also use the B wire to indicate byte-level framing. If the B circuit is not used, two synchronization bytes (SYN) are transmitted from DCE to DTE to allow the DTE to synchronize and calculate the byte-frame boundary.

As explained above, X.21bis handles the activation and deactivation of the physical medium connecting DTE and DCE devices. It supports point-to-point connections, speeds up to 19.2 kbps, and synchronous, full-duplex transmission over four-wire media.

4.29.3 X.21-bis

X.21bis is a physical-layer synchronous serial protocol which X.25 uses for communication with analog terminals. The physical X.25 connector is 15 pins with some pins used as NULL. X.21bis uses only four wires for actual communication (one pair for transmit, one pair for receive) but uses several more wires for signalling and synchronization. X.21bis is therefore capable of full-duplex synchronous operation at speeds up to 19,200 kbps between two devices.

4.29.4 X.21-bis Pinout

Table 4.9

Pin	Function	DTE/DCE
1.	Protective Ground	
2.	Transmit Data	
3.	Control	
4.	Receive	
5.	Indication	
6.	Signal Element Timing	
7.	Byte Timing	
8.	Signal Ground	
9.	Transmit Data	
10.	Control Signal	
11.	Received Data	
12.	Indication	
13.	Signal Element Timing	
14.	Byte Timing	
15.	Protective Ground	

As the pinout describes, each bit and each byte are simultaneously signaled on the timing circuits and transmitted on the data circuits. This allows the system to indicate clocking over the circuit, allowing the receiver to determine when to sample the line and retrieve a bit. When eight bits have been transmitted, the transmitter raises the byte timing wire. This acts as a double-check, making X.25 very reliable.

Since both sides have their own wires for all these functions, transmission works in both directions simultaneously and is thus, full-duplex.

4.30 X.25

X.25 is a **packet-switching** wide area network protocol developed by ITU-T in 1976. X.25 is an interface between data terminal equipment (DTE) and data circuit-terminating, equipment (DCE) for terminal operation in the packet mode on public data networks.

Fig. 4.73 gives a conceptual overview of X.25. Although X.25 is an end-to-end protocol, the actual movement of packets through the network is invisible to the user.

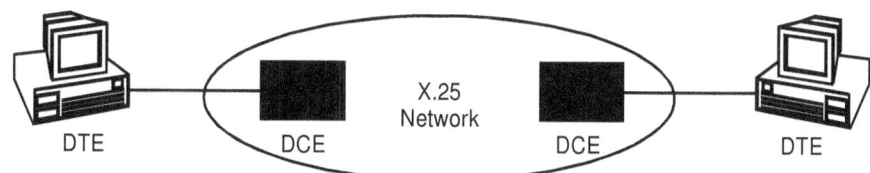

Fig. 4.73: X.25

It defines how a packet-mode terminal can be connected to a packet network for the exchange of data. It describes the procedures necessary for establishing, maintaining and terminating connections. X.25 describes a set of services, called facilities, to provide functions such as reverse change, call direct and delay control.

X.25 is what is known as a subscriber network interface (SNI) protocol. X.25 defines how the users DTE communicates with the network and how packets are sent over that network using DCEs. It uses a virtual circuit approach to packet switching and uses asynchronous TDM to multiplex packets.

4.30.1 X.25 Layers

X.25 protocol specifies three layers:

1. Physical layer,
2. Frame layer, and
3. Packet layer.

These layers define functions at the physical, data link and network layers of the OSI model. Fig. 4.74 shows the relationship between the X.25 layers and the OSI layers.

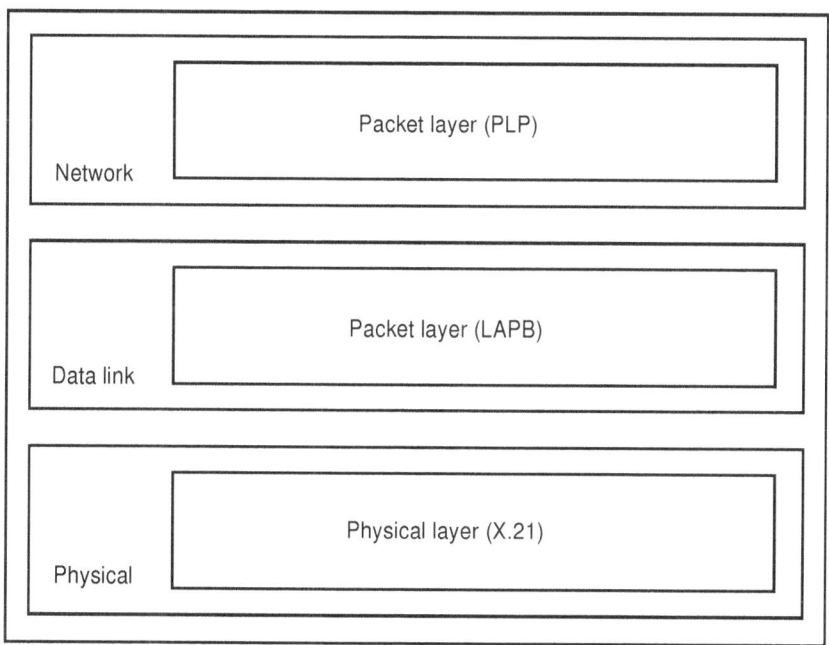

Fig. 4.74: X.25 layers in relation to the OSI layers

1. Physical Layer:

At the physical layer, X.25 specifies a protocol called X.21 (or X.21 bis), which has been specifically defined for X.25 by the ITU-T. X.21, however, is similar enough to other physical layer protocols, such as EIA-232, that X.25 is able to support them as well.

2. Frame Layer:

At the frame layer, X.25 provides data link controls using a bit-oriented protocol called **link access procedure, balanced (LAPB)**, which is a subset of HDLC. Fig. 4.75 shows the general format of the LAPB packet.

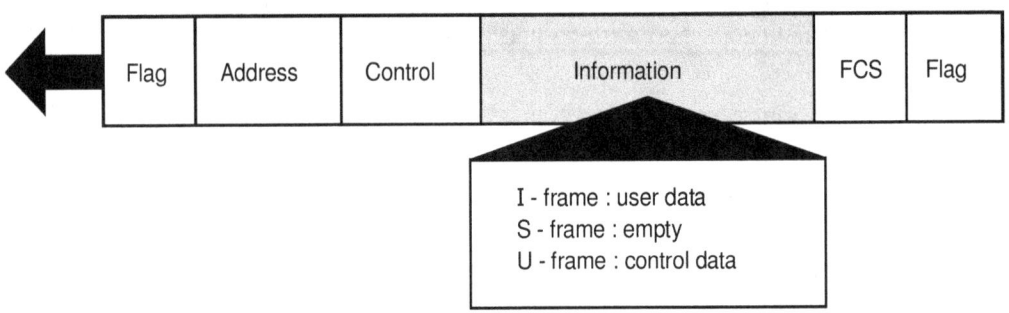

Fig. 4.75: Format of a frame

Categories of Frames:

1. I-Frames

I-frames are used to encapsulate PLP packets from the network layer.

2. S-Frames

S-frames are for flow and error control in the frame layer.

3. U-Frames

U-frames are used to set up and disconnect the links between a DTE and a DCE.

EXERCISE

1. Classify the different switching techniques.

2. Write short notes on:

    (a)   Circuit switching networks

    (b)   Phases in circuit switching

    (c)   Delay in circuit switching

3. Write short notes on:
   (a) Datagram switching networks
   (b) Delay in datagram networks
   (c) Types of datagram packet switches.

4. Write short notes on:
   (a) Similarities of VC switching with circuit switching and datagram networks
   (b) VC switching between source and destination
   (c) Virtual Circuit Identifier (VCI)
   (d) Phases in VC switching
   (e) Delays in VC switching networks.

5. What is Virtual Circuit? What is SVC and PVC?

6. Explain the different applications of VC switching.

7. Compare the following:
   (a) Circuit switching Vs. Packet switching
   (b) Datagram switching Vs. Virtual circuit switching
   (c) Circuit switching Vs. Datagram switching Vs. VC switching Vs. Message switching

8. Classify the different switches.

9. Write short notes on:
   (a) Circuit switches
   (b) Packet switches.

10. With neat diagram explain multiple access communication.

11. Write short note on: ALOHA

12. Describe carrier sense multiple Access Protocol.

13. Explain (DMA/CD).

14. Describe:
    (i) Performance of CDMA/CD.
    (ii) Ethernet capture.

15. List out various collision free protocols.

16. Explain WDMA.

17. With neat diagram explain TDMA.

18. With neat diagram explain CDMA.
19. With neat diagram explain FDMA.
20. Explain IEEE 802.3, 802.4, 802.5 standards.
21. Compare TDMA, CDMA and FDMA.
22. Draw frame structure of IEEE 802.3.
23. With the neat diagram explain SDLC.
24. Write short note on:
    (i) X.21, (ii) X.25

UNIVERSITY QUESTIONS

NOVEMBER-DECEMBER 2011

1. Write a short note on circuit-switched networks.   (10)
2. Explain in detail. (i) Random access, (ii) Controlled access.   (10)
3. What is the role of telephone network? Explain with 4 neat diagram and the major components of telephone system.   (10)

MAY-JUNE 2011

4. Write a short note on CSMA and CSMD.   (10)
5. Write short note on: (i) CDMA, (ii) TDMA.   I(10)
6. Explain analog and digital services in telephone networks.

NOVEMBER-DECEMBER 2010

7. Write a short note on: (i) Channelisation, (ii) Controlled access.   (10)
8. Write short note on CSMA/CA.   (10)

MAY-JUNE 2010

9. Write a short note on: (i) CSMA/CD, (ii) CDMA.   (10)
10. Write a short note on virtual-circuit networks.   (10)

NOVEMBER-DECEMBER 2009

11. Explain CSMA/CD with neat diagram.   (10)
12. Explain FDMA and TDMA.   (10)

MAY-JUNE 2009

13. Compare the following: (10)
    (i)   FDMA with TDMA
    (ii) CSMA/CD with CSMA/CA
14. Write a short note on efficiency and delay of both circuit-switched and datagram networks.   (5)
15. Explain datagram networks in the internet.   (5)

✲✲✲

Unit V

ERROR CONTROL AND DATA LINK LAYER AND SIGNALS

5.1 Introduction

- Physical layer takes care of transmitting information over a communication channel.
- Information transmitted may be affected by noise or distortion caused in the channel.
- Hence, the transmission over communication channel is not reliable.
- The data transfer is also affected by delay and has finite rate of transmission. This reduces the efficiency of transmission.
- Data link layer is designed to take care of these problems i.e. data link layer improves reliability and efficiency of channel.
- We can also say that the services provided by physical layer are not reliable.
- Hence, we require some layer above physical layer which can take care of these problems. The layer above physical layer is Data Link Layer (DLL).

Following are some of the functions of a data link layer.

(i) **Error control:** Physical layer is error prone. The errors introduced in the channel need to be corrected.

(ii) **Flow control:** There might be mismatch in the transmission rate of sender and the rate at which receiver receives. This mismatch must be taken care of.

(iii) **Addressing:** In the network where there are multiple terminals, whom to send the data has to be specified.

(iv) **Frame synchronization:** In physical layer, information is in the form of bits. These bits are grouped in blocks of frames at data link layer. In order to identify beginning and end of frames, some identification mark is put before and/or after each frame.

(v) **Link management:** In order to manage co-ordination and co-operation among terminals in the network, initiation, maintenance and termination of link is required to be done properly. These procedures are handled by data link layer. The control signals required for this purpose use the same channels on which data is exchanged. Hence, identification of control and data information is another task of data link layer.

(vi) Services provided to network layer: Data link layer provides services to the layer above it viz. network layer. The basic service is transferring packets from network layer on source machine to network layer on destination machine as shown in Fig. 5.1.

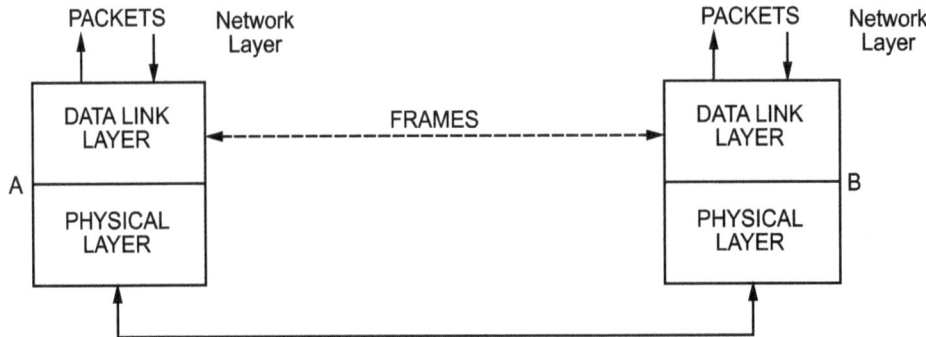

Fig. 5.1: Service provided to Network Layer

The service model describes the service provided by a protocol.

There are two categories of service models:

   (i)   Connection-oriented service.

   (ii) Connectionless service.

In connection-oriented service, connection is established between the peer entities first and then data transfer begins. There will be connection setup, data transfer and connection release procedure required to be carried out.

Connectionless services do not require a connection setup procedure. Information blocks are transmitted using address information in each Protocol Data Unit (PDU).

Acknowledged connectionless services provide acknowledgement for each PDU so that data transfer is reliable.

Unacknowledged connectionless services do not provide acknowledgement for each PDU. This is also called best effort service. In such case, network layer has to provide reliable service i.e. acknowledged service.

The service model specifies the Quality of Service (QoS). It includes expected performance level in transfer of information. Examples of some QoS parameters are:

   (i)   Probability of error.

   (ii)   Probability of loss.

   (iii) Transfer delay.

5.2 Types of Errors

Whenever bits flow from one point to another, they are subjected to unpredictable changes, because of interference. This interference can change the shape of signals. In a single bit error a0 is changed to a1 or a1 to a0. In a burst error, multiple bits are changed. For example, 1/100s burst of impulse noise on a transmission with a data rate of 1200 bps might change all or some of the 12 bits of information.

1.   Single Bit Error: It means that only 1 bit of a given data unit (as a byte, character or packet) is changed from 1 to 0 or 0 to 1.

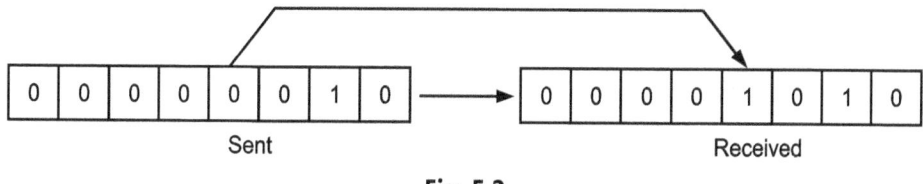

Sent   Received

Fig. 5.2

Fig. 5.2 shows the effect of single bit error on a data unit. To understand the impact of change, imagine that each group of 8 bits is an ASCII character with a0 bit added to the left. In Fig. 5.2, 00000010 (ASCII/STX) was sent, meaning start of text but 00001010 (ASCII LF) was received, meaning line feed.

Single bit errors are the least likely type of errors in serial data transmission. To understand imagine data sent at 1 Mbps. This means that each bit lasts only 1/1,000,000s or 1 μs. For single bit error to occur, the noise must have a duration of only 1 μs, which is very rare. Noise normally lasts much longer than this.

2.   Burst Error: The term means that 2 or more bits in the data unit have changed from 1 to 0 or from 0 to 1.

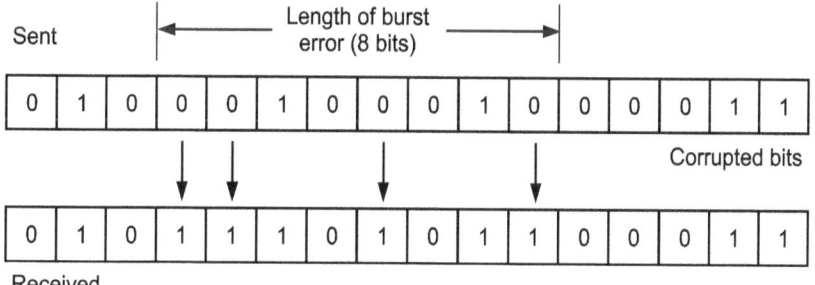

Fig. 5.3

In this case 0100010001000011 was sent, but 0101110101100011 was received. A burst error does not necessarily mean that the errors occur in consecutive bits. The length of the burst is measured from the first corrupted bit to the last corrupted bit. Some bits in between may not have been corrupted.

A burst error is more likely to occur than a single bit error. The duration of noise is normally longer than the duration of 1 bit, this means when noise affects data, it affects a set of bits. The number of bits affected depends on the data rate and duration of noise. For example, if we are sending data at 1 kbps, a noise of 1/100s can affect 10 bits, if we are sending data at 1 Mbps, the same noise can affect 10,000 bits.

Redundancy:

The main concept in detecting errors is redundancy. To detect errors we need to send some extra bits with our data. These redundant bits are added by sender and removed by the receiver. Their presence allows the receiver to detect corrupted bits.

Detection Versus Correction:

The correction of error is more difficult than detection. In error detection, we are looking only to see if any error has occurred. The answer is a simple yes or no. We are not even interested in the number of errors. A single bit error is the same for us as a burst error.

In error correction, we need to know the exact number of bits that are corrupted and more importantly, their location in the message. The number of errors and the size of the message are important factors. If we need to correct one single error in an 8-bit data unit. We need to consider eight possible error locations. If we need to correct two errors in data unit of the same size, we need to consider 28 possibilities. You can imagine the receiver's difficulty in finding 10 errors in data unit of 1000 bits.

Forward Error Correction Versus Retransmission:

There are two main methods of error correction. Forward error correction is the process in which the receiver tries to guess the message by using redundant bits. This is possible, as we see later, if the number of errors is small.

Correction by retransmission is a technique in which the receiver detects the occurrence of an error and asks the sender to resend the message. Resending is repeated until a message arrives that the receiver believes in error-free.

Coding:

Redundancy is achieved through various coding schemes. The sender adds redundant bits through a process that creates a relationship between the redundant bits and the actual data bits. The receiver checks the relationship between the two sets of bits to detect the errors. The ratio of redundant bits to the data bits and the robustness of the process are important factors in any coding scheme.

We can divide coding schemes into two broad categories:

1. Block coding.
2. Convolution coding.

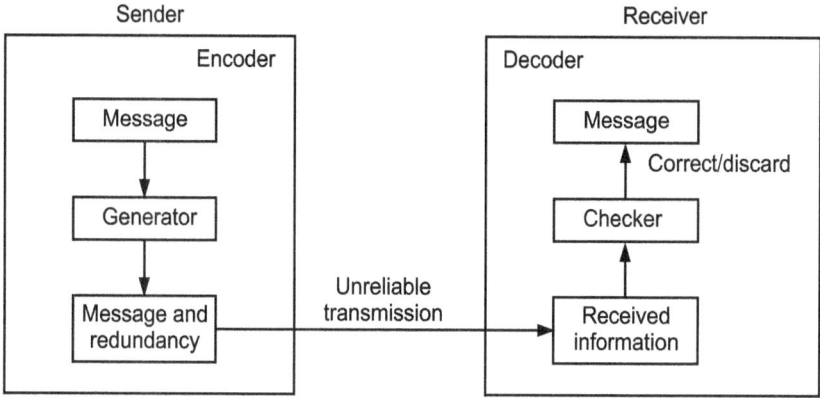

Fig. 5.4: The Structure of Encoder and Decoder

Modular Arithmetic:

In modular arithmetic we use only limited range of integers. We define an upper limit, called modulus N. We use only the integers 0 to N – 1, inclusive. This is modulo-N arithmetic.

For example, if the modulus is 12, we use only the integers 0 to 11, inclusive. An example of modulo arithmetic is our clock system. It is based on modulo 12 arithmetic, substituting the number 12 for 0.

In a modulo-N system, if a number is greater than N, it is divided by N and the remainder is the result. If it is negative, as many Ns as needed are added to make it positive.

Consider our clock system again, if we start job at 11 a.m. and the job takes 5 hrs., we can say that the job is to be finished at 16.00 if we are in the military, or we can say that it will be finished at 4 p.m. (the remainder of 16/12 is 4).

Addition and subtraction in modulo arithmetic are simple. There is no carry when you add two digits in a column. There is no carry when you subtract one digit from another in column.

Modulo-2 Arithmetic:

In this arithmetic, the modulus N is 2. We can use only 0 and 1. Operations in this arithmetic are very simple. The following shows how we can add or subtract 2 bits.

Adding: 0 + 0 = 0   0 + 1 = 1   1 + 0 = 1   1 + 1 = 0

Subtracting: 0 – 0 = 0   0 – 1 = 1   1 – 0 = 1   1 – 1 = 0

Notice particularly that addition and subtraction give the same results. In this arithmetic we use the XOR operation for both addition and subtraction. The result of an XOR operation is 0 if two bits are same, the result is 1 if two bits are different. Fig. 5.4 shows the operation: XORing of two single bits or two words.

0 + 0 = 0   1 + 1 = 0

1. Two bits are the same, the result is 0.

$$0 + 1 = 1 \quad 1 + 0 = 1$$

2. Two bits are different, the result is 1.

$$\begin{array}{r} 10110 \\ + 11100 \\ \hline 01010 \end{array}$$

3. Result of XORing two patterns.

Other Modulo Arithmetic:

We use modulo-N arithmetic through the book. The principle is the same. We use numbers between 0 and N − 1. If the modulus is not 2, addition and subtraction are distinct. If we get a negative result, we add enough multiples of N to make it positive.

5.3 Block Coding

- A digital communication system must have higher data rate, minimum signal power, reliable transmission and minimum bandwidth requirement.

- The channel over which the transmission takes place is usually noisy and it will have limited bandwidth.

- If we have to keep the signal power minimum the signal to noise ratio will be lower. This will lead to increase in error probability (p_e), as it depends on E_b/N_0 ratio. Hence, reliability of the system suffers.

- Hence, in order to improve reliability for given E_b/N_0 ratio, we can use error control coding techniques.

- Error control coding techniques can correct errors, so that messages which are likely to go wrong in a noisy channel can be retrieved correctly at the receiver end.

- This is also known as Forward Error Correction (FEC).

- For a fixed value of error probability, it is also possible to reduce E_b/N_0 ratio (signal power) using error control coding.

- Since this technique tries to overcome channel noise, it is also called **channel coding.**

- The error correcting codes are generated by adding redundancy to original message before transmitting it on a noisy channel. The channel encoder block in the transmitter does this as shown in Fig. 5.5.

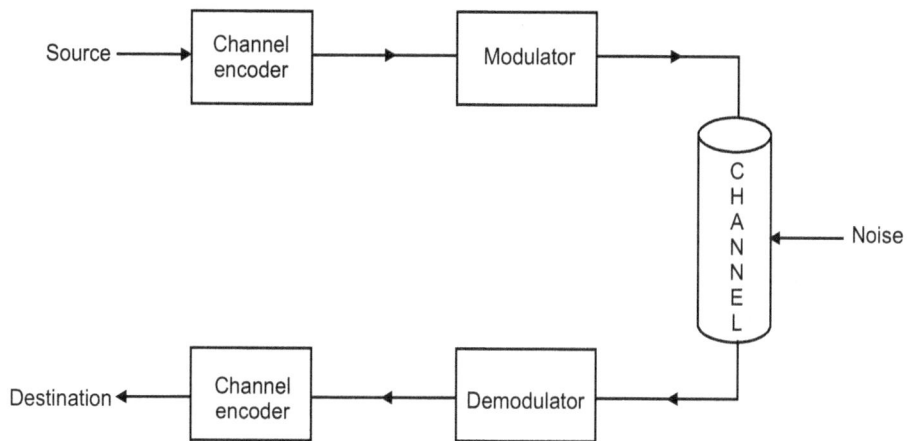

Fig. 5.5: Channel Coding in Communication System

- At the receiver we can recover the original message if the errors are within the limit as per the design of code. The channel decoder block does this recovery.
- A good error control coding technique should have
  - (i)   Better error correcting capability.
  - (ii)   Faster and efficient method of coding and decoding.
  - (iii)   Maximum transfer of information in bit/sec. (or less overheads).
- If we try to increase error correcting capability, information rate will reduce and coding and decoding will also be slower. Complexity of design increases in order to achieve better coding technique. The addition of redundancy also increases the bandwidth requirement. Thus, reliability is at the cost of bandwidth and system complexity.
- Reliability can be increased by designing error detecting systems. In these systems, we add redundancy at the transmitter end in the message. The code is then transmitted. At the receiver end we will detect whether the code received is correct or not. If not, we request the transmitter to retransmit the code. The overheads required in this case are lower than that of FEC. This technique is called Automatic Repeat Request (ARQ).
- There are number of error correcting codes. They are classified as:
  - (i)   Block codes.
  - (ii)   Convolutional codes.
- In block codes a block of k-bit message is encoded into n bits by adding n–k redundant bits.
- Convolutional codes are generated using a sliding window where, incoming message slides forward in the window. The window length is usually small and output code consists of encoder output corresponding to the message bits in the window.
- The memory requirement for linear block code encoder is more than convolutional code.

Basic Definitions

In digital communication, we use binary symbols (I/O) for transmission of message hence, we will be using the word bits instead of symbols in our discussion. But correct and general word should be symbols as a message may generate more than two types of symbols.

Let us first discuss some frequently used terms with coding.

1. **Word:** *It is a sequence of symbols.*

   e.g. Suppose we have a message consisting of 1010, then it is called a **message word.** Similarly, there will be code corresponding to this message called as **codeword.**

2. **Code:** *It is a set of vectors called as codewords or code vectors.*

3. **Parity bits:** *The bits which are added to the message bits are called parity bits.*

4. **Systematic code:** *Code in which codewords consists of message bits and parity bits separately is called systematic code.*

5. **Block codes:** *These are fixed length codewords generated from a block of message words.*

6. **Block code specification:** *The block code is specified in terms of number of code bits and number of message bits. If there are k bits in the message word and n bits are generated to form codeword, the block code is called (n, k) block code.*

7. **Code rate:** *For an (n, k) block code the code rate is defined as the ratio of message bits and code bits (k/n). Code rate is always less than one.*

8. **Parity check codes:** *These are simplest possible block codes. These codes are generated by adding one bit to the message bits. They can be even parity check codes or odd parity check codes. Even parity check codes add 1 to message if number of 1's in message are odd and 0 if number of 1's in message are even.*

   e.g.

Message	Code	Parity bit
100101	1001011	
110101	1101010	

   Similarly,

   Odd parity check codes

Message	Code	Parity bit
010011	0100110	
010001	0100011	

If single error occurs in these codewords, it can be detected at the receiver end.

9. **Weight of a codeword:** *The number of non-zero symbols in a codeword is called weight of the codeword.*

   e.g.

Codeword	Weight
10101	3
11110	4

10. **Hamming distance:** *It is a number of symbols in which two codewords differ.*

    e.g.

    $$c_1 = 10101$$
    $$c_2 = 11010$$

    Hamming distance between c_1 and c_2 is 4, denoted as $d(c_1, c_2) = 4$.

11. Minimum hamming distance between any two codewords of a code is called minimum hamming distance of that code. It is denoted as d_{min}.

12. **A linear code:** *It is a code which has following properties.*

    (i) *The sum of any two codewords in the code will yield another codeword of that code.*

    (ii) *There is always all-zero codeword.*

    (iii) *The minimum hamming distance between any two codewords is equal to minimum weight of any non-zero codeword.*

Example 5.1:

Consider the following code.

$$C = \{000, 111\}$$

Solution:

It consists of the two codewords.
Weight of 000 is 0
Weight of 111 is 3.
Hamming distance between two codewords = 3.
Minimum hamming distance of the code = 3.
It is a linear code since addition of the two codewords yield one of the codewords 111.

Example 5.2:

Consider a code.

$$C = \{000, 010, 001, 111\}$$

Codeword	Weight
000	0
010	1
001	1
111	3

Solution:

Minimum hamming distance = 1

It is not a linear code as addition of 001 and 010 does not yield valid codeword   i.e. 011 is not a valid codeword of this code.

13. **Minimum hamming distance (d_{min}): Minimum Hamming distance** of a linear code is equal to minimum weight of the non-zero codewords in that code.

Consider a code C = {000, 010, 101, 111}

Codeword	Weight
000	0
010	1
101	2
111	3

Since, minimum weight of non-zero code is 1.

Minimum hamming distance d_{min} = 1.

5.4 Linear Block Codes

Consider an (n, k) block code in which there are k message bits (or symbols) and n code bits (or symbols).

Let the code bits be,

$$C = (c_1, c_2, c_3, ... c_n) \qquad\qquad ... (5.1)$$

Let the message bits be,

$$d = (d_1, d_2, d_3, ... d_k) \qquad\qquad ... (5.2)$$

For general case, n bits of code C are generated by linear combinations of k message bits. This is called non-systematic code.

For a special case,

If $c_1 = d_1$ $c_2 = d_2$ ... $c_k = d_k$

and c_{k+1} to c_n are generated from linear combinations of $d_1, d_2, ...$ d_k then the code is called systematic code. First k bits are message bits and (n – k) parity bits added to the message.

As we have seen in earlier section, any code C is a subspace of $GF(q^n)$ and any set of basic vectors S can be used to generate code space C = <S> by linear combinations of basis vectors. Hence, m can put all basic vectors in a matrix which is called generator matrix (G). This matrix is used to generate the codewords of C. If we have to generate the codewords of length n from k message bits we will need the generator matrix of the order k × n. Hence, we should have k basic vectors in the generator matrix. The code is generated by,

$$C = d \times G \qquad\qquad ... (5.3)$$

Now, if we have to generate systematic code we should have relationship between   c and d as follows:

$$c_1 = d_1$$
$$c_2 = d_2$$
$$c_3 = d_3$$
$$\vdots$$
$$\vdots$$
$$c_k = d_k$$
$$c_{k+1} = p_{11} \cdot d_1 \oplus p_{21} \cdot d_2 \oplus \dots \oplus p_{k1} \cdot d_k$$
$$c_{k+2} = p_{12} \cdot d_1 \oplus p_{22} \cdot d_2 \oplus \dots \oplus p_{k2} \cdot d_k$$
$$\vdots$$
$$\vdots$$
$$c_n = p_{1n-k} \cdot d_1 \oplus p_{2n-k} \cdot d_2 \oplus \dots \oplus p_{kn-k} d_k \qquad \dots (5.4)$$

Hence the generator matrix will be,

$$G = \begin{bmatrix} 1 & 0 & 0 & \dots & 0 & \vdots & p_{11} & p_{12} & p_{1n-k} \\ 0 & 1 & 0 & \dots & 0 & \vdots & p_{21} & p_{22} & p_{2n-k} \\ \vdots & \vdots & \vdots & & \vdots & \vdots & & & \\ \vdots & \vdots & \vdots & & \vdots & \vdots & & & \\ 0 & 0 & 0 & \dots & 1 & \vdots & p_{k1} & p_{k2} & p_{kn-k} \end{bmatrix} \qquad \dots (5.5)$$

Thus, generator matrix G consists of two parts Identity matrix I_k and Parity matrix P.

Order of I_k is $k \times k$.

Order of P is $k \times n - k$.

i.e. $\qquad\qquad G = [I_k \ P] \qquad\qquad \dots (5.6)$

The generator matrix provides a concise and efficient way of representing linear block code i.e. a code can be written as,

$$C = dG \qquad\qquad \dots (5.7)$$

Thus, we need not store all codewords corresponding to all messages but we can generate them with the help of generator matrix which stores only few codewords.

Example 5.3:

Generate all codewords of (7, 4) Linear Block Codes (LBC) for following generator matrix.

$$G = \begin{bmatrix} 1 & 0 & 0 & 0 & 1 & \vdots & 1 & 0 \\ 0 & 1 & 0 & 0 & 0 & \vdots & 1 & 1 \\ 0 & 0 & 1 & 0 & 1 & \vdots & 1 & 1 \\ 0 & 0 & 0 & 1 & 1 & \vdots & 0 & 1 \end{bmatrix} \qquad \dots (5.8)$$

$$\qquad\qquad I_k \qquad P \qquad \vdots$$

Solution:

We know that,

$$C = dG$$

Here, n = 7, k = 4.

Hence, there will be $2^k = 2^4 = 16$.

To generate code we take each message word and multiply with G.

e.g. For message word d = [1 0 1 0]

$$C = [1\,0\,1\,0] \times \begin{bmatrix} 1 & 0 & 0 & 0 & 1 & 1 & 0 \\ 0 & 1 & 0 & 0 & 0 & 1 & 1 \\ 0 & 0 & 1 & 0 & 1 & 1 & 1 \\ 0 & 0 & 0 & 1 & 1 & 0 & 1 \end{bmatrix} \qquad ... (5.9)$$

$[1 \cdot 1 \oplus 0 \cdot 0 \oplus 1 \cdot 0 \oplus 0 \cdot 0 = 1$

$1 \cdot 0 \oplus 0 \cdot 1 \oplus 1 \cdot 0 \oplus 0 \cdot 0 = 0$

$1 \cdot 0 \oplus 0 \cdot 0 \oplus 1 \cdot 1 \oplus 0 \cdot 0 = 1$

$1 \cdot 0 \oplus 0 \cdot 0 \oplus 1 \cdot 0 \oplus 0 \cdot 1 = 0$

$1 \cdot 1 \oplus 0 \cdot 1 \oplus 1 \cdot 1 \oplus 0 \cdot 0 = 0$

$1 \cdot 1 \oplus 0 \cdot 1 \oplus 1 \cdot 1 \oplus 1 \cdot 0 = 0$

$1 \cdot 0 \oplus 0 \cdot 1 \oplus 1 \cdot 1 \oplus 0 \cdot 1 = 1]$

$= [1\,0\,1\,0\,0\,0\,1]$

Similarly, we can generate code for all message words which are given below.

Message word	Code word
0 0 0 0	0 0 0 0 0 0 0
0 0 0 1	0 0 0 1 1 0 1
0 0 1 0	0 0 1 0 1 1 1
0 0 1 1	0 0 1 1 0 1 0
0 1 0 0	0 1 0 0 0 1 1
0 1 0 1	0 1 0 1 1 1 0
0 1 1 0	0 1 1 0 1 0 0
0 1 1 1	0 1 1 1 0 0 1
1 0 0 0	1 0 0 0 1 1 0
1 0 0 1	1 0 0 1 0 1 1
1 0 1 0	1 0 1 0 0 0 1
1 0 1 1	1 0 1 1 1 0 0
1 1 0 0	1 1 0 0 1 0 1
1 1 0 1	1 1 0 1 0 0 0
1 1 1 0	1 1 1 0 0 1 0
1 1 1 1	1 1 1 1 1 1 1

From given generator matrix we can write code bits in a code word as,

$$c_1 = d_1$$
$$c_2 = d_2$$
$$c_3 = d_3$$
$$c_4 = d_4$$
$$c_5 = d_1 \oplus d_3 \oplus d_4$$
$$c_6 = d_1 \oplus d_2 \oplus d_3$$
$$c_7 = d_2 \oplus d_3 + d_4 \qquad \qquad \text{... (5.10)}$$

Hence, the generator circuit for above code is shown in Fig. 5.6.

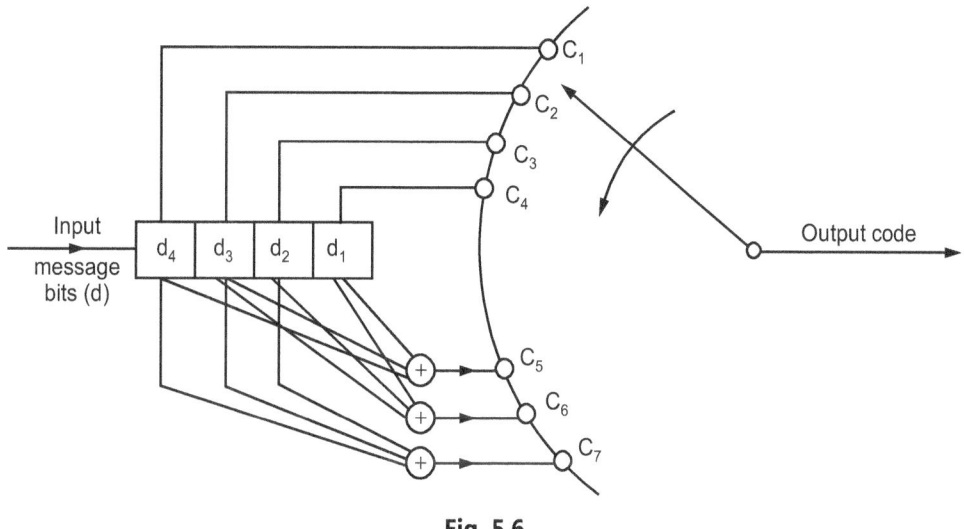

Fig. 5.6

Parity Check Matrix

We have seen that generator matrix is used to generate codewords from message words. These codewords will be transmitted through a noisy channel. At the receiver end we have to validate these codewords i.e. they are to be checked whether they are correctly received or not. If not the codewords should be corrected with the help of redundant bits that we have added at the transmitter end. For this, consider a matrix H called parity check matrix which is given by,

$$H = [P_T \mid I_{n-k}]_{n-k \times n} \qquad \qquad \text{... (5.11)}$$

i.e. H consists of two parts. Transpose of parity matrix whose order will be $n - k \times k$ and identity matrix whose order will be $(n - k) \times (n - k)$.

It can be verified for any codeword C.

$$CH^T = 0 \qquad \qquad \text{... (5.12)}$$

i.e. if we multiply any codeword with transpose of parity check matrix H result will be zero-vector.

Thus, the received codeword at the receiver is multiplied with H^T and we get zero vector if the codeword is correctly received. But if multiplication results into non-zero codeword, there will be error in the received codeword.

Substitute $C = dG$ in equation (5.12),

$$d\,G\,H^T \; = \; 0$$

Thus, for equation (5.12) to hold true we should have,

$$G\,H^T \; = \; 0$$

Now consider,
$$G \; = \; [I_k \vdots P]$$

and
$$H \; = \; [P^T \vdots I_{n-k}]$$

$$G^T \; = \; \begin{bmatrix} I_k \\ \hline P^T \end{bmatrix}$$

$\therefore$
$$H\,G^T \; = \; [P^T \; I_{n-k}] \begin{bmatrix} I_k \\ \hline P^T \end{bmatrix}$$

$$= \; P^T \oplus P^T$$

$$= \; 0$$

$\therefore$
$$G\,H^T \; = \; 0$$

The process of coding and detection is shown in Fig. 5.7.

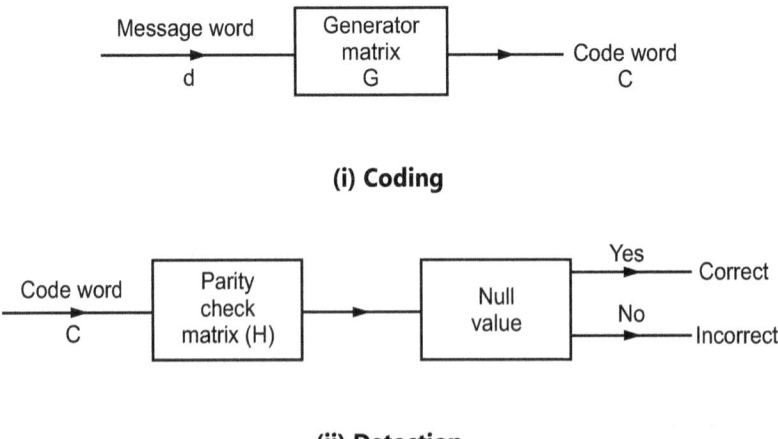

(i) Coding

(ii) Detection

Fig. 5.7

Example 5.4:

Consider a generator matrix given in Example 5.3.

$$G = \begin{bmatrix} 1 & 0 & 0 & 0 & 1 & 1 & 0 \\ 0 & 1 & 0 & 0 & 0 & 1 & 1 \\ 0 & 0 & 1 & 0 & 1 & 1 & 1 \\ 0 & 0 & 0 & 1 & 1 & 0 & 1 \end{bmatrix}$$

Find parity check matrix and check whether following codewords are valid or not.

(i)   1000110   (ii) 0101011

Solution:

The given generator matrix is of the order 4 × 7.

Hence, $n = 7$

                          $k = 4$

The parity matrix in the generator is,

$$P = \begin{bmatrix} 1 & 1 & 0 \\ 0 & 1 & 1 \\ 1 & 1 & 1 \\ 1 & 0 & 1 \end{bmatrix}$$

Now parity check matrix is given by,

$$H = [P^T_{,} I_{n-k}]$$

$$= \begin{bmatrix} 1 & 0 & 1 & 1 & 1 & 0 & 0 \\ 1 & 1 & 1 & 0 & 0 & 1 & 0 \\ 0 & 1 & 1 & 1 & 0 & 0 & 1 \end{bmatrix}$$

∴ $$H^T = \begin{bmatrix} 1 & 1 & 0 \\ 0 & 1 & 1 \\ 1 & 1 & 1 \\ 1 & 0 & 1 \\ 1 & 0 & 0 \\ 0 & 1 & 0 \\ 0 & 0 & 1 \end{bmatrix}$$

To check whether given codewords are valid or not we find CH^T.

(i)   Given: $C = [1000110]$

$$\therefore \qquad CH^T = [1\,0\,0\,0\,1\,1\,0] \begin{bmatrix} 1 & 1 & 0 \\ 0 & 1 & 1 \\ 1 & 1 & 1 \\ 1 & 0 & 1 \\ 1 & 0 & 0 \\ 0 & 1 & 0 \\ 0 & 0 & 1 \end{bmatrix}$$

$$= [0\,0\,0]$$

Hence, given codeword is valid.

(ii) $\qquad\qquad C = [0\,1\,0\,1\,0\,1\,1]$

$$\therefore \qquad CH^T = [0\,1\,0\,1\,0\,1\,1] \begin{bmatrix} 1 & 1 & 0 \\ 0 & 1 & 1 \\ 1 & 1 & 1 \\ 1 & 0 & 1 \\ 1 & 0 & 0 \\ 0 & 1 & 0 \\ 0 & 0 & 1 \end{bmatrix}$$

$$= [1\,0\,1]$$

Hence, given codeword is invalid.

Minimum Distance and H^T

- Hamming distance between two codewords is the number of positions in which their symbols differ.
- Hamming weight is number of non-zero elements in the codewords.
- The minimum distance d_{min} of a linear block code is the smallest distance between any pair of code vectors in the code.
- From the closure property of linear block codes the sum (or difference) of two codewords is another codeword.
- Minimum distance of a linear block code is the smallest hamming weight of the non-zero codeword in the code.
- Parity check matrix H and in turn generator matrix G are also related to minimum distance d_{min} of a code.
- Since $CH^T = 0$, the number of 1's in code vector C should be such that, corresponding rows of H^T add to zero i.e. corresponding columns of parity check matrix H must add to zero.

Consider the H^T discussed in earlier example.

$$H^T = \begin{bmatrix} 1 & 1 & 0 \\ 0 & 1 & 1 \\ 1 & 1 & 1 \\ 1 & 0 & 1 \\ 1 & 0 & 0 \\ 0 & 1 & 0 \\ 0 & 0 & 1 \end{bmatrix}$$

Now consider a valid code vector.

$$C = [1\,0\,0\,0\,1\,1\,0]$$

There are three non-zero elements at positions 1, 5 and 6 and the sum of 1st, 5th and 6th row of H^T is,

$$\begin{bmatrix} 1 \\ 1 \\ 0 \end{bmatrix} + \begin{bmatrix} 1 \\ 0 \\ 0 \end{bmatrix} + \begin{bmatrix} 0 \\ 1 \\ 0 \end{bmatrix} = \begin{bmatrix} 0 \\ 0 \\ 0 \end{bmatrix}$$

- The number of non-zero elements in the code is 3. If you check other codewords in the (7, 4) code discussed earlier, the minimum number of non-zero elements is 3 which is nothing but minimum weight of that code and it is also minimum hamming distance.

- Hence, the minimum distance of linear block code (d_{min}) is equal to minimum number of rows of H^T (or columns of H) whose sum is equal to zero vector.

Decoding of a Linear Block Code

Decoding is a process of detecting and correcting errors when messages in the form of codewords are transmitted on a noisy channel. The important question here is how many errors can we detect and correct. It will depend on the design of the code. The number of errors the code can correct or detect errors is called error correcting or detecting capability of that code.

A code contains certain number of codewords which are at some distance from each other which is specified in terms of hamming distance.

e.g. Consider the following code.

Message word	Code word
0	0 0 0
1	1 1 1

There are two codewords in the code whose hamming distance is 3.

When one of the codewords is transmitted the noise or distortion is likely to change some bits. e.g. when 0 0 0 is transmitted we might receive 0 0 1. As long as one codeword is not transformed into another codewords we can detect whether there was error in transmission or not. Thus, the number of errors that can be detected depends on minimum hamming distance of the code, as it is the minimum distance between any two codewords.

i.e. if a code has hamming distance d_{min} the number of errors that can be detected is,

$$\boxed{t_d \leq d_{min} - 1}$$ ... (5.13)

The number of errors that can be corrected also depends on minimum hamming distance. When a codeword is received with error we have to find which codeword was actually transmitted? Obviously, the codeword nearest to the valid codewords will be the answer. But then the received codeword might be at same hamming distance from two or more valid codewords. Hence, it is not possible to correct the code with this criteria. Also, if more errors occur, the received codeword will go near to another valid codeword which was not transmitted.

e.g. If 0 0 0 is transmitted and 0 1 0 is received we can make decision in favour of 0 0 0 as 0 1 0 is nearer to 0 0 0 than 1 1 1. But if 0 0 0 is transmitted and 0 1 1 is received we will make decision in favour of 1 1 1 as 0 1 1 is nearer to 1 1 1 than 0 0 0 which is not correct. Hence, this code cannot correct two errors. For error correction capability any two codewords in the code should be separated such that the number of errors (t_c) should result into a received word which is closest to original codeword and away from all other codewords. The condition for this is,

$$\boxed{t_c \leq \frac{d_{min} - 1}{2}}$$ ... (5.14)

This can be well understood using pictorial view. We can consider the codewords to be placed in spheres separated from each other as shown below.

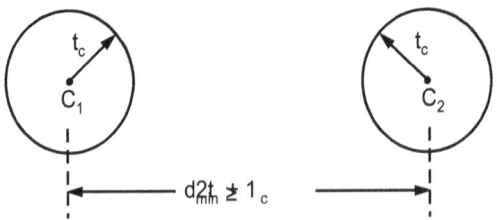

Fig. 5.8 (a): Decoding spheres

The sphere are of radius t_c, where, t_c is number of errors that can be corrected. If t_c errors occur in code c_1/c_2, the new codeword will be within their spheres and remain nearer to the valid codeword. Hence, the minimum hamming distance has to be greater than $2t_c + 1$.

If we consider the code C = {0 0 0, 1 1 1}, the codewords will be placed from other possible distortions as below on the vertices of a cube.

If (0 0 0) is transmitted and (0 0 1) is received we find 0 0 1 is near to 0 0 0 than (1 1 1). Hence, we can make the correction in favour of (0 0 0).

But if (0 0 0) is transmitted and (0 1 1) is received we find (0 1 1) is nearer to (1 1 1) than (0 0 0), hence we cannot correct the two errors here. Thus, this code has error correcting capability of 1 error. This can be verified from the formula also. The code has d_{min} = 3.

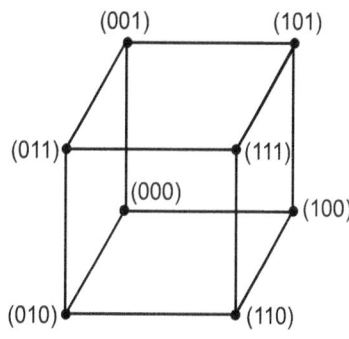

Fig. 5.8 (b): Decoding cube

$$\therefore \qquad t_c \leq \frac{d_{min} - 1}{2}$$

$$\leq \frac{3 - 1}{2}$$

$$\leq 1$$

Note that, if 0 1 1 is received when 0 0 0 was transmitted, decision will be made in favour of 1 1 1, even though it is incorrect. Here, we assume that probability of occurrence of 2 errors is far less than that of 1 error.

Example 5.5:

Find the error correcting capability of code generated in Example 5.5.

Solution:

Code word	Hamming weight
0 0 0 0 0 0 0	0
0 0 0 1 1 0 1	3
0 0 1 0 1 1 1	4
0 0 1 1 0 1 0	4
0 1 0 0 0 1 1	3
0 1 0 1 1 1 0	4
0 1 1 0 1 0 0	3
0 1 1 1 0 0 1	4
1 0 0 0 1 1 0	3
1 0 0 1 0 1 1	4
1 0 1 0 0 0 1	3
1 0 1 1 1 0 0	4
1 1 0 0 1 0 1	4
1 1 0 1 0 0 0	3
1 1 1 0 0 1 0	4
1 1 1 1 1 1 1	7

Since minimum weight of the non-zero codewords is 3.

$$d_{min} = 3$$

∴   Error correcting capability

$$t_c \leq \frac{d_{min} - 1}{2}$$

$$t_c \leq \frac{3 - 1}{2}$$

$$t_c \leq 1$$

If the code is such that there is ambiguity in deciding closest codeword, then it is called incomplete decoder. A complete decoder can decode every received word even if there are not more than t_c errors. They will make a good guess about the codeword.

There will be limit on maximum distance, on the code which will be,

$$d_{max} \leq n - k + 1 \qquad \text{... (5.15)}$$

       where, k is number of message bits.

              n is number of code bits.

This is called Singleton Bound.

Syndrome Decoding

Minimum hamming distance d_{min} of a code decides error correcting capability of a code. Now, let us see how these errors can be corrected.

The generator matrix (G) is used at the transmitter to generate the code corresponding to message. The parity check matrix can be used to decode the received codeword.

-   Let r be the received code vector.
-   This code vector may or may not differ from transmitted code vector C.
-   Let there be another vector e which will be called error vector defining the corresponding error pattern.
-   Hence, $r = C \oplus e$ ... (5.16)
       If there is no error, e will be having all zero symbols. If there are some errors, then there will be that many number of 1's in the corresponding location.

i.e. $e_i = \begin{cases} 1 & \text{If an error has occurred} \\ & \text{in the } i^{th} \text{ location} \\ 0 & \text{Otherwise} \end{cases}$ ... (5.17)

The received code vector is multiplied with H^T to get syndrome vector. As we see if received codeword is same as transmitted codeword, this multiplication will result into 0 as $CH^T = 0$.

       Since the received code vector is $1 \times n$ and H^T is of the order $n \times n - k$.

       The syndrome vector will have $n - k$ bits.

       Thus, $S = r H^T$ ... (5.18)

If r = C, S will have all 0 vector.

If r ≠ C

$$S = r H^T$$
$$= (C \oplus e) H^T$$
$$= C \cdot H^T \oplus e H^T$$
$$= e H^T \qquad \qquad ... (5.19)$$

Thus, the syndrome depends on error pattern e.

Another property of the syndrome is that all error patterns that differ by a codeword have the same syndrome. Let us look into this.

Let there be k message bits.

Hence, there will be 2^k codewords $C_1, C_2, C_3, ... C_{2k}$.

Let there be some error pattern e which will also have 2^{k-1} distinct vectors $e_1, e_2, ... e_{2k}$.

∴ $$e_i = e \oplus C_i \qquad \qquad ... (5.20)$$

Set of vectors $\{e_1, e_2, e_3, ... e_{2k}\}$ is called coset of the code. There will be 2^{n-k} possible cosets of an (n, k) block code.

Now, $$e_i \cdot H^T = (e \oplus C_i) H^T$$
$$= e H^T \oplus C_i H^T$$
$$= e H^T = S \qquad \qquad ... (5.21)$$

Thus, each coset of the code is characterised by unique syndrome.

The vector having minimum weight in the coset is called coset leader.

A standard array is constructed using these coset leaders.

In the first row all valid codewords are written starting with all-zero codewords.

In the second row we write vector e_2 which is not in first row as coset leader and then write the cosets $e_2 + c$ below each valid code vector. We continue this till all the cosets are listed.

e.g. $$C = \{0\,0\,0, 1\,1\,1\}$$

Standard array:

Syndrome	Coset Leaders	n-tupes
0 0	0 0 0	1 1 1
1 1	1 0 0	0 1 1
1 0	0 1 0	1 0 1
0 1	0 0 1	1 1 0

← Code vectors (pointing to row 1 n-tupes)

} Single errors (bracketing rows 2–4 n-tupes)

The decoding procedure for a linear block code will be as below.

1. Compute $S = r H^T$, where, r is received code.
2. Identify the error pattern i.e. coset leader corresponding to the syndrome. Let it be e.
3. Compute code vector.

$$C = r \oplus e$$

Example 5.6:

Decoding procedure for (7, 4) block code whose generator matrix is given in Example 5.4.

$$G = \begin{bmatrix} 1 & 0 & 0 & 0 & 1 & 1 & 0 \\ 0 & 1 & 0 & 0 & 0 & 1 & 1 \\ 0 & 0 & 1 & 0 & 1 & 1 & 1 \\ 0 & 0 & 0 & 1 & 1 & 0 & 1 \end{bmatrix}$$

Also find the corrected codewords for following received words.

(i) 1000110   (ii) 0101011   (iii) 0001100

Solution:

Step I:

The given code has error correcting capability of 1. Hence, there will be $2^{n-k} = 2^3 = 8$ single error patterns.

Step II:

The parity check matrix is given by,

$$H = [P^T \ I_{n-k}]$$

$$= \begin{bmatrix} 1 & 0 & 1 & 1 & 1 & 0 & 0 \\ 1 & 1 & 1 & 0 & 0 & 1 & 0 \\ 0 & 1 & 1 & 1 & 0 & 0 & 1 \end{bmatrix}$$

$$\therefore \quad H^T = \begin{bmatrix} 1 & 1 & 0 \\ 0 & 1 & 1 \\ 1 & 1 & 1 \\ 1 & 0 & 1 \\ 1 & 0 & 0 \\ 0 & 1 & 0 \\ 0 & 0 & 1 \end{bmatrix}$$

Step III:

We find syndrome vectors corresponding to each error pattern using,

$$S = e \, H^T$$

e.g. for error pattern 0 0 0 0 0 0 1 the syndrome will be,

$$S = [0\,0\,0\,0\,0\,0\,1] \begin{bmatrix} 1 & 1 & 0 \\ 0 & 1 & 1 \\ 1 & 1 & 1 \\ 1 & 0 & 1 \\ 1 & 0 & 0 \\ 0 & 1 & 0 \\ 0 & 0 & 1 \end{bmatrix}$$

$$= [0\,0\,1]$$

Following table gives all syndrome with their error patterns.

Error pattern	Syndrome
0 0 0 0 0 0 0	0 0 0
1 0 0 0 0 0 0	1 1 0
0 1 0 0 0 0 0	0 1 1
0 0 1 0 0 0 0	1 1 1
0 0 0 1 0 0 0	1 0 1
0 0 0 0 1 0 0	1 0 0
0 0 0 0 0 1 0	0 1 0
0 0 0 0 0 0 1	0 0 1

Note: If you observe above syndrome they are nothing but matrix H^T itself.

Thus, if there is single error in i^{th} bit, the syndrome will be i^{th} row of H^T.

Step IV:

Once above table is ready we can now correct the errors in the received codewords.

(i) $r = [1\,0\,0\,0\,1\,1\,0]$

∴ $S = r\,H^T$

$= [0\,0\,0]$

Hence, there is no error.

∴   Corrected codeword

$C = r$

(ii) $r = [0\,1\,0\,1\,0\,1\,1]$

$S = r\,H^T$

$= [1\,0\,1]$

Corresponding error pattern from above table,

$e = 0\,0\,0\,1\,0\,0\,0$ [Error in 4th bit]

∴   Corrected codeword

$$C = r \oplus e$$
$$= [0\ 1\ 0\ 1\ 0\ 1\ 1] \oplus [0\ 0\ 0\ 1\ 0\ 0\ 0]$$
$$= [0\ 1\ 0\ 0\ 0\ 1\ 1]$$

(iii) $$r = [0\ 0\ 0\ 1\ 1\ 0\ 0]$$
$$S = r\ H^T$$
$$= [0\ 0\ 1]$$

∴   Error pattern is,

$$e = [0\ 0\ 0\ 0\ 0\ 0\ 1]$$

∴   Corrected codeword

$$C = r \oplus e$$
$$= [0\ 0\ 0\ 1\ 1\ 0\ 0] + [0\ 0\ 0\ 0\ 0\ 0\ 1]$$
$$= [0\ 0\ 0\ 1\ 1\ 0\ 1]$$

5.5 Cyclic Codes

Cyclic codes are subclass of linear block codes. Generator matrix is used for generating linear block codes. Hence, for higher order codes we have to use large memory requirements and circuit becomes complex. Cyclic codes are linear block codes with an additional constraint. Cyclic codes are very easy to encode. Cyclic codes possess a well defined mathematical structure which makes them efficient in decoding.

Thus, cyclic codes are simple for implementation which is an important feature of cyclic code.

A binary code is said to be cyclic if it satisfies following two fundamental properties.

   (i)   **Linearity:** The sum of any two codewords in a cyclic code is also a valid codeword.

   (ii) **Cyclic property:** A cyclic shift of bits in a codeword gives rise to another valid codeword.

   As per the cyclic property if $(c_1, c_2, c_3, \dots c_n)$ is a codeword, then,

$$(c_2, c_3, \dots c_n, c_1)$$
$$(c_3\ c_4, \dots c_n, c_1, c_2)$$
$$\vdots$$
$$\vdots$$
$$(c_n, c_1, c_2, \dots c_{n-2}, c_{n-1})$$

are all codewords in that code.

Example 5.7:

   $C = \{0\ 0\ 0\ 0, 0\ 1\ 0\ 1, 1\ 0\ 1\ 0, 1\ 1\ 1\ 1\}$ is a cyclic code.

As this code satisfies both linearity property and cyclic property.

Example 5.8:

$C = \{0\,0\,0, 0\,1\,0, 0\,0\,1, 1\,0\,0, 1\,1\,1\}$ is not cyclic code. It satisfies cyclic property but does not satisfy linearity property.

Polynomials

Cyclic code can be represented in polynomial form. e.g. given a codeword of code C,

$$c_1, c_2, c_3, \ldots c_n$$

We can write it as,

$$c(x) = c_1 x^{n-1} + c_2 x^{n-2} + c_3 x^{n-3} + \ldots + c_{n-1} x + c_n \qquad \ldots (5.22)$$

In general, if $a_1, a_2, a_3, \ldots a_n$ are elements of GF(q) then a polynomial of these sequence of elements is expressed as,

$$p(x) = a_1 x^{n-1} + a_2 x^{n-2} + a_3 x^{n-3} + \ldots + a_{n-1} x + a_n \qquad \ldots (5.23)$$

- If $q = 2$, coefficients $a_1, a_2, \ldots$ will be 1 or 0.
- a_1 is called leading coefficient.
- $n - 1$ is called degree of polynomial.
- If a_1 is unity, it is called monic polynomial.
- Let p[x] represent a set of polynomials in x with coefficients in GF(q). It is called a ring e.g. c[x] will be a set of polynomials of all valid codewords.

These polynomials satisfy first seven of eight properties that define a field.

e.g. addition or multiplication of two polynomials will result into coefficients in GF(q) only.

Consider 2 polynomials.

$$a(x) = x + 1$$
$$b(x) = x^3 + x + 1 \text{ defined over GF(2)}$$

Then,

$$a(x) + b(x) = (x \oplus 1) \oplus (x^3 \oplus x \oplus 1)$$
$$= x^3 \oplus [x \oplus x] \oplus [1 \oplus 1]$$
$$= x^3 \oplus [1 \oplus 1] x \oplus [1 \oplus 1]$$
$$= x^3 + 0x + 0$$
$$= x^3$$

$$a(x) \cdot b(x) = (x^3 \oplus x \oplus 1) \cdot (x \oplus 1)$$
$$= x^3 \cdot x \oplus x^3 \cdot 1 \oplus x \cdot x \oplus x \cdot 1 \oplus 1 \cdot x \oplus 1 \cdot 1$$

$$= x^4 \oplus x^3 \oplus x^2 \oplus x \oplus x \oplus 1$$

$$= x^4 \oplus x^3 \oplus x^2 \oplus (1 \oplus 1) \, x \oplus 1$$

$$= x^4 \oplus x^3 \oplus x^2 + x + 1$$

$$= x^4 + x^3 + x^2 + 1$$

(A) Division Algorithm for Polynomials:

Consider two polynomials $a(x)$ and $b(x)$.

If divide $a(x)$ by $b(x)$ $[b(x) \neq 0)]$

we can write,

$$a(x) \;=\; q(x) \, b(x) + r(x) \qquad\qquad \text{... (5.24)}$$

where, $q(x)$ is quotient.

$r(x)$ is remainder or residue whose degree will be less than $b(x)$.

e.g.   Let $a(x) \;=\; x^4 + x^2 + 1$

$b(x) \;=\; x + 1$

$$
\begin{array}{r}
x^3 + x^2 \quad \leftarrow q(x) \\
x+1 \enclose{longdiv}{x^4 + x^2 + 1} \\
\underline{x^4 + x^3} \\
x^3 + x^2 + 1 \\
\underline{x^3 + x^2} \\
1 \quad \leftarrow r(x)
\end{array}
$$

Note that in GF(2), $1 - 1 = 0$ and $0 - 1 = -1 = 1$, $1 - 0 = 0$ and $0 - 0 = 0$ which is equivalent to modulo-2 addition. Hence, the subtraction is equivalent to modulo-2 addition.

$\therefore$ $(x^4 + x^2 + 1) \;=\; (x^3 + x^2) \cdot (x + 1) + 1$

$\qquad\qquad\qquad\quad \downarrow \qquad\quad \downarrow \quad\; \downarrow \quad \downarrow$

$\qquad\qquad\qquad a(x) \qquad q(x) \quad b(x) \quad r(x)$

A polynomial $p(x)$ in $p[x]$ is said to be reducible if $p(x) = a(x) \cdot b(x)$, where $a(x)$ and $b(x)$ are elements of $p[x]$ and degree of $a(x)$ and $b(x)$ are smaller than degree of $p(x)$.

A monic polynomial is a polynomial whose leading coefficient is one.

A monic polynomial which is irreducible and has a degree atleast one is called prime polynomial. Some examples of prime polynomials are x, $x + 1$, $x^2 + 1$, $x^2 + x + 1$, $x^3 + x^2 + 1$, $x^3 + x + 1$, etc.

(B) Representation of Cyclic codes using Polynomials:

We have seen that a codeword can be represented using polynomial as,

$$c(x) \;=\; c_1 x^{n-1} + c_2 x^{n-2} + c_3 x^{n-3} + \ldots + c_{n-1} x + c_n$$

e.g. if you are given a code word C = (1 0 1 1 0), it will be written as,

$$C = (1 \quad 0 \quad 1 \quad 1 \quad 0)$$
$$\downarrow \quad \downarrow \quad \downarrow \quad \downarrow \quad \downarrow$$
$$c(x) = 1 \cdot x^4 + 0 \cdot x^3 + 1 \cdot x^2 + 1 \cdot x + 0 \cdot x$$
$$\therefore \quad c(x) = x^4 + x^2 + x$$

We have seen that cyclic code satisfies cyclic property. We can verify that if c(x) is a code polynomial corresponding to a codeword then the remainder after dividing x^i c(x) by $x^n + 1$ also represents a valid codeword.

e.g.　　　　$x^i \cdot c(x) = c_1 x^n + c_2 x^{n-1} + c_3{}^{n-2} + \dots + c_{n-1} x^2 + c_n x$　　　... (5.25)

Divide x^i c(x) by $x^n + 1$ and find remainder.

$$
\begin{array}{r}
c_1 \\
x^n + 1 \overline{) c_1 x^n + c_2 x^{n-1} + c_3 x^{n-2} + \dots + c_{n-1} x^2 + c_n x} \\
c_1 x^n + c_1 \\
\hline
\end{array}
$$

Remainder　$\Rightarrow c_2 x^{n-1} + c_3 x^{n-2} + \dots + c_{n-1} x^2 + c_n x + c_1$

The remainder represents the codeword

$$C_1 = (c_2, c_3, \dots c_{n-1}, c_n, c_1) \qquad \text{... (5.26)}$$

which is a cyclic shifted version of original code word C. Similarly, you can verify that remainder after divisor of $x^2 c(x)$ and $x^n + 1$ will give rise to another cyclic shifted codeword.

In general,

$$\text{Rem}\left[\frac{x^i \cdot c(x)}{x^n + 1}\right] = c_{i+1} x^{n-1} + c_{i+2} x^{n-2} + \dots + c_n x^i + c_1 x^{i-1} + \dots c_i \qquad \text{... (5.27)}$$

It is denoted as c^i (x).

i.e.　　　　　$c^{(i)} (x) = x^i c(x) \bmod (x^n + 1)$　　　　　　　　　　... (5.28)

[Mod is a remainder after division operation].

A Method for Generating Cyclic Code

Theorem:

Cyclic code polynomial c(x) can be generated using data polynomial d(x) of degree k – 1 and a generator polynomial g(x) of degree n – k as,

$$c(x) = d(x) \cdot g(x) \qquad \text{... (5.29)}$$

where, g(x) is $(n - k)^{th}$ order factor of $x^n + 1$.

Proof:

Let d(x) represent data polynomial of k message bits $d_1, d_2, d_3, \dots d_k$ as,

$$d(x) = d_1 x^{k-1} + d_2 x^{k-2} + d_3 x^{k-3} + \dots + d_{k-1} x + d_k \qquad \text{... (5.30)}$$

Now, consider the polynomial.

$$c(x) = d(x) \cdot g(x)$$

$\therefore$
$$c(x) = d_1 x^{k-1} g(x) + d_2 x^{k-2} g(x) + ... + d_k g(x) \qquad ... (5.31)$$

Since g(x) is $(n - k)^{th}$ order polynomial, c(x) will be of degree $n - 1$ or less. i.e. degree of c(x) will be atmost $n - 1$.

Now, we have to prove that this code is cyclic.

Let,

$$c(x) = c_1 x^{n-1} + c_2 x^{n-2} + ... + c_n$$
$$x\, c(x) = c_1 x^n + c_2 x^{n-1} + ... + c_n x$$
$$= (c_1 x^n + c_1) + (c_2 x^{n-1} + c_3 x^{n-2} + ... + c_n x + c_1) \qquad ... (5.32)$$

Adding $c_1 \oplus c_2$,

$$= c_1(x^n + 1) + (c_2 x^{n-1} + c_3 x^{n-2} + ... + c_n x + c_1)$$
$$= c_1(x^n + 1) + c^{(1)}(x) \qquad ... (5.33)$$

But, $x\, c(x) = x \cdot d(x)\, g(x)$ ... (5.34)

Thus, from equations (5.33) and (5.34), we get,

$$x\, c(x) \cdot g(x) = c_1 (x^n + 1) + c^{(1)}(x) \qquad ... (5.35)$$

But g(x) is a factor of $(x^n + 1)$ and if equation (5.35) has to hold good, $c^{(1)}(x)$ also has to be multiple of $(x^n + 1)$. But $c^{(1)}(x)$ is a cyclic shifted version of c(x). Hence, the code c(x) generated by multiplying d(x) and g(x) is cyclic.

Example 5.9:

Find generator polynomial g(x) for a (7, 4) cyclic code and final codewords for following data words.

(i)   1 1 0 0

(ii)   1 0 1 0

(iii)   0 1 1 1

Solution:

Given: n = 7

k = 4

The generator polynomial should be of the degree $n - k = 3$.

The generator polynomial should be factor of $x^7 + 1$.

$$
\begin{aligned}
(x^7 + 1) &= (x + 1)(x^6 + x^5 + x^4 + x^3 + x^2 + x + 1) \\
&= (x + 1)(x^6 + x^5 + x^4 + x^3 + x^3 + x^3 + x^2 + x + 1) \\
&= (x + 1)(x^6 + x^4 + x^3 + x^5 + x^3 + x^2 + x^3 + x + 1) \\
&= (x + 1)[x^3(x^3 + x + 1) + x^2(x^3 + x + 1) + 1(x^3 + x + 1)] \\
&= (x + 1)(x^3 + x^2 + 1)(x^3 + x + 1)
\end{aligned}
$$

We have two polynomials of order 3, one of which can be selected as generator polynomial.

Let $\qquad g(x) = x^3 + x^2 + 1$

Now, a code is generated using,

$$c(x) = d(x) \, g(x)$$

(i) $\quad 1\,1\,0\,0$

$$d(x) = x^3 + x^2$$

$\therefore \qquad$
$$
\begin{aligned}
c(x) &= (x^3 + x^2)(x^3 + x^2 + 1) \\
&= (x^6 + x^5 + x^3 + x^5 + x^4 + x^2) \\
&= x^6 + x^4 + x^3 + x^2 \\
&= 1.x^6 + 0.x^5 + 1.x^4 + 1.x^3 + 1.x^2 + 0.x + 0.x
\end{aligned}
$$

$\therefore \qquad c = [1\,0\,1\,1\,1\,0\,0]$

(ii) $\quad 1\,0\,1\,0$

$$d(x) = x^3 + x$$

$$
\begin{aligned}
c(x) &= (x^3 + x)(x^3 + x^2 + 1) \\
&= x^6 + x^5 + x^3 + x^4 + x^3 + x \\
&= x^6 + x^5 + x^4 + x \\
&= 1.x^6 + 1.x^5 + 1.x^4 + 0.x^3 + 0.x^2 + 1.x + 0
\end{aligned}
$$

$\therefore \qquad c = [1\,1\,1\,0\,0\,1\,0]$

(iii) $\quad 0\,0\,1\,1$

$$d(x) = x + 1$$

$\therefore \qquad$
$$
\begin{aligned}
c(x) &= (x + 1)(x^3 + x^2 + 1) \\
&= x^4 + x^3 + x + x^3 + x^2 + 1 \\
&= x^4 + x^2 + x + 1 \\
&= 0.x^6 + 0.x^5 + 1.x^4 + 0.x^3 + 1.x^2 + 1.x + 1
\end{aligned}
$$

$\therefore \qquad c = [0\,0\,1\,0\,1\,1\,1]$

It can be observed from above example that the code generated is non-systematic code as message bits and parity bits are not in separate blocks.

Example 5.10:

Find generator polynomial for a (7, 3) cyclic code.

Solution:

Given: $\qquad n = 7$

$\qquad k = 3$

$\therefore \quad$ The order of generator polynomial will be,

$$n - k = 4$$

g(x) will factor of $x^7 + 1$.

$$
\begin{aligned}
x^7 + 1 &= (x + 1)(x^6 + x^5 + x^4 + x^3 + x^2 + 1) \\
&= (x + 1)(x^6 + x^5 + x^4 + x^3 + x^3 + x^3 + x^2 + 1) \\
&= (x + 1)[x^3(x^3 + x + 1) + x^2(x^3 + x + 1) + 1(x^3 + x + 1)] \\
&= (x + 1)(x^3 + x^2 + 1)(x^3 + x + 1) \\
&= (x^4 + x^3 + x + x^3 + x^2 + 1)(x^3 + x + 1) \\
&= (x^4 + x^2 + x + 1)(x^3 + x + 1)
\end{aligned}
$$

∴   Generator polynomial of order 4 is,

$$
g(x) = x^4 + x^2 + x + 1
$$

(A) Systematic Cyclic Code:

In order to encode message sequence into systematic form, it is necessary to have message bits and parity bits in separate block in the codeword.

Consider a message polynomial.

$$
d(x) = d_1 x^{k-1} + d_2 x^{k-2} + \dots + d_k \qquad \text{... (5.36)}
$$

Multiply above polynomial by x^{n-k}.

where,   n = Number of code bits

k = Number of message bits

∴ $x^{n-k} d(x) = d_1 x^{n-1} + d_2 x^{n-2} + \dots + d_k x^{n-k}$ ... (5.37)

Dividing equation (5.37) by g(x), we get,

$$
\frac{x^{n-k} d(x)}{g(x)} = q(x) + \frac{p(x)}{g(x)} \qquad \text{... (5.38)}
$$

or

$$
x^{n-k} d(x) = q(x) \cdot g(x) + p(x) \qquad \text{... (5.39)}
$$

Adding p(x) on both sides of equation (5.39), we get,

$$
\underset{\substack{\downarrow \\ \text{Message bits} \\ \text{shifted by } n-k}}{x^{n-k} d(x)} + \underset{\substack{\downarrow \\ \text{Remainder} \\ (k-1) \text{ bits}}}{p(x)} = \underset{\substack{\downarrow \\ \text{Code}}}{q(x) \cdot g(x)} \qquad \text{... (5.40)}
$$

where, q(x) will be quotient after division whose order will be $k - 1$ or less, p(x) is remainder after division of the order $n - k - 1$.

Since q(x) is of order $k - 1$ or less and g(x) of order $n - k$, $q(x) \cdot g(x)$ will be code polynomial.

$x^{n-k} d(x)$ represents d(x) shifted by $n - k$ digits or the left side and since p(x) is of the order $k - 1$, it represents parity bits.

Thus, procedure for generating systematic cyclic code is as below.

(i)   Write d(x) for given message bits.

(ii)   Find $x^{n-k} \cdot d(x)$.

(iii)   Divide $x^{n-k} d(x)$ by g(x) and find remainder p(x).

(iv)   Find $c(x) = x^{n-k} d(x) + p(x)$.

(v)   Write codeword corresponding to c(x).

Example 5.11:

Construct a systematic (7, 4) cyclic code using generator polynomial $g(x) = x^3 + x^2 + 1$ for the messages.

(i)   1 0 1 0

(ii)   1 0 0 0

Solution:

Given:

$$g(x) = x^3 + x^2 + 1$$

$$n = 7, k = 4$$

$\therefore$ $$d(x) = x^3 + x$$

$\therefore$ $$x^{n-k} d(x) = x^3(x^3 + x)$$

$$= x^6 + x^4$$

$$
\require{enclose}
\begin{array}{r}
x^3 + x^2 + 1 \\
x^3 + x^2 + 1 \enclose{longdiv}{x^6 + x^4 } \\
\underline{x^6 + x^5 + x^3 } \\
x^5 + x^4 + x^3 \\
\underline{x^5 + x^4 + x^2 } \\
x^3 + x^2 \\
\underline{x^3 + x^2 + 1} \\
1 \leftarrow p(x)
\end{array}
$$

$\therefore$ $$c(x) = x^{n-k} d(x) + p(x)$$

$$= x^3(x^3 + x) + 1$$

$$= x^6 + x^4 + 1$$

$\therefore$ $$c = [1\ 0\ 1\ 0\ 0\ 0\ 1]$$

(ii) $$d = [1\ 0\ 0\ 0]$$

$$d(x) = x^3$$

$$x^{n-k} d(x) = x^3 \cdot x^3$$

$$= x^6$$

$$x^3 + x^2 + 1 \overline{\smash{\big)}\,} \begin{array}{l} x^3 + x^2 + x \\ x^6 \end{array}$$

$$\frac{x^6 + x^5 + x^3}{x^5 + x^3}$$

$$\frac{x^5 + x^4 + x^2}{x^4 + x^3 + x^2}$$

$$\frac{x^4 + x^3 + x}{x^2 + x} \leftarrow p(x)$$

$$\therefore \qquad c(x) = x^{n-k}\,d(x) + p(x)$$
$$= x^3 \cdot x^3 + x^2 + x$$
$$= x^6 + x^2 + x$$
$$c = [1\,0\,0\,0\,1\,1\,0]$$

(B) Parity Check Polynomial:

For linear block code we have seen that there is a generator matrix (G) and a parity check matrix (H) pair used at transmitter and receiver respectively.

A cyclic code can be specified by its generator polynomial g(x). There can be another polynomial called parity check polynomial h(x) such that,

$$[g(x) \cdot h(x)] \bmod [x^n + 1] = 0 \qquad\qquad \text{... (5.41)}$$

or $\qquad\qquad g(x) \cdot h(x) = x^n + 1 \qquad\qquad \text{... (5.42)}$

$\qquad$ (Analogous to $GH^T = 0$)

The parity check polynomial is of the order k and is specified as,

$$h(x) = 1 + \left(\sum_{i=1}^{k-1} h_i\,x^i\right) + x^k \qquad\qquad \text{... (5.43)}$$

-   Equation (5.21) shows that just like g(x), h(x) is also a factor of $x^n + 1$.

    e.g. for (7, 4) cyclic code, let $g(x) = x^3 + x + 1$.

$\therefore \qquad\qquad x^7 + 1 = (x + 1)\,(x^3 + x^2 + 1)\,(x^3 + x + 1)$

$\qquad\qquad\qquad\quad = (x^4 + x^2 + x + 1)\,(x^3 + x + 1)$

$\therefore \qquad\qquad h(x) = x^4 + x^2 + x + 1$

Decoding of Cyclic Code

The decoding process of cyclic code is same for both systematic and non-systematic cyclic codes.

Every valid codeword polynomial c(x) is a multiple of g(x). When this codeword is transmitted there may be some errors introduced, hence the received codeword polynomial r(x) may not be same as c(x).

If received codeword is same as transmitted codeword then r(x) mod g(x) = 0. Otherwise it will be non-zero polynomial. Consider $\dfrac{r(x)}{g(x)}$. It can be written as,

$$\frac{r(x)}{g(x)} = q(x) + \frac{s(x)}{g(x)} \qquad \text{... (5.44)}$$

where, q(x) is quotient polynomial and s(x) is remainder polynomial also called as syndrome polynomial.

Degree of q(x) will be k – 1 and that of s(x) will be n – k – 1.

r(x) can be written in terms of c(x) as,

$$r(x) = c(x) \oplus e(x) \qquad \text{... (5.45)}$$

where, e(x) is an error polynomial decided by the bit error pattern in r(x).

$$\therefore \qquad \frac{r(x)}{g(x)} = \frac{c(x) \oplus e(x)}{g(x)} \qquad \text{... (5.46)}$$

$$= \frac{c(x)}{g(x)} \oplus \frac{e(x)}{g(x)} \qquad \text{... (5.47)}$$

$$\therefore \qquad \text{Remainder}\left[\frac{r(x)}{g(x)}\right] = \text{Rem}\left[\frac{c(x)}{g(x)}\right] + \text{Rem}\left[\frac{c(x)}{g(x)}\right] \qquad \text{... (5.48)}$$

But Remainder after division of c(x) and g(x) will be zero.

$$\therefore \qquad \text{Rem}\left[\frac{r(x)}{g(x)}\right] = \text{Rem}\left[\frac{e(x)}{g(x)}\right] \qquad \text{... (5.49)}$$

Comparing equations (5.44) and (5.49), we can write,

$$s(x) = \text{Rem}\left[\frac{e(x)}{g(x)}\right] \qquad \text{... (5.50)}$$

Equation (5.50) shows that the syndrome polynomial of error polynomial e(x) is same as received word polynomial.

Thus, the decoding process of a cyclic code will be as below.

If our aim is to only detect errors, then the received codeword polynomial is divided by g(x). If the remainder i.e. syndrome polynomial is zero, there will be no error and if it is non-zero then there will be error. If it is required to correct those errors, then the procedure will be,

   (i)   Prepare a table of error patterns and syndromes using relation (8.50).

   (ii)   Find syndrome after diving received word polynomials r(x) and g(x).

   (iii) Select the error pattern corresponding to the syndrome.

   (iv) Add error pattern to the received codeword.

Example 5.12:

Design (3, 1) cyclic repetition code and its decoding method. Find corrected codewords for

   (i)   0 1 0

   (ii)   1 1 0

Solution:

Given: n = 3

                               k = 1

The generator polynomial $g(x)$ order = 3 – 1 = 2.

Generator polynomial should be factor of $x^3 + 1$.

Now, $(x^3 + 1)$ = $(x + 1)(x^2 + x + 1)$

∴ $g(x)$ = $x^2 + x + 1$

Since, k = 1, there will be two message words 0 and 1.

(I) Coding:

(i) d = [0]

$$d(x) = 0$$

$$x^{n-k}\,d(x) = x^2 \cdot 0 = 0$$

∴ $p(x)$ = 0

∴ $c(x)$ = $x^{n-k}\,d(x) + p(x)$

                               = 0 + 0

                               = 0

∴ c = [0 0 0]

(ii) d = [1]

$$d(x) = 1$$

∴ $x^{n-k}\,d(x)$ = $x^2 \cdot 1$

                               = x^2

To find $p(x)$.

$$
x^2 + x + 1 \;\overline{\smash{\big)}\;
\begin{array}{l}
1 \\
x^2 \\
\underline{x^2 + x + 1} \\
x + 1 \;\leftarrow p(x)
\end{array}
}
$$

∴ $c(x)$ = $x^{n-k}\,d(x) + p(x)$

                               = $x^2 + x + 1$

∴ c = [1 1 1]

Hence, codewords are

Message	Code
0	0 0 0
1	1 1 1

(II) Decoding:

Since d_{min} = 3

Error correcting capability

$$t_c \leq \frac{d_{min} - 1}{2}$$

$$\leq \frac{3 - 1}{2}$$

$$\leq 1 \text{ error}$$

The error patterns will be,

        100
        010
        001

Find $s(x) = e(x) \bmod g(x)$ for each error pattern.

(i)   For e = 1 0 0

$$e(x) = x^2$$

$$x^2 + x + 1 \enclose{longdiv}{\begin{array}{l} 1 \\ \hline x^2 \\ x^2 + x + 1 \\ \hline x + 1 \leftarrow s(x) \end{array}}$$

∴ $s = [1\ 1]$

(ii)   For e = 0 1 0

$$e(x) = x$$

$$x^2 + x + 1 \enclose{longdiv}{\begin{array}{l} 0 \\ \hline x \\ 0 \\ \hline x \leftarrow s(x) \end{array}}$$

∴ $s = [1\ 0]$

(iii) For e = 0 0 1

$$e(x) = 1$$

$$x^2 + x + 1 \enclose{longdiv}{\begin{array}{l} 0 \\ \hline 1 \\ 0 \\ \hline 1 \end{array}}$$

∴ $s = [0\ 1]$

Hence, syndrome and error vector table will be as below.

Syndrome	Error Vector
1 0 0	1 1
0 1 0	1 0
0 0 1	0 1

Now, let us decode given received words.

(i)   r = 0 1 0

$\therefore$

$$r(x) = x$$

$$x^2 + x + 1 \overline{\smash{\big)}\, \begin{array}{l} 0 \\ x \\ 0 \\ \hline x \leftarrow s(x) \end{array}}$$

$\therefore \qquad\qquad\qquad s = [1\ 0]$

This syndrome corresponds to e = [0 1 0].

$\therefore$ Corrected codeword c = r $\oplus$ e

$$= [0\ 1\ 0] \oplus [0\ 1\ 0]$$

$$= [0\ 0\ 0]$$

(ii)   r = 1 1 0

$\therefore$

$$r(x) = x^2 + x$$

$$x^2 + x + 1 \overline{\smash{\big)}\, \begin{array}{l} 1 \\ x^2 + x \\ x^2 + x + 1 \\ \hline 1 \leftarrow s(x) \end{array}}$$

$\therefore \qquad\qquad\qquad s = [0\ 1]$

This syndrome corresponds to e = [0 0 1]

$\therefore$ Corrected codeword c = r $\oplus$ e

$$= [1\ 1\ 0] \oplus [0\ 0\ 1]$$

$$= [1\ 1\ 1]$$

Error Detecting Codes

Error detection system consists of encoding procedure similar to error correcting codes but at the receiver end the errors are detected by using pattern checking. The system has a provision of feedback which tells the transmitter to retransmit a message in error.

The number of errors that can be detected $t_d = d_{min} - 1$, where d_{min} is minimum hamming distance of the code.

The parity check code discussed earlier is an example of error detecting codes. In case of even parity code, there are even number of 1's in the code. If the receiver detects odd number of 1's the received codeword is incorrect. This system will fail if there are even number of errors.

The effectiveness of an error detection code is measured by the probability that the system fails to detect an error. It depends on the properties of communication channel.

Following are some examples of error detecting codes.

(i) **Parity check code:** A parity bit is added to the message such that number of 1's in the code becomes even in case of even parity and odd in case of odd parity. Errors can be detected by wanting number of 1's at the receiver end.

(ii) **Two-dimensional parity code:** k information bits from m messages are arranged in m × k matrix form. Even parity of each row is calculated and stored in $k+1^{th}$ column and even parity of each of m columns is calculated and stored in $m+1^{th}$ row as shown in Fig. 5.9. If there are 3 or less errors anywhere in the matrix, error can be detected as atleast one row will fail the parity check. But some patterns with 4 errors cannot be detected as shown.

1	0	0	1	0	0
0	1	0	0	0	1
1	0	0	1	0	0
1	1	0	1	1	0
1	0	0	1	1	1

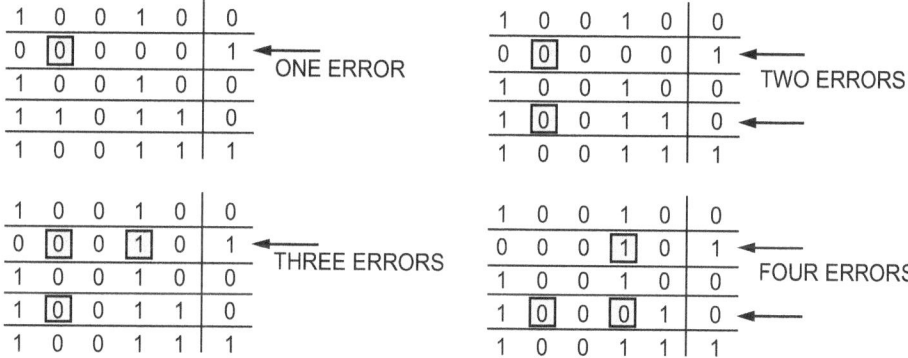

Fig. 5.9: Two-dimensional parity code

(iii) Polynomial codes:

*   They are used both in error detection as well as error correction as discussed earlier.
*   Polynomial codes are easy to implement using shift register.
*   Cyclic Redundancy Check (CRC) codes are used to generate check bits for error detection.
*   As seen earlier the message, codeword and error vectors are represented in terms of polynomials with binary coefficient.
*   The codeword is generated using

$$c(x) \;=\; x^{n-k}\,d(x) + p(x)$$

where,

$$p(x) \;=\; \text{Rem}\left[\frac{x^{n-k}\,d(x)}{g(x)}\right]$$

- Detection involves finding syndrome

$$s(x) = \text{Rem}\left[\frac{r(x)}{g(x)}\right]$$

If remainder is zero, codeword is correctly received otherwise there will be error.
- Implementation of encoder and detector using shift register is already discussed.

Standardized Polynomial Codes

Three polynomials listed below are used as standard polynomials in many applications. They are

$$\text{CRC-12} \ - \ x^{12} + x^{11} + x^3 + x^2 + x + 1$$
$$\text{CRC-16} \ - \ x^{16} + x^{15} + x^2 + 1$$
$$\text{CRC-CCITT} \ - \ x^{16} + x^{12} + x^5 + 1$$

Recently, CRC-8 and CRC-10 are also recommended for use in ATM networks. They are

$$\text{CRC-8} \ - \ x^8 + x^2 + x + 1$$
$$\text{CRC-10} \ - \ x^{10} + x^9 + x^5 + x^4 + x + 1$$

Following two polynomials are also in use.

$$\text{CCITT-16} \ - \ x^{16} + x^{12} + x^5 + 1$$
$$\text{CCITT-32} \ - \ x^{32} + x^{26} + x^{23} + x^{22} + x^{16} + x^{12} + x^{11} + x^{10} + x^8 + x^7$$
$$+ x^5 + x^4 + x^2 + x + 1$$

Error Detecting Capability of Polynomial Codes

As seen earlier syndrome s(x) is calculated by dividing r(x) with g(x). The error pattern e(x) is given by

$$e(x) = r(x) \oplus d(x)$$
$$\therefore \quad r(x) = d(x) \oplus e(x)$$
$$\therefore \quad s(x) = \text{Rem}\left[\frac{r(x)}{g(x)}\right]$$
$$= \text{Rem}\left[\frac{d(x) + e(x)}{g(x)}\right]$$
$$= \text{Rem}\left[\frac{d(x)}{g(x)}\right] + \text{Rem}\left[\frac{e(x)}{g(x)}\right]$$
$$= \text{Rem}\left[\frac{e(x)}{g(x)}\right]$$

Thus, we can formulate g(x) that will not divide the given error polynomials.

e.g.

(i) To detect all single errors.

$$e(x) = x^i \qquad\qquad 0 \le i \le n-1$$

If g(x) has more than one term, it will not divide e(x).

(ii) To detect all double errors.

$$e(x) = x^i + x^j \qquad\qquad 0 \le i \le j \le n-1$$
$$= x^i (1 + x^{j-1})$$

As seen above, x^i is not divisible by $g(x)$. Hence, we should ensure that $1 + x^{j-1}$ is also not divisible by $g(x)$.

For this, $g(x)$ should be a primitive polynomial. Primitive polynomials have the property that, if degree of primitive polynomials is N then smallest value of m for which $1 + x^m$ is divisible by the polynomial is $2^N - 1$. Since $g(x)$ has degree n–k, it will detect all double errors if codeword has length less than or equal to $2^{n-k} - 1$.

The CRC-16 polynomial $x^{16} + x^{15} + x^2 + 1 = (x + 1) (x^{15} + x + 1)$ where, $x^{15} + x + 1$ is primitive. Hence, it can detect all double errors, if $n <= 2^{15} - 1 = 32767$.

(iii) To detect all odd numbered errors: If there are odd numbered errors, $e(x)$ will have odd numbered terms. Such polynomial does not have $x + 1$ as a factor. Hence, by selecting $(x + 1)$ as a factor, $g(x)$ we can detect all odd numbered errors.

(iv) To detect all burst errors: If a burst error of length L occurs starting from i^{th} bit position

$$e(x) = x^i b(x)$$

where, $b(x)$ is of degree L–1 representing burst-error pattern. To detect this error, $b(x)$ should not be divisible by $g(x)$. For this, $b(x)$ should have degree less than $g(x)$ i.e. n–k. Thus, we can detect a burst error of length less than or equal to n–k. We can also detect a burst error of length n–k+1, if error pattern does not match $g(x)$. Even we can detect some of the burst errors of length L > n–k+1.

All the CRC polynomials contain $(x + 1)$ as a factor. Hence they can detect all odd numbered errors, all single and double errors and all burst errors of length $\le n - k$.

5.6 Checksum

- It is an error detection method used in many protocols of internet.
- It is based on the concept of redundancy.
- As the name indicates it is a method in which error is "checked" by taking "sum" of the information in bits/digits.
- For example, if we want to transmit the digits (5, 2, 8, 7) we will transmit the sum of these digits along with them as additional (redundancy) information i.e. we will transmit (5, 2, 8, 7, 22). Now, when this information is received at the receiver end we can "check" the sum of the first four digits. If it matches with 5th, the information is received correctly otherwise there will be error.

- We can have one more alternative which will make receiver's job simple. Transmit the negative of sum instead of sum so that if we add all received digits the sum will be 0.

- If you look at the information digits they will require only 4 bits for representation whereas the sum will require 5 bits and if negative sum is used we will require sign bit also. For this, we can use 1's complement arithmetic. Let us see how we can find the checksum using 1's complement arithmetic.

One's Complement Arithmetic:

In this method, a n bit number is represented in 1's complement form as below.

- If a number has more than n bits the extra leftmost bits are added to n right most bits.

- A negative number is represented by inverting all bits.

e.g.　1.　In 4 bit representation number, 22 will be represented in 1's complement arithmetic as below.

NUMBER 22 is 10110

The 5th bit which is extra is added to leftmost bit as below.

0110

+　1

0111　which is 7.

Hence, 22 is represented as 0111 or 7.

2.　In 4 bit representation, the number −10 will be represented as below.

Number 10 is 1010.

The negative number is represented by inverting the bits.

∴ −10 is represented as 0101 or 5.

Another way to find the complement is subtract the number from $2^n - 1$.

In above case, 4 bit representation $2^n - 1 = 15$. Hence, −10 will be represented as 15 − 10 = 5.

Example 5.13:

Represent the following numbers using 1's complement arithmetics using 4 bits.

(i) 36, (ii) −6, (iii) 42, (iv) −20.

Solution:

(i)　36

Binary representation of 36 is

100100

More than 4 bits are added to leftmost bits

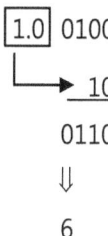

0110

⇓

6

(ii) −6

Binary representation of 6 is 0110.

Since negative number is represented by inverting bits.

0110

↓

1001

⇓

9

(iii) 42

Binary representation of 42 is 101010.

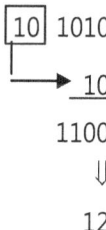

1100

⇓

12

(iv) −20

Binary representation of 20 is 10100.

More than 4 bits. Hence wrap.

1 0100

└──► 1

0101

Invert the bits

1010

10

Now, let us find the checksum using one's complement arithmetic.

Let the transmitted digits be 5, 2, 8, 7.

The checksum will be $(5 + 2 + 8 + 7) = -22$.

-22 will be represented in one's complement arithmetic as below.

$$10110$$

$$\overset{\llcorner\rightarrow}{1}$$

$$0111$$

Inverting   1000

$$\Downarrow$$

$$8$$

Hence, transmitted pattern will be,

$$(5, 2, 8, 7, 8).$$

If received pattern is same and if we add

$$5 + 2 + 8 + 7 + 8 \ = \ 30$$

Now, 30 in one's complement form is as below:

30 in binary 11110

wrap $\llcorner\rightarrow 1$

Inverting 0000

If the final result is 0, it means there is no error in the transmitted digits/numbers.

Internet Checksum:

Internet uses 16 bit checksum. The information to be transmitted i.e. message has to be represented in terms of numbers so that it can be converted into 16 bit words. The steps to be followed for computing checksum at transmitter and receiver are as below:

I.   **Transmitter end:**

    1.   Divide the message into 16 bit words.

    2.   Initialize checksum to 0.

    3.   Add words using one's complement arithmetic.

    4.   Complement the sum.

II. **Receiver end:**

    1.   Divide the received message (including checksum).

    2.   Add words using one's complement arithmetic.

    3.   Complement the sum.

    4.   If result is 0, no error. Otherwise there is error.

Let us take an example. Suppose we want to find the checksum for the word "communication". This word has to be expressed in ASCII format. The ASCII values of a-z are 97 to 122 in decimal, in hex they are 61 to 7A.

ASCII value of c is   0x63
             o is   0x6F
             m is   0x6D
             u is   0x75
             n is   0x6E
             t is   0x74
             i is   0x69
             a is   0x61

Now we add these alongwith checksum as below:

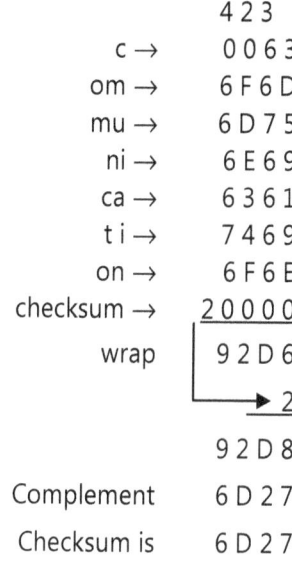

	4 2 3
c →	0 0 6 3
om →	6 F 6 D
mu →	6 D 7 5
ni →	6 E 6 9
ca →	6 3 6 1
ti →	7 4 6 9
on →	6 F 6 E
checksum →	2 0 0 0 0
wrap	9 2 D 6
	2
	9 2 D 8
Complement	6 D 2 7
∴ Checksum is	6 D 2 7

5.7 Flow Control

Any receiving device has a limited speed at which it can process incoming data and a limited amount of memory in which to store incoming data.

Incoming data must be checked and processed before they can be used. The rate of such processing is often slower than the rate of transmission. For this reason, each receiving device has block of memory, called a **buffer**, reserved for storing incoming data until they are processed. If the buffer begins to fill up, the receiver must be able to tell the sender to halt transmission until it is once again able to receive.

In communications, control of the rate at which information is exchanged between two computers over a transmission channel. Flow control is needed when one of the devices cannot receive the information at the same rate as it can be sent, usually because some processing is required on the receiving end before the next transmission unit can be accepted. Flow control can be implemented either in hardware or in software.

Flow control is a function that prevents network congestion by ensuring that transmitting devices do not overwhelm receiving devices with data. There are a number of possible causes of network congestion. For example, a high-speed computer might generate traffic faster than the network can transfer it, or faster than the destination device can receive and process it.

There are three commonly used methods for handling network congestion.

5.7.1 Buffering

Buffering is used by network devices to temporarily store bursts of excess data in memory until they can be processed. Occasional data bursts are easily handled by buffering. However, excess data bursts can exhaust memory, forcing the device to discard any additional datagrams that arrive.

Source Quench Messages: Source quench messages are used by receiving devices to help prevent their buffers from overflowing. The receiving device sends source quench messages to request that the source reduce its current rate of data transmission, as follows:

1. The receiving device begins discarding received data due to overflowing buffers.
2. The receiving device begins sending source quench messages to the transmitting device, at the rate of one message for each packet dropped.
3. The source device receives the source quench messages and lowers the data rate until it stops receiving the messages.
4. The source device then gradually increases the data rate as long as no further source quench requests are received.

5.7.2 Windowing

Windowing is a flow-control scheme in which the source device requires an acknowledgement from the destination after a certain number of packets have been transmitted. With a window size of three, the source requires an acknowledgement after sending three packets, as follows:

1. The source device sends three packets to the destination device.
2. After receiving the three packets, the destination device sends an acknowledgement to the source.
3. The source receives the acknowledgement and sends three more packets.
4. If the destination does not receive one or more of the packets for some reason (such as overflowing buffers), it does not receive enough packets to send an acknowledgement. The source, not receiving an acknowledgement, retransmits the packets at a reduced transmission rate.

Flow control refers to a set of procedures used to restrict the amount of data the sender can send before waiting for acknowledgement.

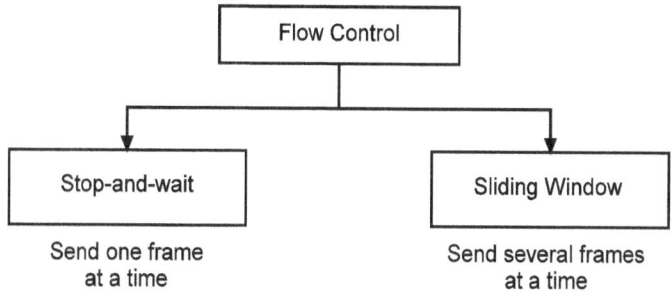

Fig. 5.10: Categories of Flow Control

5.7.3 Stop-and-Wait

The sender waits for an acknowledgement after every frame it sends.

The sender sends one frame and waits for an acknowledgement before sending the next frame.

The advantage of stop-and-wait is simplicity: each frame is checked and acknowledged before the next frame is sent.

The disadvantage is inefficiency: stop-and-wait is slow.

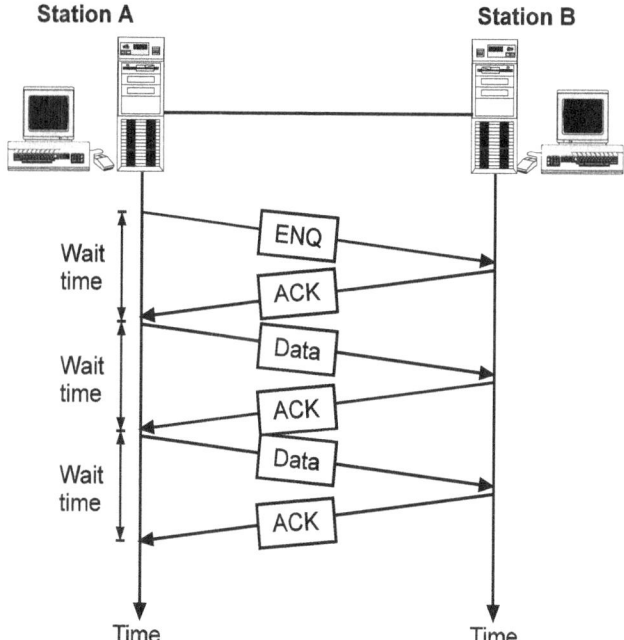

Fig. 5.11: Stop-and-wait

5.7.4 Sliding Window

The sender can transmit several frames before needing an acknowledgement. Frames can be sent one after the another. The receiver acknowledges only some of the frames, using a single ACK to confirm the receipt of multiple data frames.

The sliding window refers to imaginary boxes at both the sender and the receiver. To keep track of which frames have been transmitted and which received, sliding window introduces an identification scheme based on the size of the window. The frames are numbered modulo-n, which means they are numbered from 0 to n−1.

When the receiver sends an ACK, it includes the number of the next frame it expects to receive.

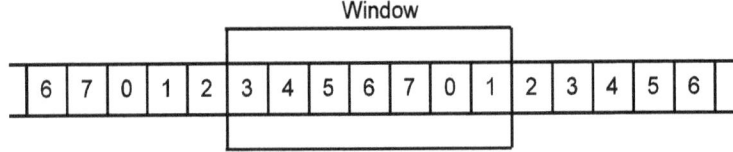

Fig. 5.12: Sliding Window

1. **Sender Window:** The sliding window of the sender shrinks from the left when frames of data are sent. The sliding window of the sender expands to the right when acknowledgements are received.

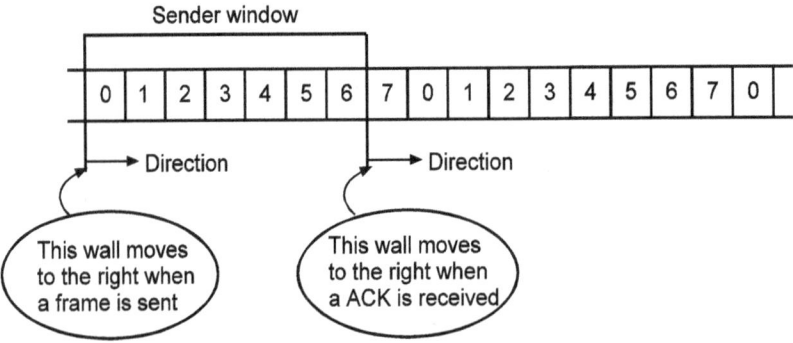

Fig. 5.13: Sender Sliding Window

2. **Receiver Window:** The sliding window of the receiver shrinks from left when frames of data are received. The sliding window of the receiver expands to the right when acknowledgements are sent.

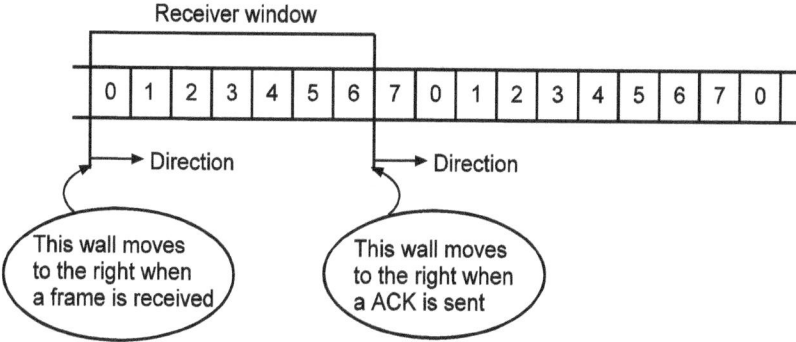

Fig. 5.14: Receiver Sliding Window

An Example of sliding window

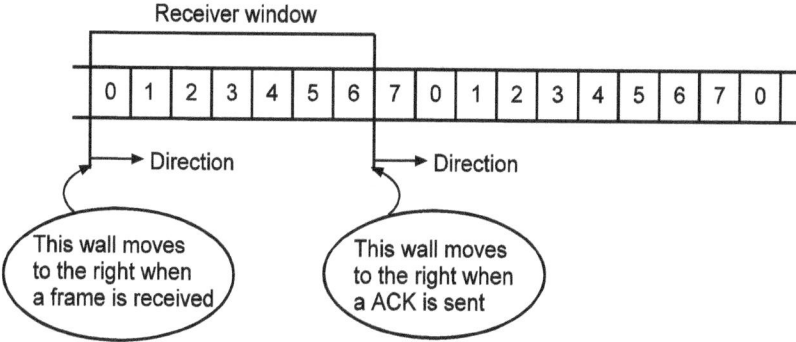

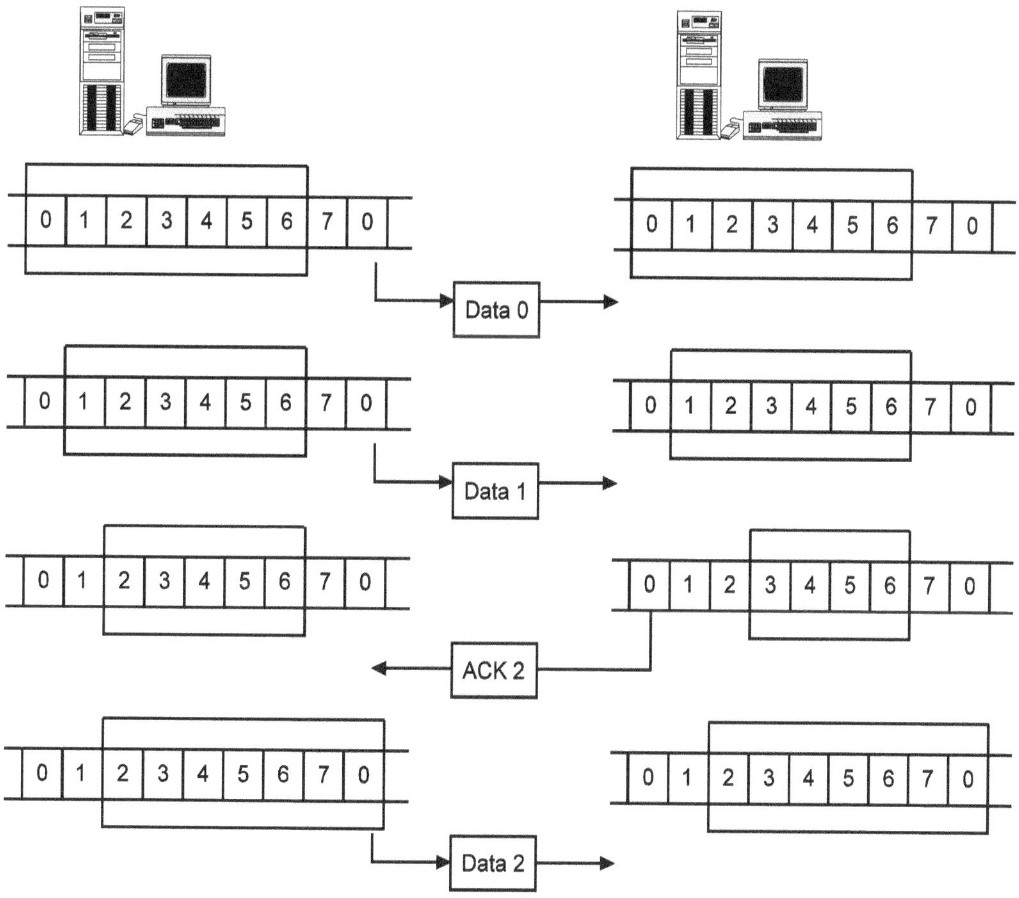

Fig. 5.15: Example of sliding window

5.8 Error Control

In the data link layer, the ***error control*** refers to methods of error detection and retransmission.

Error control in data link layer is to maintain the frames being transmitted/received are in sequence and to make sure the frames have not been distorted due to transmission error.

The Data Link layer may check for errors on the physical link between two neighbouring devices. This is link level error checking. Error checking can also be done at the endpoints of the communication. Is error detection necessary at Data Link layer? The transport layer can do end-to-end error checking. If there are no errors end to end, then there could not have been any errors on the links. If there is a high probability of error, you will want to check each packet. This does take time. Some high speed networks do not perform any error checking at the Data Link layer.

Error correction in the data link layer is implemented simply: anytime an error is detected in an exchange, a negative acknowledgement (NAK) is returned and the specified frames are retransmitted. This process is called **automatic repeat request (ARQ)**.

Error control in the data link layer is based on automatic repeat request (ARQ), which means retransmission of data in three cases: damaged frame, lost frame, and lost acknowledgement.

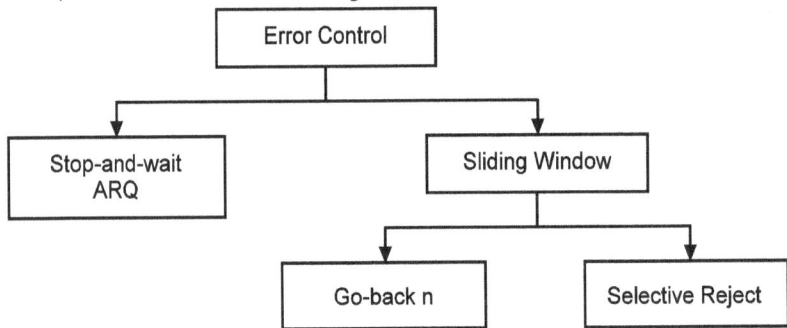

Fig. 5.16: Categories of Error Control

5.8.1 Stop-and-wait ARQ

It is extended version of stop-and-wait flow control to include retransmission of data in case of lost and damaged frame.

Following features are added to basic stop-and-wait flow control mechanism to support retransmission:

- The sending device keeps a copy of the last frame transmitted until it receives an acknowledgement for that frame.
- For identification purposes, both data frames and ACK frames are numbered alternately 0 and 1. An ACK 1 frame, indicating that the receiver has gotten data 0 and is now expecting data 1, acknowledges a data 0 frame.

- If the error is discovered in a data frame, indicating that it has been corrupted in transit, a NAK frame is returned. NAK frames, which are not numbered, tell the sender to retransmit the last frame sent.
- The sending device is equipped with a timer. If an expected acknowledgement is not received within an allotted time period, the sender assumes that the last data frame was lost in transit and sends it again.

When a frame is discovered by the receiver to contain an error, it returns a NAK frame and the sender retransmits the last frame. For example, the sender transmits a data frame: data 0. The receiver returns an ACK 1, indicating that data 0 arrived undamaged and it is now expecting data 1. The sender transmits its next frame: data 1. It arrives undamaged, and receiver returns ACK 0. The sender transmits its next frame: data 0. The receiver discovers an error in data 0 and returns a NAK. The sender retransmits data 0. This time data 0 arrives intact, and the receiver returns ACK 1 and so on.

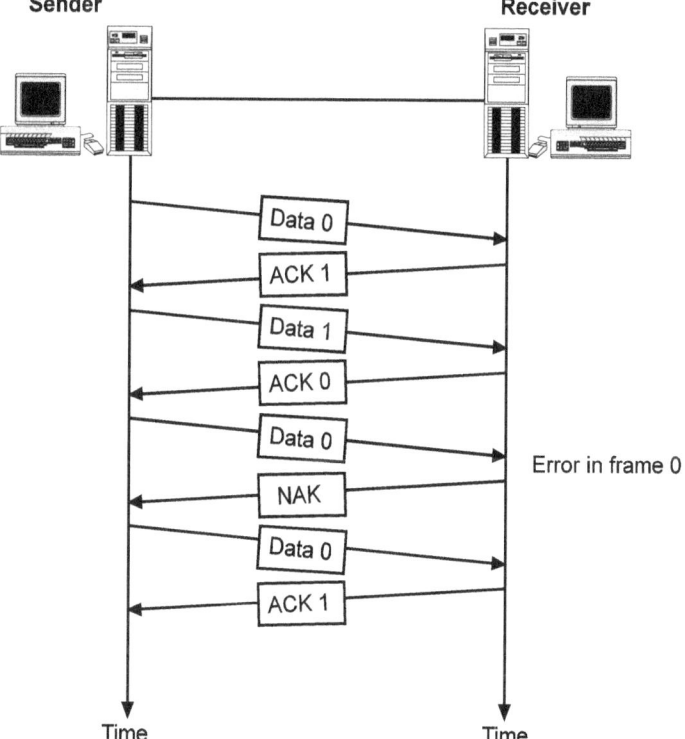

Fig. 5.17: Stop-and-wait ARQ, damaged frame

Fig. 5.18 explains how stop-and-wait ARQ handles the lost of a data frame. The sender is equipped with a timer that starts every time a data frame is transmitted. If the frame never reaches to the receiver, the receiver can never acknowledges it, positively or negatively. The sending device waits for an ACK or NAK frame until its timer goes off. If its timer goes off, and did not receive either ACK or NAK frame then sender retransmits the last data frame, restarts its timer, and again wait for an acknowledgement.

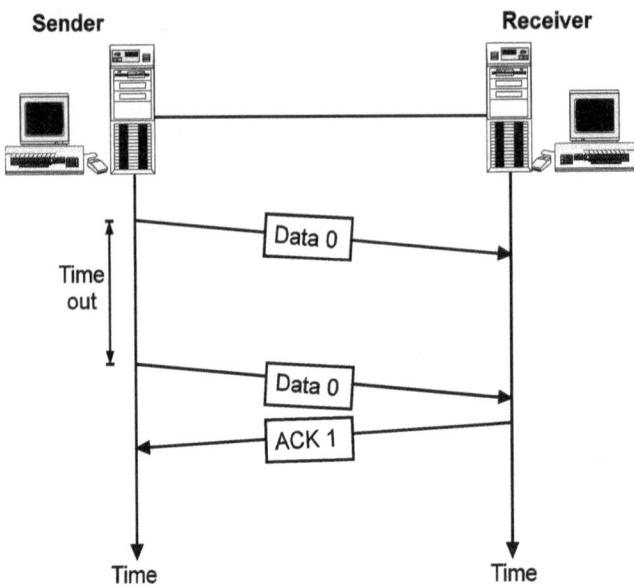

Fig. 5.18: Stop-and-wait ARQ, lost data frame

If the ACK or NAK frame returned by the receiver is lost in transit, the sending device waits until its timer goes off, then retransmits the data frame.

If receiver receives the duplicate copy of the frame then discards it and waits for the next frame.

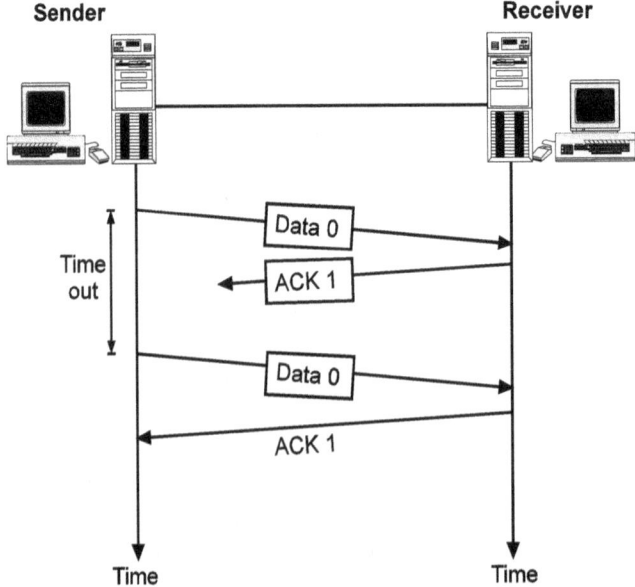

Fig. 5.19: Stop-and-wait ARQ, lost ACK frame

5.8.2 Sliding Window ARQ

It is extended version of sliding window flow control to include retransmission of data in case of lost and damaged frame.

Following features are added to basic stop-and-wait flow control mechanism to support retransmission:

- The sending device keeps copies of all transmitted frames until they have been acknowledged. If frames 0 through 6 have been transmitted, and the last acknowledgement was for frame 2, the sender keeps copies of frames 3 through 6 until it knows that they have been received undamaged.

- Receiver sent NAK frame if the data have been received damaged. The NAK frame tells the sender to retransmit a damaged frame. ACK frames carry the number of the next frame expected. NAK frames carry the number of the damaged frame itself. Data frames that are received without errors do not have to be acknowledged individually. Every damaged frame, however, must be acknowledged.

- The sending device in sliding *window ARQ* is equipped with a timer to enable it to handle lost acknowledgements / data frames.

  Two protocols are most popular:

  1. Go-back-*n* ARQ
  2. Selective-reject ARQ

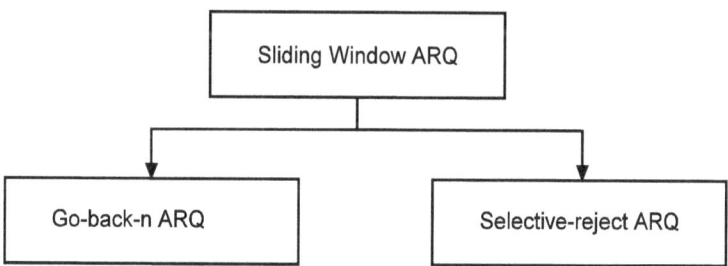

Fig. 5.20: Sliding window ARQ protocols

1. **Go-back-*n* ARQ:** If one frame is lost or damaged, all frames sent since the last frames acknowledged are retransmitted.

   A NAK means a positive acknowledgement of all frames received prior to the damaged frame. If the first acknowledgement is a NAK 3, it means that data frames 0, 1, and 2 were all received in good shape. Only frame 3 must be resent.

   What if frames 0 through 5 have been transmitted before a NAK is received for frame 3? As soon as the receiver discovers an error, it stops accepting subsequent frames until the damaged frame has been replaced correctly. In the scenario, data frame 3 arrives damaged and so is discarded, as are data frame 4 and data frame 5 whether or not the arrived intact. The retransmission therefore consists of frames 3, 4 and 5.

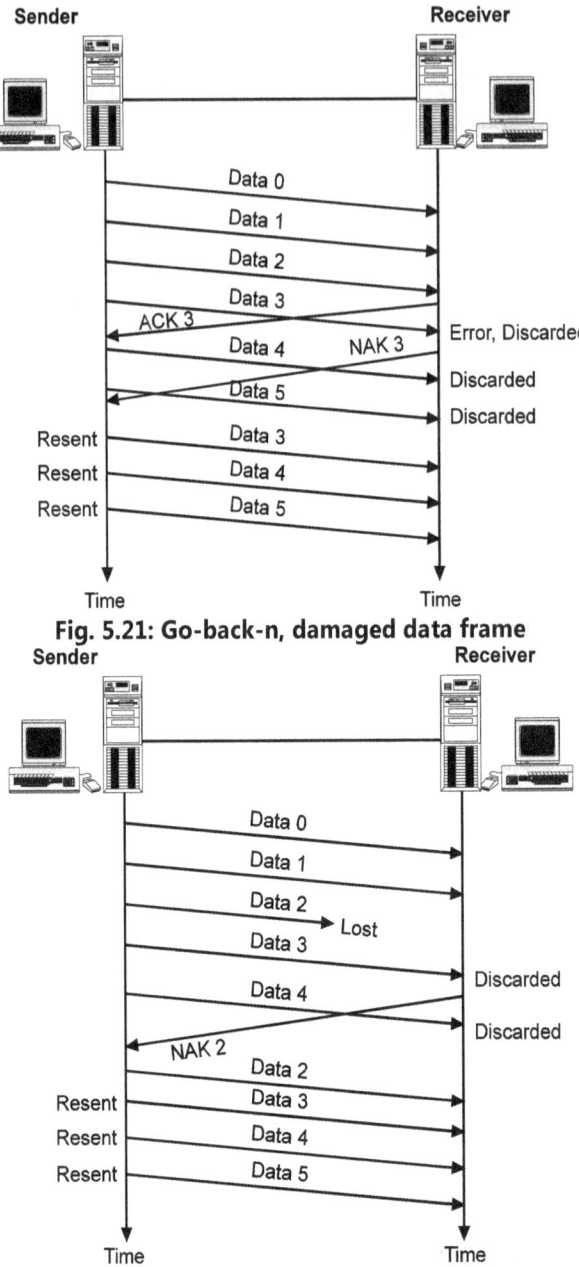

Fig. 5.21: Go-back-n, damaged data frame

Fig. 5.22: Go-back-n, lost data frame

If one or more frames are lost in transit, the next frame to arrive at the receiver will be out of sequence. The receiver checks the identifying number on each frame, discovers that one or more frames have been skipped or lost, and returns a NAK for the first missing frame. A NAK frame does not indicate whether the frame has been lost or damaged, just that it needs to be resent. The sending device then retransmits the frame indicated by NAK, as well as any frames that it had transmitted after the lost one.

The sending can send as many frames as the window allows before waiting for an acknowledgement. Once that limit has been reached or the sender has no more frames to send, it must wait. The sender is equipped with a timer that begins counting whenever the window capacity is reached. If an acknowledgement has not been received within the time limit, the sender retransmits every frame transmitted since the last ACK.

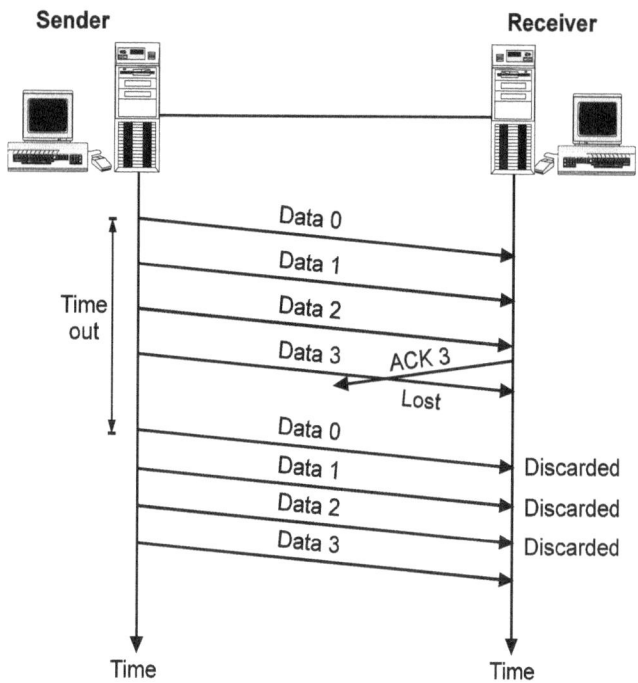

Fig. 5.23: Go-back-n, lost ACK

2. Selective-Reject ARQ:

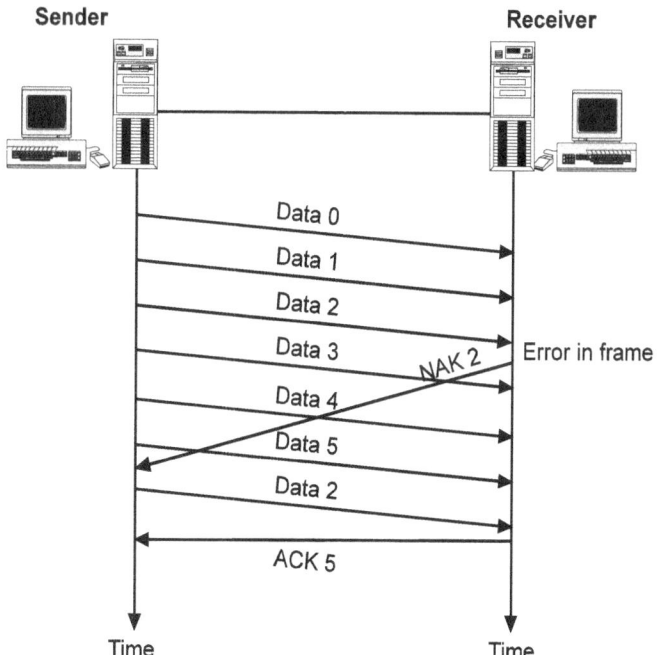

Fig. 5.24: Selective-reject, damaged data frame

- Only the specific damaged or lost frame is retransmitted.

- If a frame is corrupted in transit, a NAK is returned and the frame is resent out of sequence. The receiving device must be able to sort the frames it has and insert the retransmitted frame into its proper place in the sequence.

- When the sending device reaches either the capacity of its window or the end of its transmission, it sets a timer. If no acknowledgement arrives in the time allotted, the sender retransmits all of the frames that remain unacknowledged.

EXERCISE

1. Explain different types of errors that can occur in transmission of bits.
2. What are functions of data link layer?
3. What is error control? How it is achieved?
4. Explain error correction and detection.
5. What are linear block codes? Explain.
6. What are cyclic codes? Explain.
7. What is hamming distance? Explain with example.
8. What is generator matrix in LBC? How it is created and used?
9. What is generator polynomial in cyclic codes?
10. How is systematic cyclic code generated?
11. What is checksum? Explain with example.
12. How does a single-bit error differ from a burst error?
13. Discuss the concept of redundancy in error detection.
14. How can a parity bit detect a damaged data unit?
15. What is the difference between even parity and odd parity?
16. Explain the working of CRC error detection method.
17. Name different error detection methods.
18. Explain how checksum works.
19. Explain Hamming code with example.
20. Explain LRC and VRC methods.
21. Explain the EIA 232/V.24 interface.
22. Write short notes on: (1) Flow control, (2) Error Control.
23. With neat diagram explain categories of flow control.
24. Explain sliding window.
25. Describe briefly error control.
26. Write short note on stop and wait ARQ.
27. With a neat diagram explain sliding window ARQ.

UNIVERSITY QUESTIONS

NOVEMBER-DECEMBER 2011

1. (i) Why error detection and correction is essential for data communication. **(5)**

   (ii) State flow control and error control protocol? Explain any one in detail. **(5)**

2. Explain CRC and checksum with example in detail. **(10)**

MAY-JUNE 2011

3. Explain the concept of 7-bit Hamming code with an example. **(6)**

4. Explain the concept of CRC? Give an example of CRC checksum for message polynomial. $G(x) = x^3 + x^2$ and generator polynomial $P(x) = x^3 + x^2 + 1$. **(6)**

NOVEMBER-DECEMBER 2010

5. (a) (i) State flow control and error control protocol. Explain any one in detail. **(5)**

   (ii) What is hamming code? Show with example how a single bit error is detected and corrected using hamming code. **(5)**

   (b) Explain CRC and checksum with given example. **(10)**

   (c) Write a short note on cyclic code. **(10)**

MAY-JUNE 2010

6. (a) What is error? What are the types of error? What is ARQ and EEC? **(5)**

   (b) Compare forward error correction versus. Retransmission error correction. **(5)**

7. (a) Compare flow control with error control. **(5)**

   (b) What is hamming code? Explain with neat example how a hamming code is calculated and bit position of error is detected. **(5)**

8. Write a short note on linear block codes. **(10)**

NOVEMBER-DECEMBER 2009

9. What is CRC? Calculate checksum for the message polynomial $G(x) = x^5 + x^2$ with the help of generator polynomial $P(x) = x^3 + x^2 + 1$. **(5)**

10. Explain error detection and error coding. **(5)**

11. What do you mean by flow control? Explain any one in detail. **(5)**

12. What are the different types of error? How error correction can be done. **(10)**

MAY-JUNE 2009

13. Compare flow control and error control?   **(5)**

14. Write a short note on: **(5)**

    (i)   Advantages of cyclic code.

    (ii) Cyclic redundancy check.

15. Write a short note on block coding.   **(10)**

***

www.ingramcontent.com/pod-product-compliance
Lightning Source LLC
Chambersburg PA
CBHW081141020726
47504CB00009B/1952